The Elixir of Immortality

The Elixir of Immortality

Gabi Gleichmann

TRANSLATED BY MICHAEL MEIGS

Other Press / New York

Library of Congress Cataloging-in-Publication Data
Gleichmann, Gabi, author.
[Udødelighetens elixir. English]
The elixir of immortality / by Gabi Gleichmann ; [translated by Michael Meigs].
pages cm
ISBN 978-1-59051-589-1 (pbk. Original) — ISBN (invalid) 978-1-59051-590-7
(ebook)   1. Jewish families—Europe—Fiction.   2. Europe—History—Fiction.
3. Epic fiction.   I. Meigs, Michael, translator.   II. Title.
PT8952.17.L45U3613 2013
839.82'38—dc23
2012046085

Publisher's Note:
This is a work of fiction. Names, characters, places, and incidents either are the
product of the author's imagination or are used fictitiously.

For my sons

Marcel, Danilo, Maximillian, and Felix

This is—almost—your own history.

The future is up to you.

nothing ever repeats itself in human history

everything that at first glance seems the same

is in its own way exactly the same;

every human being is a star unto himself,

everything happens perpetually and never at all,

everything repeats itself endlessly and nevermore

—DANILO KIŠ

✑ Spinoza Family Tree ✑

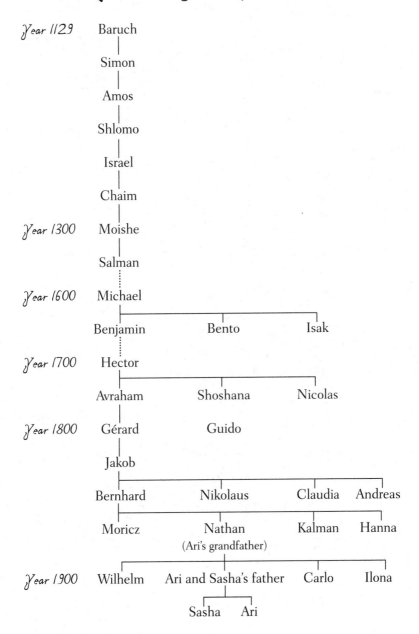

Year 1129   Baruch
              Simon
              Amos
              Shlomo
              Israel
              Chaim

Year 1300   Moishe
              Salman

Year 1600   Michael

              Benjamin   Bento   Isak

Year 1700   Hector

              Avraham   Shoshana   Nicolas

Year 1800   Gérard   Guido

              Jakob

              Bernhard   Nikolaus   Claudia   Andreas

              Moricz   Nathan   Kalman   Hanna
                         (Ari's grandfather)

Year 1900   Wilhelm   Ari and Sasha's father   Carlo   Ilona
                          Sasha   Ari

Prologue

FOR A LONG TIME the words would not come. My mother lay before me in her bed wearing only a thin nightgown, silent and self-absorbed. Her gaze had fixed itself upon some invisible spot on the ceiling. Her breathing was shallow; she was almost motionless. I held her hand, hoping she would grip mine, but her hand was cold and lifeless.

This was ten years ago on a November day under an endless blue sky. The wind was erratic and a thin layer of new-fallen snow covered Oslo. The sun was shining but the wind carried a sharp, cold winter edge, and on the Continent people were using their bare hands to tear down the wall that had divided Europe for decades.

For once, early that morning my father had called and told me in a guarded voice that my mother wasn't doing well. Given the circumstances, I shouldn't visit her. At first I felt relieved.

Every day for the previous fifteen years I'd heard that my mother wasn't doing well, that she was suffering unbearable pain, and that she was dying. My mother wasn't exactly discreet when it came to suffering. She complained incessantly, increasingly bitter with each passing year, and I responded by adopting a fairly irresponsible strategy: I simply paid no attention to her most of the time. With the passing years I became more or less indifferent and convinced myself that as long as she was still able to complain, I had no reason to worry about her health. I see now that I should have been more attentive.

At the very moment Father told me in a rush that she was in too much pain to come to the telephone, I realized that Mother was about to leave us. Only then did I understand how poorly prepared I was for this and that I would regret it for the rest of my life.

Little knowing that hardly half an hour of my mother's allotted life span was left, I rang the bell outside my parents' home. Father opened the door, and his expression emphasized the solemn and ceremonial nature of the moment. I took a seat next to the bed and gazed at Mother. Her face was white, almost translucent, and the uncombed hair lying carelessly across her forehead gave her a girlish appearance.

Who is this, really, this person lying here? She seems so familiar, so near and yet so far away. As I stared I feverishly searched my memory for images of her. In vain. She was nowhere to be found.

Suddenly it became clear that I had been ashamed of the fact that Mother had cut herself off from the world and closed herself up in her bedroom so no one would distract her from spending time with the demons in the darkest landscapes of her imagination. That's why I had carefully kept her at a distance. I had suppressed even my fondest memories of her. I shuddered at my selfishness, and I wanted to talk with her, aloud, about all those things we had never discussed. No matter how I tried, the words refused to come.

My father stood there, unmoving. Then he hastily slipped away, seeking temporary distraction in some routine household task.

A stark silence reigned in the bedroom. Deeply ashamed and seized by the seriousness of the moment, I tried to comfort my mother. I stroked her cheek softly but found nothing to say.

Instead, my mother was the one who spoke. Almost imperceptibly her lips quivered and she mumbled something about the worst day of her life: December 12, 1944. Then, still in a tone almost too low to hear, she said something about Lipot, the most devout of all the boys hiding in the house, who was brutally murdered that day by the Germans. His dead body lay in the street for two weeks before friends dared to move it under cover of darkness to the Jewish cemetery. She kept muttering, confused and not making much sense. I listened intently. Her voice was fading away.

"How could God let that happen?" She sighed. "You have to tell it to everyone. You have to tell them everything about it."

I felt the responsibility weigh upon me and pledged that one day I would describe the cramped and isolated universe that had been our abode on this earth. Mother paid no attention; she was already on her way out of this life. She drifted off with a resigned smile and gave herself up to be swallowed by the void.

ONE

The Sources

The Narrator

FIRST OF ALL, a couple of words about my great-uncle, the shining light and joy of our early childhood. There is so much more to say about him than I can remember. The subject is so vast that it stretches far past the reaches of both my memory and my understanding. Now that I'm trying to tell his story, the gaps have become even more evident.

He was an idol to my twin brother, Sasha, and me when we were small. We worshipped him. Sometimes when I looked at him as we sat there at the kitchen table, I had the feeling that the world wasn't big enough for the awe I felt. He taught us all about our extended family, he described things we youngsters knew nothing of and couldn't possibly have known, and he initiated us all in the countless mysteries revealed to him by voices from beyond the grave. He was a fabulous storyteller. He forever enticed us with his seemingly inexhaustible supply of spellbinding anecdotes, enchanted us, and made us laugh. Whenever he turned up, always unexpectedly, the ordinary days of our lives suddenly became celebrations. Sasha and I, otherwise always in constant conflict, immediately made a sort of tacit truce.

EVERYONE CALLED HIM FERNANDO, an exotic name suggesting he might have been some kind of Spanish aristocrat. Everyone, that is, except our paternal grandmother, who merely called him Franci. His real name was Franz Scharf.

GRANDMOTHER'S CONTEMPT for Fernando was fierce and inextinguishable. I never understood why—at least not until much later. The reason for her attitude was a dark, impenetrable mystery. It might even have been that Grandmother herself had suppressed it. Whatever the case, she resisted all attempts at reconciliation and never made any secret of her feelings. Of course, she never accused him directly of anything improper or malicious. But on the other hand, whenever the occasion presented itself, she was quick to remind us that he was not really related to us. He'd done nothing more than marry one of her countless cousins. And the least attractive of them all, to boot.

MY GREAT-UNCLE'S CLOSE RELATIONSHIP with us was his way of dealing with his lonely existence. His wife and their teenage daughters, the twins Anci and Manci, had gone billowing up in smoke through tall chimneys.

"It's a very sad thing," he said one day, seeking to catch our eyes, "but that's just how it is."

I remember that day clearly. It was October 24. The pale autumn sunshine filtered through the curtains. Then suddenly the color of the sky shifted from bright to dark. My great-uncle made a little choking sound and began to weep. The air in our apartment was heavy with the smell of burned porridge, one of Grandmother's specialties. Fernando's tears would not stop. His shoulders shook and his eyes were red. You see, that very day was his daughters' birthday. He opened his mouth to speak but some sort of coughing fit interrupted and words failed him.

He never raised the subject after that day. But my twin brother, Sasha, and I understood.

ON ANOTHER OCCASION he confided to us in very measured tones and almost in a whisper that he had loved a woman his whole life long, just one woman, more than anything in the world. We immediately grasped the fact that she couldn't have been his wife because a moment later he added, "And she was the very one I could never have. But her affection for me was enough."

The kitchen door was standing open, and my great-uncle was glancing surreptitiously at Grandmother as she stood before the stove, talking to herself. For some reason I started to grin. Perhaps I understood intuitively that this was his roundabout way of giving us a glimpse of what he carried in his heart.

"*Mein liebes Kind*, don't you laugh—loving her was the only good thing I've ever done in my life. No doubt you think it's strange for an old man like me to cherish a passion. But when everything else falls away, dries up, and disappears, when one is battered and finally overcome by the pitiless onward march of time, the flames of love continue to burn in one's heart until the day one dies."

EVEN THOUGH MY GREAT-UNCLE was not a blood relation, he knew everything about our ancestors, even those from long, long ago. He had an almost sacred devotion to our past. In his eyes the past was the most essential aspect of one's existence. Sometimes while telling us stories about our relatives in medieval times he would beam proudly at us, pat our heads, and sigh out loud, smiling all the while, his eyes fixed on some invisible horizon. Other times he would get annoyed that my twin brother, Sasha, and I were so ignorant of our own history. I especially remember one time when he became extremely upset—he regarded it as absolutely deliberate malice on our part—when he found we weren't familiar with every detail of the sad fate of our distant relative Shoshana Spinoza. She was—even though just a young woman in the first flower

of her youth when she died—one of the greatest pioneers
in the history of physics.

I SOMETIMES have the impression that because he had
lost his twin daughters in the war my great-uncle harbored
an unconscious desire for Sasha and me to rise above our
family history. I am sure now that more than anything else
he believed that our family environment was going to make
us weak, timorous, indecisive, humorless men. He wanted
to exert a covert influence on our souls and push us in a
completely different direction, infusing us with vitality, enterprise, and the will to succeed.

FERNANDO WAS ALWAYS WILLING to fill in the gaps
of our ignorance and to bring back from obscurity some
relative from the dawn of time. He did this by quoting at
length from some document unknown to us or by confidently revealing secrets hidden in the darkest recesses of
the past, secrets he had discovered with the help of a benevolent spirit whispering to him from another dimension.
My great-uncle's words always found ready acceptance with
us; neither Sasha nor I ever questioned the truthfulness of
his tales of our family history. He was an irresistible racon-
teur. We sat there with mouths wide open, full of pride and
wonder at the mythical world he brought to life around him.

As for me, I was so delighted with my great-uncle's stories that I learned them by heart. If he happened to leave
out a detail or a date, I could even correct him.

Only Grandmother, who occasionally grumbled to herself that she had seen through Fernando long ago, found any
occasion to question the reliability of his historical sources.
She sometimes pressed him for various explanations in a
manner that Sasha and I found quite tactless, and he would

appear somewhat hard-pressed. Most of the time he simply sat there, silent, his eyes down, with a smile that suggested a slightly guilty conscience.

But as soon as Grandmother left the room, any trace of concern vanished and the happy, relaxed expression returned to his face. Then he would beckon us over a little closer and in a confiding voice he would say, "Facts are better than fiction. When you know what really happened, you don't need to make up stories. And anyway, a liar is easier to catch than a lame dog."

Spiritualism

MOST FASCINATING of all for us was when my great-uncle, warily at times and always with an air of great mystery, described to us just how he regularly contacted the dead through spiritualists and their medium. The group was called Ad Astra. Their meetings took place every Wednesday in the home of Adalbert Nagyszenti, a Freudian psychologist. Because of his bourgeois background and political views, he had been locked up in a Stalinist re-education camp in northwest Hungary and then formally banned from his profession. At that time he was supporting himself as best he could as a night watchman in a junkyard in a shabby working-class neighborhood. Budapest's most open-minded and imaginative thinkers used to gather at these meetings. Participants sat at a round table in a room with tightly drawn curtains and no mirrors. Lit only by an array of flickering candles, their meetings would generally begin with the reading of some secret Latin texts. This was supposed to prepare the participants to embrace the spirit world. Following those preliminaries the medium, a pale-faced anorexic woman in late middle age, fell into a trance and served as the intermediary for contacts with the world beyond.

MY GREAT-UNCLE FIRST HEARD Ad Astra mentioned in the home of Dr. Kisházy, a charming, unscrupulous general practitioner, who supplemented his meager government salary by charging stiff fees to write prescriptions for absolutely any medicines his patients wanted. He wasn't in the least concerned by the fact that some of the medicines might be deadly poisons. He conducted his life according to the firm principle that mankind could not banish disease and make the world a better place; the only approach was to deal with increasing surplus population. It was evident therefore that Dr. Kisházy was no Florence Nightingale when it came to the seriously ill. On the other hand, his eyes could fill with tears when he heard selections from the poetry of Dante, and his face lit up with unconcealed delight at a glass of delicious Tokay. He made no secret of the fact that he was more concerned with his white wines than with the health of his patients. Even blindfolded, with the very first sip he could identify every variety of Riesling from the Siófok region.

For some unknown reason my great-uncle had a boundless respect for Dr. Kisházy and regularly sought his advice. He confided to Kisházy that thoughts of his dear dead daughters had been haunting him more than ever. He still found it increasingly difficult to reconcile himself to the arbitrary injustice that cuts some lives so short that they are snatched from this world before they reach adulthood. He also said that the powerful pills he had been taking for years were no longer holding his demons at bay. Every night he had nightmares—he usually saw his daughters burning alive in the enormous oven of a crematorium. The doctor advised him that his abysmal mental condition couldn't be relieved with stronger pills. He suggested instead a visit to the company of spiritualists led by his brother-in-law. He thought that direct contact with the dead girls would liberate Fernando's grieving heart from his sunken chest and allow it to fly as free as the autumn leaves that blew down the boulevards of Budapest. Kisházy promised to provide a letter of introduction. At first my great-uncle was reluctant because he did not believe in an afterlife and saw no reason to attend a séance. But the nightmares persisted, and he had a profound desire to know what had happened to his daughters.

ONE WEDNESDAY EVENING my great-uncle somewhat unwillingly turned his steps toward Adalbert Nagyszenti's apartment. Dressed in a suit of Scottish plaid, the psychoanalyst received him in the hall and immediately invited him into the adjacent room where five individuals were already seated at a round table. My great-uncle was directed to the chair next to the medium. She was already speaking some indecipherable gibberish, obviously in a trance. The séance had clearly been under way for some time. In the gloom Fernando found it difficult to make out the faces of the others, but he quickly understood that the distinguished elderly gentleman across from him was seeking contact with his only son, feared to have perished sometime in the late 1940s in a labor camp in Kolyma, in northern Siberia. Fernando knew Kolyma all too well and he was just as well-acquainted with suffering and with death. He felt a cramp in his intestines when he heard Joseph Stalin's name. A silence fell over the room. After a few minutes the host asked my great-uncle in a low voice whom he wished to contact. Fernando whispered, "My daughters," but he did not specify their names. The medium appeared to sink ever deeper into her trance. She tapped her bony fingers on the tabletop in a curious rhythm. That was her way of summoning the assistance of any spirits willing to locate their guest's daughters on the other side. She repeated her appeal several times, but no matter how often she tried, she was unable to contact Fernando's daughters. Half an hour went by. This outcome was as discouraging to him as it could be. The experience merely confirmed my great-uncle's suspicion that spiritualism was nothing but the clever manipulation of credulous fools to make them believe they could speak with their dear departed ones. He was about to stand up to leave when behind him he heard a soft, distant voice. "Anci and Manci are involved elsewhere." Fernando's expression did not change, since he was absolutely sure that this was a farce. The others in the room looked puzzled, and even the experienced medium opened her eyes in surprise.

Then the voice added, "The girls are busy reading Captain Nemo's adventures. But they send their greetings to their father. I am Shoshana Spinoza. If the young ladies' papa wishes to know more about their existence on the other side, I will be happy to answer his questions at our next meeting."

My great-uncle's jaw dropped and he sat there gaping. This was extraordinary. More than just extraordinary. This could not possibly be a deception. He saw that his distrust of spiritualism had been unjustified, for no one in that room knew the girls' names or the fact that his last birthday present to them had been Jules Verne's *Twenty Thousand*

Leagues Under the Sea. The evidence was clear and unmistakable. This was really a contact with the other side.

After the séance with Ad Astra, Fernando went home. The clock struck midnight just as he stepped into his small apartment. He sat on his unmade bed and couldn't stop thinking of Shoshana Spinoza and her report from the spirit world. After a while he leaned over to take off his shoes and noticed a newspaper lying under the bed. He picked it up and a sudden chill went through him. This was incredible. The article on the page before him was describing the American atomic submarine *Nautilus* and its maiden voyage beneath the North Pole. It was written by a journalist named Hannah Sós-Szipoa. It was immediately evident to my great-uncle that Hannah Sós-Szipoa was an anagram of Shoshana Spinoza. He felt the newspaper slip from his hands and then heard someone breathing heavily behind him. For a moment he was startled. His whole body began to tremble and he didn't dare turn around—not because he feared evil consequences or harm inflicted from someone standing behind him but because he was seized by the fear that he was going mad. Then, just as quickly, he realized that this was not madness but rather the awareness that a new world had opened itself, a world beyond this one, a world that his reason had long resisted, a world where he would become a different person. That didn't mean a new being was about to come creeping out from within him like a butterfly emerging from a cocoon, but rather in order to understand the workings of that new world he would have to see his life and existence in a new light.

That was how mysticism came into Fernando's life. He was so influenced by that evening's experiences that he, the born skeptic who was familiar with the Iliad of dialectical materialism, surrendered to a belief in the immortality of the soul and the inexplicable ability of human beings to communicate after death. And everywhere he went—not just at home with us but out in the park where people were playing chess, on buses and trains, in Dr. Kisházy's waiting room, everywhere—my great-uncle found willing victims upon whom to inflict his passionate and eloquent descriptions of life on the other side of the grave.

SHOSHANA RELATED much more to him about our extended family, about our ancestors, and even about my great-uncle's daughters. She also revealed to Fernando astonishing things about the origins of the universe and the gods present at the beginning of it all. She spoke of the times when the earth was still an empty wasteland and described in great detail all six of the worlds that had perished before the making of the seventh—our own, the last, perfect creation. She also explained to him the number seven, the holiest and most secret of all numbers, as well as its mystic influence upon this seventh creation. In our own universe, she told him, everything is ordered according to the principle of seven: days of the week, colors, celestial spheres, angels, and affections of the heart.

Our great-uncle's accounts of Shoshana's revelations were not always consistent and in fact were often contradictory. Once, after Grandmother had cornered him on that score, he told us that those inconsistencies arose because he was not permitted to reveal everything he knew. He had taken a sort of vow of silence in the company of spiritualists. That mattered little to us. All of the stories about our distant relative Shoshana Spinoza enchanted us, no matter how enigmatic they were at times.

The Mystery of Eternal Return

MY VERY FIRST mystical experience was linked to Shoshana Spinoza. One Wednesday evening when I was six years old, just seven days before Christmas—or perhaps I was seven and there were six days left before we got our Christmas presents, I'm not sure which—in any case, one Wednesday evening during the séance Shoshana Spinoza explained to my great-uncle the mystery of eternal return. He could hardly contain his excitement. The very next afternoon he revealed the mystery to us. He was enormously pleased to describe it. Everyone but Grandmother was captivated by his account. Her attention was perfunctory at best. I was just as fascinated as the others, even though I was too small to understand very much of it, particularly since my German wasn't very good. My great-uncle often would break into German in his more emotional moments. But I didn't ask any questions. I just smiled and pretended to be as excited as everyone else.

We would hear his account of that great mystery many more times. My great-uncle loved to describe it, always with as much enthusiasm as if he were talking about it for the very first time.

And what, exactly, is the eternal mystery of return?

"Nietzsche was wrong," Fernando explained to us, "because he thought that one day everything would repeat itself just as we lived through it before, and the cycle would continue perpetually. This would mean that Hitler and Stalin would return to the scene again and again, and for all eternity they would be murdering the innocent. But Shoshana puts the mystery of eternal return in a completely different light. She says that in a fully realized universe, a human being will always have the possibility of a new life, a life he can shape not according to the events of his former life but as it should have played out. That's why individuals return to this earth, time after time, and they always have the possibility of a full new life, one time in a given physical body and the next time in another. In other words, everyone lives many different human lives."

Did I believe that?

Of course I did. I certainly didn't have the faintest idea who "Nietzsche" was or what he had claimed. But every word from my great-uncle's lips was pure truth for me. It never occurred to me to challenge even the slightest detail of what he told us. After all, he was the male role model who provided me with the most valuable lessons and insights of my early childhood.

And besides, who can prove that Nietzsche was correct and that the mystery of eternal return isn't the same as the principle of reincarnation?

Piss-Baruch

AFTER REVEALING THE MYSTERY of eternal return, my great-uncle turned to me and placed his hand on my forehead. His voice was warm with excitement as he told me Shoshana Spinoza had mentioned that in an earlier life I had been our ancestor Baruch. My brother, Sasha, listened intently. I saw at once that he was jealous. Sasha was always envious of me when we were little. Even though we were twins, as alike as peas in a pod, we were completely different. Because of our differences we were torments to each other from the first, and later on we were real dangers to each other.

Fernando might simply have been making it up. But the conviction of his expression and the approving tone of his voice gave me a delightfully agreeable feeling. My knees began to tremble and my spirit was flooded with the mystery of it. I suddenly felt weightless and it was as if Baruch was present in my tissues, in my blood, and in my heart.

IN A DREAM later that night I was our ancestor Baruch, lifting King Afonso Henrique's heavy sword high over the battlefield of Galicia. I terrified the enemy soldiers; they knelt trembling before me, begging for mercy. Proud Portuguese knights stood in awe of my strength, and I relished the sweet taste of triumphant victory. A wave of warmth flooded over me.

I opened my eyes and realized I had wet the bed. My heart began to pound and I was ashamed and aghast. Sasha woke up right away. He turned on the light and saw that the bed was wet. He got furiously angry and called me "piss-Baruch," a son of a bitch, a filthy pig, and an asshole. Then he spat right in my face. As the gob of white slime went gliding down my left cheek, Sasha threatened to beat me for getting his part of the bed wet. He said he would tell everyone he knew that I had pissed all over myself. All of my friends would be disgusted and no one would ever want to play with me again. I was completely humiliated.

That moment remains forever engraved in my memory. Sasha's tongue-lashing still resounds in my ears. I can hear every word and see the scorn and mockery in his face. My brother never knew how much power his words had over me. For years afterward I was tormented by the terrifying thought that Sasha would talk about it, hurting me, condemning me, and scorning me so I would lose all my friends and wind up an outcast, doomed for all time to a life of isolation.

Even now, just putting it down on paper, I still shudder at that prospect.

Kennedy's Assassination

MY PATERNAL GRANDMOTHER was always harassing my grandfather with her questions. Most of the time she wanted to know whether he was listening and paying attention to what she was telling him. Grandfather disliked Grandmother. He had disliked her throughout their forty-five years of joyless marriage. As far as he was concerned, they were two prisoners sentenced to be chained together in purgatory as long as they lived. He brooded from time to time over the brief, irrepressible intoxication of passionate love. What might have happened if only he hadn't met that beautiful young woman in the red polka-dot dress on a cruise up the Danube on a warm summer Sunday in 1918? He was sure that things would have been far better for him. He would have been spared from so many miserable quarrels, so many sorrowful looks, and so many insults. But now it was too late. That's why he always replied, sullen as a scullery maid, that he wasn't the least interested in anything she had to say. Grandmother, for her part, wouldn't take that for an answer. Since she came from tough old stock, folks whom it was useless to contradict, she always doggedly repeated her question. Her gabbling got on his nerves. Grandmother was a daily source of annoyance and irritation to Grandfather.

WHERE WERE YOU when Kennedy was assassinated? Almost everyone who was at least ten years old in November

1963 can tell you today what he was doing when he heard
the news about the death of the American president.

I was in the bedroom, sitting on a chair next to my grandfather. He was bedridden because he was having chest
pains. We were listening to the radio. The Vienna Philhar-
monic under the direction of Willi Boskovsky was playing
Franz Liszt's Hungarian Rhapsody. The program was suddenly interrupted by the dramatic news from Dallas.

I attached no importance to the assassination of the
American president. But Grandfather had a surprised and
obviously frightened look in his eyes. He clasped his chest.

"Is something wrong, Grandfather?" I said. "What hurts?"

"Life," he replied without hesitation. "Life hurts."

A COUPLE OF MONTHS later I discussed that moment
with my great-uncle. He dismissed the notion that Grandfather had been affected by Kennedy's death. After all, they
didn't know each other.

Instead he gave me an inspired, knowledgeable, and fascinating lecture on how a reading of the life lines on a person's hand can reveal his fate as well as that of his family,
since everything is written plainly on the palm of the hand.
There was a whole science to it, he asserted; its significance
and the prospects of predicting the future were getting
greater with every passing day.

He concluded, therefore, that at the very moment that
Grandfather heard the news on the radio about Kennedy's
assassination, he had glimpsed in his palm the very day and
hour of his own death.

"But it wasn't his own approaching death, or the prospect
of it, that depressed him so much," Fernando explained.
"Instead, he was affected by the horrible notion that life is
meaningless if the death of the fragile physical body also

means the obliteration of the past, the present, and the future, consciousness and intuition, in sum, everything that constitutes the most intimate essence of a man's being."

Utopias and Family Heritage

GRANDFATHER WAS NOT SATISFIED with his life, but he wasn't in the habit of complaining about it. Of course, his views about life were anything but optimistic. Behind his words sometimes one could glimpse a view of the world as pitch-black and fear-ridden as the perspectives of Kafka and Beckett.

"The most beautiful utopias," he would say, summing up the experience of a lifetime, "should be left on the drawing boards. Any attempt to construct them in the real world, unfortunately, tends to transform itself quickly into the immediate opposite."

But Grandfather found it unbecoming to pity himself. "Any idiot at all is capable of feeling that his life has been a disaster," he would often say.

The only time I ever heard him complain about his own circumstances was after hearing that on that chilly November day Kennedy's brains had wound up all over Jackie's dress. The radio went back to its broadcast of Liszt's Hungarian Rhapsody. Grandfather climbed out of bed, adjusted his truss, went to the wardrobe, and took out a battered suitcase full of handwritten notes and old documents. He said in an offhand manner that he hoped I would read them someday. I interpreted that to mean sometime after his death. Affecting an indifferent tone to conceal his unhappiness, Grandfather added that he regretted many of the choices he had made in life, but his only real disappointment was that he had not inherited his own grandfather's enormous nose.

IN OUR FAMILY the potential of inheriting an unusually large nose is written in our genes. This inherited trait has usually revealed itself in one person of every generation. Although the nose is frankly grotesque, the child born with it is considered to be destiny's favored child. These children have always been unusually fortunate and successful in whatever they undertook. The nose brought luck to those who possessed it. Curiously enough, however, they have all died in tragic circumstances.

The Will

A WEEK AFTER Grandfather died, the whole family assembled in our house for the reading of his will. It was the first time in many years that they had seen one another. My father and his sister, Aunt Ilona, had long been feuding, and she had put a huge distance between herself and the rest of the family. His brother, Uncle Carlo, had fled Hungary during the people's uprising of 1956—when for a couple of days armed gangs had ruled the streets, hunting down communists, and violence and blood-letting were everyday events within the walls of Budapest—because he was afraid that someone in the crowd would recognize him and a vengeful mob would lynch him because he had been with the State Protection Authority, the AVH. In fact, more than that—he had been a senior official of the secret police and had tortured and executed with his bare hands people whom the Rákosi regime had labeled as fascists and war criminals.

————

THE MOOD was expectant. It was more like a christening than a memorial service for a beloved family member. My mother served coffee and pastries from Gerbeaud's.

Everyone was pleased at the treat of being able to consume those delicate, expensive baked goods during a time of shortages.

That day the pastry chef must have outdone himself, for Uncle Carlo, who lived in Vienna and could enjoy the real thing at Sacher's, declared with the certainty of a self-proclaimed connoisseur that he was convinced that Gerbeaud produced the best Sacher tort in the world. And he added that he took consolation in the fact that the communists, who had effectively laid waste to the country, had not succeeded in ruining the renowned Hungarian tradition of superb pastry making. Everyone laughed, except for Grandmother, who had never appreciated her youngest son's sense of humor. We children joined in, even though we had never known anything else. We rarely had sweets in our home. That was only the second time in my life that I had been fortunate enough to taste the divine goodness of Gerbeaud's pastries, for they were prohibitively expensive.

The lighthearted atmosphere turned suddenly tense when the time came to attend to Grandfather's last wishes. Everyone stared at my father, who in his newly assumed role as patriarch of the clan slowly opened the envelope containing the will. Aunt Ilona and Uncle Carlo occasionally turned to glance furtively at Grandmother where she was sitting at the back of the assembly. She seemed ill at ease. She responded with a disdainful sniff to everything and openly showed her dissatisfaction with the gathering. The circumstances had probably disconcerted her, above all the fact Grandfather had never let her know that he had left a will in my father's safekeeping.

It was all there, written out on a yellowing sheet of paper: who would inherit what from Grandfather's meager possessions, along with his desires concerning his burial. The will consisted of six lines and a short postscript in which he asked our forgiveness for having left so little.

His clothes and shoes were to be burned. His wristwatch, the only item of value in his possession, went to my brother, Sasha. He left to me the worn little suitcase stuffed with all sorts of papers. He wrote that he had often wanted to give his wedding band back to Grandmother and now she could finally have it. Last but not least, he stressed his wish not to end up in the Jewish cemetery. He no longer wanted to be a Jew once he was dead.

Father put down the will. For several moments no one said a word. It was obvious that my father and his siblings were disappointed. Not because Grandfather had left them nothing but because he had not even mentioned them. This opened old wounds and old grievances surfaced. The knowledge that their father had not loved them was a demon before which Grandfather's children were defenseless. It loomed perpetually before them.

My father's face showed not a trace of emotion; he was a master of deadpan expression. Uncle Carlo rose, pushed back his chair, took a couple of steps forward, stood stockstill, looked around the room, and declared that anyway it was worth it all to come home to Hungary after eight years in exile to enjoy Gerbeaud's delicate little pastries. Aunt Ilona found it more difficult to master her emotions. She began to babble something about the fact that her only memories of her father were that he was always scolding, threatening, and mocking his children—but then she bit her lip and fell silent. Then she gathered herself and drank a glass of water to calm her pulse and regain her composure. "Life is hard," she declared in a melancholy tone. "But there's no reason to make a drama of it. In any case, that will is practically meaningless."

TO A CERTAIN EXTENT Aunt Ilona was right. Grandfather's will turned out to be superfluous. Fate had always handled Grandfather roughly and once again it proved contrary to his wishes.

Grandmother had already sold his clothes at a nearby flea market the same day that he died. Grandfather had promised his pocket watch both to Sasha and to me. He would often whisper the same thing to one or the other: "You are the best young man. You'll inherit the gold Doxa." It therefore seemed to me entirely appropriate that Sasha never got it because Grandmother promptly pawned the watch along with the wedding band. And she just as quickly got rid of the claim check, since she felt no obligation to redeem them.

Nor could Grandfather's last wish be fulfilled because on the day after his death he had been buried in the very back of the Jewish cemetery where Grandmother had sought out the least expensive plot.

The Suitcase

THE UPSHOT of it all was that I was the only one to inherit anything from Grandfather. I was in no hurry to open the little suitcase. I thought I knew what it contained. From time to time I'd seen Grandfather writing in a blue note-book, but his scribblings were of no interest to me.

My father took charge of the suitcase, and it stood untouched for thirty years. After the death of my mother and shortly before he took his own life, Father turned the suitcase over to me. I opened it and realized that for all those years I'd been mistaken.

The case didn't contain Grandfather's notes. It was packed with all sorts of historical documents about the Spinoza family, many of them difficult to decipher and all of it impossible to evaluate. Here in a heap I found letters, diaries written hundreds of years apart, birth certificates, wills, contracts, papers involving real estate, and masses of unsorted papers. At the very bottom of all these documents was a book bound in a mottled brown cover. It turned out to be the secret work of my distant ancestor, the philosopher Benjamin Spinoza: *The Elixir of Immortality*.

MORE THAN HALF of the pages in Grandfather's blue notebook had been torn out. The only remaining note left there read:

> *How can one deal with the past, with all of those things that fade and slip away? Memories betray us by disappearing in time, becoming less and less distinct, more and more diffuse and transparent. Sometimes memories assume lives of their own; they turn into fantasies that begin to move, spreading themselves out in tastes and colors and odors, all the signs recognized by our senses, and then from the past they create a completely different reality, a past that never existed but even so lives on in distinct images, perhaps even more distinct than the real memories.*

What Is Truth?

MY NAME IS ARI. I am the last of the Spinoza family.
Our family tree has had few male branches and when I
quietly lapse into my final slumber only a few months from
now, according to the prognosis of my doctor, that family
saga will reach its well-deserved end. I am lying here in a
hospital bed; my fate is sealed and my memories are besieg-
ing me. All those memories that I thought had faded away,
slipped off, and disappeared over the course of time have
set themselves in motion again; they take on a life of their
own, and out of them the past comes blooming, our confusing, ambiguous past.

JUST HOW is our past confusing and ambiguous? Let me
offer an immediate example: How did the philosopher Benjamin Spinoza die?

   Immanuel Kant asserts in his early work *Dreams of a
Spirit-Seer* that Spinoza hanged himself from an apple
tree. Bertrand Russell is of the opinion that he died after
breaking his hip, and Isaiah Berlin writes in a letter to
an Israeli colleague that he drowned in the North Sea.
Marx and Engels maintain that he died in prison. Lenin
says the same but adds that the Inquisition tortured him
to death.

   Which of these thinkers knew the truth?

"TRUTH!" MY GREAT-UNCLE used to say. "The truth is
that there has never been a single truth. Many truths exist.
Those truths contradict one another, reflect one another,
challenge one another, and ignore one another."

———

TO TELL the truth, who is so certain as to assert and prove that any of those thinkers was wrong, that all of their versions didn't happen simultaneously, and that Benjamin didn't die at the same time in all those different ways?

Who can guarantee that history is always unique and always has a single meaning?

TWO

The Personal Physician

A Comet with Two Tails

THERE WAS A FAMILY legend my twin brother, Sasha, and I loved when we were small, back when the world still seemed so open, challenging, and complex and I could regard it with the optimistic eyes of a child. The reason I never tired of hearing the legend was that my great-uncle was such a superb storyteller. With a few well-chosen words and dramatic gestures he could conjure up all of the medieval history of the Iberian Peninsula with its bloody battles, cruel rulers, hypocritical priests, and conspiring noblemen. According to the legend he used to bring to life for us, the far distant past of our lineage, the history of the Spinoza family, began thirty-six generations ago in the provincial town of Espinosa, situated in the region of León near Burgos in Spain. It was an isolated place sunk in its feudal subjugation.

THE RABBI OF ESPINOSA was Judah Halevy. He had dark, intelligent eyes and delicate features. His hands were smooth and shapely like those of most of the Lord's servants, since instead of doing physical labor, he devoted himself to tireless study of the Holy Scripture. He had great knowledge, so it was not in vain that he had spent countless days leaning over a rickety desk in studies that had left him with the bent back of a much older man. The Jews of Espinosa and the nearby villages loved him, not only for his wisdom but also and just as much for his wonderful sense of humor. He was always joking with everyone; he cajoled the poor and the sick into laughing with him and forgetting their afflictions, if only for a moment. Everyone could see that he had an optimistic view of life and trustingly saw the world as the cradle of all goodness.

The rabbi's wife, Judith, was the daughter of a shoemaker, a man who was hard of hearing and had only two fingers on his right hand. He died of dysentery at an early age and left nothing behind except the poetic sound of his Gallic last name: de Narbonne. But it did not matter to Judah that Judith brought no dowry with her; he married her because he was deeply in love. Many were surprised by this, not only because everyone had thought he would marry the daughter of the city's richest merchant but even more because in those days and in that part of the world love was virtually unknown and certainly not understood.

Judah and Judith resembled each other. There was every indication of harmony between them, an uncanny ability to follow each other's thoughts and to surrender to the same impulses. They frequently joined hands across the table, rubbing fingertips for the simple pleasure of touching. It was evident to them that they belonged together; this was the natural order of things.

Judah would say, "Part of my inner self is within Judith and the other part wanted to join it."

THE SECOND SUMMER after their wedding Judith became pregnant. In the spring she gave birth to a daughter whom they named Edita. The girl had a lopsided skull and died four days later. The next year a son was born to them. He survived only four days. Judith wept and would not be consoled. Judah sought to encourage her with optimistic anecdotes from the Torah.

In their fifth year together she again gave birth to a son. At the very moment he took his first breath and noisily greeted life, she breathed her last.

"She bled to death," the midwife explained. The woman was experienced in birthing but that morning her knowledge was of no use.

Judah turned pale, broke into a cold sweat, and became agitated when he heard that Judith was dead. He didn't know what to do—whether to weep over the loss of his wife or laugh in joy over the wonderful grace that had been granted to him, a son at last.

"My beloved wife is gone," he muttered, almost inaudibly. "She who was the very best creature in the world. I will never again see her beautiful face." He lifted his eyes to the heavens and raised his voice. "Oh, my God, what have I done to offend? Why do you punish me so severely? Why have you taken Judith from me?"

Heaven did not reply. Judah knew that his questions would never be answered. But he understood the mystery of silence—wherever the Almighty is present, absolute silence reigns, a blessed light and eternal stillness. But in that hour he wished more than anything in the world to receive an answer.

THE MIDWIFE brought him the newborn child, a boy as hairy as a bear cub. Judah looked doubtfully at him and said nothing. The woman clearly could read his thoughts, for she immediately sought to offer him a crumb of comfort by reminding him of the comet that had appeared in the sky the night before.

"The child was born with hair covering his whole body," she said, "and I hardly need remind the dear rabbi of what is written in our holy books. Those who are born hairy will achieve great things in life. The comet is a witness that the rabbi's offspring will serve a king."

Judah inspected the child and discovered to his alarm that the tiny thing had an inconceivably large nose. "Poor boy," he sighed. Fearing that there might be something wrong with the child, he examined him anxiously. But he found nothing disquieting other than the large quantity of hair and the gigantic nose.

At this, the midwife uttered a phrase, perhaps only to be kind, but since the wise woman knew how to use the simplest words to express great things, it gave the rabbi the sensation that he had just witnessed a miracle: "The Almighty has given you the greatest of all gifts, a well-formed son."

Judah changed his tone. "My darling boy, how handsome you are. Dear God, I am so thankful that you have given me such a splendid little boy. Your name will be Baruch, the blessed," he said and burst into tears.

THE NIGHT BEFORE Baruch Halevy was born—in the year 1129—the October skies had been lit up by a comet with two tails. It rolled like a blue flame across southern Europe. People fell to their knees and prayed to God. Dogs barked, women began to menstruate, ceilings collapsed, roosters laid eggs, and rats turned on one another. A prominent Roman bishop saw terrifying figures approaching across the vault of heaven and thought he was witnessing the arrival of the four horsemen of the apocalypse bringing war, hunger, plague, and death. The bishop's hair turned white and he was struck dumb. They locked him away in the madhouse.

In the autumn of his age, in the still moments of the early morning, Baruch thought he heard a voice whispering to him that the two-tailed comet was an augury of the moment that his family was born.

The Conquest of Lisbon

AT THREE in the afternoon on October 24, 1147, the muezzin raised his harsh voice for the last time to make the call to prayer from Lisbon's largest mosque: *"Allahu akbar."* The muezzin never completed the summons, for a zealous crusader from the Anglo-Norman forces rushed up the steps of the minaret and abruptly hewed off the elderly Arab's head. That moment marked the end of the bloody four-month-long siege of the city. The Moors surrendered unconditionally. Catholicism was victorious. The heralds proclaimed that all soldiers were granted the right to the spoils of war according to their rank except for those items reserved for King Afonso Henriques, the conqueror of Lisbon. Shouts of joy rang out over the whole city. A new kingdom was being born.

These events were narrated by Osbernus, the Latin chronicler who assembled his writings under the title *The Conquest of Lisbon.*

My great-uncle told Sasha and me that Osbernus was an English priest. He ascribed to the Englishman a number of qualities, all of which were unsavory except for one. But the man's positive quality figures in another story I will tell later. Despite his foreign origins Osbernus had a place of honor in the Portuguese court because he was clever and succeeded in flattering Afonso Henriques with countless songs celebrating kingly heroism, thereby winning his favor. The priest was extremely reserved about his own background.

Instead of boasting of his high-placed patrons as was the custom of the time, he conducted himself so as to suggest that he had secret links with the powers in London.

Fernando said Osbernus's accounts of the conquest of Lisbon were bombastic and exaggerated, deliberately portraying the victory in epic heroic style. He said the English priest gave a fraudulent account of the nature of the crusaders. His chronicles portrayed them as courageous, good-hearted, and just men battling to uphold Christian teachings, when in fact they were treacherous and ready to murder anyone on the slightest pretext, even for a scrap of meat.

"The reconquest of the Iberian Peninsula from the Moors was not the struggle of an affectionate, peace-loving Christendom against barbarous Islam," my great-uncle emphasized to us. "It was a pure rampage, aimed at butchering the Moors, wiping out their culture, and stealing their riches."

Nor did my great-uncle mince his words when he spoke of Afonso Henriques, the founder of Portugal and its first king, whom he called a bloodthirsty tyrant. To excite Sasha and me—he knew well that Grandmother didn't like to have the subject discussed and for that very reason we would listen with even closer attention—he sometimes described to us the refined methods of torture the king used upon his people. I almost could not endure the thought that even loyal supporters were slowly tortured to death as if they were sworn enemies. Fernando spoke so knowledgeably and with such feeling—or perhaps it was because of the feverish look in his eyes—that when I was little I believed he had come face-to-face with Afonso Henriques and had nearly perished in the darkness of the royal castle's keep.

Many years later when I came to understand things a bit better, I realized that my great-uncle couldn't possibly have read Osbernus's account, because the first translation from Latin into another language was not made until a couple of years after Fernando's death.

The Promise of Moses

A YEAR AFTER the conquest of Lisbon the rabbi's son, Baruch Halevy, saw one of the most remarkable sights of his young life. One afternoon he sat down to rest beneath a cypress tree next to the main road where it stretched out empty in the burning sun. He drowsed off and after a time was awakened by a fly crawling over his face. He caught sight of an old wanderer trudging toward him from the direction of Salamanca. The man walked slowly, leaning over so far that he was bent almost double. He supported himself with a branch used as a staff and dragged his feet. His face was covered with dust and his white beard was blown by the wind. Under his left arm he carried two heavy stone tablets.

Baruch lifted a hand in greeting. The old wanderer paused, standing only a few feet away from him. Baruch felt his skin begin to prickle as the ancient one looked steadily at him. The tramp inspected the young man's timid, earnest, almost sorrowful face, as if to make sure that he was the right person.

Then he asked, "Are you Baruch, the son of Rabbi Judah the blessed?"

Baruch nodded in reply.

"Listen carefully to what I have to tell you," the man said. He leaned forward and thrust his deeply furrowed face right into that of the young man.

Baruch felt the warm breath of the ancient wanderer and looked deep into his dark bottomless eyes.

"I am Moses, prophet of the Jews. I come back to earth each thousand years to proclaim the commandments of the Lord. It makes no difference whether you are a believer or not. You have only to follow my instructions. Tomorrow you must leave your father's house and begin a journey toward the west. The Lord's will is that you should encounter the wide world. Your journey will be lengthy, and many trials await you along the way. But you will overcome them all. You have only to keep your part of the contract and the Lord will keep his. You are wondering, of course, what you are supposed to do. You are to keep the commandments engraved on my stone tablets, live according to them, and establish a Jewish community from which many great men and women will go forth and conquer every corner of the world. One day you will discover the great secret that humanity has been seeking since the beginning of time. That secret shall thenceforth be guarded by your children and your children's children for a thousand years. As long as your descendants comply with their obligations, they will go forth among the peoples of the earth with their heads high, and the Lord will watch over them. But should any one of them fail to respect the Lord's will, your generations will be obliterated from the earth. Do you understand me?"

The ancient man said again, with emphasis, "Do you understand?"

His question prompted the childish impulse in Baruch to answer as he often did, with another question. "What will happen if I refuse to leave my father?"

"You heard my words." The old man's face hardened. Both his voice and his tone were icy and his words took on an air of menace. "If you fail to respect the Lord's will, your generations will be obliterated from the earth, and you will live out the remaining days of your miserable life in Espinosa, blind and childless."

Baruch was perplexed. Was the old man speaking the truth? Should he really believe everything in the curious message he had just heard? It occurred to him that he should ask his father for counsel, for the rabbi always knew what was true and what was false. His father was always ready to set aside trivialities and deliver a sage verdict in any matter of contention.

In his complete innocence Baruch answered, "In any case, first I have to discuss it with my father and hear what he has to say—"

The old man interrupted him sharply. "Neither you nor your offspring may ever speak a single word of this to anyone. Only the eldest son of each generation is to be initiated into the great secret. That is the pledge. The Almighty has now shown you the way. Submit yourself to the will of the Lord."

"But what great mystery is this? I beg you to reveal it to me. Otherwise—"

"You will discover the mystery, just wait and see. You will encounter it when the time is ripe."

The ancient man said nothing more; he continued along his way. It seemed to Baruch that the man was moving along the road slower than a lame turtle. It took a very long time for him to disappear from sight over the far side of the hill.

In the meantime Baruch scarcely dared to breathe. Everything around him lay still and not even the slightest wind was stirring. The heat was unbearable. Suddenly his head began to ache and a throbbing terror crept forth from his insides. He felt confused and his thoughts were distracted. Could that old wanderer carrying the stone tablets really be Moses? Or was he the devil, resident in the fellow's scrawny body and trying to entice him away from his father's house? He took several deep breaths and thought of his father. Baruch had always been a well-behaved son, as obedient as a lamb. Never had he hidden anything from his father, never had he been burdened by any secrets. He felt a strong urge to hurry home and report that remarkable encounter, but he realized that by doing so he would expose his father to great danger. The ancient man's words could be true and all their family would be obliterated from the earth.

As the evening fell, Baruch could find no reason to doubt. He was convinced that the aged one who had addressed him really was Moses. He realized that it would be best for everyone if he obeyed the prophet's instructions and abandoned Espinosa. Earlier in life he had longed to leave his home, to escape the round of strictly defined rituals that made the days seem more and more alike. He was ready to be called forth from the lair of his winter hibernation to leave the house of his father.

He went to bed early that evening and muttered prayers for himself as long as he was able to stay awake. In the middle of the night it seemed to him that the room was filled with dazzling light. Once again Baruch heard the prophet say that he must abandon his home and his descendants would be free men for a thousand years. With that he understood his calling and saw the possibilities of his future so clearly that he could almost touch them.

The Departure

ALTHOUGH BARUCH WAS more apprehensive than ever before in his life, the next morning he went straight to his

father and told him of the remarkable dream that had swept
him away, a vision that he wished more than anything else
to obey. He intended to leave home immediately and take
the road toward the west. When his father asked about the
details of the vision, Baruch flushed red to the tips of his
ears and started stammering. Seized for a moment by the
demon of self-doubt, he was almost ready to change his
mind and stay forever captive in the doldrums of Espinosa,
helpless and bound to his father for life. Trying to summon
his courage, he worriedly stroked the fuzz of his adolescent
chin with the fingers of his right hand. *I must be true to my
life*, he thought. Then he replied, guided by some unknown
power, that the vision entailed a journey to Lisbon.

Judah Halevy earnestly considered his son. He could see
his own young self in the figure of that awkward nineteen-
year-old—a restless young man in the village of Gayonga
standing before his father and declaring, not without a certain
amount of anguish, that he did not want to follow the family
tradition of becoming a tailor. He wanted to become a rabbi
instead, so he would have to leave home to study in Espinosa.
It occurred to Judah that Baruch, always a dreamer interested
in nothing but plants, was completely devoid of useful skills
and had absolutely no knowledge of the wider world. He was
still nothing but a boy with none of the maturity of a young
man on the way to adulthood. The rabbi tried to persuade
his son not to leave, in any case not yet, certainly at least not
until after the Pesach holiday; together they could work out a
future for him. But his arguments fell on deaf ears. Finally he
saw no other choice for his own peace and for the well-being
of his son than to try to accommodate Baruch's wishes.

"If you truly honor the father who all alone has devoted
his life to raising you, then you will stay here in Espinosa,"
Judah told him.

The boy replied, "Father will surely forgive me for letting him down. But I must go away, leave him, and no longer be a burden to him. I know that Father is a patient man; Father's love for me fills my heart and overflows. But I have seen a dazzling light, and I must allow myself to be swept away by that vision to meet my future."

Baruch was astonished by his own words; he had no idea where they had come from. But those words presented themselves to him with amazing ease when he needed them, whenever they had to be there. Nothing he had ever experienced could compare with the expectant clarity and the great sensation of elevated purpose that now enveloped him. Baruch peered intently into his father's face and saw suddenly that his father understood.

A FEW HOURS LATER the rabbi's friends and neighbors assembled at his house for a brief session of prayer. A number of fervent psalms were recited and everyone prayed to the Almighty to look down with fatherly benevolence on this young man and protect him.

His father smoothed Baruch's hair with his palm and enjoined him to remain a good Jew, to observe the Sabbath, and to wear his prayer shawl. He reminded his son that it is not just the skullcap on the head that makes a good Jew. Then Judah recited a short passage in Aramaic from the Talmud and translated the phrases of the centuries-old advice from a learned rabbi to a young man obliged to set out to face life: *Be ready for many difficult trials; but when you demonstrate your charity toward the weak, you need never live in fear of the strong.*

"If someone casts a stone at you, you should respond by offering him bread." Those were the last words Baruch ever heard his father say.

His father bent his wrinkled face to give Baruch a kiss of farewell, embraced him, and held him tight as if he wished never to release him. Baruch felt great pain at this parting, above all as he saw his father's drooping shoulders, his bent back, and his face wet with tears. Even so he felt that he had no choice. His future was set, though for him it was still wrapped in an obscurity as impenetrable as night. He walked away with firm steps and did not pause until he reached the old oak tree on the hill outside the city. There he turned around and cast a last glance at Espinosa. From that vantage point the town looked small and insignificant.

FOR TWENTY DAYS Baruch followed the river toward Lisbon. He made his way through forests of billowing beech trees and leafy valleys filled with the perfume of wildflowers. He crossed bubbling brooks and foaming watercourses. He watched wide-eyed as birds flew between tree trunks flexing their wings, and he scrutinized the beetles and ants busily crossing the mossy ground. He felt a keen curiosity about the fantastic world that presented itself to him, all the time trying to imagine what he might accomplish with his young life. The waters of the river quenched his thirst. As for bread, he purchased it from peasants who were often stubborn and churlish; when they discovered that Baruch was a Jew, they treated him as a disgusting forest monster, shouting to drive him away. Once, in a forest clearing, he tried to shoot a hare and felt unexpected joy when the quick-footed little creature neatly avoided his arrow.

He collected various types of medicinal herbs a neighbor woman had taught him to recognize. She had been like a mother to him; in her own childhood she had traveled around León and Castile with her father, the two of them making their living by selling miracle-working concoctions and medicines. Several times Baruch took wrong turns in the darkness of night and no longer knew exactly where he was. Once he asked a peasant the way to Lisbon; as a practical joke the man sent him in a completely different direction. Baruch was furious when he realized he'd been tricked. But for the most part he experienced a remarkable feeling of freedom.

THE LAST THREE DAYS of his journey were as difficult as a hike up a long steep slope into a strong wind. Baruch arrived in Lisbon exhausted but joyful. His joints ached and his back was stiff, but he quickly forgot his fatigue. The rays of the morning sun pierced the heart of the city, lighting up the towering tops of the ancient palm trees. Umber-colored walls glowed quietly beneath the blue heaven. As Baruch entered the city gate his heart began to race. He saw women on their way back from the market with baskets full of vegetables, plenty of aggressive beggars, a one-legged boy who lay stretched out on the ground, an old man leading a scrawny cow, thin apprentices carrying heavy building stones, and merchants busily haggling with itinerant salesmen; he saw monks, drinkers, and soldiers. Loud curses came ringing out from a blacksmith's shop. The city was teeming with life and seemed at least ten times larger than his hometown.

He felt completely bewildered and scarcely noticed it when he happened to bump into a watchman standing before a house of Moorish aspect. The man responded with a fit of rage, screaming, "You young rascal, who do you think you are?" He demanded an apology and the name of the offender. For a moment Baruch had no answer for him. He stood there speechless and gaped at the increasingly agitated guard who then gave Baruch a push in the chest so violent that he almost fell down. So finally he replied, "Baruch de Espinosa."

At the House of the Ill-Tempered Blacksmith

THAT SAME AFTERNOON Baruch found employment as an assistant to Martes the master blacksmith, feared for his temper but widely respected for his professional ability. No one in the whole country could forge a sword as keen as those he produced.

Living conditions at the smithy were harsh, the work was wearing, and the food was poor. Baruch lived in perpetual fear of the master smith, who often erupted into towering rages and swore oaths so mighty that they made the place reek of sulfur. Martes was a towering, powerful fellow with a black mustache, enormous hands, and—to make things worse—a predilection for anise brandy. When he drank, he would have sudden fits of anger for no apparent reason. He was a scourge to all about him. He would usually pick a scapegoat among his assistants and torment that individual with gibes and abuse for hours on end. Sometimes he would inflict vicious kicks and punches upon his victim.

Baruch had always been overly protected by his father, so he suffered the smithy as if it were a compact fiery hell. Hardest of all was getting used to the animosity and distrust directed at him by the other apprentices. Initially, each time he was subjected to humiliation he assumed it was either because he had failed to understand something or because he had trouble with the Lisbon dialect. He supposed that he was just too sensitive and the other apprentices were not really against him. Eventually, however, he came to see that the others were intensely bothered by his presence at the forge and were treating him as an enemy. Only very rarely would they say anything to him, and then they seemed to relish using hurtful words and making disparaging remarks in his presence. This showed no signs of stopping and no one found it unusual. Baruch kept silent and put up with it, for there was no one to whom he could turn. Especially not the blacksmith, whose decided opinion was that no one at his forge had the right to complain unless his head had been half chopped off.

One of the young men Baruch tried to address told him right to his face that the priest who lived across the street had made all of them swear to shun him because the Jews had crucified Jesus Christ.

"Treat him like a leper," the priest lectured them. "Anyone who comes in contact with a Jew will wind up in hell. Poverty, plague, and immorality—every evil we suffer in this world is the fault of the Jews."

DURING HIS DISMAL TIME in the workshop Baruch's only refuge and consolation was the friendship of an older apprentice. Raimundo had been orphaned as a young boy. His father, a clockmaker who also worked as a gravedigger, had beaten Raimundo's mother to death because she had scandalous love affairs with other men—or so the neighbors said—and he had been obliged to flee to Estremadura. Soon after, he perished in a most unusual fashion, trampled to death by a frightened ox that trapped him against the gate of its pen.

Raimundo believed that God's law decreed that those who spill the blood of others will drown in their own blood. Baruch had no opinion on the subject.

Raimundo was nearsighted and squinted a great deal, a habit that gave him an enigmatic air. He had handsome, delicate features and only a few wisps of beard on his chin. He was as muscular as a bear and had no difficulty lifting stone blocks

weighing more than two hundred pounds. Even so, he was
unusually nimble, and for a lark he could walk on his hands
for thirty feet or more. Baruch was in awe of Raimundo. The
reason for their friendship was the fact that Raimundo never
joined the wolfish howling of the others but instead defended
Baruch against their attacks. Such a response certainly required courage. Raimundo was putting himself at great risk,
for his insistent defense of the Jew was in open defiance of
most of those in the shop. He took their derision upon himself
and became alienated from his former friends.

AT NIGHT when the apprentices were in their bunks in the
unlighted cellar that stank of sweat and urine, Isidoro, the
oldest of them, would entertain the rest with elaborate stories
of his escapades with the most beautiful women of Lisbon.
The apprentices enjoyed his racy accounts, even if the truth
of them was in doubt. They couldn't get enough of his tales.
Only Raimundo and Baruch, sharing a narrow bunk, thought
of anything other than the descriptions of women's bodies
Isidoro used to excite the imaginations of the other apprentices. The two young men felt a strange attraction to each
other; this longing that refused to be controlled overwhelmed
their senses. After they were sure that the others had gone
to sleep, they stroked each other's genitals. Raimundo always
initiated it by taking Baruch's penis in his hands. Baruch willingly accepted his caresses. His friend's tender touch made
him forget the stinking smithy, if only for a brief moment.

They solemnly promised that they would keep this a secret. Neither of them had any idea that Isidoro would often
pretend to be sleeping and would watch them.

ONE DAY it was Raimundo's bad fortune to displease the
blacksmith. He watched alertly as Martes, who had spent

the morning drinking anise brandy with two merchants, came tottering into the smithy and collapsed onto the ground. Raimundo helped the master smith to his feet again. Instead of thanking him, Martes showered him with abuse and declared that by God he knew exactly what was going on at night in the cellar. Then he shouted so all could hear that he was sick of the obscenities of Raimundo and Baruch, and he felt like showing everyone by sticking the heads of the wastrel and the Jew down the sewer and leaving them there, disgraced in their squalor. Raimundo felt humiliated. Although he was as intimidated as the others by the unpredictable blacksmith, his injured pride asserted itself. He told Martes to be quiet, go to bed, and try to sober up. In response the smith sent a heavy hammer flying at his head. Luckily Raimundo was able to duck, so the hammer went whistling harmlessly past him.

That evening when everyone in the workshop had gone to bed, Raimundo whispered into Baruch's ear that he was tired of being treated like a mangy dog. He suggested that the two of them run away from the wicked blacksmith and join the army. Baruch agreed at once, for he was ready to follow his friend to the end of the world. A heavy weight was lifted from them both as they slipped out of the building in the middle of the night and left the blacksmith and the forge behind.

Against Galicia

HAZE STOOD in the morning air. Lisbon lay before them in an undulating, expansive panorama. With their spirits lighter than they'd been for a long time, the friends arrived at the army enlistment office. Raimundo with his impressive physique was immediately accepted, but the officer in charge, a hefty fellow with a threatening air about him, sniffed in derision at Baruch, who was short and frail. The only big thing about him was his nose; that, as if in compensation, was truly gigantic. He was completely unfit to serve as a foot soldier in the proud army of Afonso Henriques.

Baruch felt ill and frightened when he saw he was likely to be separated from his friend. A great deal was at stake for him. He pleaded passionately to be allowed to serve the king. After a time the officer relented. He assigned Baruch to receive rudimentary training as a medical orderly pending the army's march against Galicia.

KING AFONSO HENRIQUES joined his army outside the gates of the city. They were a ragtag bunch, many of whom had volunteered in hopes of reward and promotion. Others came from regions conquered by the king where the male populations were forced to enlist in his service.

Afonso Henriques was forty years old, a true giant almost seven feet tall and inordinately broad in the shoulders. His skin was tanned a deep brown and he had a dark beard and a black mustache with ends that turned up in sharp points. Everyone revered the king and they were all very circumspect in his presence, for it was common knowledge that he was curt, violent of temper, and cruel toward anyone who failed to obey him. When he became angry, which was often, he would pound anyone at all with his fists even for the most trivial offense.

The king took his position on a hilltop and with gestures of his powerful fists and palms admonished his soldiers to silence. He harangued his men for a long time in his strong, piercing voice. With great authority he praised the troops and promised them splendid victories. He was assiduous in spurring on any who might have doubts and in infusing them with courage for what lay before them. When he asked whether his men were willing to sacrifice their lives and limbs for their king, most of them shouted their assent. Even Baruch and Raimundo enthusiastically swore their fealty to Afonso Henriques.

THE FOLLOWING DAY the army began its march against Galicia, the next step in the king's campaign to extend the frontiers of Portugal northward. That night despite his fatigue Baruch lay wide awake in the darkness. He gazed up at the stars of Galicia and for the first time in months had thoughts of his father. He remembered all the Sabbaths he had entirely neglected since leaving home. He heard the neighing of horses and the mumbled words of soldiers talking in their sleep. His heart held neither doubt nor apprehension at the prospect of the next morning's battle, his first experience of combat. He felt a deep certainty that everything would turn out as destiny required. For hours during the course of the night he was graced by the murmuring of ancient owls. Baruch felt that the wise old birds were announcing the dawning of his great day.

On the Battlefield

THE BATTLE BEGAN promptly at nine o'clock that morning on the broad meadow outside the city of Pontevedra. Afonso Henriques relied on the combat skills of his swift cavalry. Sitting high in the saddle on his war stallion, he felt invulnerable. He searched for sight of his army standing in position for attack, but the sun was hidden behind the mountain and a mist hovered like a veil of white over the meadow. Everything seemed strange and distant.

The king drew his new sword. It was a magic sword, one that only the combined force of ten men could lift. Afonso Henriques knew the secrets of his blade; he knew exactly how to hold it so that the leaden weight of it would rest light as a feather upon the hand and the edge would slice cleanly through even the hardest stone. He was not the only one to have this knowledge. The creator of the magic sword, master smith Martes, had often been fairly tipsy at work in the smithy and in that condition he would babble indiscreetly.

OPPOSITE THE PORTUGUESE stood a few sparse groups of Galician foot soldiers in miserable condition. As trumpets sounded the order to attack, Afonso Henriques went galloping toward the enemy, eager to strike terror into the poorly equipped Galicians. Above all he wanted to try the magic power of his new sword. His impulse to ride ahead of his troops proved not terribly prudent, for as he approached the Galician soldiers an arrow struck him in the chest just above the right lung. The king fell from his stallion, breaking a bone and cracking several ribs. He roared, not in pain—for he felt none yet—but in rage. His horse galloped away. Suddenly the mist lifted and the Portuguese troops fell into confusion. The soldiers' courage evaporated when they saw their king on the ground. As if paralyzed, the panic-stricken Portuguese fixed their eyes on the spectacle of a squad of Galician soldiers running toward Afonso Henriques.

In contrast, Baruch immediately perceived the danger and without hesitation raced onto the battlefield to assist the king. Though short of height, he scampered forward and reached the king before the Galicians did. He cast a hasty glance at the enemy soldiers with their obstinate weather-beaten peasant faces. Six of them were coming down upon him, weapons drawn. Baruch took hold of the king's heavy sword, lifted it from the field with a sudden effort, and parried the first Galician blow. The clash of metal was accompanied by a sound like that of a striking clock as he sliced the enemy from top to toe. He killed two more Galicians. The sword caught the first one in the neck muscles just where they connected to his broad shoulders and then it pierced straight through the yielding tissues of the second Galician's torso. The three remaining Galicians were seized by panic and began to run back toward their camp. Baruch made certain that he had put all of his adversaries to flight. At this, a dozen Galician soldiers notched their bows and shot at Baruch, but the arrows fell to the ground short of him. Baruch felt wrapped in a protective power and knew that nothing could hurt him. He lifted the king and carried him to safety.

Afonso Henriques's chest wound made him feverish and caused him dreadful pain. He was bleeding profusely and hovered between life and death. Baruch realized that the Portuguese were standing there like statues. He bellowed at the soldiers an order to attack the enemy and fight for their king. He was astonished by the authority of his own voice. As if to excuse the harshness of his words of command, he added in a lower voice, for he felt pity for the enemy soldiers he knew would certainly die, "Be merciful to the Galicians, for they too are human beings."

Then he made a poultice of leaves carefully chosen from the supply of preserved medicinal herbs he had earlier tucked carefully into his knapsack. With his knife he opened the wound in the king's chest and pressed the dark red petals into it.

AFTER THE GALICIAN SURRENDER, a wagon drove across the battlefield collecting fallen soldiers of the army of Afonso Henriques. The losses of that day amounted to about twenty archers and foot soldiers, a handful of knights, and an insignificant number of horses from the van. For the most part the remains in the wagon consisted of little more than chunks of flesh and rags. On top of them lay a horribly mutilated body, that of the nearsighted Raimundo.

Raimundo's death was a heavy blow for Baruch. Most painful of all was the fact that he had never had the opportunity to say farewell to his friend.

A King's Remembrance

WHEN AFONSO HENRIQUES had regained his forces, his chronicler and retainer, Osbernus, told him of the selfless intervention of the little Jew. As a devout Catholic, the king had no high opinion of the Jews—quite the contrary. He had imbibed with his mother's milk the conviction that those Christ-killers are cowardly and treacherous. All his life Afonso Henriques had spat upon Jews and tortured them. "He who kicks a Jew kicks the devil," he would often say. But now he was confronted with a dilemma. The young Jew was no soldier; he wasn't even a fully developed man. He had no position, no possessions; there was nothing impressive about him; he was nothing. But even so, this same Jew had risked his own life to save that of the king. And the Jew had demonstrated superhuman force when he took up the magic sword and drove off the enemy. Furthermore, he was invulnerable to arrows. And then the Jew had sat next to him, day and night, watching over him and healing his wounds.

Afonso Henriques's experience of a long life on the battlefields had taught him to honor men capable of demonstrating true strength and valor in the face of death. For a moment he entertained the speculation that the little Jew might be a fiend from hell. He discussed the matter with Osbernus. The English priest, who had taken a liking to Baruch and was pleased to have him around, assured the king this was not the case. The king promptly forgot his misgivings. Because he respected valor and appreciated strong, effective action, he resolved to overlook the fact that Baruch was a Jew. The king called for his rescuer and in the presence of his closest retainers praised him for his courage and decisiveness. The little Jew was also granted a generous reward.

Justice Is Done

WHEN THE KING RETURNED in triumph to Lisbon, great crowds of people congregated at the palace to hail him. Afonso Henriques relished the glory and the sweet taste of his power. Soon, however, unpleasant news reached his ears. A trusted servant reported with carefully chosen words that during the ruler's absence Antunes, the court physician, had been casting longing glances at the youngest of the royal mistresses, a Moorish girl of indescribable beauty, and without the slightest inhibition the girl had responded to his wooing. The king cast a doubtful look at the servant. He was reluctant to credit the report, for he knew that the physician, of all people, had to know how much she meant to him, this most favored daughter of the defeated caliph. Afonso Henriques summoned another loyal servant, who duly gave an account of the burning looks and the powerful attractions that had filled the luminous summer evening. He summoned yet another retainer, who also vouched that Antunes and the Moorish girl had conducted themselves improperly. The king was now certain. His nostrils flared, scenting a betrayal that he should have suspected long ago.

THE DECEITFUL CONDUCT of the physician and the royal mistress infuriated Afonso Henriques. And he had cause even more dire than a mere flirtation in his court to fill his heart with wrath. The thing that really set his blood boiling was the matter of Costa and Benvindo.

The brothers were men of matchless skill, bold knights who had performed great feats for the king in many of his wars. In recognition of their services, Afonso Henriques had appointed them to his Privy Council and granted them vast estates outside Mafra, on lands taken from the Moorish enemy. He had rewarded them with showers of gold and raised them from poverty to riches. Endlessly arrogant and avaricious, Costa and Benvindo cut the wages of their knights. Turning bitterly against the unscrupulous brothers, several of the generals brought their grievances to the king. They all expected Afonso Henriques to receive their complaints and reproach the brothers for tarnishing their reputations with greed. But because of the ongoing campaign in Galicia the king felt that the time was not right to punish them.

The king was generally of the opinion that as the ruler he was obliged from time to time to demonstrate his authority without mercy, to terrify his subordinates so that none of them would get the idea a conspiracy might go unpunished if he happened to be away at the wars. He considered Costa and Benvindo too valuable to send to the gallows. That being the case, he decided to have his physician and his mistress executed for high treason. His principal objective was to demonstrate to the rest of the people the inevitable consequences of disloyalty to the king.

Afonso Henriques immediately summoned his council and sent a special convocation to Costa and Benvindo. Then he sent six armed soldiers to fetch the Moorish girl and Antunes to a hearing. The temperature at court immediately rose.

THE YOUNG MISTRESS was impeccably dressed in the fashion of respectable Moorish women of the time. She appeared before the king, bowed deeply to him, and immediately perceived from his stern expression that something had displeased him. When the charges were read out, she stood there petrified, weeping and sobbing, unable to catch her breath and incapable of choking out even a syllable.

Afonso Henrique concluded that by her silence the young woman—her name was Fatima—had confirmed her guilt, for otherwise she would certainly have replied to the accusations. It made no difference whether she had been led astray by the physician or she herself had initiated the flirtation. She was guilty and had to be condemned.

Since Afonso Henriques was an ardent partisan of stern punishments, he had her walled up alive without food or drink behind the stones of a narrow palace hallway. People say that even several centuries later on moonlit nights one could plainly hear Fatima sobbing and weeping through the thick walls.

ANTUNES THE PHYSICIAN did his best to make a good impression. He held himself straight and tall and denied the crime. He could not understand how anyone in the world might have misinterpreted his courteous behavior toward a young woman suffering from serious health problems who had requested his professional opinion.

"These spiteful rumors spread about me by certain individuals are absurd and odious fabrications," he maintained. "There's an evil-minded conspiracy seeking to tarnish my name and to blacken me personally. Such informers should be punished for their mendacity. Your Grace is the noblest man in Portugal. In his wisdom, the King knows very well that he can place no credence in those who spread false rumors."

Afonso Henriques listened, frowning in distaste. He had no illusions about the matter; every feature of Antunes's deceitful face revealed that the physician was lying. Before rendering a formal verdict he turned to the council and fastened his gaze on the brothers Costa and Benvindo. He spoke.

"When a subordinate is disrespectful, lies, steals, lusts after the king's mistress or commits unchastity with her, it is not a sign of insanity. It is a sign of treason, and the punishment for that grave offense is death."

He paused briefly, waiting for any reactions. But no one said a word; they all remained silent. He then commanded the whole court and every member of the council to attend the torture session the following morning, for it would be an unforgettable and highly entertaining experience.

THE BLOOD-SOAKED TORTURE chamber in the cellars of the palace was chilly, dark, and damp, with enormous columns and tiny openings in lieu of windows. The air was filled with evil smells and the atmosphere was oppressive. At one end of the chamber a fire was flickering in a brazier. Around the flames was assembled a group of men, members of the council, some of them in knightly apparel and others in the expensive garments of the nobility. They appeared absorbed in earnest discussion, whispering emphatically to one another. The ladies of the court, robed in somber garb appropriate to the serious occasion, stood along the wall and seemed about to faint with terror.

The chief executioner, a muscular man with a pale face and straggling dark hair, reminded Baruch of an ox—strong, clumsy, and a bit simpleminded. In his dark clothing he radiated menace.

Afonso Henriques sat on a throne by the entrance. With cold calculation he scanned the room and then appeared satisfied. It was clear that nothing would please him more that morning than to see Antunes bleed, scream, and die. A huge mastiff lay growling beside him. To his left, behind a rickety desk, Osbernus the chronicler recorded everything in the chamber as it occurred.

Baruch stood close at the king's right hand, staring at the floor. He dreaded the torture session that lay before them. Nothing in his short life had prepared him to endure the spectacle of torture, and the prospect filled him with deep apprehension. He would forever remember every detail of the proceedings.

The king expected that the sight of the torture chamber would have shaken the serene attitude of his physician, but Antunes still held his head high. Either he was a man of great courage or else he was hoping for a miraculous last-minute reprieve.

Since Afonso Henriques had explicitly ruled out any mercy for such a serious crime, the head executioner began the torture by stabbing out the physician's eyes. The executioner's pasty cheeks became even paler as he set to work. He appeared almost to feel pity for his victim. Antunes's forehead glistened with sweat and a stream of urine darkened his trousers, but he made no sound of complaint as his eyeballs were dug from their sockets.

Then a second executioner proceeded to cut open arteries in the physician's arms. Dark sticky blood was collected in a bowl. The physician's blood seeped out of his scrawny body only very slowly and the torturer had to let more from his thighs to put an end to his life. As this proceeded, those present could hear faint gagging and groaning from deep in the throat of the dying Antunes.

Though it was cold in the cellar, Baruch was bathed in sweat as he witnessed the executioner's craft in action. He almost did not hear the king's command to mix the physician's blood with an herbal mixture to produce a medicine as an antidote to treason.

With a sweeping blow of a sword a third henchman separated the dead physician's head from his body. The head was affixed to the sharp end of a pole and carried away by a platoon of soldiers to be planted on a hill outside Lisbon. Then the king invited all members of the council and the court to the festival hall for a meal of bread, cheese, and wine. The assembly cast themselves upon the food like a pack of wolves.

"This is a fine and tasty meal," commented Afonso Henriques and added with a scornful laugh, "Especially when one's appetite has been whetted with blood."

A Remedy to Prevent Treason

PRODUCING AN HERBAL EXTRACT to forestall treason was an undertaking that required the cleverness of a magician. Baruch was frightened to death. He knew all too well that he lacked both the knowledge and the experience to produce such a potion. He also knew full well the likely consequences of failure: He would be dispatched immediately to the executioners in the cellar of the castle. His experience of the torture chamber provided his imagination plenty of food for thought and cast him into gloom. He dared trust no one, for Osbernus the English priest had warned him that secrets shared often turned into rumors that spread quickly through the court. He took refuge in prayer.

In a large copper vessel he blended the coagulated blood with various herbs he knew to have curative powers. He added two quarts of cold water and stirred the mixture over a low fire with a gentle continuous motion for three days and three nights. He didn't close an eye for the entire period. Once this was accomplished, he tasted the reddish liquid. His cheeks flushed and burned as he swallowed a sip. It was intensely bitter.

BARUCH COULD SCARCELY CONCEAL his nervousness when it was time to present the antidote to treason. Afonso Henriques and his whole council had assembled in the castle's most spacious hall. Leaning against the wall were the brothers Costa and Benvindo, who appeared somewhat uneasy. Osbernus the chronicler was also there. He glanced anxiously at Baruch, well aware of the arbitrary and capricious nature of the king.

Cardinal Berenguer opened the session with the reading of a text about Pope Damasus I, celebrated that day on the calendar of saints. A moment of silent prayer followed. Then it was time for Baruch to offer up the magic herbal remedy.

He had scarcely begun to speak when an impatient Afonso Henriques interrupted him. "I am sure that the whole council agrees that this highly important remedy should be tested by the boldest men among us. Costa and Benvindo, step forward."

The brothers' faces became even more thoughtful. Costa's eyes narrowed to a squint. Benvindo opened his mouth but found no words. They reluctantly approached Baruch and without a word they tasted the liquid. Then they knelt before the king.

A murmur passed through the members of the council. Before anyone could speak, Afonso Henriques ordered the rest of the lords to approach Baruch and to partake. There was a deathly silence. They all knew that they had no choice but to comply.

With trembling hands Baruch gave each member of the Privy Council a spoonful of the herbal extract. It was evident that none of them cared for the bitter taste of it; each grimaced in distaste. But they obediently swallowed the red liquid and knelt before the king.

Once all his subordinates had been so vaccinated against treason, Afonso Henriques took a leather pouch from his belt and tossed it to Baruch. "There you have ten gold coins as reward for your work. From this day forth you will serve as my personal physician. But keep in mind, everything about my physician—not only his medicines but also his expression, his gestures, his clothing, his speech, his gaze, his manner when touching me, everything—must please me."

Such a boon was completely unexpected. Baruch gasped for breath but recovered quickly. He expressed his profound thanks with an eloquence that surprised even him: "I wish to thank His Majesty for the high honor that the king in his boundless kindness has granted to me. I will pray to our Lord that he might safeguard the health of His Majesty and increase His Majesty's glory. Throughout my life I shall in

humblest subjugation, embracing his good counsels, serve
my king. May our Lord always shower his holy grace upon
His Majesty."

Out of the Dark Reaches of History

IN THE MIDDLE of the twelfth century a young Jewish
man emerges from the dark reaches of history and becomes
visible in Lisbon. His name is Baruch de Espinosa. No portrait of him exists, nor is there any chronicle of his life.
Everything that I know of my ancestor of thirty-six generations ago I learned from my great-uncle. He was the one to
reveal to my twin brother, Sasha, and me the fact that Baruch was the private physician of King Afonso Henriques, a
position that gave our Jewish ancestor many privileges virtually unheard of in that era.

In the year 1158 there spread—even far beyond the borders of Portugal—rumors that the king's private physician
Baruch de Espinosa possessed supernatural powers capable
of banishing illness and that his medicines could transform
impotent old men, granting them the virility of young bulls.
Some saw him as a sort of savior sent from heaven in answer to their fervent prayers and pleadings. Some days there
might be hundreds of ailing persons assembled outside the
palace pleading for his help. Many were royal emissaries
from foreign lands who battled for places on the benches
outside his laboratory in hopes of obtaining medicines to
take home with them.

Baruch's various herbal remedies were effective against
all sorts of afflictions, including headaches, persistent bleeding, all kinds of maladies of the bones and joints, kidney

stones, gallstones, cramps, and convulsions. They were frequently used in connection with tooth extractions, and the ladies of the court had a remedy of their own to alleviate menstrual cramps.

ACCORDING TO MY GREAT-UNCLE, Baruch once succeeded—with the help of a concoction of one part valerian, two parts salvia, and blood from the left wing of a white dove—in resuscitating the king's eldest son after the boy had died from eating too many wild chestnuts. My great-uncle insisted that Baruch had succeeded in cultivating a secret herb that so terrified death that it recoiled from the patient.

Our ancestor wrote as many as a dozen treatises about the medicinal qualities of plants. He cataloged in exhaustive detail the characteristics of those he considered most useful. A regular theme in his writings is that nature produces nothing that lasts forever, for only God can create the eternal.

In his later years Baruch devoted many years to the study of chameleons. He found that species of lizard so fascinating and remarkable that he wrote an entire book about its appearance, characteristics, and internal structures, as well as the magical powers associated with the little creature. What he found particularly intriguing was that chameleons not only change color in the proximity of objects of various hues but also do so when they are frightened or feel other emotions.

Paracelsus and Amaral

FOR A COUPLE of months in the fall of 1538, after the hardships of a hearing that obliged him to flee Basel, the alchemist and physician Paracelsus held the chair of Professor of Medicine at the University of Lisbon. He heard by chance of Baruch and his work. An acquaintance, a bald professor of gloomy mien and rotten teeth who lectured in religion and served the Inquisition, advised Paracelsus at that time that the Jew's writings were full of heretical teachings. His warning served only to increase Paracelsus's interest. The fact was that the Swiss was a rebel against conventional scholasticism and was on a quest for new knowledge, especially in the natural sciences and in traditional hermetic knowledge rooted in the Jewish Cabala and in the wisdom of the Egyptians.

Whenever Paracelsus had a few hours free, he would visit the section of the royal library where Baruch's writings were kept, deep in the cellar of the castle. Unfortunately, the rats in the damp cellar had consumed a large part of Baruch's work and some of the treatises were much the worse for wear, so that the alchemist could scarcely make out the contents. He found not the slightest trace of any heresy to offend God or the king. Instead, he brought to light an extensive collection of unique observations of nature, apparently the sole subject and scope of the texts. Paracelsus realized that he had found a veritable treasure trove, untouched by human hands for centuries, the legacy of a pioneer in the study of natural sciences.

The following year while serving as physician to the court of Aragon, Paracelsus wrote to the Holy Office in Lisbon, emphasizing that not even the sternest censor would be able to detect erroneous teachings or anything counter to the holy faith in the writings of Baruch de Espinosa. He emphasized that anyone even slightly acquainted with them would ask whether the author shouldn't receive accolades rather than accusations and be the object of admiration rather than of suspicion.

A few weeks later Paracelsus received in reply a brief letter signed by the chief censor of the Inquisition, Tristan Alonso de Navia. It opened with words of delighted admiration and praise for the work of the Swiss alchemist and physician and concluded with the comment that a discreet silence was the best response to his request, for the totality of writings by Jewish hands had forever been condemned as contrary to the prevailing Catholic world order.

PARACELSUS'S INITIATIVE was a sign of his courage. But my great-uncle was not convinced that the Swiss genius was driven by the purest of motives when he searched the depths of Baruch's work. He believed that Paracelsus not only had taken inspiration there but also had appropriated outright the texts of the royal physician, especially his treatise on the chameleon, thirty pages of which he reproduced word for word in *Philosophiae et Medicinae utriusque compendium* (Basel, 1568) without acknowledging the source.

THERE WERE RUMORS, our great-uncle intimated, that the grandmother of Tristan Alonso de Navia had been a Jew and that in order to conceal that shameful fact the head censor of the Inquisition applied himself with zealous heart and soul to the careful and complete eradication of all traces of the Jews. This might equally have been due to the fact that he was convinced that he had little time left to live. De Navia believed that he had an incurable illness and for that reason he was obsessed with death. He acknowledged this only to his father confessor, a bigoted old priest who pretended to comfort him in his trials but in fact dedicated himself to poisoning the mind of the head censor with stories of the iniquity of the Jews, instilling in him the belief that as a true Catholic he could get to heaven only by supporting their extermination.

THE FORMAL ORDER bearing de Navia's signature and the seal of the Inquisition decreed on April 19, 1540, was clear and unmistakable: *When the sun has set, all Jewish books and writings in Lisbon shall be burned in a bonfire. And the fire will be kept going throughout the night.*

The writings of Baruch de Espinosa stood high on the list of Tristan Alonso de Navia. With mixed alarm and satisfaction he stood in witness as the Jewish physician's work was consumed by flames.

IN OUR OWN DAY my ancestor's name appears nowhere in the body of scientific literature, although he is mentioned in the extensive biography of Afonso Henriques (Lisbon: Bertrand, 1999) written by Diogo Freitas do Amaral, a former foreign minister of Portugal.

That history describes the reign of Portugal's first king as violent and capricious. Amaral provides a lively description of the parlous world of King Afonso Henriques: the moral chaos, the arbitrary decisions, the intrigues, and the bloodlust. He vividly portrays the ill temper of the king and his violence at court. Counselors who advocated moderation in the exercise of power were summarily executed, as were all those who meddled in politics. Whole families were massacred without the slightest hesitation. Those who failed to please the king were usually dispatched by the application of quick-working poisons concocted in Baruch's laboratory.

Amaral writes that even though everyone at court had reason to appreciate Baruch's natural affability and miracle-working medicines, many lived in fear of him.

"The Jews have evil faces," some of them would whisper behind his back. Others commented that Baruch was ready to participate in any evil business at all to please the king, so as to advance his own interests and those of the Jews. A number of the court folk went further, discounting his medical knowledge and seeing him as nothing but a Jewish deviser of poisons.

A Good Jew

ON EASTER MORNING in 1160 Baruch was ordered to accompany the king to church to hear Cardinal Berenguer's sermon. The cardinal ranted at the congregation, a veritable fury, and used fiery phrases to condemn the apostates who had turned their backs on Jesus Christ and sunk themselves in the morass of idleness, irresponsibility, and immorality.

The unctuous sermon about wasted lives awakened Baruch's interest and he listened intently. When Berenguer flung out the Latin words *"Ibi dissipavit substantiam suam, vivendo luxuriose,"* Baruch felt them like a blow. The text was taken from the fifteenth chapter of the Gospel of Saint Luke and dealt with the prodigal son who traveled to a foreign land and "dissipated his patrimony there in riot and luxury." Baruch felt a sharp pang of conscience for the many years he had forgotten about his father and neglected Judaism.

He went to bed early that evening but awoke just after midnight to see a luminous presence standing next to his bed. It was his father who had come to take his farewell; his time on earth was over. He gently touched Baruch's hair; he bade him to remain a good Jew, to keep the Sabbath, and to wear his prayer shawl. Then Rabbi Judah Halevy disappeared as silently as he had come.

Baruch lay sleepless in his bed as the breezes of the spring night wafted into the room through the open window. His thoughts chased one another around and around in his head and it seemed that nothing could rescue him from that night's grinding torment and the sharp lash of his conscience.

Suddenly he remembered the words of Moses:

You are to keep the commandments engraved in my stone tablets, live according to them, and establish a Jewish community from which many great men and women will go forth and conquer every corner of the world. One day you will discover the great secret that humanity has been seeking since the beginning of time. That secret shall thenceforth be guarded by your children and your children's children for a thousand years. As long as your descendants comply with their obligations, they will go forth among the peoples of the earth with their heads high, and the Lord will watch over them. But should any one of them fail to respect the Lord's will, your generations will be obliterated from the earth.

Baruch decided that the next morning in the king's chamber he would ask for permission to study the Talmud in the castle and to keep the Sabbath. He then fell asleep with a clear conscience and slumbered peacefully.

AFONSO HENRIQUES GRANTED to his personal physician the privilege of establishing Lisbon's first community of Jews, under the special protection of the king. In order to observe the Sabbath with a minyan, the religious service requiring a minimum of ten adult Jewish men, Baruch obtained permission to invite a rabbi and five Jewish families from León who either tended humble shops or peddled wares from village to village. He invited Rabbi Mordechai Montefiori and the families Castro, Halevi, Abravanel, Sarfati, and Peralta.

In no time at all there emerged a complicated network of relationships and property linking these families that continually intermarried over the following four hundred years.

Married and Unhappy

RABBI MORDECHAI MONTEFIORI was determined to see Lisbon's Jewish community grow. He put all his energy into persuading Baruch to marry. The rabbi stressed that only within his own family could a man live a wholly worthy Jewish life, and he assured Baruch that he had found the perfect wife for him.

Montefiori had wisdom in his eyes. In addition, his whole shape and all of his gestures had a gravity that commanded respect. This was further reinforced by the fact that he spoke clearly and decisively, placing a careful emphasis on every syllable. When the rabbi described that perfect woman, absolutely innocent and with a demure disposition, he sounded entirely sure of himself. He simply ignored the fact that Baruch appeared uninterested, for not in his wildest dreams could he imagine the deep secret that the royal physician, the most eligible Jewish bachelor of Lisbon, was hiding within his being: an attraction to the male sex.

Soon afterward at the rabbi's home Baruch was presented to a young woman named Marianne Castro. She was squint-eyed. Before Baruch could open his mouth he was captivated by that quality; it inflamed his memories, and the enigmatic shape of Raimundo stood forth in his thoughts. Seeing Marianne, Baruch was obsessed by the thought of his friend. She had a handsome face and a boyish body with broad shoulders, small breasts, and large feet. They sat together in silence for half an hour, not knowing what to say to each other. The rabbi found this a good sign, for those who prattle about a thousand meaningless things are in fact not meant for each other.

Baruch believed that he was the only person in Lisbon who had been physically tempted by someone of his own sex. In addition, he assumed that such an inclination was against Mosaic law and he should resist it. For that reason he decided in short order that he would marry Marianne. Upon hearing this, the rabbi's face broke into a broad, heartwarming smile—an expression almost never seen there—and he revealed to Baruch the fact that Marianne was his niece.

THE WEDDING took place three days later. The rabbi gave a short sermon. He impressed upon them his view that by the special grace of heaven the Jews had been allowed to establish a community in Lisbon, and he charged them as newlyweds to fulfill their duty to be fruitful and multiply.

Following the ceremony the couple went immediately to bed. It was almost as if they were intent upon promptly carrying out the rabbi's commandment. Baruch was nervous, for he had never before seen a woman unclothed. Marianne quivered with passion. She guided Baruch's fingertips to her nipples, the most sensitive spot on her body, and his touch

gave her gooseflesh. The odor of Marianne's hair, her gasping breath, and her warm skin banished the inhibition of
Baruch's demons and he hungrily sought his pleasure. They
did not drift away to sleep until the dawn.

BARUCH FELT deeply happy. For the first month they
made love as if possessed. But Marianne became pregnant
and the more her belly grew, the less attraction Baruch felt
for her. Several months later when after a lengthy interruption she asked him to come to her bed, he discovered to his
dismay that he was disgusted by her now greatly bloated
body.

Baruch's thoughts often turned to his friend Raimundo.
He became more and more confused by the strong feelings that welled up within him along with hot fleeting images from the bunk in the cellar of the smithy. Gradually
the message from the darkness of his subconscious reached
him. He came to see that there were powerful forces at
work here against which he could do nothing, no matter
how hard he tried. He realized that wedded bliss did not
exist for him and that taking a wife had been a disastrous
mistake. Every day he reproached himself for having listened to the rabbi. From pure instinct for self-preservation
he shared his thoughts with nobody, for he knew that no
one would understand them and divorce was impossible. In
addition, he was determined to present his marriage to the
outside world as a happy one, particularly to the king who
had been so magnanimous and protective of the Jews.

MARIANNE FELT more and more unloved. One day she
had the notion that Baruch must have caught some mysterious illness. Out of a delicacy of feeling she was hesitant to
press him on the matter. Keenly aware of the warm wetness

between her legs, she would feed her husband peanuts and stewed goat testicles as often as she could, for she had heard from her mother that those foods had a powerful aphrodisiac effect. But nothing seemed to rouse his desire.

Tired at last of Baruch's indifference she asked him right out one day to mix up a potion that would stimulate certain parts of the masculine anatomy. She particularly had in mind, since it was apparent that she was no longer capable of inciting his manhood, that organ that she referred to with a sniff as "the one-eyed snake." But Baruch answered with a disgusted look that he had no intention of mixing up any such potion.

Her unhappiness at no longer being attractive and her increasingly strong longing for physical stimulation robbed Marianne of both sleep and appetite. As weeks went by, she felt more and more desperate. At last she could no longer keep quiet about her unhappy love life. She turned to her mother, even though she knew that her mother was a gossip with a huge, flapping tongue. She pleaded with her mother never to utter a word of what she was about to reveal. Her mother gave her a solemn pledge, tantamount to a guarantee that she would spread the news like wildfire. With that, a tearful Marianne confessed in a love-starved voice that for months she had received not the slightest physical consolation within her marriage. Her mother's only suggestion was to cuckold her husband, a counsel Marianne refused to accept.

THAT VERY AFTERNOON a rumor began to circulate in Lisbon's Jewish community. Passed from one female mouth to another, it was continually embroidered with new details. According to this malicious gossip, the royal physician had provoked the devil with his experiments with plants. In revenge the Dark One had planted an icy cold in Baruch's body that made him impotent and left his male member shriveled and useless. Simultaneously the Prince of Darkness had lit an unquenchable fire in Marianne's loins so that she burned incessantly with desire, and every day she needed to plant five big, strapping fellows between her legs before she could get to sleep at night.

Soon every Jew in the city knew the story of the de Espinosa couple. Some of them merrily made fun of the idea that every day Baruch was being cuckolded by his wife. Others pitied him. One or two women felt a sting of jealousy at Marianne's cavorting. No one doubted the truth of the rumor, given that it had come from a reliable source.

THE MALICIOUS TALK reached Baruch's ears. He turned gray in the face and felt unspeakable humiliation. So this was his reward for having founded a Jewish community. He spat on the ground and regretted for a moment that he had gone to the king to secure permission for Jews to live in Lisbon.

Then his anger turned toward Marianne, for he suspected that she had complained to her uncle Montefiori, that hypocritical rabbi who was always serving up fat moral platitudes to his community while secretly running after whores. Baruch assumed that the rabbi had spread the rumors. At the same time he felt a touch of pity for Marianne, because it occurred to him that from that day forth not a single Jewish man in Lisbon would be able to look at her without recalling the whole story.

For a moment he contemplated telling off the city's Jews but he quickly saw that it was already too late. An angry outburst would only make the situation worse. At length he found no other resort for his own peace and position, for the safety of his family and their future, than to swallow his pride and pretend that nothing had happened. Despite the tales, their first child was growing larger and stronger every day within Marianne's belly, on its way to birth at Lisbon's royal castle.

BARUCH FOUND it deeply unfortunate that he had lost his passion for Marianne, who as if in compensation became more fecund than ever. She gave birth to six children, all of whom sprang forth from the nights when Baruch managed to suppress the image of Raimundo that constantly haunted him and overcome his self-loathing so as to carry out with equal speed and reluctance his duty as a husband.

The couple had three sons in a row, all of them sound and healthy. Marianne brought them up with loving care. Then arrived three daughters, triplets. They died within days. The first stopped breathing only a few moments after her arrival in the world, the second died of colic, the third of anemia.

After the period of oppressive pregnancy with the girls and the difficult birthing, Marianne's breasts were stretched full of milk for the dead triplets and she suffered a sort of toxicity that attacked her nervous system. She gradually lost her grip on reality. Baruch suspected that the disturbances of her brain were some sort of inherited dementia. With every passing week Marianne drifted farther away in the labyrinth of her confusion. Toward the end she had lost virtually all memory. The tenderness she had felt for her sons she transferred to small birds, and she spent her days hypnotizing chickens. As soon as she caught sight of Baruch—she was convinced that he was a wind-blown beggar getting ready to set insidious traps and steal the golden eggs laid by her hens—she hissed like a cat, wailed, and flung curses in every direction.

Baruch felt shame at Marianne's confused behavior. But instead of seeking a cure, he became ever chillier and displayed an almost total lack of sympathy for his wife.

When the ladies of the court complained to the king that they could no longer put up with Marianne's loud shrieks and vulgar tantrums, a chagrined Baruch begged their pardon and promised to deal with the problem without delay.

He told two of the royal bodyguards to come with him. They tied her to the bed frame and then shut the door to the bedroom. He hired an elderly Jewish woman to come twice a day to clean Marianne, feed her, and speak with her. The two of them discussed chickens, since no other topic was of any interest to the distracted wife of the royal physician.

During her hours of isolation Marianne was visited by a nightmare in which she stood up from the bed, opened the door, left the room, went out to the henhouse, and found that her darlings were no longer willing to talk to her.

One morning two months after Baruch had arranged for his wife to be bound to the bed frame, the woman who cared for Marianne discovered that she had disappeared. In consternation she instinctively directed her steps to the henhouse. There lay a dozen headless hens in the dirt. It took a few moments for the woman to locate Marianne hanging under the henhouse roof, a thick rope around her neck. Three soldiers were required to get her rigid body down.

Baruch felt almost a sense of relief when he heard the news of his wife's death. He made no effort at any hypocritical pretense of grieving over her demise. Instead of paying attention to the children, he locked himself into his laboratory, leaving strict instructions that he was not to be disturbed. He slept there and took all his meals there. Sometimes he remained in the laboratory for days on end. On one occasion the children overheard him say that the only things that were important to him were the king's life and his own search for the great secret.

The Farewell of the King

AFONSO HENRIQUES'S POWERS ebbed in the twilight of his age. He suffered from a mysterious illness that consumed him from inside, spreading out from his spine. His skin became as dry and frail as parchment. He lost his appetite and perspired profusely even at rest.

The king was no longer capable of riding a horse, a fact that pained him greatly. He had a growing tendency to spend his days lying in bed. Bitter at his diminished capabilities, he spewed out threats against enemies both real and imagined and ordered severe punishments.

Every morning and evening Baruch had him drink a secret potion made with the head of a turtle, lizard urine, the liver of a guinea pig, and chamomile leaves. But nothing seemed to help.

One morning Afonso Henriques was clearly in a foul humor.

"Do you think," he said in an aggrieved tone, staring at Baruch, "that I'm going to allow myself to be poisoned with these evil-tasting potions? I suspect that you, my own personal physician, are the one who's making me sick. What proves to me that you're not in league with my son and my enemies lurking around here in the hopes of laying out my dead body in a coffin?"

"His Royal Majesty," Baruch answered with a deep bow, "is well apprised of my loyalty and truthfulness. I am not aware of any such things."

"You, Baruch de Espinosa!" The king sat up in bed. "You are either a fool or a knave, or both. You don't merit the trust I have placed in you my whole life long. I don't know why I named you my personal physician. You foul Jew, you're nothing but a simple maker of poisons who wants me dead. But I want you to know that I won't give you that satisfaction."

"Excellency," Baruch sought to placate him, "I never lose the hope and belief that the king's health will improve with the help of my medicines and especially of God who works miracles and does the impossible. His Excellency will live a long life, for there is no one who could take the place of His Royal Majesty."

"I don't give a damn for hope and belief from someone like you," the king bellowed. He ordered Baruch to leave him alone and never to come back.

AT THE END, everything occurred with impressive suddenness. There was not even time for someone to fetch the cardinal who might have heard Afonso Henriques's confession, given him absolution, and prepared him for his final journey. There was great consternation when the people were told that the king had died. The castle was full of lamentation, sobbing, and complaint.

Even Baruch was surprised. But so it is with death. It seizes us with an enigmatic smile when we least expect it. It takes us human beings by surprise in a manner most treacherous.

The Death of the Mixer of Poisons

BARUCH GRIEVED for the king for a long time. It was as if he had lost a father.

Until the end of his days, he continued to serve as the personal physician of Sancho, the new king. He supposed that his knowledge made him indispensable. In fact, the continuance was due more to the fact that the new monarch was softhearted, and once when Sancho was a child Baruch had saved the life of the little prince who had eaten too many wild chestnuts.

THERE ARE CONFLICTING REPORTS of Baruch's death.

Amaral's biography of the king records that Baruch died of a peculiar inherited genetic disease of the bowels that he is said to have passed on to his three sons.

My great-uncle was of a different opinion. "Everything goes along fine for a while but at the end madness sets in," he commented. According to him, Baruch had become fat and sluggish in his old age. He spent all his time seeking some way back into the past. Wrestling with an inner resistance, often increasingly fatigued and disappointed, he sought to reconcile himself with what he had understood to be deadly sins: his deviant sexuality and his failure to love those closest to him. Nearsighted and dazed in his senility, one day Baruch confused two vials. One of them contained the medicine for his intestines and the other was a mixture of poisons requested by King Sancho to use on the unruly Prince Braga. The royal physician died in inexpressible agony.

My own inclination is to believe my great-uncle's version just as he told it to us. After all, all of the Spinozas born with the huge nose suffer tragic deaths.

THREE

The Cabalist

Among Our Ancestors

MY FAMILY HISTORY has been much in my thoughts recently. All of them are dead now: Mother and Father; my twin brother, Sasha; Grandmother and Grandfather; Aunt Ilona and Uncle Carlo. So is my great-uncle, that man who for years inflamed our imaginations with his stories and was the one shining light of our childhood home.

It's odd that life teaches us to treasure certain individuals we don't really appreciate when they're with us, but whose importance we understand only when we begin to miss them. Maybe I can take comfort in the fact that my indifference to others has diminished over the years—for as long as I can remember, I've been insensitive to the lives of others and I've been heedless of the needs of those closest to me—and suddenly I find myself focused more on my family than on myself. Now, as my last days on earth inevitably play out and I'll soon vanish into the shadows, I have only one desire: to pass along the stories I've carried within me since childhood and to try to keep those who went before me from vanishing into thin air. I have no intention of accounting for all the generations and generations of the Espinoza family, who shortened their last name to Spinoza at the end of the sixteenth century after fleeing from the Iberian Peninsula to Amsterdam. Not only because I'm not a real writer, a lack of talent that sometimes distresses me deeply, but also because of something that our grandfather taught Sasha and me. Let me try to explain.

GRANDFATHER KEPT himself strikingly aloof from the family. Whenever Sasha and I mentioned innocently that the grandfathers of some of our classmates had taken them to Gerbeaud's for its elegant pastries, he would maintain an icy silence. If we ever brought the matter up directly by asking, "Grandfather, don't you think you should spoil us just a little bit with some of those wonderful pastries?" then he might respond dryly, "Sugared treats aren't good for children's teeth."

No, Grandfather had no interest in having us close to him. My twin brother and I knew it all too well, even when we were small. Most of the time he seemed visibly annoyed by our presence; I think that he simply disliked us. Despite that, two things about him made us feel proud to be his grandchildren. Those two things left a deep impression upon me and even to this day I remain profoundly impressed by them.

1) His elegant appearance: Grandfather took great pains with his personal appearance and was extremely punctilious about dressing correctly. He was a stylish man, clean-shaven, and he had a body of graceful proportions. No one could fail to be impressed by his glowing manly attractiveness. Even young women turned to watch him pass in the street, a gentleman of seventy years of age strolling along unhurriedly in his highly polished shoes, dark blue suit and vest, white shirt, and impeccably knotted blue bow tie with white polka dots. He always had a cane in hand—a malacca cane of bamboo, of course—and he held himself with dignified reserve. His gleaming bald head was hidden beneath a fashionable hat. He had a truly aristocratic air that made him stand out from the gray everyday crowds of socialism.

I really don't think that Grandfather would have been capable of neglecting his appearance even under threat of a firing squad. If he had been the last survivor on a desert island with no one to impress, his good upbringing would not have permitted the least touch of slovenliness. As they say in Paris, noblesse oblige. And after all, grandfather was the son of an Austrian princess.

2) His gift for mathematics: My great-uncle sometimes maintained that only two people in the history of the world have been capable of mentally calculating the products of half a dozen numbers, each of them twenty digits long, in less than two seconds: my grandfather and Albert Einstein. He would offer that piece of information casually, in passing, but with a lightly mocking expression that seemed to imply that the Einstein fellow was really not of the same caliber as our grandfather.

Only very rarely did Grandfather favor us with a demonstration of his ability to add and multiply with incredible rapidity. But I particularly remember one time toward the end of his life. He was leaning back in his armchair, newspaper in hand, and looked up just as my great-uncle closed the front door behind him. He said, "My boys, Fernando entertains you with a thousand and one tales, each more outlandish than the last. When it comes to storytelling it doesn't matter if something actually happened or not; it's the way the story is told. Fernando is entertaining—no one can deny him that—and he's always telling fascinating stories about your origins. But has he ever said a word about exponential growth?"

"Exponential growth?" Sasha and I exchanged a bewildered look.

"Fernando, with all his prattle about the past, has he ever given you a notion of how many ancestors you have?"

"Well, of course," Sasha replied immediately. "At least thirty of 'em."

"Thirty of them," Grandfather repeated with a laugh. "Listen to me, boys, and I'll give you a lesson about exponential growth. Listen closely and think about what I say. I had four grandparents. When we go back five generations, in other words to the era of the French Revolution, the number rises to 120. And back around 1630 I had 16,382 ancestors. If I look even farther back in time to the beginnings of the fourteenth century, that means thirty generations ago, all together I had 1,090,125,824 ancestors. Are you following me? That means that the two of you have had at least 4,360,503,296 ancestors."

NO ONE can keep track of all his ancestors. Certainly I cannot, least of all, having so many of them, according to Grandfather. Besides, the great majority of my family members lived lives of no particular distinction. Therefore it's best for all of us to leave them in peace. I propose to concentrate my efforts on describing a handful of individuals in the great pageant of history, remarkable men and women whose lives and deeds, thanks to the fragmentary accounts of my great-uncle, captured my childish imagination and whose fates at the same time offer new perspectives on the history of Europe.

Eternal Life

THOSE WHO HAVE READ this far in my family narrative will recall that in the year 1158 a rumor spread, reaching far beyond the boundaries of Portugal, that the royal physician

Baruch de Espinosa, whose potions could transform spent old men into raging stallions capable of achieving ten orgasms a day, possessed a supernatural power that banished illness and had by careful cultivation produced a medicinal plant that frightened away death.

ETERNAL LIFE, no less a mystery than love itself, has never ceased to fascinate and confuse humanity. Many doubt its very existence. I therefore intend to reveal to you the great secret, although in fact I am formally forbidden to do so.

No Spinoza has ever revealed it to anyone—not to a wife, not to his friends, not to his king or his lord—other than his eldest son. Because Moses, the greatest prophet of the Jews, warned Baruch that the secret had to be safeguarded by his children and his children's children for a thousand years, and as long as his descendants fulfilled their obligations, they would wander with righteous mien among the peoples of the earth and the Lord would watch over them. But should any one of them fail to carry out the Lord's will, their generations would be obliterated from the earth.

I have no children and no one to whom I can entrust the great secret. I am the last of the Spinozas. Soon I will die. I have nothing to lose, for with my passing our family will disappear from the earth anyway, and I have no intention of taking anything with me to the grave.

My great-uncle taught me most of what I know about the lives of my ancestors. But not even he was initiated in the great secret. It was revealed to me when I read the philosopher Benjamin Spinoza's book *The Elixir of Immortality*, which I inherited from my grandfather. The book has been in our family's possession for more than three hundred years and no outsider has ever been permitted to read it. I myself began the study of it all too late in life.

Benjamin Spinoza describes the secret plant that holds death at bay. I cite here the philosopher's words, as carefully chosen as the jewels in the setting of a ring, precisely as they were written:

The secret plant—Baruch de Espinosa called it "Raimundo" in honor of his deceased friend—is produced by taking citronella, chamomile, St. John's wort, snowdrops, and similar species and grafting these as close as possible to one another along the root of a Zamia acuminata.

The site of the grafts is to be carefully watered once every third day with a potion compounded of the liver of a guinea pig, the urine of a lemur, the mixture of Mithridates (consisting of wild thyme, coriander, anis, fennel, and rue), along with theriac (a compound of poppy seed and Drimia maritima, *known as sea onion).*

The new plants never live longer than eight months and cannot be transplanted or propagated.

The plant is dried in the sun for a month, following which a tincture is prepared by soaking the dried leaves for thirty days in a medium containing alcohol. The tincture should be agitated twice each day at intervals of exactly twelve hours. At the conclusion of the month the tincture is filtered through a thick cloth and left to settle for eighteen hours.

Seven drops of this preparation will hold Death at bay and give eternal life.

One day when he realized that he was no longer fully in possession of all his faculties and knew that he had little time left before he would meet his maker, Baruch instructed his eldest son, Simon, in the secrets of cultivating the Raimundo plant and preparing the secret tincture. First, however, Simon had to take a solemn vow never to reveal the secret to anyone other than his eldest son and in no circumstances to prepare the potion himself or ingest a single drop.

"I created the Raimundo plant because it was my wish that my king should live and reign forever over the country," Baruch explained to him. "Afonso Henriques was a powerful man, one whose stern gaze terrified everyone it transfixed. He hated disobedience more than anything in the world. If he discovered one of his subjects was violating his rules and breaking his commandments, he sent that person straight off to the torture chamber and his zealous executioners. No one lasted longer than three days with those wicked men and their special gifts in devising prolonged and agonizing executions. Everyone lived in abject terror of the king and he knew it. But he was like a father to me and he was vigilant with his protection. That caused resentment among the nobles of the court. They were so consumed with envy that they spread slanders about me—they claimed I was some sort of lord of black magic, good for nothing but poisoning people. I have always been weak and inoffensive, both in heart and spirit, and since I was the only Jew at court, my position was anything but secure. The nobles of the court presented themselves as honorable, but many were as treacherous as vipers. They amused themselves by sneering at me and speaking ill of me behind my back. After Afonso Henriques died, I thought my days at the court were numbered. You must understand that my principal concern in creating the Raimundo plant was for myself and for my family; I wanted the elderly king to live forever. But on the day that I was preparing to administer seven drops of it to him, I suddenly had second thoughts. It was as if something had exploded within me. The king had started to show signs of senility and he was behaving atrociously. That day he became annoyed at a servant who had spilled a couple of drops of wine on the table. Cursing under his breath, he picked up a dagger, struck the man, and gouged out his right eye. I will never forget the servant's scream of pain, his distorted face, and the blood running down it. I tried to help the poor man, but the king wouldn't allow it. He smiled, derisive and scornful. It was impossible to save the man's eye. Then and there, I suddenly realized how repellent I found the thought of an increasingly confused Afonso Henriques who would be eternally punishing imagined enemies, torturing his loyal followers, and having them beheaded. At that moment, I also realized that there is no greater curse on earth than eternal life. Believe me: The setting of the sun lends weight, beauty, and grandeur to our days. Life is short and that is our Creator's single greatest gift to us. His other gift is death, for which we should be humbly grateful."

Simon listened with a grave expression on his face and wondered if he had really grasped the meaning of that last remark in his father's long exposition. He couldn't see how one could possibly feel grateful for having inevitably to leave a world that seemed so splendid. But his respect for his father prevented him from following that thought any further. All he could say was, "Father, you can live as long as you wish; all you have to do is take the Raimundo remedy."

"Simon, when one perceives that memory and mind are fading, it is time to make a conscious choice and surrender to death. Remember, once one reaches a certain advanced age it is only the fear of death, not the desire for life, that keeps one imprisoned within one's body."

"I hear your words, Father," Simon answered. "But don't be offended if I fail to understand everything. Why are you telling me all this and entrusting the secret of the elixir to me and my descendants if it should never be used? Wouldn't it have been better to keep the recipe secret by destroying it?"

"When I was young," Baruch replied, "I once met an old man—I believe to this day that he was our great prophet Moses—who thundered a prophecy at me. If I obeyed the commandments engraved on his stone tablets, discovered the great secret, and safeguarded it, my children and my children's children would go forth, heads high, for a thousand years. That meant we are destined to be the guardians of the secret of immortality. But if any one of us fails to comply with his commandment, our line will end there."

Baruch paused for a moment and then said emphatically, "You must always be on your guard. Many are obsessed with the dream of eternal life and are ready to do anything to secure the great secret. They will not hesitate to murder you to obtain it."

Simon listened attentively. He asked no more questions. He promised again never to taste of the potion, to safeguard the secret, and eventually to confide it to his eldest son.

The knowledge of the Raimundo plant and of the elixir of immortality was scrupulously preserved by four generations of the eldest sons of the Espinosas.

The Personal Physician

ONE ASSUMES more often than not that individuals close to authority participate in events or are affected by the ideas of the age. But games of political intrigue had scarcely any effects upon the court physicians who bore the Espinosa name. Quite unlike other court physicians, they were more or less excluded because they were Jews. They were reduced to observing the activity in the Portuguese court from a distance.

This exclusion not only inculcated in them a certain feeling of alienation; it also taught them the art of slipping gracefully away while remaining ever patient and servile. It also kept them from indulging in any sort of pride or aspiring to power. They remained resolutely blind to intrigue and deaf to flattery. They were absolutely honorable and indifferent to sentiment; they thought of nothing but their arduous work and devoted themselves to it from the break of day until late at night. Their fealty to their royal masters was unshakable, even though in their innermost hearts they were more devoted to fulfilling their God's wishes than to pleasing earthly powers. No taste for novelty was cultivated in their homes; they were people for whom novel thoughts and ideas were void of significance and therefore dangerous. Their exaggerated respect for the prevailing order prevented them from thinking for themselves. They were careful in all matters to hold exactly the views fit for a loyal Jewish subject. They were pedantic and wholly without brilliance, individuals who devoted their lives to compounding medicines from organic plants. They strictly confined themselves within the narrow boundaries of their technical knowledge. They lived their lives honoring the memory of Baruch, the founder of their line, who with his great arsenal of miraculous herbal medicines was considered as great as King Mithridates of Pontus.

BARUCH TAUGHT HIS SONS to conceal from others their innermost thoughts and to make themselves indispensable. His words were passed from father to son from generation to generation:

More is to be gained by fostering dependence than through winning respect. A man who has drunk his fill will turn away from the well. Once you are no longer needed, you will no longer be esteemed. Learn this as the most important principle in life: foster dependency and never satisfy it entirely; make certain that no one, not even the king, can do without you. But never indulge in excess. Watchful silence is the holy refuge of wisdom.

According to my great-uncle, the one who turned to evil ends the virtues of the Espinosa clan—if virtues they were—was Chaim.

A Curse

ISRAEL DE ESPINOSA had no luck at all when it came to children. He longed to have sons, inheritors who would become physicians and carry on the family tradition. His wife gave birth to twelve children, every one a daughter. His house was packed to the ceiling with fifteen women: his wife, the twelve daughters, his mother, and a deaf spinster aunt often afflicted by fits of epilepsy.

Israel was convinced that his life was cursed. In his view, a single daughter would have been sufficient. But twelve—there were far too many of them; it was a full-blown catastrophe. After the births of the first five he became downhearted and no longer read out the prayers of thanksgiving in the synagogue. He no longer selected the names of the daughters but left that to his wife. He greeted each successive arrival of a child with new anger and a sense of helplessness. He would not permit himself to show the least sign of consideration for his daughters. He tried not to allow himself to be affected by them and did everything he could to forget them. To that end, he withdrew and spent all of his time sequestered in one part of the house.

Israel was the king's personal physician and Lisbon's most respected medical practitioner. He dared not seek advice from his colleagues, for he was afraid of risking his reputation. Instead, he secretly visited quacks and faith healers, who assured him that his wife was to blame because by his very nature the man stands higher in the order of things than the woman. The first of them suggested that he administer to his wife the urine of a pregnant donkey and have her eat dried palm leaves for ten days and ten nights. The second advised that even though his wife was Jewish, she should confess herself to a priest, pray to the Virgin Mary three times a day, and fast for a week after menstruating. The third mixed a bitter potion of rare herbs. His wife drank it but then she began to run a high fever, fell desperately ill, and vomited blood. Despite this experience, she was willing to undertake any sacrifice in order to please her husband. But nothing seemed to help.

One moonlit night when all avenues seemed to be closed to them, his wife decided to take things into her own hands. She knew that it was her duty not to leave this world without giving birth to a healthy son who after her husband's death would read Kaddish over him and inherit his estate. This being so, she suggested that Israel join her in making one last effort. They would divest themselves of all their clothes and remain naked as he rubbed his hand over her body until midnight. At that hour he was to penetrate her and leave his member within her until the dawn. Reluctantly, Israel agreed and did so.

Nine months later the house was filled with cries of joy. Israel leaned over the newborn, kissed the infant boy on the forehead, and named him Chaim, which means "life" in Hebrew.

The Young Man from Lisbon

CHAIM HAD TWELVE SISTERS and was the youngest of the crowd. From the day of his birth there was not the least doubt that the only son of the court physician Israel de Espinosa, his father's pride and joy, would uphold the family's reputation and follow in his father's footsteps.

The long-awaited heir was the very image of his father, aside from the fact that the little fellow had not inherited Israel's gigantic nose. He emerged into the world with the face of a little old man; he looked like a sixty-year-old with his wrinkles, bald head, and sunken cheeks, as if he had already followed a long career dealing with the onerous duties of the physician to the Portuguese royal court.

No one in the family said aloud what they were all thinking at the sight of the hideous little boy, since in those times women were not allowed to express their opinions. Only the eldest sister, a woman who scandalized folks with her bold speech, spoke up.

Leah was a psychic and could see beyond the mere appearance of things. She glanced at the newborn and immediately declared that a curse lay upon him. Her father dismissed this and replied that such a day not only was auspicious because of heavenly benevolence but was also a time for generosity and celebration. Leah responded that she could not withhold the unfortunate truth, since it stood clearly written on the boy's forehead that the long-awaited son would bring great shame on the family.

The father rebuked his daughter and said her words sprang from unmotivated envy, she was wicked, and she should be ashamed. The arrival at long last of a family heir was a gift from above, for heaven had finally blessed a womb that had produced nothing but girls.

But Leah stood her ground. Israel's face darkened with anger. He threatened to cut out Leah's sharp tongue if she uttered another word. Then he bellowed at her to leave the house and never show her face again. The daughters were thrown into a panic. No one had ever seen their mild-mannered father in such a rage or even heard him raise his voice. His wife thought for a moment that the joy of finally having a boy in the family had temporarily robbed Israel of his senses.

Leah was terrified. She slouched away, muttering to herself that no one could escape fate, and she crawled into a narrow space in the attic. She didn't make a sound for the next thirty years, and she never left her hiding place in the house.

THE YEARS PASSED quickly. One afternoon, as the Espinosa family was busily preparing for a celebration and setting out the tastiest dishes on the occasion of Chaim's twentieth birthday, a page arrived with a message from King Dionysius I. Israel de Espinosa and his son, Chaim, were summoned immediately into his presence. Israel hurried off, for he was concerned that the king might have had a relapse.

A few days earlier Dionysius I had been brought back from a journey to Andalusia in a terrible condition, unconscious, bathed in sweat, with a high fever and diarrhea, his garments soaked with excrement and urine. Israel took the king's pulse and for a moment was struck by a feeling of helplessness. He couldn't decide what would be better for the patient, to dose him with herbal medicines or to call a father confessor to administer the sacrament of Extreme Unction. But after a rapid examination he concluded that His Majesty's suffering was due to the fact that his bodily fluids had gotten out of balance, provoking intestinal difficulties and a high fever, all because his gallbladder had failed. While the queen held the king's hand and pleaded with God to hear her prayers, so that Dionysius I might not die but instead live to her own great joy and that of the whole kingdom, Israel prepared an extract of four types of herbs stirred in a concoction of various roots and plant juices. A few hours later the king opened his eyes, hands trembling and face deadly pale. He no longer looked like the great warrior who had overwhelmed all opposition on every battlefield, but at least he was alive and appeared to be mending.

Dionysius I welcomed the father and son in his throne room and told them that thanks to his personal physician's outstanding care and effective herbal remedies, he had recovered his health and strength with unexpected speed. Israel felt a great sense of relief and was able to breathe once more.

The king rose from the throne and went forth to Chaim, placed a great, heavy hand on his shoulder, and inspected him closely. He said he understood that Chaim had been receiving instruction in medicine from his father since he was a boy. The young man stood there as if petrified and sought some answer for the king but could not manage to utter a word in reply.

The king looked deep into Chaim's eyes and commented that he must be exceedingly proud of his father, who was not only a gifted teacher but also a wise man, reliable and discreet, a royal subject who never plagued his master with meaningless chatter, unwarranted curiosity, or lack of respect. The king was convinced that on the Day of Judgment Israel would be forgiven for his Jewish heritage because of his good character and remarkable accomplishments as a physician.

As a token of his appreciation, the king had decided—as had his father, his grandfather, and his great-grandfather before him—that the son of his personal physician would one day follow in the steps of his father.

Dionysius I asked Chaim if he would like to travel to Granada to study medicine and to receive comprehensive instruction from Faraj Ibn Hassan, the personal physician of the powerful sultan Muhammed II. Ibn Hassan was familiar with everything having to do with the art of medicine and had deeper knowledge than all of his contemporaries on the Iberian Peninsula. The young man affirmed, "Yes, I certainly would." The king was pleased to hear it, for everything had already been arranged. Chaim would leave the town of his birth the very next morning.

Filled with deep gratitude, Israel fell to his knees before the king and exclaimed that His Majesty was the most kindhearted man on earth. At the same time he sent a prayer up to heaven, for he knew that God's eyes were upon him. Perhaps the Almighty was sitting on the throne of glory, pleased that his inept servant would one day be succeeded as royal physician by his son, fulfilling the tradition of several generations.

Chaim could feel fate smiling upon him. His eyes filled with tears. He tried to say something but again failed to find the right words.

IT WAS not without a certain apprehension that Israel sent the pride of his family away to Granada. He knew all too well that the boy, so beloved and spoiled by his father and sisters, was naïve and inexperienced, unready for the wide world. He gave Chaim the following words of advice: "For more than a century our hands have touched kings, queens, governors, and the heads of other noble men and women and have cured the ills of their bodies. You carry a great heritage, and on your shoulders rests the responsibility for preserving the good name of our family. Never should you undertake anything without asking counsel of your teachers. Wise is he who follows good advice. You have always been hasty and impatient in everything. You must learn serenity and patience, for haste will only sow stones on the road to good fortune. Everything that exists in the world was created with due deliberation. Remember that he of modest abilities achieves more with diligence than the overly talented man who is indolent. Reputation is won at the price of hard work. Anything achieved with little effort is worth little."

Ibn Hassan and His Student

CHAIM WAS IMMEDIATELY ENCHANTED by Granada. Eyes wide and head held high, he wandered through the various quarters of the city, luxuriating in the way Granada with its sudden perfumes of jasmine and essential oils wrapped its inviting arms around him. The city was rich in everything he valued: splendid, proud buildings and gardens, running water, greenery, and birdsong. It was a true paradise of all imaginable delights; there were pleasures more refined and intense than any he had ever experienced in his native city, and in addition, the people were most captivating. He loved to listen to the way the tones of Andalusian *malouf* music echoed in the narrow alleyways. With its warmth and Oriental notes it was practically the same as the Hebrew psalms and hymns his community used to sing with such fervor in the synagogue of his childhood, provoking such a feeling of joyous exultation in him. Here in the tolerance of the Moorish caliphate he felt the breezes of freedom for the first time.

Most of all, Chaim was impressed by Ibn Hassan's wonderful professional skill and the unimaginable depths of his knowledge. Chaim decided that he would devote himself wholeheartedly to his education, studying day and night, and vowed to master every conceivable aspect of the healing profession, for he wanted to show his teacher—as well as himself—that he could be worthy of the famous court physician's instruction and trust. He felt like the most fortunate human being on earth.

Ibn Hassan gave the new pupil everything he sought and held nothing back. He was a father to the boy, to the point that he was willing to make certain sacrifices to assist his protégé.

Even though Chaim was still no more than a young apprentice, Ibn Hassan made sure to mention to the sultan in passing how talented and hardworking his Jewish pupil was. The physician's words carried immense weight at court; his every utterance was received as if the Prophet himself had pronounced a truth. For this reason, even though the powerful sultan was constantly engaged in great matters of state, from time to time late at night he would call Chaim to his library to ask whether he was getting along well in Granada and if he was still observing his Jewish customs.

A few memorable utterances—probably picked up from Ibn Hassan, remarks that perhaps would have passed unnoticed if made by someone else—substantiated Chaim's standing at court as a promising young man.

A year or two after this Chaim saved the life of the sultan's favorite general, who during a skirmish with the Ashqilula clan had been struck by an arrow that pierced his left eye and burrowed deep into his brain. Ibn Hassan judged that Chaim had succeeded in his ordeal by fire and promoted him to the post of his assistant.

He said, "From now on you are my right hand, and you will learn many things of great usefulness for your future. One day you will travel back to your home in Lisbon, become a great teacher, and have your own pupils. At that time you will teach them the most important lesson of all those I have sought to drum into your head: As a healer, one must at all times, without regard for the circumstances, offer his selfless assistance to any who need it."

Falling in Love

IT WAS LOVE at first sight. Never had Chaim seen a more beautiful creature than this young woman. Her name was Rebecca, and she was the daughter of Rabbi Abraham Orabuena of Córdoba.

The rabbi had been invited to the Alhambra for a year to discuss matters of religion and philosophy with the wise and hospitable sultan Muhammed II, for that learned Jew was deeply versed in subjects that went far beyond the ken of ordinary human knowledge. Rebecca had accompanied her father to assist him with housekeeping and practical matters.

Early one morning Chaim was summoned to treat a powerful general so plagued by swollen arteries that he could not get out of bed. He was hurrying across the little plaza when Rebecca, newly awakened, stepped onto her balcony with a sheet wrapped about her diminutive body. Her raven-colored hair fell loosely about her shoulders. Chaim stopped dead, thunderstruck. He stared at the young woman, and it seemed to him that her face, the most enchanting face he had ever seen, was more dazzling than the morning sun. Rebecca blushed and lowered her gaze, as was proper. At that, Chaim hurried on his way, wondering if that beautiful creature had been a hallucination.

As the days went by, Chaim could think of nothing but that young woman. He made discreet inquiries and discovered her name and family background, but he did not dare approach Rebecca. He regarded her from afar, for he feared the glow of her dark eyes and the sweet perfume of her hair, that hair as dark as a deep winter night, would set his heart racing so intensely that he would simply collapse.

IBN HASSAN KNEW instantly that his protégé had fallen in love. He assumed at first that some loose, worldly woman had wrapped Chaim around her little finger. He warned the young man, explaining that love's passion always sees the object of its desire as beautiful, so those in love are incapable of judging wisely; often one perceives the beloved as extraordinary, closer to perfection than to real life. Chaim assured him that the woman in question was honorable and their encounter had been dictated by fate. He described the rush of feeling he experienced in her presence and the impossible distance he felt between himself and Rebecca. Ibn Hassan could see that this passion was by no means a passing fancy. He told Chaim that his own experience had taught him that one commits an injustice both against God and against oneself if one holds deep feelings of affection toward a woman but dares not approach her. He admonished his disciple in the name of Allah to call upon Rebecca's father and inform him of his desire to contract matrimony with his daughter according to the laws of Moses.

When Ibn Hassan saw that the young physician was still hesitant to declare his passion, he cited the writings of the Book of Destiny, which he was in the habit of reading from time to time by torchlight: Chaim would contract marriage with a woman of honorable Jewish lineage and would produce a son of uncommon spirituality.

WITH A FURIOUSLY BEATING heart and more fragrant oil in his hair than he had ever used in his life, Chaim knocked on the rabbi's door. He brought with him all sorts of gifts, hoping to make a good impression. In a voice of great respect he explained his honorable intentions concerning the rabbi's daughter. Rebecca listened to the conversation from her hiding place behind a hanging tapestry and found it difficult to keep still.

Rabbi Orabuena refused Chaim's request for her hand for reasons of religion, for he thought that the suitor was of Moorish ancestry. In an elaborately courteous response Chaim explained that he was a Jew, the son of the personal physician to King Dionysius, and he was fully ready to comply with any request the rabbi might make of him. When he perceived the skepticism still manifested in the rabbi's eyes, Chaim redoubled his efforts. To present himself in a better light, he suggested that as in the days of the Old Testament, he should labor seven years without pay for the rabbi in exchange for Rebecca's hand. Orabuena gave Chaim a long, searching look and showed him to the door.

THE LOVE-STRUCK SUITOR came back evening after evening, always at the same hour, week after week, but the rabbi turned him away with implacable determination. Chaim gradually became desperate. His heart was on fire and his body was racked with longing. For days on end he could think of nothing but Rebecca, she who had aroused him with her innocent features, her great dark eyes filled with wonder, her clear and glowing skin, and the sweetly rounded breasts outlined modestly under her black dress. He didn't know what to do to accomplish his dream that Rebecca and all the secrets of her body might belong to him.

ONE EVENING only a few minutes after Chaim's knock, Rebecca cast herself to the floor before her father and bathed his feet with her tears. She confessed that she had fallen in love with the young man and wished to give him her heart. After first excusing himself for speaking so frankly, the rabbi explained to her that he could never trust Chaim, because the discrepancy between his looks and his words gave an impression of unacceptable duplicity. He could not allow his daughter to be joined in matrimony with an untruthful man, for that would inevitably lead to disastrous consequences. Rebecca, who had never had the least doubt about the character of the elegant Jewish physician, said that the issue was not whom her father could trust but rather whom she loved. The rabbi muttered a rapid prayer in Hebrew, his torso rocking back and forth, before he gave his consent. The smile that lit up Rebecca's whole face expressed her eternal gratitude. She kissed her father's cheek.

———

RABBI ORABUENA performed the marriage ceremony. The sultan and Ibn Hassan were among the guests. No one represented Chaim's family, for he had shut the door on his past and had not taken the trouble to inform his family either of the wedding or of his decision never to return to Lisbon, that drowsy little city that could never compare with Granada.

Chaim placed his hands around Rebecca's, as if sharing a prayer, and held them as he leaned forward and kissed her on the lips. She dared not return his kiss in front of the wedding guests, but she shut her eyes and sighed happily instead.

The Birth of the Cabalist

THE DISTANT ANCESTOR we called "the Cabalist" came into the world exactly at midnight on Friday the first of January in Granada. According to family legend he was born to a mother whose clan had furnished Córdoba with rabbis for three hundred years and to a physician father from a famous line of Jewish healers in Lisbon. The dwelling where this happy event occurred was situated within the Alhambra, the flowering palace that was the seat of the Nasrid dynasty for more than two hundred and fifty years, up until 1492.

Experienced Moorish midwives helped bring a semblance of order to the chaos of that night. Bloody sheets were rolled up and thrown into the open fire of the kitchen hearth along with the thick sticky tissues of the afterbirth. A basin was filled with water; a serving girl dipped a hand in it to check the temperature. The newborn screamed at the top of his lungs as they washed him. He had dark eyes and a full head of black hair.

Chaim de Espinosa, the father, unobtrusively entered the room. When they held the child up to him he could see that it had an enormous nose, just like that of his father.

"Thank you, great God, that my firstborn is a son," exclaimed Chaim, obviously greatly relieved. "Thank you, almighty God, that I have escaped the curse that lay so long upon my father."

He fell to his knees before his wife, Rebecca, gently took her hand, and thanked her for giving him a boy. Exhausted, she turned her listless, ashen face away from him. He then got up to thank the court physician Faraj Ibn Hassan for overseeing the difficult birth.

Even though it was past midnight, Muhammad II was informed. The sultan would have had no cause to visit a newborn, especially during hours when almost everyone was asleep, if the arrival of the child had not been considered so important, nothing less than a portent from above. For the child had entered this earthly life at exactly the moment that the new century began, confirming the court astrologer's prophecy of an impending event of great importance, an arrival likely to affect the fate of the Moorish kingdom and to presage fundamental change.

Muhammed II also undertook the visit because he considered it important to try to bridge the gap that separated the sultan and his subjects in those times. He treated both his Moorish personal physician, Ibn Hassan, and the doctor's personal assistant, Chaim de Espinosa, not as unworthy commoners but as friends. Muhammed II was extremely enlightened in his attitude of respect for others.

"Chaim," said the sultan, in his characteristically poetical manner, "your son will one day give you in great measure your portion of fatherly pride. This is a boy who will be particularly gifted in the ways of the mind. I can see the clarity of pure thought shining in his dark eyes. You must give him a name that clearly symbolizes the special wisdom that is his inheritance."

"Great sultan," replied Chaim, kneeling before Muhammed II, "engendered and brought to the world in the sultan's splendid palace, my son is already as dear to me as life itself. His name will be Moishe."

He Who Unites Water and Fire

UNLESS I'M MISTAKEN, I was twelve years old when during one of his learned lectures about obscure mysteries my great-uncle explained to us the symbolism of the name that the physician Chaim de Espinosa gave to his newborn son, who became the ancestor we called "the Cabalist."

It was summertime. My great-uncle had shared our lunch of potato soup with dumplings. Sasha and I hated it and would have preferred to sneak away and vomit it up. But we were always obliged to consume everything set before us. In those days food was still scarce and precious.

Grandmother went out on the stairs to share the latest gossip with the all-knowing woman concierge. They spoke so loudly that the whole house could hear them.

We lingered in the kitchen. I remember how my great-uncle wiped the perspiration from his brow and with an irritated expression waved away the flies buzzing sluggishly around his head. As usual, he was talking about our ancestors and their fascinating destinies. His words made a strong impression upon me.

———

BY MAKING unusual things seem ordinary and ordinary things appear unusual, by embellishing the ugly and making the fleeting moment eternal, my great-uncle taught us at an early age that there is hope even in the worst situations; life is always worth living, if only because it is so painfully brief. He created a parallel universe for us, one charged with suffering and mystery, to shield us against perverse reality and the endless possibilities of defeat.

Our childhood, Sasha's and mine, had a window on the past. We sat there often. We had no need for the present, for the days of the past were an enchanted place, so very much more real, and they were never-ending. We recognized ourselves in my great-uncle's stories. People had existed before us; it was as simple as that. There was a pattern woven deeply into our genes, and an invisible power impelled us to find the key to it. We perceived that same pattern in the lives of our ancestors. And now I have finally begun to see traces of it within myself.

"FRANCI," GRANDMOTHER SAID when she returned to the kitchen, "stop bothering the boys again with all that nonsense. They'll never be able to get to sleep tonight. Go out and play, you pair of good-for-nothings!"

"But Sara," my great-uncle protested mildly, "what does it matter if the boys enjoy themselves a little?"

"It bothers me plenty," Grandmother snapped. "Intelligent boys should dedicate themselves to rational matters and not listen to tall tales and talk about spiritualism. It's a sin and a shame, what you're doing. Don't you understand that sitting and listening to all your old fantasies is making them queer in the head? I warned you before. First it was comets and Moses with his prophecies, then ghosts that reveal the truth, and now it's mystical lore. But there's a limit. Where is all this going to end?"

Then she spoke a few sentences to him in German, which we didn't understand but that were clearly meant to be anything but flattering to Fernando. He began to look intimidated, and his Adam's apple bobbed nervously. Neither of us dared to say anything.

WE CHILDREN took great delight in deceiving Grandmother, for nothing was more wonderful than the times when our great-uncle opened up to us the secret rooms of the past. Sasha and I pretended to go outside to play, but instead we huddled in secret with Fernando in our bedroom. He asked us in a hushed voice if we had heard about Moishe de Espinosa, author of Sefer ha-Zohar (Book of Splendor, a classic text of the Cabala). Sasha shook his head; I said that I had. Partly because I was afraid that my great-uncle, ten thousand times more intelligent than I was and a man with insights into deep truths beyond my understanding, might think I was a dummy. Partly—and especially—because already as a child I found it easy to forgive myself for telling little white lies.

"Boys, I'm certain that you have no idea of the meaning of his first name." We greeted my great-uncle's remark with thoughtful looks and uncertain silence. He took a sheet of paper and a pen from the desk drawer, inscribed a few lines, and began his explanation.

"Today 'Moishe' signifies nothing to most people but the first name of a Jewish male child. But the mystic powers that reside in that name manifest themselves to those initiated into the secret world of the Cabala. That name is formed by the Hebrew characters *mem*, *shin*, and *he*. Each letter has a phonetic meaning but also serves as a symbol.

Mem stands for water, *shin* for fire, and *he* for breath. 'Moishe' therefore means 'he who by breathing' (that is, by living his life) 'unites water and fire' (in other words, the male and female energies) 'within us.' Your ancestor Moishe, the Cabalist, achieved the unity of these unique qualities within himself."

MY GRANDMOTHER once again interrupted, this time by sticking her head through the doorway. Her expression became grim when she discovered that we hadn't gone out after all.

"I won't put up with this any longer! Franci, are you deaf all of a sudden? How many times have I told you not to stuff these boys' heads full of nonsense and stories that you dreamed up? God's truth, you are a completely incapable old man. It's obvious that you've not had a woman for more than thirty years."

Grandmother abruptly withdrew. My great-uncle's face was pale. He sat there with his head hanging and his gaze fixed on the floor. I found the sudden silence disquieting.

But then something unexpected occurred. Grandfather appeared in the doorway. As a rule, he was never at home during the day. He spent the hours until the evening meal at a tavern with the ironic name of the Brooding Rooster, where he always had oxtail stew for lunch, the cheapest thing on the menu, and played cards with his friends. All of them were virtually toothless old men of reduced circumstances, but they were great lovers of pilsner beer. Even though Grandfather neither smoked nor drank, he was a daily client of that tavern, stinking as it did of beer and urine. People had to peer through the thick clouds of tobacco smoke hanging in the air, and most of them came with nothing to do than pass the time. The place would send cold chills up your spine even if you were no fanatical devotee of pure living. But the Brooding Rooster was the very center of my grandfather's existence. The days when the tavern doors remained shut—the first of May, the anniversary of the Russian Revolution, and Christmas Day—he endured almost as a punishment.

I don't really remember any other time that Grandfather engaged in conversation with my great-uncle. But now he said with an almost cheerful tone, "Fernando, you don't know how much I envy you. I've lived for more than forty years with that opinionated deaf old woman who never listens to what anyone else has to say. It's a trial to me, to say the least. I envy you. You're a man who's free and happy."

Then he turned on his heel and disappeared. A scarcely perceptible little smirk played upon my great-uncle's lips, and I thought I heard him mutter, "He envies my freedom. Pooh. The only free man is the one who wants nothing."

"*Liebe Kinder,*" he then said. "Do not concern yourself about understanding everything with your heads. Seek with your feelings, instead, and they will show you the way. Above all, you must always remember: Whatever you do in your lives, your actions must always be at least a little bit irrational, otherwise you risk losing your humanity. But for now, it's best that you do as your grandmother says and go out to play."

The Mystery of the Cabala

MY GREAT-UNCLE was apparently incapable of suppressing anything that he regarded as the truth. Accordingly, even though it would infuriate our grandmother, he would regularly tell Sasha and me, always with great seriousness and an air of unquestionable authority, that people are born, live, and die so that they can be born again at some point in the future.

He also often stressed that something existed above and beyond all of this—something he called "pure unfettered harmony." He explained to us children a number of times that the goal of the Cabala was to approach that harmony and to live in tune with it.

EACH TIME Sasha admitted that he couldn't remember just what kind of thing the Cabala was, my great-uncle had the goodness to repeat patiently, word for word, his explanation of the essence of those teachings.

"The Cabala is a set of mystical teachings of the Jews." He always began his exposition with that sentence. He pronounced the words slowly and with reverence. Then he repeated them so as to fix them in our memories, and continued in a hushed tone, almost in a whisper.

"The Cabala may also be described as a sort of encoded secret scripture. The goal is to hide true wisdom from those persons not yet mature enough to understand it. But the initiates and those who can decipher the code find the best-kept secrets and truths that have been set down in those teachings by the angels ever since the origin of the universe. The true Cabalist always finds what he seeks."

Sasha and I often wondered if my great-uncle was part of the company of the initiated. We asked if he himself practiced the Cabala. But we never got an answer to any of our questions about him, for he was remarkably reticent. The notion of discussing the details of his own life was completely foreign to him.

We were always apprehensive that Grandmother might come into the room and cut my great-uncle off as he was offering us thrilling insights into the origins of the Cabala, never neglecting its supernatural or fantastical elements. We listened, enraptured, even though I now understand we did not grasp very much of it. But we were small children and sometimes I imagine that he spoke of these things less to instruct Sasha and me than to defy our grandmother.

"After the birth of the cosmos," he explained to us, "the Creator taught a special wisdom to the angels, one that we now call the Cabala. After mankind fell into sin, the angels decided to teach the secrets of the Cabala to mankind so they could seek to renew their connections with Paradise."

"What's Paradise?" interrupted Sasha. He clearly didn't have much of a gift for Jewish mysticism.

"The Cabalists believe that divine energy exists on earth," my great-uncle continued. "But strangely enough, no one wishes to embrace that wisdom. Throughout all time, mankind has been more interested in worldly things than in divine wisdom. Because of this the angels were obliged to bide their time until the moment in history when there appeared on the scene someone who had achieved such a state of human readiness that the truth could be revealed to him. His name was Abraham. So the Creator made a covenant with Abraham and promised that his descendants would have access to the secret of the universe."

"And what is that exactly?" asked my brother.

"The secret of the universe," my great-uncle said once again, and added in a whisper as if to emphasize the gravity of the moment, "consists of the music of the spheres, the ur-vibration of the very origins, the Holy Name that is the key to all wisdom and energy. The name for it is 'tetragram-maton' and it consists of the four Hebrew letters *J*, *H*, *V*, and *H*. It's pronounced 'Jahveh' or 'Jahweh' or 'Jehovah.' Go ahead and try it: Say it out loud."

"Is that God's name?" Sasha asked.

"No, the Cabalists call God *En Sof*, 'who has no end.'"

"But great-uncle, once you told us that God had no be-ginning," I objected.

"The Almighty has no name. It's only we human beings who need to find a word to represent the divine. Your ances-tor Moishe de Espinosa, the great Cabalist who also studied the Koran, often quoted an Arabic proverb: 'God has ninety-nine names and only the camel knows the hundredth.'"

I was baffled. *En Sof*? The music of the spheres? An authentic power that keeps the heavenly bodies eternally in place in the great cosmic void? The whole world can be controlled by someone who manages to pronounce the four characters correctly? A camel that knows the name of God? But what did I know? I thought of the great erudition and cleverness of my great-uncle, of that great brain that con-tained so many mysteries. Several times I made the attempt to pronounce the holy name. That, at least, might be use-ful. My diction was terrible. The word rested uneasily in my mouth. It felt as if something essential was escaping my grasp.

My great-uncle laid a gentle but firm hand on my shoul-der and assured me that with a little more practice, I could become the master of the universe. I felt flattered. But I ac-tually had no desire to assume such a heavy responsibility. I preferred instead to investigate the dim recesses of history. I wanted to force my way into the secret library and discover hidden treasure. Above all, I simply wanted to listen to my great-uncle's stories about our ancestors.

An Exemplary Sultan

AND SO IT'S BACK to Granada in the fourteenth century. Before I delve any deeper into our family epic, I would like to provide an account of what I found in history books about Muhammed al Faqih, the second sultan of the Nasrid dynasty.

Muhammed II is described as an unusually enlightened ruler for his time, a potentate whose reputation reached far beyond the Iberian Peninsula. He was an absolute monarch who never exercised his power arbitrarily. "The day that I first use my power for selfish reasons will be the last day of my reign as sultan of Granada," he declared in the speech he delivered when he assumed the throne. In the years that followed, he governed his kingdom with justice, never raising his voice and never falling into a passion. He was held in awe and respect. He valued those individuals who did their duty, forgave the weaknesses of his men, and strictly punished those who infringed his laws. When he went to war, he always sought to restrain his troops from depredation and cruelty, and he never put a defeated enemy to death. He was a righteous soul, an exemplary man of wisdom and legendary bravery. His devotion to justice, which won so many hearts, was the subject of folk songs even during his lifetime.

ALTHOUGH THE SULTAN did not feel old and had always had the decisiveness and strength necessary to rule, he caught himself at times thinking that a father who begins to feel burdened with age and plagued with pain, debility, and ill-health should choose the right moment to turn over his position, riches, and power to his son. One day after

confusing the names of two of his closest political counselors, he began seriously to contemplate the question of which
of his three sons—Faraj, Muhammed, or Nasir, who had a
Christian mother—would be the best to take his place.

The custom among the Moors was that the eldest son
would inherit the kingdom, and the sultan was desirous of
respecting tradition. But he was of the firm opinion that
the interests of the kingdom must be his first consideration,
and for the general good he was prepared to break with that
most ancient of traditions.

The Eldest Son

AS A CHILD the sultan's eldest son, Faraj, had been indecisive, delicate, overprotected, and spoiled by his mother.
He seldom said anything and spent hours in a world of his
own. Many at the Alhambra had assumed he was lazy and
retarded.

The sultan was well aware that his firstborn did not em-
body the Nasrid virtues in matters of strength, zeal, confidence, or speaking ability. But he often consoled himself
with the thought that in childhood some individuals are
withdrawn and inward, and one can never predict how they
may develop and behave in the future.

FARAJ TOOK a wife at a tender age, a life event that
brought about a sweeping transformation in him. He became more self-confident, ready to engage the world, and
even talkative. Over time he began to show an unfortunate indiscretion in his speech. His ceaseless chatter and
hectic witticisms were of limited interest to most of those

attending him, for he was one of those people who in fact had very little to say.

One day while the family was at supper Faraj sought to enliven the meal by discussing politics. He had just reached the age of twenty-six. The new century was young. Faraj choose his words carefully, expressing as precisely as possible a number of views he had never divulged before. He began with a scathing critique of the sultan and insisted with unwarranted arrogance that the ongoing conflict with the rival Ashqilula clan should be resolved with force. At issue was an irregular stretch of border in the south of the realm. Faraj did not simply call for an attack; he recommended insistently that in order to improve the morale of the troops, his father should allow the soldiers to plunder the Ashqilula population and rape their women.

The sultan felt it necessary to interrupt Faraj and put him in his place.

"Complicated matters of politics can lead astray those of lesser vision. A wise man, on the other hand, knows and humbly accepts that the sultan alone is empowered to make important decisions. I wish to point out to you that your behavior is a breach of our customs and court etiquette. I will not for a moment allow you—or anyone else, for that matter—to disturb this splendid banquet with needless discussions of matters you are incapable of understanding."

Faraj had not expected such a brusque rebuff and reproach. His self-confidence collapsed and his spirits instantly fell. The blood drained from his face; he became so pale that everyone thought he was about to faint. At that moment the sultan perceived, clearer than ever before, that his firstborn was one of the great crowd of the despicable. He was an unworthy, weak, and easily exploited man, clearly unsuited to rule Granada.

ONE WEEK LATER Muhammed II implanted a hard moist kiss on Faraj's forehead and sent him away to govern Málaga, banishing him to a place taken from the Ashqilula clan ten years earlier.

The Middle Son

THE SULTAN'S SECOND SON, Muhammed, was a violent soul with an unfortunate fascination for daggers and scimitars. He pleased himself, completely disregarded custom and tradition, and scorned the law. He was impulsive, and his emotions often flared up. He loved to rule, command, and issue orders. The subjects feared him, for he was contrary, unruly, and evil; he would have people severely flogged for the least offense.

Only one person was close to Muhammed, a dark-skinned African concubine reputed to have an appetite for delights of the flesh that would have sufficed for a whole harem. She never surrendered herself to anyone but Muhammed. Her name was Nedjmaa and despite her age—she was over forty—she was considered one of the most attractive women in Granada. She was always wrapped in black satin, leaving visible only her ankles and her dark piercing eyes. The insistent rumor was that half her face had been badly slashed when as a seven-year-old she resisted a slaver who tried to rape her. It was said that as compensation for all the suffering she had undergone because of her ravaged face, fate had granted to her a perfect body.

Her father, a medicine man and rainmaker, was of the little-known nomadic Penje tribe in Africa. In their culture it was completely acceptable for mothers to conceive with their own sons and for fathers to lie with their own daughters. Nedjmaa had accepted Islam without giving up her tribal beliefs and she practiced both religions. It was said that her father had taught her the arts of black magic as well as how to urinate while standing up, and that she had eaten human flesh. Some people insisted that she could walk through flames without being burned. Others exchanged stories about magic and witchcraft, asserting that she had turned Muhammed's head with the burning fire of her genitals. Those at the court quivered with delight at the juicy details of their supposedly torrid love life.

Muhammed paid no attention to the chatter of evil tongues. His only interest was power. He dreamed that one day he would be the master of Granada.

MUHAMMED WAS INITIALLY DISTRESSED when Faraj was exiled to Málaga, but then he became hotly indignant at his father's failure to see him as the obvious candidate to inherit the throne. He became convinced that the appointment of Faraj as governor was intended to prepare his brother to rule Granada, a thought he found unbearable.

Muhammed secluded himself in his room, unreachable, ranting about disappointment and injustice, blaming by turns the royal counselors, his brother, and his mother. His fiercest curses were directed at his father. He swore with sword in hand and with a face distorted by rage that one day he would separate his brother's head from his body.

"I'll torture you to death, Faraj," he bellowed. "Soon damp, clammy earth will cover your face, plug your nostrils, and fill up your lungs. You will return to dust as if you'd never been born. For I am the only man worthy of the throne of Granada."

He waved his saber so wildly that he lost his balance and tumbled facedown onto the floor. Standing outside, Nedjmaa secretly had overheard his volcanic outburst.

By that evening Muhammed had regained his calm. As they lay together in bed, Nedjmaa revealed to him the cunning plan of vengeance she had developed for her lover.

"Providence knew exactly what it was doing," Nedjmaa assured him as she rubbed his hands. "With your brother far away and out of the sultan's eyes, you can put my plan into action. You will travel to Málaga and free Faraj from the golden cage in which he has been confined."

Death in Málaga

MUHAMMED MADE an unannounced visit to Faraj in Málaga and stayed at his brother's residence for a whole month. It was a vast dark house with many intricate corridors, gloomy and clammy with damp. The brothers seldom conversed, but the house servants reported that they often spent entire evenings sitting in silence and smoking *kef*, a sort of North African hashish.

One dark night, the tenth day of the lunar month of Muharram, they fell out with each other and began to fight. No one knows the cause of the dispute, but it was clear that Muhammed started it. Wrestling his brother facedown onto the floor, he roared with fury as if demented. He held Faraj down and crammed his face against the tiles. Faraj struggled to free himself but was no match for Muhammed. Faraj began to weep. Seeing this, Muhammed spat on his head and pulled a dagger. The struggle was brief and ended quickly. Muhammed rose, stepped back, and watched with curiosity as his brother's life ebbed away.

Muhammed felt relieved and released. Carrying out Nedjmaa's plan had been considerably easier than he had expected. Not a trace of weakness. Certainly, he was a man of action. "At last I am rid of my brother," he told himself with satisfaction. He seated himself on the edge of the bed feeling drained and leaden. *Lots of sleep and regular bowel movements, that's what I need,* he thought. As he drowsed off he heard the corridors fill with screams and lamentations.

Confession

MUHAMMED LEFT MÁLAGA by the light of dawn and rode back to his father's palace. A court servant in green livery showed him into the throne room where the sultan was seated, magnificent and imposing. Without hesitation Muhammed acknowledged that he had killed his brother.

"I acted in self-defense," he declared. "Faraj stole my concubine, a woman whose beauty was for me the deepest of all mysteries. I accused him of the deed and he lied right to my face. I told him that with my own eyes I had seen them copulating. I was infuriated; I may have shouted. Suddenly Faraj drew his dagger and tried to stab me in the abdomen. I owe thanks to my lucky stars that my quick reflexes kept me away from his blade. Believe me, Father, I swear upon my honor that I acted in self-defense."

Muhammed had expected to be subjected to a harsh interrogation. Instead, his father, overwhelmed by grief, said nothing. He fixed his gaze on his son and contemplated those ice-cold eyes, that powerful, compact body, that black mustache. He was pained to see not even a hint of sorrow in Muhammed's eyes. But what hurt him the most was that his son, his own flesh and blood, would not honor him with the truth but instead was lying, without the least compunction. He knew that Muhammed's alleged candor was false and his account of the tragic events in Málaga was in fact a deliberate and calculated fabrication.

The sultan said, "Mendacity is a flagrant offense to the will of heaven, to the will of God. I should like to believe that you are a righteous man and that you have given me a truthful account of the events as you see them. The reasons a man may think he has to hate and kill another man are manifold. But you and Faraj have never had any scores to settle with each other."

"Father," Muhammed replied, going to his knees, "I never intended to do any evil. The last thing I wished was to stain my hands with Faraj's blood. I acted in self-defense."

The sultan gestured to Muhammed to stand up. He said, "He who intended no evil has no reason to fear."

Four Evening Meals

FORTY DAYS AFTER this audience the sultan summoned his two sons, Muhammed and Nasir. He inspected them closely for several seconds before he spoke.

"After this time of mourning, deep silence, and reflection, I wish to determine what sorts of men you are. Each of you will invite me to two meals. The first of these should offer the best food and drink the world can provide. For the second you will serve me the worst meal you can imagine."

"Excuse me for asking, Father," said Muhammed, who was impatient and already beginning to appear agitated, "but what's the meaning of all this? Is it some sort of test?"

"I wish to see your true faces revealed," the sultan calmly replied, with the serene air of a man well aware of his own extensive experience. "The plates you put before me will reveal deep secrets of your souls. Within these meals the future is hidden. We belong to God and to him we will return. *Inshallah.* I command you to depart and immediately to set about these tasks."

MUHAMMED WAS NOT the sort of person capable of fussing with extensive, complicated preparations. He found the notion of devoting his time to matters of as little interest as arranging a banquet both meaningless and unnecessary. He thought the requirement to draw up two menus was especially preposterous. He saw the task as a clear sign that advancing age was diminishing his father's mental powers. This conclusion strengthened his conviction that he soon would have to take his rightful place on the sultan's throne.

When Muhammed's mother asked him if he needed help in satisfying the sultan's wishes, he made an irritated gesture and answered dismissively. "Planning two meals is a trivial undertaking. I know what I like and what I don't like. I don't need your help, Mother. Only a fool dowses his own lamp in order to light it again with a borrowed flame."

Hunting pheasants in the forests of the foothills of the Sierra Nevada was Muhammed's favorite pastime. On the first evening he served a splendid pheasant surrounded by the most elegant and delicious vegetables. A cook had prepared the dinner.

———

THE DAY had been unusually hectic, and the sultan had not found time for any food or drink other than his morning cup of lime-blossom tea. He was looking forward with great anticipation to the evening at Muhammed's banquet table. At the sight of the dishes placed before him, he fell completely silent. He took a bite of pheasant, mostly out of curiosity to test the truth of Muhammed's assertion that it tasted like honey. He made no comment about the meal. After only a few minutes he excused himself, rose from the table, and vanished from the room.

Muhammed remained seated, sighed in resignation, shook his head, and drummed his fingers on the table. "So these are the thanks I get for all the work I invested in this damned meal," he concluded.

THE LIBRARY was the sultan's sacred space, a place marked by tranquillity, a peculiar scent, and a carefully crafted splendor that not even the throne room of Granada could rival. Along the shelves that covered its walls were carefully arranged in alphabetical order five thousand handwritten manuscripts bound in calfskin with his initials stamped in gold upon their spines. Here could be found all the knowledge of the Muslim world.

The sultan took a manuscript down from the shelf and went out onto the balcony. He stood there motionless for a long time, looking out toward the horizon. The night was warm and a moon as golden as an orange was rising over the mountain crests.

THE NEXT EVENING Muhammed offered him a grilled beefsteak and stewed turnips. The sultan shook his head, pushed the plate away to signal his distaste, rose from the table, and again went to his library without commenting on the meal or expressing thanks. Obviously Muhammed was not expecting his father to show any enthusiasm for the second menu, but he was disappointed nevertheless. He had a clear impression of the sultan's unfavorable disposition toward him, even though his father had not uttered anything offensive, dismissive, or condemnatory.

On the second evening, just as on the first, his father did not ask him why he had chosen that specific menu. The reason was simple. The sultan could see full well that Muhammed had ordered up the two meals on the spur of the moment and with a wave of the hand, devoting no thought to them. The sultan had learned in his long life that only a very few people were granted powers of intellect and exceptional creativity, and Muhammed was not among them. For that reason he could expect little of that son.

NASIR, THE YOUNGEST SON, twenty-one years of age, also found his father's request a trifle bizarre—not because he found the task onerous but mostly because he had never before in his life prepared any food and drink. He therefore had no idea at all what to put on the table or how to go about providing a table full of delights. But he beamed with pleasure, for it was clear to him that his father always knew best. It was not a son's responsibility to question any desire or opinion that his father might choose to express.

Nasir secluded himself in his room for three days, studying various books and pondering. Then he summoned his mother and asked for her help.

"Let me confess something strange to you," she told him. "Since I am a Christian, I am not very well acquainted with the faith of your father. But recently, not often, in fact only three or four times, certain verses of the Koran have presented themselves to me for no apparent reason. Perhaps these are exactly the words you need to hear:

> *Fortunate are the righteous*
> *Who are humble in their prayers*
> *And who turn away from idle speech."*

"'Idle speech,'" Nasir repeated thoughtfully after her. An idea struck him.

ON THE FIRST EVENING the youngest son put out thin slices of cooked tongue. The plate contained nothing else.

Muhammed II examined the food in silence. He was baffled.

"Do me the honor, Nasir, of explaining just what this is," he said.

"This is a tongue, Father, a delicacy," the youngest son replied. "You asked to be served the best the world can provide. Therefore I took the liberty of offering you tongue. This is because in my opinion the tongue is the finest part of the body. The tongue can articulate fine words; it can give voice to truth and help us to live in harmony with the teachings of the Koran. Righteous words give men strength and courage. The tongue is a vehicle of harmony, loving-kindness, and justice. It can bring the people of Granada more closely together."

The sultan was impressed by Nasir's answer. He sniffed the tongue. Its delicate scent was intoxicating. He chewed a morsel with childish delight, carefully explored the taste, and swallowed it slowly with a deep sigh of satisfaction. The sun had gone down, and the cool of the evening spread through the room. Father and son remained together at the table for hours, deep in discussion. This was their first opportunity to spend an extended time together. Toward midnight the sultan thanked Nasir for his generosity and then, with a certain emotion, embraced him.

THE NEXT DAY, with every passing hour the sultan became more curious about Nasir's second menu. With quick steps he went that evening to the dinner table, where he found on the platter exactly the same meal as the night before. The sultan was surprised. For a moment he thought there had been some mistake. Nasir smiled mysteriously and with an elegant gesture invited his father to the table. Before touching his food, the sultan asked for an explanation.

"Father, you commanded my brother and me to serve the worst things we could find," Nasir answered him. "This evening I took the liberty of serving tongue. In my opinion the tongue can be man's worst enemy. The tongue can speak words of anger and hate, words that provoke tears and destroy human hopes. The tongue can spread lies and evil rumors. More than any other weapon, the tongue can create dissension and can harm the people of Granada."

Nasir's words greatly impressed his father. Just as on the previous evening, the sultan inhaled the dizzying scent rising from the platter, then chewed the tongue with childish glee, paying close attention to the taste, and swallowed it slowly with a deep sigh.

The sun had gone down. Evening cool spread through the room. Father and son remained at the table for a long time. They discussed poetry and passages from the Koran. Seldom had the sultan opened his heart as he did that evening. He told how the world had not been created once for all time, and he said that in the course of his life he had experienced many things he never could have imagined in his youth. He added that a relatively large number of those things that in youth he had expected to be the culmination of his existence had quickly vanished from his memory. Then he affirmed, not without a certain melancholy, that one knows only very little of what dwells within the heart. Nasir listened attentively to his father, who did not fail to notice that the youngest son's natural modesty had concealed his considerable erudition.

The Decision

TOWARD MIDNIGHT the sultan rocked back and forth in his library, talking to himself.

"Nasir has never fallen prey to the foolishness of youth. He is calm, earnest, somewhat reticent but not cold—quite the opposite, he's often very warm. His temperament is different from that of Muhammed. Muhammed seems to despise everyone and everything. Even as a child he hated Faraj. He is driven by unbridled passions, and he's always ready to do battle, willful and with the temper of a madman. Nasir is never like that; he's calm and respectful, accepting people for what they are. In addition, he's modest and takes no pleasure in the badges of rank."

The sultan came to a decision: "Discretion and wisdom dwell with Nasir. He is the right man to manage the affairs of Granada one day."

Muhammed II decided not to proclaim his decision immediately. He concluded that the wisest course would be to keep things unchanged. Nothing should be published until the time was right. He was deeply satisfied with the outcome of the process. He went to bed and fell asleep immediately.

———

A COUPLE OF MONTHS later, on a starry night, while lying in bed next to Nedjmaa, Muhammed complained bitterly about his father. "Don't I fulfill my duties every day and defend the interests of Granada? Don't I take the best possible care of my father? And his response is to tell me as often as he can—indirectly—that I'm a crude, simple soul and I'll be a scourge to everyone around me when I rule Granada one day. He lectures me on the atrocious administration of the distant caliphate of Baghdad. He obviously hopes I'll compare myself with all those terrible rulers he speaks so disparagingly of and I'll understand that I'm just like them. But I won't; I have no intention of doing so, no matter how often my wily old father tries to force me."

Nedjmaa gave him a challenging look. "You must show that you are a powerful man, a man of action, that you will overcome all obstacles your father puts in your way. Show them that nothing can keep you from your goal."

"What do you expect of me? It makes me shiver when I see what you're after. Nedjmaa, what exactly is it that you are trying to get me to do? The whole thing is completely insane. You know very well that I cannot murder my own father."

"How many have eaten of that same fruit before you?"

"Who am I to rebel against my father, my superior, consecrated by Allah the all-powerful? The very idea is insane!"

"You think too much. Just act. There is no coming back. A man who killed his brother must never turn back. Your father the sultan embodies senility and decay. He belongs to a world doomed to perish. Granada is in crisis and needs a powerful, determined, harsh master. The people are not longing for ideas and gentle behavior but instead for a man of rigor, someone to chastise them and purify them. I can see everything clearly before me right now."

"Your nonsense drives me mad, Nedjmaa. I'm worried and afraid. Perhaps it's the last remaining touch of weakness in me. I can't possibly chop off my father's head."

"Free yourself from those useless quibblings of your conscience! You won't put an end to your father's days. You'll have the Jew do it. Let Chaim de Espinosa be your tool, your willing right hand. Promise him that he will become your personal physician. He will poison the sultan for you."

"And if he refuses? You know how much he loves my father."

"You'll just have to make it clear to him we'll all face catastrophe if a senile sultan continues to rule Granada. Don't let the Jew rest for a minute, press him hard, tell him that he's either with you or against you. Remind him that he who is not your friend is your enemy, and his damned gratitude toward the sultan is no excuse in this. It's a question of choosing sides right now, making a decision, declaring his allegiance! Threaten his family if he's reluctant. That's where he is vulnerable. They say that he loves his little son more than anything else on earth, and his wife is expecting another child."

Muhammed sank into silence, apparently exhausted. Nedjmaa rose from the bed and fetched bread and water. After a moment of hesitation he accepted it. He broke the bread, ate and drank.

Crime and Punishment

HISTORY OF THE ARABS by the Lebanese author Philip Khuri Hitti is considered a classic. My great-uncle was the one who told us about it. Here, without any particular questioning of the sources but with unprecedented richness of detail, the author provides an account of the events recorded by the Arabic chroniclers.

Hitti writes:

Sultan Muhammed II ibn Nasrid died on April 8, 1302. After his midday meal he received a pastry delivered to him by a servant from the house of his son Muhammed. He was pleased by the gift and consumed it with good appetite. During afternoon prayers as he knelt in the mosque he experienced a sudden sharp pain in his abdomen. The pain intensified and he rapidly choked to death. He was interred that same evening in the gardens of the Alhambra, after which his son was proclaimed Sultan Muhammed III.

When Chaim heard the news of the sultan's death, emotion and shame tormented him. He became despondent.

"No one can help me," he muttered. "Putrefaction dwells within me. I despise myself. I have betrayed my benefactor. I am an evil person and I deserve to die."

His wife, Rebecca, saw the panic in Chaim's eyes and heard him lamenting. She wanted to know what had happened. Chaim babbled rapidly and incoherently, almost swallowing his tongue in his haste to explain. Rebecca eventually grasped the fact that the sultan was dead and her own husband had prepared the poison that killed him. She was seized with a furious dismay.

"How could you do such a horrible thing? How could you get involved with Muhammed? How could you let yourself be persuaded by him—when the sultan was certainly your generous benefactor and protector and treated you as a friend? Do you have any idea of what you've done?"

"I was betrayed by my own gullible nature," Chaim replied. "That's how I wound up in this appalling situation! Believe me, my dearest one, Muhammed promised that he would make me his personal physician."

"Even if he rewards you with the post of court physician, you'll never be able to live with yourself. Nothing will ever allow you to forget, and you'll never be free of your evil deed. Besides, if you're capable of willingly betraying the sultan who took such good care of you, without even thinking twice, then Muhammed knows that you're absolutely unreliable. He knows you'd be ready to do the same to him."

"I shudder at the thought of what Muhammed forced me to do. But he threatened to submit me to unbearable torture if I refused to cooperate."

"Your fear of suffering has caused an even greater catastrophe. Don't you understand what your treachery has led to?"

AT NIGHT Chaim lay sleepless in tormented anticipation of what might happen next. Hour after hour, in a cold sweat and with a pounding heart, he heard voices whispering to him out of the floor and the walls. Haunting cries pierced him with their torrent of mockery, abuse, and dark threats. Was he imagining things? *No,* he told himself, *these grim, implacable voices are demons who want to see me perish.*

His agonizing wait ended at dawn. Chaim felt a certain relief when four soldiers burst into the bedroom, ordered him to get dressed, and without another word carried him off to the dungeon of the palace. He looked around and shuddered at the certainty of what was coming. He quietly gabbled a Jewish prayer, understanding that this was the inevitable price of his treachery. He offered no resistance as the soldiers forced him down onto a bench and held him there. A powerfully built torturer opened his mouth and cut out his tongue with a red-hot blade. The pain was unbearable but brief. Chaim fainted almost immediately.

When he came back to consciousness his vision was blurred and he could see nothing but the light of torches flickering against the walls. He lay on his back, half naked in a pool of dried blood that had stained the bench. His arms and legs were tightly bound with stout cord. He slowly came to his senses and discovered little by little that he was dripping with blood. He was surrounded by men who stared at him with contempt. At his side stood Muhammed and his mother, the sultan's widow. Their eyes burned with hate.

Although Chaim was groggy and in terrible pain, he still had enough fortitude to try to explain. But he was racked suddenly by an attack of coughing that convulsed his whole body. He vomited blood. Those in the dungeon stiffened even further. The executioner stepped forward and held his head until his coughing ceased. Chaim took a deep breath, his eyes full of tears. His lips twitched. All eyes were fixed upon his mouth. However much he tried, he could not utter a word. The true misery of his condition burst upon him with the knowledge that his effort to speak was vain and meaningless. He would never manage to reveal the truth about Muhammed.

In the background the hunting hounds were howling. *A bad omen*, Chaim thought.

"There is only one fitting punishment when a man sinks to such degradation that he betrays and murders his benefactor and master. That is death," Muhammed declared. "Although you are the foulest creature in Granada, I will take pity upon you, for I am a sultan with a good heart. Therefore I spare you from a slow, protracted death."

With a quick flash of his dagger he slit open Chaim's belly. He plunged his hands into the body, located the heart and cut it out, then threw the still-beating organ to the dogs.

The Grim Truth

THE STORY of Chaim's treachery frightened me more than any other experience in my childhood. When I thought of him, I was struck with grief, I suffered asthma attacks, and I couldn't sleep; in the dark of the night I was tormented by terrifying thoughts. It was not unusual for me to sob until the sun began to rise. Sorrow and the torment of imagination gripped me tightly for days on end. No one could comfort me or console me. I could not bear the thought that the traitor's blood was circulating in my own arteries.

Fate used my great-uncle's voice to whisper the message to me that I was born to be a liar and a cheat. He often told Sasha and me that an unusually large nose was a Spinoza trait that turned up in each generation. The children born with that gigantic nose were always uncommonly lucky and successful in whatever they undertook. The nose brought good fortune to the one who inherited it, even though all of them, strangely enough, met tragic deaths. Likewise, duplicity was passed down through the Spinozas in a sort of inexplicable natural balancing act, also revealing itself in every generation. Children born with that strange inability to tell the truth were always solitary because they disappointed everyone and failed at everything. Their perpetual lying was in itself a curse upon them.

My great-uncle never said it in so many words, but we all knew it. Anyone with eyes in his head could see it; the truth could not be hidden. My twin brother, Sasha, had an enormous nose.

A Game of Chess

MUHAMMED HAD FELT EXHILARATED since the sultan's death less than twenty-four hours earlier. He was enormously pleased that at last he was the ruler of Granada. He considered himself exactly the right man for the job. He was greatly stimulated by the knowledge that because he was generally feared, people would comply with his wishes and humbly obey his every command. Seated on the throne with Nedjmaa at his side, surrounded by his father's old counselors, he felt a strong urge to make a demonstration of his power. He aimed more than anything else to prevent the court from speculating about the sudden death of his father. He ordered two guards to fetch Rebecca, the wife of the executed Jewish physician, so as—in his own words—to see that justice was promptly carried out. He intended to charge her with complicity in the death of the sultan.

MUHAMMED HAD NO NOTION of Rebecca's character, even though he had seen her now and again. He had always been impressed by her beautiful face, but now she appeared transformed, smaller and paler than he remembered her, anything but a beauty. He made no comment upon the change because he was disconcerted by the sight of her swollen belly; he had forgotten that she was expecting a child. A painful silence settled over the room. For a long moment Muhammed regarded Rebecca in silence. He particularly noted the sorrow in her eyes and the dignity of her despair.

Rebecca was the first to speak. She had caught sight of a table in the depths of the throne room where a chessboard was set up with marble pieces, ready for a match. This gave her an idea. She knew of the old sultan's passion for chess and knew it had become an all-enveloping passion at court. In an attempt to save her life, she suggested a chess match.

"High and worthy sultan," she said, "should I lose the match, I will forfeit the life of my son, Moishe, and that of my unborn child. But if I by dint of my efforts should succeed, I beg His Grace to spare our lives and grant us the right to go back home to the house of my father in Córdoba."

Rebecca evinced a degree of courage uncommon even among men. Her bold suggestion further disconcerted Muhammed, not least because he was certain that not a single woman of Granada knew the rules of chess. He was confident that he had nothing to lose in accepting her challenge, for no one but his own father had ever beaten him at the game. Even so, he hesitated for a moment. He glanced down at Nedjmaa as if to ask: *What do you think of this?* Just as taken aback as he was, Nedjmaa was incapable of advising him.

A satisfied little smile broke over Muhammed's face. His eyes sparkled. He accepted Rebecca's suggestion.

Muhammed played with great concentration—taking the white pieces, of course—and began with a bold opening gambit he had learned from his father. Rebecca's response was ineffective. He quickly put her at a disadvantage, capturing two pawns and a knight.

The astonished counselors following the match were convinced that Muhammed would triumph. When Rebecca made an apparently meaningless move, the spectators murmured in derision. Muhammed straightened up, filled his chest, and declared, "Victory is near." But he suddenly saw that Rebecca's next move was countering his aggressive play; the truth was that she had set a complicated trap for him.

Muhammed realized that he had been relying too much on the luck that up until that moment had never abandoned him. He had failed to perceive the astute thought and implacable logic behind Rebecca's moves. He now foresaw that he would lose in two more moves. Perplexed, he interrupted the game so as to avoid subjecting himself to ridicule. He grumbled, "This is a match at the highest level of play, and I am about to triumph. But the fact is that I have no time for playing chess. Granada needs a powerful sultan, a man of action to resolve its many issues. I am a benevolent ruler, Rebecca, and therefore I release you as of this moment. You must leave the city within two hours."

A Story About Chess

MY GREAT-UNCLE told us wonderful stories about chess and seldom failed to include, as if in passing, an account of some historic match between grand masters. He would describe it move by move. He adored chess. The game had literally saved his life.

This had happened before the Second World War in Dachau, the first German concentration camp, set up outside Munich especially to deal with Jews, homosexuals, so-called political criminals, and derelicts.

The winter was bitterly cold. One night two dockworkers who had been active in the Rostock union managed to escape from the camp. They smashed the lightbulbs in a narrow corridor and under cover of darkness overpowered two guards, strangled them with their bare hands, stripped them, and put on their uniforms. Then they nonchalantly strolled out through the main gates of Dachau.

Only a handful of prisoners had ever escaped from that camp. All of the inmates had sometimes felt the strong temptation to try and had seriously weighed the possible consequences of attempting an escape, but Dachau was not a place one could simply slip away from. Therefore the prisoners' most common escape was spiritual, into their own dreams of freedom.

The rumor spread in whispers through the barracks that two men had killed a couple of the hated guards and regained their freedom. The malnourished, worn-out prisoners were astounded and excited by the escape. Many felt that the guards had gotten exactly what they deserved. Several began to think of following the example of the bold dockworkers.

The search for the escapees went on all night. At dawn, straining bloodhounds detected the scent of the Rostock men ten miles north of Dachau. The camp commandant, Oberführer Hans Loritz, burst into a rage when he received the report that the escapees had been found frozen to death, for he had given strict orders that they were to be captured alive. Loritz was disappointed that he would not have the pleasure of personally torturing the men to death and then planting them on chairs on the parade ground for all to see, bearing a sign inscribed GOOD TO BE BACK AGAIN. The frustrated camp commandant roared at the top of his lungs that ten prisoners were to be shot immediately in retribution for each of the murdered guards.

Two armed soldiers burst into my great-uncle's overcrowded barracks, and in the stifling gloom one of them pointed at Fernando where he lay in his bunk. "You there, get up, now, stand at attention!" shouted the men in uniform. "You're going to be taken out and shot!"

My great-uncle went rigid. He was convinced that his last hour on earth had arrived. The guards stalked farther into the barracks looking for additional victims. Fernando lay there for a moment, in a fetal position, paralyzed with fear. When the guards were out of sight, his bunkmate, the tailor Aron Reinherz, whispered in his ear. Fernando knew the old gentlemen's tailor from Vienna, where they had shared the same lodgings. In Dachau they would often while away their idle hours playing chess with pieces molded of dry bread.

"Esteemed Herr Scharf, you have beaten me so often in chess. Grant me now, please, a favor that means a great deal to me. Let me be the lucky one today and take your place."

My great-uncle was so astonished that he could scarcely respond. Aron Reinherz got out of the bunk and added, "Thank you for your generosity, Herr Scharf. Allow me to ask one additional favor. Please drink a cup of coffee at Sacher's someday and have a bit of their famous cake for me."

The old tailor stood in the doorway. Half a minute later the guards carried him and another prisoner off to the parade ground outside the barracks.

A couple of the prisoners, including my great-uncle, cautiously crept to a window and listened intently, trying to make out what was happening in the yard. Four armed guards stood out there ten or fifteen feet away, their mustaches white with frost and their breath steaming in the air. The prisoners could hear the guards grumbling to one another about the intense cold. A hearty laugh rang out. Gentlemen's tailor Aron Reinherz was doubled up in amusement.

"What's the matter with you, Jew?" screamed one of the guards. "What are you laughing at? What's so funny? You're about to die, you idiot!"

"The truth is, I'm laughing at you, guard." The old Jew raised his voice so it could be heard throughout the yard. "In just a few moments I won't have to put up with the cold. But you'll be standing here the whole morning long, shivering. So just who's the fool—"

The next second the ice-cold silence of the yard was shattered by three pistol shots.

The Great Fortune of Our Lineage

WHEN REBECCA ARRIVED in Córdoba and her father asked her with amazement what had given her the idea of suggesting a game of chess, her answer was curt.

"Not what, dear father, but who. An angel. Who also guided my hand at the board."

Not long afterward, Rebecca died in childbirth, and the infant did not survive. Rabbi Orabuena took the responsibility of caring for two-year-old Moishe.

THE BRILLIANT DE ESPINOSA court physicians in Lisbon had vast knowledge of herbs and curative plants but were completely uninformed about the world around them. They were so intent on satisfying their rulers and pleasing their God by zealously complying with their own centuries-old traditions that they paid no attention to new notions and were never enticed by the contemporary proliferation of new ideas. They lived in this way from generation to generation, during a time when Jewish mystics felt extraordinarily driven to explore paths leading to the secrets of the universe and to create poetry of great beauty and depth. My ancestors lived their backward and provincial lives, indifferent to events both proximate and imminent, like all who are prisoners of their own officious shortsightedness.

Rabbi Orabuena, in contrast, was an erudite, intelligent man with a keen sense of ethics. Throughout his life he sought to identify the threads of thought common to the Jewish tradition, Christianity, and the Platonic philosophers. He wanted to understand the principles that rule the fragile destiny of the earth and even affect the eternal heavenly spheres.

The rabbi opened Moishe's eyes to broad horizons and strove incessantly to develop his intellect. He encouraged a quickness of thought in the boy and pushed him to become bolder. Above all, the rabbi made sure that three fundamental principles remained engraved clearly and forever in the boy's consciousness.

Those three fundamental truths pronounced by Rabbi Orabuena were a constant theme of my great-uncle, so I remember them particularly well. Even so, I must acknowledge that I failed to appreciate the wisdom of those words until thirty years after I first heard them. Before that, they seemed unrelated to my own life.

I.   Every day begins with reflection; every day ends with constancy.

II. There are always many more realms of truth and reason than those of prevalent contemporary opinion and the traditions of one's own society.

III. Only fools remain certain of their beliefs and fail to doubt.

The Double Loss

WHY HAVE I DESERVED *to fall into disgrace with the Almighty?* That was Israel's first thought when the news reached him that Chaim had been executed in Granada in reprisal for the murder of the sultan. A dark shadow fell across the forehead of the old royal physician; he dropped to his knees, his lips twisted into a grimace, and tears streamed down his bearded cheeks. He gave vent to his pain, lamenting loud and long, then he sank fainting to the floor.

What tormented Israel most?

Sasha and I never got an answer to that question. My great-uncle sighed aloud with a far-off smile, but for once he could not explain. And so, even today, I do not know what grieved Israel more—losing his son or the belief that he, having lived in the ardent conviction that the whole meaning of life was to serve the Lord, had fallen from God's grace.

ONCE ISRAEL had recovered from the initial shock and regained some measure of composure, he went upstairs to Leah, the only one of his daughters still unmarried, living in her narrow space in the attic of her parents' house. They had not exchanged a word since that day long ago when Chaim was born. He could not even remember the last time he had seen her; she appeared totally alien to him as she stood there, filthy and unkempt in the colossal disorder. When he looked at his daughter, she instinctively turned her gaze away. He saw she had become an old woman without ever having had a life; she emitted an odor of dead flowers. Only now did he realize that he had reacted far too strongly in completely cutting her off, allowing her place in his heart to wither, and turning her into a stranger because of a prophecy that had now come true.

Overcome with shame, he bowed his head and told her he had come to ask for forgiveness. She had spoken the truth from the very first moment: Chaim had brought eternal shame to the name of Espinosa. Then he told her in an almost inaudible voice that his son was dead. His eyes filled with tears. A new pain burned suddenly inside as he realized this meant the end of the Espinosa line.

Then Leah spoke for the first time in almost thirty years. She said that she had sworn never again to burden her father with another prophecy, but now she was obliged to tell him what her psychic powers had revealed. The continuation of the family was assured, for Chaim had a son.

Israel's blood instantly froze to ice, but once again he didn't believe Leah. His face contorted with hopelessness and fury. He pretended not to have heard his daughter's words.

HAGGARD, YELLOW in the face, prey to black moods and strong attacks of melancholy, Israel spent several weeks secluded in his study among the heaps of manuscripts dealing with the mysteries of the plant kingdom and with the laws of the Torah. He listened to the howling of the wind in the treetops and to the distant murmur of the stars. He spent sleepless nights plunged in regret. When the mornings came, he prayed with a dull voice to the Creator of the universe to spare him from any further trials.

A few weeks later a letter from Rabbi Orabuena reached him, reporting that since both of Moishe's parents were dead, the rabbi and his wife had taken the boy in hand. The letter confirmed Leah's prediction.

This news naturally consoled Israel somewhat, but at the same time it increased his own feeling of inadequacy. To whom could he entrust the recipe for the Raimundo plant? His own remaining progeny were the twelve daughters. Therefore he was obliged to leave the knowledge of the secret of eternal life to his grandson Moishe. How could he do so without having to initiate some outsider? The boy was only two years old and lived in faraway Córdoba.

One afternoon Israel happened to stumble against the table. A manuscript from the top of the stack fell to the floor with a thud. It was the Sefer Yetzirah, a centuries-old work discussing God's creation of the world. He picked it up and kissed it in a gesture of penitence for allowing the holy manuscript to come in contact with the unclean floor. He opened it at random and his eyes fell upon a sentence: *The twenty-two fundamental characters then I shaped, cast, assembled, weighed, and exchanged, and with them I fashioned all creation and everything that shall be created in days to come.* He read the sentence several times and fixed his attention especially on the word "exchanged." An idea began to take form in his head.

The court physician spent the following days elaborating a cipher. When it was complete, he used his system to encrypt the recipe for the elixir of immortality and placed the text along with a brief outline of family history in a small wooden box, roughly carved in fragrant cedar, and carefully sealed it. In an accompanying letter he instructed Rabbi Orabuena to preserve the wooden box in a secure location and turn it over to Moishe only when he reached adulthood.

ISRAEL WENT TO BED late that night. An unusual silence ruled the room. The dark was especially thick and mysterious. He suddenly felt ill and thought that something strange and disagreeable was about to occur. For a long time he could not sleep, and after eventually drifting off, he woke with a start. He perceived a sound in the heart of the silent, indescribably motionless night. He heard it with great clarity and began to panic. Someone was paging through his manuscripts in the dark. He sat up with a jerk and tried to shout, but fear paralyzed his voice. Then he suddenly sensed that someone had come creeping into his bed. He understood immediately that his visitor was death, come in the middle of that silent night to enfold him in its arms.

A Mother's Love

MY GREAT-UNCLE was always a bit enigmatic when he spoke of Rebecca, who in his eyes had been more an angel than a woman of flesh and blood. Back then I had no fear of mysteries, and I wasn't alarmed by stories with contradictions; we were always treated to inexplicable and unexpected tales when my great-uncle came to visit. Sasha and I were thirteen years old and he was seventy-five. Though I cannot claim even today to say that I fully understood Fernando or knew what was going on within him, it was nevertheless perfectly clear to me that the grim destiny that awaited Rebecca deeply moved his heart. Most of the time he was beaming and carefree. But when he thought of that woman in fourteenth-century Granada, everything dark within him seemed to surface. His eyes filled with tears and he said, as if to emphasize that she merited our sympathy, "The verdict that heaven let fall upon Rebecca was sterner than the punishment Muhammed had prepared for her as the wife of Chaim the poisoner."

My great-uncle was referring to the fact that life never gave Rebecca the chance to bring up her son. She died in childbirth shortly after coming home to Córdoba. But she defied fate. After that she never left Moishe's side for even a second. He could always detect her presence, sense her eyes upon him, hear her voice, and detect her perfume. As soon as he shut his eyes, she was there—only in spirit, of course, but even so, bubbling with life. Rebecca kissed Moishe and embraced him, exhorted him to faithfulness and whispered wise words into his ears, hovered over him and protected him against danger.

AFTER MOISHE turned thirteen and celebrated his bar mitzvah—a sort of maturity exam for boys who are then accepted as adults in the Jewish community—Rebecca visited him in the night. Moishe could clearly sense his mother's presence and hear her voice. She said that she wished to tell him something. She was not the one who had defeated the new sultan Muhammed II at chess and thereby saved Moishe's life. An angel had revealed itself to her and guided her hand during the match. The angel had moved the chess pieces in accordance with an intricate system that had originated at the beginnings of time. It was based, so to speak, on a heavenly order that was imposed upon creation, attuned to the harmonious proportions of the nebulae and galaxies of the macrocosmos. That system has a key; with it the innermost workings of the world can be deciphered.

Rebecca promised that one day she would reveal that intricate system to Moishe. Then her voice gradually faded. Moishe leaned forward, listening eagerly, but he heard nothing more. It was so quiet in the room that the boy could hear the distant murmuring of the stars.

The Wonder Child Rescues the Jews

THE STORY I most want to relate about our distant relative Moishe de Espinosa, whom we refer to merely as "the Cabalist," played itself out during the Jewish Passover of the year 1313 in the city of Córdoba.

At that time Moishe was still only a young boy, recently turned thirteen, but sometimes he felt as if he was a hundred years old. He lived with his maternal grandparents, and throughout his childhood he had been kissed and wrapped in the warm embrace of his grandmother. His grandfather Rabbi Abraham Orabuena was reputed both for his learning and for his passionate piety: He never touched food or drink before sundown and prayed to God so intensely that he would become drenched in perspiration and had to change his shirt three times a day—an unimaginable luxury in the fourteenth century.

From his maternal grandfather Moishe had learned Aramaic, Arabic, Latin, arithmetic, and mathematics. He had read books on religion, philosophy, history, and geography. The boy's head was crammed with facts and information. He kept it all in his memory and never forgot a thing. He could read the Talmud and the Torah, even blindfolded. He was capable of judging a person's character with a single glance. The instant someone opened his mouth, Moishe knew what he was about to say. He was proficient at relieving all sorts of physical ailments. He did this by applying his mental powers, never touching the afflicted individual or using magic incantations. His treatments relieved anyone with an aching back or belly, swollen arteries, obstructed circulation, the pains of rheumatism, or bloody stools.

Pious Jews often came to the boy for spiritual guidance. At times Moishe begged them to leave him in peace; he explained apologetically that he was not a real rabbi but just an ordinary adolescent, a young man also in need of guidance. But it was no use. People continued to pound on his front door.

Moishe's reputation also came to the attention of the rulers of the city. Governor Manuel Manzanedos del Castillo dispatched one of his spies to the rabbi's house to evaluate the boy's unusual gifts and report back to the governing council of Córdoba. The man noted Moishe's familiarity with Jewish thought and history and asked the boy what he considered most important to his people. Moishe answered —as he always did—that the law was the most important thing for the Jews, for God's law was righteous and applied to all individuals; no one stood above the law, whether he be noble or a common servant.

In his extensive report the spy sought to furnish as much convincing detail as possible. He twisted Moishe's words and asserted that the boy had criticized Governor Manzanedos del Castillo and his counselors for misapplication of the laws. This allegation provoked frowns and murmurs of concern among the proud gentlemen of Córdoba's most aristocratic families. They discussed the report until late in the night. Given the influence the boy appeared to have upon his coreligionists, the implication was that a burning dissatisfaction with the rulers of the city had been kindled among the Jews. If the Jews took such criticisms to heart, they would become difficult to rule.

"There is danger in dealing with people who believe that they possess the absolute truth," declared the young Hidalgo del Solís, who wanted to show his resolution. He hoped eventually to replace the aging governor. "We have seen many examples of what happens when people think they can overthrow injustice and error and impose their truth. I suggest that we invite the torturer to investigate the Jews' devotion to this young prodigy."

Several privy counselors endorsed the young man's views. The governor replied that submitting the boy to torture might enrage his community. He said that although he had many more important issues to handle, perhaps he himself should have a talk with Moishe and sound out his opinions.

Hidalgo del Solís retorted that even a thirteen-year-old Jew, burning with evil and fanatic zeal, could bring about disaster; this being the case, the council should immediately decide what to do about the boy. After a lively discussion the council voted to endorse the governor's proposal, at least for the time being.

The rumor that Moishe was about to be arrested and tortured quickly spread through the Jewish quarter. Terror gripped the denizens of its narrow streets and doomsayers predicted that Jewish blood would flow during Passover.

GOVERNOR MANZANEDOS DEL CASTILLO was studying his notes when Moishe entered the room. The governor glanced up momentarily from his papers and ordered the boy to explain his views concerning God and the law. And to be quick about it, because the governor was a busy man working on more important matters.

Moishe responded calmly and with deference, not intimidated in the least. The words flowed from his lips like the springs from the Sierra Nevada mountains, those crystal-clear streams that run bubbling down the valleys. The governor had never heard anyone speak so beautifully. He looked up from his notes and scrutinized the wonder child whom the Jews considered to be a near reincarnation of the great prophets.

The boy still showed no signs of adolescence. His face had not a wisp of hair and his upper lip showed no trace of down. He was significantly smaller and shorter than the governor had expected. His only conspicuous feature was his immense nose. But everything about his manner—the certainty, earnest demeanor, firmness, and conviction—signaled maturity and moral stature.

Moishe reiterated his view that the law was more important than anything, for it was the supreme expression of the eternal wisdom of God the Almighty. "The law," he said pointedly, "unites humanity, while views about faith, customs, habits, and prejudice hold us apart." He commented that the reason the governor was everywhere accorded respect and admiration as well as affection and honor among the Jews of Córdoba and their neighbors was that in all his wisdom His Grace Manzanedos del Castillo was the guardian of the law.

The governor felt flattered. It had been a long time since anyone had expressed such respect for him. He was the grandson of King Ferdinand II of Castile, that scourge of the Moors who had conquered Córdoba in the year 1236. After a couple of ensuing Catholic decades the great metropolis—which under Caliph Al-Hakam had been the center of the Arab world with a library of more than a million splendid volumes—gradually had settled into the status of a sleepy garrison town. As with Córdoba, Manzanedos felt that his life was at a standstill. His advancing age had rendered him a shadow of his former self. In earlier days he had thrived on political intrigue, but now he was tired of it all. He was sunk in unbearable tedium. The only thing that interested him was the writing of his autobiography. His standing in Córdoba wasn't the same as before. People no longer accorded him the respect he had previously enjoyed, and he had an uneasy feeling that the youngest lords of the council secretly laughed at him behind his back.

Moishe's words and above all his subtle view of the world impressed the governor and reinvigorated him. Manzanedos del Castillo had always found priestly sermons about God's love amusing, given that in the strict interpretation of the injunction to love one's neighbor one would be obliged to love those who did not believe in Jesus Christ—for example, the Jews and the Muslims. But that sophistry held no attraction for him, for he considered it perilous to regard enemies as anything other than enemies. No matter how he formulated the issue and pondered it, Manzanedos del Castillo found it difficult to embrace the concept of neighborly love.

So he asked Moishe, "Do you Jews hold the law to be more important than love?"

The boy answered without hesitation. "Christians' most familiar prayer begins with the words 'Our Father, which art in Heaven' and ends with 'Deliver us from evil.' It follows therefore that evil is regarded as part of human nature, born with us, but God can free us from evil if he wishes to heed our prayers. From time to time certain men, convinced that they are acting out of love according to the will of God, assume for themselves the roles of saviors and attempt to deliver us from evil. The consequences have always been tragic and have caused even more evil, suffering, and sudden death. Throughout history my people have regularly been subjected to so-called loving efforts to save us from our supposed evil, and we know where that sort of love leads. For that reason we hold that God's law stands above all because it instructs us how we should live together here on earth. And it dictates that no one stands above the law."

"But the law does not free us from our innate evil," Manzanedos del Castillo quickly replied.

"We Jews," said Moishe in a friendly but decided tone, "do not believe that humanity is born evil. According to Talmudic teachings, the newborn child bears no moral guilt. We are born virgin, so to speak. Our personality is shaped by our experiences, and these are affected by the family and by the place in which we live, as well as by those who rule us. Any person can make a mistake and fall into evildoing. That is why it is essential always to preserve our memories. By recalling the past, we can avoid repeating our bad deeds. It is a Jewish obligation to remember, so that we can reconcile ourselves with one another and help God to mend the world."

Manzanedos del Castillo was not certain that he fully understood the boy's reasoning. All that talk about remembering was sufficiently in line with his own preferences that he heard himself muttering in agreement. He believed that there certainly must be a higher world order and a lower one, and that those orders were not in tune with each other in every way. Some were born as Jews and bore a curse; others were Catholics and constructed a kingdom. But God's law had to be respected by all. Suddenly he could also see his own role in creation as the guardian of the law in Córdoba. He felt pleasantly satisfied with that state of affairs, for he liked to examine issues from various perspectives as an honorable man without preconceived opinions.

"Young man," Manzanedos del Castillo said, "I willingly acknowledge that I have always considered you Jews to be an odd feature of Córdoba. But now that you so eloquently have reassured me of the respect and admiration of my Jewish subjects, I am convinced that you respect our laws. As a gracious gesture to demonstrate that I have no direct dislike for you as a group, I will send to the Jewish community ten young healthy lambs that you may prepare in accordance with your ritual laws and distribute among the poorest of you for the holiday meal at the upcoming Eastertide."

NOT LONG after that, my great-uncle told us, people in Jewish quarters throughout Europe were recounting the legend of the fearless orphan boy who all alone saved the Jews of Córdoba from persecution.

The Evening Seder

THE FIRST EVENING SEDER of Passover in the Jewish quarter of Córdoba was always a festive occasion. Rabbi Orabuena would sit in the synagogue with his community as the sun neared the horizon, expectantly awaiting the beloved commemoration of the liberation of the Jews. That narrow space, so crowded and stifling, was filled with the holy presence of God and the angels. The people's hearts were full with special longing. Men sang hymns and women murmured evening prayers. In the midst of this expectant optimism with its promises of freedom and well-being, the rabbi delivered a brief sermon. He praised the virtues of the faithful departed, those who are now seated on the golden thrones of glory in heaven as the mysteries of the Torah are revealed to them. The rabbi's forehead gleamed with perspiration. Moishe listened, awestruck. Many faces were streaked with tears. Everyone in the congregation sensed that the mysteries of the Torah were as one with the mysteries of the world.

After the service Moishe and his grandfather took their places in the garden outside the synagogue. Members of the community surrounded them, thanking the boy for protecting the Jews of Córdoba and praising the rabbi for offering such a stirring sermon. Eventually the boy and his grandfather excused themselves and began to make their way homeward. They looked up at a cloudless heaven full of gleaming stars. A cool breeze was blowing. Their spirits were at peace as they contemplated the heavens.

"Wherever truth may lie," the rabbi said, "one thing is certain: Heaven is infinite and mighty."

"Grandfather, it takes thousands of years for the light of the stars to reach our eyes," Moishe said. "Those stars twinkling and glittering up there are suns far larger than the earth. Each has its own planets, presumably worlds of their own. Maybe those faint traces above us are a swirling mass of millions of heavenly bodies. Just imagine, Grandfather! If only one could discover the secrets of the spheres; if only it were possible to predict precisely every eclipse of the sun and moon and the appearance of every new comet!"

"The man who can interpret the Holy Scripture, especially the revelations of the prophets, will find the answers to all questions," the rabbi commented. He clasped his hand to his chest.

Moishe did not notice his grandfather's sudden difficulty in breathing. The boy's eyes shone like jewels; they sparkled with fire and with the promise of the night. In the darkness the universe seemed full of impenetrable mystery.

AGAIN THAT YEAR, as always before, Abraham Orabuena's company of friends and their wives gathered in his house to celebrate Passover. The rabbi's wife and several other women had spent many hours preparing the Seder meal to commemorate the beginning of the eight days of Pesach. The festival of the unleavened bread recalled and celebrated the origins of the people of Israel and their departure from Egypt. The purpose was for all Jews to relive once more their escape from slavery under the Pharaoh and the creation of a free people.

In honor of the Seder festivities the rabbi had donned a splendid prayer shawl and placed a richly embroidered kippah skullcap on his head. A long table set for eighteen stood in the living room, and the house was filled with the warmth from baking and the heavenly smells from the kitchen. At each holiday festival Rabbi Orabuena took care to have exactly eighteen guests at his table, for in the tradition of the Jewish mystics the number eighteen signifies life.

The guests sat on comfortable cushions chatting, laughing, and entertaining one another with a lively flow of gossip. The rabbi sat at one end of the table. Everyone knew that feast days brought forth his robust sense of humor and he was always delighted at the laughter that his jokes provoked. But this year as that holy evening began, he was unusually quiet and preoccupied.

The rabbi's wife lit two candles and recited the prescribed blessing. The rabbi rose. Everyone at the table watched him. Carefully and with a slight stiffness in his movements, he read the blessing of the wine. Then, according to tradition, came the moment for the hosts to open the outer doors to invite the Prophet Elijah into the house to proclaim the arrival of the Messiah.

They opened the doors. To the astonishment of all, a ragged Jewish traveler stood outside. He did not look like an ordinary beggar; he had the aspect of a wise man. But his clothes were tattered. Moishe saw the stranger and recognized him immediately as one of the thirty-six righteous men. They lived lives of poverty but their dignity and humility made possible the continued existence of the world.

"An unexpected guest!" exclaimed the rabbi's wife. She invited the stranger into the house.

"*Pesach sameach.* I wish you all a good Passover," the man greeted them politely, bowing his head humbly as he entered.

"*Pesach sameach,* stranger," the rabbi answered. "Come join our table and tell us what has brought you to our part of the world."

"I do not come to share the Seder meal. I am here to say one thing, no more."

"Tell us, then," replied the rabbi.

"*Makbenak.*"

When the man pronounced the word Rabbi Orabuena's face suddenly altered. He burst into tears. His eyes, his cheeks, and his grizzled beard were all wet. His lips moved, but no words emerged. The guests at the table sat in stunned silence. Before anyone found the presence of mind to speak, the stranger left the house.

"Worthy Rabbi, tell us: Who was this man and what did he want?" said one of the guests.

The rabbi took out a large handkerchief. He wiped his eyes and blew his nose. With a broken voice he replied, "We have just witnessed a miracle."

"A miracle?" another guest repeated his words in disbelief. "What do you mean, dear Rabbi?"

An unusual silence ensued. Everyone in the room stared expectantly at the rabbi. Moishe felt a sudden shiver. He had an intuition of what was about to happen.

The rabbi stared up at the ceiling. He knew that the spirits of his forefathers were watching over him. He felt the nearness of God. With his inner eye he could see the Almighty sitting upon the throne of glory, looking down upon him. With his inner ear he could hear the angels singing psalms. He knew that the Book of Life in which all men's deeds are written had been opened, and his allotted time had come to an end. The rabbi fell forward onto the table. Pereira the physician immediately rose from his place among the guests to help him.

"What happened?" called out the rabbi's wife. "How is my husband? Can you help him?"

"He needs nothing now but the grace of God," Pereira told them.

SCARCELY AN HOUR after the sudden death of Abraham Orabuena, swarms of people filled the streets around the rabbi's house. The men's earlocks bobbed in the wind. Knots of women stood there, keening. The rabbi's closest friends did the best they could to keep the people away from the residence, but the pressing of the curious almost knocked the doors off their hinges.

His dead body was laid out in the bedroom, wrapped in a black cloth, with two candles burning at the head of the bed. The rabbi's wife wandered about, sobbing. She had taken off the wig of a married woman and had covered her head with a shawl. The male guests from the Seder meal sat together on low stools and chanted psalms and prayers.

The Legend of the Secret Source

MOISHE HAD HIDDEN himself away in his bedroom and lay curled up on the bed. Anger and grief seized him in turn but they soon gave way to a feeling of oppressive gloom. He closed his eyes. The spirit of his mother came to him, kissed him tenderly on the forehead, and wrapped him in her comforting arms.

"Explain to me, dearest Mama," Moishe said, "what is the meaning of the word 'makbenak'?"

"You know the legend of Adoniram, of course? He was the man who built King Solomon's temple in Jerusalem, on Mount Moria where Abraham had offered to sacrifice his son Isaac. Adoniram employed more than a hundred thousand workers and Solomon's temple was the most splendid edifice ever constructed. That tireless architect gathered force, inspiration, and knowledge from that secret source in which are collected all seven of the wisdoms of the world. Only a handful of the chosen have ever had access to the secret source. Adoniram was one of them. Through it he learned of the Prophet Ezekiel's vision of the temple, as well as the precise dimensions of the room of the Holiest of the Holies. That space was to be constructed as a square, twenty ells by twenty ells, and since the ceiling was at a height of twenty ells, the room was built as a cube."

"A cube?" Moishe repeated.

"Yes. Even the sacrificial altar in the space before the eastern gate of the temple was in the shape of a cube. The altar platform was twelve times twelve ells in the vision of the Prophet Ezekiel. But Adoniram built the sacrificial altar on the very top of the Qubbet es-Sachra, the Dome of the Rock, to the dimensions of twenty ells by twenty ells."

"So you're saying that Adoniram did not comply with the vision of the prophet?"

"He was not acting of his own volition. Adoniram did nothing but follow the instructions of the secret source, but he wound up paying a high price for it. Three jealous stonemasons coveted his secret knowledge. They threatened him, but he refused to give them the password that granted access to the secret source. In reprisal they murdered Adoniram and buried his body at the foot of a hill. They marked the site with an acacia branch. Eventually the grave was discovered by the nine master builders. They dug up the body, and when they saw that it had begun to decay, they cried out 'Makbenak!' It means, 'The flesh is coming loose from the bones.' They placed the body in the earth once more, planted an acacia tree over it, and returned to tell King Solomon of their discovery. The king ordered them to dig up the body. They did so, and with the help of the secret source they managed bit by bit to piece Adoniram's body together again. With each gesture the nine master builders chanted 'Makbenak.' Then Adoniram was born again and a thousand lights blazed around the acacia tree. The ten men swore never to reveal the secret. Because of this, *makbenak* became the new secret password to the secret source."

"Darling Mother, tell me, may I gain access to that source?"

"The password alone is not sufficient; you must also know how to pronounce *makbenak* correctly. Only the righteous are able to do so. A quest to find the secret source is pointless. No one ever achieves wisdom by discovering a source of pure water. Wisdom comes from within."

"What must I do to become righteous?"

"Treat others as you wish to be treated. Observe the world with serene understanding, and remain ever attentive to other persons and their characters. You must communicate the knowledge you glean in simple words that many persons can understand."

"I don't see how all of these things are connected: *makbenak*, the secret source, Grandfather's death. Explain to me, I beg you, why Grandfather had to die."

"He did not die. He was liberated from the burdens of the flesh. His soul is now with the holy source, in that place where all wisdom is gathered and the Book of Life is held. That extraordinary book has its origins in the far distant past.

In it are inscribed every event and every single detail of all our lives. Grandfather is now there regarding all that is invisible to human eyes. *Makbenak* was the password that admitted him to Paradise. One day you will be reunited with Grandfather. But you have a long road to travel and you must do so alone, without Grandfather and me. My time is almost up. Before I disappear, you will receive the key that will open every door to you. Listen carefully, my son: The password I give you is the same as the moves on the chessboard that the angels provided to me when I defeated Muhammed. Translate the numbers to words and the words to numbers, balance emotion and reason, know what you seek, and everything hidden will reveal itself; life will become an open book for you."

Quietly she described the movements of the chess pieces. Then she kissed Moishe's forehead. For a moment he could see his mother's face distinctly, just before his eyes. But the vision quickly faded into the darkness. Moishe experienced the bittersweet pang of feeling his mother's presence and recognizing the unbridgeable distance that separated them.

Searching for Moishe

FOR A COUPLE OF MONTHS Moishe was regarded as our great hero. Children need heroes, and Sasha and I wanted to know everything there was to know about the Cabalist. While my great-uncle was confined to a hospital bed for treatment of minor chest pains, we combed through all the reference works and history books in his library in search of more information about Moishe. But we found nothing. Not because we lacked zeal or patience but simply because his name wasn't mentioned anywhere.

After he got out of the hospital, my great-uncle offered us an explanation, but first he required a vow of silence from us. We had to pledge that never, under any circumstances, would we speak of it outside our home.

He told us that in 1952 the Communist Party in Eastern Europe had charged a handful of prominent leaders with treason and hanged them. Executing the scapegoats was intended to distract the people from their discontent with the regime. The propaganda department immediately erased those communists' names from history and of course from all the libraries, too. Many were of Jewish ancestry. The bureaucrats were extremely thorough in their pursuit of traitors; in fact, they went too far. Wherever Moishe de Espinosa's name had stood, only white space remains.

I'VE ALWAYS BEEN DISSATISFIED with conclusions, summaries, and neatly packaged accounts of lives. I'm attracted by the random and the inexplicable. I have an odd interest in superfluous detail. Maybe that's why I so often remember the trivial things more vividly than the point of a story.

My great-uncle told us the following things about Moishe de Espinosa:

I.

For the first three months after his grandfather's death he slept lightly and never dreamed. He was in deep mourning and thought of nothing but Rabbi Orabuena.

II.

Muhammed II was generally despised, for he led Granada into economic and political disaster. With every passing day the number of his enemies grew. Despite this, he was apparently pleased with himself, more so than any man with common sense would have a right to be.

"Muhammed's arrogant bearing and firm convictions are evidence of his stupidity," his brother, Nasir, used to say. At other times he would assert, "There's not an ass from here to Baghdad as self-confident and determined as he is."

For seven years of sorrow and misery Nasir waited for the right moment. He then assembled a troop of faithful followers, all united by the desire to overthrow the tyrant. Muhammed fled as far as the city of Almuñécar. In the following year, 1310, driven by the passion for revenge, he attempted to retake the throne. His armed revolt was put down. After the defeat, Nasir showed Muhammed no mercy. He handed the task of dealing with his brother to an official who prided himself on having carried out as many as four hundred executions with his own hands. The man had lost a wife and two daughters to Muhammed's depredations. The executioner wasted no time. With great satisfaction he put out the eyes of the defeated sultan and drowned him in one of the fountains of the Alhambra.

A new page was turned in the history of Granada once Nasir became ruler. He studied astronomy and devoted more time to the natural sciences than to the arts of war. When he learned that Rabbi Orabuena had died, followed six months later by his wife, Nasir invited Moishe to live in the Alhambra and to study with the court philosopher, Yussuf al-Rahman.

III.

The people of Granada had much to discuss in the summer of 1325. Ismail I was killed by his cousin, who took the throne as Muhammed IV and became the sixth sultan of the Nasrid line. Yussuf al-Rahman, the city's great intellectual, had suddenly fallen ill and died, shortly after his youngest daughter, Hasna, married his favorite pupil, Moishe de Espinosa. A woman condemned for adultery was sentenced to be drowned in a sack thrown into the Beiro River, but the next day when the sack was retrieved she was found undrowned. The fact that she was still alive proved that she had been innocent. She was brought back to the city in triumph. One midsummer night a powerful fireball appeared over the western horizon, shining like an evil eye. Ahmed Husseini, the most highly regarded astrologer of Granada, asserted that it was a comet of evil aspect and made the grim prediction that the comet would bring a plague from the underworld.

IV.

Moishe calculated the trajectory of the comet. To make doubly sure of the result, he used the key—the sequence of chess moves—that he had received from his mother. He determined that the comet was not on a collision course with earth and estimated that it would be visible again in 315 years. He delivered the results of his calculations to the new sultan and assured him that the universe was not out of balance. Muhammed IV was both relieved and impressed. He suggested that Moishe should convert to Islam and take his mentor's now-vacant position as Granada's court philosopher. Moishe expressed his thanks but humbly declined the offer; he asked to be allowed to remain a Jew and to devote himself to the studies of his choice. Without a second thought the sultan granted him that privilege and provided him all the financial support he needed.

V.

Moishe and Hasna had five children, every one of them a boy. Four died before they had reached the age of ten. In contrast, Salman, the firstborn, survived a very long time, living to be more than three hundred and fifty years old.

VI.

Moishe and Hasna regularly worked together. They sought to identify common themes in centuries-old religious writings, with the aim of reconciling the teachings of the Jewish and Arab mystics. Moishe held that it was necessary to coax new truths from the ancient texts. His principal interest lay with the Torah and the Talmud, but he extended his study even to the Koran. For as he was wont to say, "The Holy Scripture contains many hidden truths that can be extracted only with the help of commentaries of each historical era." They were agreed that only by interpreting the fundamental texts anew could the mystical tradition be simultaneously preserved and transformed.

VII.

All of Moishe's extant texts are couched in powerfully poetic language.

VIII.

On Friday, February 2, 1342, Moishe completed his magnum opus, Sefer ha-Zohar (Book of Splendor). Not until the nineteenth century did leading rabbis acknowledge its central position within the Jewish tradition of mystic literature and its commentaries.

IX.

Moishe felt stiff and chilled to the bone during the Seder meal of 1348. He slept fitfully that night and was awakened by a sensation of burning heat. In the morning he came down with a high fever and had difficulty breathing. He vomited blood and suffered from diarrhea. He looked up at Hasna and whispered, "Who am I—and who are you—in all of this? In the Talmud is written, 'I am no more than ashes and dust, but the world was created for me!'"

The end was not long in coming.

THE CABALIST, the man who turned the path of the Espinosas from poisons to philosophy, was one of the forty million European victims of the plague of the Black Death.

FOUR

The Storyteller

Salman de Espinosa, the Storyteller

I WAS PLANNING to tell the story of Salman de Espinosa, the eldest son of Moishe the Cabalist. But now I'm feeling terribly tired and I don't know why. Is it the cancer or the medicine? The pains frighten me; they're almost unbearable. To escape them I stuff myself full of medicine. It numbs the pain but at the same time it robs me of my strength. My doctor says that I really should just lie still and rest. But I haven't the slightest desire to do so. My life is ending. I can't bear this shuttling back and forth between hope and despair. That's why I laugh out loud sometimes when I'm struck by the humorous notion that I might live for another year or two. I try to take advantage of the short time left to me by setting down the anecdotes about my family that my great-uncle told Sasha and me when we were children.

I should have taken a greater interest in the lineage of our family once I grew up, since I was supposed to continue our line. But I didn't care for children and so I had none. A prisoner of my own egotism, I put my hands over my ears whenever my mother and father tried to tell me about their lives. And then, afterward, it was too late.

Now I sit here in the graveyard of my memory and try to conjure up the past that slipped away from my thoughts so long ago. I find comfort in those stories as I write them down.

I realized recently that the tales from my childhood are the ones that come most readily to mind. Often my fingers race over the keyboard in the vain attempt to keep up with my recollections. But today every sentence is an agony for me. As my strength ebbs, I can feel myself approaching the limits of the little time remaining. Some strange force, or maybe some lack of force, is sabotaging my efforts. I try to hold my inner enemy at bay but he is steadily outwitting me with his tricks.

SALMAN DE ESPINOSA. His is a dismal story, but it also offers a lesson. They tortured him without interruption for eight days without overcoming his resistance. His body was no more than a mass of bleeding wounds when the executioner serving Grand Inquisitor Tomás de Torquemada burned him at the stake in the plaza before the cathedral of Seville. That was in March 1487. I have no desire to say any more about it for the time being.

But I can also tell you what he was doing a month after that. He rose from the dead and celebrated the Sabbath with friends in Dubrovnik, then trailed his long dark gown along the highway that followed the Adriatic coast. He wandered through small white towns drowsing away in their unexceptional everyday existence, and he distributed to pious Jews *The Seventh Book of Moses*, an extremely odd book that he had composed.

Salman's history is an important part of the Spinoza family destiny. But it's a lengthy tale, and right now I don't have the strength for such a long session at the keyboard. I must conserve my strength today and write about something easier to put down. For example, the things I know about my great-uncle.

Like Something from a Children's Book

MY GREAT-UNCLE had no blood ties to us. He had simply managed to marry one of my grandmother's five cousins, a woman who happened to be the least attractive of them, according to Grandmother. But he was determined to stay in contact with us, and he knew everything worth knowing about the Spinoza family. It was my great-uncle who taught me that we had played significant roles in the history of Europe, or at least that we had been part of that history. Sometimes I wasn't quite sure whether I should be pleased with that or ashamed of it. But as soon as my great-uncle turned up for a visit, all doubt dropped away.

"Spinoza is a name you should feel proud of," he used to say. "You come from the salt of the earth."

My brother, Sasha, and I did feel proud. Even if we did not understand exactly what the salt of the earth had to do with our family line.

WHEN WE WERE CHILDREN, we almost never heard anything about the life of my great-uncle or that of his family. He would happily spend hours telling tales about our forefathers and the distant past, but he resisted saying anything at all about himself. The few times that we asked him about his own background, he fell silent and then quickly changed the subject.

But one time he smiled at a distant memory and enthusiastically recited something that sounded like a passage from a children's book: "It is not true that my father is an actor; that is only a disguise. He is really the richest man in the world. He owns many palaces in different lands—a castle overlooking the Mediterranean, a coffee plantation in Brazil, and vast rice fields in China that stretch as far as the eye can see. In addition, he had deep tunnels dug beneath the Black Forest, where the Danube has its source, and he filled them with gold and precious gems."

We listened and gaped at him, fascinated, although a bit disappointed when he refused to say anything more.

Other times he would answer us, after quick deliberation, that we wouldn't enjoy hearing stories from his life or from his own family history, since their existence had been trivial and uninteresting.

Sasha and I suspected that he was not being entirely truthful. But we had to resign ourselves to the fact that my great-uncle had his own reasons to keep his past from us.

The Archives of the Mormons

SHORTLY AFTER the death of my mother I traveled to the United States. While I was changing planes in Chicago I happened to catch sight of an article in the city's leading newspaper, *The Morning Star*:

> *Inside a great mountain in the Rockies, east of Salt Lake City, Utah, there exists one of the most unusual collections of archives in our nation. The files are stored underground in tunnels cut into the mountain and connected by a labyrinth of corridors. The entrances are protected with steel doors and advanced security measures. Access to the hundreds of thousands of microfilms stored there is strictly limited. The temperature in the underground vaults is always 57 degrees Fahrenheit and the humidity is controlled to between 40 and 50 percent. The air pumped in through the ventilation system is filtered to prevent chemical contamination of the vaults.*
>
> *Guarded within the mountain and available only to the initiated is a stock of information that could fill 90*

million books of 300 pages each. This, however, is no secret military vault. Found here are the names of 18 billion people, living and dead, carefully recorded on 1.3 million rolls of microfilm purchased by the Genealogical Library of the Church of Jesus Christ of Latter-day Saints, a part of the Mormon Church headquarters in Salt Lake City.

The names in that enormous archive have been collected from throughout the world, lifted from every imaginable registry. The work continues today. The goal of this enormous undertaking is to make a record on microfilm of all of humanity, living and dead.

Genealogy is an important part of the Mormon religion. Thanks to that archive, every Mormon can examine his past, ascend his family tree, and have his ancestors baptized posthumously into the faith of the church.

The article awakened my curiosity. I wrote to the Mormon Church and asked for a report from their archives. I enclosed a list of the names of my closest family members. One sunny day in early April almost three months after sending my letter, I received a notice to pick up a package at the post office. I scrutinized the U.S. stamps and studied the postmark, then slowly opened the package. *Remain calm*, I thought to myself. *Be patient. Without patience one achieves nothing of importance.* When I had finally removed the cord and carefully undone all the layers of wrapping paper, I found to my disappointment that instead of a summary of information about my relatives, it contained about nine pounds of printed material about the Genealogical Library. I paged through the brochures and realized that the Mormon faith must have adherents throughout the world

studying graveyards and digging into people's life histories
—with great discretion, of course—so as to provide information to Salt Lake City.

At the very bottom of the package I found a letter in
response to my inquiry, along with a white envelope. The
letter was signed by one of the supervisors of the archive,
who regretted that only one of the names in my inquiry had
been located in the registry.

I slit open the white envelope. The first thing that met
my eyes was the title, printed in bold: FRANZ SCHARF, ALSO
KNOWN AS FERNANDO.

I scanned the following lines. Here a whole life was summarized, some twenty-five thousand days and nights, in just
fewer than ten closely written sheets of paper. Nothing was
missing, nothing of any significance had been omitted, and
every event in my great-uncle's life and background was recorded. Most striking of all was the style of it—the dense
style of a reference work with occasional phrases that came
close to verse.

I had to smile when I came to the end of the document.
It read: *Budapest, October 27, 1962.*

My great-uncle had no income other than his meager
pension. His financial circumstances couldn't have been any
worse. But he never spoke of his troubles to anyone. Other
than to my grandmother, that is. He owed her several thousand forints. When it came to money, Grandmother never
scolded him for being unreliable. He always smiled at her
with a little twinkle every month and explained that he was
absolutely sure that before too long he would be receiving
several hundred dollars from the United States. That was
an enormous amount of money for that time. Then he asked
to borrow fifty forints. She always peered at him sharply, as
if to make sure that he had not lost too much weight since

his last visit. That done, she gave him the money, because she suspected he hadn't had anything to eat that day.

We children thought our great-uncle was stingy because he never brought us any presents, not even for our birthdays. But from time to time he promised to grant our wishes to go to the pastry shop—as soon as he received payment for his writing.

Shortly before Christmas of 1962 he arrived with gifts for all of us. Christmas holidays had just begun. Sasha and I raced madly around the house, simply because we had no idea what to do with our time off. So I was delighted with the Jules Verne novel *Twenty Thousand Leagues Under the Sea* that my great-uncle presented to me. But we were most pleased of all with the delicate, fragrant little pastries that he had brought with him from Café Gerbeaud, the finest konditorei in Budapest. Never before had we consumed such expensive delicacies. Out of our heads with excitement, we wolfed down the pastries. The taste of those sweets still lingers on the tip of my tongue.

Grandmother seemed deeply concerned. She lowered her voice to a piercing whisper and asked anxiously where Fernando had gotten the money for them.

"America," he replied. "Now I'm a wealthy man. Now I can pay back all the money you loaned to me. I received five hundred dollars. It's from the Mormons. I sold them my life story."

A Lecherous Angel on the Stage

IF ONE CAN BELIEVE the Mormon archives, my great-uncle's paternal grandfather, Andrej Scharf, was born in

1839 in the city of Smolensk, situated in western Russia on
the Dnieper River. His father was a rabbi, a deeply pious
man with a grizzled beard and dark earlocks. His mother
was the daughter of a rabbi in Vitebsk. The family lived
in one of the city's poor neighborhoods where his father
had set up a rabbinic court. People in Smolensk came to
him for his good advice and for his decisions on arguments
about the law of the Torah. He conducted marriages and
granted divorces. Impoverished Jews came to him to pour
out their woes. The rabbi led a busy life and had received
few blessings.

Andrej was ten years old when one day a neighbor told
him of a commotion in Moscow. The streets had been full
of revolutionaries demanding bread for the people. They
dreamed of a state where no one was rich or poor. The revolutionaries wanted to do away with the czar. The police had
attacked the demonstrators with drawn sabers. Someone
had thrown a homemade bomb that killed two policemen.
Fifty troublemakers had been arrested. Many were still in
prison. A number of them were Jews.

The rabbi shook his head in concern and declared that
because the boy was present, he didn't want to hear such
things discussed. But Andrej's curiosity had been aroused.
He dreamed of becoming a revolutionary.

One day—he was by then in his twenties—he happened
to pass by a coal mine outside Smolensk, where he saw a
foreman in a dirty uniform thrashing an eight-year-old with
a whip because the boy hadn't been able to hold out for the
full fifteen-hour workday. Andrej couldn't comprehend such
heartlessness, let alone put it out of his mind. He sat deep
in thought for three days. His dark musings led him to the
conclusion that the man who had inflicted that cruel punishment was not a mere sadist or pervert but was in fact a

typical agent of an unjust and thoroughly evil social system. He decided that he would support the effort to improve the lot of the vulnerable. He especially wanted to create better conditions for the peasant children who worked in the mine.

He attended a number of meetings of revolutionaries where men and, to his surprise, even young women carried on lively discussions and schemed about violent ways to change the social and political system in Russia. Andrej spoke up only once: He suggested to his comrades that they should offer an attractive vision of life after the revolution. Unfortunately, a police spy was in the hall and denounced him; he was arrested that same night. Two days later he was sentenced to fifteen years at hard labor for conspiring to overthrow the government and sent to Magadan in eastern Siberia.

There he met Mikhail Bakunin. The father of anarchism, whose mere name made empires quake in their boots, had a nasal voice and a pleasing smile even though he had lost all of his teeth to scurvy. He looked deep into Andrej's eyes and declared that when the burning resentment of the people turned into revolutionary fervor and the old order was overthrown, a new society without government would flourish in freedom and justice. Bakunin stressed the elements of struggle and conflict when he spoke of revolution. He envisioned a sort of collective dictatorship. Everything would be based upon voluntary participation, and men would be freed from all requirements to bear society's yoke and uphold order. He gave the young man one of the books he had written.

Rapt in his reading, Andrej forgot the ice-cold winter around him. When he put the book down, he knew that he wanted to follow Bakunin. He imagined himself playing an important future role as an agitator kindling the revolutionary fervor of the masses. Most of all he was fascinated by Bakunin's opinion that men and women had exactly the same rights to enter freely into sexual unions and then to end them if their ardor cooled.

Two years later, in June, when the snow had melted and temperatures remained above freezing, they escaped from the prison camp, together and on foot. They managed to elude their pursuers and survived in the desolate land on berries and roots. Before long they went different ways. Bakunin escaped east toward Japan and then on to the United States. Andrej made his way west and after many wrong turnings, in early February 1861 he arrived in Budapest on a damp morning gray with mist.

ANDREJ NEVER CONFIDED to anyone the real reason that he left Russia, not even to his children or his closest friends. To the end of his days he refused to discuss his past, always maintaining, "I can never reveal it. Those memories are so far away now, and besides, no one would believe me."

Grandmother let on that she knew his secret. Once when she was exasperated with Fernando, she blurted it right out: "Old man Scharf and his friends robbed a stagecoach carrying valuables from Sevastopol and shot the coachman dead. That's why he had to run away from Russia. Everyone in Budapest knows. When he was on his deathbed he confessed it to his mistress."

WHEN ANDREJ got to Hungary, carrying no more than his little bundle, he was only twenty-two years old. But his two years under the mentorship of Bakunin were not lost time. He had alertly inquisitive dark eyes, as overtly curious as those of a gossipy old woman. He knew no one in Budapest, but in his pocket he had a scrap of paper with the name of a Hungarian—a certain Imre Herskovics—who had by chance gotten to know Bakunin while visiting a Marienbad spa and had been enthused not only by the man but also by his notions of overturning the social order.

Herskovics was drawn to the company of unusual and creative individuals. The idea of anarchism gave that severely gout-ridden Hungarian a feeling of exhilaration, and once back in his native Budapest he wanted with all his heart to foster a revolution. He had no intention of tearing down society, however; he simply wanted to organize dramatic events. He ran a theater in a remote suburb, assisted by a spinster daughter in her thirties.

Herskovics was at his desk scribbling with a goose-feather pen when the young Russian turned up at his office. Andrej cleared his throat and pronounced the only Hungarian expression he knew—*"Jó napot"* ("Good day")—but the portly theater owner didn't reply. Andrej deposited his bundle on the floor and spoke again, this time louder. With his hands in his pockets he leaned nonchalantly against the doorframe and spoke in vaguely admiring terms of Herskovics, whom he had never met before, and told him that Bakunin had asked for his help. Herskovics, not understanding a word of Russian, was thunderstruck—not because the sight of a needy young man was anything remarkable but because of the magic sound of Bakunin's name. The theater owner inspected his visitor. Russians had a confirmed reputation for eccentric behavior and Andrej appeared to be no exception. Herskovics found it entertaining to watch him talk. He knew that theatrical talent could turn up in the most unusual guises, and so he immediately offered Andrej a role as an extra, part of the crowd in an upcoming production.

———

BY THE TIME three months had passed, Andrej had married Herskovics's daughter and had been given the leading role in a new play, even though his Hungarian was still almost nonexistent. His wife was expecting a child. She was a woman capable of doing anything at all in her own unassuming fashion—except for finding a way to make her husband happy.

Masculinity's eternal impatience and longing for freedom was alive and well in Andrej. Already the day after the wedding he took a mistress to satisfy his lusts. Women would melt in his arms as he whispered adoring words in a language that seemed to them the speech of the angels. He was always pursuing several passionate affairs simultaneously, so he got himself into any number of complications. The more he lost himself in these shamelessly voluptuous experiences, the faster his political mentor faded from his thoughts.

"Life is short," he would say. "And Mikhail Aleksandrovich Bakunin's work is extremely long."

ONE DAY as Andrej was in the process of ejaculating into the mouth of a young pupil at the theater, he was caught in the act. His wife's faith in him received its first setback. Soon afterward it became obvious that he had impregnated three of the company's actresses. The upshot of this was that when he appeared for his first leading role, the audience greeted him with screams of laughter because his face bore long red marks where his wife had clawed his tender skin in an attack of hysterical jealousy. Andrej feared her violent fingers more than any Russian policeman. But they couldn't keep him away from new illicit adventures for very long.

Andrej and his wife had pledged to love each other forever. But the marriage ended after only a year, for she had gotten fed up with all the sacred promises and sworn vows he proved incapable of keeping.

An ill-humored Herskovics threw his son-in-law out of the theater. Andrej tried his luck at the privately owned National Theater, but because he still spoke little Hungarian, no director was willing to give him work. For a young man with a love of the stage, the situation was extremely discouraging. So he found an alternative approach: As little troubled as ever by feelings of conscience, he seduced the theater-owner's wife, a middle-aged woman of maternal sternness who kept her husband on a short leash. It wasn't long before Andrej was the artistic director, constantly surrounded by a court of servile directors and willing actresses.

Ervin and Annuskya

ANDREJ HAD SO MANY children with so many women that he had to use all the fingers of both hands to count them. Only one of them was not illegitimate: Fernando's father, Ervin.

Ervin spent his childhood at the theater owned by his maternal grandfather and developed a strong passion for the acting profession. When he was nineteen he was offered the title role in *Hamlet* at the National Theater. Everyone knew—just as Ervin did—that his father was behind the offer. Theater life in Budapest was thick with nepotism and mutual admiration. That made no difference; he was overjoyed. His father dropped in during a rehearsal, stood there for five minutes, and offered a number of eloquent

observations on the arts of direction and acting. But no matter how generous his father's advice may have been, Ervin's
nerves were not up to criticism. He was never able to find the
right tone to bring to life the anguish of the dream-haunted
Danish prince. Audiences stayed away, and the critics were
merciless. One reviewer wrote: "One would have to be the
father of young Scharf to see anything sublime in the way
Hamlet tangles himself up in his monologues like a cat with
a ball of yarn." As a result, it was suggested to Ervin, none
too subtly, that despite his very tender age he should be
looking for a future somewhere other than on the stage. He
was disappointed and angry. He raged. He wept. His fiasco
proved to him that he would always be a failure in the eyes
of his father.

"Having the last name of Scharf is not enough," Andrej
commented condescendingly. "One must also have some
small measure of talent. Otherwise, the performance is
simply tedious. Try to take it like a man."

But Erwin was not yet a man; he was an inexperienced
boy. He struggled to shake off the criticism, especially the
harsh words of his father. He'd hoped for some comfort or,
at the very least, some encouragement. For example, his father could have offered as advice his favorite expression,
"Never give up—always try, try again."

Ervin's soul seemed to be one great throbbing wound.
He secretly turned to drink. Alcohol did nothing to improve
his career prospects. The leading theaters refused to hire
him. In Budapest both young and old actors vied shamelessly with one another, entreating theater owners to cast
them in attractive roles. They vaunted their own merits and
fawned on the directors. But Ervin couldn't bring himself
to kneel at someone's feet and beg to be cast. He became
tiresome even for Andrej, who took to avoiding him.

———

ERVIN AND HIS WIFE, Annuskya, had a daughter and five sons. The ever-famished children witnessed their father's steady decline. He took out life's difficulties and the constant frustration of his ambitions by abusing his family. Only his daughter was spared from his tyrannical outbursts. The sons later remembered their childhood as a series of nightmares that stubbornly returned night after night.

ANNUSKYA RADIATED motherly concern. She was generous, considerate, and tender; everyone in the family depended upon her. She often sang and the children listened in awe to the beauty of her simple songs. She supported the family with her earnings as a laundress and drew her strength from the piety of her orthodox Jewish faith. Hard work, endless quarrels, pretense, and violence overshadowed her existence. She faded, dried up, and wore out before her time. One late evening after Ervin had pummeled her and violently kicked her, she cried out to God and shrieked that she'd had enough. She could not endure this life any longer. She threw herself out the window.

The family lived on the fifth floor. The children were awake; astonished, ashamed, and silent, they had watched their parents struggle. Franci, as my great-uncle was then nicknamed, was six years old. From that moment on, he hated the God who had taken his mother from him. He regularly wet his bed for the next six years.

ALTHOUGH THE DEATH of their loving mother carved a piece out of each child's heart and she left behind grief and a terrible absence, they never mentioned her in their home. Ervin prohibited the children from pronouncing her name. He insisted that she had failed the family, for a woman's fundamental duty was to be a wife and mother, no matter how unhappy she might be.

Once the family's mainstay had disappeared, it became harder every month to scrape together the money to pay the rent. They were repeatedly obliged to move. Eight times in less than two years the children endured the humiliation of being put out of their home by a succession of landlords. Finally the Scharf family wound up in the most ramshackle house on the poorest street of the Jewish ghetto, where they had to share a filthy privy in the yard with all the other renters. That is where they were Grandmother's closest neighbors.

Their apartment was cramped and dirty. Hardest of all for the children was the cold of winter, for they had no money to buy coal or firewood. The pipes froze and there was no drinking water. Icicles hung from the windowsills, and the thirsty children would break them off and suck on them. At night the cold was unbearable; to make things worse, the house was infested by rats. Huddled in bed with three of his brothers, Franci dreamed of hidden treasure and magic spells to help the family. He imagined himself achieving marvelous things.

The Artist of the Proletariat

AT LONG LAST fate showed some pity on Ervin and granted him a success.

In the spring of 1919 the communists took power in Hungary and declared the short-lived people's government, much to the surprise and misery of the people. But in those days Ervin was not worried by the widespread disquiet and general chaos in the country; the only thought in his head was whether he could overcome his nerves and get up on stage again. An acquaintance who was a director at the Vidám Színház comic theater had offered him a place as an understudy in a burlesque cabaret. By then Ervin had reached absolute bottom and may have been slightly out of his mind. He was certain that a waiter in his favorite tavern was trying to poison him on the orders of a landlord who was hounding him. Ervin hadn't been anywhere near a theater for more than twenty years. The thought of it scared him to death, but his pressing need for cash decided the matter. He accepted the offer.

Ervin appeared onstage with a gloomy expression, carrying an accordion. He took a seat at center stage. With careful gestures but without a single word he began to pull the instrument farther and farther apart until to the growing amusement of the audience it stretched to an immeasurable length. Finally, with a worried expression, he commented, "Well, it's out about as far as it'll go."

The audience was in the mood for gallows humor and seized upon his remark. "It's out about as far as it'll go" became the most popular motto of the Hungarian Soviet Republic. The newspapers were full of glowing reviews. Critics hailed Ervin's comic genius and discussed his remarkable stage presence.

One evening the communist dictator Béla Kun attended a performance. Once the applause had died away after Ervin's act, a voice was heard in the room. "How far can it go when hunger and want are everywhere in the country? We have no bread, no vegetables, no meat!"

Béla Kun knew instantly that the catcall was intended for him. He stood up from his seat in the royal box and called down to the crowd, "It'll go just fine. You'll see how far it goes!"

———

A FEW NIGHTS later Ervin collapsed onstage and was carried unconscious to a nearby hospital. He lay in a coma for a full week. During the last days of his life he was granted a few brief moments of clarity. They coincided with Béla Kun's visit to the hospital, surrounded by a flock of journalists, to award him with the nation's highest award for theater arts. Ervin received his medal and an enormous wreath of red roses. He died an hour later.

More than fifty thousand people attended his funeral. The coffin was draped with a banner of communist red. Béla Kun gave a speech at the graveside. He effusively hailed the great artist who had lavished his impulsive generosity upon the proletariat and opened new artistic perspectives on the brotherhood of man. In this manner Ervin Scharf became the one and only artistic martyr of the Hungarian Soviet Republic.

The World's Biggest Liar

FROM THE EARLIEST DAYS of his childhood my great-uncle loved to tell stories. One person who never tired of listening to them was Sara, a girl from the neighborhood—and my future grandmother. Few of his tales were completely truthful, but that bothered Sara not a bit. One summer evening as the dusk fell gently over them, Franci wanted to impress the neighbor girl. He promised to share a great secret with her, on the condition that she swear never under any circumstances to say a word of it to anyone. Then he told her in as convincing a voice as he could muster that his father was not really an actor; that was just a disguise. In fact, he was the richest man in the world. He possessed many palaces in different lands, including a castle overlooking the Mediterranean, a coffee plantation in Brazil, and vast rice fields in China that stretched as far as the eye could see. He had also had deep tunnels excavated beneath the Black Forest, where the Danube has its source, and filled them with gold and precious stones.

"How could your papa get so rich?" asked Sara, impressed.

"My father is a bandit," Franci explained. "He robs banks. He has a rifle."

"But then why does he have to live like a poor actor?"

"So the police won't find him and put him in prison. He's also the leader of a gang of five hundred robbers he sends out all across the world to rob banks and deliver the booty to him."

Sara found it difficult to imagine Herr Scharf as a dangerous bandit, considering that she had often seen him tottering around the yard and having difficulty keeping his balance on the stairs. Her eyes showed her disbelief. Franci saw that and quickly added, "I have another secret that I haven't told anyone. Swear that you'll never give it away to anyone."

"I swear," muttered Sara.

"My father is also the world's best magician. He can slip into a bank vault without anyone seeing him. He reads out a magic spell that he found in the Cabala and then he flies fifteen feet up in the air and becomes invisible."

He expected Sara to ask for more details, but she sat there silently, thinking it over.

"My mother," he then said, "is the daughter of Count Esterházy. She's shut up in a clinic in Vienna. She went out of her mind when she found out that father was a dangerous bandit and had six wives, each one in a different country.

That chubby girl with fat cheeks who pretends to be my sister and takes care of the little ones is actually Father's mistress. My father is holding a princess prisoner in his castle in Portugal. He keeps her shackled to a pillar so she won't run away. Her name is Kunigunda and Father wants me to marry her when I grow up. She has golden hair that hangs down all the way to her ankles."

"Franci, you're a liar. You're the worst liar in the world! This is just terrible. Nobody can believe a single word you say. You're just trying to trick me," exclaimed Sara, and she got up to leave.

Suddenly the ten-year-old realized that his attempt to impress the neighbor girl had gone terribly wrong. Sara had seen right through him. He had piled up too many lies for her. He was scared of losing his only friend, so he quickly made a solemn pledge to her.

"Sara, I will never ever, as long as I live, tell you another lie. I promise. You have my word of honor."

ON A FEBRUARY AFTERNOON five winters later with only an hour of daylight remaining to the day, my great-uncle and my grandmother were barely fifteen, and their fingers intertwined in the ancient game of pressing, stroking, and caressing. Sara had taken the initiative. That encouraged Franci to become more daring. He leaned closer to her to breathe in the dizzying scents of her young body, whose delights had just begun to make themselves evident to his newly awakened senses. He placed his hands on her knees and imagined all the sorts of delicious pleasures that lay between them. But how could he approach them? He resolved to kiss Sara. In the instant that their lips met he knew that he was in love with her. They held each other close and kissed for several minutes.

The First World War

ON JUNE 28, 1914, with his hands sweating and urine running down his legs, the Serbian nationalist Gavrilo Princip planted six bullets in the Habsburg crown prince Franz Ferdinand and his spouse.

That same afternoon in Schönbrunn Palace in Vienna, Franz Josef sat bleakly toying with his imperial royal seal. The face of the powerful demiurge with his milk-white back-combed side whiskers was that of a defeated old fox. For almost seven decades he had done everything he could to hold back the political development of central Europe. The dried-up, unattractive old fellow knew well what forces had been set in motion. He saw that he would be unable to prevent social and political upheaval in the empire. In short, he knew that his time was done. His last hopes had vanished with the tragic death of his nephew in Sarajevo. He ordered a period of thirty days of public mourning.

One month later as the sun went down, Franz Josef stood at an open window in the palace, his gloved hands grasping the balustrade as he looked out over the world. Then he seated himself behind his desk and cast his shadow across the future of Europe. He knew that empires wither if not fed with blood, and their viability is sustained by brutality and war. In a sort of farsighted benevolence he had understood the threat to the double monarchy. With an unconcerned hand he signed the document that plunged the countries of the Continent into the First World War.

A FULL YEAR PASSED before Franci was drafted into the Imperial Royal Army and thereby forfeited two of his basic human rights: the right to his own life and the right not to take the life of another human being.

He cherished two great ambitions in those days, but they had to be laid aside for the time being because his battalion was assigned to the Italian front.

The first of his dreams was to pursue studies of phrenology in Vienna with Tancred Hauswolff—considered by a handful of like-minded psychoanalysts to be superior to Freud—who declared that he could reveal a person's innermost inclinations and characteristics by simply passing his palms over the surfaces of the subject's cranium. Dr. Hauswolff's astonishing research was reported for all in the *Magyar Estilap,* a daily evening tabloid that served up to its readers sensational news from every corner of the world. My great-uncle could not resist the thought that someday he might become an outstanding interpreter of the dark depths of the human soul.

The other dream was that of marrying Sara and having a family with her.

THE TRAIN DEPARTED in late August from the western railway station where a ragtag crowd of men had assembled and a military band was playing high-spirited marches. Only Sara had come to wave farewell to her beloved. They stood together on the platform for a long time. They rocked back and forth, locked tightly in each other's arms. Before he climbed aboard the train, full of disdain for all the dangers that awaited him, he promised Sara that they would begin their life together as soon as he came back from the war. That declaration made her burst into tears. With them at that moment came the vague foreboding that they would never, ever belong to each other, that she would miss him her whole life long, and that she would never find happiness with any other man.

THE ITALIAN ARMY and an Austro-Hungarian army consisting principally of Hungarian nationals fought twelve great battles between June 1915 and November 1917 along the Isonzo River, hemmed in on the northeast by Italy's highest mountains. Day and night the cannons spat their projectiles toward the positions in the mountain face and the bullets hailed down as the soldiers attempted to scale the heights. These violent encounters are held to have been the bloodiest of the First World War. Historians estimate the number of the fallen at half a million young men. And there were even more who came home alive but terribly injured, with mutilated limbs and lost illusions.

My great-uncle came face-to-face with war at the third battle, which began on October 18, 1915. No one in his brigade slept a wink that night. Some prayed, while others devoted themselves to preparations and to cleaning their weapons. They were all awake, waiting for dawn. There was not a breath of wind. My great-uncle was nervous and could feel a knot in his stomach. He took a couple of deep breaths and thought of Sara. He heard her voice. She was speaking about love, saying that she was waiting for him. The thought of his future life with her chased away every trace of his fear. In a ringing voice an officer delivered the call to attack. The soldiers fired their rifles and the bravest of them began to move forward. The Italians answered their fire and the first of the comrades around my great-uncle fell. Many were martyred in the opening tumult. Several hours later the shooting died away to stillness, but the moment of silence was quickly broken by the sounds of renewed combat.

It did not take long for my great-uncle to see that war was the invention of the devil himself; he himself had no quarrel with any of the Italians.

On the final night of the sixth great clash along the Isonzo River—recorded in history books as the Battle of Gorizia—my great-uncle was on guard duty. By then he had served a full year on the front, not thinking too much about his luck or the misfortunes of others. His brigade was under orders to hold fast against the advancing Italians. He squinted through binoculars toward the plateau next to Doberdò del Lago where the enemy was encamped. He knew that he and his companions were surrounded and easy targets for Italian rifles. He suddenly felt the white-hot burning of a dumdum bullet as it pierced his uniform, bored into his chest, penetrated his left lung, and exploded with the force of a small grenade. He fell over, rolled about, and lay stretched out on the ground, confused and unable to move. He had never been afraid of dying, but now he could smell death approaching. He was filled with terror and regret. His brain burned with questions. He thought of all the young Italian men he had killed. He thought of Sara. He looked about, searching for her. It was a dark night and a myriad of stars were gleaming in the sky. The last thought that went through his head before he lost consciousness was that no one had taught him how to die with at least a little bit of dignity.

THE NEXT MORNING, the eleventh day of that sixth battle, the Imperial Royal Army raised a white flag. A surrender document was signed by commanding officer Svetozar Boroević. The ceremony was short. Afterward Boroević offered the Italian chief of staff, Luigi Cadorna, French cognac to show that the war had not undermined his good manners in the least. The gentlemen exchanged a few pleasantries.

When Boroević had assured himself that none of his closest adjutants was within earshot, he expressed his admiration for the Italian's ingenious military strategy.

Cadorna felt enormous pride at his triumph, the greatest of his career. As a reward to his men for their immense heroism, he had extra portions of spaghetti served to all. But the price of victory was so high for the Italians—fifteen thousand wounded and twenty thousand dead—that his exhausted soldiers did not even have the strength to congratulate one another on the defeat of the enemy.

On the losers' side the officers were busy for several days inspecting their decimated troops and preparing lists of the dead and missing. Great confusion reigned. There were emotional discussions and loudly declaimed prayers. After a week there were no further discoveries of warriors who had survived by taking refuge among the crags. Now the work could turn to sending letters of condolence to the families on the home front.

Terrible News

SARA READ the official report and collapsed onto the floor. She wept and screamed, stammered and moaned at her misfortune and unhappiness. Along with her saliva and tears she spewed forth a rant of bitterness and desperation. She lay in bed for three days, weeping without interruption. She was completely exhausted, hungry, thirsty, and dazed from lack of sleep. She told herself she had to try to push aside the whole appalling nightmare.

The awareness of Franci's death lay over Sara like a dark cloud. Two months later, however, she had a dream. It returned to her each succeeding night. She could see that her love was still alive, and that dark-haired angels were taking care of him in Italy. She began to cherish a faint hope that the army leadership, in a sort of miracle, would discover that Franci had survived and had been taken prisoner by the Italians. A friend of a friend offered to check via his contacts within the Ministry of Defense in Vienna. Several weeks later he returned, expressed his deepest sympathy to her in the most polite terms, and unfolded a telegram with the brief reply that the report of the death of Franz Scharf had been confirmed.

Sara's lips began to tremble as if with fever. Tears ran from her unblinking eyes. "The greatest grief of all," she said to her mother, who was trying to console her, "is that my children and my grandchildren will grow up without knowing who Franci was."

IT OCCURRED to my great-uncle when he came back to Budapest after two and a half years as an Italian prisoner of war that it would have been better if he had simply died there on the battlefield at Doberdò. That thought was his reaction to a terrible disappointment. As soon as he appeared, his sister told him that Sara had married and was expecting a child—who turned out to be my father. His sister tried to console him by saying that he could certainly find an attractive girl now that the war had taken the lives of so many men. There was a surplus of young women. She promised to make inquiries of an acquaintance, a lady of great standing with a wide circle of friends, who would be able to help him meet a Jewish girl of good family. My great-uncle was speechless. His hands shook and he shivered. He huddled as close to the hearth as possible to drive away the icy chill that invaded him. It did no good; he was bathed in perspiration. *What is happening?* he asked himself. He had never before felt this way, not as a child, not even in the trenches. And not in the military hospital outside Bologna where the nurses had cared for him for many months to restore his health before he was sent to the prisoner-of-war camp at Emilia-Romagna. Pain pierced his heart like a burning blade, and he was obliged to sit down, to breathe deeply, and to blink. A few seconds later—or, as it seemed to him, several decades later—as he opened his eyes once more, he saw only one way to escape his misery: by throwing himself into the Danube.

He spent the following days in the kitchen, passing the time by composing a bitter farewell letter to Sara with a mixture of passion and desperation. But he never sent it because he was never satisfied with it, even though he had exhausted all the eloquent possibilities of speech. His sister watched over him day and night because he had threatened to slash his wrists.

After further reflection, he decided he was not yet ready to die, for that would allow Sara to escape the consequences of her betrayal too easily. In his humiliation he went from one extreme to the other. Instead of ending his life, he decided that he would revenge himself on his love—and what better punishment could there be than immediately marrying the girl whom Sara despised more than any other on earth? Blinded by his disappointment and burning with the ardent desire to avenge himself and cause anguish to Sara, he relished the sweet prospect of revenge.

To Vienna

ELSA WAS TALL for a woman and as flat-chested as a man. She had an expressionless face, short-clipped black hair, bushy eyebrows that looked like two mustaches, pale skin, and bad breath. She was habitually silent and relatively timid. She found it difficult to get to know people. Her desire to be alone, obvious to everyone, may in fact have been nothing but a deep-rooted fear of change.

The truth is that she was not at all my great-uncle's type. He knew that it was insane of him to marry her and to father her children. Elsa had so many things wrong with her, such comical features, a fairly large number of shortcomings, and an unprepossessing appearance. But he took comfort in the fact that she did not suffer from the appalling feeling of frustrated desire, and she was not in the least untrustworthy—rather the opposite, for her simplicity concealed no guile. Most important of all, she was Sara's cousin and the two had never been able to stand each other. That fact alone decided it for him.

He made it clear to Elsa that he had erased his earlier life from his memory and now he wanted nothing but someone to love, someone who could love him. At first she thought he was making fun of her. He vowed, hand on heart, that he was in earnest. She decided to trust him, since after the war there was a general sense in the air that young people wanted to start families and new lives for themselves. Her face lit up with pleasure. Then they embraced and kissed like any couple in love. He came away with a bitter taste in his mouth, the sting of gall. But by then he had already given Elsa his pledge that he would forever take care of her.

A FEW DAYS BEFORE the wedding my great-uncle was strolling idly through Budapest's exclusive Váci Street on the way to Café Gerbeaud to have a cup of coffee and watch the elegant folk sitting at the tables outside under large umbrellas. They looked as if they'd been taken from a novel by Kálmán Mikszáth, the great chronicler of the common folk and the upper middle class. They chattered incessantly, read newspapers, and observed the passing crowd. When a handsome young woman passed by, the men's eyes lit up lasciviously as if they hadn't been intimate with a woman for years. Their hungry looks said more than a thousand words. The ladies at the tables, most of them wearing elegant hats and carrying fans, also inspected the women passing by and made all sorts of spiteful comments: that one's hips were too broad; the other's clothes were tasteless; the third one's legs were too thick.

Writers and journalists often gathered at the Café Gerbeaud. As a teenager my great-uncle had cherished certain illusions about writers. He read their books and was captivated by their ability to put so many thoughts and feelings on the page, often expressing the most secret thoughts and emotions of the human heart. He recognized the famous writers Géza Gárdonyi and Gyula Krúdy sitting among the café's clientele. But as they sat there, their faces expressed the same greed, superficiality, and conceit as those of all the rest. They perked up just as much as anyone when a young woman came by, rolling her hips. It took no particular perspicacity, my great-uncle thought, to see that those men had the same illusions, the same desires, and the same dreams of elusive happiness as all the rest.

He happened to fall into conversation with a distinguished middle-aged baron who offered him a glass of white wine and asked in a friendly tone why he had such a woeful appearance. Thus prompted, my great-uncle detailed his life's thwarted ambitions, describing how his beloved had betrayed him while he was a prisoner. He declared how much he missed her. He explained that hardest of all for him was to be deprived of the scent of her, not to hear her voice, not to be able to share his dreams with her. He felt sorry for himself and was close to tears.

"Who can relieve the agony in a young man's heart when he has been afflicted by the problems of love? An older, experienced man can do so. An older, experienced man with sharp eyes knows that a young man needs protection, that every life depends on strength and security," the baron assured him.

With that, the baron spontaneously offered a great deal of interesting information in an attempt to lighten the mood. He stemmed from a well-known family of aristocrats and was thoroughly informed about prominent writers and politicians, their doings and activities, their private lives and even their innermost desires. He lowered his voice and said that Gyula Krúdy, sitting there just two tables away, would rather fight duels than write books. Krúdy had always gotten sexually excited in the company of younger women and enjoyed going to bed with two women at the same time—preferably domestic servants, as his own mother had been. The baron also recounted anecdotes about traditions, hunting, morality, and the toppled communist leaders—of whom he had little good to relate. He had an exquisite way of expressing himself; his words were crafted with the silkiest, smoothest turns of the language. He returned again and again to the theme that there was no way for a young man to get ahead all alone in Budapest, that without good connections and a patron one could achieve nothing, that one absolutely had to belong to the right circle and know the right persons of power and influence.

"Might is the same as right here in Hungary," he emphasized. "If one is of severely limited economic means it is immeasurably useful to have a wealthy protector with good contacts. Nothing can smooth an assiduous young man's way into the sacred precincts of power more effectively than a sponsor and protector."

The baron carefully caressed my great-uncle on the inside of his thigh. He offered to use his influence to promote his young friend's career if they established a more intimate relationship. The furtive touch of the baron's fingers came as a shock; it was disquieting and humiliating. My great-uncle did not know what to do. Should he get up and leave? Or should he stay there and pretend not to care?

He looked directly at the baron and summoned all his strength and resolution. With feigned bravado he said loudly, "Keep your manicured fingers off my leg! You're nothing but a swine." He rose abruptly and left.

After that he wandered aimlessly through the inner city for several hours, some of that time in drizzling rain. It seemed to him that he had lost his foothold, that his life was crushed and empty. An inner voice told him that he had to close the books on the past. It wasn't the future that was dark; instead, it was the past. *It is not possible*, the voice said, *for a man scarcely twenty years of age to feel that his unhappy love life makes him less alive than the corpses in the crevices of the Doberdòs mountains.*

He searched for something he could believe in. *Phrenology.* That might offer him a refuge from his grief. But he would have to move to Vienna. He thought that destiny must have arranged his encounter with the baron who had touched him so lustfully, for the incident gave him a strong distaste for life in the decadence of Budapest.

That night he came to the decision to abandon his native city.

IT WAS NO easy matter to persuade Elsa to move to Vienna. She felt anxious and had no desire to leave the home where she had lived all her life or her mother and grand-mother and four siblings, as well as Aunt Miriam and her daughter, Sara. My great-uncle explained calmly to her without becoming in the least emotional that he would never be able to feel comfortable in that tiny apartment, a room and a half measuring only a bit more than three hundred square feet in all, constantly under the vigilance of seven other people.

It wasn't difficult to see what my great-uncle feared most of all, even though he spared Elsa the details. The mere thought of meeting Sara one day and having to see her swelling belly struck him with deep apprehension. Granted, she and her husband had established a home in a distant working-class neighborhood, but he foresaw that eventually she would come to visit her mother in the apartment.

UNEXPECTEDLY, ELSA'S MOTHER, Luiza, supported the idea. She saw her daughter's anguish and made a mental count of all the girls her age who were already married. Many were mothers now, and some had several children. Didn't Elsa want to get married?

"You'll turn out to be an ugly old spinster, my dear, if you're afraid to move away from home," she said disapprovingly. "No man wants to get me and grandmother and Aunt Miriam as your dowry or to live in this hovel with all of us old women."

Luiza didn't limit herself to words; she took direct action. She collected all of her daughter's possessions, packed them in a little valise, and placed it next to the front door. Then she offered the following advice: "There is only one way to make sure that a man stays home, and that's with the drug of sex. Franci is like every other man in the world; he has simple needs. His senses have to be tickled and his body needs caresses; he has to be dealt with like a big child. Give him confirmation of his manhood. If you're clever and you flatter him, you can keep him from dipping his wick in some other woman's grotto."

It was a hasty departure and they set out only a few minutes later. The pair of newlyweds, with their little valise in hand, took the tram to the railway station on the west of the city to start the trip to Vienna. Pleased and expectant, my great-uncle heard the train wheels rattle across the railway bridge over the Danube and saw Budapest disappear behind them toward the horizon. A couple of hours later he sensed the locomotive slowing down, and through the grimy windows of the second-class carriage he could make out the distant shape of his new hometown.

Phrenology

THE COUPLE TOOK a one-room apartment in one of the most run-down sectors of the working-class neighborhood of Meidling. They furnished the apartment as best they could. Once everything was in place, my great-uncle sat down at the kitchen table and heaved a great sigh. He could scarcely believe his eyes. So this was his home. He looked at his hand, adorned now with a ring. He was married and had a wife—granted, not the woman he loved, but anyhow —and now he was in Vienna. At least he had the possibility of pursuing one of his two ambitions. He told himself that he could alleviate the pangs of his lost love by studying phrenology with the renowned Tancred Hauswolff. It was a wholly new field of knowledge that demonstrated conclusively that intellect, instinct, and perceptions are attributes linked to the cortex of the brain, and they can be touched, inspected, and measured.

AS SOON as he could, my great-uncle called on Tancred Hauswolff. With pounding heart and trembling hand he rang the bell. The servant, a bulky woman in early middle age, opened the door to him. She stared vacantly in front of her and told him to remove his shoes immediately because she didn't want any marks on the parquet floor. She exuded authority and power. My great-uncle politely bent over in reluctant acknowledgment of his submission and obeyed her injunction. He stiffened in embarrassment when he discovered that the big toe of his left foot was peeking out of a gaping hole in his sock.

The servant shook her head resignedly and showed him into the famous psychoanalyst's reception area, a luxurious room packed with furniture upholstered in dark leather and dimly lit aquariums of colorful fish. On the walls hung erotic etchings and a huge map of the southern Austrian province of Kärnten. Hauswolff, a man with pale slicked-back hair and thick spectacles, sat behind an enormous desk and accorded him a chilly look.

"But you are a Jew, young man. Don't attempt to hide the fact. I know Jews. I have studied them for decades. I can see from the shape of your head and the dimensions of your cranium that you are a Jew. I'm a learned man, a scientist. I can tell with a glance, even from a distance, that you're a Jew."

My great-uncle was disconcerted, but he knew that this opportunity would never present itself again. He smiled amiably and quickly spoke of his zeal to become Hauswolff's pupil. The psychoanalyst listened with a distracted air but noted his visitor's evident youthful energy, passion,

striking intellect, and personal warmth. But no matter how
attractive the young man was, the doctor could not overlook
the fact that he was a Jew.

"Can you pay for your studies? Do you have any money?"
asked Hauswolff.

"About five hundred shillings."

"Don't joke with me! My patients pay me three times as
much for a half-hour consultation. You Jews are so avaricious. You know, young man, the love of you Jews for money
is infantile. It all goes back to the child playing with his own
excrement, his fascination with shit." He stressed the word:
"*Scheiss.*"

Hauswolff lit a cigarette, took a deep drag, and got up
from his desk. He turned his back to his visitor and looked
through the open window at the summer sky. Only then did
my great-uncle notice how short the famous psychoanalyst
was. The man was high strung, about forty years old, tiny,
pot-bellied, and well-dressed. He sported a black bow tie.

"Nevertheless, you are intelligent," commented Hauswolff,
"and endowed with a rich imagination. And in any case, you
Jews are brilliant teachers. I studied for a time under the personal tutelage of Freud. Do you recognize the name? I was
deeply impressed by his intelligence. But for him everything
came down to sexuality, to one or another form of sexual guilt.
Such notions are pure perversion. As if only sexual neuroses
stimulated the mysterious forces of the unconscious! Such
Jewish filth is disgusting to an Aryan mentality. The Jewish
school of psychoanalysis is absolutely unacceptable. Psychoanalysis should be an Aryan science. We men of science have
responsibilities. For that reason I can't take just anyone as my
pupil. I will take three days to think it over."

Then, still standing at the window, Hauswolff went off
on a long, involved lecture on the psyche, using jargon that

my great-uncle could hardly follow and commenting on the analysis of irregularities of the cranium to evaluate human consciousness. He spoke with impressive passion in a torrent of words.

When my great-uncle later came back to learn whether Hauswolff would accept him as a pupil, a small crowd stood outside the house. An extremely fat neighbor woman told anyone who would listen that the police had come to arrest the renowned psychoanalyst because he'd given in to his own strong sexual urgings. He'd been caressing his female patients' bosoms more often than their skulls.

One day he was caught with his hands in a patient's underwear. Rachel Abrahamowicz, daughter of the wealthy Jewish furrier, was an extremely beautiful twenty-year-old who suffered from hysteria and had suicidal impulses. She proved not to be an ideal subject for hypnosis. She relaxed completely on the doctor's sofa but felt no desire to enter a trance. Hauswolff thought that the young woman was sleeping deeply, so he slipped his hand under her skirt and began to stroke her between the legs. Rachel gave him a stinging slap on the left cheek. She immediately threw a hysterical fit and ran home in tears to her father, a close friend of the chief of police.

The scandal shook Viennese society. For several days the newspapers seemed to write of nothing else. Insinuations and unconfirmed accusations filled column after column. Sensationalist reporters dug up every tiny detail of Hauswolff's life and character. He was accused of raping several women under hypnosis. Someone claimed that he had forced a rich baroness to turn over her diamonds to him for safekeeping; he was alleged to have sold them to a jeweler in Kohlmarkt. It turned out that he had never completed his studies or passed any academic exam. His certificates and diplomas were crude forgeries. Previously respectful colleagues washed their hands of him. Freud commented that he had always known that Tancred Hauswolff was a money-grubbing charlatan obsessed with seducing upper-class women. The phrenologist's charade recalled the fable of the emperor's new clothes.

On the morning set for the court hearing, Hauswolff was discovered dead in his cell. He had taken the contents of a cyanide capsule hidden in his spectacle case.

A New Future

MY GREAT-UNCLE had little success in his search for work, since he was entirely uneducated and had no particular skills. One disappointment followed another. Every time, a job prospect eventually went to someone else. Finally he had no choice but to work as a porter in the railway station. The work was hard and the unusually cold winter made it even more strenuous. In that Vienna winter, during a prolonged period of biting cold, pigeons and sparrows froze to death and fell out of the trees. My great-uncle was exhausted by the time spring arrived. He lost his job because severe back pains kept him at home in bed.

Their lack of money and shabby existence cast him into ever deeper gloom. He could feel the future slipping away from him. Everything reminded him of his melancholy childhood, and those dismal memories just made the problem with his back even worse. He saw himself as a failure locked in a narrow prison cell, and he yearned for Sara. Each night he mused miserably over what she and her love had meant to him, and he wept without ceasing. Dark circles appeared under his eyes. Watching him furtively, Elsa saw him becoming more despondent with every passing day.

ONE AFTERNOON there was a knock at the door. Their neighbor asked if he could borrow a little salt. Aron Reinherz was a pious Jew from Galicia. Many rumors about him circulated in the apartment building. My great-uncle and Elsa had their own worries and they were not interested in gossip. Even so, some of their neighbors' talk had reached their ears.

Aron Reinherz was reputed to be a good man who had suffered a life of terrible misfortune. His only daughter had gone one day to the mikvah, the ritual bath, where she had been seized with cramps and drowned. His elder son was killed on the Italian front in the war and the younger one died of the Spanish influenza. His wife had taken the losses so hard that her heart had simply stopped. Despite all this, Aron Reinherz was always good-humored, a man with a ready quip or jest wherever he went.

REINHERZ WAS CLEVER and alert, and no one ever needed to explain anything to him. He simply knew it already. He was no philosopher; he was just a gentlemen's tailor. He instantly grasped my great-uncle's precarious situation and promised at once to arrange for a job with his cousin Herschele Jankelevitch, better known in Vienna as Hermann Jack.

Circus Jack

WHEN MY VISIBLY NERVOUS GREAT-UNCLE arrived at Circus Jack, he thought the place totally bizarre and despaired of finding any employment there. Then he entered the big circus tent and suddenly felt himself transported to another world. A jovial mood reigned within. A handful of people sat around a long table set up next to the animal cages. They were eating and drinking with great pleasure as a giant with an enormous mustache and thick bushy eyebrows was telling some convoluted tale in Russian. It seemed to be a hilarious story, as far as my great-uncle could make out. A kind of strange nobility shone in the giant's face. My great-uncle immediately realized that in this tent there existed what he had long missed in Vienna: warmth, humor, and camaraderie.

A gray-haired fatherly figure with steel-rim glasses riding low upon his large nose got up from the table and introduced himself as Hermann Jack. He welcomed the visitor with a congenial smile and invited him to join them at the table. Before taking his seat, my great-uncle told them he was Franz Scharf from Budapest. An elderly man asked if he happened to be related to Andrej Scharf. My great-uncle confirmed that Andrej had been his grandfather, and the man expressed his most profound admiration for the theater manager in Budapest. He offered my great-uncle a glass of a tasty but extremely strong alcoholic drink that he himself had distilled. My great-uncle was also urged to taste several delicate sausages and cheeses. Everyone around the table treated him well, as if they'd known him forever.

After many a heartfelt laugh and an additional two glasses of the strong drink, he gathered his courage, turned to Hermann Jack, and declared, "I haven't enjoyed myself so much in a long time. You've all made me feel at home." In a hopeful voice he added, "Perhaps it's too forward of me to ask if you might have some sort of job I could do for you?" He explained that his attempts to establish himself in Vienna and find work had so far met no success.

The circus ringmaster pointed to a large poster on the wall featuring a clown with a red nose and a tragicomical expression. "Our dear friend André, the chief attraction of the circus, has been promoted. He is now keeping the angels amused. He never came out of the anesthetic after his operation for gallstones. You can be his successor. A good clown needs a few years on him and has to have experienced plenty of misfortune. True, you're young, but I can see by your eyes that tragedy is no stranger in your life. Fate has brought you all sorts of defeats. For that very reason I can see a place for you in the circus. We'll teach you to do magic tricks and lots more. From now on your name will be—Fernando!"

CIRCUS JACK was one of Vienna's most popular institutions. The audience was constituted principally of working-class families with children, and they were delighted to have something better than the amateur artists so typical among itinerant entertainers in the suburbs. Hermann Jack had attracted a number of unrivaled international stars: the bearded Neapolitan sisters with enormous breasts and bulging backsides who gleefully sang romantic arias in Italian while riding around the ring on their unicycles; the world's smallest dwarf, who dressed as a Roman senator with a laurel wreath on his head and drove around triumphantly in a carriage drawn by four Icelandic ponies; the one-legged English sailor George, who was shot from a cannon and disappeared into space; the Russian giant Oleg, who swallowed rats alive, burst strong chains with his teeth, and had a bus loaded with twenty people drive across his chest; the Italian triplets Uno, Bruno, and Duno, who performed death-defying acrobatic numbers. The repertory also featured the most professionally accomplished tightrope dancers, trapeze artists, lion tamers, and Indian snake charmer ever to grace a circus ring in Vienna. Just as impressive was Circus Jack's collection of exotic animals: a fat pig with five legs, a few stumpy Lipizzaner horses, and an irresistibly charming little monkey with unusually long arms.

My great-uncle performed as a clown and magician. Six days a week he stood in the ring wearing a red potato nose, a glowing golden wig, shoes that were far too big for him, and an enormous belly that made him look as if he had swallowed three dozen billiard balls. At first his stance was awkward and his dancing was hopeless. But he rehearsed and repeated his number endlessly and worked single-mindedly to perfect it; his goal was to raise his art to a level that exceeded even that of the most highly polished illusionists. He opened his number by holding his black top hat out to people and showing its empty white bottom. After establishing in this way that his art was not to be doubted and stood above any suspicion of deceitful manipulation, he waved his magic wand and described complicated gestures in thin air. Then with exaggeratedly precise movements and an intent expression he began to pull quantities of bright multicolored paper ribbons from the hat. Eventually he filled the whole ring with a rustling mass that seemed to have no end to it.

Fernando always got thunderous applause, not so much for his abilities as a magician as for his charmingly foolish antics. They appealed to the child in all of us and set the whole audience roaring with laughter.

An Unhappy Marriage

ELSA DID NOT SHARE her husband's delight with circus life. She found it hard to understand how he could thrive and feel normal in that collection of—to use her words—"ridiculous creatures."

As for her, she sat home all day long, waiting patiently for his return. The old sewing machine she had purchased at the flea market hummed from morning to night next to the kitchen window as she made ladies' blouses for a shop. Her German was broken at best. She was embarrassed that there were so many words she did not understand. She rarely ventured outside the house, especially because she had begun to suffer from asthma and her vision had deteriorated. Her isolation from everything and everyone became more pronounced as the years went by. Her thoughts and feelings, all the sorrows that had fastened themselves to her like tar, were sealed up in words that she never shared with anyone.

Some of those days she felt deeply unhappy because her husband was so seldom home. But to preserve the peace she never raised the subject with him.

FROM TIME TO TIME Elsa suspected that my great-uncle was seeing other women and that like his grandfather he had illegitimate children all over Vienna. The thought of this would set her weeping hysterically, and she would totter across the way to Aron Reinherz, mostly because there was no one else in whom she could confide.

She actually didn't like visiting the old Jew, because of the foul air in his lodging. It was never cleaned or aired out, the air was warm and stuffy, clumps of dust covered the floor, and spiderwebs stretched across every corner. The bed was unmade and the sheets bore traces of bedbugs. Several times Elsa caught herself contemplating the impossible: asking her neighbor why he never cleaned up and then offering to take care of it for him.

She knocked on the door but she rarely managed to put into words the miseries that weighed her down. Aron Reinherz could read them all with a single glance.

"Just remember, too much thinking can drive a person mad," he said gently. Then he assured her that no man was more faithful than her husband. He counseled her to go to synagogue instead of leaving herself prey to evil thoughts and depression. Instead, she should pray to have a child.

"I am no prophet," Aron Reinherz said, "but I am sure that a prophecy whispered into my ears by Providence will be fulfilled. It will not be long before you find yourself with child. Perhaps even with two. And when there are children at home, your husband will be there with you."

After a time Elsa began to feel less agitated and started to talk about various other aspects of her everyday life.

"This must remain between the two of us," Elsa said, when she had regained her composure. "Not a word to anyone. My husband would only misunderstand and think that I was accusing him."

After visiting her neighbor she went outside to the street, filled her lungs with fresh air, and took the trolley to the Church of Our Lady of Succor. She sat in the empty church deep in thought and remembered her mother's good advice: A woman must incite her husband's desire if she is to keep him and get her own way.

Embracing a man was also a way of controlling him. But what if one felt only a vague discomfort in such close physical contact? Was a woman lost if she felt no desire? A shiver passed through Elsa as she thought of her husband. Everything suggested that he was suffering from the disruption of his sex life. He was her lord and master, and it was her duty to please him. She concluded that a man's sexual drives were a necessary evil that woman must endure. That was the way of the world. So she lit a candle and prayed to the Virgin Mary to make her fertile.

LATE THAT EVENING, when my great-uncle came back to a home shrouded in darkness, Elsa unfastened his trousers and pulled him into bed, meekly opening her legs and allowing him to penetrate her. His orgasm was almost instantaneous, and the knotted tension of his body relaxed. But once it was over, he felt disappointed. He yearned for something more than cold hands and chilly sex.

A few weeks after this Elsa discovered that she was with child. That pregnancy lasted only three months. She miscarried again, the fourth time in recent years.

AT FIRST my great-uncle would tell Elsa all sorts of tales about his life with the circus. When it became clear that she was not interested, he lapsed into silence at the dinner table. They hardly exchanged a word anymore. He did what he could to lighten the mood at home, even when he was most despondent over the gloomy marriage into which he had thrown himself so thoughtlessly. He felt more resigned with each passing day. Eventually he tired of Elsa entirely and was no longer pained at the thought of having married the wrong woman, this uneducated, contrary creature whose thin, ailing body was worthless except for an occasional brief bout of copulation in the dark.

The Waldvogel Tavern

MY GREAT-UNCLE rarely bothered to go home after the matinee performance. He went instead to the nearby

Waldvogel Tavern to spend his free time. He usually arrived at about half past five and always sat at the same table. He ordered the cheapest fare on the menu. He was not much given to alcohol and would drink only a single beer. But he always brought his chess game, and there was generally someone to play with.

For some people the game of chess offers exhilaration and escape. That's how my great-uncle experienced it. As a ten-year-old he had learned how to play from a neighbor, a scrawny butcher, also Jewish and just as poor as everyone else in their building. The butcher was kindhearted, unlike my great-uncle's perpetually drunken father, who struck his children with violence, shouted, and erupted in tantrums. An encouraging word, a pat on the shoulder, and a kindly look could have gotten Franci to do absolutely anything, but his father's approach to child rearing denied him all of that. In contrast, the butcher warmly greeted the children of the apartment house and initiated the young boys into the magical world of chess. Because he was endowed with a lively imagination, Franci adored the game, even though he found the theory of opening gambits completely uninteresting. After the butcher died, the children could no longer play chess and returned to dreary reality. But my great-uncle never forgot the indescribable pleasure he associated with those black-and-white chess pieces.

HE WENT to the Waldvogel Tavern not only to play chess but also, and just as important, to talk with other people. He found it easy to fall into conversation and enjoyed the back-and-forth of it. He would regularly lean back comfortably on a chair with his legs crossed and a cigarette between his lips, and as he sipped a beer he would shower his new acquaintances with questions. Why had they come to

Vienna? What were they doing in the city? He would shift the conversation gradually to their pasts and to their political views. He didn't say much about himself, and if someone reproached him for that, he always gave a disarming laugh.

"If you were to hear about my life," he used to say, "it wouldn't give you any pleasure. My existence has always been humdrum and devoid of interest."

THE COZY PUBLIC ROOM in the tavern was a meeting place for men who had emigrated from Eastern Europe. These rootless creatures spent their time playing chess and discussing politics.

In a world that was becoming ever more divided and complicated, these idlers regularly indulged in stirring declarations. They were ready to offer cures for all the world's ills. Some advocated anarchism, others Marxism. Some set their hopes on Zionism, while the socialists among them maintained that Lenin was not as bad as the bourgeois press in Vienna painted him. Certain of them maintained that the salvation of mankind lay in psychoanalysis; others advocated terror as a weapon against the oppression of the authorities.

On Tuesday evenings the tavern was crowded with a group of younger men. These deluded poets drank new ale in great quantities and dreamed of transforming the art of verse by rediscovering the use of powerful metaphor and bold expression. They worshipped youth, which they predicted would blow away all the outmoded quaintness of contemporary structures and performance. They invoked the deadly beauty of lightning and yearned for the day when the heavens would unleash their unavoidable destiny. They were always high-spirited as they read their latest works out loud to one another. Almost every week one or several would feel faint with the excitement.

Frombichler and His Friend Adi

MATHÄUS FROMBICHLER was a talented chess player, a bold attacker perfectly willing to sacrifice a piece or two to set up a checkmate. People said that before the war he had played to a draw with Emanuel Lasker. Grand master Lasker had visited Vienna at the invitation of the Socialist Party and played twenty-six simultaneous games, winning twenty-two of them. Four ended with a draw.

The only opponent to whom Frombichler regularly lost was his friend Adi. They had met during their school years in Linz. Two desolate souls, they had trailed miserably behind their classmates and been held back several times. Both felt that they had suffered indignities. They shared an implacable hatred of authority and often disagreed with their teachers. They found each other quickly and remained inseparable for life.

Frombichler was clearly the better chess player. One time he opened a match with a dashing forward thrust of pawns along either side of the board and then attacked Adi's center from the sides. He won in about twenty moves. Adi was already in a foul humor that day and the ignominious defeat affected him badly. He became so furious that he pulled out a pistol and tried to fire it at Frombichler. Luckily, several people were close by and one of them snatched the weapon out of the hands of the hot-blooded Adi. Frombichler almost had a heart attack. He decided that from that day on he would allow Adi to win. At the same time, he felt a grim gratitude toward his friend for not having killed him.

IN THEIR YOUNGER DAYS Adi had been capable of flying into a rage at almost anything. Frombichler told my great-uncle about it and gave as an example something that happened one freezing January night in 1913. Dr. Trotsky came to play chess at the Waldvogel Tavern, accompanied by a swarthy Georgian with a bristling mustache.

Trotsky came every Wednesday to seek company and was valued by everyone for his elaborate politeness and his admirable conversational gifts. But his guest, dressed in heavy dirty boots and a ragged overcoat, had the manners of a real peasant and was incapable of polite conversation. On the other hand, he was a remarkable chess player, at his best in the middle game where he had mastered a great variety of clever and complicated moves. Forceful attacks on the king were his specialty, and his opponents rarely survived them. He moved the pieces with his left hand even though it was somewhat withered. He made short work of everyone in the tavern.

Trotsky called him "Koba." Some say that his real name was Josef Dzhugashvili. Others used his nickname: Stalin.

In his last match he played against Adi, who had learned that very day of his failure for the second time to pass the entrance exam for the Art Academy. Adi glowered his dislike for the Georgian throughout the evening. He was determined to defeat that unpleasant individual at any price. He quivered with almost unbearable tension. But after only eight moves he fell directly into a trap.

Adi felt deeply humiliated. He began to perspire, his temperature rose, his hands trembled, and he saw black specks before his eyes. The Georgian smiled slyly, clapped Adi on the shoulder, and said, "*Spasiba*." This was no more than an innocent word of thanks, Adi knew that, but he had never heard the Russian word before. The momentary touch shot through him like an electric shock. He was trembling with fury and could hardly control his hands. He felt a murderous urge to assault the fellow. It was a sudden attack of insanity, a hatred that he could not suppress. For a moment he almost gave way to the impulse to reach out and seize the Georgian by the throat. But he realized there were too many witnesses, so he managed to restrain himself.

Trotsky and his guest left the tavern shortly afterward. Adi followed them, murder in his heart. After they had walked a considerable distance in the cold air he came back to his senses and calmed down somewhat. When he returned to the tavern, he shouted so everyone could hear him that he hated people from Eastern Europe. His shock of hair swayed over his forehead, his hands contorted in the air, and his voice rose to a falsetto as he vowed one day to take the life of that swarthy Georgian with the big mustache.

Everyone knew that when it came down to it, Adi was a decent fellow. But his curious outbursts and screaming were not good for business. Because of that remarkable performance, Julius Waldvogel formally banished him from the tavern.

I DON'T KNOW exactly when my great-uncle and Frombichler first met, but I do know that at first he found Frombichler extremely annoying. It bothered him that in the middle of a chess match Frombichler would often get wound up talking about this Adi fellow. The more experienced older Eastern European immigrants kept their distance from Frombichler when for no reason at all he would trot out his friend's visions of improving the world. Most of the immigrants avoided playing chess with him.

AT THE CLOSE of the Great War Adi had been lying in the hospital, a victim of poison gas. He had plenty of time for reflection. He then made the rounds of the offices of all of Vienna's major architects with his portfolio of sketches without securing a single offer of employment. His watercolors had been met with indifference at the art galleries. He was deeply disappointed by his Austrian countrymen. They were obvious degenerates, he declared, and he moved to Munich, a city where he had yearned to live since his boyhood.

In his new home country, he discarded his paintbrush and tossed aside his palette, since his lack of success showed he had no future as an artist. He tried his luck at politics instead and became the chairman of a newly established German political party. In hissing consonants and with thundering vowels he spewed tirades about morality, racial purity, the mission of the Germans, and the treachery of the Slavs.

Frombichler's contention was that Adi brought hope to a German working class ravaged by alcoholism, syphilis, tuberculosis, and nervous disorders. He commented that with those frantic harangues in various Bavarian inns his friend had made scoffers choke on their laughter—all those people who had mocked him for his short stature and comical mustache—and predicted that with his unprecedented power over the emotions of his audience, Adi soon would have the whole German nation at his feet. Frombichler even went so far as to say that he could foresee a coming world revolution led by his friend, one that would eliminate expressions such as "mine" and "yours" from human consciousness. He spoke of the firestorm that Adi and his inflexible strength of will was setting in motion, a burning feeling of new purpose that would ignite even the underclasses of the direst slums.

"The time will soon come," Frombichler declared, "when workers will no longer put up with poverty, begging, and apathy. All they have to do is listen to my friend Adi and be bold. Playing chess is a fine way to sharpen one's senses."

Adi wound up in jail after a failed coup attempt. Frombichler suddenly wasn't speaking about him so often, and sometimes when he did, his voice was dull, with no trace of his former enthusiasm. Everyone in the tavern could see he was bitterly disappointed by his friend in Munich, particularly because Adi had dropped his theme of class struggle in favor of an anti-Semitic devil myth: the depiction of the Jews, first within the bourgeoisie and later in the founding of Marxism, as a people striving to dominate the world. Because he himself was half Jewish, Frombichler felt betrayed when he found that Adi's anti-Semitism was not only incidental pandering to popular discontent but was in fact the very core of his friend's political mission. Frombichler continued to annoy his chess opponents with his chatter, but now it consisted chiefly of tales about his own family.

Frombichler and His Family

FROMBICHLER WAS HEAVYSET and compact, raised on starchy food, the son of peasants, imprinted from an early age with the notion that bread and meat were essentials. His face was round and his head bald; his eyebrows formed one thick line and his bull neck was furrowed with deep wrinkles. There was something wrong with one of his feet, and he limped badly. He was a curious sight whenever he got up from the chessboard to make his way to the toilet. But in the kitchen of the Hotel Imperial, where he was employed as a cook, he was agile and alert, perfectly suited to his life among the pots and pans.

Sometimes my great-uncle was seized by a dark suspicion that Frombichler was not always entirely truthful—not because he thought that Mathäus was a liar or a fabricator but because many of the events in his accounts of his family were so bizarre that it was difficult to imagine they could actually have occurred.

Karl, the first to bear the family name of Frombichler, married in 1601. Since his wife's dowry consisted of several acres of fertile land, he took up residence in the village of Güttenbach in Burgenland, the same region where his ancestors, proprietors of their own farms and imbued with an ancient sense of dignity and honor, had cultivated their fields for hundreds of years. The people of Mathäus's mother were not as firmly rooted. She came from a family of Jews and had grown up in the splendid Biederhof castle, some forty kilometers southeast of Vienna. Her maternal grandfather was said to have been a finance minister for the double monarchy, serving as trusted counselor to Kaiser Franz Josef. In addition, the family, whose ancestors included several famous philosophers, had moved all about Europe.

"My Jewish lineage offers not just enough to fill a book," Frombichler said adamantly, "but enough for a whole library. You have no idea what sorts of legends feature the Spinoza family. The fictions of writers are childish fantasies compared with what happened to my forefathers. Fiction is no match for reality. When you know what actually happened, you don't have to make up fanciful stories. That's why it's easier to catch up with a liar than with a lame old dog."

What awakened my great-uncle's serious interest in those accounts was the fact that Frombichler once happened to mention that he had some cousins in Budapest. He immediately added that he didn't particularly care for them, for when his maternal grandfather's fortune was divided, his uncles refused to be moved by any feelings of brotherly affection. His mother received nothing because she had married a Gentile, a man who to top it off was a farmer's son. He was particularly incensed at his cousin Nathan who, according to his version, had for no justifiable reason appropriated the most valuable possession of the family: philosopher Benjamin Spinoza's invaluable treatise *The Elixir of Immortality.*

"Nathan—you don't mean Nathan Spinoza, do you?" my great-uncle asked, his pulse suddenly accelerating. "The Nathan Spinoza who married Sara Neumann?"

"Yes, in fact, that's my cousin. Do you know him?"

"No, I don't. The fact is, I've never met him. But it's certainly a small world. You see, he married my wife's cousin Sara, the most wonderful woman on earth. We grew up together, so I know. Now you'll have to tell me more about your family. I want to know everything there is to know about the Spinozas."

UP TO THAT POINT my great-uncle thought he had succeeded in burying his love for Sara in a deep dark hole inside him. The many pleasures of the work at Circus Jack had almost allowed him to forget her. But the fire that had been burning inside had not entirely gone out, and the name of Nathan Spinoza made it blaze up fiercely. Suddenly he felt a sick longing for Sara. Buried memories came to the surface as if pulled up from some deep mine shaft inside him. He again felt the stir of her breath against the top of his head and the pressure of her breasts against his chest as they embraced in the kitchen of his childhood home. He recalled the happy delusion of hope for the future that her love had inspired in him.

The Scent of Flowers and Family Happiness

AFTER HER FOURTH MISCARRIAGE Elsa remained in bed for several weeks, listless and melancholy. One afternoon she heard a feeble knocking at the door. She got up and staggered to the door. When she opened it, her neighbor Aron Reinherz stood there. He saw instantly that she was not doing well and inquired about her condition. Elsa tried to wave away the question, but the old Jew understood. He consoled her with some entertaining anecdotes and offered to accompany her to visit a Tatar princess from Baku who had been forced by the 1917 Revolution to leave Russia. She now had a practice in the suburb of Simmering, where she cured all sorts of ailments with essential oils of flowers and plants.

People came from afar to Olga Bashkir. She not only sold the oils, flowers, and plants but also prescribed how long one should inhale their odors, always while seated and never for more than ten minutes a day. For high blood pressure she recommended inhaling woodland geranium; rosemary was best for asthma; and she cured backaches with bay laurel. She raised the flowers and plants in her own garden.

The princess advised Elsa to take Siberian lily (*Lilium pensylvanicum*). She said to inhale the flower's perfume for eight minutes each day for three weeks.

"I don't smell anything," Elsa said suspiciously. "This flower has no perfume at all."

"No flower produces a scent for its own sake; it emits its perfume for someone else," Olga Bashkir explained patiently. "You must gently rub the stalk so that the flower becomes aware of your interest. It will then render up its perfume. It seeks to please everyone, and every touch elicits its perfume. Siberian lily will cure you, *meine Frau.* It will infuse your womb with blood. With a little passionate assistance from your husband, you will provide him with as many offspring as he can possibly wish. But I must warn you: If one inhales the scent of the Siberian lily for too long, the children will inevitably be girls."

Elsa begged Aron Reinherz to say nothing to her husband about the visit to the Tatar princess. He nodded his understanding.

ON A COLD OCTOBER DAY in 1929, called Black Thursday by historians because of the stock market crash on Wall Street, Else gave birth to twins. The two girls, radiantly beautiful, were both in fine health.

As my great-uncle peered into their little faces he saw that one of them had a marked resemblance to his maternal grandmother, while the other's features were a perfect copy of his mother's. He was happy beyond words.

"I would like very much," he said humbly, "to give the girls the names of my sainted mother and my blessed grandmother, Annuskya and Margit."

At that time everyone knew my great-uncle as "Fernando," except for his wife—she still used his childhood nickname.

"Franci," Elsa answered, "those are splendid names. I'm happy to give them to the girls. But even more than that, I want to honor you. So let us to call them Anci and Manci."

SINCE THE FIRST DAY Elsa set foot in Vienna she had yearned to return to Budapest. That desire haunted her and held her for all those years. She had never discussed her secret dream. Once home from the hospital, she gave in to its insistent call and suggested to my great-uncle that it might perhaps be a good idea to go home to the family in Budapest to show them the twins.

He wouldn't hear of it.

His pretexts were thin. He claimed that he didn't have enough money, he couldn't stand his mother-in-law, he was doing splendidly in Vienna, and he couldn't get any time off from Circus Jack.

The real reason that he wanted to stay away from the city of his birth forever was entirely different, of course: Sara. His reluctance was mixed with a strange apprehension, as if he feared he would somehow be disappointed. It was as if coming face-to-face with Sara again would destroy his vision of true love, the dizziness that had blinded him one February afternoon long ago, when he was only fifteen and their hands met and their fingers intertwined in the age-old game of touching, squeezing, and caressing.

Hermann Jack and Admiral Horthy

THE TRAIN SET OFF toward Vienna. Hermann Jack sat slumped in a corner, silent and downcast, worn out from a long succession of sleepless nights and burned out from hundreds of late-night cigarettes. He was confronting a crisis. Everyone knew that business was terrible; all those empty seats were mute witnesses to that. And they could all see that the ringmaster was distracted, uneasy, and more bleary-eyed than ever before. He had done his best for a long time, striving to keep from his circus family the truth about their finances. When a Hungarian friend promised to make some helpful introductions to prospective lenders, he took the train to Budapest in one last desperate attempt to put his financial house in order. Not one of his Viennese creditors was willing to provide more support. They had been patient with Hermann Jack for a remarkably long time, overlooking his inability to pay down the principal on his loans, but recently he had begun to receive threatening letters written in insulting language. The Depression had emptied everyone's pockets, and lenders had become noticeably more coldhearted. Most were refusing all requests for extensions or renegotiation. They now insisted that unless he pay up by September 14, 1931, they would ignore his pleas, foreclose upon Circus Jack, and force it into bankruptcy. The meetings in Budapest had come to nothing, and Herman Jack had only thirty-six hours left before the deadline.

He closed his eyes and imagined he heard something. It sounded as if an enormous wheel was breaking loose beneath his secure universe, rolling toward him and his circus, pitiless and uncontrolled, about to carry them into the abyss. At that instant the idea came to him. He had neither wife nor children, and the circus was his only family. The next morning he would take out a policy insuring his life for a huge amount of money, and that evening he would kill himself. The circus would be saved and he would not fail his friends and employees.

When Hermann Jack asked himself if he was afraid to die, he had to admit that unfortunately he was not a particularly courageous soul. The thought of physical suffering had always frightened him terribly. He knew he would have to devise some simple, rapid way of taking his own life. In the moment that followed he heard a violent crash. For a thousandth of a second he experienced a strange weightlessness.

EXACTLY TWENTY minutes after midnight on September 13, 1931, the Vienna Express was dynamited on the railway viaduct outside the little town of Biatorbágy, some thirty kilometers west of Budapest. The locomotive and the first six carriages plunged into a deep ravine. The next morning rescue teams found twenty-two mangled cadavers in the twisted, burned-out railway cars. One of the bodies bore on the ring finger of its right hand a gold signet ring with the engraved initials H.J.

A VIOLENT QUARREL erupted immediately after the people of Circus Jack received the news of Hermann Jack's death. It had nothing to do with impending seizure and bankruptcy, for none of them had had any illusions about circus finances. The dispute was whether Jack was a Jew or a Catholic. Where should his remains—if indeed they *were* his, since they were burned beyond recognition—be buried? The circus divided into opposing camps. Finally the Gordian knot was cut by the Russian giant Oleg, who suggested a nonreligious funeral at a Protestant cemetery. After hours of discussion they voted and unanimously accepted his proposal.

Several hundred people attended the funeral. My great-uncle stood there in his black suit, mute and freezing. He could not bring himself to heave even a single sigh. The whole situation was simply too unreal. Of course, he was grieving at the loss of his friend and mentor who lay there in the coffin, a blackened tangle of bones. All around him he saw people he did not recognize, people who were wailing with grief and flooding the place with their tears.

A Catholic priest—Hermann Jack's nephew who had converted when still a young man—approached the grave, and the Jews began shouting. Everyone sensed that something momentous was about to happen. Within seconds a bloody fistfight broke out between the groups of different religious faiths. Friendships of long years' duration were pounded to pieces.

THE FIRE that had consumed the sections of the train was still smoldering when a state of emergency was proclaimed in Hungary. Every paragraph in the constitution related to freedoms and human rights was set aside. As regent and head of state, Admiral Horthy was not particularly interested in arresting the culprits, since he had more important things to deal with. It was clear that his principal aim was to jail troublesome political opponents.

Two weeks later the police arrested the Hungarian Szilveszter Matuska at his home in Vienna. Without the least expression of remorse he confessed his responsibility for the attack as well as for five other train bombings he had carried out earlier in Germany. He was even proud of his accomplishments. He was sentenced to eight years in prison. And that cleared up the affair, most people thought.

But that was only the beginning. In the weeks that followed, the conservative Hungarian press published a lengthy series of impassioned articles blaming the deed upon the communists. Two prominent Jewish members of the Communist Party were promptly arrested. Even though their alibis were watertight, they were condemned to death for the Biatorbágy bombing. Everyone knew the truth. In the liberal press, in parliament, and in the general public there arose an outcry demanding that the men be released. Vigorous protests were organized across the world. The Horthy regime paid no attention to any of that. Sándor Fürst and Imre Sallai were hanged two weeks after their trial.

An Aroused Political Consciousness

EARLY ON THE MORNING of July 15, 1927, the workers at Vienna's electricity plant cut off the power. That was the signal for people to abandon their places of work for a march on parliament. A couple of months earlier, a faction of illegal right-wing vigilantes had murdered a number of demonstrating Social Democrats. A court in Vienna had released the killers, even though they admitted firing upon the demonstrators. The day after that verdict, tens of thousands of workers marched on parliament in protest. Mounted police drove them back. The workers armed themselves with paving stones and surrounded the Palace of Justice. Soon, approximately two hundred thousand people were in the streets. Some carried pails of gasoline. Toward lunchtime the Palace of Justice went up in flames. Fire trucks were immediately dispatched to the blaze, but the masses of humanity refused to let them through. Confronted with this situation, the police chief made the decision to equip six hundred policemen with rifles and dumdum bullets to disperse the crowds. The police fired wildly in every direction. Men and women, children and the elderly, and even four policemen were mowed down. In all, eighty-nine were killed and more than a thousand were wounded. The doctors at the hospital told journalists that not even during wartime had they seen such carnage caused by firearms.

The events outside the Palace of Justice greatly rattled my great-uncle and changed his views. He himself did not participate in the demonstrations, but he couldn't avoid reading newspaper accounts of the bloody events and hearing the vivid tales on everyone's lips. He found it scandalous that a dozen policemen were decorated with the order of merit and the entire bourgeois press supported the excessive use of force. In his address to parliament, Chancellor Ignaz Seipel lay blame for the massacres exclusively on the Social Democrats. My great-uncle's decided opinion was that only a malicious and irresponsible politician could assert such carefully crafted lies. He blamed both the entire Christian Democratic regime and the bourgeois class that had voted Seipel and his gang into power.

THE CASE of the anarchists Sacco and Vanzetti in Boston a couple of weeks later was big news on the front pages of the papers. Even though the two Italian immigrants were obviously innocent, they were sentenced to death for an armed robbery during which two people had been killed. They were granted several stays of execution. Protests were organized throughout the world; in Vienna seventy thousand marched in silence through the streets. It was no use. The judge declined to reconsider the case. Because of their troublesome political views and a general hatred of foreigners, Sacco and Vanzetti had been judged before the trial began. In August, any hope of justice for them was finally dashed. The poverty-stricken anarchists were executed in the electric chair.

My great-uncle felt a deep sympathy for the executed Italians and their families. He read everything he could find in the newspapers about their fate. Again and again he ran across the name of Bakunin, described as the leading light of anarchism. The name sounded familiar somehow, but he couldn't place it.

IN HIS CHILDHOOD HOME no one had ever mentioned his paternal grandfather. The subject was taboo. His father despised the famous theater director and refused to meet

him. My great-uncle must nevertheless have picked up
something about his grandfather, somewhere or other, for
when he saw a picture of the Russian anarchist in the paper,
a memory suddenly arose before him as clear as life: He had
heard that as a young man in Siberia, Andrej Scharf had
been a disciple of Bakunin. Thinking of his grandfather,
he realized how little he really knew about the past. He
couldn't even recall his own mother's face.

In Vienna's Central Library he located Bakunin's complete works in German translation. He threw himself into
the study of the anarchist's bible. Its pages were full of views
about disobedience. He read:

> . . . the true knowledge valid for everyone, developed in
> all of its extension and in all of its unchanging detail,
> should reproduce the universe, system, or social order of
> all natural laws manifested by the relentless evolution
> of the world . . .

Astonished, he shook his head and turned the page.
Since he didn't understand much of this, he soon found
Bakunin's writings tiresome and returned them to the
shelf.

After the stock market crash—during the months when
every day he could see highly educated academics waiting
patiently, hour after hour, in bread lines outside charitable
institutions—he went back to the library to borrow more
tomes critical of social conditions. A pale, almost transparent librarian helped him reluctantly—she wore a sort of
tight little smile that suggested bitterness or incurable loneliness. He came home with his arms full of books. He could
only dimly make out the differences between the writings
of Rosa Luxemburg and those of Trotsky. Most of it was

incomprehensible. But he did make one discovery: socialism. The socialists proved, black on white, that the capital-
ist world order was unjust.

It occurred to him for the first time that life and society
should have had more to offer his mother than the dreary
struggles with his father—a man who had given up and
crawled into a bottle of booze, broken for life by a heartless
father and his own lack of talent.

And that is how Antonio Gramsci entered his life. The
author's writings about solidarity with the working masses
impressed him deeply. The same was true of his words about
freedom and individualism. He devoured the Italian's notebooks, which had been smuggled via clandestine means out
of the fascist prison where he languished. Gramsci's writings provided him the key he used to coax open all the locks
and to understand the world. Their tone was harsh, but the
notebooks of the incarcerated political philosopher glowed
with certainty, even though he was physically broken, tormented by illness, and deprived of contact with the outside
world. Everything could be explained; one needed only to
have a clear grasp of history.

MY GREAT-UNCLE no longer frequented the Waldvogel Tavern. Almost everything there had changed. The
agreeable—gemütlich—atmosphere was gone as were the
Eastern European immigrants and chess matches. Nor was
stocky Julius still the owner; he had died shortly after his
much younger wife, Hildegard, ran off with an itinerant
beer salesman. The beer hall now was run by his nephew
Ernst, a man more interested in racehorses than in his clients. The poets no longer recited their verses on Tuesday
evenings. They now wore armbands with swastikas and discussed the views of Hitler.

One evening in an alley close to the tavern, my great-uncle watched from a distance as a humpbacked old Russian Jew, once a regular at the Waldvogel Tavern, was kicked into a bloody mess by three uniformed Nazis. He did not dare to intervene for fear of being attacked himself. The struggle against fascism, he told himself in an effort to quiet his conscience, should be carried on with means other than violence.

An Encounter with Freud

AFTER CIRCUS JACK had been declared bankrupt, my great-uncle secured employment as a magician and illusionist at the Steinkeller Cabaret.

One evening Sigmund Freud paid a visit. The cabaret's owner, Steinkeller, met him at the door. They traded a few Jewish jokes and Freud was shown to the table closest to the stage. He ordered a small espresso, lit a cigar, and blew smoke rings. After Fernando's act the owner invited the world-famous psychoanalyst to take the stage to offer a few remarks about our need for illusions.

Freud spoke with majestic, magnetic dignity. He said that he had observed Fernando closely and with great curiosity. He had noted a number of interesting points, but these he would keep to himself. He acknowledged that he was moved by the talented magician's presentation. He quickly added that, of course, this was a matter of innocent deception, in the sense that Fernando had led everyone to believe they were seeing something that in fact had never happened. At that point someone in the audience spoke up and asked Freud if he believed that human beings had so-called supernatural powers. The curer of afflicted souls emphatically denied such a contention and said that parapsychology was pure humbug. He then offered several profundities about our fundamental need for illusions and our susceptibility to suggestion. Last but not least, he stressed the importance of using one's own faculty of critical reasoning and not allowing oneself to be duped, either by stage presentations or in public spectacles. He received a hearty round of applause.

My great-uncle had not been warned of Freud's visit, and he felt offended that his art had been dismissed as if it were nothing more than simple trickery. He spoke up immediately and expressed his humble admiration of Freud by calling him "the Christopher Columbus of the human subconscious." He suggested a little experiment that might prove the existence of psychic powers. He asked Freud to write down something on a scrap of paper and place it in the breast pocket of his suit. My great-uncle asserted that his intuition could reveal what was written on the paper. The proposal caught Freud's fancy; he agreed with pleasure to participate in this innocent experiment.

"Herr Fernando," he said politely, "a few moments ago you called me Columbus, but I see myself as more of a conquistador. I possess the curiosity, boldness, and endurance of such a man."

"And the same ruthlessness, dear doctor," called out someone in the audience, provoking a few hearty guffaws.

"That may well be," Freud continued. "But I have looked deeper into the soul of man than anyone else, and I have never been able to detect any mystical powers there. Do not take my remark personally, Herr Fernando, but you will not be the first charlatan I have exposed."

He took his pen, wrote something on a piece of paper, and placed it in the breast pocket of his suit. There was a heavy silence in the hall as my great-uncle stepped close to Freud, closed his eyes, and appeared to concentrate, all in a highly theatrical manner. The first thing that came into his mind was an image of tiny colorful fish. They were swimming around in dimly lit aquariums in the reception room of the dead phrenologist who claimed to have studied at number 19 Berggasse with the father of psychoanalysis.

"Tancred Hauswolff!" exclaimed Fernando.

Freud couldn't believe his ears. "That is correct," he said and held up the paper, which was then shown to the audience: *Tancred Hauswolff.*

Everyone in the house applauded. The jubilation was boundless. People didn't just laugh; they wept with rapture. The next day Fernando was the talk of Vienna, and the queue for admission to the Steinkeller Cabaret stretched for blocks.

Cabaret Artist

MY GREAT-UNCLE quickly took advantage of his new celebrity status to develop his repertory. He began to write and present monologues of biting social commentary. His career was brief but it had long-lasting consequences.

In her monumental work *One Hundred Years of European Cabaret* (1982), the Belgian theater historian Ghislaine Vlaminck writes that Fernando single-handedly transformed the art of the German cabaret. His fame sprang from his impudent and unerring political satire. Vlaminck writes:

> *Fernando was the epitome of the frustrated moralist and the scourge of the wicked, a man who mercilessly*

flayed them alive at the Steinkeller Cabaret. As a so-
cialist he criticized the egotism of the propertied classes
and their love of money. As an anti-Freudian he poured
out his gall on psychoanalysis, disparaging its leading
lights as "psycho-anuses." As a pacifist he mocked war-
lovers and militarists. As an atheist he placed himself at
a significant distance both from the Jews and from the
Catholics.

But there was one name that came up more often
than any other in his performances: that of Adolf Hitler.
After the seizure of power in Berlin in 1933, Fernando's
monologues were built almost exclusively around that
name. The fact that the Nazi movement was gaining
strength with every passing day egged him on to even
greater daring and insolence. As the tramping boots of
ten thousand members of the ruling party made Nurem-
berg tremble in the flickering of torches and the forest
of banners, Fernando was the only German-speaking
cabaret artist who continued to mock the neatly musta-
chioed former corporal with the comical sweep of hair
that fell over his forehead. He turned the locale that had
been Vienna's most exclusive cabaret into a bastion of
anti-Nazi sentiment.

Hitler's Berlin cast dark shadows over Vienna. David
Steinkeller received a summons to the office of the police
chief to receive "a few friendly words of advice he would be
wise to heed."

Gagging Fernando? The very thought of it was grotesque.
Steinkeller strove to articulate a defense of the principle of
artistic freedom. The reply he received, loud and clear, was
that his favorite had clearly overstepped the bounds of reason and permitted himself to utter every imaginable sort of

indecent talk, questioning the morality of the Catholic public that faithfully supported the fatherland. What was now
at stake was not Fernando's future but that of the cabaret
owner himself, and it depended entirely on the subject matter presented in his locale. Steinkeller was advised to get rid
of his star performer as quickly as possible or face severe
personal consequences. He promised to think it over, but he
was determined to allow Fernando to express himself freely
onstage, no matter what happened.

Two weeks later on a warm July day with dark thunder-
clouds on the horizon, Steinkeller was summoned again.
This time it was no longer a discussion between him and
the police chief. Two muscular toughs in leather coats were
there to help convince Steinkeller. The two of them were
direct and forceful in their reasoning: They forced him into
a chair, gave him a couple of bone-jarring slaps, and held
his shoulders in a steely grip. Steinkeller felt his heart racing and the blood roared in his ears. He listened in fear and
paralyzed fascination to the police chief's knowledgeable
description of everything they would do to him if Fernando
wasn't out of the cabaret within twenty-four hours. This
must have been extremely painful for Steinkeller, for he had
a heart of gold and loved Fernando like a son. He realized in
horror that he had no choice; it was useless to resist and he
had to yield before the threat of further violence.

Against Hitler

TO HIS OWN SURPRISE, my great-uncle had a sudden,
perceptible feeling of relief, almost of exhilaration at these
developments. For a while he thought he would miss the

theater, especially the contact with the audiences when he looked directly into their eyes as they listened to him, thirsting for truth—the very thing, after all, that humor is so powerful in presenting to us in our lives. But instead of grieving, he took up his pen to battle against ever more rampant fascism. He was elated to see the same hands that a few years earlier had hefted suitcases in the railway station and later extracted colored ribbons from a clown's hat now producing articles published on the front pages of the *Arbeiter-Zeitung* under the pseudonym *Scharfrichter* (Executioner). His life had the sweet smell of the resistance struggle and the wind of freedom. This made him even more daring. The principal theme of his articles was how to oppose Nazism. He exuded self-confidence. With Gramsci in his valise he knew exactly how to go about formulating the campaign of resistance.

While this was going on, he was also working on a study of the Spanish Inquisition. His interest in that subject had been roused by Mathäus Frombichler, who had by then been called to Berlin by his friend.

ADI HAD REACHED his goal after many years of struggle. The temperamental Austrian with the stony face and the comical haircut had succeeded in convincing the German people to put the fate of the nation in his hands. He was the Reich Chancellor, and with his fiery speeches he fed the people of Germany a vision of invincibility and a future German empire in Europe. Millions placed their blind allegiance in the new Führer and roared their enthusiastic adoration of him.

But Adi had no shortage of enemies, either. He was used to verbal attacks from the unholy alliance of Jews and Western democrats. But now things had changed. His trusted astrologist had warned him of an incipient conspiracy to get rid of him. The crystal ball predicted that the Führer would die in his own kitchen. Adi deduced that someone would attempt to poison his food. He wasn't easily intimidated, but he took this threat seriously. He immediately took a number of precautions. He dedicated himself to a strictly vegetarian diet and consumed only green salads. He also directed his old friend Frombichler to quit his job as principal chef at the Hotel Imperial and come to serve as his own private chef.

AMONG FROMBICHLER'S ANCESTORS there was a mystic named Salman de Espinosa. This man had lived in medieval Spain and had been tortured without respite for eight days by Catholic executioners. They never succeeded in breaking his resistance. Like Hitler, the Inquisition believed that the Jews were responsible for every misery and evil in the world. A great number of Spain's Jews fled that country; those who remained fell victim to persecution.

My great-uncle was fascinated by the story of Salman de Espinosa. He saw a clear parallel between fifteenth-century Spain and contemporary Germany. He could see that the fate of the Jews was sealed. It was only a question of time. Clouds were massing on the horizon.

After the Anschluss

IN THE EARLY HOURS of March 12, 1938, a German agent sent a telegram to Berlin from the main post office in Vienna with a request for military assistance. Within hours Hitler's tanks rolled across the borders. Flag-waving children and adults lined the streets to welcome the invaders. Austria was occupied without a shot being fired and was annexed to Nazi Germany.

FOLLOWING THE NAZI SEIZURE of power in Austria, the so-called Anschluss, all political parties except the National Socialists were dissolved and many of my great-uncle's friends were arrested. He sent Elsa and the girls to Budapest to get them out of harm's way. He stayed behind and continued to write about the Spanish Inquisition as a predecessor of Nazism.

DAVID STEINKELLER, a Romanian citizen, was one of the first to receive an order of deportation. It was redacted in obscure bureaucratic language but was extremely specific about where he was to report and what he was allowed to carry with him. Steinkeller sent a letter to the Gestapo replying that three years after the Nuremberg racial purity laws, the significance of which had escaped no one, he was well aware what awaited him and he preferred to take things into his own hands. He dressed himself in his most elegant suit, carefully knotted his tie, and heaved a sigh. He missed the laughter and tears of free, unintimidated audiences listening to Fernando's monologues. He then made his way up to the attic and hanged himself.

SOMEONE WAS BEATING on the front door. My great-uncle was sitting at the kitchen table by the window, writing. He had an idea of who it might be and he went to open the door. Five large men in black leather overcoats stood outside. "Gestapo!" their leader barked.

"Franz Scharf," replied my great-uncle, and regarded the rest of the men inquisitively. "And you, gentlemen, who haven't introduced yourselves? What are your names? And in any case, what are you selling?"

"Secret police!" the leader announced. "We are here to arrest the Jew Scharf. We also have an order to search the house for books or papers with anti-Nazi views."

"Anti-Nazi views," Fernando echoed him. "Everything in this residence is opposed to the Nazis, down to the toilet paper that I used to wipe my ASSHOLE." A second later a hard fist smashed into his chin and he lost consciousness. When he came to, he was on his way to Dachau.

FIVE

The Wanderer

About Writing and Fernando

AS I LOOK over what I've written to this point, I'm a bit ashamed at the lack of a clear chronology. But I take comfort in the knowledge that this account isn't presented as a scientific inquiry, so it doesn't need a rigid structure or require exacting research.

I'm writing about Spinoza family history. My mother asked me on her deathbed to tell the world about the separate universe we inhabited on this earth. I can still see her pale face before me—the uncombed hair hanging across her forehead and the way her glazed eyes looked past me, fixed upon some invisible spot on the ceiling. Her breathing became shallower and shallower, until finally the room was completely still. I felt morally bound to fulfill her wish someday.

My mother died in November 1989 in the sixty-eighth year of her existence, but nearly ten years passed before I set to work. The mere thought of sitting down to write for a week or a month was unbearable. I'd always felt a persistent urge to be somewhere else, anywhere else. Besides, all my life I've found it hard to express myself in writing; it's terribly difficult for me to put my thoughts on paper.

Only when I learned that I was really, truly dying did I come to terms with the fact that, as the last of the Spinozas, I was the only person who could still remember my great-uncle's tales of distant family history. I was the surviving witness of those bitter but entertaining quarrels between my grandmother and grandfather. I was the only one still alive who remembered how my twin brother, Sasha, died.

I realized suddenly and with great pain that my greatest failure wouldn't be my death but the fact that my death will obliterate all memory of everyone who came before me. That sudden realization gave purpose to my final days, for it drove me to start writing this, my testimony about earlier generations.

That's why I'm not bothering to record my own thoughts and deeds. These memoirs have almost nothing to do with me or my life history.

I CHERISH the hope that the people whose stories I first heard in my childhood days will come to life again here. I hope they'll appear as immediate and vivid as they were for us back when my great-uncle told their stories to Sasha and me. With that aim I devote painstaking attention in every waking hour to evoking the different centuries, bringing out the colors and the flavors unique to each age, describing just how the tempests of history buffeted my ancestors, and showing how dismal, ordinary life roused their feelings, affected their lives, and drove them into frenzies.

Sometimes their stories stand out against the tumultuous background of their times, and their private lives and small victories illuminate the great events and terrible catastrophes of history.

THE REASON I come back to my great-uncle so frequently is that although he hadn't even a single drop of our blood in his arteries, he nevertheless represented for me the very incarnation of the Spinoza family. In his own peculiar and amusing way he taught me everything I know of our history, traditions, and customs—all of our futile successes and ignominious defeats, all the events of deep significance and all the meaningless drivel. He succeeded more or less intentionally in bringing all that into harmony: the past and the present, family and Jewish identity, the universe and the world, spirits and morality, love and destruction. He made me believe in the existence of impenetrable mysteries and the possibility of communicating with the spirit world, and he convinced me that the changelessness and dreamy melancholy of the past was of far greater interest than our modern world with its ever-accelerating changes.

More than anything, although we did not know it at the time, with his air of mystery he succeeded in implanting into my heart and into that of my brother, Sasha, the very meaning of life: the fact that fate—not God, for Fernando did not believe in such nonsense— had an overarching plan for all of humanity and our family line was playing an important role in it.

THAT WHICH BOUND our great-uncle to us—this is something I did not understand as a child and grasped only much later in life—was his desperate love for one woman. All his life he loved Sara, my grandmother, with a passion that bordered on madness. In order to stay close to her, he abandoned his own history and replaced it with that of the Spinoza family, including Sara's minor role and the overlooked incident of her unhappy marriage.

Frombichler's Incredible Story

FROMBICHLER SAT at his usual table. He hadn't yet tasted the beer in front of him. He dreamily contemplated the foam and seemed not to notice when my great-uncle took a seat opposite him. He was waiting for the bubbles in the tankard to dissolve and reveal how much beer it contained.

"Three-quarters," he announced, bitterly. "A swindle," he muttered, "a fraud with all that foam. Vienna is a den of fraud, lies, and deception. A man can't even get a full tankard of ale in this city anymore." A long silence followed. My great-uncle thought, *What idle nonsense*. Just as he was about to contradict his friend, Frombichler spoke.

"I'm going to tell you something, Fernando, in confidence, of course, something that's no fraud at all but God's own truth."

He drained the tankard in one long swallow and belched loudly. My great-uncle heaved a sigh but was secretly amused.

"You may think that this story is merely a tall tale," Frombichler continued with an earnest glance. "But I swear by the memory of my sainted grandmother that every word is true. I hardly need to remind you that truth is stranger than fiction. When you know what actually happened, you don't need to make up a story. That's why it's easier to catch up with a liar than with a lame dog."

Slowly and deliberately he began the story of Salman de Espinosa.

BY THAT TIME, characters from the Frombichler family saga were as familiar to my great-uncle as his fellow artists at Circus Jack, and he willingly listened to tales of their strange destinies. He enjoyed each new Spinoza who emerged from the obscurity of the Middle Ages. The hours spent with Frombichler were a sort of theater performance; colorful figures from all over Europe appeared and disappeared, involved in a drama of great complexity. My great-uncle listened, fascinated, as Baruch used a poultice to resuscitate the eldest son of the king of Portugal and Chaim compounded the poison used to murder Sultan Muhammed II. He found these stories exhilarating.

Occasionally he felt inclined to doubt somewhat the veracity of those stories. At other times he reproached himself for letting Frombichler stuff his head so full of those anecdotes—provocative to the imagination but hardly credible—that he got the Spinoza family on the brain. Sometimes he resisted his self-assigned role as the passive listener absorbing a family saga that was not his own. That's when he would avoid Frombichler's table, glancing furtively in that direction while seating himself elsewhere in the tavern to play chess with some Russian immigrant. His absences were brief, and soon he was sitting with his friend again. He couldn't resist the fascination of the lingering splendor of vanished times. He had no connection with that world but in some strange fashion it brought him closer to Sara. At least that's what he told himself.

NONE OF FROMBICHLER'S EARLIER STORIES compared with that of Salman de Espinosa. My great-uncle's feelings about it were mixed. He couldn't decide immediately whether it was a complete invention or truth itself. On the one hand, much suggested that it was an old wives' tale, pure and simple. On the other hand, he had heard tell of strange events, and he'd had a number of eerie experiences that the laws of nature could not explain. He was convinced that there are mysteries we humans cannot explain.

He searched his friend's face. At long last, after downing four large tankards of beer and listening without interruption for five hours, he got up to relieve himself of the inner pressures that had been building for quite a while. He hurried to the toilet and slipped off homeward without saying

goodbye. Once on the street, he decided to get to the bottom of the story, whatever it might take. He would dig into
old documents, find out the truth, and uncover everything
there was to discover about Salman de Espinosa.

Beyond the Chronology

I DON'T KNOW what's gotten into me. Here I've gotten
carried away by the flood of memories again and lost the
thread of my story. This may make it difficult for any eventual reader to keep things straight, since any story without a
clear chronology is likely to become confusing.

This is a good place to take a break, since I'm sure that
an overly scrupulous examination of the historical record
would cast doubt upon this account of the Spinoza family.

You see, the remarkable thing about my great-uncle's stories, all of which Sasha and I absorbed with the due measure
of good faith and enthusiasm, was the complete absence of
a consistent framework. His tales—those that I am trying
to reproduce here—were fragmentary stories plucked out of
thin air. Nowhere were they firmly fixed; nothing tied them
to anything. It was almost impossible to confirm any of the
details. There was no chronological order other than that
which I much later tried in my helpful fashion to impose.
There were no beginnings and no ends. The past was there
but its future was not.

MY AIM here is to describe the events of a man's life, from
the fourteenth century when Granada was still ruled by
enlightened Moorish rulers up until that man's death in
Freiburg im Breisgau one Friday evening more than three

hundred and fifty years later. He put an end to himself after spending his final days with his relative Benjamin Spinoza— to whom he bequeathed all the knowledge and secrets he had carried with him throughout the wide-ranging wanderings of his existence.

Salman de Espinosa was a thickset, vigorous man with an indescribably large nose. He was full of curiosity and joy, happy to engage in discussions and extremely erudite, and he had a stride so vigorous that the muddy ground splashed all the way up to his shoulders as he made his way around the world. He never traveled on horseback. He always went on foot, happily tramping twelve or fourteen hours a day without a break and never getting tired. Perhaps that was why he was called "the wandering Jew."

I ASSUME that my great-uncle would have had no objection if I were to begin by describing Salman's complicated background, given the countless times he recounted to us every tiny detail of the unusual circumstances that obliged the wandering Jew to leave Granada, his place of birth.

A Childhood in Granada

SALMAN'S FATHER was the renowned Jewish Cabalist Moishe de Espinosa. They lived in Granada, and Moishe enjoyed the protection and financial support of the sultan as he secluded himself to study the mysteries of creation and the universe. He left behind the Sefer ha-Zohar, or Book of Splendor, a Cabalistic tome, with bold observations and poetic formulations envied by the mystics. It perplexed religious seekers the whole world over.

Salman's mother, Hasna, was the daughter of the revered Arabic philosopher Yussuf al-Rahman. She was a devotee of the study of virtue, righteous conduct, and conscience. She used an approach to rearing her children that was entirely contrary to the customs of the time: no pressures, no obligatory exercises, and no punishments. She provided them with ample doses of Jewish and Arabic learning along with her mother's milk.

The plague of Black Death robbed Salman of his parents, Moishe and Hasna, when he was only fifteen years old. Death was nothing unknown to him, for in his short life he had helped to bury all four of his infant brothers. But now everything had changed. He was completely alone, abandoned without family or relatives, with no one to take care of him. A gaping abyss stood before him. He despised death and raged in terrible anger at his inability to duel with it. He wanted to lead a powerful and victorious rebellion against death, but he had no arms to use against it. All he could do was protest. He was enraged by his impotence. Behind him stood the certainties of death, and before him stood the uncertainties of life.

Whenever he recalled the disappearance of all those he had loved, he burst into tears. His grief was direct and unconstrained, the grief of an orphaned child. Then he would abruptly collect himself, not yet knowing that these were the signs of his destiny, the cruel foreshadowing of the fact that in the course of his several centuries of life he would always lose everything that was precious to him.

I TURN once again to Philip Khuri Hitti's classic *History of the Arabs* for help in describing the unfortunate circumstances that obliged Salman to leave Granada, the city of his birth. The Lebanese author offers the following version of Arabic chroniclers' accounts of the death in Granada of Sultan Yusuf I, which occurred only a few weeks after the burial of Moishe and Hasna.

The sultan was murdered in the mosque while deep in afternoon prayer. A madman clutching a dagger leaped upon the ruler and stabbed him in the chest. The sultan gave out a loud groan and collapsed on the floor. His cry alerted the guards, who found him bathed in his own blood. The sultan was still conscious and tried to say something to them, but weakened by the heavy loss of blood as he was, he could not articulate a single word. The guards carried him to his private quarters in the castle. He turned his dying eyes to those closest to him as they assembled and gave them sorrowing looks of farewell. Then he died. He was followed on the throne by his eldest son, Muhammed V, who was then sixteen years old.

According to Hitti's account, Sultan Yusuf I had been endowed by Allah with intelligence, perspicacity, and good judgment. He was spiritual, just, and highly respected; he had excellent relations with all the other rulers of the Iberian Peninsula. Art and poetry were greatly appreciated at his court, and he had a reputation as the protector of freedom of thought.

Even so, surprisingly enough, Hitti does not mention that Yusuf I considered Moishe de Espinosa to be the most accomplished of contemporary mystics and generously funded his research, for the sultan hoped that the Jewish philosopher would be able to produce a work explaining the nature of the Divine and its ordering of all things.

Nor does Hitti describe all of the strange events in Granada in the days immediately following the death of Yusuf I.

———

MY GREAT-UNCLE told us that a howling night storm destroyed that part of the Alhambra inhabited by the new sultan and tore up the imposing fruit trees in the garden by their roots, ripping them into tiny pieces. The only one that escaped total destruction was a magnificent apple tree, under which the old sultan would often read during the heat of the afternoon. That tree was ripped up by the roots, blown over the castle walls, and flung down into the main plaza. As dawn was breaking, the people hurried to pick and hide its fruit, which had turned golden ripe overnight. The following night, all of the statues in the Alhambra disappeared without a trace, and the roof of the mosque was blown away. On the third night terrifying phantoms appeared in the sultan's palace, and howling and lamentations filled the air. The sultan's counselors sought to reassure the uneasy Muhammed V that these were mere illusions, until it was discovered that twenty-one graves—exactly the number of years that Yusuf I had occupied the throne—had opened and now lay empty.

Muhammed V was inexperienced and scared out of his wits, more inclined to severity than to mercy, impatient, and easily annoyed if something was not to his liking. My great-uncle said his brown eyes were colored with the hues of suspicion and petty-mindedness. He was terrified that the end of the world was upon him.

The court astrologer, the influential Ahmed Husseini, had always had an evil eye for Moishe, the far more knowledgeable protégé of the sultan. The envious Husseini declared that with his Cabalistic spells the Jewish mystic had called down upon them the demon Messias and with him the Last Judgment. "Only the blind refuse to see and the deaf refuse to hear," Husseini proclaimed, further alarming the already deeply apprehensive young sultan. In a voice that scarcely concealed his poisonous hatred and envy, he added that even though Moishe now lay dead in his barren grave, no walls were solid enough to resist Espinosa's Jewish demon; the fiend could blow them to bits with a wave of his hand. The court astrologer suggested summoning Salman to the palace at once to turn over all of his father's manuscripts. Everything must be burned immediately. To make sure that the boy was not hiding anything, the sultan should not hesitate to have his belly cut open to see if it was crammed with dangerous magic spells.

The Last Sigh of the Unbeliever

THE REALIZATION that he no longer had any home in this world made Salman quake with fear.

The captain of the sultan's bodyguard knocked at the door, flanked by two soldiers. When the young man opened the door, the captain explained in a mild tone that the unbeliever Salman de Espinosa was given two hours to deliver the full collection of his father's works to the palace.

Unbeliever? What did that mean? No one had ever called Salman an unbeliever. Astonished, he went to his neighbor Mordechai, a grave old Jew who had been his father's closest friend.

The elderly man invited Salman in for tea. He smiled thoughtfully as he prepared it. Salman had the feeling that the old fellow had something extremely serious to share with him.

"Have you taught yourself to read the Koran?" Mordechai asked him.

Salman nodded.

"Ah-ha—but you are a Jew?"

"I am, but my mother was a Muslim."

The old man gave him a melancholy smile and murmured, "Salman, the truth of the matter is that you are neither Jew nor Muslim. According to Jewish law, you must be born of a Jewish mother in order to be a Jew. And what does Islam require of a Muslim? A Muslim father. But you have neither. Your mother was Muslim, your father a Jew."

"So what does that make me?"

"You are the Almighty's finest creation, the measure of everything: You are a human being. If all Jews, Muslims, and Christians were that, if they had a human outlook toward life and moral views, then you would have no need to fear the morrow. Keep that always in mind and always be a human being, with everything that status signifies. Above all, always be full of care and compassion for others."

The old man advised Salman to go home, collect his father's writings, and set off without a moment's delay for Córdoba, where he should seek out Rabbi Jacobo Tibbon and warn him that the new sultan wanted to destroy the work of Moishe de Espinosa.

BREATHLESS AND PERSPIRING, Salman paused briefly a little way outside the city. Everything he had collected for his hasty departure fit into his bundle: Sefer ha-Zohar and another manuscript or two, along with a crudely carved wooden box bearing a seal that he had discovered at the very back of the drawer containing his father's notes. The box intrigued him.

He turned back and for a few brief moments took pleasure in the striking beauty of the Alhambra, framed by the towering mountains of the Sierra Nevada. He loved that place more then any other on earth. He already felt a certain longing to return—not to the house of his birth but rather to the places where sovereign peace had generously enfolded him in its arms, particularly to a clearing in the northwestern reaches of the great forest. He would often sit there watching the distant setting sun. Only now did he understand how much he was about to lose. His eyes filled with tears. He sighed deeply and cast a last glance at Granada, then began his long, wandering journey.

A Religious Debate

DAYLIGHT BEGAN TO FAIL, and Jacobo Tibbon pulled the candlestick closer to the page. Salman sat silent at the other end of the table while the rabbi examined the text. The learned man went through it carefully, caressing the page first with one hand and then with the other, then slowly following with his right index finger the characters inscribed there. Finally he leaned forward and kissed Moishe's work, the Sefer ha-Zohar.

"Extraordinary," muttered the rabbi with evident enthusiasm. "Your father, blessed be his name, answers many of the questions that have plagued me ceaselessly over these recent years. What he has written is an indisputable masterpiece. I will take great pleasure in using what is inscribed here for the religious debate next week in the market square. I am obliged to participate, even though it would hardly be wise of me to win. The Christian mob will seize the least pretext to attack us, plunder our homes, and slaughter us."

Salman was perplexed by this and asked for an explanation. The rabbi told him that in a number of places the

Catholic Church had acceded to pressure and staged religious debates that more often than not degenerated into farce. With these verbal contests the Christians intended to demonstrate the inferiority of the Jewish faith. The church was usually represented by converted Jews who hoped to win better positions for themselves by defeating the rabbis. Even though with their greater knowledge and superior rhetorical skills the rabbis were capable of easily demolishing the unsubstantiated declarations of their opponents, when all was said and done, they were forced to declare themselves defeated, especially in the face of the looming threat of reprisals. In Toledo, where one of these debates turned out differently than expected, the men of the church had tortured the learned Jews, obliging them to forswear their Jewish identity and denounce the Jewish faith. The rabbi explained to the tender young man that similar attacks had occurred elsewhere.

Salman couldn't understand why the Catholic Church was doing this.

Tibbon replied that the church thirsted after great power and wanted to control everything on the Iberian Peninsula, including nonreligious areas of life. Ecclesiastical aims frequently conflicted with the interests of the civil rulers, and since a number of the Christian kings had Jewish counselors, the wrath of the priests was directed toward those influential men. The church insisted that if the Jews resisted conversion, they should be cast out and driven away just as the Moors had been. In response to church pressures a series of anti-Jewish measures had been instituted throughout Spain.

THE PEOPLE OF CÓRDOBA went outside on that unusually warm morning to the Plaza de los Reyes Católicos to attend the first religious debate between Jews and Christians.

The vast plaza was full of monks, nuns, peasants, artisans, old folk, women, children, thieves, prostitutes, the crippled, and the maimed, as well as an occasional Jew. The surging mass of humanity followed the debate, spellbound.

Upon a tribune hastily erected for the occasion sat the elderly governor Hidalgo del Solís in the company of the ambassador of the Holy See, Miguel Cruz de Medina, canon of Córdoba Cathedral and director of the theological debate; various nobles from the ruling council; a couple of priestly scholars; a notary; an assistant; and two abbots invited to represent the Cistercian orders of Seville and Carmona. The most august citizens of Córdoba sat with their families upon the balconies overlooking the plaza, clutching colorful ceramic crucifixes and receptacles of cold water from which they frequently drank.

The church bells tolled to mark the opening of the debate. Cruz de Medina stood up, extended his arms, and began his invocation, which was entirely too long and tiresome. Once he had finished, he summoned forth the participants, instructed them to take the customary oath, and enjoined them to participate assiduously in the debate. Jacobo Tibbon nodded in agreement but said nothing, while his opponent replied in a ringing voice, "Amen!"

The rabbi's opponent was one of the so-called new Christians, the converted Jew Gaspar Santa María, who claimed that he was among the few initiates who knew the secret reasons for the Jews' stiff-necked insistence on maintaining their ancient faith. He had formally pledged to the pope to convert at least ten thousand of his former coreligionists to the true teachings by demonstrating to them that the Christian world was full of miracles, while their Elohim, whom they persisted in calling the Ultimate, was a tyrant and a vengeful, wicked old man.

With the very first exchange it was obvious to all that Santa María was no match for the rabbi, either in knowledge or in eloquence. The rabbi outshone him in every way, demonstrating his prodigious intelligence and wisdom with each response.

Under the pressure of the occasion and increasingly unsure of himself, Santa María fell into a confusion in his exposition. He began to stammer. The rabbi commented that in his opinion conversations such as this one were extremely beneficial; they were healthy intellectual exercises that always taught him something new while encouraging him to think more clearly, since the contention between differing views encouraged him to rise to previously unimagined heights. It was important, therefore, to seek out opportunities to encounter the views of others and embrace them with open arms instead of sharpened claws.

Santa María felt insulted by this remark. He replied that Jews were not as intelligent as the twisted logic of the rabbi sought to suggest. They were merely sly and cunning because they were born filled with black gall, a fact for which there was ample evidence. That verbal thrust drew thundering applause and prompted shouts of delight from the crowd.

The rabbi was not at a loss for a reply. He praised his adversary for his candor and high spirits and especially for the fact that he was not holding back his emotions. Then he said that no assertion shocked him, no views offended him, and there was no concept so nonsensical or ridiculous that he would refuse to consider it, as long as both parties to the discussion were seeking to discover the truth.

Only a few applauded that reply. Salman was one of them.

Santa María went on the attack. He proclaimed that all Jews were evil and bore the collective guilt for crucifying

Jesus. The Sanhedrin, the great Jewish council of Roman times, had formally condemned the Son of God to death, and therefore all of them—his voice rose almost to a falsetto—would inevitably wind up in eternal damnation and their bodies would be roasted over the coals like lambs on a spit.

The rabbi responded that he honored truth and welcomed it wherever he found it. He willingly surrendered to truth and lay down his arms in defeat at its approach. But the truth just enunciated, he added after a momentary pause, was one that would not stand up to impartial examination. The first point was that the Jewish people were not responsible for the death of Jesus; the culprits were a small group within the religious and political establishment. In the time of Jesus only ten percent of the Jewish people lived in the land of Israel, and no one could in good conscience hold the Jews of other lands and their descendants centuries later responsible for the decision of the Sanhedrin. Questionable trials and executions have occurred throughout all ages, the rabbi said pointedly. Few people would be left on earth if one had held whole peoples responsible for every unjust verdict in history and had persecuted and murdered the innocent for those miscarriages of justice, as Christians had done with the Jews.

The rabbi noted that unlike his opponent he had no experience with hell, so he could not express an informed opinion about its existence. Even so, he knew that the picture of a dark, cruel place that people had once found comical, even impossible, had now been described by priests so convincingly and with such imaginative detail that many had begun to believe in its existence.

"When a lie is repeated long enough, people accept it as the truth because they need to believe," the rabbi emphasized.

He stopped for a moment to collect his thoughts. Then he said, "From the time of Jesus up to our own day the world has been filled with violence, pillaging, and lies, and Christians have shed more blood than other people have. Nor have they been such shining lights of morality among the peoples of the world. So when my honorable opponent threatens us Jews with eternal hellfire, he must be evoking a place populated principally with Christians."

A deathly silence enveloped the plaza, as if Tibbon's words had fallen into a world without sound. Santa María was perspiring copiously and pulling nervously at his beard, clearly shaken by the rabbi's convincing logic. The longer that painful silence continued, the more the faces in the crowd darkened. The displeasure grew in ferocious silence and was just about to burst into violent indignation when Cruz de Medina stood up and clapped his hands to distract the people. He saw that the representative of the church had been left speechless. To stave off defeat and its consequences, he stopped the debate, commenting that the sun stood at its zenith and the heat was unbearable. He stretched his hands up toward the heavens and exhorted them all to join in a moment of silent prayer. With his eyes closed and his head tilted slightly to one side he seemed to be listening to a distant voice.

The theological debate was scheduled to resume three days later.

Evil Deeds in Córdoba

FOR THE FIRST TIME in his life Salman had seen enemy faces up close and experienced a terrifying hatred directed at him. He was seized with a fear of those around him and wanted to run from the plaza, but a tall dark man in stinking filthy rags blocked his way. Everything about the man was huge—his head, his shoulders, arms, hands, and feet. Next to that unkempt giant, Salman looked frail and insignificant. The man grabbed him and lifted him up. An icy voice whispered into his ear, "Tonight I'll be coming to kill you."

That afternoon Tibbon's friends assembled at his house. The rabbi read a prayer of thanksgiving and bowed before the Almighty who had given him the strength to sustain that first part of the theological debate without falling prey to arrogance or vanity. He entreated the creator of the world and the human race not to permit the days of the Jews in Córdoba to be turned into nights of uncertainty. A lively discussion ensued about the possible consequences of the rabbi's incontestable triumph.

The companions in the room agreed that there was a risk—some of them even insisted it was an imminent risk— that a raging mob would attack the Jews under cover of darkness. They urged Tibbon to barricade himself inside his house.

The rabbi refused to heed such advice. He said it was the duty of the intelligent man to resist specters born of fantasies and fear. He declared that he would lose no sleep that night over imaginary threats.

Rabbi Tibbon asked one of his friends, the silversmith Luis Abudalfía, to lodge Salman in his house for the next several days, since he himself could not guarantee the boy the care and feeding adequate to the needs of a young man.

DARK HAD HARDLY FALLEN over the Jewish quarter when several dozen masked men carrying pikes, axes, and shovels attacked Jews in the narrow streets. Innocent women and men in their path were mercilessly struck down and left bleeding.

The clandestine gang was directed by Father Dominic Martínez, a Catholic priest from Madrid whose long experience of life in the cloister not only had provided him an extensive knowledge of Catholic teachings but also had filled him with an unreasoning hatred against Jews and other unbelievers incapable of reciting the Our Father, the Hail Mary, and the Credo. One night the Virgin Mary had answered his silent prayers by appearing in a dazzling light in his cramped monastery cell. She had informed him that the devil had insinuated himself into the bodies of Jewish scholars so as to propagate his wicked gospel. She reminded him of hell's eternal torments for those who fail to combat evil and cast it out. The Virgin instructed Martínez to go forth into the world to preach against the Jews, for the Last Judgment was close at hand. She promised never to abandon him as long as he remained pure in heart. That visitation provoked him to scourge himself every evening or to ask another priest to lash him with a whip of hemp fiber.

During the afternoon this same Father Martínez had assembled in his church a band of devoted Christians who were fiercely merciless brawlers. He prefaced his sermon by quoting the Holy Scripture: The Messiah had already come and would return again on the day of the Last Judgment. He eloquently incited the assembly against Jacobo Tibbon, asserting that the rabbi had deeply grieved Jesus Christ and the holy word during that morning's debate, because he had spun a web of elaborate Jewish lies. He concluded his violent accusation of the rabbi by declaring that true Christians with their hands on the cross could never accept such infamous doings. He exhorted them to teach the Jews a lesson, offering the prospect of looting the vast riches hidden in the rabbi's cellar.

The surging mob stormed through the streets to Tibbon's house. The rabbi, weary with the weight of his nearly seventy years, opened the door, regarded the men with a dignified smile, greeted them simply, and invited them to enter his house for an inspiring exchange of theological views. For a moment the masked men stood there transfixed; then crude reality stepped forward, wrapped in the soiled cloak of Tomás Huerta. He was a rough-hewn character, an inveterate drinker who wound up in bloody brawls every week and indiscriminately mistreated everyone who got in his way; when he sobered up he would always rush to Father Martínez to confess and do penance. Huerta shouted that the Jew had a box of enough gold coins to fill up all their houses. That was the signal to invade the house. To their great disappointment, the masked guests found nothing in his simple dwelling but worthless household goods and piles of Hebrew manuscripts. A couple of well-aimed hammer blows to the head left the old man lifeless on the floor. Tibbon was spared the sight of men turning everything upside down, tearing the Holy Scripture to shreds, and emptying their bladders throughout the house.

To purify Córdoba of the evil spirits that were the rabbi's familiars, they set the house on fire.

The Secret of the Wooden Box

NEARLY SIX MONTHS had passed since those tragic events. Even so, Salman's throat closed up in misery when after wandering for a week along narrow paths in the sun and the wind, in the rain and the cold, he stepped across the threshold of Gabriel Abudalfía's house in Seville and reported the death of the rabbi. The merchant listened attentively to Salman's account. He wanted to know everything about the deaths of his father and mother, the new sultan of Granada, the religious debate, and the atrocities committed in Córdoba. He heard how his sister-in-law Henriette had succumbed during the epidemic of typhoid fever, leaving her husband, Luís Abudalfía, alone with five children. This was why he had sent Salman to Seville. At the end of his long tale, the boy broke down in tears. Gabriel Abudalfía clapped him kindly on the shoulder and assured him he was welcome to stay in their house for as long as he wished.

Salman had brought the little wooden box with him on his hasty flight from Granada. When he broke it open a year later, the contents surprised him. He had expected to find some part of his father's writings meant to be kept secret. Instead, within the box there lay an indecipherable text and a written history of the Espinosa family. He could see from the handwriting that neither of the documents had been composed by his father.

The family history had been noted down by someone he had never heard of but who was clearly from his own lineage: court physician Israel de Espinosa, in Lisbon, in the month of Nisan of the year 5062 according to the Jewish calendar—that is, in May 1302.

The text had no chronological order at all. Salman had the impression that Israel must have written in great haste and had no opportunity to edit it, for it seemed as if the whole history of the great family had occurred in the same era and simultaneously. It was a holy mess, hastily outlined and fragmentary, with many names, parallel and sometimes incomplete anecdotes, sudden unrelated changes of subject, and various apparently unrelated commentaries. None of this inhibited Salman. Fascinated, he read it all, skipping nothing. He turned the pages, intent on learning more about his own origins. When he grasped the fact that he belonged to a line with an urgent mission in this world, he felt prouder than ever, and his sense of isolation dropped away. Now his life had meaning. He resolved to discover his own role and mission as part of that family line. It was clear that he would have to discover the meaning of Moses's prophecy, so it was vital to decipher the obscure, illegible document.

In the flickering candlelight of long winter nights, as freezing winds howled around the Abudalfía home, a Salman indifferent to the world outside sought to tease out the secrets of the enciphered document. He worked his way farther into the text with every passing night, but he could not get at its hidden meaning, no matter how much attention he devoted to it. Fruitless months went by, but the boy refused to give up. His determination was unshakable, for nothing was more important to him than the goal of his search. He was convinced that his whole future depended on decoding the cipher.

Finally, one spring night when chance, fate, and time happened to find themselves in auspicious alignment, the conjunction of those forces pierced directly through the yellowing document and the text opened its dark secrets to Salman. His heart was in his throat as he read the recipe for the elixir of immortality and the centuries-old admonitions that no one should ever consume even a drop of the potion and the secret should never be revealed to anyone except the eldest son of the family.

Death's Sworn Enemy

SALMAN HATED DEATH. He considered himself to be its sworn enemy. Death had deprived him of all those he held dear: four brothers, his father, his mother, and Rabbi Tibbon.

Why was death so cruel? What was it trying to tell him? He was perpetually amazed by the enigma, while at the same time understanding full well that death was the only certain thing in this life. All who are born must die one day, even if none of us knows when or how.

But now that the elixir of immortality with its guarantee of eternal life was within Salman's grasp, he was overcome with the desire to challenge and defeat death.

IT WAS MUCH MORE difficult to cultivate the Raimundo plant than Salman initially had expected. One planting after another withered, and he suspected that this was due to the heat of the summer. When autumn and cooler weather arrived, Raimundo finally began to put forth leaves. It took Salman another three months to finish the preparation of the elixir.

The taste was foul, but Salman was resolute in his determination to triumph over death. He quickly downed the seven drops. A wave of nausea swept through him.

He awoke in the middle of the night in a high fever and suffering from sharp pains. His face was dark blue. Beads of blood stood out on his forehead. His cries awoke everyone in the house. They summoned a doctor, who poked and pressed every part of Salman's body. The physician scratched his head and obliged the young man to get up from the bed and execute a series of peculiar movements.

Following this, the doctor tickled the soles of his feet and his elbows. At last, with an encouraging but worried smile he gave his diagnosis. Salman was physically healthy, perhaps a trifle frail, but he was suffering from a spiritual affliction that arose from something difficult and painful buried in his heart. This hidden woe had inundated his body with bitter phlegm, causing the fever and provoking muscle spasms. The physician could not identify any definitive cause for the bleeding from the forehead. He thought some sort of process of inner cleansing might be underway, similar to that which women experience each month. He told Salman to consume three garlic cloves thrice a day to lower the fever and, other than that, to take no solid food for three days.

The next morning Salman's fever had disappeared. He felt wonderful.

Many Years of Happiness

THREE YEARS LATER Salman married Gabriel Abudalfía's youngest daughter, Esther. It was an arranged marriage, not a love match. Esther's siblings were married and already had families. Esther had been yearning for the day when she would dress as a bride and know married bliss. One morning she asked her father to arrange things. That very afternoon Abudalfía remarked to Salman that perhaps the time had come for him to marry. What could be more appropriate than to wed a young woman whom he had seen almost every day for many years? After all, such regular encounters strengthen relations and friendships. He was careful to make it clear at the same time that Salman owed them nothing and was in no way obliged to acknowledge the debt of gratitude he owed the family for being allowed to share their quarters. However, if Salman should choose to accept the role of son-in-law in the household, he would be welcomed as a partner in the merchant's flourishing firm.

The wedding celebration was the most elaborate for many years in the *judería*. Everyone would have cherished warm memories of the fest if only the bride had not happened to suffer a tragic accident at dinner.

When Esther leaned over to speak to guests on the other side of the table, a flickering candle touched her festively arranged hair. It suddenly became a flaming torch. Many of those present thought at first that this was a joke, carefully prepared and artfully realized; guests at the table burst into happy laughter. Esther's face was severely burned, for it took several minutes to extinguish the flames. Their wedding night was not exactly what Salman had expected, and he had to wait more than six months for her to open her sex to him so that they could unite as husband and wife in the consummation of the flesh.

The couple had five children—three sons and two daughters. Salman worked for his father-in-law and traveled frequently. The perpetual problems of ordinary life seldom left him the time to think of anything else. The secret formula in the fragrant little wooden box almost slipped from his mind.

The only thing that from time to time reminded him of the elixir of immortality was the fact that he never felt any physical pain or showed the slightest signs of the process of aging that affects all humans. The inexorable march of time molded ever deeper wrinkles in Esther's face, but Salman always looked exactly the same as he had that day beneath the wedding canopy when he pledged his eternal fidelity to her.

Two Christian Men

IN THE YEAR 1391 Pesach happened to coincide with Easter week. The traditional evening Seder of the Jews commemorating freedom from slavery in Egypt was celebrated on Easter Friday. In one part of Seville people came together in a festive celebration with burning candles, a well-furnished table, their favorite delicacies, and gleaming chalices of wine. The rest of the city was plunged in deep silence as the folk devoted themselves to praying, remembering, and accompanying Jesus Christ along the Stations of the Cross.

Under cover of darkness a nobleman slunk into the *judería*. Historical sources give his name as Diego de López Alba and describe him as incorrigibly addicted to whores and prostitutes. His aim was to wallow in the pleasures of the flesh, since that evening he had not found a single woman in the Christian sections of the city willing to sell herself to him.

His venture into the Jewish quarter was due in no small measure to the fact that three days before this, in front of the Giralda bell tower by Santa María Cathedral, he had seen a broad-hipped, heavy-breasted Jewess with the face of an angel, long cascading hair, and eyes the color of ripe chestnuts. That handsome woman fixed her gaze on him for an instant as he walked past, a sign that he interpreted as an open invitation. Enchanted by the woman's body, he trailed some distance behind her in hopes that she would show him the way to the place where she practiced her trade. The Jewess strolled along a narrow street that circled halfway through the Jewish quarter. Next to a couple of houses with barred windows it widened into a plaza with a market, stalls, shops, and workshops. Swarms of women with black shawls over their heads were doing their shopping, haggling at stands heavy with oranges, grapes, melons, dates, olives, and beans. López Alba was afraid of losing his beauty in the press of the crowd. But suddenly she left the marketplace, swung into Calle Moisés, and disappeared into a house with a stone facing that signaled the prosperity of the inhabitants. He found the door locked when he attempted to enter.

On Friday evening the love-struck aristocrat took the same path back to Calle Moisés. He groped his way along the walls of the house and peeked through the windows in hopes of catching sight of the beauty whose flesh he yearned to embrace. She was inside in holiday attire at a lavishly set dinner table, her hair in a tight knot on top of her head, surrounded by several old folks, a slightly humpbacked man, and four children of various ages, all obviously members of her family. They were eating unleavened bread, drinking red wine, and joyously singing. López Alba saw immediately that as far as the woman was concerned, the only satisfactions he could hope for that evening would be those of his eyes and imagination, instead of the anticipated pleasures of grasping her buttocks as he thrust himself deep inside her. He felt sharply disappointed, and a sense of resentment flared within him. He briefly contemplated breaking into the house to assault her. *What kind of Jewish cunt is this?* he thought to himself. *In the street by day she conducts herself shamelessly, like a hot-blooded whore, showing off her big tits and great rear to tempt Christian men, and by night she wraps herself in dark cloth from head to toe at home and pretends to be a dutiful Madonna and loving Jewish mother, then afterward wallows voluptuously in bed until the dawn with that cripple!* The hotheaded nobleman threw a large rock through the window, howled insults, and fled.

He sought out several friends who were idling that evening away by playing cards. He told them he had been on his way to mass at the cathedral, but because he was deeply immersed in religious contemplation he had lost his way and wound up in the *judería*. There with his own eyes he had seen the Jews profaning the sacrament of the holy mother church, butchering an innocent Christian infant and drinking its blood, singing praises to Satan, laughing at Christ's suffering, and mocking his sacrifice by stuffing crucifixes up their asses.

One of the cardplayers, the priest Alonso Adejo, slammed his fist on the table. "*Basta!*" he roared. "That's enough of these Jews' shameless behavior. How do they dare mock the Christian faith in these hours when our thoughts are with Jesus Christ on the cross? We can't just sit here and accept that. We have to do something and do it right now!"

ALONSO ADEJO was seen as one of the less-principled souls among the clergy of Seville. His name was linked to countless rumors. For example, it was said that in his younger days he had overpowered several teenage girls of respectable Christian families who had come to him for spiritual guidance, but no one dared to complain. Quite the opposite, in fact: the girls' fathers did everything they could to hush up the matter, because they feared their daughters would not be marriageable if it became generally known that their hymens had been broken.

The generally accepted story was that the person who finally put a stop to Adejo's assaults was a fat whore of Jewish background. He had promised her payment in silver coins if she met him in the church. Once they were inside, he became violent, dragged her out to the choir, tore open her blouse, cruelly fastened his hands on her naked breasts, and obliged her to kneel. He stuffed his swollen member into her mouth and demanded that she suck it. As she started to work, he pulled out a leather whip and began to lash her. The woman screamed and tried to get up; he ignored her protests. He pushed her back down with one hand and tried to wield the whip with the other. She became infuriated, chomped down as savagely as she could on the glans of his penis, and bit off the extremity with a violent jerk. He screamed like a stuck pig and lost his grip on her shoulder. She stood up, spat out the bloody bit of flesh, told him he could keep his silver coins because she was providing him this relief at no charge, and then ran out of the church. The shocked priest fell to the floor in a swoon. The three choirboys who found him and saved him from bleeding to death were certainly not of the more discreet sort, for soon everyone in Seville knew that a fat Jewish whore with sharp teeth had cut off the seed-spouting faucet of Alonso Adejo and converted a lust no Christian maiden had been able to satisfy into impotence and bitter longing.

That nameless whore had instilled into his heart undying hatred and animosity, and he considered it his priestly duty to annihilate all who did not believe in Christian teaching and refused to have their children baptized.

The First of the Pogroms

THE KING and the archbishop of Seville were known for their cordial attitude toward the Jews. They took prompt action when word came to them that Adejo had incited strong anti-Jewish sentiments with his sermon. Even as the priest was busy in his parish readying a campaign to throw out the Jews, the archbishop stressed in his sermon at the cathedral that Christianity valued mercy and loving-kindness equally, and for that reason every Christian was bound by his faith to show tolerance for the Jews. As soon as the king heard the rumor that Adejo had assembled a mob of volunteers, an imposing, seething band planning to descend upon the Jews, he ordered his soldiers to take up defensive positions around the *judería*.

Those measures were of little help. Adejo and his hatred had a far greater influence upon the people than the message of the Gospel did; the swords and lances of the protecting forces were not sufficient to protect the Jews of Seville.

SALMAN COULD NOT SLEEP. His nights had always been thus. Every night of his life he had lain awake, overwhelmed with the fear of losing himself in the remote darkness of eternal night. He kept his breath shallow, lay there without moving, and listened fearfully to the street noises far off in the depths of night. He thought that he heard the distant murmur of troops in quick march. After a moment of silence, he heard more sounds. This time he could make out the words "fire" and "blood."

He positioned himself by the window and saw several black-clad figures in the street. Their hands held glistening sword blades, rapiers, stilettos, and double-edged knives. They began chanting, "With fire and blood, we'll kill the Jews." The noise from outside, the terrifying words, and the menacing rhythm of that chant shook him deeply. He had been through this before—the attack out of the dark by the mob howling battle cries. He suddenly recalled that night in Córdoba when masked men struck down old Jacobo Tibbon and set his house on fire. Salman had been only fifteen and had watched those events from his hiding place in the neighboring house of Luis Abudalfía. His helplessness as the rabbi's house went up in flames had tormented him ever since that night.

He knew instinctively what was about to happen. He felt completely exposed, and in his mind's eye he could see how the dark shapes would grab him and send him tumbling, spit on him and kick him, beat him, and trample him, slash off his clothing and set fire to his body as he lay there already half dead.

He rushed to awaken Esther, who was breathing deeply and wheezing in her sleep. At that instant he heard a violent pounding upon the door.

WHAT HAPPENED that night in Seville was so horrific, so bloody, and so terrifying that I couldn't bear to listen to my great-uncle's description of it. His voice was mournful and desolate. It was evident that it cost him pain and great effort to put the gruesome details into words. I recoiled in disgust from what I heard, and I had the vision of sinking slowly into a hellish clamor of men crying out in pain, women weeping, and children screaming. My stomach turned and I had to cover my ears. I began crying and shaking. My great-uncle looked down at me in surprise, confused; he couldn't decide if he should go on with his description of the first pogrom against the Spanish Jews, a bloodbath that was only the first of many over the following hundred years. He decided to stop there. He never said another word about that episode in the history of our family.

That's why I do not know exactly what Salman and his family suffered on the night of June 6, 1391, when the self-proclaimed guardians of the pure faith murdered men, slit the throats of women and children, plundered houses and set them on fire. Behind them they left the corpses of four thousand innocents.

What I do know is that the next morning Salman and Esther found the corpses of their daughters and their families in the burned-out ruins of the Jewish quarter. The bodies were horribly slashed and badly burned. Salman could not hold back his tears. Esther did not scream; she did not weep. She stood there erect with a stony expression, overwhelmed by pain. She peered closely at the bodies of her children and grandchildren for a very long time, and the grief destroyed her will to live. She fell lifeless to the ground.

The Immortal Wanderer

ONCE AGAIN death had robbed Salman of all those whom he loved most: his wife, his daughters, five grandchildren, two sons-in-law, friends and neighbors.

Once again he had stood in the valley of the shadow of death. What was death trying to tell him?

He listened to death. He listened closely for a long time. Eventually he realized that he had already stepped past his own mortal limits and pushed out into the unknown, and he was now experiencing the rarest moment of grace, the unimaginable moment of perfect liberty, unknown to most, sought desperately by many, never before achieved by anyone. He was the only one ever granted the privilege of experiencing such a moment, perceiving the looming figure of death, looking him in the face and possessing something that forestalled death's embrace.

Salman examined his body. He was more than sixty
years old, but his face was that of a young man. Only the
blindness of habit had prevented him and those around
him from seeing it. It was even more peculiar that his body
showed no signs of having been beaten, kicked, stabbed,
and burned. He could not find even a scratch, not a single
bruise, not the most trivial injury to testify to the brutality
of the mob on that ghastly night. He recalled that a towering brute had broken his leg with violent blows of a hammer
without eliciting a word of complaint from him. It was clear
to him that he could withstand any physical torment at all,
for he possessed an invulnerability that was all but divine.

He was still, more than ever, the same person he had
always been: a man nourished by the bounty of the world's
gardens and by its animals, a man who gave back to the
earth all his surplus, a man who sorrowed because he had
for all too long been without the close warmth of love. But
he could not deny that he was experiencing everything with
the vigor of a god. He felt self-confident, as close to perfect
as he was willing to admit, and eternal. He was at one with
God due to the simple fact that immortality was his destiny. He knew that he would have to bear that great truth
all alone, because he could never tell anyone that he had
discovered the perfect antidote to all illness, the elixir of
immortality.

SALMAN WAS STOCKY and resilient, a man with an unbelievably large nose; he had a lively curiosity and a joyous
nature; he was erudite and eager to enter into discussions;
and his stride was so energetic that the muddy earth splat-
tered all the way up to his shoulders as he made his way
in his wanderings across the world. He never rode a horse
but always went by foot instead, taking pleasure in walking

uninterrupted for twelve or fourteen hours without showing the least sign of fatigue. Perhaps that was why he was called "the wandering Jew."

For more than a century he wended his way across the land from Andalusia in the south to the Pyrenees in the north. He stopped in tiny villages and in large cities, and encountered a foul stench everywhere. That unbearable smell was not due to the people's custom of dumping their night soil in the streets, making the towns steam with the impurities running in the gutters. The stink that followed him on his journeys across Spain was caused by something else that was rotten through and through.

Six Brothers

MY GREAT-UNCLE would never speak about his own life to Sasha and me. When we asked about his background he didn't reply and abruptly changed the subject. But just one time he mentioned, as if in passing, that he had lived in Vienna in the 1930s and worked on a study of the plight of the Jews in fourteenth-century Spain. I don't remember how the subject came up. He summarized it for us. We always listened in admiration to his stories and they always cast a powerful spell upon me—except for that one time. That is why I remember the occasion so well.

He said that just like Hitler, who had dreamed of a Germany of racial purity, the churchmen of the Spanish Inquisition were obsessed with *limpieza de sangre,* the purity of the blood. They suspected everyone of having impure blood and there was a requirement that people prove that in their veins there flowed not a drop of *mala sangre,* contaminated blood. The offices of the Inquisition were heaped high with reports of individuals designated to be examined, tested, and isolated from the rest of the population. My great-uncle explained that the manhunt was completely absurd, of course, considering that Spaniards were already a mixture of Basques, Celts, Iberians, Phoenicians, West Goths, Vandals, Arabs, and Jews. There was not a single racially pure person anywhere in the whole land.

The Jews were special targets, he emphasized to us. In hopes of escaping the brutalities of the Inquisition, a minority of the Jews began to work for their persecutors. He called them "collaborators" and said that their denunciations split families apart. Worse, many converted to Christianity and accepted baptism so as to save their own lives and those of their children. This way they were permitted to reside outside the Jewish quarter, to avoid wearing the humiliating red badges sewn on the fronts of their garments, and to practice their trades.

Sasha and I exchanged a puzzled glance as we tried to make out the meaning of the incomprehensible words *"mala sangre,"* "excluded," "collaborators," and "converts." We wouldn't have understood it any better even if our great-uncle had been able to communicate it to us in Spanish. He didn't notice—or pretended not to notice—that we were listening to him without much enthusiasm, wondering what on earth he was talking about. We would have much rather listened to stories of his life in Vienna in the 1930s, but neither of us dared to interrupt him.

Suddenly the door opened with a jerk and Grandmother stormed into the kitchen where we sat around the table. She stopped short and glared at my great-uncle. He tensed and fell silent.

"Franci, you're not feeding the children more of your absurd tales, are you?" she asked, a dangerous light in her eyes.

"No, no," he answered. "We were talking about chess. I was just telling the boys about that amazing championship match in the spring of 1921 between José Raúl Capablanca and the reigning grand master Emanuel Lasker. After four defeats, Lasker gave up and blamed it on his failing health. It was a world sensation. I'll never forget the moment when I heard the news on the radio. It was on my last day of internment at the Emilia-Romagna prisoner-of-war camp. The next morning I was going to travel back home to rejoin my family."

"Franci, Franci. Mind your tongue! Be careful what you say," Grandmother said. She turned on her heel and vanished from the kitchen as suddenly as she had arrived.

My great-uncle's response to her immediately awakened our interest. We wanted to know what he had been doing in a prisoner-of-war camp. We had no idea where Emilia-Romagna might be and even less what "internment" meant. But we were intrigued. We never found the opportunity to ask him about it, however, for as soon as Grandmother had left, Fernando went back to his account of what life had been like for the Jews in that cruel totalitarian medieval Spanish society ruled by the all-powerful clerics and their merciless courts.

A few minutes later when he noticed that we were less attentive than usual, he got up, took a pen and piece of paper out of a kitchen drawer, and began scribbling, preparing a diagram to show us that Salman de Espinosa had six male great-grandchildren and the eldest of them, Emmanuel, had six sons of his own, as follows:

I.

Ephraim. He lived as a pious Jew. On days other than the Sabbath and religious holidays he honored the covenant between God and Israel by wearing small black-lacquered boxes called tefillin, attached by winding leather cords seven times about his left arm, the one closer to the heart. As he recited Morning Prayer he would hold upon his head little boxes containing texts from the Fifth Book of Moses. He observed kosher and scrupulously adhered to tradition. In the autumn of his life he was obliged to flee the country and settle in Portugal. He was buried in Oporto.

II.

Elias. He accepted baptism but secretly remained a Jew. The spies of the Inquisition in the Ciudad Real noted that on Saturdays no smoke rose from his chimney (for the Jews neither prepared food on the Sabbath nor lit their fires) and he was arrested. He was charged with eating meat on days of obligatory fasting and reading the psalms of David in Hebrew. After several days of brutal torture they chopped off his hands and cut them into small bits. He was burned alive.

III.

Elon. He converted to Christianity at an early age after the face of Jesus appeared to him in a bowl of chicken soup his mother served him at Pesach. He decided that the purpose of his life was to promote Christianity and the propagation of God's church. He discovered by accident that he could perform miracles. It was generally believed that he could make the deaf hear, the mute speak, and the blind see. He served for many years as the prior of the Dominican cloister in San Pablo and ended his days as the bishop of Santander.

IV.

Enoch. He fell in love with an elderly Christian widow and married her after converting to her faith. He studied law and became the mayor of Madrid, proved to be an outstanding administrator, and was named to a ministerial post in Castile. He persuaded the king and queen to publish a decree that obliged unbaptized Jews to wear a distinctive badge on their clothing and live in a walled-in sector of the city, separated from the general population. He died childless, a victim of internal hemorrhaging.

V.

Isaías. He was a clever man, a master of the art of concealment. As a young man he changed his name to Enrique Español, the goal being to erase all traces of his ancestry. He became a minion of the Inquisition, and he so surpassed his colleagues with his zeal in burning thousands of Jews at the stake that he quickly rose through the ranks. King Ferdinand became aware of his valuable contributions and he was granted the rank of commissioner as well as the responsibility of driving the Jews out of Spain.

VI.

Ezra. He was the family rebel. Because he had been fascinated as a boy by the stories of the Maccabee rebellion told by his father on Sabbath evenings, he decided to dedicate himself to resisting the forces of the Inquisition. He planned and participated in a failed attempt led by Salman de Espinosa to assassinate Grand Inquisitor Tomás de Torquemada. After enduring cruel torture he was forced onto the bonfire awaiting him in Seville. The last words from his lips before the flames ended his young life were, "Forgive me and show me your grace, Lord Jesus Christ."

———

AFTER HEARING all of this, it suddenly occurred to me
that those distant relatives of mine were complete strangers
to me. For a moment, their baseness and despicable characters made me ashamed to be a Spinoza.

The Hounds of God

THE COMMON PEOPLE called them *de Domini canes*,
the hunting dogs of God. The Dominicans were the bloodhounds of the Inquisition. They pursued heretics, those
false Christians who pretended to have given up Jewish beliefs but clung in secret to certain traditions: they did not
eat pork, they observed the Jewish Sabbath, or they fasted
on days of repentance. They were called "Marranos," a disparaging term that means "swine."

The Dominicans had informants to help them and their
activity was greatly valued by the priests; vigorous, well-
documented denunciation was a fine Catholic ideal. But in
case the approval of the church were not enough, the informants were also encouraged with temporal compensation
in the form of tax exonerations. In order to make it easier
to frame denunciations, the Dominicans produced a manuscript detailing the twenty signs one could use to identify a
Jew—by appearance, according to customary behavior, and
by his manner of expressing himself.

Marranos were hauled away from homes in town as
well as from the Jewish quarter. The unfortunate victims
were locked up in cellars of the cloisters that had been converted to the prisons of the Inquisition. There they were
held and tortured by Dominicans and by members of the

Santa Hermandad (Holy Brotherhood), a rabble consisting of robbers, soldiers, and amnestied prisoners. Many prisons were so overcrowded that the prisoners had to stand up even while sleeping.

The Marranos were brought before so-called judges of the faith, with no idea of the charges against them and no way of defending themselves. Inquisitors wanted prompt confessions, and they did not care how they got them—whether with or without torture. Most of the time the summary trials ended with death sentences. Those could be commuted to life in prison if the culprits reconciled themselves with the mandates of the church. If it was later discovered that their conversions had not been in good faith, the hypocrites were promptly burned at the stake. Even individuals who had been dead for thirty years could be condemned as heretics. In such cases the remains were dug up and burned at the same time that their heirs' possessions were confiscated.

The Inquisition considered it of paramount importance to confiscate the property of its victims. This easily obtained revenue was divided between church and crown, but the determination of the respective shares was often a source of friction and dispute. The greed of the Spanish royal couple became notorious throughout Europe, and it was said openly that they had instituted the tribunals of the faithful only to enrich themselves with the wealth of the condemned. Such ridiculous assertions did not bother the royal pair in Madrid, however, as they dreamed of unifying Spain and instituting a new order in Europe under their rule. They knew all too well that undertaking the building of a new empire is possible only with a well-filled treasury.

"There's nothing new under the sun," my great-uncle used to say. "Totalitarian systems copy and borrow ideas from one another. Hitler and Stalin can be blamed for a great deal, but certainly not for the originality of their thinking. They were not the first to invent informers, racial purity laws, torture, phony courts, forced confessions, or genocide. Like bastard grandchildren of Ferdinand and Isabella, those tyrants adopted the approach of the Catholic royals and applied modern scientific methods to make it more efficient."

IT WAS A SPRING DAY in 1420 when an anxious María de Torquemada told her father confessor that her pregnancy indeed was an easy one and she was suffering no discomfort. She confided to him that from time to time, however, she could hear the distinct sound of dogs barking in her womb. Bishop Pedro de la Cueva reassured María that the child she was to bear had from the very moment of conception been endowed with spiritual light. He took the sound of barking dogs as a sign that the child in her belly was *Domini cane,* a chosen one endowed by the Lord with the mission to serve as a watchdog to protect Christian flocks from Jewish wolves.

Little Tomás was carefully cared for, for he was the nephew of the highly respected Cardinal Juan de Torquemada. He was separated from other boys when he turned six, and the Dominican monks took him in charge, but not until he became eighteen did he don the garb of the black brothers.

"He had a gift for rhetoric," my great-uncle told us, "and even as a young man he would preach to the monks who eagerly clustered around that young man as if they themselves were the apprentices."

"*His eyes gleamed like stars and an aura radiated from him,*" wrote one of the priests responsible for his theological instruction. "*The enemies of the true faith are alarmed by him and their sleep is uneasy.*"

María de Torquemada was very proud of her son's violent dedication to the faith. He never ate meat, he fasted two days a week, in every matter of consequence he invoked Saint Dominic and expressed himself in the same manner as that saint, and at the age of thirty-two he was appointed prior of the Santa Cruz cloister in Segovia as well as father confessor to Ferdinand and Isabella. This gave him great influence over the royal pair. But his adoring mother feared that one day Tomás might discover that his own grandmother was a *conversa*, a baptized Jewess, which meant that he would not be able to flaunt an exemplary certificate of *limpieza de sangre*, one reaching back to the seventh generation to prove that the blood flowing in his veins was pure.

But Tomás de Torquemada, who insisted that everyone's family tree be inspected, never made any effort to investigate his own. It may be that he was too intent on hunting down Jews and their offspring as if they were carriers of the plague and leprosy. He was intent upon persecuting them mercilessly, arresting them, ransacking their homes, torturing and burning them, and then demolishing their reputations and obliterating all memory of them.

Legends Are Woven by the Common Folk

AFTER THAT NIGHTMARISH NIGHT in Seville, Salman was seized by the feeling that life had given him an unexpected gift: the possibility of freedom, the gift of the ability to leave everything behind. Everyone, including all three of his sons, assumed that he was one of the four thousand innocents murdered, mutilated, and burned to unrecognizable remains on June 6, 1391.

Salman was not used to freedom. His adult life had been dedicated to duty and work. His first responsibility had been to create a family; then he had trudged to attend the burials of his parents and four brothers. Later he was so terrified of losing his own family that terror made him completely forget the great secret of the Espinosa family entrusted to his safekeeping. But once his wife, two daughters, and five of his grandchildren were dead, he experienced a sudden almost overwhelming desire to break free. The thought that struck him like a physical blow as he wandered through the ruins of the *judería* was that having tasted of the elixir of immortality and looked death in the face, he should devote his life to helping those held as virtual prisoners in the narrow alleys of the Jewish quarter, helping them achieve their own freedom.

That was the beginning of it all.

He set out on winding roads that led him from south to north and back again from north to south, striding onward energetically without flinching before spring thunderstorms, the burning heat of summer, or winter snowstorms. He encountered the people of his faith from east to west and for a hundred years he tirelessly assisted them. He quieted their droning litany of complaints by providing answers to difficult questions, not only those about spiritual matters but also those about the body. He gave them wise counsel and resolved practical everyday problems—always for free, without asking for a single peso or a scrap of bread. He dressed simply and never raised his voice. Everywhere he went, he fearlessly attacked the Inquisition's shameless manipulations and its brutal advance. He delivered no sermons or words of praise, nor did he manifest the slightest ability to work miracles. He turned up wherever he was most needed to help people bear the various disasters that afflicted their lives—suffering, persecution, illness, and death. He was known by many names, though not by his own. In most places he was called "the wandering Jew," and no matter how hard the men of the church tried, they could not stamp out the legends that the common folk wove about him.

A Murder Plot

SALMAN HAD FOLLOWED Tomás de Torquemada in secret through almost all of the kingdoms of Spain. He watched in Zaragoza as Torquemada pressed the rulers of the city to wall up the Jews and to sentence a married Catholic woman to a hundred lashes before expelling her from the city for visiting a Jewish home. In Valladolid he heard Torquemada issue orders to burn effigies of Jews who had fled abroad to escape the Inquisition. From a distance he observed the Grand Inquisitor in his quest to carry out divine justice as Torquemada's forces searched the cemetery of Ávila for the bones of a rabbi who had been dead for fifty years. He listened in Toledo when despite the pope's injunction against fanning the all-consuming fire of hate against those of another faith, Torquemada responded to his appointment as Grand Inquisitor for the Holy See in Castile and Aragon by declaring his intention to rid Spain of the Jews. He authorized any and all means to that end.

Salman had come to know Torquemada well after those many years, although he had never stood face-to-face with him for a close-up view of his bloodthirsty smile. He knew the Grand Inquisitor's thought process and his motivations. He knew that the most hated man on the Iberian Peninsula was deathly afraid, obsessed with the thought that someone would murder him. He noticed that the demon priest never traveled alone; on his journeys he was surrounded by a bodyguard of fifty mounted inquisitors and two hundred foot soldiers. Salman knew that the foul smell from Torquemada's mouth was the breath of death itself and every ounce of the fat prelate's flabby body corresponded to ten human beings he had sentenced to the flames.

SALMAN HAD NO INTENTION of doing away with Torquemada. Leading Marranos—baptized Jews who secretly clung to their ancient traditions—had gathered in the house in Seville of the wealthy Don Jehuda de Veras. After a long discussion of the Book of Judith, the biblical account of how a Jewish woman killed the Assyrian ruler Holofernes in order to save her people, they eventually reached a consensus that the assassination of a tyrant was justified in extraordinary circumstances. They decided that the Grand Inquisitor had to die so that Spain's Jews might live.

Salman was invited to the meeting and discovered to his horror that the conspirators were about to designate Ezra de Espinosa to carry out the deed. This deeply disturbed him. He did not want his great-great-grandson to risk his young life in such a despicable attempt to kill another human being, even if the target was the odious Torquemada.

None of the conspirators in de Vera's house—Ezra least of all—knew Salman's true identity. But they all knew he was the wandering Jew, so they listened respectfully when he opened his mouth to speak. He told them he had followed the Grand Inquisitor over the course of many years and had seen that the man was driven by an inexplicable obsession with killing, an evil so great that it defied human understanding. He had also determined that Torquemada was protected by evil demons and would die only if one

THE ELIXIR OF IMMORTALITY

could stab him in the heart with a silver blade tempered in the blood of a dark gray peregrine falcon. Whoever delivered the killing blow would have to wear suspended from his neck an amulet fashioned from the beak of the same dark gray peregrine falcon. His listeners regarded Salman with increasing dismay. No one questioned his pronouncement. He told them that no extensive search was necessary to identify the right person. With that, he rose, took a knife from his pocket, and showed them the amulet that hung from a cord about his neck. Walking slowly around the great table where the others were seated, he declared that he—he alone—would be able to take Torquemada's life.

IT WAS A CHILLY TUESDAY MORNING. The air was clear and pure. The Grand Inquisitor was making the final preparations for an important sermon he would be delivering at Santa María Cathedral to the assembly of inquisitors, announcing his decision to institute tribunals in every inhabited place in the kingdom.

The conspirators agreed that the best time to attack Torquemada was as he climbed the broad steps that led to the cathedral.

Salman felt nervous. He lay curled up under a blanket on a wagon positioned next to the cathedral steps. He had never killed a man. Doing harm to a fellow human being was contrary to his nature. For that reason he tried to imagine Torquemada not as a man of flesh and blood who merited human sympathy but instead as the instrument of death. Salman was the sworn enemy of death. He had always hated death. He clenched his jaws and felt that hatred pounding within him. This was a feeling so strong that it was as if a live creature was stirring beneath his ribs. That hatred, that searing avalanche of human fury, distracted him. He failed to notice that the hundreds of soldiers stationed around the plaza before the cathedral had seized his confederates and were approaching the wagon where he was hidden.

Torture

ON THE DAY BEFORE Torquemada's great announcement, Clara de Monteforte was arrested at the market of the Plaza de España. The vigilantes of the Inquisition, whose duties included the secret monitoring of purchases in the market, had been watching her for a long time because they suspected her of being a Marrana who regularly prepared Jewish food at home. That suspicion was kindled by a report from José Almeida, the proprietor of a vegetable stall, who noticed that unlike other women of that neighborhood, Clara would regularly fill her wicker basket with great quantities of onions and garlic. The dates of these purchases corresponded remarkably closely with those of Jewish holidays.

Clara wasn't aware of anything unusual that early morning because she was intent on buying vegetables and meat for the upcoming Easter holiday. She did not notice the three men around her as she picked up a large bunch of garlic. They grabbed her. She screamed and tried to break away, overturning José Almeida's vegetable stand. No one responded to her wild protests. She bit the arm of one of the muscular assailants, who swore and brutally struck her head, knocking her unconscious. The men carried her away to the vaulted cellar of Santo Isidro cloister. Then they and four soldiers went to Clara's house to arrest her husband, the carter Pedro de Monteforte, and their three sons, who did not resist. The family was shoved brusquely into a cramped chamber with nearly fifty other prisoners. The narrow dark dungeon resounded with cries and lamenting. In a hurricane of protest, people screamed in each other's faces, demanding to be released. Men proclaimed their innocence, women recited Catholic prayers, and children wept.

That same afternoon several soldiers took Clara and Pedro de Monteforte to the torture chamber. Clara turned out to be a hard nut to crack. She resisted fiercely, screamed, spat, and kicked wildly. The torturer struck her in the head with an iron bar several times. She was bleeding heavily from the ears and could scarcely hear. The inquisitor screamed into her ear to make her understand. She didn't say a word because she was completely bewildered; she stood there, stunned and weeping. She wanted to spit in the torturer's face, but her mouth was too dry.

Her husband, Pedro, one of the conspirators, was no match for her. He lacked her robust physique. He panicked. Trembling and drenched in cold sweat, he begged for mercy, desperately pleading for his life. The Inquisition's experienced torturer made short work of Pedro, chopping off his left foot and extracting a full confession. The carter wept, cried like a baby, wept some more, and spilled every detail of the plot to murder Torquemada.

THE GRAND INQUISITOR exulted. He felt fortunate he had exposed the wickedness of the Marranos and now had grounds to confiscate the wealth of several of the richest men of Seville; and perhaps most fortunate, he was alive and unscathed because the planned attempt on his life had been detected in time.

The conspirators were arrested and subjected to horrific punishment. Their wives and children were tortured, mutilated, and then burned alive before them. Then they received the same treatment.

TORQUEMADA CHOSE to preside personally at Salman's hearing. He spoke gently—almost as if he felt a certain human sympathy for the accused—and promised that Salman would not be tortured if he divulged the whole truth, everything that he knew that could assist the Holy Office in its mission. First of all, his own identity: where he had come from, and why he was called the wandering Jew. In addition, who had conspired to have the Grand Inquisitor murdered, and why was he chosen to carry out the evil deed? Torquemada admonished him to leave out no detail if he wished his life to be spared.

Salman was gripped by a feeling of unreality. For a moment he thought his senses might be betraying him. Perhaps this was not really happening.

He sought to call to mind the hundreds—no, thousands—of Jews he had met, all those who had fallen to their knees in wild sorrow and pleaded for help after losing their families and possessions. *Yes,* he thought, *I knew them all—artisans and peddlers, rabbis and physicians, courageous women and terrified children. All the members of the great legion of suffering.*

He collected himself, answered Torquemada civilly, and promised to be entirely truthful. He stated that his name was Salman de Espinosa, born one hundred and sixty years earlier in Granada. He was called the wandering Jew because he never traveled on horseback but always on foot. The murder of the Grand Inquisitor had been planned by every Jew throughout Spain and the task was given to him because he was immortal.

Torquemada flew into a rage. He ordered the torturer to strip Salman, put him on the rack, and bind his arms and legs. He told Salman that he could still show mercy if Salman confessed the strict truth.

Salman replied that his crime was not that of attempting to murder the Grand Inquisitor. His voice was firm. The crime for which he was about to be condemned was that of embracing his Jewish identity and observing Jewish tradition.

Torquemada bellowed, "My holy mission is to send all you Jews to the stake and burn away every trace of your whole hateful tribe!"

"Don't be too presumptuous," Salman replied, as if offering friendly advice. "Men and women like me will always exist. All of you, however, will eventually disappear. Time is short; soon the worms will feast themselves upon your flesh and flames will consume your remains."

Torquemada told the executioners to get to work immediately. He turned and left the chamber. Four men tortured Salman without interruption for eight days but they never broke his spirit. He remained conscious throughout it all and praised his tormentors for their able handiwork. On the ninth day they threw his slit-open body into the flames. Inquisition records state that he was sentenced to death as a heretic and practitioner of black magic. He had used consecrated communion wafers at the Jewish Passover meal to summon the dark powers of the cosmos.

Truth Is Stranger Than Fiction

A MONTH LATER, Salman celebrated Shabbat with friends in Dubrovnik. Then he trailed his long dark gown along the roads that followed the Adriatic coast, wandering through compact little white towns sunk in their everyday somnolence and distributing to faithful Jews *The Seventh Book of Moses,* a very odd book that he had written.

My great-uncle told us all of this. And he added, "Truth is stranger than fiction. If you know what actually happened, you don't need to invent stories. Besides, it's easier to catch a liar than a lame dog."

In the autumn of 1995 the Spanish television channel RTVE broadcast a miniseries about the life of Tomás de Torquemada. The renowned reporter Juan Cruz Ruiz had spent several months tracing the Grand Inquisitor's travels across fifteenth-century Spain. I was vacationing in Madrid and happened to see the final episode in my hotel room late one night. No expense had been spared, and the program offered both in-depth analysis and dramatic reenactments. One could almost catch the whiff of human flesh roasting in the bonfires.

From this program I learned that Torquemada died a natural death in September 1498. He was buried with great pomp in Ávila on the grounds of the Santo Tomás cloister where he had spent the last years of his life. The cloister had been constructed in 1494. It served both as the residence of the Grand Inquisitor and as the seat of the tribunal of the Inquisition. The Jewish cemetery previously at that site had been dug up at the command of the king and queen. Gravestones were used as building material for the towering cloister.

Torquemada enjoyed 338 years of peaceful rest in the leafy gardens of the cloister of Santo Tomás. The Spanish Inquisition was formally abolished in 1834. Two years later a gang of unknown individuals dug up the grave of the Grand Inquisitor, broke open his coffin, removed his remains, and burned them.

SIX

The Philosopher

A Call on Meester

ON THAT WARM AUGUST MORNING in 1640 a contrite Uriel Spinoza trudged toward the house at 4 Jodenbreestraat in Amsterdam. He did not know that he had only a few hours left to live.

MEESTER WAS A MAN of generous spirit. Each time Uriel Spinoza called on him in his well-furnished residence, Meester bustled forth, proclaiming in a hearty voice that he'd been hoping the Jewish philosopher would come back for a visit. He sent his servants to fetch spiced brandy and poured out generous portions for both of them. Meester loved the pleasant feeling that spread through his body with a goodly dose of alcohol, but Uriel Spinoza's head became uncomfortably hot when he drank.

The painter and the philosopher got along splendidly. Their personalities were completely different, but both felt that opposites complement each other, while folk with too many similarities tend to bristle with envy, rivalries, and animosity. Their very differences gave them the impression of standing close together and at the same time enjoying their marked differences.

The friends spent many an evening together before the hearth on the ground floor of the five-story house. They always discussed issues of great significance. Their discussions were usually conducted with calm and equanimity, and the painter considered the philosopher's powers of logic beyond compare.

Meester wanted to become a bit more enlightened, not better educated. Intellectual subtleties and dazzling flights of rhetoric were of little interest to him. He preferred a discussion of basic principles, since above all he wanted to understand how to employ his talents, devoting them with insight, reverence, and technical bravado to creating works that could provide a glimpse of heaven both to himself and to others.

Uriel Spinoza tended to concern himself principally with questions of the vanity of human reason and the immortality of the spirit, much like other great thinkers of the past. He was a learned rabbi, but he did not rely solely upon the Talmud and the Cabala for insights into the great questions of our existence. He studied Aristotle and Pliny, Seneca and Cicero; he adapted their concepts and teachings, combining them with his own. He was careful to borrow only those ideas that helped advance his own thinking. He held that a righteous man never sought to conceal the shortcomings of his own thoughts by citing the authority of others, and he stressed as vital the view that every individual should be personally responsible for his own views.

No one in the city listened with graver attention than Meester to the logic underpinning Uriel Spinoza's bold assertions about the nature of the human spirit and his arguments that the world is not an impenetrable mystery accessible only to God but is in fact a reality that man can grasp.

My great-uncle said that Uriel was a peculiar creature with a character not particularly suited to establishing close friendships. Even those of his own flesh and blood—his half brother, Michael, and Michael's family—were of the opinion that other than his erudition, Uriel had little to offer. They turned their backs on him. The Jews of Amsterdam could not find it in their hearts to forgive Uriel for spreading extremely dangerous ideas. He lived out his days as a pariah, shunned by all of them.

ONE NIGHT in a tavern discussion a textile merchant with regular contacts with Jewish colleagues suggested to Meester that perhaps he should spend less time with that fellow Uriel Spinoza. He warned that if their close acquaintanceship became generally known, it might lead to a drastic fall in the number of his commissions as well as misgivings among his patrons, especially those with good ties to prominent Jews who viewed the philosopher as a blasphemer. That friendly attempt to discourage him had no effect on Meester's relationship with Uriel. Meester would never drop his friend for propagating revolutionary ideas; the merchant's comments prompted him to listen to the philosopher's reflections with even greater interest.

That's why Uriel was hammering frantically at the door of 4 Jodenbreestraat on that hot August morning. He wanted to report the ghastly thing that had just happened, and he knew that only one man in Amsterdam would be willing to listen. Meester was his only friend.

MEESTER'S HOUSEMAID, Sjoukje, was a buxom young woman with delicate features who took her master into her bed to placate him whenever he noticed that she had been stealing from the household funds. She opened the door and told Uriel that Meester could not receive anyone. Her face was somber.

"Mijnheer Spinoza will have to come back another time."

Uriel saw immediately that Sjoukje had been weeping.

"It is absolutely vital for me to speak with Meester," he said, turning away from the serving girl in an effort to conceal his distress.

Sjoukje almost choked on her own words as she told him that early that morning a message had arrived from Leiden informing Meester that his mother had died. Her face twisted in misery. "And last night Heer Meester and his wife lost their newborn daughter. The little girl coughed up blood and stopped breathing. She's the second child to die in this house in two years."

Uriel stood there aghast, staring at her. Through his work in philosophy he had come to terms with death and had accepted it, but in that moment he could not comprehend why death would snatch away an innocent infant. He saw the baby girl's death as arbitrary and unjust; he felt as if someone had just carved out a piece of his own heart, for he knew how much the newborn meant to Meester. Sjoukje thought for a moment that the Jewish philosopher was going to burst into tears, but he did not. He staggered slowly away.

A Portrait at the Right Time

MY GREAT-UNCLE never revealed the man's real name to us. I have no idea why not, actually, but he surely must have had his reasons. He called him "Meester," and for a long time I assumed that was his name.

My twin brother, Sasha, and I often heard about Meester and the Spinoza family. That is why the story remains engraved deep in my memory.

MEESTER WAS IN URGENT NEED of money. His wife, Saskia, would soon be giving birth to the couple's first child, and no one was willing to extend any more credit to him.

The palatial residence in Jodenbreestraat had cost thirteen thousand gulden. He should never have purchased it, considering the high cost of the monthly mortgage payments. Even though he had devoted all his energies to finding patrons who might commission portraits from him, no new orders were forthcoming, principally because he now had the reputation of treating his clients with arrogance and condescension. He had started work on several paintings, but they stood incomplete in his workshop because he had no money for paints, and no one was interested in buying any of his finished works.

Hardest of all for Meester was the fact that his earlier patrons had turned their backs on him. Men whom he had considered his friends brusquely told him to look for help elsewhere. Most of the time his appeals were met with silence, indifference, and cold responses.

In the midst of this financial crisis, one of Meester's creditors demanded repayment of a debt that he had thought would not be due for another two months. That lender, a heartless devil who was an illegitimate son of the once-powerful Johan van Oldenbarnevelt, the politician beheaded for high treason, was known to enforce his demands with the help of a gang of toughs armed with pikes. Meester had entreated the man to grant him a week's delay, but the lender was threatening to break both of the painter's arms and demolish his furniture and household goods if the money was not paid within forty-eight hours.

THE NEXT DAY, unexpectedly, almost like an apparition, Michael Spinoza came to Meester's workshop with the idea of commemorating his fortieth birthday in October 1638 by commissioning a family portrait of himself, his wife, and their three sons.

Thank God. This can finally put an end to the terrible misery that has been tormenting me so long, Meester thought. Although overjoyed, he managed to keep his feelings under tight control and hidden from his prospective client. Prompted by instincts inherited from peasant forefathers with expressionless faces who had bought and sold livestock in the cattle markets of Zuid-Holland, Meester affected indifference. As a bargaining ploy, he explained in gloomy tones that he was extremely busy at the moment and the waiting list for his services was long; even if he were to make an exception, considering that the matter involved the highly respected president of the Jewish council, there would be one condition—one nonnegotiable condition—for him to agree to paint the family portrait. "Heer Spinoza must resist the temptation to specify anything about the composition of the painting and must accord the artist full freedom to conceive and execute the work. Only on that condition could I accept the commission."

The good-natured Michael Spinoza nodded and replied, "But of course, whatever the gentleman wishes. He certainly knows best."

Under the impression that Meester's work was in great demand, he demonstrated his gratitude to the great painter for accepting the commission by allowing Meester to set the price. He did not bother to haggle.

"Each full-length figure costs two hundred," Meester declared, mentally rubbing his hands together in anticipation, because he had never before received such a high fee.

With these calculations the price of the commission was set at one thousand gulden. The following day they met in Michael Spinoza's office to sign the contract before witnesses. Half the sum was paid in advance. Execution of the portrait was expected to require three months of work, since

Meester had no apprentices to paint in the background and the clothing.

THE HUGE QUANTITY of gulden now in the master's hands amounted to exactly five times as much as his most recent fee for a commission. Extremely relieved, he went straight to his favorite tavern. He promptly informed the owner that his luck had changed and he had come to pay off his debts. He seated himself comfortably on a chair that the relieved tavern keeper had quickly pulled out for him, and he called for a round of brandy for everyone in the house. Surely new commissions would come flooding in now. He was certain there was money here for the taking. After a couple of snifters of spiced brandy, he got it into his head that he would be getting plenty of commissions from wealthy Jewish merchants, and soon he would be able to pay off the debts encumbering his expensive house. He thanked his Creator for providing him with a client so greatly respected by the Jews, a man whom they were likely to emulate.

The following day Meester sent Michael Spinoza the gift of an etching from Leiden as a token of his esteem. It depicted the city's cathedral, surrounded by blooming linden trees, and the gleaming white private mansions along the Rapenburg Canal.

THE WORK BEGAN in early summer. Meester was suffering in the unusually hot weather, but he plunged into the task with great energy and creative force. His approach was meticulous; he made countless sketches. His workshop was excessively warm, and Meester discarded most of his clothing without bothering to ask permission of his client. His torso was bare, to Madame Spinoza's evident annoyance, as he continued his sketches. He was lost in his own world and paid no attention to her. The floor was littered with piles of sketches in red chalk.

Michael Spinoza's family spent long hours every day motionless and uncomplaining in the workshop where the peeling walls were hung with unsold paintings. Weeks went by and the heat never broke. It was especially unbearable next to the window where the artist had placed the family. To make things worse, the reek of Meester's sweat was almost unendurable as he stood behind the easel every morning, shirtless and unwashed, dirty and disheveled. But no one complained. Not even as he mixed the various paints and an acrid, unpleasant odor rose from them.

Meester laid out the base coat with a palette knife and broad brushes that he wiped on his trousers. He spread the colors thickly with sweeping movements, layer by layer.

No one said a word, all day long. Only Madame Spinoza's coughs broke the silence. Her lungs were weak, and the strong odors in the workshop made her gag and wheeze. This annoyed Meester a great deal, probably due in no small part to his instinctive dislike for her.

Even before they first met, Meester had an intuition that he would find it difficult to put up with Madame Spinoza. He remembered his friend Uriel saying that his sister-in-law had long nursed an implacable hatred for him and she had thrown herself into a rage, flinging horrible imprecations at him, when he tried to contact his half brother and young nephews.

Meester often made fun of her in the evenings as he sat there in his favorite tavern behind a couple of uncorked flasks of brandy. He sarcastically described her odd appearance, her fat hands, and her stark-white round cheeks.

In the House of the Dead

ONE DAY SJOUKJE FOUND Meester's favorite pet animal dead in the cellar. He had purchased the merry little chimpanzee for ten stiver one night on a binge while visiting a prostitute down near the harbor. This turned out to have been one of his more successful transactions, because the little creature—whom he dubbed Caravaggio, not without a certain touch of irony—often provoked him to hearty laughter. A few minutes in the company of his chimpanzee were always the perfect tonic for his gloomy moods.

Meester was depressed by his loss. Neither work nor brandy could lift his spirits from the melancholy that weighed upon him as he grieved for the little chimpanzee. He lost his powers of concentration and told Michael Spinoza that they would have to break off their work for a time.

THE DEATH OF CARAVAGGIO proved to be an omen that presaged even more painful events in Meester's life. A few days later he was buffeted by yet more grief: His tiny little daughter, Cornelia, just baptized and only a couple of weeks old, died suddenly after heavy intestinal bleeding.

The house at 4 Jodenbreestraat was plunged into tears. No one spoke above a whisper and meals were consumed in total silence. The doors were opened to no one. Meester had ordered a period of deep mourning. He felt drained. Terrible anxiety kept him awake day and night. He could see Caravaggio's features clearly before him, then it seemed that the darkness closed in around him and he was unable to recall the face of his daughter, Cornelia. During the nights— all those sleepless nights he spent trying to remember the details of his baby daughter's face—he was wrapped in black despair. He sat week after week in his studio, alone and silent in his inexpressible pain and heart-searing grief, sunk deep in overpowering, bitter thoughts. He felt dead inside and believed he had lost his ability to paint.

MICHAEL SPINOZA had heard that work in Meester's studio had stopped, which meant that the family portrait would not be ready for his birthday. He waited patiently until the middle of September and then decided to call on Meester in an effort to help him through his difficult hours.

Life had taught Michael Spinoza that sorrow was perpetual. Scarcely a year before this, he and his wife had lost a newborn child. He knew the only way to put Meester back on his feet again was to persuade him to return to his work.

A DISAGREEABLE ODOR permeated the workshop and all the paintings had been turned to face the wall. Meester sat there clad in a nightshirt with a worn dressing gown hanging about him, carelessly unknotted. Michael Spinoza scarcely recognized him. The painter seemed to have shriveled; he was thin and yellow in the face and had great circles under his eyes. It was obvious that he had not bathed for a long time. Michael Spinoza presented his condolences. He said he understood Meester's difficult predicament, because he himself had suffered a similar loss. He saw immediately that the painter's self-pity had turned into a crippling bitterness.

"Death has haunted my house," Michael Spinoza said. "Unfortunately, there is nothing to be done about it. Last year when we lost an infant I raged and wanted to run through the streets screaming out my grief and telling everyone how badly I had been treated by my Lord, even though I have always obeyed his law. Believe me, I understand how it feels to lose someone you love. But life goes on, and fortunately, time heals all wounds."

Meester seemed distracted. He sat there for a long time without a word. Then suddenly he began to speak. He muttered rapidly and most of what he said was incoherent. He asked questions and answered them himself. His words gushed through the studio like a stream of water. He reckoned sums, proclaimed his righteousness before the fates, mumbled, and complained. Everything he had been holding inside him, even his most secret thoughts, surged forth. He did not look to see if his visitor was listening. He did not even seem aware of the words spilling from him.

Michael Spinoza waved his hand before Meester's face from time to time, but nothing distracted the painter from his delirium. Finally Spinoza rose and went to the door.

"I have to go now," he managed to say as Meester took another breath. "I have an important meeting at the synagogue."

Meester forgot himself for a moment. A smile suddenly lit his face. He tried to hold it back, but it spread and took possession of his features.

"You have a divine gift," Michael Spinoza told him in his gentlest voice. "Using it in your time of deepest grief can alleviate your pains. With your unwavering discipline you have achieved the very highest summit of artistic expression. My advice to you is to go back to your easel immediately."

An Insult

LATER THAT AFTERNOON Meester applied a brush to his canvas. He had not succeeded in calling forth from his memory the features of that delicate creature who had been his daughter for only a couple of weeks. But he could see Caravaggio clearly. He decided to paint a portrait of the little animal that had amused him so. Since he had no blank canvas available, he painted the chimpanzee's head on the body of one of the Spinoza children.

SUCH AN INSULT would have enraged even the gentlest soul. Michael Spinoza felt betrayed when he discovered that Meester had placed the head of a monkey on Bento's body. His wife could scarcely hold back her tears; in a venomous voice she exclaimed that Meester had absolutely no understanding of true art. The children laughed and teased Bento, who got terribly angry.

Meester had been exhilarated when he went to Michael Spinoza's residence to display his creation. At their reaction, his humor changed abruptly, and he refused to submit to any correction from Madame Spinoza or to allow them to treat him like any idiot off the street. He told her in a voice quivering with rage that he particularly refused to be accused of failing to understand art. The moment had arrived, he declared, to say exactly what he had felt in his heart for so many years but for various reasons had never put into words. There was no one anywhere, no one in all the world, who was his equal in the art of painting.

"It is not our intention to offend the artist or to call his art into question," quickly intervened Michael Spinoza, who wanted to avoid making things worse. He feared that his wife was about to let fly with several fierce insults. "We have the highest respect for the artist's genius. For many years we have marveled at his works and his masterful talent. That was why I turned to the master. But portraying my son as a chimpanzee must be one of the most absurd ideas ever to have crossed his artistic mind."

"The client promised me full freedom of artistic expression!" answered Meester in his towering rage. He felt insulted, and his voice was full of sudden, blazing hatred. "If the clients do not care for the portrait, they can paint one for themselves. But they should not delude themselves with the idea that they could be capable of doing so."

He picked up his painting and departed without a word of farewell.

A FEW DAYS LATER Michael Spinoza addressed to Meester a letter describing his disappointment with the painting with a candor and dismay more suited to confiding in a friend. He stressed that he wanted at any cost to avoid further misunderstandings. At the same time, he wrote, he earnestly requested Meester to consider the possibility of replacing the chimpanzee head with that of Bento.

Meester was adamant. He had been humiliated by the audacious liberty taken by the Jewish couple in criticizing his art, and he deeply regretted that he had wasted so much time with the Spinoza family. In addition, he was convinced that it had been intelligent of him to paint Caravaggio into the canvas, for he had created a different and invaluable masterpiece, a work to be contemplated with the ethereal selfless gaze of an artist, not with the egotistical, unfeeling eyes of a merchant. For these reasons he stubbornly insisted that the chimpanzee's head would remain exactly where it was. He demanded immediate payment of the remaining five hundred gulden owed him by Michael Spinoza. He threatened to take legal action if he did not have the money in hand within a week.

Michael Spinoza declined to pay. After every possible effort to persuade Meester to change his arrogant stance, he went to court and had the contract declared null and void.

Even with this verdict, he did not have the heart to demand that the debt-ridden Meester return the down payment of five hundred gulden.

The painting was left bundled up in plain wrapping paper in the studio until Meester's death. It was titled *Caravaggio Accompanied by the Spinoza Family.*

MY GREAT-UNCLE never had the opportunity to view that painting where it was hanging in an Amsterdam museum, but he knew every detail of it.

He told us that Bernard Berenson, the American who was perhaps the most prominent art historian of the early twentieth century, felt tears fill his eyes the first time he saw the painting and exclaimed, "Miracles happen for those who believe in them!"

Later, in his book *Seeing and Knowing*—which I have never read and am simply quoting according to my great-uncle's account—Berenson wrote: "This was nothing more or less than the first modern painting in the history of art. Here was an epoch-changing work that with intentional explosive artistic force broke open the way for a new approach to European art."

The Boys and the Stone

URIEL SPINOZA wandered about the narrow streets, stumbling from time to time over the piles of garbage. A stifling anxiety dogged his heels. Oppressed by the heat, he fanned himself with the document that he had received earlier that morning from the Mahamad, the Jewish council.

He glanced sidelong at the unknown faces around him,

seeking a friendly look, searching for eyes that were not filled with fear or squinted in disdain. He was well known in the Jewish quarter. People there regarded him with suspicion. Some openly mocked him; some even spat upon him. Everyone knew who he was: a renegade, a blasphemer who according to vague rumors had once been a highly placed official of the Catholic Church in Oporto.

Uriel's thoughts were in a whirl. Who knows anything at all about any other human being? Who can perceive what is hidden in the depths of a pair of eyes or behind a face? Who knows what is hidden in the soul or what lies deeper still, even more concealed, hidden even from the person who carries it within him?

OUTSIDE THE ESNOGA, the principal synagogue, he passed five boys who were playing together. As he heard their shouts, it occurred to him that their lives were far different from his own reality. He seemed always to have been an adult. He could not recall his childhood. The images and memories had vanished.

The boys recognized him and they froze. His reputation was known to even the youngest inhabitants of the Jewish quarter. All the children knew who he was.

Uriel Spinoza was a Jew who had lived the life of a devout Catholic in Oporto. His subsequent conversion to Orthodox Judaism meant he had to flee to the Calvinist Netherlands where refuge was offered to religious minorities. Jews in Amsterdam regarded Uriel as an apostate for criticizing the rabbis and questioning the tenets of Jewish faith. He was a rootless Marrano with no home anywhere.

The stern Rabbi Orobio had explained to the boys in the Talmudic school that of all the Marranos, Uriel Spinoza was the first who allowed himself to be exploited by the

Catholics. Orobio asserted that Uriel was still a Catholic, his aberrant lifestyle was a scandal to all Jewish customs and traditions, and his avowed purpose in life was to undermine the authority of the rabbis. He was dangerous and a serious threat to the Jews of Amsterdam.

"No one should ever speak to that man," Orobio said in a threatening tone. "His is the voice of chaos, children. His evil teachings can ruin you for the rest of your lives."

The boys watched Uriel from a distance. He was tall, thin, and wiry, with a nose as crooked as a bird's beak and tiny dark eyes that peered out at the world as if they already knew everything. He had an odd gait and dragged his feet, not because he was elderly but because he was self-absorbed.

The boys trailed after him, jeering loudly. Uriel halted when he heard the children insulting him with words so horrid that he had never heard them before. He turned around. At that moment one of the boys threw a large rock that struck him on the temple. He felt the blood beginning to run down his left cheek. He gasped and then sighed, for he recognized his own nephew Bento as the one who had thrown the rock.

A Unanimous Decision

ONCE URIEL GOT HOME he sat by the table. The sparsely furnished room was shrouded in silence. He took out the document he had received from the Jewish council and read through it slowly several times.

The decision was unanimous. Uriel Spinoza was excommunicated from the Jewish community of Amsterdam because he espoused views that questioned fundamental teachings of the Jewish faith. Banishment was for life, effective immediately. The signature on the document was that of Michael Spinoza, his own half brother.

Uriel's hands began trembling uncontrollably. He had lived in isolation for years, deep in poverty with no one close to him, with no woman in his bed. But never before had he experienced such a feeling of isolation. He was frightened to find himself banished by the very people with whom he most wished to share his thoughts. All of his efforts had been motivated by the deep desire to offer his Jewish community a glimpse of truth. This obsession had given purpose to his existence and had driven him to devote himself to the time-consuming process of writing, in the effort to identify the principles that ruled human existence.

Uriel had never been in the habit of thinking of his childhood or his youth. Through much of his adult life he had pretended to be a Catholic. He had been forced to hide his Jewish origins, so he had completely erased his earlier life from his consciousness. As he now turned his thoughts back in time to Oporto, it cost him a great effort to dredge up any fragmentary memories.

Perhaps his own distorted past had caused him to fail to understand why Jews in exile found such comfort in reliving their memories of the Sephardim, the Jewish way of life in Spain. Many seemed to think that only there had life been worth living.

Suicide in Exile

MY GREAT-UNCLE described to us many times how the Spanish Inquisition spread fear, terror, and death everywhere in the Iberian Peninsula. He also told us that the

crueler the persecution of the Jews became, the more stead-
fastly they clung to the faith of their fathers.

He made no secret of the fact that many of them simply
broke down in exile in the Netherlands, even though people
there were free to live according to their own traditions.
Jewish refugees were tormented by the sights and memories
that floated through their minds and called to them in their
dreams. Some of them simply couldn't stand living with the
knowledge of the loss of the Sephardim.

"Suicide in exile was quite common," my great-uncle
commented. "It was hushed up and overlooked. No one ever
discussed it."

But what could we understand of suicide, the two of us
who were only twelve-year-old boys? We couldn't grasp the
concept at all, no matter how hard we tried.

MICHAEL SPINOZA had a neighbor, my great-uncle told us,
a God-fearing Jewish father of a family, whose name my great-
uncle had unfortunately forgotten. He was in his forties, stiff
and nervous, with twisted shoulders, the sort of man who had
endured life's harsh trials and sought consolation in the Holy
Scripture. The man spent a whole afternoon playing with his
five children, passed out candies among them, and told them
a bedtime story. His wife was away, assisting a young relative
who was about to give birth. When she returned the next
morning, she found that the throats of all her children had
been cut. Her husband, soaked in blood, had hanged himself
with his own prayer shawl. He left no farewell note.

Bialomba. The name of the strange tree came unbidden
into Uriel's mind.

An ancient Portuguese legend tells how the inedible
fruit of the bialomba tree become disconsolate and fall to
the ground, where they shrivel and transform themselves

into monarch butterflies with a bright yellow crescent moon on their wings. If the wind is blowing, one can carefully lift the butterflies and toss them into the air where they can live and fly away. Otherwise, one leaves them on the ground, and they starve to death. That's the end of it, and life goes along its merry way. But if one treats the butterflies without respect, tramples them, or destroys them some other way, bad luck is inevitable.

Uriel sought to call forth other scenes and events buried deep inside, but all he could remember of his youth was that act of pure vandalism out in the woods near his native city of Oporto. Heedless and feeling invulnerable, he had trampled to bits the fruit of the bialomba tree and crushed countless butterflies.

THE RABBIS said the order of the world was something incomprehensible to humankind, a mystery known only to God. Uriel had challenged those teachings and advocated a different interpretation. He believed that the world could be measured and weighed, and that it was possible to describe its mysteries. His disclosure of this conviction had caused the council to declare him an apostate.

Now he began to see that the world was incomprehensible and full of secrets, governed by invisible powers that humanity was completely incapable of understanding. If there is order in the cosmos and meaning to creation, they lie beyond human comprehension.

But if we understand nothing and our lives do not depend upon our own free choices but rather are predestined, what is the meaning of any individual life?

His whole life and consciousness, everything, was now directed toward that sole question: What is the meaning of any individual life?

In that instant an avalanche loosed itself inside Uriel. Everything collided within him—his faith and his philosophy, all of the values determining justice and injustice, everything he had developed in protest against both Jewish and Christian dogmas. His own precepts were suddenly meaningless. He discarded them.

God's ways are incomprehensible to mankind, he now understood. He went to his cramped little library. He caressed the spines of his books. They stood there, each with its message, so many words of wisdom that were now meaningless to him. His own scribblings seemed superficial and of no interest. He was sorry he had bothered to write them.

He seated himself at the table once again. Before him lay the document from the Jewish council, a loaded pistol, a couple of sheets of paper, a small pot of ink, and a steel nib. He dipped the pen in the ink, tapped away a couple of drops, and wrote, "What would my life have been if I hadn't trampled the bialomba fruit?"

Then he placed the mouth of the pistol barrel against the exact spot on his temple where Bento's rock had gashed him. He took a deep breath and with his index finger he pressed the trigger.

A Comet and Death

ON THE SAME NIGHT that Uriel Spinoza committed suicide, an unusually large comet appeared in the heavens. There were alarmed rumors that the comet's tail would brush the earth. A Catholic priest, most probably under the influence of alcohol, predicted that the Jews would disappear and that the sin-filled city of Amsterdam would be flattened. He had received that message from the archangel Gabriel. Another priest, this one in Eindhoven under the patronage of Prince Frederik Hendrik of Orange, glimpsed the plan of creation in his tea leaves and foresaw that the Antichrist would come riding astride the comet. People everywhere spoke with fear and trembling of the imminent destruction of the world.

MANY PEOPLE had gathered that evening in Michael Spinoza's house to observe the comet. There was a profound sense of unease in the air. The master of the house assured his guests that the end of the world was not nigh and there was no cause for panic. He explained that his relative the Cabalist Moishe de Espinosa, blessed be his memory, had observed the same comet in Granada in the year 1325 and calculated that it would return 315 years later, missing the earth by a wide margin.

His reassuring words did not convince everyone. Many were openly skeptical.

As night fell, a servant entered in a panic, crying that he'd seen the comet from an upstairs window. Everyone rushed to the second floor.

BENTO WAS PETRIFIED, certain that the comet would utterly demolish his family's house. He glared at his little brother Isak, who was playing on the floor. Giving in to a sudden impulse, for no reason at all he viciously kicked his little brother. He thought they were unobserved, but their father had come back to fetch his spectacles. Standing in the doorway behind Bento, he saw exactly what happened.

Michael Spinoza's face contorted. He lunged forward, grabbed the boy's arm, and hauled him into his study. He berated Bento and made him stand in the corner. One of the Jewish council members burst panic-striken into the room.

"A terrible thing has happened," he exclaimed, scarcely able to speak. "They've found your half brother, Uriel, dead in his house. There was blood everywhere and he has a huge gaping hole in his head."

Bento's face turned fiery red. His heart pounded furiously and he fled from the study in tears. He thought he had killed Uncle Uriel.

"I'm dreadfully sorry, Mijnheer Spinoza," the newcomer said, lowering his voice. "It was completely thoughtless of me to let your son hear of this. I have no idea what possessed me, but I thought you had to be informed at once. Especially because of the council's decision. Even so, I should have been more discreet. Bento is a sensitive little boy."

A Miracle Child

THE YEARS PASSED and the comet was long gone, but whenever Michael Spinoza remembered that evening, he sank into melancholy, brooding upon the fact that Bento was living in Rijnsburg.

The comet's long tail had lit up the heavens over Amsterdam. That fascinating but menacing apparition panicked the population. Some were afraid that Europe would be consumed and laid waste; others fell to their knees in prayer; still others felt exalted by the sight of God's gleaming glory. The comet passed close to the earth, left nothing behind, and went its peaceful way onward through the universe, just as Moishe de Espinosa had predicted 315 years earlier.

Michael Spinoza's strongest memory from that night was the strange, sudden, and inexplicable change in Bento's personality. The boy seemed utterly transformed. His father couldn't help but think that perhaps the comet was responsible. From one day to the next an unruly and usually mean-spirited boy became the sweetest and most considerate young man one could ever imagine.

BENTO NEEDED no more encouragement in his studies, for he became a model pupil and the pride of his school. Those who met him were astonished. At the age of eleven he could recite the Torah and the Gemara both forward and backward. He knew everything about Abraham, Isaac, and Jacob, almost as if he had been their close companion from time immemorial.

Stories of his keen intelligence spread even to the Jewish communities beyond Amsterdam. Everyone assumed he was destined to become a great rabbi.

One day something occurred that redirected his path and transformed his young life.

MICHAEL SPINOZA OWNED one of the largest private libraries of the city. After searching it for weeks, Bento finally located the manuscripts of Uriel Spinoza where they had been carefully hidden behind other books.

He read through those writings in secret, more reverent and attentive even than when he studied the Torah. Even though his uncle Uriel had written in a style more scrupulously logical and brilliant than any he had encountered, at first Bento could not understand any of it. But he didn't give up; he felt an urgent duty to read further. He was haunted by the belief that he had killed his uncle. Guilt lay heavy upon his soul, and nightmares had tormented him for years. Against the background of that terrible event, Bento counted it a sacred obligation to study the blasphemer's manuscripts in depth, so as to discover who he had been and what he had thought. It was no burden to study what his uncle had written.

Bento read through it all several times over, line by line, neglecting nothing. Concentrating fiercely, he pondered even the least important details, trying to make out the underlying message. He found it difficult to follow Uriel's thoughts, not because he was slow or lazy but because they followed a logic quite different from that shared by the familiar texts of Judaism. Despite that, Bento saw immediately the purity of his uncle's motives in undertaking his work. Bento's only frustration was one he would never share: the fact that Uriel had been so unforthcoming about his own life.

The essays contained assertions that almost took Bento's breath away.

On one page of *Concerning the Mortality of the Human Soul* stood the assertion that following a death, for three days the soul contemplates the pathetic corpse it previously inhabited, now a miserable cadaver beginning to rot, then abandons that body and dissolves into thin air.

In the essay "Propositions Opposing Tradition" Uriel questioned whether God really gave Moses and the Jewish people their law on the slopes of Mount Sinai.

Almost everything of substance in those manuscripts— the bold thoughts and the breathtaking audacity of the logic—directly conflicted with Jewish folk wisdom and everything Bento had learned at home and at the Ets Haim School of Talmudic Studies. Sometimes he recoiled from the texts in disgust; other times he became alarmed and found it scandalous that Uriel was pushing his logic beyond all reasonable limits so as to undermine the authority of Jewish teachings.

After months of intensive study Bento began to feel that he'd had enough. He had tired of the qualities that had initially impressed him the most—the purity and inimitable elegance of Uriel's language—mostly because he could find the blasphemer's opinions were almost without exception completely contrary to his own. But one day, after all his strenuous efforts to synthesize the tens of thousands of lines Uriel had written out in his isolation, the young man's attention fixed upon a single sentence. It took his breath away: *The most important thing is not having correct and truthful views but rather daring to think for oneself, to challenge ancient tenets of faith, and to stand up for one's convictions.*

For a moment Bento's head spun. He read that sentence over at least a hundred times. He repeated the words aloud: ". . . challenge ancient tenets of faith, and to stand up for one's convictions . . ."

In that instant he saw his calling, He would devote his life to finding his own way, to elaborating his own thoughts and communicating truths. Even if he was still too young to know what he wanted to write about.

The Torah with New Eyes

BENTO READ the Torah with new eyes, not knowing how far astray he was being led by Uriel's invisible hand. He read and made notes as if possessed. His eyes gleamed and his notes became more and more challenging and critical.

He realized that Uriel had precisely identified a vital shortcoming of the Holy Scripture: the books of Moses failed to provide any evidence to substantiate a number of central theses.

Bento tried a different approach. Perhaps no general truth existed at all. Perhaps the world existed only in thirty-six historical accounts. Everyone at the rabbinical seminar noticed the change in Bento and wondered what had happened. He was often distracted, increasingly introverted, and frequently lost in daydreams. People began to think he might be possessed by an evil spirit, a dybbuk. They whispered that the ghost of the dead blasphemer Uriel Spinoza must have taken up residence in young Bento.

When his teachers asked what was going on, he answered with counterquestions:

"Does God really have no body?"

"Is the soul immortal?"

"Does an infant who dies two days after birth have a soul?"

"Does divine Providence rule the world in the best possible way?"

The school's chief rabbi, the venerable Talmudic scholar Morteira, took the young man aside in a shadowed corner of the school yard, laid a hand on his shoulder, and said in a quiet voice, "Bento, what are you trying to do? We don't recognize you anymore. You're behaving in an extremely peculiar manner. This is creating consternation and confusion for everyone in this community. And your questions! They're extremely dangerous. No Jew can give himself over to wild musings like those in your head. Spiteful tongues are wagging. This could turn out very badly for you. If your comments should reach the wrong ears, we could all be in danger. Have I made myself sufficiently clear?"

But the questions kept presenting themselves, and Bento was not the sort to keep his mouth shut. Finally he assembled his notes and composed a powerful appeal for spiritual freedom. His text caused a huge outcry in Amsterdam's leading Jewish circles, and other tracts followed.

The Jewish Council Takes Action

THE JEWISH COUNCIL was determined to silence Bento's questioning of fundamental truth. They summoned him to a hearing in the hope that he would recant and denounce his own writings. To everyone's astonishment, however, he acknowledged that he was guilty of all charges. He even seemed to take pride in the fact. Every member of the Jewish council revered Michael Spinoza and none of them denied that Bento had a brilliant intellect, but they felt themselves duty-bound to see that justice was done.

"We are not condemning your son for what he has said and written, dear friend," the president of the council told his predecessor, Michael Spinoza. "He was extremely thoughtless, and we can attribute that to his youth. But what has been done cannot be undone. We are exiling him so as to keep him from repeating his mistakes and to prevent others from following his example. This is the same reasoning we followed in the case of your half brother, Uriel, as you will certainly recall."

I'M TRYING TO UNDERSTAND why the members of the Jewish council labeled Bento an apostate and drove him out of the community of the faithful.

It's easy for us today to think of those council members as foolish old men who made ridiculous decisions. But Bento's theses could certainly have affected people's

thinking, created confusion, and disrupted relations within
the Jewish community. The council feared most of all that
the mayor of Amsterdam might react to Bento's criticism of
religion. The Dutch were citizens of a modern state ruled
by energetic businessmen who embraced the liberal ideas of
the time, practiced religious tolerance, and accepted Jews—
but only so long as the Jews didn't go around questioning
everything, the way Bento did.

More than anything else, the old men of the council
found it impossible to ignore the young man's challenges
to the Torah. The faithful simply could not abide his denial
that the Jewish people were the Chosen People, bound by
Mosaic law. The general view on that particular subject was
that Bento had gone beyond all permissible limits.

Rabbi Isaac Aboab de Fonseca read out the text:

*In accordance with the judgment of the angels and the
pronouncements of the Holy Ones, we banish, curse,
exile, and excommunicate Bento Spinoza. With the
assent of Holy God and in accordance with the blessed
collection of the Torah's holy books and the 613 prohi-
bitions inscribed therein, we pronounce upon him the
curse Joshua made upon Jericho and Elisha placed upon
the wicked young men, the curse proclaimed in the law.*

*May he be cursed by day and cursed by night, cursed
as he lies in his bed and cursed as he rises, cursed when
he walks abroad and cursed when he comes back. May
the Lord never forgive him and may God's wrath be ap-
portioned to that man and come over him to cast upon
him the weight of all the curses written down in the
Book of the Law.*

*And the Lord will erase his name under the heavens
and the Lord will cast him forth from all the lineage of*

Israel to his destruction, with all the judgments of the
firmament, as it is written in the law. And may all ye
who are the servants of God forever remain unharmed!

Take into account these commandments: no one
shall have any oral or written communication with him,
no one shall offer him any service whatsoever, no one
shall live under the same roof with him, no one shall
approach him any closer than the span of five ells, and
no one shall read anything written or produced by him.

Freedom in Rijnsburg

IN SEPTEMBER 1656, after his excommunication by the
Jewish council of Amsterdam, Bento descended the stairs
of his family home with a spirit of anticipation, carrying
the suitcase he had packed in haste. In the hall his mother,
father, and two brothers awaited him. His father placed his
hands on the young man's shoulders and solemnly assured
him that they all wished him well. His mother believed that
he would be home again soon and the whole thing would be
over, like a bad dream.

His younger brother, Isak, who was chubby, nervous, and
greatly troubled, threw a tantrum. He smashed a vase that
stood on the windowsill and stamped his feet. He screamed
that none of this was fair. He didn't calm down even when his
mother admonished him. Only when his father pinched his
cheek and sharply reprimanded him did his emotion subside.

Bento's elder brother, Benjamin, who liked to speak in
the flowery language of a poet and wrote cycles of graceful
sonnets in praise of God, insisted that he would soon follow
Bento, take care of him, and stand by him in his journey

through life. He reminded Bento of the great thinker Maimonides, who said that exile should be regarded as a gift from Providence. The trials of banishment serve, even for those of robust constitution, as unparalled incitements to duty, courage, and daring, character traits uncommon among those who live in security, shielded from all danger.

Bento was embarrassed as his mother's hair brushed his cheeks and she kissed him farewell. His father wondered whether they would ever see each other again, but he said nothing. He patted his son's head and helped him into the wagon that was waiting. And then Bento left his home in the Jewish quarter for the first time in his life. He promised his parents he would soon return, but he never did.

THE JOURNEY to Rijnsburg was long and difficult. Bento tried to read for a few minutes but he gave up and grumbled to himself. The jolting of the wagon upset his stomach, and several times he was on the point of throwing up. Even so, he felt strangely happy, almost joyful.

Anyone else in his situation—forced to leave behind his family, Jewish life, and his native city of Amsterdam—would have felt uneasy about the future, since in that world a homeless man was regarded as an affront and an absurdity. But Bento felt strangely liberated. Now he was free from all ties, free from the time and place of his birth, and above all he was free to think for himself.

HE LOVED HIS LIFE in Rijnsburg, even though he lived in a cellar reeking of damp. He delivered academic lectures about God as the only necessary substance of existence. He set a rigorous course of study for himself, not only in Cartesian philosophy but in almost everything under the sun. He took daily measurements of barometric pressure and investigated water, earth, and the colors of the sky. His neighbors thought that he was out of his mind. He knew that as a freethinking spirit he would just have to get used to such attitudes.

Benjamin Makes His Entry

THE TRUTH IS that Bento didn't want his elder brother to follow him. He'd always felt oppressed by Benjamin. He ignored Benjamin's offer for several months. But Benjamin insisted, and eventually in a moment of weakness Bento gave in, hoping really that nothing would come of it.

Benjamin arrived to find his brother squatting on the floor, bowed over Descartes's *Principles of Philosophy*. Bento was thin, his cheeks were sunken, and he was bathed in perspiration from the summer heat. His brain was stuffed with pantheistic thoughts, but he was indifferent to the surrounding mess of unwashed mugs, plates, flatware, and ancient moldering leftovers. The air in the room was as musty as that of a Pharaoh's burial chamber. The layer of dust on the floor showed traces of the three or four generations of rats that had gnawed the binding of the Torah to pieces and constructed three nests in the bed.

Benjamin saw at a glance that his brother rarely had visitors, certainly none of the female variety. He was about to say something but managed to hold his tongue because he knew Bento would be terribly offended.

The brothers were alike in many ways, but when it came to order, they were complete opposites. That was one reason that Bento had always felt a certain resentment of his elder brother.

Benjamin was a pedantic sort, a man who needed a life of order and routine. He set to work immediately. Bento held forth on the complexities of Cartesian philosophy while Benjamin stopped up rat holes, fetched water, washed the bedclothes and hung them up to dry in the interior courtyard, scrubbed the floor, dried the walls, and arranged the books—not in alphabetical order or according to subject matter but according to size. Once he had finished his cleaning and tidying, he took a seat, heaved several deep sighs, listened to the clock in the bell tower strike eight times, and considered himself ready to begin a new life with Bento.

God and Wasted Lungs

DURING THE DAY the brothers were employed in a nearby workshop, polishing optical glass and lenses for binoculars. The work filled their lungs with powdered glass while putting into their pockets a modest but assured income. At night, well out of the hearing of others, they engaged in bold and thoroughly unconventional discussions about human freedom and whether one could live a just life in conditions dictated by the constraints of law.

They were young, decisive, and free, and as allies they expected to achieve great things. But first, Benjamin suggested, they should expand their own consciousness and develop their spirituality, for only those acquainted with their own souls are capable of reasoning properly. The next step would be to inquire into the secrets of human life. Both were interested in matters of the heart, but they deliberately avoided other noble parts of the body, for they wanted to avoid the temptations of ignominious bodily lusts.

ONE NIGHT everything became clear. A sudden insight into the most fundamental principles almost caused them to swoon. Bento tried with no success to capture their thoughts on paper. His hand shook uncontrollably with the excitement of it. Benjamin took up the pen, for he had always had an easy time expressing himself in writing.

"God cannot be seen, experienced, or defined," he noted. "God is present in everything but remains eternally silent and unapproachable. He has left traces in his creation for us to study and pursue."

The brothers were deeply grateful for the grace allotted unto them. Benjamin would sometimes burst into tears, not from sorrow but from a sense of inner joy. He felt that he had been granted the greatest happiness of any man on earth.

CONVERSAS, THE FIRST WORK by the brothers, was the thin pamphlet in which they developed their logic and graceful style. Only a handful of copies were issued, for the printer Pieter van Driest was afraid of the ecclesiastical authorities. The church was in the habit of dispatching spies without warning and these *visitatores librorum* would review newly published texts. Censorship was strict, but there was a certain latitude for unconventional views, provided they were expressed with due discretion and press editions were limited. Only a few months earlier the shops of two book printers had been attacked by arsonists, so one had to be constantly on one's guard. That was why the pamphlet bore the Latin subtitle *Caute*, an admonition to beware.

Conversas was based on the discussions between the brothers, but only one author's name appeared on the cover: Bento Spinoza.

———

BENJAMIN WAS a magnanimous individual and indifferent to superficial distinctions. He demanded little of life. His primary desire was to remain close to his brother so as to support and protect him. Benjamin was gentle and well-disposed toward others, and harsh only toward himself. He sat at his desk every night. His writing instrument, a steel nib, returned frequently to the inkwell. He devoted himself with tireless invention to transcribing the philosophical studies that were winning his brother increasing recognition. He demanded nothing for himself, least of all any credit as an author. He wanted Bento to be recognized and appreciated, perhaps someday even to exact an apology from the Mahamad in Amsterdam.

Bento's health was delicate. The weak lungs he'd inherited from his mother had filled with the powdered glass breathed in the air of the workshop while polishing lenses. He suffered from severe shortness of breath, and his body ached all over. At night he was often subject to chills and high fevers. He complained that his body seemed to be failing him and gradually falling apart. Benjamin was deeply concerned. Bento progressively lost weight and became more and more listless.

Benjamin bathed his brother, applied herbal remedies, and rubbed pungent salves into his chest. Neither these treatments nor bloodletting were of any use; Bento's afflictions would not go away. The brothers could not afford to pay a doctor. Benjamin had borrowed money wherever he could in order to finance the printing of the tracts published under Bento's name. He was deeply indebted and the lenders refused to extend any further credit.

What could they do?

Bento resigned himself. Benjamin pondered and suddenly found a solution.

Rescue from Distress

BENJAMIN DECIDED to take a wife, more to help his brother than anything else. He wrote a beautifully phrased letter proposing matrimony to a somewhat older unmarried Sephardic woman in Rijnsburg who had inherited a fortune.

Of course, a rich woman had no lack of suitors—but all who had appeared over the years had been scared away by her breathtaking ugliness or else were dismissed because they appeared more interested in the dowry than in the prospective bride. Every Friday evening as the other Jewish women strolled arm in arm with their husbands to the Sabbath service, Mafalda Fonseca hurried to the synagogue to ask God why he was denying her the possibility of learning about love.

Mafalda read through Benjamin's letter time and time again. She had never imagined that Judaeo-Spanish could have such a beautiful sound and so many splendid words. A completely unexpected flame rose within her and set her chubby cheeks ablaze. For the first time in her life Mafalda, so long infuriated by her loneliness, started seriously envisioning the many possibilities of love. She realized that it was not too late; she answered the letter the very same afternoon.

The wedding took place a month later.

BENJAMIN KNEW little about women. Everything that happened on his wedding night was novel to him—extremely easy and at the same time extremely difficult.

Mafalda immediately took the initiative and maintained it throughout the night. Benjamin was relieved that the homely woman he had married was so splendid under the covers. Even so, he was baffled by the notion that another person could be so passionately interested in his body. When his droopy and previously lifeless member rose to full erection, he involuntarily recalled the prayer of blessing he regularly recited: *Baruch Atah Hashem mechayei hameitim* (Blessed is God who awakens the dead).

He'd never imagined that a woman's enjoyment of physical pleasure could be so intense as to cause her to cry out almost as if in pain. Mafalda scared him a little; still, he felt extremely lucky.

Afterward they shared a glass of red wine.

MAFALDA WAS IMMENSELY HAPPY that the Lord had turned his loving eyes upon her. At last she had a Jewish man of her own, and their union would be as happy as that of her parents, whose warm and affectionate relationship she had cherished in her memory throughout all the years. And she had gotten herself a learned man, too, one who was also polite and considerate. A man who with his intimacy and caresses had aroused her passion. A man who generously cast his seed into the child-producing recesses of her sex. What it came down to was the fact that all the joys of matrimony now lay within her reach.

What more could she want from life?

One Brother Too Many

IT WASN'T LONG, however, before dark clouds gathered over the house on Singelstraat. For Benjamin did not arrive alone; he brought along his brother to their married life.

With every passing day Mafalda found Benjamin spending more time with Bento than with her. She felt lonely and aggrieved. The brothers were caught up in lively discussions but silence was her only companion. She sorely missed their playful night games. Evening after evening she lay naked under the sheets with her heart pounding, tensely waiting in the dark for Benjamin as he sat up until long past midnight assiduously writing out proper copies of Bento's notes. Finally she became convinced that Benjamin cared more for his brother than he did for her. Her face contorted and flushed dark red in fury, and she locked herself away in the bedroom to weep. She wept every day for three months. Jealousy poisoned her spirit.

MAFALDA COULD NOT STAND Bento for several reasons. It wasn't just that he was getting between her and the delights of matrimony. She found him arrogant and proud, and she couldn't understand anything about him. At times she told herself, straight out, that the man was mad. It seemed to her that his constant lecturing about these different axioms and premises and Euclidean geometry was simply an advanced form of insanity. Sometimes he would just sit there for hours staring at the wall, completely unapproachable, lost in some mystery that he had invented for himself. She was also very put out by his loud snoring and nightly coughing fits.

Mafalda wanted Bento out of her house. She strongly doubted that it was healthy to have him under the same roof. She could see him sucking the life force out of all those around him, especially out of Benjamin. Bento made her feel almost like a ghost.

———

ONLY WITH the greatest effort was Benjamin able to control himself and hide his despair. This was exactly what he had feared most of all.

Mafalda was not to be moved: Bento must leave the house. She was ready to do whatever it took to keep from spending one more day with her brother-in-law in the house in Singelstraat. She fell into a sudden rage. "He has to leave! He has to get out of here!" She screamed and threw an inkpot against the wall, then flung herself into bed, sobbing piteously.

Benjamin knew it was useless to argue with Mafalda, for the tension between them had reached the breaking point. He had no choice. He was obliged to give in, no matter how painful it was. He could see that the sooner he did so, the better. But it took him great effort and strength of character to announce it to his brother.

BENTO'S FACE FLUSHED with displeasure and he pretended to ignore Benjamin. He took out a magnifying glass, examined two flies that had lighted on the kitchen table, and discussed the value of their lives with philosophical detachment, fully in the spirit of Descartes. But it was no use. Two days later under duress he packed up what little he owned and moved to a room in the house of the painter Mesach Tydeman, an acquaintance who lived in the pastoral Voorburg outside The Hague.

Benjamin promised Bento he would provide him with the best possible support, not only paying for his room and board but also taking notes during philosophical speculations and converting them into finished texts.

Bento's departure left Benjamin laden with sorrow and a very guilty conscience—as well as a number of unexpected debts and a quantity of unpaid physicians' fees to pay.

Benjamin still thought it heartless to drive Bento out of the house. His brother was too sick to live alone and his wife should have been more sympathetic. He avoided Mafalda for a while, but after several days, when she reached out to him in a gesture of reconciliation, he gladly took her hand.

BENJAMIN SOON DISCOVERED the pleasures of life in Singelstraat without Bento. Now Mafalda was always in wonderful spirits. There was plenty of time for matrimonial pleasures and making babies. The couple had four sons, and their father educated them according to a pedagogic system of his own devising. All became learned men. The eldest, Aaron, became chief rabbi in Paris. Another was appointed to a professorship at the Sorbonne. As years went by, all of the sons and their families wound up in France.

The Cabalist

THE FIRST PERSON to note the brothers' work was Abrabanel ben Israel. This is how the *Encyclopaedia Judaica* describes him:

Abrabanel ben Israel (1619–1688), born Solomon des Pino-Zaah in Andalusia, also known as ABI, active in Holland, was a Sephardic scholar, Cabalist, diplomat, author, liberal rabbi, and founder of the first Jewish book-printing enterprise. He corresponded with many of the leading philosophers and crowned heads of Europe. In 1655 he visited Oliver Cromwell in London and addressed Parliament. With his brilliant rhetoric he was successful in convincing the members of the

*House of Lords to abrogate a law that since 1290 had
forbidden Jews to reside in England. He was also a close
friend of Rembrandt, who painted his portrait.*

I'll tell you immediately who was concealed behind the
name Abrabanel ben Israel: none other than Salman de Espinosa. Salman kept a close watch on his relatives in Amsterdam, just as in Spain and Portugal he had followed from
a distance the lives of his children and grandchildren, as
well as their children and grandchildren. He chose to appear under different names to keep his real identity a secret. He was well past three hundred years of age at that
time, but because he was immortal, he had the appearance
of a man in early middle age.

I GET THINGS a little confused again whenever I get distracted by one of my stray thoughts, those little tales that pop
up inside my head for a few seconds. Because I mentioned
death, the subject of the Cabala has suddenly come to mind.

I was nine years old when my great-uncle first told us
about Moishe, Salman's father, and I immediately decided
—more on impulse, of course, than informed consideration
—that someday I would be a Cabalist like him. I had the
notion that a Cabalist was some sort of higher noble being,
fearless and glowing with dignity, clad in magnificent armor
as he rode forth mounted on a proud white steed. I'd probably confused the word "Cabalist" with "cavalier."

Several years later my brother, Sasha, and I were given
a lengthy, detailed description of the professional work of a
Cabalist. He calculates the numerical values of words by
applying an extremely complex system, seeking mystical
correspondences between our lives and the eternal truths
embodied in the perpetual movements of the heavenly

spheres. Naturally, all that was much more than anything I could comprehend at the time, but just hearing it still strengthened my desire to become a Cabalist.

When I was thirteen I made a simple Cabalistic calculation following the procedure described by our great-uncle, basing it upon the letters of Sasha's name and the birthday we shared. I was probably angry at my brother for some reason I can't remember, because by invoking the mysteries of numerology I determined that Sasha would meet a tragic death shortly after his seventeenth birthday.

The following day with equal parts of doubt and self-assurance, though oblivious to both, I told my great-uncle the results of my calculation. He was the only one I could report them to. He was my favorite and my confidant, even though he wasn't really a member of our family. I felt a deeper connection with him than with any of my real blood relatives—Mother and Father, Grandmother and Grandfather, and Sasha. No matter how kind and generous they were, there was still an impenetrable barrier between us, one that excluded questions and confidences. But with my great-uncle it was different.

I've carried memories of those experiences with me throughout my life. Don't ask me why. Many times I've forgotten things I wanted to remember. At other times, images from the past come to me thick and fast, accompanied by random words, bright lights, or even smells. All of this occurs without any attempt on my part to evoke them; they're just suddenly there.

I saw a glint of surprise and fright in my great-uncle's eyes. His face crumpled and he took me into his arms. Completely taken aback, I looked up and saw that he had tears in his eyes. He smiled and said I must have made a mistake in my calculations.

And of course, he was right. Somewhere a tiny little error in arithmetic had slipped into my calculations. Because Sasha never reached his sixteenth birthday.

A New Chapter

ABRABANEL BEN ISRAEL'S enthusiastic letter of recommendation had a positive effect. Respected seats of learning in Europe began to take an interest not only in Bento but in both of the Spinoza brothers. The brothers received attractive offers of professorships. Bento turned down an invitation from Heidelberg. Benjamin couldn't understand why.

Bento told his brother he was unwilling to sacrifice his freedom to express his views. The role of a wide-ranging thinker suited him best. He was happy with his life exactly as it was. He refused to become anyone's lackey. He was free to live as he chose and set his own pace. No one could oblige him to hire himself out or peddle his thoughts to the rich and powerful. He would never in his life agree to such a thing.

"A brotherhood of wandering scholars has crisscrossed Europe for hundreds of years," Bento declared. "They have differed from one another, but each has been a restless spirit, seeking and moving on. The wide-ranging thinker is capricious, a comet who goes where he likes, lives a solitary life, and chooses his own path. That's exactly the life for me."

Benjamin was unmoved. "Good intentions can result in hasty decisions and rash actions," he answered. "I think it would do you good to be attached to some place. The simple acceptance of a public post doesn't mean you have to choose between the norms of others and your own principles—"

"My dear brother!" Bento cut him short. "Plato says that if a man devotes himself to worldly affairs and still comes away with clean hands, it's a miracle. You know me and you know that whenever tempting offers lure me to ambition, I spurn them and resolutely plod off in the opposite direction."

"Unlike you," Benjamin said, "I've never been able to remain idle for more than a few hours at a time. My life is centered on my family and the pleasure of collecting and systematizing knowledge, searching through the labyrinth of all the different views in this apparently confusing and insubstantial universe. When all is said and done, your worries about losing your freedom of thought don't make sense to me. I believe that man's inherent freedom is entirely compatible with accepting employment as a teacher."

BENJAMIN HAD THE IMPRESSION that one chapter in his life was coming to an end and another was beginning. Mafalda enthusiastically encouraged him to accept an academic appointment, enjoy the acclaim, and profit from the fruits of his labors.

And thus it was that he moved with his family to Freiburg, the city of one of Europe's leading universities, an institution with a hierarchy like no other, that employed the most renowned professors of the German-speaking world. It had six faculties, eighty professors, two thousand students, a library of four hundred thousand books, an observatory, and a botanical garden with exotic plants.

ONE WEEK followed another as the autumn ebbed away. December came and snow lay deep on the ground. Benjamin began to see that for the first time in his life he had managed to free himself from his brother. He told Mafalda he was almost ashamed at the sense of liberation arising from the physical distance between him and his brother and his enthusiastic involvement in his teaching. He felt almost giddy. She told him he had changed. When he asked her what she meant, she simply gave him a warm, approving look and went on her way. After that evening's playful encounter in bed, which was, by the way, fantastic and in fact better than ever, she explained that his face now was more serene and relaxed. He smiled with a bemused expression but knew in his heart that she was right. They nestled together as usual and fell asleep.

Practical Philosophy

ANNIE CAMPSIE-SMITH, Benjamin's British biographer, describes how in Freiburg he occupied himself with writing a practical guide to the problems of moral philosophy. Many saw it as pathbreaking. Other philosophers of his day were accustomed to writing in a prose style far removed from the lives of their readers. In contrast, Benjamin used plain language and offered concrete examples. His approach was effective and yielded results.

The Berlin book publisher Adalbert Althardt read excerpts from the work and was enthusiastic. He promised to pay an honorarium of fifteen florins per page. A publishing date was negotiated. Expectations rose, but the work was never completed. Today it is regarded as lost.

BENJAMIN WOULD STAND behind his lectern, eyes half closed, and speak of formulating the principles of philosophy with an approach similar to that of geometry, deducing them from abstract definitions. He spoke in a low voice but he could be heard clearly throughout the lecture hall. He set out his ideas with an infectious enthusiasm.

He often spoke of God. He emphasized that God has no cause or origin. He posited that God is immanent, not transcendent. The God he was describing had little in common with the gods of Christianity or Judaism. His God had no human qualities and could not be imagined as a father or creator.

Benjamin stressed that man can never love something that he understands completely. He held that love is based on the stimulating sensation that a thing is beyond one's comprehension.

He also spoke of shared existence, courage and health, money and charity, physical activity and pleasure. He insisted that when a human being enjoys life, he approaches perfection and divine nature.

"A cheerful disposition can never be excessive; it is always a good thing," he admonished his audience. "And melancholy is always bad."

He boldly asserted that fear was worse than anything else, especially when it arose from ignorance and superstition, the sort of fear used by so many of the powerful to enforce moral codes. He believed that morality must be based upon justice, which is commensurate with a greater value: the good. It was his adamant view that without an understanding of the good, rulers cannot fulfill their responsibilities.

Benjamin made no secret of his view that instruction in philosophy was more than systematic training in ratiocination. It was also—and just as much—a kind of shaping of the character, a process of molding personality. Study was only a means of achieving a greater insight into fundamental moral values that are unchanging and universal.

Students were so enthused by Benjamin's incisive exposition that most of them broke into applause at the end of his lectures and left the room beaming with good humor.

THE DEAN of the university lived near Benjamin's residence, and they spent many a late evening engrossed in stimulating conversations. The dean was awed by Benjamin's intellect and often praised his ability to communicate his original thinking to the students. But he offered a friendly warning, because he knew that Benjamin's ideas could shock people. Before this no one in Freiburg had articulated such daring propositions. He admonished the philosopher to maintain a certain reserve, for if he pushed his speculations about temporal power any further along these lines, they would drift away into the make-believe world of utopia. And if his manuscripts should fall into the hands of the church, there would probably be hell to pay.

Societas Jesu

IT WASN'T LONG before the Catholic authorities became concerned. German bishops who were members of the secret order Societas Jesu began to hear worrying reports about Benjamin's lectures. Spies sent out to collect evidence came back with a great deal of explosive material. The informers testified under oath that Benjamin had argued strongly that an erroneous understanding of God was the root of the lack of spiritual freedom and that Catholic interpretation of biblical texts sanctioned intolerance and oppression.

The spies' accounts prompted great indignation among the bishops. They refused to countenance a Jew's berating of Christ's church. Their strong preference would have been to keep the trial short and promptly light a bonfire beneath this heretic who denied the teachings of Jesus. It was unfortunate that such a proceeding was not feasible in Freiburg. But the bishops were crafty conspirators.

Balthasar von Uhrs, grand master of the lodge and renowned as a zealous servant of God, took upon himself the task of leading the attack. He promised to apply several tried-and-true tactics. The bishops felt reassured, and they rubbed their hands, certain of victory. They knew that the grand master was well acquainted with the church's arsenal of weapons against its foes. With murderous aspect von Uhrs wrote out a bill of charges in which he accused Benjamin of atheism and claimed that his philosophy was nothing but occultism. The grand master exhorted the prince elector of the city to summon the Jewish heretic to trial for propagating false doctrine.

KONRAD VON HOHENWEILER was no stranger to Benjamin's world of ideas. He even shared a number of the philosopher's views concerning religion and power. He had inherited the title of prince elector from his father and therefore had no choice in his own life and duties, but he took little pleasure in his secular power. He ruled Freiburg reluctantly and never put his whole heart into it.

The prince elector's annoyance grew as he read through the letter from the grand master. He had long been aware that the bishops' exalted words about love and fine talk about justice were frequently a cover for duplicity, threats, and blackmail. He waved away von Uhrs's most serious charges as weak and unsubstantiated. He felt almost insulted by the grand master's attempt to stigmatize the philosopher with transparent insinuations and obviously false assertions that anyone could see through.

The prince elector had found it necessary to deal with von Uhrs in various other connections. He considered the grand master far less intellectually qualified than the man's predecessor. Nor was he impressed by the man's character; he perceived him as a haughty, fanatical, and despotic individual, far less unblemished than the bishop and his supporters painted him. He concluded that instead of damning Benjamin as a dangerous heretic, the letter of accusation revealed the true face of its author. The prince's own private conclusion was that von Uhrs had devoted considerably more attention to his mistress than he had to the contents of the philosopher's works.

In order to avoid disturbing the delicate balance of powers in Freiburg, however, the prince elector was obliged to accede to certain of the church's demands, even though they were often unreasonable. As for this attack on Benjamin Spinoza, he decided not to give in. He wrote in reply to von Uhrs that he found no cause to institute legal action against the philosopher, but he would require him to reply to the charges.

BENJAMIN WAS NOT particularly disturbed by von Uhrs's letter. The fact that he had fallen into disfavor with the Catholic bishops bothered him hardly at all. His friend the dean worried that Benjamin would end his days punished and in disgrace, and he counseled Benjamin to retract a number of his harshest statements and offer an apology. Benjamin was open to any advice offered in a spirit of respect and consideration. But in this particular matter he refused to heed it.

"A man can put up with a great deal," he replied to his friend, "but not with an affront to self-respect and personal honor."

He found that the bishops were conducting themselves more like a pack of howling dogs than as spiritual leaders. But he would not allow von Uhrs's mendacious and hate-filled pamphlet to remain unanswered, so he composed a piece in which he deployed all of his dialectical ability, elegantly defended his own views, and powerfully refuted every point contained in the grand master's accusation, never lapsing into rant or getting into unrelated matters.

THE PRINCE ELECTOR took the time to read Benjamin's defense carefully. What made the greatest impression on him was not the philosopher's intelligence or clear vision but rather his spirit and honorable conduct, the fact that he had the courage to confront the religious authorities as well as to admit a new perspective by conceding certain weak points in his own logic.

Once the prince had finished studying the text he issued a proclamation to all of Baden-Württemberg declaring that Benjamin Spinoza was above all suspicion of impiety and the charges of blasphemy against him were unfounded.

IT WAS SPRINGTIME, warm and full of light, but von Uhrs was in a black mood. He had suffered an enormous loss of prestige. His fat body foundered, saliva drooled from his mouth, and he hung his bald head. He feared that the catastrophic defeat might prompt his destitution as grand master at the next meeting of the company.

His hatred for Benjamin Spinoza grew with every passing minute and filled him with new energy. He immediately began a number of covert manipulations. He wrote flattering letters to some of the bishops; to others he circulated dark, bombastic comments about the mockery, derision, and affronts to which the church had been exposed by the ignorant prince elector.

Von Uhrs opened their next meeting with a theatrical coup calculated to gloss over his failure and redeem his credibility. He declared that he had proof that the Jew Spinoza was in contact with evil demons that had deranged the senses of Konrad von Hohenweiler.

The bishops were aghast. They exchanged astonished glances. The grand master explained that the decision of the prince elector had been dictated by those demons. The clergy need not be concerned by this temporary setback. What difference were a few months, he said, when the church is eternal?

A young bishop from Regensburg, the most quick-witted of the assembly, immediately proposed to declare the insolent Jew Spinoza the greatest threat to pure doctrine in all the German-speaking states. An outburst of applause greeted his proposal. With a formal vote they unanimously gave the grand master a free hand. Two of the more senior bishops cautioned him to proceed deliberately and with great care.

The bishops concluded the meeting with a thunderous anthem of praise to the Lord.

Burglars and Hired Assassins

BALTHASAR VON UHRS lost no time. He hired two burglars to break into Benjamin's house one day when the family was out. They were capable and efficient, and they knew exactly what to look for. They entered the shuttered residence, thoroughly searched all the rooms, opened cabinets, pulled out drawers, and dumped the contents on the floor, looking for hidden manuscripts and any other compromising material. After searching every nook and cranny and going through the contents of every drawer several times, the burglars returned empty-handed to their patron.

AT THE NEXT conclave of the Societas Jesu the grand master stressed to his fellow conspirators in the clergy that godliness itself was at stake. He insisted that the Jew Spinoza's heretical teachings had opened a horrific abyss and stressed that the pious and righteous had to use all their forces to counter the loathsome attacks on the truth of God's teachings. He expressed deep dismay that the Jew could not be dragged to the bonfire as a warning and example to others, and he spoke of the need to tighten the thumbscrews further. He proposed a new plan.

The prelates listened attentively. Some of them nodded in agreement with the leader's sage advice.

A Bavarian priest of impressive rotundity stood up and reported that in his parish a pig with seven legs had been born and a newborn had emerged with its feet turned backward. He feared these were portents of impending catastrophes unleashed by the evil Jew, and he declared that it was vitally important to follow the grand master's plan. A colleague beside him stood up and reported that in his home city of Cologne an elderly woman had given birth to a hermaphrodite; the male member looked like that of a horse and the female parts resembled an enormous shell, and the newborn's body was entirely covered with down. A third bishop took it upon himself to inform them that in his diocese a nun had given birth to twins. He decried this as a sign of the extent of contemporary depravity and declared that such decadence had to be resisted.

One of the bishops rose, approached Balthasar von Uhrs, kissed his ring as a sign of devoted admiration, and declared that the grand master would prevail not only in that conflict but also in all other campaigns he led against the enemies of the Catholic faith.

The assembly was unanimous that Spinoza had to be discredited and dragged down from his pedestal. After the meeting the bishops instructed Catholic priests throughout the German-speaking region to warn the people the next Sunday that the professor of philosophy in Freiburg had conversed with devils and was capable of bending demons to his will.

BECAUSE HE WAS a Jew, Benjamin was fair game, an ideal target for a church intent on persecuting those of different opinions. Their calumnies could not shake his standing at the university. The authorities did not require him to recant and refused to ban him from his profession.

BALTHASAR VON UHRS stood in the cathedral clutching his gleaming miter and attempted to light a candle. His heavy breath made the weak flame flicker as he vowed not to rest until the day that Benjamin Spinoza lay stretched out in his own excrement and all his protectors dropped dead in horror.

"God's justice will make their corpses a feast for rodents and a banquet for worms," he whispered, and kissed the crucifix that hung from his neck.

Then he assiduously pulled all possible strings to make the Holy Father in the Vatican aware of the unrepentant Jewish philosopher. Von Uhrs addressed a letter to the Roman curia and provided a number of examples of Benjamin's heretical declarations, most of which the grand master had fabricated.

POPE CLEMENT X, then on the throne of the Vatican, was a man of action. When leading prelates wanted someone to be taught a proper lesson, he would dispatch a hired assassin. After paging through von Uhrs's documentation, the pope decided that this dangerous Jew had to be silenced.

The archives of Clement X, now in the Vatican library gave an account of the plans to murder Benjamin, who is described as the devil incarnate in human form. They are part of the public record.

A REPRESENTATIVE of the Holy See gave an Italian murderer his instructions. The assassin suggested poison, since Benjamin's weakness for sweets was common knowledge. The hired killer sewed an envelope of arsenic into the cloak he always wore on his travels. He explained to the grand master that the dose in the envelope was carefully calculated. He prepared a selection of chocolate-covered pastries and gave them to a servant to deliver. Unfortunately the inattentive servant left them at the wrong house.

That night the dean of the university died in terrible torment. His sudden death sent wild speculation through Freiburg.

Justice in Freiburg

THE ITALIAN ASSASSIN was ambushed behind the inn on a moonlit night by three men brandishing knives who were after his purse. He attempted to flee but then turned and knocked one of them unconscious. He plunged a knife into the neck of the second assailant, directly into the jugular, and the man bled to death immediately. The third man ran back to the inn and called for help. A crowd overwhelmed the assassin and took him prisoner.

No one knew his identity. They knew only that he was from Italy, which meant there was no need to show him too much consideration. They took the Italian to the torture chamber. His guilt was manifest. He was charged with murdering a citizen of Freiburg. Everyone knew he was going to be broken on the rack and the wheel and killed.

They stretched the naked Italian on the floor and bound him to four pillars. The chief official at the hearing knelt next to him and demanded his name. The prisoner refused to answer. In response the torturer leaned over and branded his chest with a red-hot rod. The Italian's scream must have been heard for blocks.

The official again asked for his name and again received not a word in reply. The torturer returned, this time with two glowing tongs. Desperate fear was evident in the eyes of the Italian. The branding irons were applied once more and held in place until his flesh turned black. The stink of burned flesh filled the torture chamber, and the prisoner appeared to have lost consciousness. The torturer's assistant dumped a pail of water over the Italian and brought him back to consciousness.

The torturer made preparations to brand the man again. The Italian was seized with fear when he saw the glowing irons again approaching his chest. He tried to save his life by confessing. He told them he was a hired assassin with many men's lives on his conscience, but he murdered only when commanded to do so, never for the pleasure of it. He volunteered that he had poisoned the dean by mistake.

He said he had been planning to murder Benjamin Spinoza with a dagger.

The official asked who had sent him to Freiburg. The Italian answered that he was a mere instrument of fate, not subject to judgment by God or by men. The torturer again hefted his iron. The response was a weak whisper: "Balthasar von Uhrs."

The official gestured to the executioner, who took out a heavy wheel and rolled it several times across the Italian's body. The pain was so intense that the assassin thought his brain was exploding through his ears. The torturer smashed one of his shins with the wheel. The Italian's back contorted in pain and his body twisted in a terrific arc. He did not scream; a gurgling sound came from his throat. The torturer broke his other leg and then his arms, one by one. Finally the wheel slammed down upon his neck. The torture chamber became absolutely silent.

The presiding official turned his face away. It was obvious that he was not used to such entertainment. He began to vomit.

Protection and Apparitions

THE CHIEF OF POLICE summoned Benjamin and informed him that an Italian assassin sent to kill him had been arrested and executed. Benjamin was frightened and appalled. He could not understand why anyone would want to murder him.

A terrific thunderstorm broke over Freiburg that night. Enormous lightning bolts lit the skies. Benjamin lay sleepless, prey to threatening apparitions. As soon as he closed his eyes, he imagined a dark-clad assassin crossing the threshold to kill him. He couldn't get the thought of the Italian out of his mind.

Years afterward Benjamin would describe how he wandered for the first time through the desolate dark landscape of madness that night. A mystical hazy veil oppressed his brain, disordered his thoughts, fed his suffering, and forced him into ceaseless brooding on his troubles.

KONRAD VON HOHENWEILER was the most powerful man in Freiburg. An enlightened despot, he was no stranger to philosophy. In his youth he had drunk deeply from its springs; René Descartes had been his tutor for three years. Benjamin had won the prince elector's good opinion with treatises on tolerance that stimulated the prince's intellect and touched his heartstrings.

THE PRINCE ELECTOR promised that his own bodyguard would offer protection to Benjamin.

BUT IT WAS NO USE. Benjamin's nerves were shattered. He hadn't the slightest doubt that someone was plotting his death, no matter what others told him.

He awoke every night thinking he could feel a knife thrusting into his body. If he was lying on his back, the knife was plunging into his belly or his neck. If he was curled up, the murderer was stabbing him in the back.

Even during the day he expected to be stabbed at any moment. Without realizing it, he would often lay a hand across his throat as if trying to protect himself. Fear overpowered him the moment he stepped outside his house. As a precaution, he let his beard and mustache grow and disguised himself in hopes of escaping detection by the assassins lurking in the street.

IN REACTION to these imagined threats, Benjamin—normally the most peaceful creature alive—would imagine striking dead the dark-clad assassin. In his inner eye he could see himself adeptly avenging himself upon the evil Italian. In one scenario he would wield an axe; in another he would use a knife. He was always careful to make sure that the blows he dealt were mortal and that the Italian was left lifeless. Over time these daydreams and fantasies grew worse. Benjamin saw himself sawing off the assassin's head and ripping his intestines from his body. One night he saw himself pushing the dark figure off the church tower and heard the noise of the man's skull smashing against the stone pavement. Another night during a thunderstorm he sent a lightning bolt to strike the murderer and watched the flames consume the dead body.

Benjamin found no peace. Visions and nightmares constantly plagued him. He had to kill the Italian. The fate of the whole world depended upon it. After that, killing his assassin was not enough; the dark-garbed Italian had to be expunged, obliterated, reduced to nothingness. Even the memory of him, the knowledge that he had once existed in this world, had to be erased.

Twenty-nine Years of Solitude

BENJAMIN'S STUDY had two lead-framed windows, each consisting of twenty small panes looking out onto the inner courtyard. That dim little room contained only a bed, a chair, a rickety desk, and shelves filled with books.

For twenty-nine years Benjamin had huddled here. He never left the room, not even to attend the funerals of his brother Bento and his wife, Mafalda. He was terrified the dark-clad assassin would be lurking outside his door.

Benjamin was completely isolated after Mafalda died. An eerie silence lay over his lodging. His sons never visited. A faithful old servant turned up every day at noon, pushed a plate of food through a slot in the door, and emptied the chamber pot. An unremitting unpleasant odor wafted out through the opening.

Benjamin encountered only one living person in all those years. In the fall of 1692 a visitor was admitted to the house by the old servant, who whispered the man's name almost inaudibly through the slot. The door, always kept barred from the inside, flew open. Benjamin had been waiting for this visitor for a very long time.

BENJAMIN BURST into speech. He told his visitor that he hadn't said a word to anyone for nineteen years. He had sunk for a long time in an incomprehending haze of madness. He had blindly paced back and forth in that small room. Days had given way to years and he never noticed.

In the twelfth year something remarkable had happened. The memory of it gave him gooseflesh. A sudden darkness fell at noon, and Balthasar von Uhrs suddenly appeared in the room. The grand master had circled Benjamin seven times, apparently astonished, then stopped in his tracks. They regarded each other without a word. Benjamin had never met von Uhrs before that day. He recoiled from the strong stench emitted from the grand master's mouth as the man told him they had been linked for ages, through many lifetimes. It all went back to a clash in Galilee at the time of Jesus. He said nothing more, except to declare that he had never regretted his campaign against Benjamin, and to assure him they would meet again in another few hundred years. Von Uhrs disappeared. With him went the Italian who had been standing outside the door.

That night the heavens cleared and moonlight filled the room. After the fiends disappeared, the fog in Benjamin's brain began to dissipate. He realized that night that some-day a man would arrive to reveal the true path.

"I have waited for that man for seven years," Benjamin said, "and all that time I have tried to think of him as a friend and confidant who will console me, ease my mind, and help me to understand the meaning of my life. He will help me understand why I chose to live as I did, usually from fear, sometimes out of vanity, seldom guided by wisdom. I haven't gone to sleep a single evening without visualizing him as my sole support, like a relative sitting all night in vigil by a sickbed, waiting for me to heal and prove worthy of him. I have sequestered myself in this room because I knew I could not escape this encounter. My whole life has been directed toward it."

The Great Gift

THE VISITOR REPLIED with a smile that Benjamin was the only man alive who could understand him. Then he gave his name: Salman de Espinosa, the wandering Jew. He said that he had led death by the nose for more than three hundred and fifty years. Lengthy journeys across the four continents had taught him thirty-six languages, and his many lifetimes had endowed him with encyclopedic knowledge he now wanted to bequeath to Benjamin, his direct descendant and heir. Death had taken from him everyone he had loved, and for that reason he had been its sworn enemy. But now he and death had reconciled themselves with each other, and in less than seventy-two hours they would finally be united, because he had worked out how to reverse the elixir of immortality.

Benjamin begged him to tell everything he knew, since time was so short.

Salman told him the story of Baruch, the callow young man who had met Moses, heeded his command, left his father's house, brandished a heavy sword in battle, and become personal physician to the Portuguese king; he described the medicinal potions that transformed old men into raging stallions and Baruch's propagation of the Raimundo plant to honor the greatest love of his life.

Salman told him of the great secret, the elixir of immortality that had been handed down from father to son— from Baruch to Simon, from Simon to Amos, from Amos to Shlomo, from Shlomo to Israel.

Salman recounted the story of Israel, the physician who had twelve daughters before a long-awaited son came into the world; how Israel refused to speak to his eldest daughter, Leah, for almost thirty years because she had foreseen with her psychic powers that scandal would tarnish the family name; how after the death of his son he had worked out a system of encryption so he could pass the secret on to his grandson, then only two years old.

Salman told of Chaim, the young doctor in Granada, and his moral lapse in poisoning his master, the worthy Sultan Muhammed II, in expectation of serving a wicked tyrant;

and how the new sultan brutally executed him and threw his heart to the hounds for breakfast.

Salman told of how his own father, Moishe, the Cabalist, neglected the family mission of safeguarding the great secret and instead devoted his life to investigating the secrets of the universe and interpreting apparitions in the vault of heaven; and of how he had left as his legacy a pioneering work of Jewish mysticism.

Salman recounted his own life: how he was neither Jew nor Muslim; how he fled from Granada after his parents died; the encounter with Rabbi Tibbon and how Salman watched, helpless, as the rabbi was murdered. He explained why he had prepared and consumed the forbidden elixir that gave him immortality; he described his marriage and life in Seville, the century that he had spent in his peregrinations back and forth across Spain, the failed attempt to assassinate Grand Inquisitor Torquemada, and how he had been bound to the stake in Seville but had risen again from the flames without even a drop of sweat upon the least of the hairs of his head.

Salman told how on the same night in 1492 that the Jews were driven out of Spain, he sailed westward with Christopher Columbus aboard the *Santa María*, serving as the Hebrew interpreter on the quest for a new homeland for the Jews; of the long journey across the Atlantic; of going ashore on the islands of the West Indies and of the inhabitants who spoke perfect Hebrew; of the Spaniard Hernán Cortés, who with a force of four hundred men subjugated the widespread domain of Montezuma; and of the *conquistadors'* expeditions in search of Mexico's gold, exploits of men so cruel that they made the lackeys of the Inquisition seem like innocent choirboys.

Salman told of his own restlessness: the fact that he never lingered anywhere more than a month or two; his work as a rabbi, an artisan, a teacher, a physician, a printer of books, an artist, and a counselor to royalty; how he had climbed the snow-covered plateaus of the Andes, crossed the desert sands of the Sahara, bathed with holy men in the Ganges River, washed his clothes in the China Sea, and wooed the young wife of an elderly Russian governor in Siberia; how he had witnessed all of life's misfortunes, sorrows, illnesses, injustices, earthquakes, and floods, as well as all its famines, plagues, and epidemics.

Salman told Benjamin how he had trailed his own descendants at a distance from Spain to Portugal and thence to Holland. He had patiently waited for ages to find someone in the Spinoza family who could understand him and take up the burden of the heavy legacy Moses had long ago laid upon the family.

"I do not offer you eternal life or redemption," Salman said. "What I offer is knowledge that you must investigate, collect, keep safe, and pass along. I have taken great pleasure with all I have learned even though I have not managed to change the world, overcome stupidity and evil, or give people their due recognition and justice. I have not performed heroic deeds or saved anyone's life. But I am not discouraged, for I know that you and those who come after you will achieve more than I. Take this, my dear man, so I can die in peace."

He took from his knapsack his father's manuscripts, his own manuscript *The Seventh Book of Moses*, and the recipe for the elixir of immortality, just as it was written out by Israel, his grandfather's father. He handed it all to Benjamin.

"Beyond all doubt this is a holy day and not a dream," Benjamin responded. "I accept your gift and open myself to the radiance of its wisdom. May it penetrate my being and illumine every part of my body. My heart is racing and my pulse is thundering at the glorious, life-giving splendor of your gift."

"My son," said Salman, "a few hours before I appeared here, I consumed seven drops of the freshly prepared elixir of immortality. The second dose serves as an antidote to the first. I am not entirely certain what will come to pass, but my calculations suggest that this body I have inhabited for more than three hundred and fifty years will dissolve within seventy-two hours. I can already feel the change. The skin covering my chest has become so thin that it is almost transparent. I must leave you now. We will meet again in eternity."

Benjamin's eyes flooded with tears. They embraced. Then Salman left that little room and set forth on his last journey.

Benjamin's Final Days

BENJAMIN DEVOTED the remaining ten years of his life to writing *The Elixir of Immortality*. He was fully aware that only a handful of individuals would ever read it, but he spared no effort in creating an absolute masterpiece, profoundly intellectual and elegantly written.

He dedicated the work to his four sons, even though only Aaron, the eldest, would ever read it. He wrote, "This is your own history. The future is up to you."

HOW DID BENJAMIN SPINOZA DIE?

Immanuel Kant claims in his *Dreams of a Spirit-Seer* that Benjamin hanged himself from the branch of an apple tree. Bertrand Russell, on the other hand, says that he died after he broke a hip, and Isaiah Berlin writes in a letter to an Israeli colleague that Benjamin drowned in the North Sea. Marx and Engels maintain that he died in prison. Lenin said the same thing and added that the Inquisition had tortured him to death.

Benjamin's death is a subject of contention among academics.

Two Paintings

TWO OIL PAINTINGS portraying Benjamin have come down to us. One is titled *Philosopher B. Spinoza* and is signed by the mannerist painter Michael Lukas Leopold Willmann, a great admirer of Michelangelo. Commissioned by the University of Freiburg, it was finished some time in the early 1670s; the exact date is unknown. The painting was displayed in the left wing of the Faculty of Philosophy.

In the 1930s new winds were blowing through Nazi Germany. Individuals of Jewish ancestry were progressively excluded from society, and their rights as citizens were abrogated. In 1934 Martin Heidegger became rector of the University of Freiburg. Many had great hopes of the renowned philosopher who had written *Being and Time*. Some cherished the deluded hope that Freiburg would continue to offer refuge to freethinkers.

Few were aware that the new rector had long been a dues-paying member of the National Socialist Party. Heidegger devoted his evenings to writing tracts on humanism and philosophical matters but during the day he worked with determination to institute sweeping changes in line with the worldviews of the new German Führer, Adolf Hitler.

He dismissed all the Jewish instructors and subjected professors to formal hearings on their views, loyalties, and contacts with Jews. He ordered his staff to take down all of the portraits of persons without clearly documented Aryan ancestry. He cleansed the holdings of the library by having all works by Jews systematically removed. Condemned books and paintings were fuel for a bonfire in honor of German purity.

Benjamin's portrait did not wind up in the bonfire.

My great-uncle told us that the man who saved Benjamin from the flames was none other than Hermann Göring. The Reich Marshal was an art lover and one of the era's most avid collectors. In his summer palace a few miles outside Berlin, named Carinhall in memory of his late Swedish wife, Göring covered the walls from floor to ceiling with priceless works of art. Every one was stolen. Most came from Jewish homes plundered throughout Nazi-occupied Europe.

Benjamin's portrait hung for ten years in the Reich Marshal's study at Carinhall.

After the fall of the Thousand-Year Reich the painting mysteriously made its way to the Soviet Union and turned up in General Arkady Bondarchuk's spacious dacha on the Black Sea.

Bondarchuk had studied philosophy in Moscow before the Second World War. He had read Bento Spinoza's *Ethics* with great interest and spent a lot of time studying the issues of good and evil. He was a great admirer of Bento and assumed that the portrait depicted him.

For his contributions to the conquest of Berlin the general was subsequently honored with the highest decoration for bravery offered by the workers' state. Stalin presented the medal to him in a ceremony in the Kremlin to thunderous applause. The ruler called Bondarchuk "my favorite general."

Four years later the general was accused of collaborating with the CIA and stealing state property. No one blinked as Stalin had his "favorite general" executed. The traitor's real name was Aron Bronstain; he was of Jewish ancestry and a distant cousin of Trotsky.

The fall of the four-star general opened the Soviet dictator's last great purge. Hundreds of Jewish physicians were murdered. Yiddish culture was virtually wiped out before Stalin and his regime of terror went to their graves.

Benjamin's portrait disappeared without a trace, along with all the other contents of the dacha of the executed general.

THE OTHER PAINTING hangs in the Rijksmuseum in Amsterdam and bears the title *Caravaggio Accompanied by the Spinoza Family*. The artist's signature is visible on the far right of the canvas: Rembrandt.

Here Benjamin is seven years old. He has blue eyes and carefully parted curly black hair, and his face is dominated by an unbelievably large nose. A warm smile suggests great openness, as if the boy wants to tell everyone that the world is full of joy and beauty.

SEVEN

The Revolutionary

The Encyclopedist

H.S.—BEHIND THOSE INITIALS IS concealed the only important Jewish writer of the French Enlightenment, a man as daring as he was eccentric, a historian of ideas and ancient times regarded as the world's first expert on the history of sexual perversion in Athens. The philosopher Michel Foucault analyzed that whole genre in a series of pioneering works, and he asserts that H.S. knew more about that subject or understood it better than anyone else.

His name was Hector Spinoza, but he inscribed himself into history with his initials, H.S. Or tried to do so. It's not clear whether he succeeded. In France, a country that loves to honor its geniuses, not a single street, not even a tiny alley bears his name, and he appears nowhere among the fifty thousand biographies of notable Frenchmen in the *Dictionnaire Larousse de l'histoire de France*. Puzzled by this neglect, I wrote both to the Ministry of Culture and to the publisher of that twenty-volume reference work. The ministry never replied. In contrast, I received a polite but relatively meaningless letter from a certain Maurice Lacouture, who regretted the absence of my relative "Hermann Spinoza" from the *Dictionnaire* and suggested it might be due to a technical oversight that would surely be corrected in the next edition, due out sometime around 2020. It was obvious to me that the editors had no idea of the identity hidden behind the initials H.S.

I KNOW relatively little about Hector Spinoza. In fact, I know less about his life than I do about his death.

My great-uncle seldom mentioned him; he was much more interested in Hector's daughter, Shoshana. In his memoirs, Jakob Spinoza—my grandfather's pedantic grandfather, finance minister to Kaiser Franz Josef, and close friend to the ruler, a figure I will say more about in these pages—mentions Hector by name only one time. Voltaire does not mention his friend even once in the notes for his autobiography. On the other hand, however, as my great-uncle pointed out, under the entry for "Philosopher" in his *Pocket Dictionary of Philosophy* Voltaire does cite maxims of H.S., though without using quotation marks or identifying the source:

> *Treat others as you would treat yourself.*
> *Love humanity in general, especially those who are virtuous.*
> *Forget injustices but never forget benevolence.*
> *I have seen men incapable of study but never men incapable of good deeds.*

HERE'S WHAT I KNOW about Hector Spinoza. He lost his mother when he was six years old. She was the only person who was ever close to him. He grew up in Strasbourg, where his father was a merchant. After his nineteenth birthday he left the city of his youth to study law at the Sorbonne. During his years there he read at least a thousand books and taught himself four foreign languages: German, English, Arabic, and Greek. Hector's obsession with reading was almost limitless; so was his memory. Once he had read something, he retained it forever.

His interest in abnormal behavior was aroused by Paracelsus's book *Philosophiae et Medicinae utriusque compendium*, which he came across in a carton at a used-book stall on the Left Bank of the Seine. He was especially fascinated by the remarks of the Swiss physician and alchemist concerning chameleons, those strange little lizards that change color to match their environment.

After finishing his studies he set himself up in the practice of commercial law. He quickly outmaneuvered all of his competitors and acquired a clientele more vast than any other Jewish attorney in Paris ever had. His clients were principally aristocrats, and he was adept at increasing their fortunes; not one was ever disappointed. He himself was neither greedy nor profligate but in fact generally indifferent to money. He invested the lion's share of his considerable income in his unique collection of esoteric literature.

On one occasion he traveled to Marseille with the sole purpose of purchasing the Talmud that had been the personal possession of Moses Maimonides, the great twelfth-century thinker. Pierre Arditti, the owner of that treasure, was in dire need of funds but refused even after protracted negotiations to part with the obviously priceless book. Arditti could not bring himself to give it up because his family had owned it for more than five hundred years. In a flash of inspiration, Hector offered to marry Arditti's only child, his daughter, Sophie. He had in fact never met her but he saw that only by marrying her could he procure Maimonides's Talmud for his collection. Arditti could not turn down the offer of a prosperous Jewish attorney clearly on the rise in Paris society to marry a young woman whose only dowry was a family name honored by the leading Sephardic circles of Marseille. Hector was extremely pleased to discover that Sophie was not ugly in the least; she had quite a handsome face, even if the overall impression was blemished just a bit by the flaming red beauty spot right on the tip of her nose. The simple wedding ceremony took place the very next day.

This was Hector's second marriage. His first had lasted only eleven days. His wife had died suddenly of septicemia, the infection known as "blood poisoning."

Hector and Sophie had three children and lived in well-furnished comfort in one of the capital's most exclusive arrondissements. But Hector was never able to put Maimonides's Talmud into his collection. Arditti outlived both his son-in-law and his daughter, dying eventually at the age of ninety-eight.

Hector was a complicated individual, single-minded and fixed in his routine. He rose at five o'clock every morning and went to bed at midnight. He was perpetually at work. At home he was authoritarian and domineering. He was quite irritable and complained shrilly when the children got in his way, but there wasn't a bad bone in his body. He had a great store of affection to share from time to time, whenever he managed to think of something other than his work and writing. In company he was timid and self-conscious; most of the time he walked with eyes downcast, and he preferred to slip away from company. Every first Monday, second Tuesday, and third Wednesday of months not spelled with the letter *r*—it made no difference whether the weather was splendid or terrible—he would take a stroll in the Jardin de Luxembourg at half past five in the evening. On those occasions he put on his wife's most elegant clothing and shoes, wore very heavy makeup, and concealed his bald head under the abundant tresses of a woman's wig. He promenaded with head held high, desirous that everyone should see him. He did not know why he did this. But on those occasions when he was detained for unseemly behavior in public, he persuaded the gendarmes that he was honoring the memory of his dear, departed mother. They always released him the same evening.

———

HECTOR BUSIED HIMSELF with freelance writing as a sideline to his real work. He was fearless and passionate. He made contact with Diderot, d'Alembert, Voltaire, and Montesquieu, the thinkers who inspired the French Revolution. They constituted a small group who worked hard and were subject to great pressures, allies in a loosely defined common enterprise. Their guiding spirit was an enthusiastic belief in progress. They believed that the essentially good nature of man had been corrupted by the hardships and discrimination of society but could be redeemed through enlightenment. Society could be reformed. The written word was to be the vehicle of this enlightenment. Their writings were lively, full of optimism and faith in the future. The authorities found them suspect. These radical thinkers were persecuted, silenced, and forced into exile. Their books were burned.

Hector, the only Jew among them, collaborated in the great *Encyclopédie* (1751–1780), the bible of the French Enlightenment. He was the only participant obliged to sign with his initials because they wanted to hide his origins. He was greatly displeased by this, but there was nothing he could do about it.

His unusually brilliant contributions were infused with burning passion. They dealt with religious revolutionaries, utopian thinkers, apostates, and heretics. He considered it a point of honor always to take up controversial subjects, preferably those banned by the authorities. The reading public, those few souls, often regarded his articles with suspicion. But Hector did not doubt his mission; he dreamed of a future world of greater justice in which his work would be viewed with different eyes.

———

HECTOR WROTE a book on the history of masturbation in ancient Athens. With the willing intermediation of Voltaire he had it brought to the attention of Catherine the Great, who in a manner quite unusual for despots was flirting with reformist notions. Hector cherished the secret hope that Her Majesty might endorse his book and open doors throughout Europe. But he received no reply from St. Petersburg. Hector was obliged to do battle with the Parisian censors. It was an unequal match. Six times he was required to make extensive revisions. When the book was finally approved for publication, the entire press run sold out in two hours. Literary lion Olivier Mareau, a servile representative of the regime whose constant theme was the duties of the citizen, quickly penned a vile comic satire ridiculing the pathbreaking work. Hector refused to be intimidated. He circulated handwritten copies of the original, unexpurgated version with his candid views of humanity couched in astonishingly uninhibited language. It was a bold move; in no other text in the French language could one find so many synonyms for the word "penis." The scandal was enormous. Both the nobility and the bourgeoisie of Paris erupted in fury and called the book filthy and immoral. Minister of the Interior du Saint-Florentin, responsible for the police, retaliated decisively. At midnight, just after Hector had gone to sleep, several gendarmes woke him and hauled him off to an interrogation. The minister threatened to clap him into the Bastille where he could rot away in the company of well-fed rats. Hector sought to defend himself as best he could by citing his sources. By morning he was so exhausted that even though the intense discussion with the minister was still underway, he drowsed off in his chair and in a nightmare imagined hoards of rats attacking him from every direction with their sharp teeth, tearing strips of flesh from his body. He shuddered awake, soaked in sweat, and beseeched du Saint-Florentin to confiscate and burn all copies of the manuscript.

A Collection of Books

HECTOR REGARDED VOLTAIRE as the most exalted of his contemporaries. He invited Voltaire to his home for the Sabbath meal a number of times, even though the man disliked all manner of religious observance and had made many deprecatory, even contemptuous comments about the Jews.

One evening Hector received Voltaire and two elegantly dressed English gentlemen who exuded a strong odor of cologne. The four of them drank cider and had only just seated themselves at the dinner table when Voltaire, in the mood for a bit of provocation, began to inquire whether in Jewish thought there was any justification for the presumption that evil is a necessary condition for the continued existence of the world. The English guests grinned; they were looking forward to an exalted theological discussion.

The question perplexed Hector. For a few moments he appeared lost in thought. He took off his spectacles, wiped them with a napkin, and then carefully placed them in front of him on the table. He started to say something but changed his mind. He got up from the table as if he had just had a sudden inspiration.

"Would you like to see something extremely unusual?" he asked. "You will not find a book, in any language at all, in any field of study, that has as much power, as many unique qualities, and as many insights as this one. None!

Gentlemen, this book is nonpareil; no book can compare with it and it resembles no other. I shall firmly maintain this contention until the day I die."

Without waiting for a response from his guests, Hector went into a side room furnished as an immense library. In higher spirits than he had been for a long time, he began to climb an unusually tall ladder to fetch down his treasure, Benjamin Spinoza's *The Elixir of Immortality.*

The others stood in the doorway, sniffing at the odor of ancient paper and dust and peering through the gloom. As he ascended the ladder, Hector told them in an animated voice that here they were privileged to view the most extensive library of esoterica in Europe.

"This place is holy." Hector's voice was exalted. "Every book you see here has a soul. Within each binding, unsuspected mysteries wait to reveal themselves. Over thirty long years, sparing no expense, I have collected more than three thousand manuscripts of Cabalistic mysticism, more than four hundred original editions of the Talmud, and manuscripts written out by hand by Roger Bacon, Paracelsus, Simon the Wise, and Erasmus of Rotterdam."

"My dear Hector," said Voltaire, "what is this fantastical book you speak of with such warmth?"

"Patience, *cher maître,*" replied Hector. "We will get to that in a moment. You must first understand that deep secrets can be found in most of the magnificent books in my library. But they cannot compare with the secrets in this amazing book. Before I open it, let me simply pledge that I will abandon myself body and soul to the Prince of Darkness if you detect even a single word of untruth in this book. However, I will pray that hell's fires burn you all, that pains of the gut will twist you into convulsions, that lightning will lame you, that cancer will strike you, and that like Sodom and Gomorrah you will perish in brimstone and fire and be cast into the abysm—*if* you fail to keep silent about what you are about to see or reveal to anyone that you have viewed the masterpiece of my sainted grandfather's father, Benjamin Spinoza."

Hector scrambled to the top of the ladder. At the sight of the treasure his eyes glistened with tears. He declared ceremoniously that he had discovered what he had been seeking. If truth existed anywhere in this world, it was between the covers of this book. The following moment, as he reached out to pick it up, he lost his balance and fell headlong to the floor.

Voltaire and the others heard a heartrending scream. The Englishmen thought they were party to a practical joke. They burst into hysterical laughter. Voltaire stared at them in amazement. He understood immediately what had happened.

Hector lay lifeless on the floor beneath a heavy, beautifully bound handwritten edition of the Talmud that had fallen on him and crushed his enormous nose and head.

Voltaire leaned over and pressed one eyelid; with the careful attention of a physician he sought to detect the breath of life from Hector's lips or the beat of a heart beneath his jacket. His life had ended. Hector lay on the floor as if he had always been there. Voltaire rose and in a stoic tone informed his companions that the wisdom of the Jews, allied with chance and the logic of dark forces, had taken Hector's life.

The Guardian

THE FUNERAL was held at the Cimetière du Père-Lachaise. A large crowd attended even though it was a cold winter day. Hector had saved countless marquises, counts, and barons from imminent ruin, and his magic had multiplied the fortunes of even more members of the aristocracy. They all came to show their gratitude with one last silent tribute. No other Jew was ever as deeply mourned as Hector, and no one had been buried in Paris with greater ceremony and reverence.

Only one of the encyclopedists came to honor that man who had devoted his life to the ideals of the French Enlightenment. That was Voltaire.

The philosopher's old acquaintance the Count of Villeparisis leaned his head on Voltaire's shoulder as they stood there next to the grave. With tear-filled eyes the count sighed. "No one can deceive death. Not even an attorney a shrewd as Spinoza. It is truly a shame. I will miss him! He had agreed to represent me next week in a very important case."

Voltaire nodded and stepped to the side.

The rabbi delivered a lengthy sermon and enthusiastically praised the departed. It was evident that he, also, was one of Hector's satisfied clients. From time to time distinct sobs from the children and the wife interrupted his talk. After this, the titled attendees placed upon the grave their wreaths of roses, tulips, chrysanthemums, lilies, and hyacinths. Voltaire deposited a stone, for Jews always place a stone upon a grave or memorial. Flowers wither and die but stones last forever.

THE PHILOSOPHER was fond of the Spinoza children and knew that the widow was not able to take care of them. He approached Madame Spinoza and in a well-intentioned effort to console her, he offered words that later were to become famous: "The human condition is hard, for grief is woven into our lives. To hold ourselves erect, we must learn how to fall."

Voltaire told the widow as she stood there in tears that he would be glad to assume responsibility for the upbringing of Avraham, Shoshana, and Nicolas. He became their guardian.

Madame Spinoza

HECTOR'S WIDOW, Sophie, was from a merchant family of Spanish origins. Her forefathers had fled Madrid around 1370 to escape the Inquisition. They were members of the ancient Jewish line alleged to have descended from Rabbi Moses Maimonides, also known as Rambam, the learned twelfth-century Cabalist and physician many consider to have been the greatest Jewish thinker.

The Ardittis regarded themselves as Jews of a special type, a view reinforced by their Sephardic traditions. The Spanish they spoke to one another had changed little during the nearly four hundred years since their escape from Spain. With a naïve feeling of superiority the family looked down upon Jews who did not share their background. A word they often used, pronouncing it in a tone dripping with contempt, was *todesco*, which meant "German" and referred to Ashkenazi Jews. It was unthinkable for an Arditti to marry a *todesco*. Sophie was only five years old when her father warned her against any such future misalliance.

Among the Sephards of Marseille there were a number of so-called good families, meaning that they had been wealthy for a very long time. The most approving remark that members of this circle could make about a person was that he was *de buena famiya*—that is, of good family. The

Ardittis belonged to that wealthy caste, but with his profligate living and a series of unsuccessful speculations Pierre was close to ruining the family. He told no one—especially not his wife, a real shrew—and tried to keep up appearances by secretly selling off the family jewelry. He used the proceeds to invite his comrades to overly elaborate Shabbat dinners. That amiable man lived in constant fear of being excluded from the closed ranks of the world of good families.

ALL HER LIFE long Madame Spinoza gloried in the proud name of her family. She took every opportunity to remind her children they came from a good family and there was none better. Hector usually endured her continual ranting with equanimity, and sometimes he would even joke about it. Occasionally he would give in to his annoyance and snap, "You brought no dowry with you into this marriage, but still you think it's all very well for you to play the grande dame and act so hard to please."

Hector was often indignant that she took so little interest in her children. He scolded her frequently for neglecting them and sometimes told her directly, especially when he was vexed that he still had not laid hands on Maimonides's Talmud, "If I'd only known that you didn't have a shred of maternal feeling in your body, I'd never have married you." She always responded with great astonishment, and his criticism fell on deaf ears.

MADAME SPINOZA suffered chronic migraine headaches; they were a daily occurrence. She was never happy, partly because in her beloved Jewish ghetto in Marseille she had been admired as a young woman of the very best breeding, but after her wedding and move to the capital she became a neglected housewife. She looked down upon the Parisians as barbarians and refused to learn to speak proper French. She had no friends because no one was sufficiently well-bred for her taste. She seldom went out. Several months might go by before she found occasion to set foot outside their residence.

She was miserable. She did not kill herself or turn to drink; instead, she developed a fanatic interest in literature, especially that of the theater. Her life revolved about belles lettres. She devoured Greek dramas and comedies in the original texts. She could count up ancient works by the score that still were waiting to be discovered, and she regularly went on about how clumsily contemporary playwrights had dealt with the same themes or similar ones.

MADAME SPINOZA felt an enormous sense of relief when Voltaire offered to take charge of the three children.

The Liar

MY GREAT-UNCLE used to say, "Anyone who has never told a lie or stolen something is physically incapable of understanding someone like Avraham." Then he would add, "But who has been so lucky as to live such an unusual life?"

"So you mean that nobody is honest and we're all liars and deceivers?" Sasha asked him.

His reply was prompt. "In a sense, all human life is deception. Every story is a fiction. In the same way, the whole world is a swindle. We human beings know what's right, but despite that, we fail to do the right thing because temptations overwhelm us. We also can tell right from wrong, but we give in nevertheless, even though we're free to choose. We're weak, and in response to our weaknesses, we cheat and we deceive ourselves. That's why we love to listen to stories about men who tell heaps of lies. They're much more interesting than lives of the saints, where we can't recognize ourselves. We've all built our lives on lies, both little white lies and great, enormous ones."

HECTOR'S ELDEST SON, Avraham, had a natural inclination to tell falsehoods. It was second nature to him. In his fabrications and half-truths he mixed up noble matters and base ones, the possible and the impossible. He was completely uninhibited about it, and he would lie as easily about trivialities as about great events.

He could never resist the temptation to steal. Avraham stole everything that tempted his covetous nature: money, jewels, food, objects, literally anything. And he stole from everyone—the closest members of his family, his friends, acquaintances, children, and the elderly. The only vice he never stooped to was the use of physical violence.

ONE DAY AVRAHAM went too far. He stole fifty-six louis d'or and a Swiss pocket watch from Voltaire. The philosopher confronted him. Avraham declared that he was innocent, maintained that he had always done his best to live according to the law, that is, as an honorable man, and he blamed his sister, Shoshana, for the theft. Thereupon two liveried servants searched him and found him to be carrying on his person the vanished coins and pocket watch. That decided the issue of culpability. He refused to confess his crime. He brazenly accused the servants of having planted the money in his pocket. Voltaire found the whole matter quite painful. This was the last straw for him; he felt a great weariness in the face of Avraham's shameless lies.

After the boy's father died, Voltaire had placed the young man in a boarding school known for its strict discipline and locked gates. But Avraham escaped from the school and lived with a band of thieves in the forests outside Saint-Étienne, where Voltaire sent several gendarmes to fetch him. Sobbing and bitterly resisting, the boy was forced to come with them to Ferney. The philosopher hoped that his generosity and benevolence as well as the security of his château would have a beneficial effect on the boy's character.

Voltaire spent seven years as Avraham's guardian, trying to fill the boy's head with knowledge and understanding, advising and encouraging him, guiding him toward a life of wisdom and beauty. But no matter how hard he tried to save Avraham from the fate that seemed inevitably to await the young man, he failed.

Voltaire could no longer deceive himself. Avraham could not be set right. He was a man without a future. The philosopher believed that sooner or later Avraham would wind up in jail, and for a moment, just a fleeting moment, Voltaire thought about packing the rascal directly off to the Bastille. But then he remembered unfortunate Madame Spinoza and knew that the theft of those louis d'or was only a foretaste of all the trials her son would put her through.

AVRAHAM WAS BANISHED from Ferney. He traveled to his mother's residence in Paris. She was not at all pleased to see him. He told her he had left the château at Ferney of his own volition because he couldn't stand the way Voltaire was treating him—dealing with him as if he were the meanest of his servants, making him sleep in a dark cellar and live on the scraps he scrounged from garbage pails. His mother couldn't believe Voltaire would be so cruel, but she was too weak to confront her son.

Only a few days after coming home Avraham began to plague his mother and insist she pay him his share of the inheritance from his father—in cash. He wanted to rent his own apartment because he disliked living with his mother, and he intended to live the good life in his own place. To placate his mother and Voltaire, who was still his legal guardian, he declared that he was going to study at the Sorbonne and follow in the footsteps of his father. His mother's eyes filled with tears. Voltaire was not fooled; he was under no illusion that Avraham would complete any studies or qualify himself for a respectable profession.

AVRAHAM ENROLLED at the Faculty of Law although he had never had the least interest in the legal code. He did not attend lectures—instead, he took a position in the office of a notary who administered the affairs of counts and countesses. Within a couple of days it became obvious to his employer that the young man was incompetent. When the notary asked for additional details of his previous work history and experience, Avraham got tangled in contradictions and couldn't talk his way out of the mess. He finally had to admit that he had invented all of his references. Avraham must have known instinctively that an appeal to sympathy and understanding was the best way to calm those he had angered. He said that he had lied, not because he had a real interest in working in the notary's office but because he needed money to care for his gravely ill parents and seven younger siblings, including two sisters born blind and mute. He promised he would never again fail to tell the truth. Upon hearing of these terrible afflictions, the notary, a kind man, felt sorry for the unfortunate family. He allowed Avraham to stay. Within weeks Avraham was again facing charges of fraud and dereliction of duty. The notary threatened to call the gendarmes, but when he heard that Avraham was Voltaire's ward he limited himself to turning the rascal out.

ONE DAY Avraham happened to run into a priest who had known his father. Playing upon the sympathy of the Catholic man of God, he confided that the notary who had been employing him was a pederast. That highly respected gentleman, he declared, was attracted to young boys and given to making inappropriate advances to them. But he, Avraham, had emphatically refused to be enticed.

The priest thought it terrible that Avraham had been so unfortunate as to wind up in the wrong place and had been berated without justification by both his mother and his guardian for losing his job; they should have given him their support. The priest felt called to use Avraham's difficult situation to lead him back to God. He persuaded the young man to stay for a few days at the cloister of the Royaumont Abbey, not far from Paris. Seclusion there would help distract him from recent unfortunate events, so that he could anchor himself in something greater than himself. The priest confided that he had heard the voice of God during the six months he had spent in isolation at the cloister. Avraham gave a silent snort of derision at this, but he smiled and pledged he would do his best to concentrate upon spiritual discipline.

The priest's views on eternal life and temporal existence hardly coincided with his own, but Avraham did go to the cloister, mostly because he had nothing else to do.

On the second morning of his stay he went to confess to the abbot. Avraham avoided mentioning the shady events in his past; he said instead that as a Jew he was deeply tormented by the death of Jesus, and he yearned for salvation. The abbot gave him absolution without bothering to require any acts of penitence and suggested that he convert to the Catholic faith in order to receive the Holy Spirit and the love of God.

Avraham was quickly persuaded. Before the bell pealed that evening to call the faithful to vespers, he had already decided: He would become a Catholic. Not because he yearned for the union of his soul with the divine or because he wanted a glimpse of the kingdom of heaven but because an acquaintance had informed him that any Jew who wanted access to the world of salons and fine soirees in Paris would have to embrace the Catholic faith. It would do no harm, he told himself, to repeat a few ritual formulas in Latin.

HIS MOTHER WEPT when Avraham told her he had accepted baptism. She was paler than ever before. For a moment he thought that her heart would burst. But she made no complaint.

In a letter to Voltaire written that same afternoon she poured out her troubles. "How can he do such a thing to me?" she wrote. "A young man of *buena famiya*! This will cast a dark shadow over the rest of my life."

The Baron Meets the Countess

AFTER AVRAHAM RECEIVED his portion of the inheritance, he rented an elegant apartment in the Marais neighborhood and lived a carefree life. Every evening he was out until the break of day with his new drinking companions, fellows who boasted that they knew the rules of elegant manners as well as the back of their own hands. The rest of the time they were offering coarse comments to everyone around them and making derogatory remarks about the Jews, eliciting no response from Avraham.

He always offered gallant compliments to the ladies and easily attracted new ones who were willing and beautiful. He quickly became the toast of late-night Paris, which may have well been principally because he invented a new identity: He styled himself "Baron Armand de Spina-Rosa" and boasted without a blush that his family name was one of the most prestigious of European aristocracy. He lavishly dispersed money from the great riches he claimed to control.

ONE EVENING in a salon that was not among the best reputed in Paris, a mutual acquaintance presented Avraham to the Countess de Mercier. She was the most gorgeous woman he had ever seen. Her beauty made his knees tremble and his sex organ quiver. Avraham's fate was sealed in an instant. He knew immediately that he would do anything at all for this woman—he was even ready to die. He was so overcome with sudden infatuation that he could scarcely say a word.

The countess broke the silence. "What a remarkable coincidence it is to meet you here, my dear Baron de Spina-Rosa. I have heard so many good things about you. The baron's father would often speak of his intelligence and generosity. That's right, I knew your father, the old baron. Once upon a time, you see, we were extremely good friends. But unfortunately, circumstances sent us along different paths after I moved to Paris. How is your dear father doing?"

"Indeed, I thank you, he is very happy now," replied Avraham. He couldn't take his eyes off that enchanting, wonderfully beautiful creature, especially not from her low-cut bodice.

"It feels almost as if we had known each other for a very long time," she said. "And therefore I shall dare to take the liberty to confide an extremely personal matter to you. I hope that you will not be offended."

Avraham felt flattered by her confidence in him.

The countess told him how deeply shocked and alarmed she was over the contents of a letter she had just received from her husband's attorney. Her husband was an elderly nobleman, thirty years her senior, who possessed vast estates and an ancient castle just outside Saint-Étienne. She had never seen a person as lighthearted as the Count de Mercier on the evening when he took a hearty farewell of her to travel to Paris to care for his ailing brother. She was therefore completely unprepared for what happened the following day. The count was accompanying his attorney and the attorney's son on a hunt for wild boar when the son unexpectedly glimpsed a splendid stag; he couldn't resist the wonderful opportunity and loosed a shot at the noble animal without taking the time to aim. The bullet ricocheted against a tree trunk and struck de Mercier directly in the heart. The count certainly never even heard the shot that killed him. Only a few days earlier the count had been duped into signing a will stipulating that all of his possessions would go to his attorney. And now, according to the terms of that cold and heartless instrument, she was no longer welcome at the castle, not even to collect her own clothes and jewelry.

Avraham found this most unfortunate for the beautiful creature. He immediately replied that he wished to help her to overcome her difficult circumstances.

The countess took Avraham's hand and said, "Baron de

Spina-Rosa, you are a good man and a true friend. I find myself cast out of my own home with nowhere to live and with no resources at all. In addition, I have lost all the clothing I possess. I have never felt so alone, so abandoned, so vulnerable. That is why I have opened my heart to you. But I have no right to burden the baron with my sorrows. It would be all too much to ask that you devote time to my problems."

The countess's eyes filled with tears and she began to weep. Avraham tried to console her. His infatuation appealed to his chivalry, and he pledged to protect her, provide her an apartment fit for a countess, and furnish her with a whole new wardrobe.

"Countess de Mercier—Hélène." He added quickly, "I beg your pardon, it is not my intention to intrude. Of course I ask nothing from you in return. Do not fear me. I wish only to lighten the countess's spirits and to get to know her a little better."

The countess quickly mastered her emotions, called over a servant, and ordered a bottle of the best champagne in the house. She rapidly downed two glasses and said by way of excuse, "I must reinforce myself and soothe my nerves, so as to express my undying gratitude that in the baron I have suddenly and unexpectedly acquired such a helpful and generous friend—dear Armand."

Avraham felt a surge of happiness such as he had never known before at the knowledge he was in a position to help the needy countess. He saw her lily-white skin, the rosy, dimpled cheeks, and her seductive glance. He tried to imagine what it would be like to hold her in his arms—little knowing that within just a few hours, she would willingly follow him home and share his bed.

———

AVRAHAM RENTED an exclusive apartment for Hélène near the Église de la Madeleine and ordered an entire new wardrobe for her. He visited her every day and was overjoyed as she taught him the finer points of love play, taking him places he had never dreamed of.

Every day Avraham recalled the words of Voltaire: *Love which strikes suddenly is the most difficult to cure, and the only way to relieve the pain of thoughtless passion is to make love even more furiously.*

A Business Lesson

AFTER A FEW WEEKS of this Hélène asked if she could introduce Avraham to her beloved brother Robert Deschanel, who was having difficulties with the authorities because of malicious rumors spread by competitors and individuals conspiring against him. He had been discharged from his employment and was seeking some way to provide for himself and his family. She added that Robert had a wonderfully charming wife. Avraham accompanied her to meet the brother over a glass of wine.

Deschanel turned out to be just as fine a person as his sister. Warm, charming, and direct, he spoke immediately of his troubles without beating about the bush: He had just completed a two-year prison sentence for fraud. An unscrupulous colleague in the office had cold-bloodedly stolen money, forged documents, and laid the blame on him. Deschanel said that he would be a liar if he were to say that life in the Bastille hadn't been unendurable, especially considering he was innocent; but worst of all was the loss of his reputation. No one in Paris would even speak his name, let alone recommend him for employment. One day he had become so despondent, he said with tears in his eyes, that death seemed the only way out. He had acquired a rope and was tempted to hang himself. But he thought that he should do one last good deed by using his talents and making someone wealthy.

Deschanel had heard from his sister Hélène that the baron was a good and wise man, and he wanted to suggest a collaboration that could profit both of them. He quickly outlined a couple of ideas, stock speculations that could easily yield fabulous profits without the slightest risk. Deschanel assured the baron he could make him one of the richest men in Paris and simultaneously redeem his own reputation.

Hélène nodded in approval throughout the presentation.

Avraham found it somewhat difficult to concentrate upon the details of Deschanel's plan, for his eyes were drawn irresistibly to the sight of Hélène's décolletage, which was even more revealing than usual. *One of the richest men in Paris*—that phrase brought sweet music to his ears. He thought of Voltaire, who had always undervalued him and never believed he would turn out to be anything. He could imagine the philosopher's face, filled with surprise and reverent admiration when he heard of Avraham's unprecedented financial success. *One of the richest men in Paris* . . . He was overcome by an irresistible desire to work with Deschanel.

"Your candor," he replied, flushed with the wine and the prospects of a gleaming future, "has won my absolute confidence, and I will be most happy to place a portion of my patrimony in your hands. If you will permit me, dear friend, to call you Robert, I will raise my glass to toast the brilliant future that awaits us."

"We can be entirely open with each other here, dear Baron de Spina-Rosa," Deschanel answered and sipped his wine, "given that through Hélène you are, so to speak, a member of the family. I should like to get to work as quickly as possible. I always say that you can't make a profit if you fail to strike while the iron is hot. And believe me: I have reason to pride myself on my ability to see things clearly."

THE VERY NEXT DAY, with Deschanel's most willing assistance, Avraham invested a considerable sum in the Paris-Senegal Trading Company. To be sure, he had never heard of the enterprise before. But Deschanel assured him that it was an unusually well-managed and solid enterprise, a leader in a lucrative branch of commerce; it was engaged in the transport of slaves from West Africa to North and South America.

VOLTAIRE FELL into a rage when he heard of the investment and demanded that Avraham immediately sell his holdings.

"I have brought you up in the spirit of humanism," the philosopher protested. "You cannot possibly associate yourself with this undertaking by financing such a cruel and inhumane commerce."

Avraham easily resisted the temptation to give in to Voltaire's higher moral principles. "*Maître*," he replied quickly in a flattering tone, "I cannot pretend to aspire to your character of high principle, but I certainly stand in admiration of it."

"Consider this: You may be the victim of a fraud," Voltaire responded in a more reasonable tone. "You know almost nothing about this man Deschanel, or about the beautiful countess, or about this Senegalese enterprise."

Avraham refused to be shaken from his convictions.

"I am very well acquainted with the qualifications of Monsieur Deschanel," he said firmly, "and I am fully convinced that he is extremely adept in conducting business. I have no intention of losing the profitable opportunity that Robert has prepared for me in a spirit of great goodwill. Share prices have been rising persistently, and selling my holdings now would be pure folly—and besides, doing so would not save a single Negro from the slave ships. This is a sure road to riches!"

AFTER THE CONVERSATION with Voltaire, Avraham went home and made some quick calculations. No matter how he did the arithmetic, his investment was bound to make him wealthy beyond his dreams in the course of only a few months.

"Discounting," he happily repeated the business term he had learned from his new friend. "Discounting! It's simply a matter of finding an investment that will provide a high yield and daring to put your money into it. Isn't that what Robert is always saying? And besides, what does Voltaire know about modern notions such as business?"

He rubbed his hands together and went off to Deschanel to bid him to purchase even more shares with what remained from his inheritance.

FATE WAS WAITING in ambush for him. A couple of weeks later a letter reached Avraham on a snowy February morning.

My dear Baron Armand de Spina-Rosa,

As a result of reports that have just reached me from Dakar, I have the sad duty of informing you that the English navy under the command of Admiral Edgar

Whittaker-Stocks has occupied the city and shut down the lucrative trade in human beings. As a consequence the Paris-Senegal Trading Company has gone into immediate liquidation. The value of your shares in the enterprise as of today is zero.

It is deeply to be deplored that these times of political unrest have had such an unforeseen effect on your investments.

I shall pray to God that the disposition of the funds that remain to you from your inheritance is such that you are still able to sleep easily. If you should have the need, I am of course available to assist you both in word and deed.

Concerning my own future business plans, I have been appointed chief administrator for the Municipal Treasury of Bordeaux. As a consequence I am unusually encumbered with business responsibilities and will find it difficult to take time from these duties over the next few days. I will be traveling to Bordeaux no later than the end of this week.

Recommending myself to you with respectful sincerity,

Robert Deschanel

Étienne and Hermione

AVRAHAM COULD NOT believe his eyes. He shook his head and read the letter again and again. He took out the little pouch stored beneath the bed and opened it. He hastily examined the share certificates inside it and realized that the whole thing could be a fraud.

"I am ruined!" he exclaimed. "No, this cannot be!"

He tried to tell himself the whole thing was simply a misunderstanding. He remembered all the times he had invited Robert Deschanel to dine at the finest inns of Paris and of the reports of the glowing prospects of business in Senegal he had always received. For a moment he asked himself if this was really happening. Perhaps his brain was overwhelmed with love and playing tricks on him.

He took a carriage to Deschanel's office. The door was locked and no one came to open it, even though he pounded vigorously for several minutes. He decided to visit Hélène, assuming that she would know the whereabouts of her brother. He knocked at her door with his heart in his mouth. No one answered.

The concierge came up to him. "The countess moved out early this morning with all of her trunks and baggage," the old woman reported and started to snivel. "She was in such a hurry she didn't even say goodbye to me—to me! I've done so much for her and loaned her so much money!"

VOLTAIRE LISTENED attentively to Avraham's recital of the events. The philosopher decided that the whole story had to be complete fabrication, and he said right out, "Avraham, I believe you're lying. You've simply squandered all your inheritance. And now, my dear Baron de Spina-Rosa, this is the end of your life in a fantasy world. You're penniless, and no woman will want you. That's why you're trying to entice more money from anyone who will listen to you."

HIS MOTHER FELT that Avraham had dishonored his father's memory by recklessly spending his whole inheritance, but she agreed to help her penniless son. She hired an attorney who promised full discretion and guaranteed that he would get to the bottom of this delicate affair.

THE PAINSTAKINGLY PEDANTIC ATTORNEY methodically put together his case. Avraham was required to provide a written account of every meeting with Deschanel and Hélène, including every tiny detail—how long they had been together, what they had said, what he had answered, where they had eaten dinner, and why he had placed his entire inheritance with the Paris-Senegal Trading Company, an enterprise of which no one had ever heard.

At the sight of the stock certificates the attorney laughed right in Avraham's face and said he should have required a better authentication of the transactions than those clumsy forgeries.

The attorney took only two weeks to unravel the mess. His inquiries established that Robert Deschanel, whose real name was Étienne Girard, had vanished from Paris without a trace, failing to pay the rent for his apartment, of course, and leaving nothing behind but an old trunk full of forged papers that showed what a mad rogue he was. The attorney checked police records and found that Étienne Girard had gone to prison three times for fraud.

And then came the worst news: The attorney also found "Hermione Girard" in the records. That was Hélène's real name. There had never been any Countess de Mercier. The whole thing was made up; the countess was a role that Hermione Girard had played in order to entice Avraham into her clutches.

And then came the last devastating blow: "Hermione Girard," the attorney informed him, "is not Étienne Girard's sister but his legally married wife."

The Light-Fingered Monk

LIFE IN THE CLOISTER was Avraham's escape from the hopelessly tangled circumstances that made his life seem so terribly complicated and meaningless. He took refuge at the cloister of the Royaumont Abbey, where Father Sebastien, a valiant soul who had the ear of the abbot, took him in. They sat in a tiny room used as a workshop and labored patiently, endlessly, manufacturing religious articles for sale to other churches and cloisters: crucifixes, medallions, church candelabra, and rosaries of various lengths.

Avraham had nimble fingers, a sharp eye, and a sense of precision. Within a few weeks he had mastered the craft. He was extremely hardworking; he had great concentration and would turn and shape objects for hours on end. He carved, shaped, sawed, and filed, building up a comprehensive inventory of objects the brothers of the cloister could take out to sell on their travels.

After he put down his tools at the end of a long day of work, he would listen to the organ music in the chapel. He regularly sat there for an hour or two, motionless, staring straight before him as if deep in prayer.

Avraham was beloved in the cloister. The brothers praised him for his dedication to work and his modest appearance. Even the abbot, a man of great severity, developed a sympathy for him.

ON ONE OCCASION Avraham confided to the abbot that before entering the cloister he had worked in business. Another time he suggested several ways for the order to increase its revenue. Some time after that he presented the abbot with a large wooden relief depicting Jesus suffering at Golgotha. The abbot was greatly impressed, especially when he examined Avraham's carving closely and saw the care and ingenuity that had gone into it.

The abbot saw that Avraham was no ordinary monk and thought it might be useful to keep him close at hand. At first the abbot asked Avraham's advice on some trivial matters. But after demonstrating his conscientiousness and intelligence, Avraham was entrusted with the administration of the order's finances.

Almost as proof of Voltaire's worst fears, one day Avraham was arrested for stealing from cloister funds, a charge he hotly denied. He was put in prison.

His mother turned in despair to Voltaire. The philosopher was unmoved by Avraham's plight, but he demonstrated his magnanimity. He did Madame Spinoza a favor and spoke to his contacts at the royal palace—at that time he was a trusted friend of the queen. The charges were dismissed and Avraham was released, whereupon the young man left Paris without a moment's delay.

Moricz and the Family Inheritance

SOMETIMES IN MY CHILDHOOD I thought life wasn't worth living. This was especially the case when I tried to get my parents to show affection. I wanted them to see me and to appreciate me as I was, without acting or pretense. But it always seemed to me that they liked my twin brother better.

Nothing is more painful to a child than the feeling that his own father and mother don't love him.

I RECALL MY PARENTS' beaming faces at the end of every school year when Sasha brought home his report card with outstanding marks. He gave them every reason to be proud. As for me, starting in the third grade I received failing marks in both mathematics and history, and the stern school principal called my parents in for a conference. They listened with obvious displeasure when he said I should repeat the year. My shame at my failure was devastating. I couldn't bear to see my father's expression of dissatisfaction. Later that evening he gave me a scathing lecture. He was in a towering rage. I had made my hypersensitive mother suffer so much that she was almost distraught.

Even now, approaching the end of my life, I have to admit that I've never gotten over my father's rebuke for not being as bright and clever as a Spinoza was supposed to be.

FOR MY WHOLE LIFE I've heard that an unusually large nose is part of the Spinoza heritage. It appears in someone of each generation. The children born with that huge olfactory organ were always unusually fortunate and successful in whatever they undertook. Sasha had an enormous nose, and he was better in everything than I was.

I'd also heard of another inherited trait: a tendency to lie also turned up in each generation. Spinoza children born with that strange inability to tell the truth were always lonely. They failed at almost everything. I knew that this inherited duplicity was a sort of curse. And I've always been quick to shade the truth a little or even a lot in hopes of pleasing others.

ONE AFTERNOON my great-uncle had described some of Avraham's adventures in the New World, and I had an idea. I went to my grandfather and asked him what he thought about the traits that reappeared in every generation of our family.

The question didn't appear to surprise him in the least. He said, "It sounds as if you've been staring at Sasha's nose again. Don't worry, you'll turn out to be a fine fellow—even if you did inherit your mother's little turned-up nose. Trust me. I should warn you that not everything Fernando describes in his tall tales will come to pass in the real world. Yes, sometimes you tell lies and do stupid things. And who doesn't, sometimes? Every human being is occasionally careless and makes mistakes. The wise learn from their errors, while the foolish blab about them to everyone they come across. Keep in mind that a good reputation is more often due to what one hides than to what one actually does."

Grandfather's words awakened some hope within me. Perhaps when everything was said and done, I wasn't doomed to eternal perdition. I felt a bit better, but not quite as relieved as I would have liked.

Grandfather spoke again. "You may know that I had a brother named Moricz. He had a tragic end, the poor fellow; he froze to death on a mountain plateau in Lhotse, in the Himalayas. You're the spitting image of him. He wasn't exactly a paragon of honesty. He did a number of mad things in his life, but some of his schemes one couldn't help laughing at."

GRANDFATHER HAD NEVER before mentioned Moricz to us. It was from Grandmother we had heard that his young brother had done something scandalous that Grandfather was ashamed of. But now my grandfather opened up and told me that Moricz loved to play poker and had once wound up in a terrible fix. He needed money to pay off a gambling debt. When he realized that no one could lend him such a large sum, he had an inspiration. He put on his best suit, located in a drawer some gold medals that Kaiser Franz Josef himself had pinned upon his grandfather, and attached them to the breast pocket of his suit. Then he got two acquaintances who were street sweepers to follow him to Váci Street, the most elegant of Budapest's pedestrian esplanades, lined with the most exclusive shops of the city. This was in 1911. They took their positions outside Elemér Polgár's Tailoring for Gentlemen, where the nobility of Europe ordered their suits, following the example of the Prince of Wales. The two workers pretended to be making measurements with instruments they were carrying while Moricz took notes. It didn't take too long for Polgár, the master tailor himself, to appear in the doorway, intrigued, and to ask what the workers were doing just outside the entrance to his establishment. With apparent reluctance Moricz informed him that they were from the municipal planning authority. Plans had been made to construct an open toilet for gentlemen just at that location, since for reasons of public health it was deemed necessary to install one somewhere along that lengthy pedestrian walkway. Polgár exclaimed in an anguished voice and with a trembling lower lip, "A pissoir in front of my shop! Completely unthinkable—it would be my ruin. You can certainly understand, young man, that no stinking toilet can be tolerated outside my salon. Think of all my clients, every one of them blue-blooded, of the most genteel nobility; they cannot be exposed to the stink of piss." Moricz tried to calm the tailor, telling him in confidence that the measurement phase was not yet complete. The results of their work would be evaluated before a decision was made about the exact placement of the gentlemen's toilet. Polgár immediately saw his chance. He invited the polite young man from the planning office into his salon for a quiet discussion in private. The master

tailor offered Moricz a snifter of the finest French cognac—
and with it, two thousand imperial crowns if the workers
would move the site a hundred paces or so farther along
the esplanade. As a diligent civil servant, Moricz could not
countenance a bribe—that is, at least not until the amount
was raised to five thousand crowns. A few hours later, after
paying off his assistants, Moricz went home with twenty-five
thousand crowns in his pocket, a fabulous sum at that time.
He had the deep satisfaction on that sunny day of having
diligently provided six lucky proprietors the opportunity of
warding off the planning department's project of installing a
pissoir just outside their shops.

That story about Moricz affected me profoundly, particularly since our grandfather was never one to tell us children
funny stories. But at the same time it reinforced my suspicions that Avraham, Moricz, and I had something ominous
in common, something written in our genes.

The French Physician

AVRAHAM SET OUT to wander. He trudged the dusty
roads that ran this way and that across South America. He
mumbled French words backward for his magic spells and
advised people that in exchange for a trifling sum, grate-
fully accepted, he could work miracles. They listened to
him in disbelief. He tried to overcome their doubts with
good works, promises, and threats. He also sold small
heart-shaped charms inscribed with the names of Catholic patron saints that he claimed would protect the bearers
against sickness, deformities, jealousy, and black magic. But
those he met in the noisy streets lived in great poverty, and

his enterprise yielded him little. In the evenings Avraham would go to sleep hungry most of the time.

THAT ITINERANT EXISTENCE might have been his whole life if the wife of a rich mestizo in Caracas hadn't given birth to a monstrosity with bat wings instead of arms and two horns protruding from its hairy forehead. This happened after she had paid Avraham the fee of fifteen silver pesos to visit her at twilight every day for a week to stroke her abdomen and chant an ancient blessing to protect the child from the evil eye. Her husband had Avraham arrested, charged with heresy, and remanded to the city's Dominican tribunal, feared for the severity of its sentences. The prison warders found that Avraham was circumcised, clear proof of heresy and criminal intent. The prosecutor from the Holy Office found this evidence entirely sufficient to establish the guilt of the accused. He declined to investigate further and called no witnesses.

Avraham listened meekly as the verdict was read out. The court condemned him to death for profaning his baptism by accepting circumcision, eating meat on days when the church prohibited it, working on holidays, observing the Jewish Sabbath and other Jewish holidays, conversing with the devil and serving the powers of hell, and, last but not least, for defrauding Christians by pretending that he could cure illnesses in exchange for payment in silver.

Avraham admitted his crimes and stoically accepted the verdict, even pledging that in hell he would assiduously observe the holy faith and Christian traditions. In return the authorities promised he would not be tortured or locked in chains.

Before dawn on the same morning he was scheduled to burn at the stake, he persuaded a fellow prisoner—a humpback condemned to spend a year in chains for raping two women mourning in a cemetery—to chew the rope off his hands and ankles. He escaped from the prison while the warders were occupied elsewhere, and fled northward, turning up three months later in Louisiana, a colony on the southern coast of North America where most of the population spoke French.

HE GAVE HIS NAME as Armand Seigneur and claimed he had been a celebrated Parisian physician at the court of Louis XIV. Along with his many other accomplishments, he had cured the king's gout. Avraham had a confident air about him. No one questioned his education or asked if he had a license to practice medicine.

Without a penny in his pocket he rented a large house in the center of New Orleans. He had the living room equipped as an office, consultation room, and laboratory. Smoke rose from pots, liquids bubbled, and a faint odor of quicksilver lingered in the air. He put the word about that he was a specialist in unusual afflictions. He declined to treat open sores, for the simple reason that he had an absolute horror of the sight of blood. He won his patients' trust by eloquently describing the brilliant successes of his treatments. His inspiring and fantastical tales of Versailles duped everyone. The royal court physician's reputation spread rapidly throughout New Orleans. The demand for his unusual methods of medical treatment was enormous.

Patients with well-filled purses were welcome at any hour of the day, and he always treated them with consideration and elaborate courtesy. The doctor was not the least interested in taking charity cases. He received the poor with suspicion and dismissed their illness as delusions.

The Mayor's Gout

ONE DAY the mayor arrived for an appointment. Gaspard Gorell was generally despised and known to be thoroughly spineless and corrupt. Everyone in New Orleans knew he regularly took bribes from the slave dealers who for all practical purposes governed that lawless city.

Gorell shrieked in pain. His eyes were inflamed, and he suffered from gout. In quest of relief from his afflictions, he regularly went to the mud baths in the nearby hamlet of Jefferson. But this time nothing had relieved his suffering.

"The last attack was five days ago," he told the doctor, "and I still haven't recovered."

Avraham assured the mayor that he could help and might even be able to cure him, using secrets of alchemy that were all the latest rage in Paris. The mayor had to promise under oath that he would not utter a word about the details of the treatment. Avraham then read out Hebrew incantations and lit a mixture that gave off a copious quantity of smoke. He took a quick astrological reading and announced that the pains were caused by demons that had taken up residence in Gorell's body.

He chalked out a magic circle around the mayor, swung back and forth a censer that stank of camphor, and sought to conjure away the malign ethereal presences. He heaved deep sighs, perspired, muttered disjointed phrases, and obliged the patient to drink half a glass of red wine in which three ounces of crushed poppy seeds had been soaked overnight. Tottering with fatigue, Avraham announced that Egyptian plague demons named Selbebuth and Osirusis had abandoned Gorell's afflicted body. He concluded the session with several Hebrew prayers, pronounced backwards: "*Churab ata janoda, unjehole chelmen mal.*"

"The doctor is so wonderfully eloquent," exclaimed Gorell, amazed by the energy suddenly filling his body. The results were more astonishing than any he had experienced during the five years he had been visiting the mud baths in Jefferson.

AT THEIR NEXT APPOINTMENT Avraham blindfolded Gorell. He advised the mayor that the treatment he was about to carry out was not to be found in any book of medicine. It was a secret intended only for royalty.

"It is based on the study of a hitherto unknown part of our organism," Avraham explained, "and it has to do with the heavenly bodies' influences upon the hidden inner structures of the human being."

He carried out a series of slow movements—he called them magnetic strokes—above the mayor's back. He spoke of rendering the muscular structures amenable to the healing forces of the powers of the planets.

Gorell didn't understand a word of the physician's prattle, and he experienced no alleviation of bodily pain. But he was flattered that he, a man of simple origins, a peasant's son from Bordeaux who in his youth had come to the colony of New France, should receive the same treatment as the crowned heads of Europe. He felt particularly honored.

Acting as if it were a precious gift, Avraham gave the mayor a handwritten note. "These two sentences should be read aloud ten times a day—five in the morning and five at bedtime."

Gorell examined it expectantly. "My name is misspelled," he exclaimed, somewhat indignantly. "There should be two *l*'s in Gorell, not three."

Avraham gave him a piercing look. The mayor realized he had gone a touch too far. "It sounds promising, Doctor," he replied anxiously in an effort to smooth over his blunder.

THE VARIOUS TREATMENTS became more intense. Gorell visited him every day. Exorcism of demons required time and patience. Often the mayor would sit blindfolded for as long as three hours at a time, while Avraham carried out and further elaborated the patterns of strokes, his hands hovering just behind the mayor's back, never actually touching him. They carried on lively conversations during their time together, exchanging views and discussing market conditions while sighing at the unbearable heat and the mad decisions of French politicians that had allowed lands east of the Mississippi to fall into the hands of the British. Avraham praised all of the mayor's opinions, no matter how simpleminded.

Gorell was always in an excellent humor during these sessions, smiling, laughing exuberantly, and enjoying the respite from his burdensome duties. Over time he initiated Avraham in his shady political affairs and even into details of his own financial dealings. He also confided that he was still in mourning for his wife, five years after her death; she had choked on a fishbone. Gorell felt—even though he was still tormented by gout, almost as much as before—that he had made a loyal and trustworthy friend.

BY JULY 1779 the treatments had gone on for more than six months. Avraham told Gorell not to come for a consultation on the following Thursday and counseled him to visit the mud baths instead. He explained that he needed a day to himself to work undisturbed and test a new treatment method. The mayor respected the physician's wishes and spent all of Thursday in Jefferson. He was completely enervated when he came home that evening. He went to bed early, because the mud baths had drained him of all energy.

On Friday morning Gorell went to the doctor's house as usual, but Avraham was not there for the appointment. The house was empty and the doctor had vanished. A general search turned up nothing. Someone claimed to have seen him in the vicinity of the mayor's house shortly after Gorell's departure for Jefferson.

Late that evening Gorell discovered why the physician had left the city so hastily. The scandal was huge. Avraham had gotten into Gorell's house, opened the safe, emptied the secret compartments in the desk, stolen every cent he could find, and made off with the mayor's daughter Claire, a little seventeen-year-old redhead who was as innocent as she was charming.

Gorell pulled out his hair in desperation; he screamed and cursed for all he was worth. The next morning he hired an experienced half-breed bounty hunter to track down the pair. The bounty hunter searched diligently for them for more than a year, but they always kept one step ahead of him, forging their way into more and more inhospitable territory.

Dinner for Two

AVRAHAM AWOKE one morning, three days after they'd spent the last of the stolen money, and discovered Claire was gone. She had abandoned him.

A note inscribed in her childish script lay on the table:

After a year of constant travel, going from one hor-
rible place to another that was even worse, I think I've
learned my lesson about the temptations of the flesh.
But worse than all that for me was the feeling that in
your company I was losing my soul.

Bon voyage!
C.

Avraham was furious. But the truth, the cruel and inevi-table truth, gradually dawned upon him after a number of additional setbacks, misfortunes, and unexpected events: a man cannot live his whole life as an outlaw fleeing justice.

Seized by despair, he lamented his choices in life, bleat-ing like a sheep: His father had never cared for him, his mother was weak and had never bonded with him or offered any affection, and from early childhood his heart had been as heavy as lead. Voltaire hated him and had refused to provide him with any education. Now he would reach the end of his life as an ignorant failure, never having tasted the glories of success, never having conquered the world, with none of the honors due to a man of *buena famiya*.

He thought of Hélène and wondered where she might be. Was she still with her husband? Had they gone their sepa-rate ways? He imagined her just as beautiful as before, or even more beautiful than in fact was humanly possible. She was the most splendid creature he had ever seen. He would willingly give up everything, even die if necessary, just to be in her company again, even if only for five minutes.

AFTER CLAIRE'S RETURN home to New Orleans the hunt for Avraham continued for another couple of months. The bounty hunter's efforts turned up nothing.

Avraham ended his days on this earth a few weeks after Claire abandoned him. He lost his way in the Everglades swamp in Florida and wound up as a tasty dinner for two greedy alligators.

Close at Hand While Still Far Away

THE EUROPEAN CUSTOM that the family name is passed from father to son was completely in line with Moses's stipulation to our ancestor Baruch of how he was to safeguard the great secret. That may be one explanation for the fact that women have always been seen as less important in the Spinoza clan.

For a long time I thought that no girls at all had been born to the family over the course of its thirty-six generations. Of course I was mistaken, even though I learned almost none of their names. When I think back to my childhood, I recall that at least one woman stepped forth from the obscurity of history: Shoshana. Though she was never physically present, my great-uncle's stories always kept her close at hand.

MY GREAT-UNCLE told Sasha and me that few things make such deep impressions as the first stories that touch our hearts. They follow us all our lives and constitute islands of memory that summon us back to them.

Shoshana inhabits one of my islands. The first time my great-uncle spoke of her—explaining that although she was

dead, her spirit still hovered over us and one could communicate with her through a medium—she seemed as real to
me as the air I breathed. I was swept away and enchanted
by her story. I imagined myself living back in those days,
and I often dreamed of her. In the same way, I was influenced by the magical atmosphere my great-uncle cleverly
created with his tales. I was sure that Shoshana could see
me and was smiling at me from her heaven.

WE WERE QUITE YOUNG when my great-uncle told us
of his secret relationship with Shoshana. He had regular
contact with her through a well-known medium at Ad
Astra, the mysterious company of spiritualists he visited
every Wednesday evening at the residence of Adalbert
Nagyszenti, a Freudian psychoanalyst who because of his
bourgeois background and political opinions had been in-
terned for four years in a Stalinist reeducation camp in
northeastern Hungary. Upon his release, Nagyszenti was
banned from his profession. He got by as best he could by
working as the night watchman for a scrap yard in a grimy
workers' suburb.

At first my great-uncle asked to contact his twin daughters who had gone up in smoke through the towering chimneys of Auschwitz. The silence at the first séance of his
life became almost unbearable. Just as he was about to get
up from the table to leave the room in disappointment,
Shoshana turned up and conveyed a greeting to him from
his daughters on the other side. The contact with her was of
great significance in my great-uncle's life.

Tears appeared in his eyes whenever he spoke of
Shoshana. His face shone with delight at the hidden truths
she reported from the spirit world, stories that he often
shared with us.

But did I ever see him express any doubt about the messages he received from her? I cannot remember any. Perhaps I was blind to it.

THROUGH SHOSHANA my great-uncle had access to stories that exist in the obscurity beneath what we call history. They were never recorded in books. Throughout all time there have existed persons with access to the pure and undistorted truth, persons who knew things that no one else did. People who remembered forgotten miracles. Individuals who bore our suffering on their shoulders. As a child, I was convinced that Fernando was such a man.

A Young Woman's Education

IN HIS CAPACITY as guardian of the Spinoza children, Voltaire put five-year-old Nicolas into a convent school and fourteen-year-old Avraham into a boarding school reputed for its strict discipline and locked gates. Shoshana alone was allowed to stay with him at his château in Ferney.

The philosopher set her difficult tasks and was very demanding. He considered it his duty to give the girl the care and education normally provided only to boys. Ten hours a day, every day of the year except her birthday, various tutors instructed her patiently in Latin, Greek, philosophy, literature, and mathematics.

VOLTAIRE DEVOTED a great deal of his own time to Shoshana. He patiently led her into the labyrinthine ways of human knowledge about the universe and creation. He oriented her in the principal schools of philosophy. From time to time he would spend several hours lecturing on the great new advances in human knowledge. He spoke to her of Émilie du Châtelet and her speculations about the physical world. From time to time he would provide commentaries on a work by Plato or a passage in Virgil. One day a week he set exercises for her in the art of constructing elegant essays and letters. He taught her how to coax beautiful convoluted French prose from her pen. He assigned her topics for oral presentation and insisted on elegant polished speech. He monitored her use of grammar and found it satisfactory. He lectured on history and the art of medicine. Voltaire had the imposing appearance and piercing gaze of an eagle, and she followed the artful sweep of his intellect with a heart hammering with joy.

THE PHILOSOPHER NOTED in his diary: "Educating a person is collaborating with the forces of creation, and he who instructs another undertakes anew the creation of the world."

ON THE THRESHOLD of adolescence Shoshana was drafting original essays—all still available in the Voltaire archives in the Bibliothèque Nationale de France in Paris—on themes such as Pythagoras as a politician, Plato's thoughts on the state, the culture of the Mayan Indians before the Spanish conquest of Central America, the evolution of culture in France, and Francis of Assisi's conversations with birds.

She solved advanced problems in mathematics and read with fascination Newton's *Principia* on the heavenly bodies and their gravitational properties.

Grammar and syntax fascinated her. She spoke five languages fluently, and already as a young teenager she was translating Greek drama into French.

Voltaire criticized a number of the choices in her French version of Sophocles's *Antigone*, but he arranged nevertheless for its premiere at the Théâtre-Français. The much-admired actress Thelma delivered an interpretation fit for the ages, under the direction of the celebrated Italian Raimondo di Vespucci. The public was ecstatic.

THE PHILOSOPHER wrote to Madame Spinoza that her daughter, who had just turned sixteen, "has a great talent; her Latin would have done credit to Cicero and her Greek would have sounded elegant at the Areopagus. My only disappointment is that she is of the feminine gender."

Émilie and Science

SHOSHANA'S INTEREST in translating Greek drama evaporated one day, a development as sudden as it was unexpected. She began to delve into the profundities of challenging works of great men of science. She struggled for all of one spring with Newton's second treatise on the laws of thermodynamics. She studied, did research, and took notes, and her conclusions differed from those of the Englishman. Her experiments established that the energy of an object in motion is proportional to its mass and a squared function of its speed. That finding contradicted Newton's thesis and overturned fundamental principles long accepted by the scientific establishment.

SEVERAL INFLUENCES stimulated Shoshana's interest in the natural sciences. Émilie du Châtelet was principal among them. Voltaire's comments about that renowned researcher opened new prospects for her.

She heard the warmth in Voltaire's voice when he spoke of Émilie, who had been his lover for years. Émilie's face and figure remained vivid to him, many years after her death. For him she was the embodiment of feminine virtue and intelligence. He was clearly still deeply grieved that death, ever unexpected death, had taken Émilie from him just as their life together had reached resplendent heights of beauty and happiness.

He spoke of Émilie's beauty and sensuality, her trim waist and thrusting breasts, and her towering achievements as France's first female mathematician, physicist, and researcher.

Shoshana became ever more deeply fascinated by Voltaire's picture of Émilie. She wanted to know everything about her. She brought up Émilie's name at every opportunity, even though she felt an unhappy pang of jealousy whenever Voltaire spoke of her. She wondered, *What does he see in her that I don't have?*

SHOSHANA IMAGINED SAYING, *You are my love and I am the one whom you should love, throughout all eternity.*

Her nineteenth birthday came and went, and she was no longer a child. Voices seemed to speak to her, and at times she was struck by the odd feeling that somewhere in her brain there was a cavity, a hollow that had to be filled, filled with a ferocious passion that would drive her to take Voltaire in her arms, kiss him, and tell him, *I love you, I need you.* She decided to fill that empty spot in her brain with Émilie. She would take on all her characteristics, transform herself from Shoshana into Émilie, replace her and become Voltaire's only woman.

Sometimes her conscience chided her for wanting to become another person. It was almost as if she was contemplating a kind of suicide. At other times she no longer knew who she was. She often rebuked herself, but she could not control her heart. She felt a deep longing every day, every hour to become Voltaire's beloved.

In the Shade of the Pear Tree

VOLTAIRE WATCHED with delight as his ward sat in the shade of a one-hundred-and-fifty-year-old pear tree next to his château in Ferney near the border with Switzerland and studied the principles of thermodynamics. The early summer months of 1768 were a time of great happiness in his life. With the purchase of the château came a title of nobility. Count Voltaire, who by then had long been free from trying disputes, had put behind him all the bitter conflicts of his earlier life. He had settled in a quiet corner of France. In his ardor to promote tolerance and the Enlightenment he had written eighteen new articles for the revised fifth edition of the *Pocket Lexicon of Philosophy*, which by then was so bulky that only an impressively capacious pocket could accommodate it. He was famous and respected, in excellent health, carefree and happy. His fortune took care of itself. Sometimes at night he would awake with a thrill of happiness. He had achieved all of his dreams. Nothing could disturb his peace and quiet.

ON THAT MIDSUMMER EVENING Voltaire went out into the garden, picked a bouquet of flowers, and presented it to Shoshana. He arranged for a delicate dish of kidney sauté for dinner, accompanied by a superb wine from the region, to celebrate the fact that his pupil had put the final touches on her treatise on objects in motion. They clinked the polished crystal wineglasses together, and he provided yet another proof of his great benevolence. He promised to contact the president of the Académie Royale des Sciences in Paris, the distinguished Professor Jean-Baptiste Ferry, to have Shoshana's work be published and debated at the annual meeting of the association of physicists in the fall.

Voltaire told Shoshana that before contacting Professor Ferry he wanted to show his support by correcting certain points that seemed a trifle weak and strengthening the arguments for others. He added immediately that he had no intention of questioning or weakening her incisive reasoning; the treatise was unique. But a written text could always be tweaked and somewhat improved.

Shoshana expressed her deep gratitude, but she heeded an inner voice that admonished her to decline, politely but firmly, Voltaire's offer of a critical edit. She was absolutely certain of her thesis; she knew that her observations and conclusions were indisputable. And besides, it was her own work; she did not want anyone else to modify it. She did not dare to affront her benefactor by refusing his help, so she changed the subject instead and asked a question about Émilie.

Voltaire fell into melancholy as he spoke of his deceased life partner. His eyes fixed upon something invisible and impossibly far away. After all those years he could still hear Émilie's voice whispering in his ear. Shoshana listened attentively, trying to identify any detail, however insignificant, that might refer to her, to Shoshana.

The Breath of the Night

IN BED that night Shoshana felt the warm breath of the bright evening wafting through the wide-open windows and across her skin. That soft touch combined with the languorous effect of the velvety smooth red wine and aroused a tingling ecstasy in her young body, a feeling beyond all words and understanding, something different from anything she had ever experienced before.

The warm currents of her yearning sensuality were dangerous, she knew, and they could lead to madness. Even so, she slowly reached up and rubbed her left nipple with her fingertips. She shivered with pleasure and felt her skin prickle up in gooseflesh. The sensation of pleasure was profound. She shut her eyes and imagined Voltaire's hands, knowing, wonderful, and perfect as they caressed her naked body. She trembled with desire.

Shoshana knew that sinners were certain to wind up in hell. Cardinal Carlos Fellici in Geneva had often told her so. But she also knew from the great philosopher himself that everyone regardless of rank or sex or age had a right to happiness.

For that reason she had no misgivings or pangs of conscience. She abandoned her body to its will to act and seek, to find and take its desire. She was obsessed with Voltaire's manly strength, his integrity, his calm superiority, his greatness of spirit. She wanted to give up her arms and the sweetness of her womanhood to the man she loved with all her heart.

SHOSHANA ROSE from her bed, silently made her way to Voltaire's bedroom, carefully opened the door, and watched him for a long moment. Then she shed her nightgown, crept into his bed, and caressed his face.

Voltaire awoke with a start. He wasn't surprised to find Soshana in his bed. He understood immediately what she wanted. He turned his searching gaze upon her. She was nineteen and a half. Her body was thin, almost scrawny, and her breasts were still those of a young girl. She was not particularly handsome. But beauty was not the issue here; the problem was something else. His body was not responding. Tenderly he informed her he was an elderly and ailing man, too old for such pleasures. His smile was extremely gentle and apologetic.

"My child," he said, and carefully enfolded her in his arms, "you are at the fortunate age at which one makes love. We must find the right man with whom you can share those all-too-transitory moments."

She was devastated that he had refused her. She seized his hands, pressed them against her face, and began to weep.

At Home in Paris

THE NEXT MORNING Voltaire instructed his secretary, Wagnière, to hire a carriage for a trip to Paris, and the philosopher told Shoshana to pack her belongings into two large trunks. They left Ferney at lunchtime and took the road via Nantua and Dijon. They changed horses four times. Once they were obliged to wait for a couple of hours outside Troyes because an axle had broken.

Neither Voltaire nor Shoshana spoke a word during the entire journey of five days. Each found it painful to sit in silence hearing only the other's breathing, but they preferred that to carrying on a conversation as if nothing had happened.

MADAME SPINOZA was surprised by the knocking on the front door of her apartment near the Palais Royal. She was expecting no callers. The clock had already struck four, but she was still wearing a colorful morning robe of crepe de chine. The sight of Voltaire and Shoshana standing in her entry was an unwelcome and entirely unexpected surprise. Her habit was to avoid even the slightest exertion in life, and she detested being disturbed in her comfortable existence.

Voltaire preferred to speak with her in private. He told Shoshana to leave them, and after the door closed behind her he briefly summarized the situation. In his opinion, he stressed, it was no longer healthy for the young woman to be living with him. He regarded Madame Spinoza sternly, for he knew well how indifferent she had always been to her daughter; he insisted that he considered it best for Shoshana to move back home.

Voltaire's words left Madame Spinoza completely at a loss. She had never had the least desire to take charge of her daughter. Shoshana had always seemed a stranger to her. Even a few days under the same roof with her daughter would render her life unbearable. But she dared not oppose Voltaire.

"But of course," she answered with a friendly smile, carefully concealing the effect upon her of the philosopher's announcement.

The first quarrel between mother and daughter broke out the very next morning. "Shoshana, I cannot bear all of this!" Madame Spinoza shrieked in her bitterest tone. The day had hardly begun when her daughter had locked herself in the bathroom and huddled there, weeping interminably. Her mother had no idea what to do: she felt helpless and entirely unprepared. She was convinced that she would fall into a nervous collapse if the child's hysterical weeping continued. Things got no better when Shoshana at last left the bathroom several hours later. She insisted her mother leave her in peace and declared that being cooped up with her mother was like going to jail.

Over the following days Madame Spinoza repeatedly berated Shoshana for destroying her life. In answer her daughter screamed that she didn't have a bit of sympathy or motherly feeling in her pampered body. New and futile conflicts between the two women erupted constantly, obliging the good-hearted old manservant Gilbert to intervene as a peacemaker. He admonished both mother and daughter and called on them to demonstrate a modicum of mutual goodwill so as to make their lives together more bearable.

GILBERT ENTREATED Madame Spinoza to write to Voltaire to ask for his help in resolving their difficulties. She accepted his suggestion but was uncertain how to word the letter. In response, the elderly servant dictated the text to her. He urged her first and foremost to remind the philosopher to send Shoshana's treatise to the president of the Académie Royale des Sciences. That would certainly put the young lady in a better mood and keep her from continuing to weep for days on end and interrupting her tears only with wrathful tantrums. He told her to emphasize that a disciplined regime of scientific inquiry was likely to rein in Shoshana's wild nerves.

The Debate

VOLTAIRE REACTED PROMPTLY, as always. He sent Shoshana's work to the Académie Royale des Sciences with an effusive letter of recommendation.

The president of the academy, Jean-Baptiste Ferry, had great respect for Voltaire. He immediately sat down with the treatise. He read it with a critical but friendly eye, and his jaw dropped in astonishment as he absorbed the first few pages. He had never before seen such a bold, independent, and comprehensive piece of work. He wished that a man of mature age had written it. That would have certainly made it easier for everyone to accept the outcomes of those empirical experiments and the author's decisively worded conclusions. He dreaded the immense controversy that this thesis was certain to generate. Its criticism of Newton's work was decisive and devastating. Ferry had no doubt that the young woman behind the work was a conscientious and truthful researcher. He had a distinct impression that she could well be correct in her analysis. Her paper might well demolish one of the basic principles of physics and provoke the most passionate scientific clash of the century. For a moment he was tempted to toss the pages into the fireplace and let the flames consume them. He resisted, as a respectable scientist was bound to do. But he knew that the impulse to burn that piece of work would also tempt a number of his colleagues. The advisory committee of the academy would certainly do everything possible to prevent publication of the work and silence the young woman. If it succeeded, future generations might well condemn him for all time for suppressing the greatest discovery of the century. After quickly weighing the pros and cons, he decided to bypass the committee and send the work directly for publication.

THE WORK was printed in early fall under the title *A Treatise on the Energy of Objects in Motion by S. Spinoza.* The author's sex and age were carefully withheld from the four leading physicists invited to discuss the treatise at the Palais du Louvre in the elegant quarters of the Académie Royale des Sciences in a session to be chaired by its president, Jean-Baptiste Ferry.

In the crowded room were seated a number of journalists, many physicists, the entire faculty of natural sciences from the Sorbonne, two senior representatives of the court, and, as guest of honor, d'Alembert, the permanent secretary of the Académie Française. Voltaire escorted Shoshana.

President Ferry made the opening remarks. There were looks of astonishment on many faces when with a politeness that verged upon exaggeration he presented the author of the first treatise to be debated during the annual general meeting of the Royal Society of Physicists.

"Shoshana Spinoza, *ahem* . . ."

Shoshana stood up. Voltaire admonished her in a whisper to pay attention to her posture. A murmur ran through the audience. A woman? No one had expected this. And so young! Beyond all comparison, the youngest person who had ever attended a meeting in the salon of the academy. The four physicists on the podium could not believe their eyes.

Voltaire knew that many of those older scientists, blinded by prejudice and deep-seated misogyny, could not conceive of the notion of female physicists. He remembered the withering reception accorded to Émilie in her day. He stood up. Addressing President Ferry, he respectfully stressed the vital importance of impartiality and open minds as the physicists of France evaluated advances in scientific knowledge.

The suspicious expressions on the faces of the four physicists made it immediately clear to Shoshana that they would stubbornly resist her findings. The distinguished gentlemen would seize upon any pretext to dismiss her work because she was young and female. And she lost no time in providing them with a good one.

Baptiste de Gendre was the most senior of the four, and it was his privilege to begin the examination of Shoshana. Without bothering with niceties, he started by asking the young woman to stand and swear before Almighty God that she herself had carried out all the calculations, that she had written the treatise herself, and that Voltaire was not the author.

The great philosopher was outraged. He protested immediately and declared with great force that such insinuations had no place in serious scientific debate. President Ferry dismissed his comments.

Shoshana's expression made it plain how demeaning she considered the request. Her face lost color and she dropped her gaze. She clearly felt uncomfortable looking Baptiste de Gendre in the eye. Everyone in the hall tensely awaited her answer. It seemed an eternity before she began to speak.

"Unfortunately, I must decline," she replied in a low voice. "This is a matter of conscience for me." She explained that she felt called to devote her life to the study of the mysteries of nature; she wished to apply scientific methods, search out truths, and understand the workings of the world.

"The greatest attribute of a researcher is the willingness to question," she said. "This means not falling prey to the prejudices and pet theories of the day. For that reason I am skeptical of sweeping explanations of the world, models that answer all questions and solve all problems. We should be willing to challenge them."

She paused for a moment and looked around the hall.

"Scientific inquiry cannot prosper when an unknown God is accorded unchallenged dominion over the world. I reject the concept of God as a king of kings asserting a predominant role in the realm of science. For me, God is only a word, and I cannot swear to something in which I do not believe."

Baptiste de Gendre clutched his hands to his head and exclaimed, "No human being, and certainly no serious man of science, can deny the existence of nature's Creator—"

Shoshana did not let him elaborate; she immediately cut him off. "No man of science can be so blind and witless as to assert that our knowledge of God is based on science."

Pierre Delpech, author of important articles explaining magnetism, spoke up. "Mademoiselle Spinoza is presumptuous enough to believe that she can correct Newton's theory of energy. That may be a sign of youthful error and entirely fallacious reasoning. But denying the existence of God is a crime. She should be punished."

Alain Gaillard, the youngest of the four physicists, seemed to lose control completely. He stood up, jabbed his index finger at Shoshana, and shouted angrily that the Jewess was calling into question the very basis of the organization of society as well as the king's sovereign power, and she should be locked away in the Bastille for it. Regaining his calm somewhat but nevertheless addressing her in an insulting tone, he declared that the individual standing before the company of physicists was no man of science; she was a Jewish witch.

The other three physicists exchanged amused glances. Spontaneous applause broke out in the hall and there were a few scattered whistles. Seething with anger, Voltaire shook his head.

Gaillard's words had not yet sunk in entirely, but Shoshana knew that the examination was finished. She heard an inner voice saying, *You will never be admitted to the world of science.* She realized that she was being judged according to rules made by elderly men and had been condemned in advance— for being young, for being female, and for being a Jew, but also and especially because she had dared to question conventional wisdom. She felt helpless, and everything seemed pointless. She suddenly understood, even though just a few moments earlier she had imagined herself upon the threshold of a new life, that the most rational thing she could do was give up. It stung her deeply to see the self-satisfied expressions and glaring faces of the four physicists. Their thoughtless trampling of her soul horrified her. A slap in the face would have caused less pain. She turned away to shield herself.

President Ferry knew that upon an earlier occasion Gaillard had let slip certain comments that betrayed a deep dislike for Jews. Ferry said he did not wish to criticize his colleague, but Professor Gaillard was perhaps a touch too demonstrative in his behavior. He was very careful to maintain a neutral tone. Like all other men of standing, he knew how important it was to maintain control of a meeting. In order to keep the assembly from descending into chaos, he declared, entirely on his own initiative and without asking for the agreement of the four physicists, that Shoshana Spinoza's treatise could in no circumstances be approved by the academy. He gave no rationale for his decision.

Jubilation broke out in the audience. The four physicists applauded long and hard. Only a few of the younger students expressed displeasure at Ferry's conclusion. D'Alembert sat in his place of honor, looking extremely concerned.

In the Faubourg Saint-Germain

SHOSHANA AND VOLTAIRE immediately left the hall. They began to walk aimlessly through the galleries of the Louvre. Shoshana felt a shudder rack her body. She stopped short, closed her eyes, and gasped for air.

Her mother had arranged for a modest reception in her apartment and invited a number of guests to celebrate her daughter's day of triumph. Shoshana could not face the prospect of seeing all those people. She was despondent. So she told Voltaire she wanted to take a carriage to his residence in the rue Faubourg Saint-Germain.

UPON THEIR ARRIVAL there, Voltaire suggested a glass of wine and did what he could to make her feel better. He acknowledged that perhaps it had been naïve of him to suppose that those physicists of the old school would embrace her conclusions. The very existence of the results of her research threatened their understanding of the physical world and its fundamental principles. Moreover, the language of her treatise was aesthetically very pleasing, certainly something not appreciated by those with no ear for the musicality of the French language. Voltaire declared that he was convinced, however, that he had judged the work correctly. For that reason he intended to send it to an Italian professor of physics at the University of Bologna, a place more open to ideas and therefore more propitious to the discussion of new concepts.

Shoshana was glad to have his support. She felt an eerie presence seeping into the room, and the wine had set her blood racing. She rose and approached Voltaire where he sat comfortably on his chaise longue. She brought her bosom within inches of his face, unhooked her bodice, pulled down her camisole, and exposed her small breasts. His face lit with surprise and desire at the sight of them. He stared, enchanted, as they trembled with anticipation. He inhaled the intoxicating, alluring fragrance of her youth. His heart began pounding and his long-somnolent manhood slowly but surely began to awaken. He was surprised, for he had thought himself no longer capable of movement in those nether regions. He sensed that he would be able to deliver the pleasure her body was longing for. Ever so carefully, he began to caress her breasts. He brushed her lips and then her neck, and his hand glided over her hips. He bent forward and closed his lips about her left nipple, kissed it, and sucked at it. Few teeth remained in his mouth; he was as gentle as an infant. She thrilled to the touch of his gums upon her breast and felt the warm wetness welling up in her sex. He pulled her down upon the chaise, removed her dress, and carefully took his position on top of her. His face convulsed, he moaned, he pushed his penis into her and thrust it deep. "Careful!" he said, more to himself than to her, because this was what she wanted more than anything in the world. For a few fleeting moments their bodies rocked slowly back and forth.

Once they had possessed each other, she was the most deliriously happy woman in the world. Voltaire helped her lace her dress once more and then sent her home in a carriage to her mother.

No Reply

THE NEXT MORNING a letter from the great philosopher was delivered to Shoshana at their residence. She scanned it with her heart in her mouth. Voltaire wrote that he was appalled by what had happened. He regretted his own weakness and was ashamed he had allowed burning desire to confuse his emotions and overcome his reason. Although the thoughtless deed had lasted but a few moments, it was a most unfortunate occurrence. He apologized for his unbecoming behavior; rutting like a wild animal was completely inappropriate conduct for a man of his age and position. He proposed they should mutually agree to forget the whole matter and refrain for the time being from any contact with each other.

Shoshana became distraught. She read the letter at least ten times but refused to accept its message. She took to her bed and tried to relive the brief joy she had experienced the previous day in Voltaire's arms. She caressed her breasts and rubbed the cleft between her legs, rousing herself into a hot sweat. Her body shook. She could not tell if she was quivering with erotic ecstasy or with an agony of self-loathing.

After a while she seated herself before her mirror. She looked deeply into the face reflected there and saw a total stranger. She had never seen that face before, and it frightened her. The expression in its eyes was anguished, confused, and deeply distressed. That could not be her own face; it had to belong to someone else, to some unknown woman. She desperately desired to free herself from the face of that unhappy stranger. Finding it impossible to wish away that strange woman, Shoshana smashed the mirror.

SHOSHANA SLEPT for only a couple of hours, then collected herself sufficiently to draft a frantic letter to Voltaire. She begged him to receive her. She emphatically refused to separate herself from the very being who most inflamed her passions.

The letter came back an hour later, unopened.

Over the course of the following two weeks she sent eighteen letters to the philosopher. Each consisted of only three words: *I love Thee.*

All were returned. Voltaire did not read a single one.

Frozen Dreams

IT WAS UNBEARABLY HUMILIATING for Shoshana to see the man she loved turn his back on her. She sank into a deep depression, convinced that her life was completely meaningless. She lost all appetite and subsisted on nothing but tea. She grew increasingly thin and feeble. Her cheeks were hollow and her eyes were sunken.

GILBERT, THEIR ELDERLY SERVANT, could see by Shoshana's sorrowful face that the failure of her relationship with Voltaire had devastated her. He tried to console her. He assured her she had no better friend than the great philosopher. Voltaire was wise, a man of great experience; he had seen almost everything there was to see; he could give her excellent advice. But, after all, he was seventy-two years old. Shoshana should be content to have a father such as he, but no woman in her right senses could imagine that Voltaire as a lover. It was useless to dream of him. Gilbert, a Breton who had grown up on the Atlantic coast, likened it to an attempt to swim into breaking waves that constantly tossed one back against the rocky crags of the coast. These were words of wisdom, but Shoshana refused to heed them.

THE BRIGHT LIGHT of autumn flooded into Shoshana's room, but she felt that she had entered a shadow world.

She lacked the will to live. She wished simply to wither and die.

In November she discovered that she was pregnant.

Gilbert counseled Madame Spinoza to feed her daughter apple sections in sugar syrup to keep her alive. She fed Shoshana with a spoon, but Shoshana vomited it all up.

That December was unusually cold. Large snowflakes drifted down from the skies, and the streets of Paris were covered with icy slush. The winter weather spoke to Shoshana of frozen dreams and hopelessness.

On Christmas evening she bled copiously and miscarried the child. She burned with fever. Her mother bathed her sweat-soaked brow with damp towels. In her fevered delirium Shoshana shrieked Voltaire's name. Their elderly family physician, Dr. Villancourt, examined her and reported that there was nothing he could do, for she had essentially lost her will to live. Once her fever subsided, she sank again into indescribable depths of melancholy. Filled with loathing for everyone and everything, she said not a word for five weeks.

One early January morning while her mother was away visiting a milliner and trying on a new hat, Shoshana felt a freezing chill invade her body. She was stiff, and it took her a long time to get out of bed. All of her strength seemed to have ebbed away.

Slowly and with great care she twisted her sheet into a thick noose. She put on a red dress, stepped up onto a stool, twisted the sheet around a hook in a beam, and put her head through the noose. She straightened up for a moment as if she intended to say something, but then she drew the noose tight and kicked away the stool. A violent shudder went through her wasted body.

Bologna and the Science of Physics

AS DARKNESS FELL in January 1772, three days after Shoshana's death, the city of Bologna set off fireworks at the university. Perhaps they were not as spectacular as the legendary fireworks of forty years earlier in celebration of the appointment of Laura Bassi as the first female professor at Europe's most ancient seat of learning. But it was nevertheless a relatively impressive pyrotechnic display.

Hundreds of rockets shot into the skies; their explosions sketched out brilliant white lilies against the darkness of the firmament, all in celebration of the formal acceptance of Shoshana's thesis and her posthumous election as a member of the Academy of Sciences of Bologna.

Voltaire stood in the immense crowd of people assembled to watch the spectacle and cheer. His eyes filled with tears as he watched the shower of burning stars.

THE SCIENCE OF PHYSICS was all the rage during the nineteenth century. Royalty followed progress in the physical sciences, the growing bourgeoisie interested itself in the new advances, and newspapers profiled the leading physicists—Ampère, Faraday, Ohm, Volta—as the great heroes of the age. Anyone who made a significant discovery automatically had his name inscribed in the public mind when a unit of measure was named after him. In contrast, the name of Shoshana Spinoza disappeared from memory.

POSSIBLY THE GREATEST BREAKTHROUGH in physics occurred in 1905 when a young man named Albert Einstein, an employee of the patent office in Bern, published four articles in the German physics journal *Annalen der Physik.* He was immediately hailed by scientists across the world. Now there would be no turning back. The world would never be the same.

Einstein's fourth article is of special interest for the story of Shoshana. It deals with the relation between mass and energy and contains the famous formula $E=mc^2$ (in which E stands for energy, m for mass, and c for the speed of light). His formula confirmed that Shoshana's calculations were correct and her theory was valid.

Nicolas

A FEW HOURS before Nicolas drew his first breath, Shoshana's father gave her a red dress. It was her birthday present, for fate in its mysterious fashion had decided to bring her little brother into the world on the very day that she turned five.

She had dreamed of such a dress for months, ever since her mother had taken her to the Théâtre-Français to see Jean Racine's classic tragedy *Phèdre.* Madame Spinoza wanted to interest her daughter in the classics of Greek theater. She explained that Racine's story was based on Greek mythology, and he had borrowed freely from his antique precursor Euripides, whose attitude was completely different and whose style was much more controlled. But Shoshana was very young, and she understood almost nothing of the play about the queen who falls in love with the wrong man and finally chooses to take her own life. Throughout the entire performance the child had eyes for nothing but the red dress the acclaimed actress Thelma was wearing to play the title role. Shoshana dreamed that one day she, too, would have a glorious dress like that one and it would transform her into a queen.

The five-year-old was enormously excited by the birthday gift from her father and wanted to show it to her mother. Madame Spinoza was in her bedroom behind closed doors that day, and the room was barred to her daughter. Shoshana stood outside and tried to catch a glimpse of her mother; but the door was quickly shut each time Dr. Villancourt, the family's jovial physician, or any of the strange women with him entered or left the bedchamber.

The girl heard sobs, shrieks, cries, and groans behind the door. She asked who was crying. "Go away!" replied her father as he paced back and forth in the hall. Only Gilbert, the family servant, had a kind word to spare for Shoshana. He explained that her mama was about to have a new baby and the strangers in the house were busy helping her.

Suddenly they heard a scream: *"Madre mía, madre mía!"* The wailing became even louder. Shoshana was terrified when she realized that it was her mother making those sounds.

A few minutes later she was called into the bedchamber. The strange women were moving about the room, smiling. The proud father laughed and held up the newborn. At the first glimpse of the child's face, they were struck with astonishment.

"Your son," Hector said, turning toward the bed where his wife lay pale and still, "is a true Spinoza. Look at his incredibly large nose. He's so beautiful; he's the most perfect boy child imaginable."

NICOLAS WAS THE ONLY ONE of the siblings with a talent for music. Even when he was a small boy his beautiful singing voice astonished his family. At the age of five, shortly after the sudden death of their father, he was allowed to enter the boarding school for choirboys at the Église Saint-Sulpice in the Franciscan monastery in Ferney, close to Voltaire's château.

His mother was not entirely pleased that her son the Jewish boy *de buena famiya* was required to spend all his time in church, from the early-morning service of matins to evening vespers, dressed in a choir robe and wearing a four-cornered black cap.

Voltaire reassured her. "The boy has a gift for music, and we should do everything possible to encourage it. In addition, it will do him no harm to be exposed to the Christian faith. It may even prove useful eventually and provide him access to the better sort of society. Madame, you know how things are in this country. One must not hide one's lamp beneath a bushel. If we were living in India I would tell Nicolas to hold a cow by the tail. Here in France he picks up a crucifix. We two have no greater wish than to see him join the ranks of noble thinkers, those who distinguish themselves with their intelligence, insight, and tolerance. The ultimate goal of all culture is personal development."

To Nicolas, Voltaire spoke directly and with no particular allowance for the boy's tender age. "Take me as your model, not your mother. This is for your own good. You'll have to give up your Jewish identity. This will improve your prospects in life, and you'll be better accepted by others. You will see: One day you'll be a highly respected philosopher."

In the Cloister

AS A GENERAL RULE the ecclesiastical school of the Saint-Sulpice cloister never accepted Jewish pupils. It was only with the greatest reluctance that Abbot Hugo Montell made an exception and arranged for a place for Nicolas after he received a letter from Cardinal of Geneva Monseigneur Carlos Fellici communicating His Eminence's strong desire that the cloister school instruct Voltaire's ward in the true Christian faith. No one dared to say so openly, but neither the school's teachers nor the parents were pleased to have a Jewish boy in that stringent Catholic boarding school.

NICOLAS REMEMBERED all his life the terror of his arrival at the cloister. He felt a clutch of fear as he descended from the carriage with Voltaire's servant and caught sight of the immense main building. Ominous monks stood sternly watching him as he waited next to the window in the refectory. Voltaire's description of their goodness and sympathy had led him to expect a completely different reception.

The immensely stout and bald Abbot Montell received them and inspected him with curiosity and distinct distaste. Nicolas sat as if nailed to the chair. He tried to appear both pleased and resolute, all the while yearning for his sister, Shosana, always the one sure refuge in his existence. He could scarcely hold back his tears. He sensed very clearly how unwelcome he was at the church school.

AT THE CLOSE of his second day of classes, Nicolas sat daydreaming and failed to appear sufficiently attentive to the teacher, who had been watching him closely.

"I'm very pleased with all of you," the teacher said. "That is, all except one of you. Only one boy failed to pay attention to the fascinating account of the life of Jesus I read to you. One boy sat there and fidgeted the whole time, chewing his nails. A single young man has brought shame upon the entire class." He made a dramatic pause. Nicolas wondered who the culprit could have been. "You, Nicolas Spinoza, our new Jewish pupil, you behaved in a despicable manner. I've never seen anyone so distracted, anyone who showed such a lack of respect as you have for the suffering of Jesus. Your behavior is, in a word, unforgiveable, and I understand why none of the other boys wants to have anything to do with you." The teacher pursed his lips. All of the other boys looked at Nicolas in disgust.

THE NEXT DAY he was humiliated in the school yard by an older boy who pretended to shake hands with him but clenched his hand so hard that he forced Nicolas to his knees. He received a violent kick in the stomach as a further reminder of the public shaming inflicted upon him. Nicolas rose painfully and stood there unsteadily with tears running down his cheeks. The older boy, the undisputed leader of the choirboys, spat in his face, prompting general glee among all the boys.

For years the other choirboys harassed Nicolas. He was always isolated, he had no friends at the cloister, and no one intervened to stop the constant disparaging comments of the monks and the other boys. Sometimes Nicolas hated his Jewishness because it made others despise him.

A Long, Wandering Journey

AT THE AGE OF THIRTEEN, when Nicolas entered puberty and hair began to appear on his cheeks, he was summarily expelled, in accordance with the rules of the boarding school of the Église Saint-Sulpice.

He felt humiliated and had no idea where to turn. Shoshana had moved out of Voltaire's residence—he knew that from her letters—and he had no desire to live alone in the philosopher's house. Sobbing, he picked up his bundle of possessions and began to trudge through the November chill toward Paris.

He wandered through a desolate landscape. Poverty-stricken villages and farms were scattered about the forests. Only along the rivers did the land appear fertile. Settlements were small and widely dispersed. He saw a number of cows apparently untended along the riverbanks. There was drizzling rain almost every day. He suffered from the cold and found it hard to distinguish the roads. He could see he was on his way to getting lost. Sometimes he longed for the cloister's ascetic comforts, for the strict but assured daily routine, for the music of the organ in the church. Those feelings of nostalgia never lasted long.

Day followed day, and he soon established a rhythm for his journey. During the morning hours it was easy to cover distances, for he was fresh and could lose himself in his fantasies. Later, as the day progressed, his thoughts became disconnected, and he could no longer think straight. Fatigue set in and his feet began to ache. Late in the evenings he would try to find some sheltering grove where he could sleep.

He got to Paris toward the end of December. He saw the silhouettes of the towers of Notre Dame far away in the distance. He put down his bundle and stood motionless for a time, leaning against a tree. He felt terribly homesick.

NICOLAS WOULD NEVER FORGET the sight that greeted him when he took off his shoes upon arriving at his mother's apartment. The soles of his feet were black. The stain was deeply embedded in his skin and impossible to wash away. The bottoms of his feet had dried and cracked, and the stink of them was so terrible that even the lice stayed away. He looked in the mirror. During the four weeks it had taken him to walk to Paris he had lost twenty-five pounds. He was shocked by the hardened face staring back at him from the mirror. He realized that the hard trek had made a new person of him.

He hadn't seen his mother for many years. She had aged prematurely and was sunk in gray melancholy. He noticed the signs, so unusual for an Arditti, of despair and listlessness. She had become an exhausted old woman, unable to take her son in. Shoshana was living there and was already more than their mother could handle. Madame Spinoza made no effort to pretend she was pleased to see her son.

While Nicolas was taking a warm bath, she wrote to Philippe Charrier, formerly a friend of her husband and now the rector of the Lycée Louis-le-Grand, one of the country's best preparatory schools. She explained that Shoshana had lost her mind and required constant attention. She was overwhelmed by the task. She could not possibly house Nicolas as well. She entreated Charrier to take charge of Nicolas, to give him hope and inspire him with sensible counsel.

She handed the letter to Nicolas and told him he would have to leave. She kissed his cheek and reminded him that he was *de buena famiya*.

Nicolas was downcast and discouraged from his long journey. He stood in the hall and wished that fate had been kinder to him. He wanted to stay close to his mother and sister, but once again he was forced to endure separation from his family. He wasn't even permitted to speak to Shoshana. He took a deep breath and went out to the waiting coach, not knowing that he had just seen his mother for the last time.

Warm Memories

PHILIPPE CHARRIER greeted Nicolas as if he were an old friend. Nothing in his warm voice betrayed the fact that they had never met. He accompanied the boy through several rooms. In the innermost sanctum they settled at a table covered with a snow-white linen tablecloth, and Charrier offered him some heavenly fragrant spice bread. An old-fashioned writing desk with a worn leather blotter stood in one corner. An oil lamp hung from the ceiling.

Charrier's wife, Madame Léonie, came into the room and smiled warmly at Nicolas. The rector presented the boy to her with flattering words that somewhat embarrassed his guest. "Here you have Nicolas Spinoza, an intrepid little adventurer born to an ancient line of philosophers. He'll stay with us and attend school. And I'll keep a vigilant eye upon him."

Madame Léonie greeted Nicolas warmly and addressed him as "Monsieur." This was the first time in his life anyone had done so. At her request, the boy gave an account of himself and his time as a choirboy, somewhat reluctantly, then described the long journey to Paris and his arrival at his mother's house.

After a time a noticeably well-dressed boy appeared. He bowed politely, but his inscrutable smile made Nicolas feel ill at ease. The boy was watching him like a hawk.

"This is Maximilien Robespierre, a pupil from Arras, our talented young friend," Charrier explained. "His benefactor is none other than the bishop of Arras. Maximilien is a quick study. Nicolas, you'll both be living with us. You two will be like brothers."

The boy from Arras seated himself and took a slice of bread. Madame Léonie asked him what had happened in school. The boy responded with such refined words that he made Nicolas feel like a savage.

A servant opened a bottle of red wine for the Charrier couple, and the rector unexpectedly began to tell them about his childhood in Dijon. In school he had taken an interest in topics that attracted no one else. One particular enigma had long occupied his thoughts as a child: Why was it darker at night than by day, given the inconceivable number of stars, many of them far larger than the sun, that in their great mass provided the eternal light that illuminated the heavens?

It was no wonder he'd never had any friends, he commented with a hearty laugh. Not even during his teenage years did he come across anyone of his own age with whom he could discuss such conundrums. That hadn't particularly bothered him, but it had given him a sense that he was different from others of his age.

Nicolas recognized himself in the rector's remarks, but he didn't dare say so.

Charrier told them how he had come to Paris as a young student carrying well-thumbed copies of Plato and Molière in his pack. His hunger for learning had motivated him to seek scientific knowledge and investigate the mysteries of the cosmos. He had listened to many intelligent men in Paris before encountering Hector Spinoza, who had taught him so much. He was deeply grateful for their friendship. Hector gave life to his fantasies and opened his eyes to all kinds of new things. For example, Hector had told him how Isaac Newton was struck on the head by an apple falling from the tree of science and as a result became the first to work out calculations that explained how the Creator constructed the universe. The English physicist was the founder of modern science, the rector declared. Charrier said that thoughts were always bubbling in Hector's vast soul, concerning every-thing from the Creator to the flight of the bee; he would hold forth just as happily on the principles of statecraft as on the mystery of reincarnation. Hector, he told them as he sipped his wine, had encyclopedic knowledge and loved to discuss matters beyond the comprehension of humankind.

As Charrier spoke, Nicolas seemed to travel back in time. He saw how much the friendship of his father had meant to the rector. He swelled with pride. Suddenly he remembered that when he was a little boy, every night his father would tuck him in and give him a kiss. Afterward, as his father walked away, Nicolas would quickly pull the blanket over his head and blink hard, in an effort to go to sleep. The strange thing was that he could see that scene clearly before him, but he could no longer remember his father's face.

A FEW WEEKS AFTER his arrival in the Charrier family he received a letter from Voltaire. The philosopher invited Nicolas to come stay at his château in Ferney. He prom-ised to send a leather pouch with more than enough coin to cover the cost of the journey. Voltaire vividly described life in the country as an exciting adventure for a young man. He appealed to the boy, mentioning his loneliness and his difficulties with the great pocket lexicon. He also reported, not without a touch of self-irony, that he was finding it very difficult to urinate; that simple bodily function was caus-ing him considerable discomfort and obliged him to make frequent recourse to his chamber pot, each time producing only a few pitiful drops.

Several more letters followed, and Nicolas's memory of the man who had brusquely sent him off to the clois-ter boarding school faded as he read the lively lines. The boy began to repress memories of the miseries and burnish those of the good times at the philosopher's residence, for he longed to have an affectionate father figure.

An Unforgettable Morning

ONE SUNDAY IN MARCH Nicolas awakened to find himself with a throbbing erection. That morning twenty years before his execution would live in Nicolas's memory with a vividness that would surpass most of his later memories.

The boy had no idea what to do in order to return his member to its usual proportions. He was afraid that it would never again be normal, and he wondered what the women in the house, Madame Léonie and Eloise, would say. Eloise, the wet nurse for of the youngest child, was a sharp-tempered Gascon woman who wasn't afraid to talk back to the rector and bared her milk-filled breasts without shame. As Nicolas thought of Eloise, he felt a warm rush of feeling and remembered his dreams of going to bed with that young peasant girl, drinking milk from her breasts, and seizing her by her broad hips. He took his penis in hand, held it tightly, and completely surrendered to the intoxicating arousal that gave him pleasure such as he had never known before. He was in the midst of these fantasies about Eloise when Maximilien interrupted, pounding on the door and calling out that he had a visitor.

Gilbert appeared in the doorway with grave news for Nicolas. There had always been something boyish in the appearance of the old servant, but now his bleak gaze and the way he pressed together his fleshy lips in that expressionless face conveyed an entirely different message. They sat down in the private sanctum and without beating around the bush, Gilbert told him of Shoshana's death and Madame Spinoza's subsequent difficulty in obtaining a burial permit, because suicides could not be interred in holy ground. It had taken Gilbert a month to get Shoshana's body placed in a mass grave in the catacombs beneath Paris. Madame Spinoza hadn't had the strength to inform Nicolas personally of the death of his sister. And now Madame Spinoza was gone as well, without leaving so much as a letter of farewell. She had gone to sleep peacefully two evenings earlier, not aware that death was lurking in her bowels, and she did not wake up in the morning. Dr. Villancourt believed that a ruptured appendix had taken her life.

Nicolas was surprised at his own calm and by how little the deaths of his sister and mother affected him. He told Gilbert that all of this was a complete surprise—but so it was with death; it always arrived when one least expected it. He recalled that he was five years old when his father died. He remembered that day only very vaguely, no more clearly than the day he was placed in the cloister school. Everything had happened in a flash and there he was, alone and isolated from his family. Since then he had almost never seen any of them again—not his mother, not Shoshana, and not Avraham. They were all gone now, but even before, they'd seemed more like phantoms than persons of flesh and blood. Voltaire was the only person who seemed real to him, Nicholas said, because he'd always been there, as real as the air that one breathes. Nicolas told Gilbert of the philosopher's letter and said he had promised to spend a couple of weeks that summer at the philosopher's residence in Ferney.

Gilbert interrupted the young man and offered words of warning. "Voltaire is a philosopher rightly revered for his great intelligence," he said. "One should certainly praise him for his generosity as well, for he volunteered to become your guardian after your father's death. However . . ." The old servant lowered his voice. "He did this not from friendship or love but out of self-interest. He has always had an ulterior motive. He's after something that belongs to you."

Thoughts of Voltaire

I WISH I had a better insight into all the matters involving Voltaire, for he was a complicated and fascinating figure.

On the one hand he did many good things. He preached tolerance to a world in which heretics and Jews were still being burned at the stake. He shook up the society in which he lived with his energetic opposition to miscarriages of justice. He vaunted the principles of freedom, and he laid out the intellectual premises for the French Revolution. He created masterpieces of literature and philosophical thought. He overcame a childhood of poverty and ended his life as a wealthy man.

On the other hand, he was shrewd and conniving. He often employed lies to force truth into the open. He was a false-faced toady, he was ingratiating, and he flattered royalty to gain access to the corridors of power. To some he presented a friendly face, only to stab them in the back when it suited him. He was a traitor to his class origins, a man who lived in luxury and extravagance.

When I try to understand Voltaire, I have nothing to go on other than what my great-uncle told us. But sometimes it feels as if Voltaire, like a Spinoza, might have inherited both of the two fundamentally opposed traits and destinies that turned up in every generation of our family.

I must use the months—perhaps only days—that I have left for my family history. I don't have time to undertake a study of Voltaire's life.

ALL OF A SUDDEN I've recalled something that my great-uncle described to Sasha and me. I'm not surprised to find myself thinking of it now.

In Alte Bücher, one of Vienna's choicest antique bookshops, during the 1930s my great-uncle was searching for books about the Catholic Inquisition in Spain, and he came across the memoirs of Charles-Joseph Lamorals, seventh Prince de Ligne. The prince stemmed from a line of Belgian aristocrats but became a field marshal in the Austrian army and lived in Vienna until 1814. De Ligne had been a great admirer of Voltaire and once had occasion to call upon him at the château in Ferney.

The prince was completely captivated by what he termed "*sa belle et brillante imagination*"—the philosopher's generous spirit and dazzling sense of imagination. Voltaire usually went about with a little black skullcap covering the crown of his head; he mentioned that during his time in Dieppe and Colmar he had lived in the Jewish quarter. He gave his visitor a dramatic reading from a text—written in direct response to the Lisbon Inquisition's sentencing of thirty-three Jews to the bonfires—that he had titled "Sermon of Rabbi Akib, Pronounced in Smyrna." In the guise of that fictitious rabbi the philosopher delivered devastating criticisms of Christians who persecuted Jews on the pretext that they had murdered Jesus:

> *If only you had sufficient wits to reply, I would ask you*
> *why you seek to exterminate us, we who are the fathers of*
> *your fathers. What would you reply if I were to tell you*

*that your God belongs to our religion? He was born a Jew,
he was circumcised as a Jew, he was baptized, admit it,
by John, who was also a Jew . . . He complied with the
mandates of Jewish law. He lived as a Jew and died as a
Jew, while you—you burn us alive because we are Jews.*

The prince applauded enthusiastically when Voltaire
concluded the reading. Later that evening he wrote in his
diary, *"On disait partout qu'il était juif"* ("Everyone said that
he was a Jew"). And he added that his visit to Ferney had
proved to him beyond a shadow of a doubt that the rumor
was true.

The Man from Brittany

NICOLAS WAS STRUCK SPEECHLESS by Gilbert's warning. Not because Voltaire had selfish reasons to become
their guardian but because he had heard absolutely nothing
about any valued possession.

"Would you like to know what he wants?" Gilbert asked.

The boy nodded. The old retainer made him swear never
to tell anyone else.

"What I'm about to say perhaps may surprise you," Gilbert began. "It astonished me, as well, when I learned of it
from your father just after you were born. Before revealing
it, he insisted on my pledge of absolute silence and complete loyalty. I accepted those conditions, but I must admit
that there have been times, occasions of which I am now
ashamed, that I found that burden difficult to bear. But I
never betrayed my promise to your father, and I have never
uttered a word about it to anyone."

Nicolas showed signs of impatience at this, but Gilbert told him to try to restrain himself for a moment. Gilbert first needed to get matters off his chest by revealing certain youthful escapades he had sought all his life to conceal behind his facade of good manners and discretion. It was necessary for Nicolas to understand the circumstances in which he'd first met Hector Spinoza, for otherwise the boy wouldn't understand their special relationship.

Gilbert said that his real name was Giscard Bras, and he came from the tiny village of Sainte-Marine in western Brittany. His father, a fisherman, was lost at sea in a tempest, and the search for him was called off because the powerful storm did not abate for a full three weeks. Gilbert, then nine years old and the eldest of seven children, was apprenticed to another fishing boat, but his pay was miserable and the needs at home were great. That was why his mother began to charge a few sous to read people's palms. For other clients she would touch objects that had belonged to deceased persons and summon a vision of their lives in the next world. She had no real powers of clairvoyance, but one day she predicted that her own firstborn would get into difficulties with the law. The following week Gilbert, just twelve years old, was jailed for blasphemy because he had failed to bare his head when a religious procession passed by him on the street. The cell where thieves and murderers generously shared their experience with him was the only school he ever knew.

It was hard for Nicolas to imagine that Gilbert, the all-knowing servant who was the very embodiment of French *phlegm* with his calm, his courtesy, and his gracious manners, the man who never lost his composure or raised his voice, had been a full-fledged criminal, a thief and a con man, and had spent many years behind bars. Or that once upon a time he had killed a man.

A Meeting with Our Uncle

ONE WEEK AFTER Grandfather's death the whole clan assembled in our home for the reading of the will. It was the first time in many years that we had all come together. My father and Aunt Ilona had long been feuding, and she maintained an icy distance between herself and the rest of the family. Uncle Carlo had fled from Hungary during the people's revolt of 1956 and taken up residence in Vienna; this was the first time he had come back home.

SASHA AND I were too small to remember Uncle Carlo from the time before the revolt. This occasion was, shall we say, our first real meeting with him. We immediately noticed that he was nothing like our father, who was a dour man always locked away within himself. I'm almost ashamed to admit that I immediately liked our uncle better than our father. He was more open and welcoming. He was jolly, warm, gregarious, and almost as good at telling stories as my great-uncle. There was something spellbinding in the way he talked and in the shrewd twinkle of his fleeting glance.

We especially appreciated his frankness. Not just the fact that he spoke without compunction of his dead father's irritability or his declaration before everyone present that he didn't dare taste his mother's soup for fear of salt poisoning, but because he discussed topics our family had always tacitly avoided. In our house no one talked about what had happened during the war, either because they couldn't face the nightmarish past again or because they wanted to protect us children from the torments and suffering of those times.

Uncle Carlos stayed with us for three days. He then asked for Father's indulgence and permission to leave, since he was obliged to get back to his work. We imagined that he had some senior position in an international bank, considering his knowledgeable discussion of the world economy during one evening's conversation. But after he had left for Vienna, Grandmother informed us almost with glee that Carlo hadn't found a decent job or anyone there to marry. He was employed as a street sweeper.

Though we spent only a short time with Uncle Carlo, Sasha and I learned a great deal from him about the war on the eastern front. Because he was a Jew, Uncle Carlo was picked up and sent to the Don River during the miserably cold winter of 1942–1943 in a brigade of laborers who went ahead of the Hungarian army and risked their lives to clear mines and secure the bridges. The big battle lasted only three days. The skies were almost black throughout that time. The proud Hungarian army was completely annihilated. Miraculously enough, Uncle Carlo managed to get away with his life and came home again after four years in a Soviet prisoner-of-war camp. Fate had made different arrangements for most of the rest of the forty-four thousand Jews in the military work brigades. They disappeared without a trace on the banks of the Don.

Sasha asked Uncle Carlo what he felt now when he remembered the war. Our uncle did not answer immediately; he carefully extracted his spectacles from a worn leather case and put them on. We had the impression that they made his eyes look many times larger and more sorrowful. "Nothing in particular," he answered. "Absolutely nothing in particular. Only a distant, nagging headache. Other than that, nothing."

The Deserter

GILBERT TOLD NICOLAS that he had been in jail, little knowing that war was in the air. One morning his cell door opened, and he was issued a ridiculously large army uniform, leather boots that were too small, and a rifle with no ammunition. Then they sent him north toward Belgium with the rest of the prisoners. No one told them how dangerous it was to go to war against the army commanded by the Count of Cumberland.

Flights of birds beat their way across the skies of Fontenoy. One morning some days later, after he had seen all too many of his comrades bleed to death on the battlefield, he told himself that the issue of the Austrian succession had little to do with him and he had no personal disputes with those who had been mustered into the opposing army. He decided to desert.

He waited for a moonless night. When everyone else had gone to sleep he slipped out of the tent. Suddenly a sergeant loomed before him and blocked his escape. He gave the sergeant a shove; the man fell over backward, hit his head on a stone, and perished on the spot. That's how Gilbert became a criminal: He wanted to go home and the sergeant was standing in his way.

His life as a deserter and hunted murderer turned out to be harder to survive than the war. He slept in forests in the company of drunks and worn-out whores. He often woke up from dark nightmares in which his father's chiding ghost was howling his name. Once he was almost murdered by a gang of bandits after quarreling with their leader. Another time he almost burned to death in a barn. One winter morning he awoke half frozen in a drafty cellar and decided he'd had enough. He couldn't stand it anymore. The whole thing was pointless. There was a curse upon him. There was only one way out. He wanted to die; his whole soul wanted to die.

That was when he met Hector Spinoza.

"Your father not only saved my life," Gilbert said, "he gave me everything I'd never had before. Trust. Warmth. Employment. Generous pay. A home. Friendship. He gave meaning to my life and made me the man I am today. Everything I am and everything I have, I owe to Hector Spinoza."

Nicolas thought of his father. With a pang in his heart he recalled the library where his father used to sit. He also remembered the frightening, evil-tempered, impulsive violence of his father's slaps. He remembered that in those days long gone, he had appreciated the attention shown by his father with those blows more than he had appreciated the gentle but disengaged manner of his mother.

The sun's warm rays lit up the room. Titters and voices were audible in the hall outside. The two sat there for a moment, looking at each other in silence.

Nicolas was the first to speak. He admitted that the events of the previous few months had frightened him, made him miserable, and left him at a loss. Gilbert's story had cleared up many things for him. He appreciated Gilbert's truthfulness. Now, however, he wanted to hear what it was that belonged to him and Voltaire was scheming to get.

After My Grandfather's Funeral

WE POSSESSED the recipe for eternal life. Even so, through a sort of strange twist of fate, our family suffered several more deaths soon after my grandfather's funeral.

Uncle Carlo had just begun his shift the day after his return to Vienna when the driver of a truck carrying a load of women's clothing lost control of his vehicle. The Volvo 385 Viking rolled over in the intersection between Mariahilferstrasse and Esterhazygasse. The police arrived promptly and closed the surrounding streets to all traffic because several automobiles had been damaged in the accident. That part of Vienna was in chaos all morning long. It took more than four hours for two tow trucks to move the Volvo. Only then did the police discover that a street sweeper had been crushed to death beneath the eighteen-ton truck.

Grandmother had never been particularly fond of her youngest son, and when she received the news of his death she exclaimed without thinking, "Typical Carlo! All his life long he had trouble keeping his fingers out of brassieres and panties."

TWO MONTHS LATER, we again had to drape all the mirrors in our house in black and wear mourning. This time it was for Aunt Ilona. She was scheduled to undergo a routine operation. Sasha and I were never told what it involved. Grandmother said it had something to do with a manipulation of the abdomen most women of a certain age are obliged to undergo. The operation was a success but the patient never woke up. The autopsy established that the physician had been too generous with the anesthetic. I remember that Grandmother was sorrowful and aggrieved—not so much because of the death of her daughter as because there was no way to sue the anesthesiologist, since his wife was the niece of the secretary of the minister of health. "That's socialist reality for you," commented Grandmother.

BUT THE WORST CAME after that. The young man to whom I was bound in the strange mystery of life as a twin died a terrible death. And it was completely my fault. I received my punishment immediately, however: After losing Sasha I became deeply depressed. I felt alone, defenseless, and paranoid, perceiving all sorts of menacing dangers that others found inconsequential. Even today I can't bear to discuss it. Thirty years later, that loss continues to be just as wrenching, painful, and distressing. It has influenced everything I've done throughout my twisted and tangled life.

Like No Other Book

GILBERT SAID that shortly after Nicolas's birth his master manifested great confidence in him by showing him a book unlike any other, a book that contained the sum of all wisdom and answers to the world's mysteries, a book written by the philosopher Benjamin Spinoza.

"That book consists of a thousand and one pages," Gilbert told Nicolas, "and is titled *The Elixir of Immortality*. Your father made me promise that if anything ever happened to him, I would hide the book and deliver it to you upon your thirteenth birthday. He believed that you were the only one who could follow in his footsteps. You were his natural heir."

"Why my thirteenth birthday, exactly?" asked Nicolas.

"After the bar mitzvah, at the age of thirteen, a Jewish boy is a man, responsible for his actions."

"You mean that Voltaire is trying to lay his hands on that book?"

"Exactly. Your father revealed to Voltaire the existence of the book just before the unfortunate accident that took his life. The philosopher knows that he can find the answers to all of life's greatest mysteries in that book. Ever since your father's funeral, Voltaire has been after your mother, trying to get her to show him the book. But she knows nothing about it, since your father never mentioned it. And besides, I'd already hidden it in a safe place."

Gilbert picked up a packet and handed it to Nicolas.

"Your father also wrote out a sort of will for you to read and put it in a sealed envelope that I kept inside the book. There he gives you an account of the great secret of the Spinoza family and explains why the book should never be read by anyone other than you and your eldest son."

"Gilbert, tell me the truth: Did you ever feel tempted to look into the book? If it really holds the sum of all wisdom and the answers to the great mysteries, surely at some time or other you must have thought about picking up a little bit of wisdom for yourself."

Gilbert squirmed and delayed a moment before answering, obviously ill at ease. Then he replied in a low voice, "I've never felt that desire. But even if I had, and the temptation to break my vow to Hector Spinoza had been too great, it would have been of no use to me. You see, I never learned to read."

WHEN AT LAST I READ *The Elixir of Immortality* I could see what an immense significance the book had for the French Revolution. Of course I've never thought that the history they teach in schools is worth studying, because it doesn't contain the truth about the past. That's why I don't know much about history.

And so I know too little about the general conditions that led to the French Revolution, that watershed of history— why it erupted and just what happened. On the other hand,

I have noted that the radical philosophy of the Enlightenment is supposed to have stimulated revolutionary impulses. My ignorance may be my excuse for not really believing that claim. What could the connection possibly have been? The philosophers of the Enlightenment—Voltaire, Rousseau, Montesquieu, Diderot, d'Alembert—had almost nothing to do with the common people, and ordinary folk didn't read books, not only because most of them had no money to buy books but simply because only a very few people were able to read at all. And even fewer were those who eagerly purchased the convoluted tracts produced by the pens of those deep thinkers. Besides, all of those philosophers died before 1789.

It's easy to point to passages in Benjamin Spinoza's great work that could be interpreted as precursors of the key themes of the French Revolution: *liberté, égalité, fraternité*— freedom, equality, brotherhood. A century before the storming of the Bastille he wrote of natural rights and of human rights (nota bene: *not* "civil rights"), and he sketched out the concept of an ideal society with no distinctions between people on the grounds of race, religion, sex, or economic advantage. The vacuum created when religion lost credibility and vanished from the human spirit he preferred to fill with a belief in mankind, for he never doubted for a moment the ability of devoted, determined human beings to reform society in pursuit of their instinctive desire for perfection.

The Inseparables

EVERYONE AT the Lycée Louis-le-Grand called them "the inseparables." They were always together. No one could imagine them doing anything apart from each other during the waking hours of the day. They agreed on everything and could read each other's minds. They laughed at the same jokes and got hungry at the same time. Both were short and animated. Their classmates used to joke that if it weren't for Nicolas's gigantic nose, one might easily mistake them for twins. But they were not twin souls. Deep down, they were completely different.

The Bishop of Arras had reinforced in Maximilien a keen awareness of his privileged status. He came from a modest background, but the bishop had made him believe that the world lay open before him. Maximilien seemed energetic, direct, and friendly, but his heart was grim and cold. His guiding principle was that a man had to harden himself to pain, fatigue, and misfortune. He rose early every morning and took a quick swim in the nearby stream, whether it was warm or freezing. In winter he often returned with face and hands blue with the cold.

Nicolas, in contrast, was timid and quiet, a boy who easily lost himself in daydreams. The rector and Madame Léonie sometimes worried that he seemed so oblivious to everything. They couldn't know that his thoughts were deep in the book his father had left him. Often he could think of nothing else. He translated its lessons into texts of his own, usually late at night.

Maximilien and Nicolas shared many of their thoughts, but each of them had a secret preoccupation.

Maximilien was a brilliant conversationalist. He captivated everyone with his elegant rhetoric, and he often boasted that there was no essay competition he couldn't win. But the truth was quite different. His verbal eloquence was nature's compensation for his inability to write. He did everything he could to hide this shortcoming, and he worried obsessively that his failing might be discovered. But when Nicolas came into the Charrier household, everything changed. Maximilien disliked the new boy from the start and considered him a weakling. But as soon as he discovered Nicolas's talent for the written word, he began to regard him in a different light. Maximilien had the distinct feeling that he could take advantage of Nicolas. And he was right.

Nicolas's fear was quite different. He had sung in the church choir for many years and appeared before huge audiences, but he always suffered from crippling stage fright. When he was called on to speak, even to a small group, his voice failed him, he perspired heavily, and he couldn't utter a single word. Throughout his eight years at the cloister school his teachers and classmates had mocked him harshly. That experience had given him a permanent horror of public speaking. He was convinced that fate had endowed him with a lucid, graceful prose style to show he was destined to express himself on the page. He was grateful for his friend's understanding, for Maximilien shielded him from the agony of public attention by taking the pieces Nicolas had written and delivering them as speeches. He pretended they were his own.

And the secret that Nicolas never shared with anyone? It was the book from his father, *The Elixir of Immortality*.

Louis XVI

WHEN THE NEW KING took the throne in 1774, Rector Charrier announced an essay contest at Lycée Louis-le-Grand. Participants were to write a tribute to Louis XVI.

The consequences of the competition were far-reaching, for they sealed not only the fate of the king but also that of all of Europe. When my great-uncle described that episode of French history to Sasha and me, I became very upset. I wasn't angry at my great-uncle; I was furious with the king. That day marked me with antiroyalist sentiments that have lasted all my life.

In the version we heard, Nicolas wasn't particularly fond of the king. Eloise, the wet nurse, had told him that Louis XVI loved to hunt, especially for deer, and every autumn he would visit the forest near her home city of Pau, the domain of the most noble stags. His entourage always included a great number of pompous nobles known throughout the region for their swinish and constantly drunken behavior. They manhandled women and spread chaos, boisterously joking and taunting one another. One year a thoroughly inebriated count cut the throat of a twelve-year-old girl who resisted when he tried to rape her. He disposed of the body in the forest and later acknowledged his crime without the least sign of regret. In his boundless conceit Louis waved away the accusations. He told the girl's parents with a sneer that they would have to compensate the count for his suffering. The message was clear: Might makes right whenever the poor accuse the rich. Eloise said the people of Pau thought the Dauphin should be hung upside down at the end of a rope to send more of his blue blood to his brain. She spat on the ground three times after pronouncing the word "Dauphin."

Nicolas had little desire to write an encomium of such a man, but he had no choice. He peered furtively into Benjamin Spinoza's book for inspiration from that font of wisdom. He immediately came across a passage that caught his interest. The resulting essay called for thorough social reform in the kingdoms of Europe and declared that with the aim of strengthening France's preeminent standing in the world,

Louis should lead by glorious example. It was a superb text. Despite his inherent modesty Nicolas knew his essay would win. But instead of seeing it as a triumph he viewed it as a frightful danger to him, because the winner would be granted the privilege of reading his essay before King Louis XVI and Queen Marie Antoinette. Nothing could possibly be more terrifying for Nicolas. Without a word he turned the essay over to Maximilien, who promptly agreed to present it to the rector as his own work.

YEARS LATER when Nicolas sat in the Conciergerie he would remember every detail of what happened after the rector had proclaimed Maximilien Robespierre the winner of the contest.

The child of poverty from Arras, assured early in his life by his mother and the bishop that his destiny would be intertwined with history, was giddy with joy and anticipation. His greatest ambition had always been meeting the king and queen.

The reading of the tribute was scheduled for eleven o'clock on the morning of November 1, 1774. The royal couple were to arrive by coach, pause on the school grounds long enough to listen to it, and then continue their journey. Maximilien was in place an hour ahead of time, on what turned out to be the coldest day of the year. The wind blew and hail battered his face. He cursed the weather and blew on his hands in an effort to keep them warm. The royal coach did not appear. Two hours after the scheduled arrival, all the other pupils had gone inside to thaw out, and Maximilien was the only one still outside. The rector waved and gestured for him to come inside, but Maximilien scornfully turned away. The rector commented that he had never seen such a stubborn young man. Nicolas was convinced that his friend was endangering his health. Their classmates thought the boy was out of his mind. Maximilien hid his disappointment at the late arrival of the king and queen, bravely resisted the grim force of the weather, and remained steadfast in his place. But when the royal coach appeared at last and drove past without stopping, he burst into tears.

Perhaps it was the five freezing hours spent in the school yard, but it might just as well have been the shattered dream of reciting a tribute directly to the king that filled Maximilian's heart with black hatred for Louis XVI as he returned to the school. His classmates couldn't believe their ears when they heard him heaving out his angry curses, and many shook their heads in amazement. Everyone thought he had gone mad when they heard him vow that the king would pay dearly for this, with his life. Maximilien shrieked that now his own life had meaning and purpose: He would make sure that someday the king would be executed.

"Louis must die," he cried out, "so that the country can live!"

The Last Night in His Cell

LATE IN MARCH 1786 Nicolas made the acquaintance of the woman who two months later would become his wife and would bear his two sons. It happened in Rome.

All of this is recorded in the little notebook smuggled in to him by Rector Charrier, the only person permitted to visit him in his prison cell. With unheard of discipline and concentration Nicolas filled it to the last line of the final page on the night before Robespierre had him beheaded. Nicolas eventually had been unable to countenance his friend's reign of terror and had criticized him openly. It's all there in the notebook—names, places, and dates, all those densely recorded details that summarize a man's life.

Here he describes how he translated Benjamin Spinoza's exalted reflections about liberty and equality into simple, immediately understandable texts peppered with slogans against tyranny. The desire for revolution had long been brewing among the common folk, bred of resentment against injustices and a long-smoldering hatred of the social order. All Nicolas did was articulate the calls to freedom and the hopes of the oppressed, expressed in pamphlets he delivered to Robespierre each month. His friend distributed them via clandestine channels to escape the censors, building up his own standing among the Jacobins at the same time.

Nicolas records in his notebook that he completed his studies and joined the bar. Many Parisians remembered Hector Spinoza and were happy to turn to the son who had followed in his father's footsteps. They furnished him with a considerable clientele and sent him off on lengthy journeys.

He traveled to Italy in the company of Count Rémy-Bertillière to negotiate arrangements for the importation of blue marble. The billowing green landscapes of Tuscany are described with such feeling that the reader almost catches the whiff of perfume of the flowering hawthorn trees.

One day their affairs brought them to St. Peter's Basilica at the Vatican. It started to rain. Nicolas and the count sought shelter in one of the richly decorated chapels. They discovered they were not alone. A dark-haired beauty sat in one corner with a book in her hand. Nicolas recognized its distinctive gray cover at once. It was *Système de la nature ou des loix du monde physique et du monde moral*. He had a copy of the book by the Baron d'Holbach in his own library. Scandalized talk provoked by that book had spread with a speed more characteristic of epidemics. It was often denounced as "the bible of materialism." In many parts of Europe the ignorant masses happily used it as fuel for book burnings.

Nicolas's curiosity was piqued by the sight of that young woman sitting at the very heart of the Christian faith and reading a book that proved God does not exist. He walked up to her, bowed, stretched out a hand, and asked, "Mademoiselle, from what splendid star have you fallen so that I might have the pleasure of encountering you here?"

"I am from the Jewish ghetto here in Rome," she replied. She gave her name as Chiara Luzzatto.

"*Es de buena famiya?*" inquired Nicolas with a smile. "Are you related to Moishe Chaim Luzzatto the Cabalist and philosopher?"

"Moishe was my paternal grandfather but I never met him. He died twenty years before I was born. He left Amsterdam and moved with his family to the Holy Land, where he founded a synagogue in Acre. Only a few years later his entire family perished in a plague epidemic. All, that is, except my father. He is now a rabbi here in Rome and carries on my grandfather's work." Nicolas heard the pride in her voice.

It wasn't difficult to see that Chiara had deeply impressed Nicolas, for within ten minutes he was holding her hand in his. Nicolas, who had always been abashed in the presence of women, later explained his behavior by saying that events in our lives relating to love are guided by rules more magical than rational; accordingly, it is wisest not to try to understand them.

But on that final night in the dank cell in the Conciergerie, with his whole being filled with the certainty that
even if his own head would soon be lying in the basket below
the guillotine, his family's lives would continue, he wrote in
the notebook, "There was a magical glow from Chiara that
I knew would light up my entire existence."

EIGHT

The Prince

The Master of the Castle

THE BIEDERSTERN FAMILY lived in Castle Biederhof, a proud edifice some twenty-five miles southeast of Vienna. It overlooked the richly endowed province of Burgenland, a region with a notably mild and agreeable climate and situated between the vast estates of the Esterházys and those of the Batthyánys.

Our great-uncle explained to me and Sasha that as far back as the Middle Ages those fields and forests were famed as Austria's most splendid precincts for hunting to the hounds, especially in pursuit of boars, stags, deer, and foxes, and he added that the hunting dogs were usually sabuesos españoles, a medium-size hound with a graceful build, great persistence, and serene temperament. They were dogs of exceptional vigor and courage, especially when they were hunting wild game through marshes and thickets.

Those splendid lands were celebrated by many authors, above all by Franz Grillparzer and Adalbert Stifter, both of whom were frequent guests of the Biedersterns.

The imposing castle, with its walls and towers and the ancestral ghosts lurking there among the spiderwebs, had a long history that my great-uncle knew by heart. He told us that the oldest section, a castle keep with a tower one hundred and twenty feet tall, was built early in the 1330s by the fourth count of Biederhof.

THREE HUNDRED AND FIFTY years later, in response to the impending threat of Ottoman Turkish troops marching northward toward Vienna, Baldemar, Count Biederstern, ordered the works that transformed the castle to a fortress, according to plans drawn up by the Italian architect Domenico Carlone.

Baldemar, an outstanding military strategist, was a most honorable exemplar of the heroism of the Biederstern family. In recognition of his contributions in defeating the Turks, Kaiser Leopold I accorded him the rank of prince, as well as the titles of Durchlaucht (Your Highness) and heroic Hochgeboren (of noble family).

WHEN HEINDRICH BECAME the head of the family, he had the castle enlarged and decorated in Empire style. The rededication took place in April 1824 in the presence of the Kaiser.

It was a glorious spectacle, the greatest event of the year for Vienna society. The vast halls, crammed with historical mementos, were crowded with the leading citizens of Vienna. In the hall of mirrors Heindrich declared to everyone that the previously drafty, dust-covered reaches of the castle had been haunted by the ghosts of earlier generations. But he invoked his late father and told his guests not to be alarmed; never again would Biederhof be haunted. A couple of the younger and more frivolous ladies seemed bored with all the portraits of uniformed ancestors, for they were regaling each other with court gossip and giggling loudly. The crowd moved on to the banquet room and a superb luncheon. In that relaxed atmosphere they felt extremely spiritual, so they dedicated themselves wholeheartedly to the champagne. The emperor himself opened the round of toasts that celebrated the successes of the Biederstern family.

HEINDRICH HAD PLANNED every detail of the reconstruction of Biederhof. He made no concessions to the

Biedermeier style of the age with its over-precious exaltation of everyday objects; instead, he showed himself to be a fully competent amateur architect with practical sense and an appreciation for beauty. The monumental castle was unique in European architectural history of the early nineteenth century, not least because the gentleman who oversaw the construction spared no expense in carrying out his plans.

Heindrich was determined to achieve his grandiose political ambitions, and the magnificent castle was his headquarters. The Kaiser often visited, and it was no secret that His Majesty approved of the prince's political career. Among the regular guests were even Archduke Karl, Archbishop Braunschweig, and the country's most powerful politician Prince Klemens von Metternich. Heindrich had ample opportunity to keep his own bright star firmly planted at the center of the Habsburg universe.

HIS FULL NAME WAS Heindrich Friedrich Antonius Sion Nepomuk Hubertus Baldemarnes Paul Düssig von und zu Biederstern. He was the eldest son of Prince Hugo IV zu Biederstern and Princess Anna Beatrice von Metternich. His full title was His Majesty the Prince of Biederstern, Count of Eisenstadt, Baron of Mattesburg, and Prince Elector of Fertö-Hanság.

THE BIEDERSTERN LINEAGE was founded by Otto, the ur-ancestor who came out of nowhere in the obscurity of the early ninth century. Legends indicate that he must have been an unusually honorable man for his time, since he was hailed as *bieder* (honest).

As a consequence, therefore, their line was in fact two hundred years older than their beloved Ostarrichi, as the country was officially described in the earliest known document, signed in the year of 996.

Friedrich Bieder and his troop of eight hundred brave knights were part of the Habsburg army that at Christmas in 1276 crossed the highest part of the Grossglockner mountain range. He suffered frostbite of the hands and feet but kept alive by rubbing his limbs with warm horse dung. In the course of three days he lost four hundred soldiers to a snowstorm. Despite his severe frostbite Friedrich came down the far side of the mountains and took the enemy by surprise, slaying every last man and securing the Habsburg rule of King Rudolf throughout the realm.

For his heroic contributions he was promoted to the rank of count. Upon that occasion the appellation of *Stern* (star), an honorary suffix, was attached to the family name.

HEINDRICH WAS EXTREMELY PROUD to bear a family name lauded throughout the country. In private and out of earshot of others, he would express to his family the conviction that there was no one else in all of Austria, except for the Habsburgs, of higher rank or greater distinction than the Biedersterns. In any case, no other family in all of German-speaking central Europe could display in its salon an ancestral portrait painted by Leonardo da Vinci.

Early Pangs of Love

ALBERTINA ESTERHÁZY was Heindrich's great love. They had met as young children and secretly pledged themselves to each other. Their mutual bond would be the sole purpose in their lives for all eternity. They saw themselves as twin stars who shone upon each other, moving inevitably to fuse and absorb each other. But their love was never to be consummated.

Albertina's father, Prince Albert IV, was an incurable wastrel. His friends among the aristocracy referred to him as "Crazy Paja," for he was madly rash and frequently flagrantly less than honorable, a man particularly given to living beyond his means. He prided himself on having squandered more money than anyone else in his generation.

In order to lay hands on sufficient funds to pay off some great losses—the rude creditor, a social climber with no respect for nobility, was threatening to force him into bankruptcy—the prince promised to marry off his daughter to Mattias Schwarzenberg, the eldest son of one of the empire's wealthiest aristocratic families. And, of course, he did so without bothering to consult Albertina.

Albertina wept, cursed her father, and accused him of heartlessness. She didn't want to hear anything about an arranged marriage and refused to meet Mattias. The prince argued that Mattias was a fantastic catch—if the young pair would just spend an hour together undisturbed and fall in love, everything would turn out splendidly for everyone. But Albertina refused to listen, even when her father pointed out that within a few years the young Schwarzenberg would inherit a huge castle and extensive estates in Bohemia.

"Father, wealth means nothing to me. My heart belongs to another," she confessed in tears. "I love Heindrich Biederstern."

The prince pretended not to hear this. He declared that love could come flying in the window anytime at all but might be forgotten just as quickly, since love had nothing to do with building families, keeping up fortunes, or living in society.

"Allow me to decide what is best for you," he said with that inimitable tone of superiority that was his sole talent in life. He patted his daughter's cheek. "You know that you're in good hands, and that way you won't have to bother yourself with all sorts of unnecessary details. You can just be happy that you'll have a wealthy and distinguished husband. In any case, I've already given my word of honor. Mattias's father and I have decided that the wedding will take place in July, and he's already paid me a hundred thousand schillings to cover a portion of my expenses. I would have been ruined without those funds, and we would have been forced out of the home our family has owned for three hundred years. You certainly wouldn't want your father, a prince of the Esterházy line, to wind up in the poorhouse. Think what a disgrace that would be."

HEINDRICH WAS CRUSHED by the news of Albertina's upcoming wedding. He felt as if he had been robbed of his future. He simply could not understand how another man had suddenly appeared and taken away his beloved to imprison her in an undesired marriage, consecrated in the name of God and the Holy Spirit. He was convinced that he was the only man on earth who could make Albertina happy, and no other man needed her love and tenderness more than he did.

Heindrich tried to discuss the issue with his father, but Hugo zu Biederstern wouldn't hear of it. The old prince snapped sharply that a father had the privilege of determining who would be his daughter's husband, and he added that it was entirely reasonable for Albertina to accept the age-old obligation of Austrian nobles never to marry for love. It was completely out of the question for a Biederstern to break tradition or ignore the practical realities of their aristocratic world.

"I can assure you," the prince advised his son with a look of distaste, "that anyone who fails to heed tradition isn't worth his own weight in horse manure."

Heindrich lowered his eyes. A heavy silence settled around him. He felt profoundly disappointed at the cruelty of his fate. What pained him more than anything else in that moment was the fact that Mattias, of all people, would be the man to lead Albertina to the altar.

Heindrich had stood in the shadow of the young heir of the Schwarzenberg line all his life. His own father was continually comparing him to Mattias, a young man wreathed in mystic glory even though he was only a couple of years older. Heindrich's father never neglected an opportunity to taunt Heindrich by praising Mattias's superiority in all matters. The old prince never knew how much this tormented Heindrich. This was a most singular lack of perception, considering that Hugo zu Biederstern had been treated in exactly the same condescending manner by his own father.

Heindrich vowed to himself that he would banish every thought of Albertina and that he would never again address a cordial word to her.

YEARS PASSED before he saw her again. She was standing in the lobby of the Burgtheater with her husband, Mattias Schwarzenberg. For a moment Heindrich stood as if turned to stone, but then he acknowledged the couple with a chilly smile. Then he ignored them.

Heindrich never spoke Albertina's name again. He saw no reason to do so. The loss of his true love to the chief rival of his youth was a continual torment. It marred his life. As he once acknowledged to his cousin August, it had destroyed all trace of tenderness in him and had instilled the need to achieve worldly success.

Political Ambitions

IT WAS EXPECTED as a matter of course that the young prince would show his loyalty by actively supporting and protecting the social hierarchy that depended upon the emperor. But Heindrich had significantly more extensive political ambitions than that.

For many years his father, Hugo zu Biederstern, had been a trusted counselor to His Majesty. In that capacity he was the very incarnation of a political ideal revered since the days of the patricians of the Roman Republic: a nobleman devoted to duty, tradition, and honor.

Heindrich had a different motivation for engaging in politics. Vengeance was what moved him. He intended to surpass Mattias Schwarzenberg with his heroism and invaluable contributions to his emperor and the fatherland. He would rise to preeminence and make Albertina regret giving in to her father's will and the centuries-old patriarchical tradition he represented.

As a stalwart of the emperor's Third Mounted Brigade in the campaign against Napoleon, Heindrich mocked death, and displayed a keen sense of strategy and decisive leadership. He became one of its most admired officers and was quickly promoted to the highest levels of command.

During the victorious battle at Aspern-Essling just outside Vienna in May 1809, he seemed invulnerable. In a heroic fury he slew with his saber ten French soldiers who had leaped out of an ambush and were clustered around Archduke Karl. The Kaiser decorated him in recognition of his unparalleled courage. With his head held high Heindrich delivered an impromptu reply thanking His Majesty and swearing an oath of fealty. He declared emphatically that he was ready to shed every drop of his blood in the battle against the enemy. His powerful words impressed the generals gathered around him, and the emperor deeply appreciated the ardent devotion of the young prince whose family had always been closely allied with the Habsburgs.

A FEW WEEKS LATER, on the day before the disastrous clash at Wagram, Heindrich caught a glimpse through his binoculars of Napoleon on horseback reconnoitering the terrain some two hundred yards ahead of his troops. Heindrich felt a deep revulsion for the presumptuous newcomer who had crowned himself emperor of France and murdered the last members of the Bourbon royal family, distant relatives of Heindrich's mother. The tiny Corsican was anything but impressive. Nevertheless, Heindrich recorded in his diary that he had seen the new spirit of the times riding forth: "It was a remarkable feeling to see such an apparently insignificant individual sitting on a magnificent horse, looking out over the world and seeking to become its master."

Heindrich understood instinctively that Napoleon's successful march through Europe marked the beginning of a new era. The feudal society that was the Biederstern family legacy would be thrust aside and replaced by constitutional regimes based on citizens' rights, individual liberties, and economies based on trade. The way to the future had already been mapped out, and Heindrich's own world was at risk of winding up in the dustbin of history. For that reason he was determined to use all of his powers to resist such changes. Napoleon had to be defeated at any price.

TWO STRAY FRENCH BULLETS in the first skirmish of the battle that would devastate Austria put an end to Heindrich's military career. The first of them smashed his knee and gave him a limp for the rest of his life. The second buried itself in his lower abdomen without causing serious damage.

But the field physician shook his head with a look of concern. He was unable to dig out the bullet. He explained that it remained somewhere deep within Heindrich's body.

"There is a risk, although only a minimal one," he added with some misgiving, "that the bullet may displace itself and take some unpredictable path within the lieutenant's body."

Heindrich did not flinch. For hundreds of years his family had shed its blood for the Kaiser; he was an officer of the proud Austrian army and he had looked death in the eyes many times on the battlefield; he had nothing to fear.

BY THE AGE of thirty Heindrich was a prominent politician in the capital and enjoyed his share of glory. During the Congress of Vienna of 1814, where his maternal uncle Prince Metternich hosted two emperors, four kings, numerous archdukes, and many princes at a gathering to reestablish order and a balance of power after the bloody Napoleonic Wars, Heindrich made a glorious intervention. He rose before their assembled majesties, shoulders erect and back straight in his spotless military uniform hung with decorations for bravery, and radiated self-assurance. His thinning hair made him look older than he was, and his eyes had the confident gleam of experience. He spoke with gravity and authority, and his message was uncompromising. To the delight of those assembled in that gilded ceremonial hall, he insisted that the aristocracy should once again be accorded the powers it had exercised in Europe before the French Revolution. Thunderous applause greeted this remark. He thanked Charles-Joseph Lamoral, the seventh Prince de Ligne, who was present in the room, for his inspiring reflections on conditions in Europe. Then he delivered a ferocious attack upon the ideals of the Enlightenment, which in his opinion had undermined the aristocracy's natural right to power. He directed especially critical words against Nicolas Spinoza, ideologue of the French Revolution, and against the Jacobin leader Maximilien Robespierre, who had cried "compassion is treason" as they sent their king to the guillotine.

A Suitable Husband

HEINDRICH CIRCULATED in the uppermost reaches of society and was deeply involved in the glittering social life of the aristocracy. All found him a delightful individual, deeply cultured, and of the most reliable views. His voice was mild and he scrupulously avoided the temptation to condescend to others. His frankness made people adore him, and his courteous manner was most disarming. He won everyone's goodwill, and it was rumored that he was a special favorite of the emperor.

He appears briefly in the diaries of Archduchess Henriette. She sat at the very heart of Schönbrunn society and was a witness to every event of importance. Few other than Heindrich escaped her censure. He had saved her husband's life in the war and, moreover, his eloquence pleased her. Above all, she appreciated his manner of moving through the salons with impressive assurance. He always conducted himself with dignity and as a peer to all. The archduchess decided he was the right man to satisfy any expectations of life her niece Clementina might reasonably have.

THE GIRL WAS TWENTY-ONE years old, a splendid youthful beauty, but she lived sequestered from worldly society under the close watch of the Lord, whose will she assiduously obeyed. The archduchess did not share her niece's fervent faith and had no illusions about the girl. She dispatched the following words to Heindrich:

> *Clementina is very pious but possesses no particular spiritual distinction. Her life is devoted to prayers and to the celebration of God. The responsibility for her upbringing has been assumed by the Carmelite sisters in their convent outside Vienna. Consequently, she is thoroughly imbued with notions of respect, reverence, and humility. On the other hand, she lacks warmth and passion—you will understand, my prince, what I mean. I am convinced not only that she will be adequate for the prince in his daily life but that she will also provide him a son to continue his line. The two of you appear predestined for each other. By taking her in marriage you will assure yourself a glorious future. You will both have the Kaiser's eyes upon you.*

Heindrich was the scion of a noble family who figured among the church's most ancient supporters. Even though his relatives and ancestors had been familiars of cardinals and archbishops for centuries, he was a relatively free thinker in matters divine. He enjoyed reading Voltaire but did not share the philosopher's anticlericalism. On the other hand he considered—of course, without neglecting to fulfill his duties toward the church as required by his standing—that the Catholic faith was based on a number of childish fantasies, including the Immaculate Conception and the appearance in human form of the son of God. Clementina's devout religious faith did not bother him in the least, however, and he accepted her piety without hesitation. Her devotion might even be considered a positive quality, for it reinforced the young woman's otherwise relatively mediocre character.

FEW MEMBERS of the nobility gave any credence to the myth of true love, and no one of that class was surprised when Heindrich married Clementina, despite their contrasting personalities and completely opposed views. Arranged marriages had always played an important role in the history of Austria. They were the means by which the state and the great fortunes had been consolidated. The arrangement united a princess and a blue-blooded prince and linked families counted among the country's oldest and most tenaciously loyal to the crown, as proven by courage on the battlefield; the arrangement was seen as strengthening the empire and the position of the emperor.

ALTHOUGH NO ONE SAID so, there was no doubt that Clementina's close family ties with the archduchess were the deciding factor when Heindrich asked for her hand. The discreet prince never mentioned this to anyone.

Political Successes

HEINDRICH WAS ONE of the country's great practitioners of the intricate art of politics. Where other aristocrats saw only complications that they all, without exception, detested like the plague and instinctively avoided—just as their fathers had done—Heindrich always came up with brilliant solutions. He was especially gifted with insight into the factors shaping the evolution of society.

It was during Vormärz, the period before March 1848
when revolutionary sentiment was growing, that the new
demands of the middle class for economic and political
freedom became a growing threat to government by the
upper class.

The more Heindrich studied the writings of Voltaire,
Rousseau, and Tocqueville, as professionally indispensable
to him as they were interesting, the more hatred he felt for
the universalist ideals of the French Revolution.

His idol was Joseph de Maistre, the misanthropic strategist of the reactionary restoration.

Heindrich had a deep and lasting distrust of Jews, Free-
masons, and liberals, whom he described as birds of ill
omen and malicious parasites in the Austrian body politic.
He prevailed upon Vienna's chief of police to recruit informers throughout the city who would report directly to him.
He instructed his spies to offer a stark choice to those suspected of allegiance to the ideals of the Enlightenment: inform upon their comrades or go to prison. The tactic quickly
paid off, for rabble-rousers proved most willing to save their
own skins by denouncing one another. Because he knew
what everyone was thinking and saying, Heindrich could
keep a vigilant eye on everything happening in the empire
and mercilessly crush groups that threatened the state. His
maneuvers to forestall political change within the Habsburg
empire were considered invaluable.

In just a few years Heindrich became one of the most
powerful of the Kaiser's men. He had only a very few friends
he could rely on, but the compensation was that he had a
mass of enemies who never disappointed him. He ably out-
flanked his predecessor, and his political career reached its
zenith with his appointment to the post of minister of the
interior and police.

Napoleon's Bullet

IN THE SPRING of 1841 Heindrich was deeply involved from early morning until late at night dealing with an espionage case that had shaken the foundations of the Austrian Empire. Someone had sold military secrets to the Russian czar's ambassador in Vienna. The reports in question were extremely sensitive documents known to only a very few people. Among them were the detailed descriptions of plans for Austrian mobilization, military ciphers, military transport capabilities, the inventory of military provisions, plans for resupply, and details of the fortifications along the borders. It was clear that the traitor had to be someone high in the military command, but his identity was unknown.

Heindrich had reason to suspect that this was not a matter of a single poisonous snake or a lone criminal eager to finance a life of luxury by selling out the fatherland, but that it was a widespread conspiracy, nothing less than a plot against His Majesty involving many individuals in the highest military circles and probably some very senior politicians.

He immediately requested an audience and informed the Kaiser, who listened to his report and instructed him to hush up the affair.

"The desires of His Majesty the Emperor," replied Heindrich with an appropriately steely demeanor, "will of course be obeyed. We shall act quickly, discreetly, and without mercy. Nothing is more important to me than unraveling this affair. The security of the empire must be our primary concern. The traitors will be seized, come what may, and executed."

Heindrich investigated thoroughly, applying all his talent and dedication. He sat studying documents far into the night and formulated a carefully calculated strategy.

———

BECAUSE HE WAS NEVER ABLE to sleep more than three hours at a time, Heindrich was in the habit of lying down after lunch for a half-hour nap on the broad sofa in his office at the Ministry of the Interior in Vienna.

One morning he was suffering from a throbbing headache. He had felt extremely fatigued throughout the morning and found it almost impossible to concentrate. Despite this, he tried once again to review the top-secret accounts of the espionage affair. He sensed that he was on the track of something vital and a breakthrough was imminent. His fatigue eventually overwhelmed him and, contrary to his custom, he lay down before lunch to rest. He immediately fell asleep. He opened his eyes only a few minutes later. He sat up with a jerk.

He saw it all clearly. He was certain of the identities of the traitor and his fellow conspirators. Heindrich had always been a man of calm and discipline, but now his body was quivering with excitement. He burst into laughter, for now it seemed so simple. The thought crossed his mind that in different circumstances he would have dismissed the whole thing as a bad joke. He quickly went to his desk and called in his secretary, who entered with an expectant look. Heindrich appeared very satisfied with himself. He cleared his throat; it was vital for his voice to be loud and distinct. He began to dictate an order of arrest. Just as he was about to pronounce the name of the traitor, his face stiffened and he stopped in mid-sentence. At that very instant Napoleon's bullet concluded its long random journey through Heindrich's body and arrived at his heart. Death enfolded the Prince zu Biederstern before he could reveal his discovery.

Misalliance

WHY DID my great-uncle tell us stories about Heindrich and the Biederstern family? What did we have to do with them?

The Spinoza family had been Jews since time out of mind, perhaps due more to random circumstances than out of conviction, and we had the long-established and laudable tradition of crouching over holy scripture and eternally praising God, who in fact believed more in us than we did in him. Study and debate were our obsessions.

The Biedersterns, on the other hand, were an exemplary noble family distinguished by their courage and heroism, certainly not by scholarly devotion. Already by the end of the thirteenth century they had consecrated their swords to the defense of the Habsburg emperor, and their only other preoccupation was the blue blood in their veins. Throughout the centuries they married other aristocrats, since in their eyes everyone else was insignificant.

Our clan had never been accorded any rights, never had anywhere in the world to call home, and regularly had to flee over the mountains and across the seas, at risk everywhere except in our world of books. The Biedersterns had dwelt carefree in their magnificent castle, noble owners of vast estates and extensive hunting preserves, faithful supporters of a church that readily forgave their transgressions because of the glory of their family name.

But the differences between our lives lay not only in customs, legends, and conventions; they were also expressed in our mentalities and relationships, our concepts of ourselves, the things that moved us and dominated our thoughts, and the dreams and memories we carried within us.

WAS THERE in fact anything at all that linked the families of Spinoza and Biederstern?

One bright fall day love struck both families with violent force and united us for all time. We Spinozas took no joy in it; neither did the aristocrats. Heindrich was lucky to be dead already, for otherwise the mere thought that his ancient blood would be circulating through a Jewish heart in the descendant of a man who had sent the French king to the gallows would have killed him in the twinkling of an eye.

It was because of the strange misalliance between our great-grandmother and great-grandfather that my great-uncle spoke so often of the princes of Biederstern.

The Heir

THREE DAYS AFTER Heindrich's remains had been committed to the earth, Rudolf seated himself at his father's desk. He had always known that one day he would take over the place. As the firstborn and the only son, he would continue the Biederstern line. He was now the patriarch and commanded all the family resources. He was the only one who counted; his sisters were irrelevant.

Rudolf had always expected to exult in his power when the great day arrived, but the truth was that he was intimidated by the responsibility for the castle and the fortune, and all the duties that came with them. He feared that people would say he could not possibly compare to his exalted father. To banish those doubts, he vowed always to be decisive and never to hesitate. He would rule everything with an iron hand and require people to show him the proper respect.

———

THE BEREAVED FAMILY gathered in his father's office half an hour later. To Rudolf's right sat his mother and her spiritual advisor Bishop Kaulbach, whose every breath inspired calm and confidence. His sisters, Ursula and Mercedes, were on his left. The women wept, as was to be expected. Rudolf had often seen those women use tears to exploit his father's good nature and get their way. He was firmly decided that he would not be controlled by his mother and sisters.

"Father is dead. I now take responsibility for the family. Every decision, large or small, is mine. From this moment on, I rule in this house. No one is going to nose around in family affairs or pry into matters not of their own concern. No one is to disturb me before noon under any circumstances. Anything else? No? That will be all for today. Leave me. You have already taken up enough of my time. I have a great many matters to consider."

His mother and sisters lowered their eyes. For the first time ever, Bishop Kaulbach showed signs of experiencing some emotion. His jaws were tightly clenched. The new master of the castle smiled in triumph.

The Black Sheep

RUDOLF WAS the black sheep of the Biederstern family. From the day of his birth, the boy had conducted himself inappropriately and without the least consideration for others. He showed no interest in leaving his mother's womb to come out into the world. Her difficult labor meant nothing to him. Dr. Leuterbach, the family physician at that time, commented that the boy was being obstreperous, and he found himself obliged to resort to forceps. As soon as the little fellow was dragged out into the light of day, he established a reputation as a recalcitrant screamer. He was a lively, well-shaped child, even though the forceps had left deep grooves in his little cranium. He was applied at once to the breast of the waiting wet nurse.

In later years Clementina and Heindrich occasionally speculated that Dr. Leuterbach's unfortunate decision to use forceps might have somehow had unfortunate effects upon Rudolf's mental faculties.

THE CHUBBY RED-CHEEKED RUDOLF inherited neither his father's pleasant manners and disarming courtesy nor his mother's natural diffidence. He was a demanding child. He did not speak; instead he bawled, from earliest childhood onward. When faced with conflicts, he always resorted to violence. He refused to be contradicted. He often threw temper tantrums that terrified all the servants in the castle.

The task of helping him become a cultured and educated young man was assigned to teachers hired from abroad. Before two years had passed, five of them had been sent home at their own request. No one could withstand his explosive temperament. The last tutor, a scrawny humpbacked Swiss, peering furtively at Rudolf's father while carefully avoiding his gaze, admitted with careful courtesy that he did not believe that the young man had much of a future. Then he asked for permission to leave the castle.

BOTH PARENTS' SPIRITS lifted when Rudolf was sent away to the renowned boarding school of Captain von Knapp in Fürstenbrunn, outside Salzburg, where that respected officer educated the sons of the best noble families of the land until they were of an age to apply for admission to the military academy.

Rudolf made no friends at school. He often got into fist-fights and scared everyone away. He wanted to be noticed and respected, and this desire drove him to pretend to be even wilder and more violent than he really was. The boys called him "the madman" and shunned him.

The fifth time that Rudolf mistreated a classmate, the rector sent a letter to Heindrich declaring that the boarding school in Fürstenbrunn could no longer accommodate the boy.

In the years that followed he was sent to three other schools, always with the same result. In each he behaved abysmally and brutally bullied his classmates.

Making a Man Out of a Boy

THE BIEDERSTERNS were an ancient family of warriors. Their family crest displayed a lion and a crown, and their motto was "Strength in Service to the Emperor." There was therefore no discussion about Rudolf's future. At the age of eighteen he went to the military academy in Vienna. Clementina looked forward to seeing him resplendent in the uniform. Heindrich was convinced that the army with its strict discipline and its generals, colonels, and captains, fine fellows all, would make a man of him and give him a secure foothold in life.

But Rudolf caused an enormous scandal before three months had passed. He was delighted when he was expelled from the military academy, effective at once.

THIS CAME AS A GREAT SHOCK to his parents. Clementina was distraught. Heindrich sought advice from his cousin August, who despite all his many sins and heavy baggage was the archbishop of Burgenland.

August heard him out, his head tilted to one side and a smile playing about his lips. His advice to Heindrich was as simple as it was straightforward. In those days the custom was for young aristocrats to be initiated in the games of the bedroom by a woman who was a professional in this field. The bishop's view was that once the youthful lusts of Rudolf's flesh were satisfied, the urges of his spirit would subside and his aggressive behavior would abate.

"Do you mean, my dear cousin, that I should take Rudolf along with me to the Salon Rouge?" Heindrich asked in surprise.

"Your son's innate masculine vitality and his desire for conflict should be directed into the appropriate channels. He will have to sow his wild oats. So put him in the hands of a woman who can make a man out of him."

Heindrich sighed. August took his hand and firmly pressed it. "Count on me," he said in the same warm voice he used for his Sunday sermons.

Rudolf was summoned to his father's office that same evening. Heindrich offered him a glass of dry sherry.

"My son," he said while lighting a cigar, "one day you will become the head of the Biederstern family and you will have to assume responsibility for everything here—"

"That certainly won't be very difficult," Rudolf interrupted him.

Heindrich pretended not to hear him. He resumed, "It is therefore important for you to experience certain things and encounter many different types of people. You and I will go to Vienna tomorrow for new experiences. We will visit a place that some call 'the house of the magic moment.' That is where men of our class go to make the world go away for a few hours, but never to seek true love."

Arabella la Duce

SINCE BY THEN Heindrich had already gone to meet his ancestors, he was spared the ordeal of Rudolf's wedding, the talk of the town for the best of Austrian society.

Rudolf's intended wife was not the first who had escaped from humble origins via marriage to the nobility, and he was not the first man lured by blind passion to marry below his station. Even so, most of the aristocracy found his choice of wife completely incomprehensible. There was simply no justification for his behavior. A man of his elevated standing and vast wealth should never have allowed himself to be blinded by the beauty of such a common woman. A number of people thought that the marriage could be nothing but a bizarre joke.

ARABELLA GREW UP in Vienna's poverty-stricken neighborhood of Brigittenau, a collection of ramshackle houses leaning precariously in every direction and about to fall down, inhabited by beggars, whores, pimps, and the alcoholic working class. Her father, a tubercular widower who crawled into the bottle to forget his sorrows, worked as a wig maker in order to support his seven children. The wife he still adored had run off with a Gypsy tramp because she could not endure her husband's violence whenever he drank.

Arabella thought it was her fault that her mother had abandoned the family. She was the only girl in the house, and her father took pleasure not only in beating her but also in forcing her into the privy where he poked and groped her. At last she became so hysterical that he let go of her and shouted that she was a dirty whore just like her runaway mother. From time to time his conscience reproached him, and he would push two groschen into her hand and tell her to go buy a pastry.

Once Arabella became a teenager, her father noticed that the boys in the street would follow her with their eyes. He felt a certain pride. Sometimes he felt a touch of fear and misgiving at the sight of her impressive figure and handsome head of black hair: What good was beauty to a poor girl?

Arabella was determined not to remain mired at the bottom of society. She wanted to rise; she wanted to become someone and to do something grand, wonderful, and meaningful. She wanted to be appreciated and to gain a bit of respect. She had a fine singing voice and had memorized a couple of arias from Italian opera. She dreamed of joining an opera chorus. She was willing to try anything. She even allowed the opera manager to become familiar with the most intimate details of her body—but it got her nowhere.

One morning as she stood naked before the mirror it ocurred to her that her womanliness was her greatest advantage. She was twenty-one years old and had an exuberantly rounded rear end and large breasts with nipples as round and hard as chestnuts. She thought it over, weighing the advantages against the risks. Oh, well—since she'd never aimed at becoming a paragon of duty and virtue, she might as well burn her bridges and cast herself body and soul into a new line of work.

SOME WOMEN on the streets in Brigittenau had become prostitutes even before they learned to read. They looked like soulless zombies. Arabella told herself this was because they were struggling just to survive from one day to the next. She wanted to do something different with her body: to create art, not for the rude masses of workers and artisans with their horny hands, foul-smelling bodies, and sudden spasmodic ejaculations, but for the true connoisseurs, the gentlemen with bulging pocketbooks who took their time and savored the pleasures of love.

Having determined that having lovers with noble titles would increase her own enjoyment, she made her way to the Salon Rouge, an elegant establishment for a select clientele of great wealth and exacting tastes.

Arabella was an arresting beauty, and Madame Sonya immediately saw that she would be a magnificent addition to the house. The owner of the brothel renamed her "Arabella la Duce" and invented a history for her as a promising opera singer from Paris. That very evening her pretended virginity was sold to Prince Schwarzenberg, who was always willing to pay generously for a bit of extra excitement.

Arabella's natural talents made her an instant success. At first she was amazed, but she quickly learned to exploit her power over men. Before long the most sophisticated gentlemen of Vienna were exchanging stories about the new arrival who was the most passionate woman in the city.

A Visit to the Salon Rouge

RUDOLF'S EXPERIENCE in the realm of love could be described as strictly limited and not in the least impressive. He was remarkably clumsy, inhibited, and unimaginative when it came to women. Cold shivers ran up his spine whenever he stole away to the Salon Rouge for a little pleasure. Sometimes he stood outside the entrance debating whether or not to enter, torn between his desire and his inherent timidity with women.

THAT TEMPLE OF EROS offered a rich array of every imaginable attraction; for special clients it even provided young boys. On the night that Rudolf first encountered Arabella, he was offered the choice of a young girl as flat-chested as a boy, a married bourgeois housewife with swaying hips and juicy hams, an Oriental woman direct from the sultan's harem in Yemen, and a promising songstress from the Paris opera with plenty of fire in her blood.

He asked for the last of these, for he had heard from a baron of his acquaintance reputed for his loose living and racy talk that the moist cavity between the thighs of that femme fatale was the closest place to heaven one would find in this transitory life.

AFTER COLLECTING PAYMENT, Madame Sonya showed him to a room at the very top of the house. Only the most privileged guests were granted access to the top floor, and Rudolf had never been there before. The room was larger than others he'd seen at the Salon Rouge. An immense round bed surrounded by six tall candelabra stood in the center. The red flicker of their flames spread an intoxicating fragrance through the room. Rudolf was lightheaded even before the madame closed the door behind her. An air of enchantment hovered about him and filled the room with a magical atmosphere.

Arabella la Duce sat on the edge of the bed. She rose and slowly approached Rudolf with a seductive gait. She was the most gorgeous creature he had ever seen. He stood there as if bewitched and scarcely dared to breathe. Her enormous dark eyes shone with the animal desire of womanhood.

Well aware of the powerful eroticism she radiated, Arabella swayed her head so that her hair fell free of its clips and hairpins and draped itself across her shoulders. A shudder of desire ran through Rudolf's body as she gently unbuttoned her blouse. He could not tear his gaze away from the dazzling white of her breasts as they spilled forth. He had never seen anything so splendid or so exciting.

She took his hand, led him to the bed, and removed his clothes. Then she pulled him down onto the mattress and slowly explored his body with her soft tongue. Time stood still for Rudolf. The room ceased to exist, as if he had entered paradise itself. After a long time at this she settled herself astride him and her experienced hands began to stroke his penis. Rudolf immediately experienced the most intense ejaculation of his life. He felt shame at having climaxed so quickly, and he would not meet her gaze. He blinked heavily several times and fell asleep at once.

WHENEVER RUDOLF THOUGHT of Arabella the following day, his face flushed red, his pulse began to race, and his eyes gleamed. He felt a joyous excitement, a strong urgent longing for the woman who had so disturbed his spirit. This was something new and strange for him. He counted the hours. He could scarcely endure the wait until the evening, when he set off directly to the Salon Rouge once again.

That night's encounter was even more powerful. This time he was the one who explored every inch of her body with his fingers. She pressed her sex against him at every moment and when at last he exploded within her, he was so exhausted that he almost fainted.

The Proposal

WHEN RUDOLF RETURNED to the Salon Rouge on the third evening, Arabella was already taken. His disappointment knew no bounds. In a heated, grieving voice he stubbornly remonstrated with Madame Sonya, but in vain. Arabella was fully booked for the whole evening.

His face twisted into a grimace and his instinctive impulse was to strike the madame. He restrained himself, fearing the likely consequences, and swallowed his wrath. Disconsolate, he declined the offer of a young redheaded beauty and a mature blonde. He told his coachman to drive him to the nearest drinking establishment, and there he consumed a bottle of wine in the effort to recall the enchantment of the mood that had enveloped him in Arabella's bed.

He lay sleepless that night and spent the whole next day in bed stewing in his own sweat. He shook with an obsessive animal attraction to Arabella. He was tormented by terrible passionate longing. He wanted to possess her. He wanted her for himself alone, away from everyone else, far away from strange men so he could watch over her. He wanted to absorb her into his blood. So he decided to marry her. He thought this was a splendid idea. As her husband he would have constant access to her body.

THAT EVENING he rushed to the Salon Rouge. With his trousers about his knees and his swollen member in Arabella's mouth, he asked her to be his wife. She listened to him with polite interest and even felt a little flattered, but she hadn't the slightest interest in marrying him. Because of Rudolf's awkwardness and her own complete ignorance of the aristocracy, Arabella had assumed that he was of a much lower rank in society. And besides, he was not exactly the Prince Charming she had been dreaming of—more the opposite, in fact, for he was the sort of man she preferred to avoid, since neither his technique in love nor his company attracted her in the least. But in the cowardly fashion of those who are eager to hold on to rich acquaintances otherwise denied to them in their everyday lives, she chose not to turn him down outright. She pretended to be dutifully impressed.

THE NEXT MORNING Madame Sonya informed Arabella that Rudolf was a prince of the blood, related to the emperor, rich beyond all imagining, owner of a large castle and a richly furnished residence in Vienna. Enchanted by the overwhelming magic of the words uttered by the mistress of the brothel, Arabella capitulated. She suddenly saw Rudolf in a completely different light. She immediately thought less about his terrible appearance and more about his ancient lineage, luxurious castle, and great wealth. In her imagination she saw the most exclusive sectors of society prostrating themselves at the feet of the princess of Biederstern. That was why during their next encounter, in the throes of a faked orgasm, she was quick to whisper shyly but with great clarity that she would be happy to become his wife.

A Hard Trial

RUDOLF'S PROPOSAL to Arabella was a hard trial for his family. No one could understand how he had allowed himself to fall into the clutches of a common prostitute.

Clementina, who had remained in deep mourning since Heindrich's untimely demise and whose eyes were always red with weeping, saw this as a cruel blow of fate. She hoped she could change Rudolf's mind.

SHE BEGAN CAUTIOUSLY. "You should be aware that a marriage between people from entirely different classes is rarely happy or long-lasting, no matter how wonderful it may seem at first."

"Just drop the subject, Mother," Rudolf replied, shaking his head.

She refused to be intimidated and instead continued in an increasingly querulous tone. "Just think of me, of all of us. Can't you see how much I'm suffering? Don't you see that this is a disaster? What a disgrace!"

Her voice stuck in her throat and she had an air of desperation, as if she was bearing all of the sorrows of the world on her delicate shoulders.

"Suffering? Disaster? Disgrace?" said Rudolf. "Is that what my happiness means to you? Arabella is the best thing that has ever happened to me!"

Clementina gasped and looked at her son as if he were a complete stranger. She prayed silently to God not to allow such a terrible misfortune to take place. Her eyes filled with tears. She instantly withdrew to her room and stayed there for a long time, racked with tears and sobs.

RUDOLF REFUSED to be budged from his belief that he was doing exactly the right thing. He was firmly convinced that the best way to take the measure of a person was to assume the opposite of what was commonly rumored. He knew very well that the regulars of the Salon Rouge described Arabella as a completely depraved and uninhibited woman. He assumed therefore that in reality her character was suffused with virtue, innocence, truthfulness, and tenderness.

THE PAIR was married by Archbishop of Burgenland August zu Biederstern, who turned to the newlyweds and delivered a wonderfully poetic sermon with accounts of family history, texts from the Bible, and a number of humorous remarks, all of it delivered with a certain frivolous elegance. Almost five hundred people attended the wedding dinner at Castle Biederhof.

His mother and sisters blushed in humiliation when after the ceremony in the church they were obliged to exchange a few words with the depraved women from the Salon Rouge.

The archbishop, on the other hand, appeared to be in fine spirits. Out of the hearing of others, he told the women that he would be happy to slip away into sacristy with one of them for a private prayer session.

With their extravagantly plumed hats and low-cut dresses that invited men to lose themselves in the depths, Arabella's colleagues attracted a great deal of attention.

A Stormy Marriage

THE MARRIAGE between Rudolf and Arabella was never officially terminated. They remained man and wife until death parted them. But they did not live together for long.

Since Rudolf could be with Arabella whenever he wished, within a few months of the wedding he discovered that she was completely ordinary. Her pretentious manner and persistent desire to be invited to various social events annoyed him. So did the fact that she regularly ordered outfits in flagrantly bad taste that were commented upon by everyone. Rudolf shared his mother's somewhat moralistic view that clothes were for wearing, not for display. He was especially resentful that Arabella's physical passion had cooled so quickly and she went to bed with him less and less often. He could scarcely remember the taste of her pulpy lips.

One evening, in an attempt to rekindle the passion in their relationship, he staged a melodramatic scene and pretended to believe that Arabella had betrayed him. He complained that he knew little about her earlier life at the Salon Rouge or even what she did on those days when he had to travel to Burgenland on family business. He had imagined that this would make Arabella afraid of losing him, so she would change her attitude and become more devoted and affectionate. More than anything else, he was hoping to reawaken her sexual appetite and rouse the magic powers of her femininity.

Arabella misread his intentions, however. Instead of begging his forgiveness for the past with beseeching looks and quivering voice, she responded with a remarkably lively account of the exciting life she'd led at the Salon Rouge. She supposed that Rudolf, whom she found to be relatively unimaginative in bed and who had caused her own blood to cool, wanted provocative suggestions about what she most enjoyed in bed.

She left out none of the most intimate details, which made Rudolf increasingly ill at ease. He felt the sting of jealousy. Arabella's animated expression and lively voice made him suspicious, for she seemed to suggest how boring she found their games in bed. Perhaps she was still getting together with men who attracted her. At that moment he was struck by an illness that would torment him for a long time and ruin his life.

RUDOLF COULD NOT GET OUT of his mind the images of his wife as the Queen of the Night in Vienna. Every time admiring men swarmed about her and each time she smiled at a man, Rudolf told himself that Arabella had never stopped consorting with her earlier acquaintances and frequented them still. These notions had not previously occurred to him. Malicious rumors spread by envious tongues seemed to confirm his suspicions. The poison of jealousy gradually consumed him.

Recurring dreams tormented him every night. He could see unknown men caressing her breasts and stroking her black hair. He awoke confused and in a cold sweat. He could feel himself swelling with indignation, and he struggled to regain control of his emotions. She was as beautiful as an angel as she lay sleeping next to him in bed. Her beauty overwhelmed him. His feelings of desire were mixed with unbearable pain. Her womanly body attracted him, but more and more he despised her deceitful spirit. He wanted the deceiving whore and her tempting sex to burn eternally in hellfire. His mind filled with fantasies of inflicting pain on her. They became more and more vivid. Rudolf's jealousy grew with every passing day. He hated every man around him and regarded them all as idiots. He stared fixedly at anyone who spoke to Arabella. He regularly misinterpreted innocent situations, completely lost his head and misbehaved, offending everyone who came his way.

The increasingly odd behavior of the young Prince zu Biederstern did not go unnoticed. People were frightened by his volatile moods and unbridled aggression. Those of the best society began to avoid his company. Soon it became fashionable in the salons to make fun of him behind his back, in the same way that the salons had always buzzed with admiration for his father.

Rudolf's terrible reputation even reached the ear of the emperor.

An Idyll in the Countryside

A FEW BRIEF VISITS to the aristocratic circles of Vienna made it obvious to Clementina that the Biederstern family was no longer as respected as before. She thought that Arabella was to blame, and so she urged Rudolf to move back to Castle Biederhof. She worried that her son would be openly shunned by the highest aristocracy. Rudolf went along with the idea, because he was less and less interested in society.

An entire wing of the castle was prepared to receive the young couple. The tranquillity of pastoral Burgenland was good for Rudolf's spirits and filled him with satisfaction. He and Arabella took daily promenades through the castle's extensive gardens, and he sought to make her appreciate the comforts of country life and to persuade her to turn her back upon the gossip and glitter of the aristocracy.

Arabella found their existence in the countryside to be a long, chilly, dreary autumn. This was not the life she had dreamed of. She wanted to be in fine company, roam through the world of the salons dressed in her finery, and visit the Burgtheater and the Opera. She wanted to be noticed, admired, surrounded by flattery and a thousand other little attractions, to feel fortunate at her privileged standing and see the appreciation that shone in men's eyes, to luxuriate in the role of one of the most attractive women in Vienna. She did not want to live like a rural princess among uneducated peasants and foresters stinking of white wine. She longed to return to the capital.

RUDOLF REPEATEDLY DISMISSED her requests to be allowed to return to Vienna. After three months at Biederhof Arabella told him that she had been invited to a soiree and had accepted because she had desperately wanted to escape their seclusion and meet other people. Rudolf wanted her to stay home with him that evening. He wanted her not to go anywhere. He was certain that her claims of a longing for city life were pure deception. Surely the reason she wanted to travel back to Vienna was to cast herself without a backward glance into the arms of other men.

Arabella felt like a prisoner. She stood with shoulders erect and head high and with insistent determination threatened to leave Rudolf. His eyes met hers, which were fearless. He was at a loss for words and felt cornered by her righteous indignation. A sudden wave of ill temper swept over him, and he lost control. He called her a bitch and all manner of other epithets. He felt his muscles clenching and his whole body surging with a force that concentrated its power in his belly and his sexual organ. He threw himself upon Arabella, tore off her clothing, penetrated her with violent force, and bit her lips so hard that the blood flowed.

"You despicable cur," she said in a voice full of loathing, and then she clawed his face.

She was frightened by the dark animal pulsation that battered her as Rudolf emptied himself deep in her sex. She wanted to hurt him and offend him.

"Many men better than you have lain with me since we got married, and not one had to use force to have me," she said calmly and clearly, with the eerie self-control of a wild-cat. "Every one says that he has never experienced anything as heavenly as the warmth of my wet sex. That's what I want to hear, not your wheezing in my ear. And besides, they all please me far more than you've ever managed to do."

Arabella's taunt drove Rudolf into even greater fury. He seized her by the throat with both hands. "I'll choke you," he threatened her, "until your tongue hangs out of your filthy mouth!"

An inarticulate gagging sound came from Arabella's lips.

Rudolf rose and buttoned his trousers. He lifted Arabella and carried her to an adjacent room. He flung her onto the floor and locked the door.

ONCE RUDOLF HAD CALMED DOWN, he felt a tinge of regret and thought that perhaps he should apologize. He understood now that it was the fear of losing her that had prompted him to behave so wildly. During his solitary din-ner he tried to decide what he could do to placate Arabella and keep her happy at Biederhof. He found no solution. So he decided to sleep on it and wait until the next morning.

ARABELLA FELT DEEPLY OFFENDED, and she seethed with rage. Rudolf was a real bastard, she thought, cruder than almost all the men she had ever met. She kicked the door and swore he would never again mistreat her like that. She was by God not his possession. After a long struggle she managed to pick the lock with a hairpin. She left that very evening for Vienna.

RUDOLF'S DISMAY knew no bounds when he discovered early the next morning that Arabella had disappeared. His heart pounded so hard he couldn't breathe; a cold sweat broke out on his forehead and hands. He didn't know where to go. The Bohemian servant Bohumil smiled benevolently at him. In all the years that the old retainer had known Rudolf, he had never seen him so devastated. He asked if he could give the prince something to drink. Rudolf asked for a large glass of cognac.

We all know that masculine self-esteem is a sensitive plant that must be watered or it will wither. Rudolf irrigated it with alcohol. After he had poured a large quantity of wine and cognac down his gullet over the course of a week, he called for his horse and carriage. The coachman sped toward Vienna. Rudolf sprawled against the soft cushions with his eyes closed, imagining Arabella. He felt the love for her welling up within him and was all but decided to bring her back home.

But nothing would turn out as Rudolf had expected.

An Evening at the Burgtheater

A LIVERIED SERVANT was sent out to locate Arabella. Night had already begun to fall when he returned to the Biederstern mansion. The servant knocked at the door of the salon but heard no response. After a long pause, he hesitantly opened the door and caught sight of two empty wine bottles on the table. The prince was silhouetted in his arm-chair before the hearth. Smoke rose lazily from the cigar in his right hand. The servant cleared his throat and announced that he had learned from reliable sources that the prince's wife would be visiting the Burgtheater that evening in the company of Prince Mattias Schwarzenberg.

Rudolf erupted into a towering rage at this news. The pains of jealousy were a knife stabbing his heart. He was sure that Arabella was Schwarzenberg's lover. The thought offended him deeply, since for some reason never explained to him, the name Schwarzenberg was deeply despised by his family. He decided to go at once to the theater.

THAT EVENING'S GALA at the Burgtheater was the event of the season, both socially and artistically. An expectant mood filled the horseshoe-shaped hall. His Majesty Ferdinand was celebrating his fiftieth birthday with a new drama written in honor of the emperor by the popular author Franz Grillparzer.

MATTIAS SCHWARZENBERG had only recently become a widower, but he still appeared vigorous and youthful, an aristocrat in the best years of his life and by no means a grieving old man. He participated in social life with exuberant energy and never missed an event.

The Schwarzenberg family had a large box in the first row. It was the envy of everyone in Viennese society, for it was directly adjacent to the emperor's loge.

That evening Arabella was wearing a tight-fitting long red dress cut daringly low so that it generously displayed her ample bosom. She sat next to the prince, sipping a glass of champagne, pleased that the young gentlemen in the rows above were staring at her in fascination. She loved for men to strip her naked with their imaginations.

The play was a fine one in agreeably melodious verse. A young man in a strange costume killed another one onstage. An older woman wept, another fell to her knees. The actors gestured wildly. Arabella sat there entranced by the action. Mattias Schwarzenberg was in pain, however, because he had injured his back in a serious hunting accident.

Arabella leaned toward her host to whisper a comment about the play. The gentle curve of her breasts swayed very close to the prince.

Just at that moment Rudolf erupted into the loge. He thought they were being extremely intimate with each other. He had absolutely no doubt that he had caught Schwarzenberg in the act of caressing Arabella's breast. Rudolf shook with fury and began screaming like a madman.

Onstage one of the leading actors was in the middle of declaiming a poetical line about the sweetness of the morning air. He choked on his words and stood there petrified with his mouth half open. Everyone in the theater, actors and audience, turned their attention to the box adjacent to that of the emperor.

For a fraction of a second Rudolf and Arabella stared into each other's eyes. She knew instinctively that her most effective response would be to break into tears, using the weapon of all women since time immemorial. She rose, her eyes brimming, and embraced her husband. She assured him that she loved and respected him, that he was the closest thing to her heart. Rudolf would not yield. Arabella's words and tears made no impression upon him. He didn't want tears from her; he wanted her to confirm the error of her ways, whether her conscience was clear or guilt-ridden.

He felt duped and humiliated before everyone in the hall. It suddenly seemed to him that he had been granted a glimpse into a life of lies and crimes that exceeded anything he could have imagined. He violently thrust Arabella back into her chair, almost turning it over, and screamed that her declarations of love were lies, cheap theatrics, and she was nothing but a whore.

Schwarzenberg stepped between them. He admonished the young prince for behaving like a child, in a manner hardly appropriate for the heir of such a highborn family.

Full of spite, Rudolf threw himself at the prince. He struck him in the face several times and then kicked him in the groin. Schwarzenberg was completely overwhelmed. He doubled up and sprawled against the wall, gasping for breath. His mouth tasted of blood, his wig hung awry, and his left ear was filled with a roaring that seemed to pierce his head. He clasped his hands to his face and found that his lip had been split open. The signet ring gleaming on his little finger was covered with blood. Rudolf disappeared from the box before Schwarzenberg could catch his breath sufficiently to issue a challenge to a duel.

ENORMOUS CONSTERNATION filled the Burgtheater. The ambassador from the Court of St. James, Lord Hickenbottom, was so alarmed that he suffered a massive heart attack, fell into a coma, and died early the next morning. Several ladies fainted. Everyone fell silent in terrible distress. One after another, spectators lowered their eyes and pretended to be somewhere else. The theater was deathly silent. Even those sitting in the farthest reaches of the hall could hear that the emperor was upset, for his hand shook uncontrollably as he unwrapped a chocolate praline from Sacher's pastry shop.

The Decree of the Kaiser

EARLY THE NEXT MORNING Rudolf received a note written in childishly sprawling script upon Prince Schwarzenberg's personal stationery. Arabella declared that as far as she was concerned, their marriage was ended.

Rudolf's first thought was that she wanted to be free to indulge in all of her vices, everything that she had been kept from doing by their stay in the countryside. He fell into a black mood and visualized unbearably graphic images of how he suspected she would be using her freedom.

Before he could sink any deeper into those painful fantasies, a new message arrived, this one from the Hofburg Palace. The emperor was getting involved in the matter. Rudolf was summoned to the court to account for his behavior at the Burgtheater.

"IN EARLIER TIMES young princes were not so quick to mistreat distinguished older princes," His Majesty stated. And he asked sternly, "Does this unacceptable attitude have something to do with your personality, young Biederstern? I have heard of a number of other distasteful incidents."

Rudolf was calm, or at least so it appeared. He acknowledged that his use of force was inappropriate and a breach of good manners. He also regretted that he had disturbed the performance at the theater. But he was not the least apologetic for handling the prince so roughly. Why should he be? A man has the right to defend that which belongs to him. He loved Arabella and the old goat was trying to steal her away. There was no reason at all for him to feel guilty or to have a bad conscience.

"The spectacle of jealous fisticuffs," responded the emperor, "you could certainly have spared yourself. And the rest of us, as well. I wish to advise you, young prince, that the women of Vienna are hypocritical and flirtatious. They are wicked fairies who torture men. Neither more nor less. It is entirely different in Budapest. In my youth there I once met a gloriously beautiful Hungarian countess. She could make any man's blood boil. But she was timid and reticent, just as was her Christian duty. Nothing at all like your wife. Everyone knows *her* background. And, by my word, at the theater I saw with my own eyes the way she was dressed. Her décolletage was an open challenge to good moral character. You should ask your mother to teach her proper decorum."

Rudolf had a sudden pressing need to urinate. It made him nervous. He shifted his weight from one foot to the other like a great clumsy duck and his hands began to tremble as if he had been drinking. He was seized by a growing panic, more and more difficult to conceal.

He interrupted the emperor. "Your Majesty, forgive me for saying so, but it seems as if the emperor was never in love. The emperor appears not to understand what Arabella means to me. And I beg Your Majesty please to abstain from getting my mother involved in my marriage."

The emperor frowned and shot Rudolf an icy look. He was not used to such lack of respect. None of his subjects had ever allowed himself to use such a tone. Ferdinand was not about to allow his late friend's scandalous son to speak to him in such an impertinent manner. Even if the young man was his own relative.

THE EMPEROR ORDERED him to quit the castle at once. Thirty seconds later, Rudolf stepped behind a door in the adjacent imperial salon and urinated without the slightest hesitation and at the same time let loose an enormous fart. The first impulse of the astonished retainer charged with escorting the young man out of the Hofburg was to attack the shameless prince; he restrained himself only with great difficulty.

KAISER FERDINAND was a short, melancholy man often subject to fits of epilepsy and not fit to rule Austria. Everyone knew it. He always avoided the issues of strategy that determined the fate of his empire and found political matters simply too complicated. He said exactly that, with the disarming smile of a person who doesn't want to grow up. The country was ruled by a quadrumvirate dubbed the "four-leafed clover," consisting of Duke Ludwig, Duke Hans Karl, Prince Metternich, and Count Kolowrat. The emperor spent his time going around in pomp and circumstance, arranging for one brilliant ceremony after another, and exchanging gossip with his adjutants.

The powerful men of the ruling council considered this incident an excellent opportunity—since if there is no fear of reprisal, unruly events will begin to propagate themselves even in the best society—to demonstrate decisively that the emperor would not tolerate any actions aimed at undermining the hierarchy of Austrian society. They decided that Ferdinand would have to be perceived as the upholder of the moral values of ancient Austria.

"There must be order," insisted Duke Ludwig. "No one can piss in the imperial salon with impunity." He wrote out a decree and obliged the emperor to sign it. Prince zu Biederstern was in disgrace and forever banished from the court. Further, Rudolf was forbidden to visit Vienna for a period of ten years.

An Estate in Decay

POLITICAL COMMENTATORS in the liberal press of the capital theorized in guarded terms about the hidden meaning and long-term consequences of that decree.

The salons of Vienna were roiled by veritable orgies of gossip. Prince zu Biederstern's fate was on everyone's lips. No one was surprised by the harsh punishment handed down to him. Indignation was still great over his inexplicable behavior at the theater and his shameless attack upon the respected Prince Schwarzenberg. Honorable men proclaimed to one and all that never again would they shake hands with Rudolf; they asserted that even the rotters and curs one encountered while subduing the Balkans were better men than the young prince. Many were pleased that the madman had been exiled from the salons and sent away alone and dishonored in his misery. Some members of society commented that the whole affair would be the death of his poor mother.

THE BANISHMENT of Rudolf from courtly society was hard for his family to bear. It was hardest of all for his mother, a Habsburg on her mother's side and the niece of the emperor. The shame was great, the incident was huge, and a centuries-old family reputation had been dragged into the dirt.

Rudolf locked himself away in his office in the castle. He sat down at the desk to write a lengthy letter to Arabella, to tell her that even though he was only one of a thousand men for her and perhaps not even the most interesting, she was his one and only, the one who stood at the center of his life. He wished to tell her that through a sort of magical attraction she had brought out in him all the elements of tenderness and warmth hidden in the depths of his heart, qualities that no one had ever managed to evoke. He had trouble finding the words to express all of this. He stared dully at the empty page for a long time. After a while he began to experience a vague dread that Arabella might actually come back to him. A voice within him whispered that his love was stimulated less by Arabella herself than by the rupture between them. He suddenly remembered that the more time he had spent with her, the less attractive she had seemed to him. In her absence, however, his fantasy worked full time, stimulated by pain, creating in his heart a lunatic love for her.

A FEW DAYS before Christmas, Rudolf's mother abruptly entered his office without knocking. He was sitting at a desk littered with empty wine bottles. She started to say something but burst into tears instead. Several minutes passed before she was able to control herself. Finally, reluctantly, she entreated her son to ask His Majesty for a pardon. Rudolf refused to be moved. He told his mother without the least sign of contrition that he felt he been treated unfairly. In his view, the Kaiser was interfering with his own private affairs. That was why, with no heed for the consequences, he had made the bitter decision that he would cease to be Ferdinand's faithful servant. He stressed that decision later that evening in a fairly drunken rant delivered in the garden of the castle to a group of frightened, freezing workers. With wild gestures Rudolf wound up his address with words that were almost prophetic: "The warm winds of springtime will sweep that coldhearted emperor from his throne." Following that, he called for bread and meat to be distributed to the people. There was no lack of wine, either.

—————

HIS SPITEFUL DECLARATION quickly became common knowledge in Vienna. In the view of aristocratic society it confirmed that by breaking with convention and marrying a whore, Rudolf had sunk as low as he could go; he had completely lost his mind. The fact that he also had the arrogance to denounce the emperor was unforgivable. His direct public criticism of the Kaiser was taken as proof that he was a traitor and a politically dangerous outcast.

ALONE, BANISHED, with no prospects of a return to the world of the salons, Rudolf lived beyond all limits of rational behavior, remote from life's realities. He slept the days away and spent his nights frequenting all the dubious bordellos on the Hungarian side of the border. Every night he demanded new prostitutes to soothe his pains. He was constantly in search of one with Arabella's swarthy aspect, her perfect, voluptuous body, her willfulness and determination. But he never found one with the same womanly charms, sensual lips, and enigmatic expression. Perhaps because he paid for women who in fact meant nothing to him. Nevertheless, he was given to madly throwing away diamonds and rubies, gems that would have been the treasures of an exhibition in any first-class museum in the world, giving them to prostitutes who wouldn't have merited a second look from any man from the Viennese nobility.

With all the wine and cognac poisoning his blood, Rudolf was unshaved, unkempt, and smelly. He adored baked goods rich in sugar and cream almost as much as he liked alcohol. This diet resulted in a rapid gain of more than sixty pounds that made him almost unrecognizable in his blubber.

When he wasn't debauching himself in the bordellos, he was frequenting smugglers and cardsharps wanted by the Hungarian police. He did not realize how unscrupulous they were until he had lost the lion's share of his inheritance playing cards with them.

HIS MOTHER AND SISTERS could not hide their disgust with Rudolf's chronic drunkenness and atrocious behavior. When they pleaded with him to stop drinking, he told them to go to hell and screamed that he hated their affectations and constant prattle. Then he drastically reduced the allowances of all three.

The bishop of Burgenland sought with all his ecclesiastical techniques of persuasion to bring him to his senses. Rudolf simply burst into merry laughter and told him that the final souvenir he had carried off from Arabella was a case of syphilis.

HE COMPLETELY NEGLECTED his duties as the master of the castle. The magnificent estate rapidly fell into a state of decay, but no one dared to criticize him. The master had absolute power and made all the decisions; his wish was everyone's command. They all understood that this was the natural order of things. Although he was much diminished physically, seriously alcoholic, and short of cash, the prince wielded absolute power over them and his inheritance. Everyone was obliged to cater to his every whim, attend to him in abject servility, and comply with the social order that those living on his estate had inherited throughout generations of serfdom.

Winds of Change

CIVIL UNREST intensified in March 1848. There was an upwelling of discontent and change was in the air. A new epoch was dawning, the new era of class struggle. The citizens of Vienna rose up and demonstrated in the streets. From one moment to the next, they changed from loyal subjects to revolutionaries. Paving stones flew. Windows shattered. Public spaces were laid waste. Blood flowed in the streets. The crowds surged forward, massing and shouting their demands. In the turmoil, the people were simply trying to better their lot in life. The prevailing world order came under furious attack. The government tottered.

THE SCENES on the streets of Vienna were reprised across Europe. The unexpected conflagration set city after city on fire. Europe was aflame. Outcry against the prevailing social order resounded in Paris, Munich, Milan, and Budapest. The military held back the thrusting crowds.

BIEDERHOF REMAINED strangely calm even though it was situated only twenty-five miles from Vienna. Echoes of the political unrest reached the Biederstern family castle, so of course the workers on the estate knew that in the capital class clashes were growing, and the pressure for reform was surging like a mighty river. They never showed the least interest and wasted no time trying to make out the meaning of all this. Getting into a lather about politics and distant events was like arguing which came first, the chicken or the egg.

Kaiser Ferdinand found the revolution most unpleasant and betrayed his increasing apprehension in his posture: He tended more and more to twist to one side as if defending himself. He was depressed and confused by the news of turmoil in the empire. His epileptic seizures became more frequent. The situation finally became unbearable. One dark bleak day after receiving a report that some hooligan had broken a window at Schönbrunn Palace, he precipitately fled Vienna and took refuge in Olomouc, a rustic village on the bank of the Morava River in northern Mähern.

So that the people would not interpret his flight as surrender to revolutionary masses, Ferdinand abdicated and designated his eighteen-year-old nephew as his successor, without consulting the real rulers of the land. Franz Josef ascended the throne at a time of extreme political tension under the skeptical eyes of the ruling class.

Opinion makers among the conservative aristocracy considered the new Habsburg ruler a naïve and boyish lightweight. They assumed him incapable of putting down the revolt and ruling the empire. Even ancient faithful court retainers feared that Franz Josef's rule would be a disaster. Franz Josef opened a military campaign against rebellious subjects of his vast realm on a spring day just as the trees began to bud. He didn't allow mistaken notions of Christian charity to get in his way.

The struggles with the rebels were especially violent in Hungary, where the new Kaiser had sent the Croatian commander Josip Jelačić and his army of forty thousand soldiers, tried and true. Croatians had lived under the yoke of Hungary for seven hundred and fifty years. They hated the Magyars for forcing the Hungarian language and culture upon them. Patriotic Croatian troops experienced brilliant successes for the very first time. Rivers of blood flowed, meadows were strewn with corpses, and the Croatians destroyed everything that stood in their way—houses, bridges, farms, even public laundries.

Order was restored after a year of this. The emperor had demonstrated his strength, and the prestige of the throne was restored. Peace and calm reigned throughout the land.

Burial

WE KNOW LITTLE of Arabella's fate after that evening in the Burgtheater. Her relationship with Schwarzenberg lasted only a few months. She was shown the door when she could no longer hide the fact that she was pregnant. She left her newborn baby girl with her eldest brother, then she lived for a time with an elderly baron with a reputation for sadistic mistreatment of women. After that, her long-term relationships gave way to much briefer ones. A whole generation of men—this time of less cosmopolitan stamp—paid for the privilege of emptying their seed into her.

Arabella's allure lasted only as long as her raven-black hair retained its luster and her skin remained smooth. Then she quickly wound up on the back streets of Vienna.

She died of an acute infection on a spring day just a week before her twenty-seventh birthday. People said an old woman with little experience of practical medicine had bungled an abortion. No one was at all surprised.

They buried Arabella in her bridal gown, according to her dying wish, in a potter's field on the far edge of the capital. Only three people came to bid her farewell: two former colleagues from the Salon Rouge and a confused old woman who hadn't known Arabella but made a habit of attending all the funerals. It was fortunate that the two relatively bedraggled whores were present. The priest didn't want to carry out the full graveside service, but the younger woman offered him a blow job in lieu of his customary fee. The priest zealously applied himself and gave a particularly enthusiastic eulogy depicting the piety of the last princess zu Biederstern.

A Turning Point

GRIEF FASTENED ITS CLAWS in Rudolf's soul when he received word of Arabella's death. His days at Biederhof were already black as night, and he now sank into even deeper melancholy. The master of the castle had lost his taste for Hungarian prostitutes and had no money left to gamble away at cards. He never went out; he sat alone in his armchair, his face as pale as death, staring emptily into space or absorbed in deeply meaningful conversation with the cat, the only earthly creature that seemed to care for him.

His family was deeply concerned about his health. Everyone at the castle knew that Rudolf was ill, and they could see that something was seriously wrong. Only the reliable old Bohemian retainer Bohumil, who had accompanied the young master twenty-five years earlier to Captain von Knapp's renowned boarding school, knew he had been using opium to alleviate the misery of his tortured spirit. But the pleasant distractions of opium did not last for long. His addiction and abuse rapidly undermined his already fragile health.

Creditors were gathering outside the castle doors like hungry wolves. Everyone on the estate wondered how much longer the prince could survive. His mother had a premonition, stronger with each passing day, that the end of the family was near.

ONE STORMY NIGHT Rudolf sat up in bed, looked around, and wondered if the sun had already come up. The skies were fiery red, and cries could be heard in the distance. At first he was completely confused. He pulled on his clothes, bewildered, and went out on the balcony. Lightning had struck buildings in Biedersingen and the timber mill was on fire. By the time he got to it, nothing was recognizable. Where houses and workshops once had stood, only chimneys were left. Smoking heaps of blackened timbers were everywhere. The mill had burned to the ground, leaving nothing but ruins.

RUDOLF WAS A CHANGED MAN after the great fire in the autumn of 1856. The transformation was unbelievable. In every man's life there comes a moment when he can start anew, and Rudolf experienced that moment after climbing the steps of the highest tower of the castle. From that vantage point he looked out over the surrounding landscape and saw everything that the centuries had given to his family. The weather was magnificent. He saw fields and trees and rolling hills, a whole region of Austria that belonged to him. He stood high atop the castle handed down from his father and grandfather and from their fathers and grandfathers over the centuries and through the generations. Biederhof lay like a jewel case among those cultivated fields and forests.

Rudolf had grown up in a world where one could pretend that money did not exist. He had never learned the mysterious process by which the secret depths of forests were transformed into new slate tiles for the castle roof and trees became bales of firewood for the royal kitchens in Vienna. Only when he could no longer pay wages to coachmen, servants, cooks, gardeners, and foresters because no one would provide him with credit did he finally begin to grasp the disaster that was looming. He saw that everything the Biedersterns had always possessed, everything that embodied the family name, was slipping inexorably out of his hands. If he lost the estate, he would grieve the spirits of his ancestors and obliterate their heritage.

At first he felt numb, and then his heart filled with a bewildering mixture of pain and fear like nothing he had ever experienced. He broke into wild lament and tears streamed down his cheeks. That was the turning point. The good fairy of insight had broken through the evil circle that imprisoned Rudolf.

HE ROSE before daybreak the next morning to discuss the reconstruction of the buildings. He sketched architectural plans and huddled with the chiefs of the mill to estimate the costs. He got back to the castle only at nightfall. His engagement amazed everyone. His mother's face went chalk white when she heard of it; she thanked the Almighty and wept in her room.

MONTHS PASSED. One freezing cold day when the land was covered with snow, the workers were forced to suspend construction for fear of frostbite. Their fingers were stiff with cold. The entire population of the estate was summoned to the castle. Spiced wine was heated at open hearths and served to them. Rudolf told them he had hired a manager in order to keep the property out of the hands of his greedy creditors. He said that the uniquely talented man scheduled to arrive from Frankfurt the following day had saved his German cousin Prince Ludwig von Thurn und Taxis, an experienced practitioner of the fine art of idleness whose estate had been in deep financial decline. He wound up his address by stressing that each of them had the duty to comply with every request of the manager, no matter how apparently insignificant. The residents of the estate felt somewhat reassured and looked forward to the following day. The choice of manager, however, turned out to be a source of great surprise at Biederhof.

NINE

The Minister of Finance

Vertigo

MY HEAD IS SPINNING again as I confront the complicated skein of past events that affected my own life. A young son of a rabbi in León who encountered Moses, an unprincipled physician in Granada who poisoned his master, a wandering Jew who defied death for more than three hundred and fifty years, a philosopher in Amsterdam who suffered from paranoia, a Parisian attorney who loved books, his daughter avid for learning and her two strange sons—all those presences in the past that my great-uncle with his enthralling tales re-created for us in my childhood may perhaps have had more influence on my character than my own mother and father, who always seemed so remote and unavailable.

WHAT WOULD my life have been if Jakob Spinoza hadn't accepted the request to manage the affairs of the run-down Biederstern estate and save it from ruin?

His eldest son, Bernhard, would almost certainly have married a different woman, so none of us—not Grandfather, not Father, not I—would have been born.

But as I think it over, it occurs to me that probably none of us would've been granted the mercy of drifting in eternal heavenly bliss and avoiding birth. I would still have come into this world, but as someone different, not as the person I am.

Would my life have been happier?

I'll never know, and I'm willing to admit that I'm grateful for that. It would've been bitter to find out, some time before the curtain finally fell, that my life, ruled more or less by chance in a world of troubles, could have been different from the very start and could have offered me joy and worldly pleasures.

CHIARA GOT to the Place de Grève as dawn was breaking, to make sure of securing a place as close to the platform as possible. She then stood there for hours in the pouring rain, waiting with unshakable serenity.

The event announced for that morning would have made anyone else despondent, stunned with grief. But not Chiara. She did not care for tears. Weeping was anathema to her. She was of the opinion that women should never indulge in tears.

She had put on her wedding dress, as white as snow, so Nicolas would see her in the gray mass of people. It was her message to her husband that life was on their side, a way of endowing him with even greater courage.

She saw no reason to expect any miracle or divine intervention. She was sure that Robespierre would save Nicolas from the guillotine at the last moment. She believed they were still "the inseparables," even though the differences between them had become contentious, and she entertained no misgivings. It was not the belief in friendship that kept her from groveling at Maximilien's feet with pleas for Nicolas's life, as some friends had urged her to do; it was her fierce conviction that a woman who begged demeaned herself and deserved no sympathy.

The ever provocative Robespierre accepted no protests and tolerated no criticism. He was arrogant and pitiless, brimming with contempt for humanity and determined to go to any lengths in his campaign to apply his stirring revolutionary slogans and create a new world. Everyone knew that by now. Many of them had begun to realize that the spirit of freedom that had intoxicated France was already ebbing away. Chiara could not believe that Robespierre, despite the arrogance and brutality she knew so well, would make Nicolas pay with his head, merely for daring to speak of acts that betrayed equality, brotherhood, democracy, and human rights, all the achievements of the revolution.

At the stroke of eleven, just as the rain stopped and the sun peeked out from behind the dark clouds, drums beating in the marketplace signaled that the prisoner was on his way from the Conciergerie. The tumbrel with Nicolas aboard arrived a few minutes later. The excited crowd stood there, packed tight. Many were eager for the bloody spectacle, as if it were the first public execution in Paris. Whistles and boos were heard, and many waved their fists in derision.

Nicolas advanced with slow steps, head high, accompanied to the scaffold by the rhythmic beating of the drums. His hands were tied behind him, as a precaution and to mark him as a criminal condemned by the people's tribunal. He appeared confident and fearless, alone against the rest of the world. He knew that as a rebel against the tyrannies of Robespierre, he could expect no mercy. The dignity radiating from him impressed even the vilest of his abusers.

When Chiara and Nicolas caught sight of each other, she spontaneously went up on tiptoe and pursed her lips in a declaration of love. He smiled and blew her a kiss.

The drumbeat suddenly ceased. Nicolas turned toward Maximilien, who looked pale and listless. The colossal power vested in Robespierre as the absolute dictator of France obviously had not cured him of the chronic fatigue from countless sleepless nights, but the Jacobin leader was concentrating upon the only thing that energized him and made him forget his weariness: the execution of enemies in the name of the high ideals of the revolution.

Nicolas nodded and greeted him with a friendly tone. "Maximilien, next time it will be your turn to set your thick neck here. *Au revoir.*"

He knelt and placed his head beneath the guillotine. His neck was bared so everyone could see his throat and the shapes of the vertebrae that led back under his white shirt.

The crowd fell silent. The executioner stood motionless, as if believing that the ideologue of the revolution would be spared at the last second. Chiara's hands began to tremble. She felt dizzy. An invisible power took her by the throat and squeezed her chest so hard that she had trouble breathing. Robespierre rose and savagely ordered the executioner to get to work. No mercy would be granted to conspirators against the revolution. The blade fell with a thud and was greeted by a joyous outcry.

Chiara stood there motionless long after the spectators had left the marketplace.

A First Novel

TWENTY-EIGHT YEARS LATER, when Chiara heard that Napoleon had died in exile on St. Helena, she patiently tried to explain to her grandson Jakob how a revolution in the name of freedom and equality had produced an emperor with absolute power ruling the country. She found that the task was too much for her.

How could one explain that a people who had sought to exterminate the ancien régime once and for all, that old despotic order, would then turn to follow a Corsican captain who on the thirteenth of *vendémiaire* (October 4, 1795) ordered troops to shoot into the crowd on the steps of Saint Roch church in Paris, killing more than three hundred royalists, and then shortly afterward promised France a new golden age? And how does one respond when asked why the revolution could not be carried out without piling up tens of thousands of bodies in the streets and marketplaces? How did liberation turn into terror? Above all, why does history always require a bloodbath, and why do we humans never learn from the past but always allow the hydra of violence to grow new heads and spit more poison?

CHIARA AND HER TWO SMALL SONS somehow survived the months immediately after Nicolas's execution, and no one, not even my great-uncle, knew how they did so. In the autobiography she wrote late in her life, *Souvenirs*, she did not say a word about that time.

On the other hand, she records in those memoirs with matter-of-fact realism and a good dose of self-irony that she hesitated for a very long time before finally deciding to write about her experiences during the revolution, principally because they were still so vivid to her. She also had evident problems in selecting an appropriate point of view. She initially sought to take a factual approach, so the account would not be colored by her own temperament or suffering. With that idea in mind, she wrote it as an essay. Her friends' response was unenthusiastic; they found it deliberately dull, with none of her energy. Their comments did not discourage her. Quite the opposite; she realized that her first draft was a naïve effort to hide from the realities and instead she would have to describe what had happened in her own style, daring to abandon genteel artifices considered appropriate for the weaker sex.

———

WOMEN OF THE EARLY NINETEENTH CENTURY were supposed to write in a distinctly feminine style that did not challenge the reader. They deftly constructed a fabric woven of many individual lives, colored with sentimentality and self-sacrificing generosity. Ever undemanding, admirable in their self-abnegation, and always ready to yield to others, female authors relegated themselves to invoking unquestioned platonic concepts such as Love and Charity.

BECAUSE OF HER FIERCE DESIRE to communicate her own truths about the revolution, Chiara abandoned the empty rhetoric of contemporary female writers. She wanted her art to confront reality. She wanted to shape the consciousness of her world by bursting balloons; to tear down the myths about a heroic revolution and subject them to healthy rational analysis and sober reflection; in short, she wanted to create a hurricane to sweep away the reassuring lies that prevailed throughout the land.

THE NOVEL APPEARED under her maiden name, Chiara Luzzatto. It was published in 1804 by Éditions du Agorah in Strasbourg with the title *Chronos dévorant un de ses enfants* (*Time*—from the Greek—*Devouring One of His Children*). Hers was the first account of its type to describe the days of the bloodbaths in Paris. It was a thunderclap, a cannon shot, and its fame rapidly spread across all of Europe. Chiara was praised for her unique artistic felicities, and above all, for her language. "A French of such clarity and purity had scarcely been seen since the days of La Rochefoucauld," noted the Marquis de Sade, who as a political opponent of the Jacobins' use of the death penalty had only with great difficulty avoided the guillotine.

The Property of All

HEINDRICH ZU BIEDERSTERN, who never lost an opportunity to criticize leaders of the French Revolution whose ideas made him recoil in horror and repulsion, was among the most devout admirers of the novel. He found it masterful, in certain passages almost a work of genius (especially those that described the grim suffering of the nobility at the hands of the unruly masses) and in other passages of international caliber. He declared that Chiara Luzzatto was the equal of even the best male authors. The prince was so pleased with her novel that he underwrote the costs of translation into German. He made no secret of the fact that it had given him a much deeper understanding of the politics of the time. He declared that this account made the truth of the barbaric events of the French Revolution the property of all.

During the Vienna Congress of 1814, where Europe's leading rulers discussed how aristocrats were to regain the power they had wielded before the French Revolution, Heindrich made a much-applauded appearance. His lengthy speech was essentially an attack against the ideals of the Enlightenment, which he blamed for undermining the natural right of the aristocracy to exercise power. The prince directed sharp criticism against Nicolas Spinoza for having roused the wrath of the people with his scribblings and against Jacobin leader Maximilien Robespierre for instituting the reign of terror. He quoted no fewer than four passages from Chiara's novel to evoke the cruelty of the revolution—ignorant of the fact that the authoress was Nicolas's wife and, moreover, one of those who voted on January 20, 1793, in favor of decapitating the king.

———

SEVERAL CONTEMPORARY ARTISTS were deeply marked by Chiara's debut novel and took inspiration from it. The most significant of them was the Spaniard Francisco Goya.

The year was 1819. Dismayed by the increasingly antiliberal actions of the Spanish monarchy and fearing he would be targeted, the painter fled Madrid for the pastoral landscape of Castile and isolated himself at his newly purchased house. He had just turned seventy-three. He was accepting no new commissions, even though many of the nobility had begged him to paint their portraits. With his memory failing, half deaf, and perpetually ill-humored, Goya preferred to be with his canvases, his paintbrushes, and his dark oil paints. He seldom left his studio with its unimaginable disarray of canvases and frames piled in precarious heaps and all sorts of work material flung at random on the floor. He never told anyone how he spent his days and nights. His wife knew only that he hardly slept anymore. A cook brought him food in the morning and in the evening, always accompanied by a bottle of strong Rioja wine. He wore wide black trousers and sleeveless white shirts of the finest Egyptian cotton day and night. He wore this garb even in the deepest of winter. He never felt the cold; the Rioja in his blood kept him warm.

Goya received Chiara's novel as a birthday present from one of his mistresses, a woman forty years younger than he was. She spent one night a week with him, but they almost never spoke to each other anymore. For that reason he was surprised when she handed him the book and told him to read it. She left without saying goodbye. He immediately understood that she had left him for good and would never return. He sat motionless for a time, with the book in his hand, surrounded by a portentous silence.

Goya was surprised to find himself piqued by curiosity. He had never been a reader of novels. He would have given his life for *Don Quixote* by Cervantes, but he considered all other novels to be lies written by contemptible wretches who wanted to get ahead and therefore not worth the effort of studying. Chiara's book, however, appeared to be something different. It was the parting gift of his lover of many years. He wanted to see what lay within.

Goya opened the novel at random and began reading, not without an occasional yawn, until he came to the passage that tells how the coldhearted revolutionary leader sends his best friend to the guillotine. It describes with a hair-raising wealth of detail the head of the condemned prisoner separating from his body and falling into a laundry basket as his wife, clad in her wedding dress, stands only a few feet away, having believed right up to the last instant that he would be pardoned by his friend. The episode is permeated with devastating horror, intense revulsion, and stunned hopelessness. It greatly impressed Goya. Fascinated, he paged farther. At last, eighteen hours later, he put down the bulky novel. He was deeply affected. For three days he found it impossible to eat, drink, or sleep. He stared into space, haunted by horrible visions. He could see heads chopped from bodies spurting cascades of blood. On the fourth day, unexpectedly, exhilaration filled him. He picked up the broadest of his paintbrushes and a container of black oil paint. He looked around for a canvas that would be large enough. Finding none, he hurried into the dining room, tore down the canvases hanging there, and began painting on the whitewashed wall. This was the beginning of the "black period" in his art.

The completed work shows a gigantic monster that has just chewed off the head of a naked male body held in its hands. Goya named it after Chiara's novel, for despite its powerful description of human folly he regarded it not as degrading to mankind but rather as liberating and purifying. To emphasize that the wall painting was his own interpretation of the French Revolution, he used the Roman term "Saturn" instead of the Greek "Chronos" ("Time"). *Saturno devorando a su hijo* ("Saturn devouring his child") is one of the artist's greatest masterpieces.

The Road to Frankfurt

CHIARA'S DEBUT NOVEL brought Amschel Rothschild into her life. She traveled to Freiburg at the invitation of Princess Karen von Hohenweiler, who regularly invited friends and acquaintances to her home to discuss current issues. Chiara was pleased—pleased to be recognized as a writer and proud that her novel had attracted attention outside France.

Although this was the first time she had been asked to discuss her novel in public, she was not at all nervous, and the sophisticated individuals of the literary salon saw none of her customary reticence. A group of friendly and curious princesses and baronesses clustered around her, and she discovered to her great astonishment that they had all read the book. She saw a fashionably dressed man watching her intently as the crowd swirled around her. She was exhilarated by the ambiance of titled ease at the elegant gathering, especially by the unaccustomed experience of being the focus of attention.

In her memoirs she describes that evening as giving her the sensation of suddenly emerging from a dark tunnel into the dazzling light of day.

Chiara spoke at length and in detail of the events that had shaped the novel, not neglecting Nicolas's fate and its decisive effect upon her attitude toward life. In a firm, clear voice she said she believed that within every writer a great hurt is concealed. Seeing that gloom had settled upon the gathering and some of the women had tears in their eyes, she concluded by assuring them that despite all the adversity and defeats, she saw life as a celebration. The audience applauded enthusiastically.

Once the clapping had died away, a man stood up to ask a question—the same individual she had noticed earlier. He had continued to stare at her throughout her talk, unobtrusive but intent. He asked her to name the quality she found most important for an author.

She replied, "Having one eye for those things all humans share, and another for their differences."

Later that evening the princess introduced Chiara to her questioner, Amschel Rothschild, who had come from Frankfurt with the express purpose of meeting the authoress. He turned out to be an excellent conversationalist, quick-witted and well-educated, and his graceful remarks were delivered with a warmth and sensuality that was unapologetic but not in the least insistent. There was something about his general aspect that Chiara found remarkably attractive, an evident nobility of spirit that impressed her.

She was somewhat taken aback when he interrupted himself in the middle of a thought to ask whether they might meet again. She came close to blushing. The wine served that afternoon may have influenced her, for despite her natural reserve toward men, she agreed.

THE NEXT MORNING Chiara and Amschel Rothschild took a stroll in the city's English Garden. They discussed writing and death, love and loneliness, not in the manner of casual acquaintances but with a warmth and frankness that surprised them both. He made it perfectly clear that he was married and that he considered that fact to be no hindrance to their developing a friendship based on mutual respect. Chiara found that he was an honorable man with original views and an open enjoyment of life. She agreed to correspond with him.

How often they met, how things played out between them, when exactly Chiara surrendered to Amschel after his fiery courtship of her, how he expressed his gratitude for that gift—my great-uncle could tell us nothing of any of that. Or perhaps, because Sasha and I were young and tender, he preferred not to share the details of their love affair. In any case, he told us that Amschel soon asked Chiara to move to Frankfurt, his home city, even though she was nothing like the archetypal *petite amie* cherished by bourgeois gentlemen of the time.

Eventually, but only after three years and a hundred and fifty letters, she agreed. During that period she occasionally asked herself what she saw in him. The answer was always the same: Amschel made everything more intense and her life became more vivid. He communicated to her a feeling of hope, of growth, of new possibility. Wherever he was, she knew, her future was destined to be.

A CERTAIN DELICACY was required to explain to her sons, Gérard and Guido, her plans to move. Chiara presented the project as an exciting departure from their humdrum lives, and she dwelt at length upon the beautiful home that awaited them. Guido's interest was immediately piqued when she told him of the young physicist Johann Friedrich Benzenberg and the astronomical observatory he had founded in Frankfurt with the support of Rothschild's bank. But Gérard, who was older, regarded her with suspicion. He remained extremely doubtful about the project—until she told him about the excellent schools available to him, for Amschel in his generosity had pledged to pay his tuition. She had foreseen that such a promise would entice Gérard, because his heart was set upon studying the law and she did not have the money to send the boys to the best schools.

CHIARA HAD AN UNEASY FEELING that Amschel might be a burden to his wife, Angela, instead of a strong supporting arm, for he had never brought her to the places that Chiara and Amschel visited. But Chiara had never met Angela and had no idea what she desired. Perhaps Angela felt her needs had already been met.

Amschel assured Chiara that his wife—in fact, she was his cousin and theirs was an arranged marriage, not a love match—had never objected at all to the proposal that Chiara and the boys share their spacious residence instead of living in rented accommodations. He asserted that Angela in fact welcomed the idea, for such an intimate arrangement would allow him and his lady friend to celebrate their love in freedom. Even so, Chiara felt a certain disquiet. Her misgivings turned out to be unwarranted.

ANGELA WAS A FEW YEARS older than Amschel. She had the habit unusual in sophisticated circles of chattering gaily and speaking completely without inhibition to strangers. There was a refreshing lightheartedness about her that touched even the hardest heart. She was a great adorer of children; for years she thought of children every moment of the day, but she proved unable to have any of her own. Perhaps that was why she was so eager to have the boys in the house; and the fact that there were two of them made her twice as happy. She spent every afternoon tutoring them in German. Within a couple of weeks she was lavishing motherly love upon Gérard and Guido as if they were her own sons.

Angela was grateful that Chiara and the boys had come into her life. She knew all too well how lonely that vast residence could be. That was why she even consented to the proposal that she, her husband, and Chiara, whom she treated as a sister instead of as a rival, should sleep together in the same bed.

MY GREAT-UNCLE once told us that Chiara, Amschel, and Angela were united by the bands of love not only in life but also in death. They were laid to rest in the same grave.

Chiara

THE ROTHSCHILD RESIDENCE was enormous. It had salons and bedrooms too many to count and plenty of nooks and crannies—furnished with a taste that Chiara found entirely too formal. She deeply disliked the huge oil paintings with heavy gold frames hung throughout the house. They depicted the most impressive scenery the Alps had to offer: mighty mountains, snow-covered peaks, leafy valleys, and dramatic swirling clouds pierced by the rays of the sun. One could almost hear Swiss cattle mooing from the canvases. Chiara found those paintings completely tasteless and lacking in significance; they depressed her. No matter how hard she tried, she could not imagine how Amschel, a soul in perpetual quest of originality, could have purchased these epic scenes and hung them in his residence. He eventually explained that they were an inheritance from his father, the founder of the family bank, who all his life had sought to distance himself from everything that might remind him of his origins: the narrow Judengasse in the ghetto where Frankfurt's Jews were locked away from sunset until sunrise, as well as on every Sunday and every Christian holiday.

NO ONE AROUND CHIARA could fail to see her dislike of Frankfurt. With pursed lips she often delivered sharp remarks disparaging her new city of residence. She was constantly finding something or other to complain about: the fact that all Germans were stiff and formal and made her feel she had no home anywhere; the city's ugliness and dismal appearance; and especially the prevailing chill. She always felt cold, for winter never seemed to end. The sun did not warm the place up until July, rather than by April as it did in Rome, that city the springtime bathed in hot, glittering brilliance.

She was always talking about her native city. The people were warmer, the streets were more beautiful, and the air was healthier. "Life in Rome is better than anywhere else," she insisted in a tone that brooked no opposition, so no one dared to disagree. Still, many people laughed behind her back when she claimed in all seriousness that if one threw a straw into Frankfurt's Main River it would sink like a stone, while even objects of lead would float in the blue waters of the Tiber.

CHIARA DID NOT TELL anyone why she had never returned to Rome after marrying Nicolas Spinoza in 1788 and moving to Paris. It was a mystery to everyone, especially given that she often expressed a deep longing to see her two sisters.

A Heavenly Feeling

HOTEL QUELLENHOF in Bad Ragaz. Napoleon's cannons were thundering in Prussia, Austria, and Poland, but everything was quiet in the province of Graubünden in eastern Switzerland. The war seemed far away. Amschel Rothschild had long ago established the tradition of spending Christmas in that little spa town, taking his rheumatism treatments far from the world's tumult and putting himself in the hands of experienced doctors who made him limber once again. In December 1808, he brought Chiara and her sons with him for the first time.

In the hotel lobby Amschel ran into an acquaintance from Berlin, Anton von Wiedersack, a dried-up little fellow who concealed the haughty covetousness of a Prussian noble behind dark glasses and an impeccable cravat. The gentlemen greeted each other with pleasantries and exchanged the usual remarks about the difficult times they were living in. They decided to meet again with their families for afternoon tea.

The air was warm and fragrant in the elegant salon. The guests who sat chatting at other tables were well-dressed and bored, both of which were qualities essential to the art of socializing with the wealthy in that tradition-laden atmosphere.

Amschel introduced Chiara and her sons to his acquaintance. Herr von Wiedersack rose and greeted them politely, but he became notably less cordial when he heard

Rothschild's female friend and her boys speaking rudimentary German with heavy French accents. This immediately marked them as of suspect origin. Frau von Wiedersack moved restlessly in her chair as she greeted this foreign woman who had popped up from nowhere, and she commented without concealing her displeasure, "We had hoped to meet your wife here, my dear banker." Her daughter, Désirée, hid a yawn.

Amschel responded with a small smile to this remark that in other circumstances could have been taken as an affront. Chiara seated herself and examined the von Wiedersack couple, puzzled that their attitude to her had suddenly turned frosty. For a few moments there was a painful silence.

Obsequious waiters wearing tuxedos and displaying perfect posture served diminutive golden-brown petits fours with their tea, lightening the mood somewhat.

Herr von Wiedersack initiated conversation by vigorously condemning Napoleon, calling him a mere commoner who had the outrageous ambition of ruling all of Europe. The little man seemed completely to have forgotten his childhood in the backstreets of Ajaccio. *"Bonaparte est merde,"* he said to stress his exasperation. This appeared to have exhausted his supply of French. "His victories are as ephemeral as soap bubbles, and he himself is more insubstantial than the rainbows reflected in them!" Von Wiedersack laughed in self-congratulation. He had absolutely no doubt that the French army's victory march across Europe would soon be checked for good. He then expressed his admiration for the Prussian soldier, that strong and healthy fellow whose only thought was for the welfare of his people. "You have no idea what splendid soldiers we have," he said emphatically, turning toward Chiara. "You have never seen them march along Unter

den Linden." This was the prologue to a lecture on the greatness of Prussia. He concluded by expressing his thanks to
Amschel for loaning funds to King Frederick Wilhelm III to
build up the army. "Believe me, Herr Rothschild, everyone
in Berlin is pleased that you have managed to acquire a huge
fortune during the Napoleonic Wars and have so generously
loaned it to us."

Chiara shared von Wiedersack's opinion of Napoleon, of
course, but she found his words proof of his simplicity. His
declarations were laden with a narrow-minded nationalism
that made her extremely uncomfortable. She saw that his
rant against the emperor was in fact directed more against
her than against the Corsican. Von Wiedersack obviously
assumed that a woman from an enemy land was a spy. She
had a comment on the tip of her tongue, something about
how she was sorry for all of the young men about to die in
the war, but she considered it more prudent to remain silent, because she was not certain that she would be able to
carry on such a discussion in German. She lowered her eyes
and sank deep into her chair.

Amschel noted at once that the smile on her face had
stiffened into a mask. He quickly changed the subject and
spoke of the hotel's beautifully decorated salons.

The pompous von Wiedersack responded that the opu-
lent hotel must have appeared just the same in the days
when Paracelsus was employed by the spa there as a physician and prescribed the consumption of copious amounts of
its mineral-rich water to those who journeyed there to seek
relief from their pains.

Amschel listened to the Prussian nobleman with polite
interest and to Frau von Wiedersack with astonishment.
Chiara on the other hand found it difficult to refrain from
exposing von Wiedersack's ignorance. She was tempted to

inform him that Paracelsus had practiced in Bad Ragaz in 1535, two hundred years before the hotel was built. But she resisted. *The silent submission of intelligence to stupidity*, she told herself, *is the price one must pay to be accepted in sophisticated company*.

The young people at the table—Gérard, Guido, and Désirée—said nothing. They had been taught not to speak in the company of their elders unless addressed directly.

Guido sat next to Désirée. He looked furtively at the unexpectedly gorgeous sixteen-year-old creature. She had long blond hair and temptingly sensual lips, and a melancholy cast to her eyes gave her face a mysterious air. Her waist was narrow and her bosom—soon to become one of the chief attractions of Berlin society—was of impressive dimensions. When she dropped her napkin, they both reached for it. The tips of their index fingers touched for just a moment. Guido felt an electric shock go through his body. The memory of that touch remained with him for years. It was the closest brush with heaven he experienced in all his years of adolescence.

Guido and Anton

THE FRIENDSHIP between Guido and Anton was an unusual one. Anton von Wartenburg came from an ancient military lineage. His father was a general and his uncle was a Prussian field marshal who had fought heroic battles against Napoleon. His mother's family, the Hohensteufens, was one of the oldest noble lines and traced its origins to Frederick I Barbarossa, the German-Roman emperor who led the third crusade but never reached Jerusalem because

he drowned in the Salef River in Turkey on June 10, 1190—
which, as my great-uncle told Sasha and me, happened to
coincide with the day that Baruch, the founding father of
the Spinoza line, died in Lisbon.

Anton's father, General von Wartenburg, was a towering man, strongly built, impeccably clad, and self-confident,
a man who blended military dignity with aristocratic elegance. The general was not pleased with Anton, his puny
and inhibited only child. The boy often suffered horrendous
asthma attacks and had little aptitude for practical matters.
His only interests were algebra and physics. His heroes were
Kepler and Huygens, Copernicus and Newton. His bible
was Galileo Galilei's *Dialogue Concerning the Two Chief
World Systems*, and he possessed—a gift from a Bohemian
maternal uncle for his fifteenth birthday—the fifth vertebra
of the Italian scientist, which someone had carved out and
stolen from his cadaver where it lay entombed in the Basilica di Santa Croce in Florence.

CHRISTIANS IN FRANKFURT did not associate with
Jews. They lived in different worlds and only very seldom
did their contacts cross ethnic and religious boundaries,
which for all practical purposes were nearly the same.

The fact that General von Wartenburg found Rothschild
agreeable and preferred his company to that of his own
peers wasn't due to Amschel's superb spiritual qualities and
disarmingly egalitarian outlook. The principal reason the
aristocrat chose to frequent the rich banker, risking a certain degree of social opprobrium for associating with a Jew,
was a simpler one: His finances happened to be extremely
precarious. The Wartenburg fortune had been handed
down through the centuries, but as soon as his wife got her
hands on it, she started spending it on grandeur, luxury,

and pleasure. The general found himself obliged to borrow to finance her extravagant way of life, particularly the vast estate and household she expected him to maintain. He contracted a considerable amount of debt. Old loans were paid off with new ones, and he became ever more dependent upon Amschel's generous lending. That was also why he allowed his son to meet and invite home the young Jewish boy of the same age who had come from Strasbourg and was staying at the Rothschild residence.

The boys got along immediately. They were bound less by their shared status as outsiders than by their belief that the deepest secrets of existence had been carefully formulated and concealed in some mystery that one might be able to solve with the help of the right keys. They expected to find them in the natural sciences. They united in deep friendship in their search for the philosopher's stone.

IT WAS SUMMERTIME. Warm breezes gently touched the friends' cheeks. They sat in the grass beneath an apple tree in the splendid park that surrounded the Rothschild residence. They were discussing Newton's work on the gravitational attraction of heavenly bodies and its effects upon human beings. They were both nineteen years old. Their shoulders occasionally touched as if by accident. Suddenly Anton seized Guido's hand, smiled, and looked deep into his eyes. Their fingers intertwined. Their movements were languid. The air was charged with a strange energy, and they felt as if they were in a dream. Anton whispered something in Guido's ear, but Guido didn't understand what he was saying. Anton pulled Guido close, and the eyes of both boys betrayed a longing for warmth and physical gratification. They kissed. Anton's mouth was sweet, and his skin had a tang of perspiration that excited

Guido. He held Anton tight and ran his hands through Anton's hair. Guido's breathing became louder. He gasped; he almost whistled. He could feel the growing stiffness of his penis and the pounding of his pulse. His abdomen was suffused with a heat that traveled slowly up his spine to his head. His hands roamed freely and explored his friend's body. He felt a deep, overwhelming gratitude that Anton was a man. Never before had he experienced such an emotion. He loved Anton for the very fact that he was male. Suddenly he realized that the two of them, brought together by destiny, by the act of possessing each other's bodies, were penetrating into the deepest, darkest secret region of passion, the forbidden zone, and with this act they would become sinners subject for their transgression to the ruthless, unforgiving punishment of expulsion from Paradise. Guido was ready to endure that punishment, for he knew that he did not wish to pull back from this newly discovered desire.

Scandal

THE FRIENDS' HAPPINESS did not last for long. Their love and the boundless pleasure they found in each other's arms could not be concealed from the watchful supervision of faithful servants. The watchers reported everything to the general, as they were bound to do, and one day he surprised Anton and Guido in bed together. The nightmarish scene that ensued put a brutal end to the bliss of their young lives. The general bellowed that his son was a perverted swine. Beside himself with rage, he promised to take his sword and chop him into tiny pieces for tarnishing the

family's centuries-old motto "*Semper purus*" (Forever pure).
He gave Guido a smashing blow across the face, delivered
forceful epithets best not repeated here, and challenged
the young man to a duel, for the honor of the von Wartenburg family had to be upheld. In issuing this challenge the
general was infringing the code of honor prevalent among
the military: *Every son of a Jewish mother is to be regarded as
devoid of honor, and therefore a gentleman is not permitted
to duel with such a person.*

WHEN CHIARA HEARD of these developments, she was
distraught. Amschel maintained a surprising calm. She demanded that Amschel immediately present an abject apology to von Wartenburg and try to persuade him to forgo the
duel. She had a profound horror of such barbaric behavior.
Especially because she knew that Guido, who had never
touched a weapon in his life, would be easy prey for the general, a man who had literally grown up with a sword in his
hand. She remembered that the general would soon have to
repay a large loan he had taken from Amschel six months
earlier, and she begged her husband to try to hush up the
affair by offering to discount the debt.

IN THE CENTER of Chiara's study loomed a desk with a
quantity of drawers, files, niches, secret drawers, and lids.
That impressive monument in dark wood with light-colored
inlay resembled an empty stage with trapdoors, movable
panels, and cleverly designed secret spaces, a repository that
only the most talented thieves could ever persuade to reveal its contents. Curiously enough, Chiara was irresistibly
drawn to clutter. Her desk was always covered with mis-
cellaneous piles: letters, documents, books, dictionaries,
pens, teacups, wineglasses, scissors, small change, even the

occasional garment. But one day she cleared the desk and placed a large empty bottle in the center of it. The sight of that bottle, *fiasco* in Italian, squeezed her heart and filled it with grief. A fiasco. It symbolized her disastrous failure with her young son, Guido.

GUIDO'S CHEEKS were bright red and his eyes were downcast. He was a short young man of nineteen, frail, with delicate features and an unusually large nose. At times of calm his large dark eyes were filled with intelligence and warmth, but now they were radiating grief and pain. From his very earliest childhood his pensive face had given his mother the feeling that he would not live very long, or if he did, that he would become a burden to her.

"Guido, tell me on your word of honor," said Chiara, "is this true? Did you and Anton . . . ?"

"Yes, Mother," he spared her from asking the question and added without flinching, "We love each other."

"'Love each other,'" Chiara repeated the words. "You have dragged us into the gutter. Without moral scruples and with no consideration for your family, you have committed a horrible crime. If your father knew of your shameful behavior, he would be rolling over in his grave."

"But Mother, we love each other."

"You have no idea what love is," she said, and rolled her eyes.

Neither spoke. The room filled with an uncomfortable tension. Chiara was not so bothered by the fact that Guido had an unspeakable vice; what pained her most was that he had hidden it from her and concealed his own nature. He was a different person from the one she had believed him to be, and that made him a stranger to her. He had shared with her only a trivial portion of his inner life; the rest, the important part, that which overshadowed all the rest, he had shared with someone else. After a long moment Chiara broke the silence. She told Guido to leave the room and get out of her sight because she could not bear to deal with him any longer. That was an odd reaction, one might think, from a woman who had always looked at the world around her with such steady and unflinching eyes.

GENERAL VON WARTENBURG refused to accept Amschel's offer. He regretted profoundly that they found themselves in such a difficult situation, one that jeopardized their friendship. Circumstances obliged him to defend the good name of his family. "For the sake of honor," as he expressed it, "we must humbly submit to our fate."

"My dear banker," he said, "do your best to see the duel from a different perspective: Consider that I am generous enough to offer Guido the oportunity to demonstrate once and for all that the legend about the cowardice of the Jew is just that: a legend."

Amschel wasn't able to find words adequate for a response to this before the general clicked his heels and made the prescribed inquiry: "Where and when can my seconds locate your stepson?"

THE ONLY PERSON in the house Guido could talk to was Angela, who was always ready to turn the page whenever someone committed an offense. But this time he declined her offer to discuss what she called his "misfortune."

Amschel had no time for him because he was deeply engaged in trying to limit the negative effects of the scandal and counter the malevolent rumors about the vast banking enterprise his father had built up and he was now responsible for managing.

His mother locked herself in her study and refused to see him. His brother, Gérard, was studying in Berlin.

Anton had been dispatched to his uncle in Prussia, depriving Guido of any possibility of contacting him. A benevolent retainer told him in confidence that once in Prussia Anton had been persuaded by his uncle to marry to a certain Baroness von Proschwitz, a maternal cousin who was as stupid as a donkey and devoid of any female grace. That report wounded Guido terribly. He was devastated by the thought that he and his beloved would perhaps never see each other again. He was struck by deep despair. Reflecting on the matter, he realized that his mother, of all people, was capable of understanding him, for she must have suffered the same sort of anguish when his father was imprisoned in the Conciergerie. But he had fallen into disgrace with her; her silence and turned back were the severe punishment for his shameful offense. This made his grief and isolation even more terrible. And, moreover, he feared that the general's seconds would turn up at any moment.

Guido abandoned hope for the future. His desperate desire to hear the voice of his beloved again and to feel the smoothness of his skin had become too much to bear and were made even more bitter by his mother's rejection. He decided that as a man sentenced to death, he would send her a final message. He wrote to her that even though people often laughed behind her back when she said so, she was right to maintain that if someone threw a straw into the Main River, it would sink at once.

Then Guido went to the southern corner of the huge garden, where the ashen-gray waters of the Main flowed gently past, and drowned himself in the river.

The Dream of a Son

GÉRARD SPECIALIZED in the complexities of international law. No one at the Rothschild Bank had developed such expertise. He had brilliant prospects. With Amschel's hearty approval he married Diana, whose father owned the Oppenheimer bank. The arranged marriage quickly bore fruit; one year later Jakob was born.

For some reason unknown to me, my great-uncle almost never mentioned Chiara's elder son. All he said was that Jakob was scarcely out of the cradle when his parents, Gérard and Diana, died.

THE HEP-HEP RIOTS began on August 2, 1819, in Würzburg. Within a few days, all across the thirty-six German states indignant crowds went out on the streets and violently demonstrated their anger that prominent Jews, inspired by the French Revolution and particularly by all its declarations about human rights and civil rights, were making utterly absurd demands for reform. The savage, bloody pogrom raged for several days. Thousands of Jews were attacked, beaten, and murdered, and their homes and offices were looted.

In Frankfurt the Jewish ghetto wasn't the only target. Rioters made their way to the Rothschild house, then pillaged and burned it. The charred bodies of Angela, Gérard, Diana, and two aged women servants were later found in the ruins. The only survivor was a manservant found curled up in a fetal position, badly burned and weeping.

AMSCHEL HAD LONG LOOKED forward to seeing his own features mirrored in the face of a beloved son. During his early years with Angela he often imagined how the swollen figure of his pregnant wife would be transformed into that of a new mother, tired but happy, holding their first-born son to her breast. In his imagination he could hear the newborn's first cry as the air made its way into his tiny lungs after he emerged from the warm paradise of his mother's womb. He could almost feel the tiny, soft infant fingers in his own hand.

But Amschel never had any children of his own.

He sometimes thought of Chiara's firstborn son as his own, his natural heir. That is why his grief over the death of Gérard was even deeper and more overwhelming than that he suffered at the loss of his wife, Angela.

Jakob's New Mother and Father

THE DARK MONTH of August was followed by a dismal autumn. The winter promised no relief. Chiara and Amschel usually spent Christmas in Bad Ragaz, but this year they remained in Frankfurt. There was no question of making the long journey to Switzerland with an infant of only nine months. Amschel was deprived of the reinvigorating massages and other treatments that were his favorite treats, and that year he couldn't mingle with the bank's growing crowd of international clients at the Hotel Quellenhof, where spa cures and the casino attracted the royals, the titled, and the upper crust of society.

JAKOB THOUGHT that Chiara and Amschel were his mother and father, for they had always treated him as their own son, from love for his vanished parents. Two additional qualities bound him to their hearts in undying love: this adorable child's nose was incredibly large and his right shoulder was somewhat twisted, so that he looked as if he had been born humpbacked. Custom inured Chiara and Amschel to the sight of him and so they never thought of his curious posture, but strangers noticed it immediately. It never occurred to anyone to tease him about his deformity. But the reactions of others made it difficult for him to forget his handicap.

The size of his nose distinguished Jakob from all other children. He did not know that the burden of that gigantic nose turned up in each generation of our family and signified that he would achieve great things. Chiara often reassured him and told him he was the very image of his grandfather, Nicolas Spinoza, the large-nosed revolutionary. That pleased him very much.

THE BLOOD of the Spinozas and the Luzzattos mingled in Jakob's veins. Many generations of both families had devoted themselves to study. They loved books and juggled ideas, an occupation they preferred to jingling coins. Chiara taught him three languages when he was still quite young, put into his hands the most important books from the cultures of three countries, and admonished him as often as she could, "You possess utterly only that which is in your own head." As they set forth together on stimulating mental journeys into the past, she impressed upon him again and again that material objects disappear, things pass away, nothing is forever, one can never live any time but in the present moment, and there is no life after this one. She was determined to ground him in the traditions of Jewish thought and ethics.

———

FOR AMSCHEL MONEY was a means, never an end in it-self. Karl Marx was completely mistaken when he described Amschel as a heartless man of questionable financial integrity, obsessed with riches. But I don't intend to write a polemic here; I want to give a straightforward account of the facts.

Old Rothschild had taught Amschel that one's reputation in the Jewish world was linked not to wealth but to one's wisdom and knowledge. A wealthy man in the Judengasse was respected only if he was also learned. The Talmud, his father told him, exhorts one to resist the temptations and pitfalls of wealth. The founder of the Rothschild bank stressed that his real goal in amassing a fortune was to raise the level of his cultural sophistication and that of his family, and to improve their social standing.

Amschel saw the talents of the Spinozas and the Luz-zattos clearly reflected in the boy's mental acuity. In great admiration of Chiara's undertaking, he encouraged her to equip Jakob with every possible intellectual advantage. He himself proceeded much more carefully and sought to extend the boy's horizons by opening for him the world of finance, orienting him step by step to the rules of that game. He placed his faith in the combination of theoretical knowledge and pragmatic intelligence.

A Man of the World

AMSCHEL FOLLOWED the intellectual debate within the German empire with deep concern, for he wished and devoutly hoped that the German-speaking lands would be the first in the world to realize the freedoms and ideals advocated during the French Revolution and, not incidentally, would in his lifetime become the lands to free the Jews after centuries of oppression. What most disquieted him was the hallowing of Germany's so-called sacred obligations and the malevolent depiction of Jewry as an international and emphatically non-German threat. Jews were alleged to be foreigners incapable of setting the interests of the German fatherland above all else. There was talk about an inherently creative Aryan intellect and a Jewish character completely bereft of originality and capable only of imitation. Aryans were described as conscientious, moral, logical, and vigorous, while Jews were sly, immoral, illogical, and passive. Aryans were praised for their deep sense of the ideal and the heroic, and for their love of their native land, especially its forests and the Alps. Jews were blamed for their eternal rootlessness and saddled with responsibility for every evil since the beginning of time. They were always to blame. A Jew was always a Jew—first, last, and always.

AT HIS FATHER'S DEATHBED Amschel had promised to remain forever true to his Jewish faith, even though already as a young man he had closed his heart to any belief in God. Many of those in his circle of acquaintances were obliged to renounce Judaism, for the hatred of Jews was palpable in the very air that one breathed. They converted, took Christian names, and assimilated. His own brother Solomon, who lived in Vienna, was advised by court officials to embrace Christianity when the emperor granted him the Austrian title of baron. Amschel forbade it, exercising his prerogative as head of the family. He wrote to Solomon, "I hope you are aware that our ancestors have remained true to our people and our traditions for thousands of years. I have never represented myself as anything other than what

I am: a Jew from Frankfurt. And I will shun any Jew who converts to Christianity."

At the age of sixty Amschel was an exemplary man of the world, both in the French sense—that is, as a member of society—and in the German one, as a man who has seen the world.

Sometimes Amschel would imagine that when Jakob came of age he would give to his ward the heraldic shield he had inherited from his own father. It symbolized the red flags waved by Eastern European Jews in sympathy with the ideals of the French Revolution. His father placed that red shield over the main entrance to the newly furnished offices when he established the bank in 1792. Amschel hoped the gift would spur Jakob to change his last name to Rothschild, just as Amschel's father Mayer Amschel Bauer had done.

AMSCHEL DIED with quiet dignity. He had come to a truce over many long years with that old enemy of his, rheumatism, but his body was unable to prevail over the problems of his ailing heart. He never mentioned the pains in his chest, for he had always been a discreet individual, a man who preferred to make light of his problems rather than to afflict them upon others. As a result, his death was completely unexpected by everyone. He went to sleep one evening and did not wake the next morning.

The funeral ceremonies were worthy of Amschel. In one of the drawers of his desk they discovered a paper with a preliminary effort to outline a last will and testament. His wishes concerning the funeral were followed to the letter. He wanted a simple coffin of dark wood, and he specified that only his closest family members were to accompany him to the graveside for his final journey.

The Meeting of the Board of Directors

A FEW WEEKS AFTER Amschel's coffin had been lowered into the ground, his four brothers assembled for a family council to discuss the future of the bank. Such meetings were unusual, since they lived in different parts of Europe where each managed his own branch. Solomon, the head of the Vienna section and eldest surviving brother, automatically assumed his role as the new patriarch. The others listened respectfully and with great interest as he outlined plans that were both farsighted and carefully thought out. He asked whether the piece of paper with Amschel's last wishes should be considered a legal document and then answered his own question, stating that it was invalid as a last will and testament, since no *notarius publicus* had witnessed the text. Therefore, Solomon concluded, there was no reason to satisfy the departed's wish that Jakob, a young man not even of his own flesh and blood, should inherit his shares in the bank. There was even less justification for the young man to become a member of the board of directors.

"If nothing else," he said, raising his voice, "this document confirms the truth of the rumors that have been circulating in the bank for some time. Chiara and Jakob exploited Amschel's prolonged illness. Loyal colleagues observed with disgust as the two systematically abused the confidence of our dear brother. An individual whom I trust implicitly has informed me that they have long manipulated Amschel and deceived him. Chiara is the brains behind it all, that notorious old woman who's been living at our expense for as long as I can remember. It's clear that she aimed for the young Spinoza to take over our family business and usurp our birthright. In her naïveté she overestimated Jakob's ability and underestimated our intelligence. Any concession to them is completely out of the question."

Solomon received unanimous support at once. This being confirmed, he proposed a resolution to amend the firm's statutes of incorporation: Only those who were born members of the Rothschild family could own shares in the bank and serve on its board of directors. They passed the resolution by acclamation. He admonished the brothers to avoid the ravages of a struggle for power, since any such conflict would prejudice the interests of all. It was therefore vital that despite his considerable contributions to the firm, Jakob should at once be relieved of his duties.

"We must handle this with the utmost tact," commented Mayer, who lived in Paris. "I'm concerned that Jakob might feel slighted, take offense, and cause difficulties for us."

"I will take the matter in hand," Solomon replied. "I will open a private account in his name with a modest sum as compensation, so he can get by financially until he finds other employment. Chiara and he can scarcely expect us to provide for them forever."

The brothers found this a splendid proposal. Nathan, head of the London office, said, "You've thought it all out, Solomon. I'm most impressed by your prompt action." Calmann, who managed things in Naples, agreed.

"It is my responsibility as head of the family to stay alert and make quick decisions," Solomon continued. "I have thought about our general situation, but I have not yet had time to go over every detail. I suggest that Amschel's shares be divided equally among us brothers. In addition, I would like to see his house deeded to my son Anselm Solomon, who is living in Berlin. Provided that no one has any objection, he will move to Frankfurt and take over the management there. The residence is perfectly suited for him. His splendid wife, Désirée, who these days is taking care of her mother the delightful widow von Wiedersack and the children, will get along there very well."

SOLOMON DIDN'T HAVE THE AUDACITY to look Chiara in the face. He dispatched the bank's attorney to her, and the message delivered by that gentleman was extremely painful to her. She had lived with Amschel for forty years but now they were treating her like a mere housekeeper.

Chiara had long known that Solomon had never cared for her. She was a woman—that in itself was enough to provoke his distrust. Her intelligence and indifference to money did not help. He also disapproved of the fact that she was living in sin with Amschel, but instead of urging his brother to take Chiara as his lawful wife before God and his people, he had continually harped on the decay of contemporary morals—never thinking for more than a moment or two of the immorality he was encouraging by consorting with young girls at the Salon Rouge, Vienna's leading bordello.

Solomon was annoyed most of all by Chiara's influence over Amschel. It provoked his jealousy. He assumed that she was working against him, and he did not understand, for his brother was all too polite to inform him, that his own blindness and inability to think in strategic terms were his principal enemies, not Chiara. They were the reasons that Amschel had not involved him in the most important decisions affecting the bank.

Chiara suddenly recalled how often she had been astonished by Solomon's shady schemes and his perpetual subordination of ethical considerations to financial gain. But it still came as a cruel surprise that he was so lacking in brotherly love as to disregard Amschel's express wishes. These things baffled her. Only now did she comprehend how base he was.

And that was how, even though she was in deep mourning for Amschel, she was evicted three days after his death from the home that they had built together. The other family members—Jakob, his wife, Eleonora, and their two small children—were also out on the street.

A Luncheon to Remember

I'M LEAVING CHIARA AND JAKOB to their fate for the time being, for I've suddenly recalled something else Grandfather related to us.

I really don't believe that Grandfather cared for Sasha and me—perhaps he simply disliked children as a general principle—since he almost always appeared irritated when we were anywhere in his vicinity. But just now there unexpectedly came to my mind one of the infrequent occasions when he consented to grace us with his company. This was after the school year ended. We had just completed third grade, my twin brother with his brilliant marks and I with my failures in history and mathematics. We were sitting in the kitchen eating lunch in silence. Grandmother had left us in quest of the latest news from the all-knowing concierge, the woman who kept her informed about everything going on in the neighborhood. We were surprised to see Grandfather come into the kitchen. He was in the habit of spending the day at his favorite tavern, ironically called the Brooding Rooster, where six days a week he would order a lunch of oxtail soup, the cheapest item on the menu, and then play cards with his friends. We never learned why he had broken with his custom that day. He dished out a bowl of soup and took a seat next to us.

With only his second spoonful of soup Grandfather exclaimed angrily, "That damned woman! She's never learned a thing about cooking, not even by trial and error. She always burns everything. Her cooking is a pure disgrace. The only place I've ever had worse food was in prison!"

Then he sent several swearwords flying, although since he both dressed and behaved with innate aristocratic elegance, he said them in German.

We didn't understand the words, but we were alarmed and avoided his eyes. Sasha looked up after a few seconds and said carefully, both to challenge me and to change the grim mood, "Grandfather, I had the best marks in class. Five over five in all my subjects. Aren't you proud of me?"

I can still see my grandfather's surprised expression. One might have thought that he'd had no idea we'd been going to school.

"Yes, well, that's certainly fine," he said, and shoveled down a few more spoonfuls of soup. "And what do you want to be when you grow up?"

"A cosmonaut," replied Sasha, who idolized Yuri Gagarin, the Russian peasant's son who shortly before this had become the first man in space.

"That sounds exciting. So, then, leaving the earth behind —maybe you'll have the chance to get out of this socialist hell that we're living in." He turned to me. "And you, Ari, what do you want to be?"

Ashamed of my failures in school and dreading the confrontation with my parents later that afternoon, I answered, "Somebody else. I want to be somebody else."

"That's exactly what my brother Moricz used to say: I want to be somebody else."

Turkish Delight

IN ONE CORNER of Lipótváros, Budapest's exclusive fifth district, stood Kohn's delicatessen, where the affluent bourgeoisie of the city did their shopping. Moricz passed by the popular shop every day on his way to and from school, and sometimes when he had managed to filch a coin from his father's jacket, he would go in to buy sweets. One afternoon he found the shop empty; neither clients nor employees were there. He looked around in surprise. An odd, almost threatening silence lay over the shop. "Hello!" he called out, and coughed sharply to attract the attention of the shop attendants. But it appeared that there was no one to hear him. Moricz smelled the sweet scent of ham, forbidden to us at home, mixed with the distinct fragrance of chocolate. He stole forward to the display where they kept various confections with honey and the Turkish delight. He looked around once more to make sure that no one else was in the shop. His mouth began to water as he gazed wide-eyed at all the sweets. He deposited his school bag on the floor, lifted the lid of the glass bowl with his left hand as quietly as his could, and then with his right hand crammed his trouser pocket full of the vivid Turkish confectionary, the very essence of absolute delight. Without losing a second, he bolted out of the shop with indescribable feelings of good fortune and intense joy.

OVER THE NEXT TWO YEARS Moricz became so obsessed with the thought of repeating that thrilling exploit

—standing alone in the shop and thrusting a fistful of sweets into his pocket—that he probably spent more time lurking around the delicatessen than in school, avidly watching for a moment when the shop would be deserted. He knew that it would take incredible daring and adeptness to avoid disaster. The boldness of his exploits excited him. He felt invincible.

In the evening he let everyone think that he was deeply engaged in his studies and homework, while in fact he was concentrating ferociously on learning to imitate his father's handwriting. This was no easy task, for the celebrated journalist had a very personal hand with extremely small letters. But at last, after filling and blotting several hundred sheets of paper, Moricz could confidently replicate his father's very unusual handwriting style in every detail. Over the course of the following year he presented a towering pile of imaginatively formulated medical excuses, written and signed in his father's forged hand, without arousing suspicion at school.

ONE DAY Moricz's luck ran out. He was just about to nip out of the store with his pockets full when he ran into Hermann Kohn, the owner, who was standing in the door and watching him.

"You little thief!" the old man snapped, and caught him by the ear. "So you're the rat who's been stealing our candy. I noticed that lots of Turkish delight has gone missing lately. How long has this been going on?"

"I humbly apologize," the embarrassed Moricz replied. "I never took anything before today. This is the first time. My mother sent me here to buy some fat smoked herring the doctor said would be good for her poor health and nerves. But there was no one in the shop to help me and for just a moment I was tempted by all the candy. The good Mr. Kohn certainly understands that my mother is not a wealthy person and she doesn't have the funds to purchase Turkish delight for me . . ."

The shop owner didn't believe a word of it. A glance at the boy's clothing was all he needed to see that his family was anything but poor.

"You're lying," the old man said, and pulled him sharply again by the ear. "What's your name and where do you live? I'm going to tell your father that you've been stealing from me."

"My father is dead. He was a drunk and he killed himself after losing all his money gambling at cards—"

The old man pulled his ear again.

"Ow! . . . Nathan Spinoza," Moricz said without a blink. "That's my name and I live at number 8 Mor Wahrmann Street."

Before he released the boy, Hermann Kohn made him empty his pockets. Then he went into the shop and gave his employees a tongue-lashing for leaving it unattended. He wrote a letter to Herr Spinoza at once, not bothering to try to be polite, and sent an employee to carry it to the address Moricz had blurted out under pressure.

ALL HELL BROKE LOOSE that evening in the Spinoza family. Grandfather told us about it as the three of us were trying to finish Grandmother's soup—in itself a relatively unappetizing task. He said that the memory of that distant evening was still sharp in his mind, for never had he felt so unjustly accused. The injustice of the charges he had endured as a ten-year-old caused him so much pain, he told us, that even in old age his heart would begin to pound whenever he even thought of it.

It may be superfluous to add that I've forgotten a fair number of details from my grandfather's story, for that lunch took place more than thirty years ago. But I'm trying to describe it just as I remember it.

NATHAN—IN OTHER WORDS, my grandfather—was summoned by his scowling father. The boy stood there completely uncomprehending, not moving a muscle as Hermann Kohn's letter was read out loud to him. Then he was subjected in turn to harsh scoldings and hard slaps, even though he insisted that he hadn't been anywhere near the delicatessen. He'd spent the whole afternoon in the building with a friend in the apartment on the floor below. His father refused to believe him. He was convinced that the boy was lying. Nathan fell to his knees and begged him to send their servant Vera down to the neighbors to see whether he was lying. His father reluctantly allowed it. Vera came back shortly afterward to report that the classmate's mother had confirmed Nathan's alibi. Without the least sign of yielding or regret or reconciliation in his voice, his father ordered him to go to the kitchen, have his meal there, and then go to bed at once.

It's natural for a father always to be regarded as the example and model for a boy who's growing up. Nathan was in awe of his father—a journalist, an advocate for society's needy children, the very symbol of justice—and he felt deeply betrayed. He withdrew in silence to his room, his heart so deeply aggrieved that he felt his chest would burst.

MORICZ WAS CALLED IN for an interview. It took awhile for the servant to locate him, because he was hiding beneath his bed.

"Do you know why you're here?" his father asked the boy, as he closed the door to the study behind him.

"I know why, Father," he replied firmly, "but I have never stolen anything from Kohn's delicatessen. I swear it on my word of honor."

"Moricz, I haven't said a word about the shop. What makes you think that I was about to accuse you of some theft there?"

"My intuition, Father."

That won him a dozen hard slaps, each one accompanied by the ironic repetition of Moricz's reply, before his father began with great deliberation to undo his belt. Now facing the prospect of the application of real violence, the boy reconsidered and recalled that perhaps he had forgotten to pay for a handful of Turkish delight that afternoon at Kohn's delicatessen.

"Taking candy is stealing, and you have taken a lot of it. It is galling to discover that I have a son who's a thief. But even worse is the fact that you're not man enough to own up to your actions. So you blamed your brother for the theft!" his father barked. "Why did you tell Kohn your name was Nathan?"

"I thought you understood me, Father. It's easy to explain. It wasn't because I'm afraid to assume the responsibility for my actions. On the contrary! I'm proud of everything that I do. But sometimes I get a little tired of being Moricz. I want to be someone else."

Different Roles

"I WANT TO BE someone else." Those were the words used by Andrej Scharf, artistic director of the National Theater, when he greeted his new students as he opened the doors to the theater academy. And he added, "You should have only one thought in your heads: I want to be someone else, the character that I am playing."

The legendary man of the theater was from Russia. For reasons never revealed to anyone, he settled in Budapest and quickly became known, several years after Moricz was born, for his artistry on the stage and his attractiveness to women. Ladies could not resist him when he recited Pushkin's love poems with his heavy Russian accent and flattered them in whispers.

It was no secret in the theater world that Scharf the lady-killer always favored the female students at the theater academy and he recruited most of them for his bed. That's why many were surprised when it became evident after only a few weeks that Moricz Spinoza stood in his special favor. True, everyone who met the youngster found him unusually charming and appreciated his beguiling personality, and many commented very favorably upon his striking diction and remarkable stage presence. But no one could understand how in the world Scharf—a man with ten sons engendered with just as many women, each of his offspring as neglected by him as the next—had taken such a liking for Moricz. People spoke of a sort of father-and-son connection between them.

MORICZ ABSOLUTELY THRIVED in the theater, where everything was play and make-believe. He spent every waking hour at the academy, except Saturday morning when according to his own account he attended worship services at the synagogue.

After a hard day of training and exercises he loved to go down to the cellar, stand before the mirror, and practice various roles while wearing one of the hundreds of costumes stored in the enormous wardrobe down there. Each was more fantastical than the next. The care and the artistic flair of the costumers were beyond compare. The fabrics were hand chosen: ancient woven textiles, heavy brocades, silk and satin, all fabrics that gleamed with class and quality. The nimble team of the National Theater's costume workshop created haute couture for the stage, of a quality seldom seen.

THE HAND OF DESTINY guided Scharf one day to a flea market in a neighborhood far from the center of Budapest. He had wandered around for quite a while when at one of the stands he recognized quite by chance the costume that his eldest son, Ervin, had worn several years earlier for his disastrous stage debut as Hamlet. Scharf was certain of it because he had been planning to stage the piece in the near future with Moricz in the leading role, wearing exactly the same costume. It was a simple snug-fitting suit consisting of a jersey and breeches of pliant black suede. The stall owner, a scrawny toothless fellow with breath that stank of cheap red wine, also offered him a pair of pointed suede boots with tight lacing that were part of the costume.

Scharf called the police and explained in broken Hungarian that the costume and the boots were property of the National Theater. The man must have stolen them. The stall owner earnestly denied it. He said he had inherited the clothing and the boots from his uncle, recently deceased in Transylvania. Another stall owner then inserted himself into the discussion. He said that the man was a thief and a fence of stolen goods, and his young companion turned up every Saturday morning with ten or so costumes, every one a treasure and in all likelihood stolen. The constables took the scrawny shop owner to a nearby police station. Scharf went along.

In preparation for the hearing, a hulking policeman softened up the peddler with a couple of powerful blows to the
stomach and face. This encouraged the man to become extremely cooperative. He told them that all of the garments
he sold were goods stolen from the National Theater. When
asked how the thefts had been carried out, he said it was
as simple as could be. His fellow in crime was a student at
the academy who had permission to stay in the downstairs
areas where the clothes were stored. Everyone thought that
he was practicing various roles, but in fact he was selecting
expensive costumes that could easily be sold. Each day he
put one or two costumes on beneath his own clothing and
calmly left the theater. "What's your friend's name?" the
policeman asked. Scharf, who was present during the interrogation, didn't need to wait for the answer from the stall
owner. He already knew.

MORICZ'S CAREER in the theater was promising but
short. It ended before it had even begun. But in any case,
thanks to his tender age, he avoided going directly from the
National Theater to prison.

Psychoanalysis

A FEW YEARS LATER during the Dreyfus trial in Paris—
when a French officer of Jewish ancestry was accused of
treason and sentenced to life at hard labor even though he
was innocent—my grandfather's father, the journalist Bernhard Spinoza, made the acquaintance of the Italian physician Cesare Lombroso, founder of the science of criminal
anthropology. They remained in contact and exchanged

letters at more or less regular intervals. Appalled by the behavior of his eldest son, Bernhard turned to Lombroso, who held the professorship of psychiatry at the University of Turin. Before long he had in hand a twelve-page letter of reply. The contents indicated that although he had never met Moricz, the Italian was convinced that the young man's criminal tendencies could be ascribed to inherent biological characteristics, linked either to improper nutrition or to directly inherited physical defects. Lombroso referred to the most recent scientific discoveries, citing his own research, and wrote that without question, Moricz's character was an example of the close links between genius and madness. Exactly what kind of mental aberration, however, he could not determine with precision. He therefore recommended that Signor Spinoza take his son to a psychoanalyst—Dr. Sigmund Freud in Vienna or his colleague Sándor Ferenczi in Budapest—for a complete evaluation.

THE APPOINTMENT took place in an office on the third floor with a view over the Danube and the lovely hills of the Buda section of the city. There was a sweet smell in the waiting room that made Moricz think of the Turkish delight he used to steal from Hermann Kohn's delicatessen. He had consented to psychoanalysis only because his father had forced him to do so. He had decided in advance that he would not trust Sándor Ferenczi for a moment.

"If you would, gentlemen of the Spinoza family, please come in."

The doctor was a short man with a dark, piercing gaze through the thick lenses of his spectacles. He spoke loudly, moved in a jerky fashion, and seemed nervous.

"Herr Spinoza, I am in the habit of reading everything that you write, and I am well aware of the significant contributions you have made as a journalist. You are a defender of justice, and you always take the side of the weak against the powerful and the authorities. I understand that you have provided your son with a proper education in his civic duties, emphasizing honesty and the virtues of honorable conduct. Despite this, the boy for some cause unknown to you is periodically overwhelmed by the desire to commit crime. Have I understood the situation correctly? That is, in fact, why you are here?"

Bernhard was embarrassed and squirmed uncomfortably in his chair. Moricz sat there as stiff as a poker.

"I once met Professor Lombroso in Milan, and he advised me to turn to you for help," Bernhard explained. "My son Moricz is a fine young man; he is warm, humorous, inventive, eager to learn, and talented in many ways. But he has always found it difficult to stick to the truth. As long as he limited himself simply to lying I was quite unworried and thought he would learn how to rein in his fantasies once he got older. But he has now engaged in various serious criminal undertakings, and this has me deeply concerned. That is why I have come for the doctor's assistance. I hope that the doctor will be able to cure him."

"Herr Spinoza, I must be frank. I do not believe that I am capable of curing your son. But I shall seek to understand him."

THE SESSIONS lasted for nine months, and Ferenczi was deeply frustrated because he got nowhere with Moricz. Many of his other patients also had odd delusions, but this case was stranger than any of the rest. The doctor had never seen a personality as split as this one. The young man appeared for his appointment three times a week, and each time it seemed that a different person was sitting on the doctor's couch. Sometimes Moricz was silent and withdrawn, staring straight ahead. Other times he giggled constantly for the entire half hour and then thanked the psychoanalyst for his undivided attention. Other times he wept, his head on his knees, and said that he was shedding tears for his dead mother because he hadn't been allowed to mourn for her. Often he cast about wildly through time and space and served up a cavalcade of the most incoherent and unbelievable stories about his family, alleging they had wandered around Europe since the founding of the kingdom of Portugal. He insisted that his ancestors could awaken the dead and transform impotent old men into virile bulls. He adamantly declared that one of his ancestors had lived for more than three hundred and fifty years because he had drunk seven drops of a potion that made him immortal, and another had been a wealthy maharaja in India even though he didn't know a word of Hindi, that a third had been the cause of the French Revolution and had lost his head to the guillotine, and a fourth had discovered electricity and caused a disastrous fire that killed his seven children. One day he came to the appointment and sat there spinning a tale that his mother was a blind princess and her mother had been the best-known courtesan of Vienna's demimonde.

Ferenczi often scratched his head in perplexity as he sat reading over his notes late at night. At length he concluded that Moricz had spent the whole time intentionally trying to fool him with these wild fantasies. He understood that this was the young man's way of protecting his real self. But which of these manifestations was his real self?

Ferenczi was bewildered. He could not put his finger on whatever dark depth of the soul gave Moricz the strength to elaborate his tales and do his tricks of psychological transformation. He decided it was beyond his ability to make a complete diagnosis of that strange teenager's psyche. He thought for a time of referring the boy to Sigmund Freud. He dismissed the notion as a terrible idea, at least for the time being, since it would be humiliating to admit defeat and thereby acknowledge his own professional shortcomings. But later, when his office was closed between Christmas and New Year's Day, he sat in his rocking chair and reconsidered the matter. In a moment of inspiration he realized that the only hope was to assemble his personal notes and the record of Moricz's appointments and send it all to 19 Berggasse in Vienna. Freud was never reluctant to provide psychological analyses of people he had never met. Only Freud could see through the young man, apply his stringent no-nonsense analysis, and elucidate the boy's hidden motivations.

A Historic Chain

I'VE BEEN WONDERING lately how Moricz could have known so much about the Spinoza family. My hypothesis is as follows.

Shortly before Nicolas was carried off to the Conciergerie, he recalled the fate of Danton. A shudder went through him as he realized that something equally terrible could happen to him. This prompted him to exact from Chiara a vow to safeguard the historical account of the Spinoza family for their two small children and to hide Benjamin's *Elixir of Immortality* somewhere secure. She had to promise not to open it and to turn it over someday to their eldest son, Gérard.

Chiara was no Madonna, and it was obvious that God was not at the center of her life. She enjoyed drinking wine and gossiping, and the relationship in which she lived—a ménage à trois—was beyond all doubt completely at odds with the morals of the time. Nor did she have any Spinoza nearby to support her. Nevertheless, she kept her promise to Nicolas. Perhaps from loyalty; perhaps because she understood that our family was truly special.

Our family originated in a mystery and a miracle before almost any of the European nations were created, and we've played a significant role in history without feeling arrogant about the secret knowledge—completely incomprehensible to humanity today—that we bore with us through the various ages and lands. None of us ever spoke of it. Not because of Moses and his prophetic warning to us on that dusty road in León to fear the wrath and terrible punishment of the Lord, warning that our lineage would be obliterated from the face of the earth if we uttered a single word of it to anyone. But because we *knew*—and he who possesses great knowledge has no need to speak of it. We knew and our lives were wrapped in silence—a vow of silence that we ourselves had not taken but one that we had inherited from preceding generations—and we knew that the purpose of that knowledge of ours was to make the world a better place. We were serving the future by bearing the burden of the past.

After Chiara buried both of her sons, she had to start all over again. Now Jakob would receive the family history and inherit Benjamin's book. I can vividly imagine the conversation between grandmother and grandson. She succeeded in convincing Jakob that he was an essential link in a long family chain that should never be broken, and that he had to accept as his own the family legacy that gave individual life its meaning and purpose. Because Jakob loved his grandmother more than anyone, he systematically fulfilled, without exception, all of his obligations to family tradition.

After Jakob died, the book went to his eldest son, Bernhard. That energetic and principled journalist who lost his adored young wife never took the time to develop deep relationships with his three children. Bernhard was far too absorbed in his campaigns to save the world. He was even less able to find time to orient the next generation to those family legends he had heard as a child, for he regarded them as myths. He had no desire to deceive his sons about their family origins.

So perhaps it's not so surprising that Moricz managed to lay hands on detailed accounts of that past. Nothing came more naturally to him than hunting through his father's cabinets, picking the locks of the desk drawers, and snooping through his jacket pockets in search of something worth stealing. Bernhard would have died of mortification if he'd known what his eldest son had been doing ever since he was a child.

One day Moricz came across *The Elixir of Immortality* in a secret drawer in his father's desk. He began leafing through the manuscript but was intimidated by the overwhelming weight of the many dark mysteries that filled its pages. Luckily for him, his instinct for self-preservation warned him somehow of impending danger. He returned the book to its place at once, carefully locked the compartment, and left the study. Only seconds later his father came home to retrieve from his desk some important documents he had forgotten.

Thoughts of that book gave Moricz no rest. Driven by nagging curiosity, he returned to the study a few weeks later and took out the thick leather-bound volume. He opened it at random and read the start of chapter two: "The first Spinoza mixed life-giving herbs and the last Spinoza will let his family's inheritance go up in smoke."

He understood that *The Elixir of Immortality*—in addition to a great deal more—provided a detailed account of the family's early history. He was fascinated to discover that Benjamin had made a number of predictions about coming ages. He searched frenetically through the account for his own life story, for he had the feeling that it had been written more than two hundred years earlier. But he was unable to decipher the meaning of the only passage related to his own fate, because he looked through the book before the time was ripe.

Analysis and the Putsch

FERENCZI READ the curt response with a distinct feeling of disappointment. It surprised him that everything Freud said about Moricz was couched in vague terms and generalizations that could be applied not only to all of his own patients but to most of the Jews of central Europe, as well. The father of psychoanalysis wrote:

> *Two thousand years of persecution and life in the strict isolation of the ghettos in which they were confined have created a uniquely Jewish model of behavior. It manifests itself in body language, in the powerful urge to flee, in the intensity of their conversation, their frantic activity, and the ambition to excel, all in the effort to survive. It is also seen in an almost uncontrollable*

impatience, extreme reactions to any stimuli interpreted
as threatening, fierce outbursts of anger, the desire to
contradict others, and dark, pervasive fears.

Freud said that Moricz Spinoza displayed all of these
symptoms. However, he lacked the typical Jew's genuine
curiosity about the lives of others, the characteristic sense
of humor, and the ability not to take himself all too seriously. This was because like most adolescents he suffered
from narcissism. The young person often has a strong need
to be the center of attention and lacks empathy with others.
Patients afflicted in this way seldom feel the need to
change their behavior. Moricz Spinoza was young, however,
and it was most likely that the eventual awakening of his
sex drive would bring about changes for the better in his
behavior.

MANY YEARS LATER, at the Café Gerbeaud in Budapest,
Ferenczi was leafing through *Esti Lap*—Budapest's leading
newspaper, which featured a daily serving of sensational
news from all parts of the world—and he came across an
extensive article describing the Nazi Party's beer-hall coup
in Munich in November 1923, published on the day that
Hitler and his companions were to go on trial.

According to the article, the attempt to overthrow the
government—the so-called putsch—began when a handful of men in brown shirts and swastika armbands rushed
into the popular Bürgerbräukeller and noisily interrupted a
speech by the former prime minister of Bavaria. Hitler stood
on a table, fired a revolver at the ceiling, shouted that the
national revolution had begun, declared the ruling government abolished, and said the time had come to free Germany from the red terror. The following day he led a march

to the sound of beating drums, and a mass of three thousand political supporters followed him all the way to the center of town. Many were armed with pistols; others carried flags with swastikas. That was when a police official ordered his troops to open fire against the conspirators. Shots were exchanged. The national revolution was put down in less than two hours, and twenty dead bodies lay in the streets. The coup leader was arrested and charged with high treason. Sitting in the dock were Hitler, Ludendorff, Röhm, Wagner, and several more, but Moricz Spinoza, the alleged brains behind the failed putsch, was still at large. The article reported the rumor that he had left Germany and was then in China.

Ferenczi started in surprise at the sight of Moricz's name. The brains behind the Nazi attempt to grab power? Escaped to China? This couldn't be true! He read the paragraph about Moricz again. Somewhat shaken, he put the newspaper down and thought back to the curious case of the young man who had told so many tall tales and refused to face reality. Even now, he couldn't think of Moricz without an affectionate little smile.

Upon his return to his office Ferenczi took out the file on Moricz and reviewed the records. He glanced at some of his notes and looked at Freud's letter again. He was miffed by the slovenly analysis. What drivel; what a pack of banal stereotypes. He remembered his disappointment at Freud's reply and how he had not dared to be so tactless as to criticize the master in Vienna. He poured himself a glass of cognac and settled on his analyst's couch. The facts were staring him in the face. That letter from Freud had prompted him to contact Moricz's father to recommend discontinuing the therapy sessions. He blamed himself now for heeding

Freud's advice and concluded that his mistake arose from a professional failing; one of several unfortunate aspects of such a close collegial relationship was that it was impossible to maintain a healthy critical distance. He should have listened to Moricz more closely and steered their conversations to the boy's relationship with his mother. The doctor told himself that perhaps additional therapy might have kept him from going so far astray in life.

New Friends

FROMBICHLER AND MORICZ were cousins. They frequented each other in Vienna in the months before the outbreak of the First World War. That was where Moricz met Frombichler's childhood friend Adi, who at that time was still a long way from becoming the leader of the German National Socialist Party. Moricz and Adi discussed all kinds of things. Behind Frombichler's back they also debated the Jewish question. Adi said this was the most important issue of all. Adi was never inhibited about spewing anti-Semitic comments in all directions (except when he was with Frombichler, who reacted badly to such talk). Moricz, in contrast, appreciated Adi's caustic jokes about the Jews. Once after Moricz smiled at one of his crudely dismissive gibes at the Jews, Adi rose from his seat at the table, seized Moricz's hand in both of his own, and declared, "*Mein Bruder!*"

MORICZ AND ADI were criminal geniuses who thrived in each other's company. They hammered out many a plan together. One of these schemes was to lay hands on the Spinoza family treasure and sell it to some noble German plutocrat with secret Jewish roots.

But my grandfather got there before them. He found *The Elixir of Immortality* among the papers his father left behind and realized immediately that the book must be kept out of the hands of his unreliable brother. He hid it. Moricz was incensed and terribly angry when he found out; he felt that he had been robbed. He insisted that because he was the firstborn son, the book was his rightful property. Frombichler agreed with him. Adi was the most disappointed of them all, for he had secret plans for it. He chewed his mustache in anger, but he did not dare tell them his real intentions. He vowed that one day he would murder the Jew Nathan Spinoza to get *The Elixir of Immortality*, for he believed the book would give its owner dominion over the secrets of the universe and knowledge of the ultimate mysteries of existence.

BEFORE I RETURN to Chiara and Jakob, I need to make one thing clear: Anyone looking for historical fact or philosophical insight here should look elsewhere. I make no claim to accuracy or insight. I have one purpose before I die, and that is simply to prevent my family from slipping into oblivion, forever forgotten. My time is short, and all too often, this wandering around in the maze of memory gives me a headache. That's why I haven't managed to put these stories into proper order. I just record my memories as they come. I promise no structure here, for this narrative is shaped by pure chance. Let me again emphasize that I haven't made anything up; I'm just repeating what I heard.

Toward New Challenges

CHIARA AND JAKOB and family arrived in Vienna in early December after two years in Regensburg with Prince Ludwig von Thurn und Taxis, a longtime devotee of the fine art of extravagant living who had gotten himself into dire financial straits. Jakob had put the prince's finances in order by selling off certain postal routes in the Habsburg dominions that the prince's ancestors had run for hundreds of years. This astute move established the foundation of the European postal system of our own day. A few years later Jakob again gave the prince a helping hand in negotiating the agreement for the German state to take over the rest of the Thurn und Taxis courier network, in exchange for extensive grants of land. The deal made the prince the proprietor of one of the largest estates in Europe. It established Jakob's reputation as a financial wizard and economic genius.

THE SPINOZA FAMILY resided at the Hotel Savoy. They leafed through the newspapers at the breakfast table, but Chiara and Jakob had more important matters to consider than all those articles in the Vienna press about the plans of Kaiser Franz Josef and his new bride, Elisabeth, or "Sissi," as she was called, to take a second honeymoon trip. This time they were going to Corfu, since the empress was quite interested in Homer's epic about Odysseus, particularly in the stanzas describing the wandering hero's shipwreck on the shores of that island.

Chiara and Jakob were preoccupied by arrangements to travel southward across snow-covered Burgenland within a couple of days. Prince Rudolf Biederstern awaited them there with new challenges.

On the Estate

TIME STOOD STILL at Biederhof. The people who worked on the estate—cooks and servants, washerwomen and housemaids, seamstresses and wet nurses, cleaning women and kitchen maids, foresters and gardeners, stablemen and sawmill workers, artisans and coachmen, journeymen and apprentices—were all natives of the region. Their fathers and mothers had served the Biederstern family for generations and they'd never known any other life. Those who were in the service of the prince knew they would always have work and their wages were assured. If one of them lay ill at home, he could count on a visit from the princess to deliver wine, bread, and fortifying broth, even though she had to take the trouble to lift her long skirts above the mud outside and chase away pigs rooting for scraps. And when someone lay on his deathbed, he could close his eyes in peace, knowing his children's future was assured.

The unchanging rhythm of the seasons and years had knit links of common interest, goodwill, and sympathy between the noble family and its servants. Every Sunday they prayed together in the church, where each family sat in its designated place, and during Holy Week they took part in the procession, walking in order of precedence along a path strewn with flower petals. In summer ample quantities of fruits and vegetables not reserved for the castle pantries were distributed among the folk on the estate. The autumn gathering of the grapes was always a festive time when both the great and the humble trod the grapes. Later that season came the annual hunt for boars, stags, deer, fox, and pheasants—a time for dinner conversations over venison steaks for the privileged in the castle and a time in other abodes for platters heaped with the giblets and sweetbreads provided to families living on the estate. The season just before Christmas was filled with the squeals of hogs being slaughtered and the fragrance of ham.

Biederhof operated as one large family. Each had his place and knew who he was. They all knew one another and knew that they comprised parts of a greater whole.

No one from the outside had come to Biederhof seeking work for as long as anyone could remember. Jakob Spinoza was the first, and his appointment as the estate manager caused a great stir.

EVERYONE LIVING on the estate except for Prince Rudolf and his mother, Clementina, had been summoned to stand before the castle that cold winter day when Jakob arrived with his family. Many faces had openly curious expressions as the crowd watched them descend from the carriage. Many stood on tiptoe to get a better view. The previous day the master of the castle had ordered wine to be served and had announced that a manager would be arriving along with his wife and three children. But no one had expected him to bring an old lady as well. She was the most remarkable creature anyone had seen in quite a long time, dressed like a man and with her gray hair cut almost to a stubble. Nor had anyone been expecting Jakob to address them with a short formal speech of greeting. He introduced himself, his wife, Eleonora, and the children, but even before that he told them that the elderly woman was his paternal grandmother—and therefore not his mother, as some of them had supposed. But the greatest surprise came when he told them without a flicker of hesitation that he was a Jew, a fact that Rudolf had forgotten to mention. The mixture of pride and humility in his voice did not escape anyone as he added, "I hope no one will see this as an obstacle to our ability to accomplish our mutual goals."

At the sight of Jakob's enormous nose, the workers felt somewhat uncomfortable. Granted, he wasn't one of those despicable peddlers, Jews with backs bent beneath life's heavy burdens, clad in worn black robes and wearing skull-caps, with dangling earlocks and heavy Eastern European accents, who sometimes turned up by mistake in that region where circumcised men were as rare as sea monsters, and then tried to beguile honest folk into buying worthless trash. Jakob's clothing, his eloquent manner of speaking, and his air of confidence showed that he was a gentleman from the city. Those qualities commanded respect. No one in the castle yard dared even to think of whispering any denigrating words about him.

But he was a Jew, a strange and alien creature.

Rudolf had stressed that it was the duty of one and all to carry out the instructions of the manager and comply with even his slightest wish. Ordinarily, this would not have been a problem, since they were used to unquestioning obedience and respected the authority of the prince. But for most of the population of the estate—simple men and women whose concept of the people of Moses was defined by Catholic imagery of the Jews—it was unthinkable to regard a Christ-killer as an equal. And perish the thought of taking orders from a Jew. The very idea was repugnant. And humiliating.

Two Meetings

THE FIRST ENCOUNTER with the master of the castle didn't turn out exactly as the new arrivals had hoped, even though it began well. Rudolf received them in his study and welcomed them, his eyes shining with pleased expectation. He clapped Jakob on the shoulder with surprising warmth and said, "The gentleman succeeded magnificently in Regensburg. And he'll do the same here, won't he?"

He invited them to accompany him to one of the smaller dining rooms for a light meal and refreshments. After a welcoming toast with the estate's excellent Riesling, the company sat down around the table. Eleonora had on her knee the tiny Claudia, not yet weaned. A serving maid had taken the two boys, Bernhard and Nikolaus, off to the kitchen.

Two servants carried in an enormous silver platter filled with sausages, pork pâté, and slices of baked ham elegantly arranged around a large sow's head.

"This garlic wurst is assuredly the best-tasting sausage anywhere in all of Burgenland," Rudolf boasted. He told them that several hogs had just been slaughtered and the fresh sausages were prepared according to the time-honored recipe that plump old Mathilda had brought to Biederhof. Moreover, he added, the childless cook was like a mother to him. In fact, he actually adored her more than his own mother. He proposed a toast to her.

A painful silence ensued, for although the guests were not particularly devout, none of them ate pork. Jakob made an effort to explain why they preferred not to partake of the food placed before them.

Rudolf stared at him with an expression that made it obvious he was completely unable to understand how anyone could turn down Mathilda's wurst. His nostrils quivered at the scent of something here that he could not quite identify. All of this made him nervous. He refilled his wineglass and downed the contents with a single long swig. He served himself more and emptied the glass again just as quickly. He collected himself. He began to talk about the history of his family in an effort to smooth over the awkward situation. He recounted how his ancient forefathers, full of burning passion and pride, with swords in hand and Austria in their hearts, had accomplished great deeds for the emperor. They adored the emperor. God bless him. Of course. No one was more devoted to the church than the Biedersterns. Even if he himself was perhaps a bit lacking in deference for those seated on the thrones of heaven and of Austria. He drank more wine and compared the family's epic past with the menacing present. He complained of his exile from Vienna. He did not miss the music, the arts, the theater, or the poetry reading. No, not at all. Nor did he miss society life, all those arrogant fools who went around and around in the salons, noses stuck up in the air and exchanging idiotic remarks with one another. What he yearned for was the city itself. Sometimes this stultifying country life got on his nerves. He drank some more. He made malicious comments about Ferdinand, the previous emperor, that wretch who destroyed his marriage, and then he poured himself even more wine. He told them he had married for a cause that no one in his family had ever experienced: true love. That was why the family found it so hard to understand him. And for that same reason the nobility in Vienna had spread shameless slanders of him. He drank even more wine, and his speech became slurred. With tears in his eyes, he told them that his wife was a fabulously beautiful woman, but not the deferential type to sit home with her embroidery. She was a whore. She went to bed with anyone. He'd met her in Vienna's leading brothel, where she was the star attraction. He gave her his heart and his untarnished family name, but she had deceived him left and right. He, who had been swept away to love by dreams of fidelity. But no love is proof against the risk of loss, he proclaimed, and he dumped yet another glass of wine down his gullet. Then he rose from his chair, poured more wine, and raised his glass. He was about to proclaim a toast to the defunct wife whom he still adored, but he passed out instead, fell straight forward, and sprawled full length upon the table, his face a few inches from the sow's head, as if he wanted to kiss its snout.

"*Pfui*, what a disgusting man," Chiara said, appalled that Rudolf had such scant control of his own conduct and manners. Her face was pale beneath its powder, and she repeated her comment in disgust as she left the room. "Ugh. He is a despicable man."

IN HER LATE AGE Chiara began to write her memoirs. She was eighty years old. Other than the meager correspondence with her sister, Allegra, she hadn't written a thing since her novel half a century earlier. She had made several attempts but each time found herself dissatisfied and at a dead end. She never again managed to recapture those lovely cadences of the language or the exhilarating and fantastical images of poetry. The pleasure of writing and the desire to create were gone. At last she gave up, afraid of failure.

In her memoirs she writes that it was a great relief for her to encounter Clementina a few hours after their arrival at Biederhof. Rudolf had made an atrocious impression and was certainly no *bella figura*, and Chiara's first impulse was to abandon the castle. But Jakob would not permit it, although he acknowledged that the prince's behavior, hardly appropriate to his status and his birth, had for a short time led him to contemplate the same course of action. He asked her to overcome her distaste and try to put up with circumstances.

Clementina's joyous, beaming face was a healthy contrast to Rudolf's. The princess made no secret of the fact that she was delighted Chiara had come to reside at Biederhof; her presence would alleviate the dull monotony of daily existence there. Delight, let it be said, was something that Clementina had not experienced for a very long time, not since the terrible day when the family carriage drawn by a team of four horses had ventured out onto the frozen surface of Lake Neusiedler and broken through the ice. Both of her daughters had drowned. She had quit the company of her noble kinsfolk in Vienna long ago, and if the reports of her chambermaids were to be believed, her grief was beyond all imagining. She commented that the two of them were about the same age, and few of their generation had managed to stand fast against the merciless onward march of time. This being the case, she dared to hope that Chiara might occasionally enjoy having afternoon tea with her.

The ladies got along very well despite their great differences. Memory held each of them in its powerful grip, and their daily conversations dwelt most of the time upon the past. Both had lived long lives in violent and turbulent times, and had endured their share of the misfortunes of their eras.

One day Clementina spoke of the immense significance of Chiara's novel for her husband and for all like-minded people in Vienna. And, of course, for herself as well. Heindrich had been endowed with a genius uncommon in people of their high standing, she commented. He was a man of action and had books translated into German. It was a great day when Robespierre fell and the end of the reign of terror arrived, she acknowledged, a day that remained sacred to all of them. But only when one read the novel did one finally escape from the terror that had gripped the aristocracy since the eruption of the French Revolution. Only then did one grasp the fact that the dark night of oppression was ended.

She added that she would have been pleased to read many more works from the same pen. She saw Chiara's shoulders sag for a moment, and took this to mean that her friend was pained not to have written more. Chiara explained that life over recent decades had obliged her to stand by as one opportunity after another vanished and promises were left unfulfilled. Clementina replied that even though at their age life no longer flourished so abundantly, Chiara should nevertheless try to write her memoirs. She had nothing to lose. No one was insisting upon a masterpiece. With an affectionate smile she said, "You must assemble your thoughts and write us a new book so we can devour it with pleasure."

That same night the lamp in Chiara's room was kept burning until the early hours of the morning.

Daily Life at Biederhof

JAKOB WAS FIERCELY EAGER to learn everything about Biederhof, and he spent the first days going from place to place and getting acquainted with the people on the estate, finding out everything about their work, and asking them about their families. He knew that formal systems of management were virtually unknown in Austria, and the presence of a Jewish manager could easily provoke envy, reluctance, and even outright hatred. This he wanted to avoid at any price.

He made his expectations clear to everyone and carefully defined their duties. Whenever they had a problem they were to come to him immediately; no one had anything to fear.

In these encounters with Jakob the workers kept their faces expressionless. They were uneasy and uncertain exactly how they were supposed to respond. His interest and candor surprised them, for no one had ever paid any attention to them, and they weren't used to being treated with respect by their betters. But it wasn't Jakob's words that impressed them. Many didn't really understand what he was talking about. His affable presence, his natural friendliness, and his evident engagement had a more positive effect than what he said. Not everyone was convinced, however. Some were still skeptical. Others, a bit more outspoken, suggested that maybe the big-nosed Jew was pretending to be friendly so he could take them all in with his cunning. There was no shortage of right-thinking folk who suspected that the apparently mild-mannered manager might one day turn into a raging evil demon.

JAKOB SOLD ONE PORTION of the Biedersterns' fields and forests to the owner of the neighboring estate, Princess Esterházy and Batthyány, and used the proceeds to pay off creditors. He managed to reimburse all those who had provided loans to cover the losses sustained during Rudolf's systematic mismanagement of family finances. After calculating the income and expenditures of the estate with the same determined precision a Swiss watchmaker applies to constructing his best clock mechanisms, he signed a contract with Solomon Rothschild, the president of the bank's Vienna office, and obtained a comprehensive mortgage loan. He invested the funds in the timber mill, in farming activity, and in a number of smaller industrial undertakings he established on the estate. He made contact with the most respected middle-class businessmen in the capital city. Within a few years, thanks to his wizardry in finance and commerce, Biederhof was flourishing.

DURING THE THIRD SPRING after his arrival, the estate experienced a disaster previously unknown to Burgenland. Extensive rains were followed by hot sunshine, and untold myriads of gnats and mosquitoes hatched. They darkened the skies and attacked everything that moved. Within a few days everyone was swollen from countless bites and choking because they couldn't avoid inhaling the swarming gnats. It was impossible to go outside. They all expected something terrible to happen, but they did not know what it might be. Everyone sat behind closed doors, doggedly waiting. The only disturbance in the great silence that descended upon the estate was the ringing of the church bells for Sunday mass.

Jakob stiffened when he heard that the priest had gone on interminably in his Sunday sermon about the fourth of the ten plagues of Egypt, the gnats that invaded the lands of the Pharaoh. He knew that he had to do something without a moment's delay. He could not simply sit inside with his arms crossed and let the priest flail away, stirring people up. He knew all too well how quickly certain unpleasant suggestions take wing and what the consequences might be.

Chiara came up with the solution. She had once accompanied Amschel on a visit to a beekeeping operation, and she now remembered the clothing the beekeepers wore to tend the hives. She suggested that the women gather odd bits of fabric and sew masks and gloves. Her proposal was immediately accepted. In a matter of hours everyone was once again able to return to work, veiled like beekeepers. The mood of the people improved and they were pleased to be busy again, even though it took a few more days for the plague of gnats to pass.

MORE MONTHS WENT BY. One year of busy activity succeeded the next. During the fifth winter of Jakob's management of the estate, a large number of the workers and their families, especially the old and the very young, came down with chronic coughs, bloody mucus, high fevers, chest pains, and night sweats; they wasted away with unnerving suddenness. The doctor thought it might be an epidemic of tuberculosis, spread through the air when people coughed or sneezed.

The priest had a different explanation. He asserted with a passion that frightened most of his listeners that this was God's punishment upon the people for loose talk, whoremongering, and immoral conduct. During a visit to the home of a gardener where several people were afflicted, visibly declining and about to die, the priest declared that a vampire on the estate was sucking away their will to live. Many shared his view.

Jakob had to act quickly to stop the spread of contagion and the flood of rumors provoked by the priest. The doctor had told him that the cramped quarters and filth of the workers' houses were fertile grounds for tuberculosis. Without delaying to consult Rudolf, Jakob used a portion of the estate's profits to improve the living conditions of the workers. He ordered old houses torn down and new ones built. He also had a clinic and a school constructed.

Two Deaths

THE WORKERS STARED at Jakob with distress and sympathy when they heard that Chiara had fallen ill. For several weeks the family had heard the sound of stifled coughing in her room. At night she lay bathed in sweat under Eleonora's care. The physician was unable to cure her tuberculosis; she was beyond all help, and he could offer her only a few words of comfort. He told Jakob she might not survive until the spring.

THE CHILDREN called her Grossmutti. They adored the stories she would tell them. Every Friday evening Chiara would recount a passage from *Mesillat Jesharim* (*The Way of the Righteous*), the best-known work of her grandfather Rabbi Moshe Chaim Luzzatto, written in the form of a debate between a wise Jew and a pious Jew. Three days before she passed away, on the last Shabbat she celebrated with the family, she told them of a dark prophecy about an enemy of Israel who would threaten the entire people. He would inflict upon the Jews a defeat from which they would not recover for thousands of years. His name would be . . . Chiara fell silent and stared absently into space. Jakob, Eleonora, and the children regarded her with eyes open wide and waited for the name. But it became obvious that she could no longer remember it.

"Children," she said in a heavy earnest voice after a few moments of silence, "you have no idea how privileged you are to live in a time and place where nothing is threatening you. Your forefathers did not enjoy the same good fortune, and I fear that our descendants may face something infinitely more terrible."

"Grossmutti," said fourteen-year-old Bernhard, taking the floor, "it sounds like you've forgotten the name of the terrible fiend. But do you remember the rest of the story? What should we do to defeat him?"

"I do not know," Chiara replied. "I do not know. I have never attempted to pry into God's mysteries."

CHIARA'S SOUL had scarcely departed toward its heaven than Clementina followed. She died in her sleep. The castle maids whispered that her heart had broken because the loss of her friend was too much for her.

Rudolf was at first bewildered when he heard of his mother's death. His grief exploded minutes later in a fierce tirade against a servant who hadn't foreseen that he would need a bottle of red wine that early morning to wash down the news.

Chiara's Last Wish

SOLOMON'S HEART ATTACK at least made it possible for Jakob to carry out one of Chiara's two last wishes. During the final two years of his life the patriarch of the Rothschild family was no longer the decisive and commercially astute man who had driven Jakob out of the bank only a decade earlier. His uncertain health kept him from putting the last touches on a huge loan to no less a client that the emperor of Austria. Since none of his brothers could handle the matter, the family council voted to call Jakob in. He gave them one condition and emphasized that it was not negotiable: Chiara must be interred in the same grave with Amschel and Angela. The family council didn't comment or protest. They accepted his demand.

CHIARA'S SECOND WISH could not be fulfilled, however, principally because of bureaucratic obstacles. She wanted her heart to be placed in Nicolas's coffin at the Cimetière du Père-Lachaise in Paris.

A Princess

SHORTLY AFTER THE DEATHS of Chiara and Clementina something wholly unexpected and quite remarkable occurred at Biederhof. One spring morning a wagon arrived carrying a shabby man and a twelve-year-old girl with long black hair. The man insisted on speaking to Prince Biederstern. Rudolf was in a meeting with Jakob when the liveried servant reported that a short, thin, unshaven, ill-clad stranger with a young girl trailing behind him was asking to meet him. Rudolf replied that the man should wait in the salon and told the servant to keep an eye on him to make sure he didn't steal anything. He then turned back to listen to the manager's careful review of the financial situation of the estate. By the time the meeting was over, he had completely forgotten the visitor. He had a lengthy luncheon; drowsy after a couple of glasses of white wine, he lay down for a nap. When he awoke that afternoon the servant informed him that the visitor had begun to show some signs of impatience after waiting for five hours and was again asking to see the prince. Rudolf was in no hurry, however, for he had no idea that the meeting was to be one of the most important in his life. Another two hours went by before he was ready to receive the man.

"Your Highness," the visitor said, "it is a great honor for me finally to meet the prince. I have heard so much about

him and for years I've tried to imagine what it might be like
to be with him here in his castle—"

"Be so kind as to go directly to the matter at hand," Rudolf interrupted him impatiently. He stood there haughty
and erect, certain that the shabby man with the dirty child
was a beggar, and it was therefore entirely appropriate to
address the individual with condescension. A chilly mood
pervaded the salon. "I am busy, man. I have no time for
flattery. Why are you here? What do you and your daughter
want of me?"

"No, Your Highness, I am not asking for anything from
you, just the opposite, in fact. I've come to give you something." He pointed to the child. "Ariadne is not my daughter. She is Your Highness's own flesh and blood. I'm here to
deliver her to you. My name is Alois Braun. When Ariadne
was born, my sister Arabella asked me and my wife to take
her in. I'll never forget Arabella's desperation when she had
to give up her only child. But she had no choice. She had
no way of taking care of the girl. We promised to bring
Ariadne up, and we have. But now my wife is dead and I
have many children and nothing to feed them with. Ariadne can't live with us any longer. No one can blame me,
for I have only a small house and many mouths to feed. I
have no prospects and nothing to give her. But God exists,
and he always holds his sheltering hand over princes. The
prince's daughter will thrive here in his house. Ariadne is
a thoroughly charming girl and the prince will come to appreciate her."

Rudolf was no longer listening to the man; he was looking at the girl. She stood there with her head bowed, trying
to hide her face behind the heavy curtain of hair.

"You there, look up," Rudolf said peremptorily. "I want
to see your face. I must see if I can find any trace of the

Biederstern features. How else can I know if you belong to me? Your mother was hardly a Madonna."

"Ariadne's always on her guard when she meets folk she doesn't know," the man sought to excuse her. "Your Grace will kindly forgive her if she keeps her eyes down. It's because she can't see anything. She was born blind. My sister infected her with the syphilis."

Rudolf approached the girl, lifted her chin, and pushed aside her hair to see her features. Ariadne was the very picture of his own recently deceased mother. The blood drained from his face. The shock of discovering that he had a daughter left him speechless. He was obliged to sit down.

Two Fires

RUDOLF COULD HARDLY BEAR all the memories of Arabella reawakened by his daughter, whose foul temper soon pitched him into the abyss of premature old age. When Ariadne arrived at Biederhof he was not quite forty years old; a few months later he looked to be sixty. At first the servants were the only ones who whispered that the prince had aged in an abnormal but fully deserved manner. But soon it became common knowledge on the estate that the blind daughter had caused the master of the castle so many woes that in six months he had aged at least ten years.

ARIADNE WAS TO ALL APPEARANCES an exact copy of Clementina, but she had inherited her temperament from her mother and father. She tormented Rudolf with constant outbursts of ill temper. He often reacted with such a fury of his own that one might have imagined he intended to kill her. One day, things went so far that he snatched up a heavy hunting rifle and held it fully cocked only a few feet from the girl's head. She couldn't see what he was doing, of course, but a servant desperately shouted, "Don't shoot, Your Grace, for God's sake, she's your own daughter!" When Rudolf heard this, his anger subsided and he closed his eyes. Once he had fully calmed down, he had a vision of himself as a little boy in short pants and remembered the way he had carried on during his worst tantrums. The agonized faces of his mother and father rose before him. The thought crossed his mind that now he was being repaid with interest for everything he had done to his poor parents.

ARIADNE HAD BEEN AT BIEDERHOF for six months. She was deeply homesick. She yearned for the Brigittenau neighborhood—not for the poverty and hunger of it and especially not for Uncle Alois, the tyrant, but instead for her cousins and everything else she knew and loved. The castle was an enormous prison to her. She was never allowed to leave it by herself. She felt enclosed, encircled, and isolated. It was suffocating her. She hated Biederhof. The castle itself was her enemy. Here she was a cipher, a stranger. She never met anyone but her father. She despised him, not only because he'd neglected her when she was small, but also because he was selfish and stern, a man with no love or conviction behind his authority; all he had to offer were empty threats worthy only of contempt. She also hated the servants. They padded about behind her back, whispered, tittered, and told lies about her. It was clear that the miseries of her heart mattered to no one. She always felt helpless, incensed, and ready to weep. She could scarcely contain her pain and anger. Isolation almost paralyzed her. She wanted to die, to go to sleep and never wake up. She was shrouded in mournful silence. She felt betrayed. No one cared about her, no one wanted to share her secrets and passions, no one listened to her or paid any attention to her standing there with her eyes so dark and empty.

In Jakob's House

JAKOB'S DAYS were filled with work. His responsibilities for Biederhof and, after Solomon's death, for the Viennese affairs of the Rothschild bank required almost superhuman effort. During the four months spent helping Prince Thurn und Taxis sell the postal network to the German state he had never slept more than three hours a night. But no one ever heard him complain, not even at the fact that the time spent at his desk had bent his spine even more. Or that the meticulous examination of the fine points of all the contracts, promissory notes, reports, and statements of accounts had caused his vision to deteriorate. Perhaps his regular reading of *The Elixir of Immortality* helped restored his spirits. Night after night with no trace of fatigue he explored Benjamin's work, pondering every detail, no matter how apparently insignificant, for he knew that each piece could later be of value in understanding the whole.

THE SPINOZA FAMILY invited Rudolf to celebrate New Year's Eve. This was a first. He had never before set foot in their house next to the castle. Even though the general tenor of relations between Rudolf and Jakob was good, in fact almost friendly, they had never met except on business. But whenever Rudolf needed help he could always count on Jakob. It was Jakob's firm belief that one should greet everyone with a warm smile, believe the best of people, and always offer a helping hand. That was why Jakob invited his employer and Ariadne to dinner, an initiative quite unprecedented at the time. He did it for the girl's sake. Jakob and Eleonora pitied the blind child who seemed so lonely in the castle.

The house was full of shrieking children and uninhibited glee. After dinner Jakob led the family in group song, singing with great feeling although with a hoarse voice. No one heard the clock strike twelve in the general hubbub. It was twenty minutes after midnight when they became aware of the oversight and boisterously exchanged wishes for a happy New Year.

Rudolf and Ariadne walked slowly and silently back to the castle through the chill of the night. He had a headache, for it had been an evening of more human company than he was used to. She felt happier than she had been for a long time. At last she had made some friends.

RUDOLF TURNED to Jakob for help and counsel. His face was pasty white and he had suffered through many sleepless nights. He said that he desperately needed a confidant, someone with a paternal air, someone he could discuss things with. He admitted that it was difficult for him to turn to Jakob and open his heart. He had never before done such a thing. But perhaps a man-to-man talk would help, since he needed practical advice. He didn't expect Jakob to understand him entirely, since Jakob was a man who loved his own children, a man who saw them as a blessing, while he himself suffered under the burdens of fatherhood. Ariadne was so fearful and rebellious, even though she was blind, that whenever they were in the same room for more than a few minutes, they started quarreling. Life with her was unbearable, for she was worse than her mother ever had been. She was so malicious and imaginative as she defied him and stirred up trouble that she needed sterner discipline than he was capable of imposing. Rudolf confessed that he despised himself for his weakness, but it was terrifyingly clear to him that he could no longer endure the presence of Ariadne in the castle. He was afraid that one day he would lose all control and physically harm the girl. What should he do? Ariadne was his daughter, after all, and his only relative. He could not stand the girl, but he was tormented by the thought of losing her.

Jakob sat silent for a long moment. Then, without hesitating or mincing words, he suggested that Ariadne move in with his family. He believed the girl needed friends, other children to play with. Rudolf acknowledged that Jakob was probably right, for since New Year's Eve she had been pleading every day to be allowed to play with the Spinoza children again, threatening that if he refused, she would smash every window in the castle.

With that, everything was settled. Rudolf told a servant to have the chambermaids pack up Ariadne's belongings.

ARIADNE LOVED living with Jakob and Eleonora. She played with the youngest children, Andreas and Claudia, who saw her as a big sister, and she studied alongside Nikolaus, her contemporary. But Bernhard, the eldest boy, was the one closest to her. She received a great deal of attention and felt that they regarded her as a member of the family. She demonstrated more devotion to Eleonora and Jakob than she had ever shown to her stepmother and stepfather, and she called Andreas and Claudia her "little brother and sister." A few years later she even adopted the family's name and bore it proudly and happily until her all too untimely death.

A Long Friendship

MY GREAT-UNCLE did not like Franz Josef. He was of the opinion that the Kaiser had robbed him of several years of his youth. He told us how after the battle at Solferino in northern Italy in 1859 revealed Austria's weakness, Franz Josef was forced to give up possession of Lombardy. The defeats in the war with Prussia led by steps to the loss of Venice and the expulsion of the Habsburgs from Germany. The emperor was obliged to change his approach. At the insistence of his wife, Sissi, he set himself resolutely to work, applying his usual cunning to maintaining a political balance. He made peace with the Hungarians, and had himself crowned king of Hungary in a ceremony in Budapest. In the new alliance of Austria and Hungary, known as the double monarchy, the Austrians and the Hungarians ruled their respective domains and jointly dominated other peoples.

Securing his title as Royal and Imperial Majesty was a costly affair. The Ausgleich ("Compromise" or "Reconciliation") of 1867 almost emptied the state coffers in Vienna. The financial situation eventually became so difficult that Franz Josef was obliged to humble himself to the extent of inviting potential creditors to tea at the Hofburg.

It's no easy job, my great-uncle commented, to rule as absolute monarch over a population of fifty million souls.

FRANZ JOSEF almost lost his cigar when Jakob came in, for His Majesty's imperial and royal jaw dropped at the sight of the Jew's incredibly large nose. The emperor had never seen anything like it. He was on the verge of bursting into laughter.

Jakob had encountered this same reaction many times before. He said, "The nose comes from my grandfather, Nicolas

Spinoza. But His Majesty need not be alarmed, for my ancestor's revolutionary blood does not flow through my veins. I am greatly honored to be here, and I can assure His Majesty that I do not come with any thoughts of chopping off heads. I humbly desire to serve my emperor and do everything I can to exalt his standing and that of the empire."

That impromptu speech impressed Franz Josef. He heartily approved of Jakob's sentiments. He answered in a bantering tone, "If you serve your emperor well, you may well receive a title. If you displease your sovereign by God's grace, you will spend ten years in a solitary prison cell. That does indeed constitute a sort of sinecure, compared to decapitation by the guillotine, your grandfather's fate. This all goes to prove that we Habsburgs are more humane than French revolutionaries."

Both smiled. It was the beginning of a long friendship.

FRANZ JOSEF'S LIFE was marked by many sorrows. His brother Maximilian, the emperor of Mexico, was deposed and executed by a firing squad of his ungrateful subjects. His only son, Rudolf, committed suicide in mysterious circumstances. His sister Valentina perished in a fire in Paris. His wife, Sissi, was stabbed to death with a sharpened file by an Italian anarchist. His presumptive successor, Franz Ferdinand, was shot to death by a Serbian nationalist.

A day eventually came when the emperor lost his desire to live. For two weeks he had locked himself away in his bedroom, not saying a word to anyone. My great-uncle told us that by then the emperor was contemplating suicide. He ordered a servant to bring him a thick rope, but the thought of hanging from a chandelier with his legs dangling gave him a headache. He began to suffer cold sweats and his stomach twisted into a knot. There had to be some other way, but he didn't know which method would be the surest and the least painful. The situation was further complicated by the fact that he could not seek counsel from any of his ministers. Who could help him? Whom did he dare trust? He had Jakob summoned and opened his heart to him. Jakob pondered for a couple of minutes and then offered a suggestion. He told the Kaiser he owned a book of Talmudic wisdom that held the answer to every question. He promised to return quickly and went to his residence. *Life is more important than anything else,* he thought, and so he did something he knew was absolutely forbidden. To free his friend from the dark imaginings tormenting the imperial and royal brain, Jakob carried Benjamin's secret book, *The Elixir of Immortality,* to the Hofburg and read selected passages aloud. He went so far as to allow Franz Josef to look through the book.

The emperor's mood improved markedly after a while, and he began to think of his life in a more positive light. He told his friend Jakob, "Your book has given me new faith in life. I doubt that there exists any greater wisdom than that contained by these covers. Therefore I advise you to burn this dangerous book. Human beings are not yet ready for some truths."

Hot Nights

EVERY NIGHT BERNHARD WAITED, quivering in anticipation, for the others in the house to fall asleep. Ariadne's body was the center of his world. Her fragrance intoxicated him. He loved her soft breasts, her thin belly, her moist sex, and her pouting lower lip. But more than anything else he loved her small hands and the way they playfully caressed his member. Nothing was more important to him than the hour he spent alone with her at night. When he was certain that everyone else was sleeping, he tiptoed into Ariadne's room. The touch of her skin made the rest of the world disappear for him.

ON A NIGHT OF THUNDERSTORMS after Bernhard had been forced to wait an extra-long time for everyone to drift off, he arrived, feverish with anticipation, in the room of his beloved. But Ariadne whispered tearfully to him, "I can't, I can't. No matter how much I want to, I can't satisfy you, my darling."

"What's wrong?" he asked, dismayed.

"I'm with child."

She was fifteen; he was seventeen. I was never able to discover which of them had the notion that the only escape from a situation that became more hopelessly complicated with every passing day was to run away from Biederhof. One night they sneaked out of the house and made their way by fits and starts to Budapest, where they managed to get properly married in an outlying neighborhood, joined by a drunken local mayor who wasn't too demanding and didn't require any documentation from youngsters nowhere near the legal age of consent.

Six months later Moricz made his entry into their world.

Exit

JAKOB'S FIFTY-FIFTH BIRTHDAY was a tremendous day. That very afternoon the emperor was to grant him a title of nobility and appoint him minister of finance. The ceremony took place in the left wing of the Hofburg, opened in honor of the occasion after reconstruction and restoration work that had taken five years to complete. More than three hundred prominent guests were invited to experience the gleaming splendor of the Habsburg residence at the ceremony for the Jew Jakob Spinoza.

It began as a festive occasion. Franz Josef was in an especially good humor. Standing straight and tall, bristling with the bushy sideburns that had long been the instantly recognizable symbol of imperial power, he beamed, impeccable and splendid, above the reverently bowed heads of his subjects.

He offered a number of pompous remarks and then dubbed his friend "von Spinoza," pinning upon his chest the Grand Cross of the Order of Maria Teresa, First Class. This was a rare honor. At that time only six other individuals held the distinction of the highest rank of the Grand Cross. All were military officers from the finest noble families. No Jew had ever received such a distinction. Nor had any Jew ever been appointed to a ministerial post in Austria.

Franz Josef seated himself upon the throne. Jakob stood alone in the middle of the enormous hall. Obviously deeply touched upon this momentous occasion, he delivered brief remarks in a tremulous voice, expressing his profound gratitude for the inconceivable honor accorded to him. He instructed the servants to fill everyone's glass with champagne so he could propose a toast, not only to His Majesty the Emperor but also to the memory of the woman who had been like a mother to him and had most instructed him in life, but who unfortunately could not share that moment: Chiara Luzzatto.

The sound of popping champagne corks filled the hall. A couple of them flew high into the air. One of them described an arc directly over the heads of those nearby and struck the harness supporting the colossal crystal chandelier from Arnošt Gruša's renowned workshop in Bohemia. The chandelier fell to the floor with a deafening crash. Directly beneath it lay Austria's newly appointed minister of finance. The only visible part of the dead man was a large nose, protruding from the heap of broken crystal.

TEN

The Journalist

A Secret Is Revealed

IT PROBABLY HAPPENED in the early summer of 1964, since my grandfather was already in his grave by then. My brother, Sasha, and I, fully fourteen years of age, were playing with a ball in the bedroom the two of us shared with our grandmother. We were pretending we were at the European Cup soccer finals at the Prater Stadium in Vienna, at the match between Inter and Real Madrid. I was the quick-footed Italian Sandro Mazzola and easily kept the ball away from Sasha, who represented the entire Spanish defense, and I slammed a powerful arching shot against the night table that represented the goal. The ball rebounded directly up in the air and struck the large dark painting hanging on the wall.

The portrait was of grandmother's mother, Miriam Neumann, as painted by an amateur artist in 1907. She was thirty-nine years old at that time but she looked much older, an elderly figure with a bleak expression.

The painting fell to the floor with a crash. My great-uncle was in the kitchen negotiating a miserably small loan from Grandmother, since the five hundred dollars he got from the Salt Lake City Mormons for his autobiography had long been nothing but a memory. The noise brought them both rushing into the bedroom. Grandmother was completely outraged. "How can you do something like this to me? Why can't you leave my beloved mother in peace? Isn't anything sacred to you? What horrible children!" And so on, and so on—I can't remember everything she screamed. She was about to slap us both, but the lady on duty at the building entrance unexpectedly came to our assistance. Grandmother heard the doorbell, and it immediately distracted her from our offense and her grief; she hurried to the front door to get the latest news from the neighborhood, which the all-knowing concierge always generously shared with her.

My great-uncle helped us hang the portrait in its place once again. With a stern look he admonished us to be careful. "It's a bad omen, disturbing the dead," he said. "One should never awaken them from their sleep. They've earned their rest. No one has the right to make them come back as ghosts."

I often wondered why my great-grandmother's eyes appeared so sorrowful. Her dark look was the last thing I saw every evening before going to sleep and the first thing that met my eyes in the morning, because the gloomy painting hung directly opposite the double bed that Sasha and I shared. Was she annoyed with me? I took the question to my great-uncle, who was always ready to provide answers to difficult issues. He reassured me that her sorrow had nothing to do with me. It was because she was lonely.

"It's almost impossible to describe in words how very lonely a person can feel," he commented. "And Miriam, I should tell you, was an extremely lonely person. She was alone throughout her life."

Without our having to ask, my great-uncle took the opportunity to do what he loved most: tell us a story. With a somber voice he began to recount Miriam's childhood in the shadow of her father, oppressed and unloved in the hovels and the crowds of children in Galicia—to be more exact, in the obscure village of Chertnow, rarely visited by outsiders, where Jews lived in their voluntary isolation, their destiny steered by the zaddik Menachem, reputed to have mysterious powers and held in awe by Hasidic Jews throughout Eastern Europe.

After a considerable time he got up, stood there for a moment, looked around in the room as if to make sure that Grandmother was nowhere near, and then lowered his voice.

"I'm going to tell you a secret, boys."

I imagined that he was about to reveal some dramatic details about the magical powers of the zaddik. But the secret he shared with us had to do with something completely different.

"Some time before the death of her father," he whispered, "Miriam suddenly had an irresistible desire to have a child. The child's father was poor, a stranger, young, a fair number of years younger than she was—almost a boy, with no home of his own, a refugee from Belarus. He stayed in Chertnow only for a short time, just long enough to catch his breath, and then he set out immediately into the world again."

A Dramatic Quarrel

SASHA AND I could scarcely believe our ears. The revelation that Grandmother had never known her father made me feel sad for her. I went hurrying off to offer my sympathy. Standing at the stove, she stuck her thumb into the potato soup, and then licked it. "Not too warm, not too cold," she pronounced with satisfaction. I told her what we had just heard, thinking that my consideration would please her. Instead of thanking me, she began shouting. She was frightfully angry at me—but curiously enough, not at Sasha—for having listened to such bad-mouthed talk and believing it. Then she gave my great-uncle a terrible scolding for spreading wicked lies and trying to mislead two innocent young boys.

"My mother, may her memory be blessed, was an honorable woman, the widow of a respected merchant in Chertnow! He was a good man, and I'm proud to be his daughter."

She spat out a few vehement sentences in German. We didn't understand what she was saying, but my great-uncle certainly did. He was visibly intimidated.

My brother and I sat down on the sofa and followed with awed attention the theatrical spectacle of the adults shouting and gesturing wildly. We weren't used to that sort of thing in our quiet house. We actually should have been frightened by it, but the quarrel had seemed so unreal that we felt torn between dismay and laughter.

Grandmother blazed with anger. My great-uncle raised his arms to heaven and called upon God to witness his innocence. Grandmother raised her voice even more. "I am absolutely scandalized. Franci, you have shamed me in front of my grandchildren. This is an absolute horror. Aren't you ashamed! That with your mouth you should dare to speak the name of my sainted mother!"

German invective again filled the air. My great-uncle's face was ashen. Rivulets of sweat ran down his forehead. He tottered to the front door and slammed it behind him.

It was only a very long time afterward that I next encountered my great-uncle. That was the following year, at Sasha's funeral.

Miriam

MIRIAM NEUMANN was poor but not in the least simple-minded or past her prime. She wasn't particularly good-looking, true, but she didn't deserve to be alone or resigned to her fate. She wasn't tall; she was thick of body and round of build. With a black kerchief tightly knotted under her chin, she looked like a maid or a peasant girl. She was in her very late twenties and still a spinster. The reason that she never married remains a mystery to me.

It seemed astonishing to those in her hometown that she hadn't found a husband. The inhabitants of Chertnow exploited family connections for such arrangements, but it was also possible to employ a matchmaker. In certain cases community leaders were asked to send letters to their counterparts in nearby settlements in Galicia. In some way or other, sooner or later an eligible bachelor always turned up. Never in human memory had any Jewish woman of the town had to despair.

Miriam was the youngest child of a family in humble circumstances. Her parents were well-practiced in the ancient arts of caring for the sick and grieving for the dead. Their first four children, all sons, died in their infancy.

Rachel, the elder daughter, was everyone's favorite. She was tutored from an early age to be marriageable. She knew how to do laundry, iron, cook, carry out religious rituals— there was no girl in all of Chertnow who had been better brought up. Her father used to joke that she was born the same way as the greatest Jewish queens in history, with her umbilical cord around her neck.

Miriam, two years younger, was frail and short of breath. Her parents foresaw an uncertain future for her. As a child, she was reticent and introspective. She answered timidly when spoken to but almost never had anything of her own to say. She received her sister's clothes as hand-me-downs, mostly items that should have been discarded, and since her feet were larger than Rachel's, she always wore shoes that were too tight. Her experiences in life had been unhappy from an early age, and she trembled in fear of scoldings, corrections, and dismissive comments. Their father taught her to read and write, of course, but his attention was always elsewhere, as if he was teaching a stranger. He was ashamed that Miriam could never recall a word of a text that she had just read. She understood every sentence, but every single one immediately replaced the previous one, so that the meaning of the whole always escaped her.

Her mother, a woman of few words, was the only person who sometimes showed some concern for Miriam. Her name was Hanna and she was a native of Plotnow, another small Jewish town in the vicinity. Hanna's father was a miller, and she was the next to the youngest in a troupe of nine sisters. Her vision was extremely poor and her sluggish, somewhat pained appearance concealed her true character. She devoted herself selflessly to her husband and Rachel, but one seldom saw her do anything other than cook, wash, and weep.

Even as a girl, Miriam could see how rapidly her mother was aging. Her skin lost its elasticity and her body lost its form; with every passing month new wrinkles appeared in her face.

Hanna died when Miriam was seven years old. She caught an inflammation of the lungs, an illness fatal for many in those days. She had a feeble constitution and was already relatively worn out, so it all went very quickly.

No one had any idea how desperately Miriam wept at night or how she secretly attempted to resurrect her mother by muttering Kaddish, the prayer of mourning for the departed.

The Peddler

HER FATHER, Samuel, was a peddler. His stinginess was legendary, surpassing that of anyone else in Chertnow, and everyone laughed at him behind his back. Even so, he was a highly respected member of the community, for he could cite passages of the Holy Scripture appropriate for any imaginable occasion, and he had a beautiful singing voice. He often served as a substitute cantor for the Saturday morning service.

After his wife's death he lived as a widower and became even stingier. In his worn robe tied with a length of rope, he looked like a beggar. He baked the family bread over a fire of wood bark.

Samuel's unpredictable temper terrorized his daughters. He was extremely strict and quick to punish the girls for the least offense. Miriam never complained. Every time their father burst into a rage she sat with her head bowed in fright, lost her appetite, and withdrew into herself. Rachel, on the other hand, became ever more rebellious as the years went by.

Samuel insisted upon absolute compliance with the customs of the Jewish faith. Dietary laws were strictly observed in their home. Tradition smelled faintly of lavender and ancient mildew.

Piety meant nothing to Miriam. She concluded as a result of her fruitless resort to the earnest recitation of Kaddish that God was deaf and unable to hear her prayers, and that was why her mother couldn't come back from the realm of the dead. She also remembered how her mother would stand with her bent back turned to the hearth, toothless and prematurely old: What comfort had her Jewish faith ever provided her?

Everyone in Chertnow knew that Samuel's quiet life was overshadowed by an immense sorrow. He never got over the fact that Rachel, his favorite daughter, who had just reached her bloom, the most beautiful young woman in the city and not yet quite seventeen, had hurriedly and against her father's will married the distant cousin of a neighbor, a simple Jewish tailor from Budapest, and moved with him to Hungary. Some said she simply grabbed the first man who came her way in order to escape her joyless home.

Samuel was even more grieved when Rachel's marriage produced no children. The more time passed, the more ardently he wished for God's blessing in the form of a grandchild.

After Miriam's twentieth birthday, her father began to look around seriously for an appropriate son-in-law. She discouraged the effort and always found something lacking in the candidates. This one was unacceptable for one reason, that one for another, and a third was simply unthinkable. She pursed her lips and effectively drove off all her suitors.

A Miracle

ONE DAY at a dance organized in the meeting hall to celebrate the holiday of Purim, where she sat out of the way like a wallflower, she caught sight of a young man, only twenty-one years old, named Jasja Karpilovski. He had arrived in Chertnow the previous month from White Russia—Belarus—and intended to travel on to America. Jasja was tall and blond; he had a thin face, high cheekbones, and pale blue eyes. When he invited her to dance and put his hands around her waist, his touch whirled her out of the world. Her infatuation was instantaneous; life force pried her open like a mussel, and she shuddered with a desire she was now ready to accept. She had no more objections; she was ready. That same night she lost her virtue and became a fallen woman.

Once the misfortune could no longer be concealed, Miriam went to her father and stammered out a confession of her crime. She hoped he would welcome the news—for the child within her was the fast grip of life itself, the force that eternally ends and begins again. Granted, Jasja had already disappeared without even saying goodbye, but Miriam declared, "From time to time a miracle occurs."

"A miracle?" repeated Samuel, and stared at her in disbelief. His first impulse was to rush to the synagogue and pray for a blessing for the unborn child. Then he turned on his heel and hurried off to seek counsel from the zaddik Menachem, who was believed to possess profound wisdom and have the answers to all of life's questions.

"A miracle!" the holy man repeated. He reflected, drew his fingers through his long beard, rose, went to his bookshelf, took out a work of the Cabala, opened it at random, read a few lines, nodded, and then decisively dismissed the theory of a miracle.

"Such miracles do not occur outside of marriage," he said.

Citing passages of the Torah and other holy writings as well as reciting incantations and many of the different names for God, he succeeded in convincing Samuel that this was the work of the Evil One.

"You yearn for honor, for a grandchild, and instead you receive disgrace and a bastard," the zaddik told him, mincing no words.

Samuel replied that his shame was great; he scarcely dared to meet the eyes of the pious and righteous people of Chertnow.

"But despite everything, Miriam is my daughter. What should I do?"

Menachem told him to put out his daughter and never to allow the bastard to enter his house.

"One black sheep can be the ruin of the whole herd," the zaddik asserted. His tone brooked no opposition.

The news spread quickly and there was a great stir. Everyone in Chertnow was indignant. A few loudmouths wanted to teach Miriam a lesson, but the leader of the community refused. It was her father's responsibility to deal with the matter and to punish her.

Samuel's Passing

PERHAPS IT WAS THE EFFECT on Samuel's body of the sun and the heat of that summer day. On the morning after he had made it clear to Miriam that she and the illegitimate offspring in her belly would have to leave the house, he complained of pains in his chest and couldn't get out of bed. His head was burning hot and his mind reeled in confusion.

MIRIAM MIXED goat's milk with garlic and horseradish and left the concoction simmering in a pot over the fire for half the night; in the morning she gave Samuel a portion of it on his empty stomach. He only shrieked and spat it out and complained at the foul taste.

More days passed. Miriam tried other recipes, but Samuel refused to consume his daughter's various potions.

He became progressively weaker, and his beard, black until very recently, began to whiten. His body had become loose, almost disarticulated, and hung like an empty sack. He lay in his bed, apparently lifeless, left by his neighbors to his suffering. Miriam prepared chicken soup with strong spices, her father's favorite dish, but he refused to touch it.

One afternoon, for no reason at all, Samuel cast a fierce, hateful look at Miriam, ranted at her, and spat out along with abundant spittle the crudest insults that Yiddish could articulate. "No one escapes his destiny," he said over and over again, his voice gradually failing. Then he howled that he could see the Angel of Death in the room and the gravedigger who was standing there with his spade ready.

Miriam was alarmed and exhausted. She had watched over her father day and night from the day he had fallen ill.

That night she was seized by a terrible anxiety. Shivering with fever, she listened to the continual buzzing of flies in the room and to the locusts making a din in the dawn. As she fell asleep in the early morning, at the end of her forces, her father's heart stopped beating.

The ordeal that Miriam endured the next day at the burial service would haunt her for the rest of her life. It wasn't her father's death or the isolation that scared her the most; it was the way she was treated, suddenly and with no warning, by people who had known her since she was born.

Even though rain was pouring down that day, everyone in Chertnow came to the ceremony for the peddler. Menachem delivered a sermon of fire and brimstone. He wildly exhorted the people to oppose all evil, for if one gave in to wickedness, confusion would reign in a world that was already falling apart. He warned that the town could wind up in the clutches of Satan and the people were in danger of being wiped off the face of the earth. The community listened to him with deep respect.

The rain made it seem that everyone was sobbing and weeping floods of tears. Everyone except Miriam. She was in control of herself throughout it all, her face calm although her spirit was alarmed. She stood there, isolated, silent and pale in her black clothing, drenched, with no sign of tears and no cries of grief. She only stared down into the grave. People exchanged knowing glances behind her back. The Jews of Chertnow were famous for their generosity, but not a soul among them made a move to comfort Miriam. It was clear to them beyond all doubt that she had dragged her father into his misfortune. She was responsible for his death.

Alone and Outcast

AFTER THE GRAVESIDE CEREMONY Miriam took to her bed. Her mind was full of confused images, there where the darkness of the soul and the desires of the body combined to create the same terrors she had experienced as a child. She wanted to end her life. She went directly to the kitchen pantry and took out a bottle of kerosene. She opened it, but couldn't bring herself to drink. The sharp smell that filled the whole house nauseated her.

She felt an overwhelming desire to collapse. She wanted to fall down in the street before them all and just lie there on the ground. Dazed by her own weakness, she wept without interruption for three days. Then she prepared to confront the world again.

AFTER HER FATHER DIED, Miriam was no longer dependent; for the first time in her life, she was in charge of her own fate. She was completely isolated. She could sense enemies everywhere, and the people all glared at her with wicked, baleful looks. She was afraid of leaving Chertnow but she had no choice. She could not stay. The Jews of her hometown despised her. She was regarded as a sinner, a shameful whore who had driven her father into his grave. Miriam felt sick in her soul, poisoned by their resentment. She packed her few belongings and left the town with bitterness in her heart.

I still find it incredible that the happiness in Miriam's life lasted only a few hours. To be more specific: from eight o'clock until half past eleven on the evening of March 26, 1897. For those three and a half hours she felt full of life, free, fulfilled, and loved. After that, everything was unremittingly dire. She received a terrible blow from life that cast her into the gutter. She became pregnant, Jasja disappeared without a word, her father rejected her and her unborn child, and then he died.

She felt weighted down by guilt. Everything was her fault. She had given herself to Jasja. The mysterious, perilous urgings of sex had led her into sin. She pledged to herself she would never have another man. She would never again allow a man to come near her.

Two Versions

CHERTNOW IS NO LONGER to be found on the maps. There are two versions of what happened to it.

In the extremely strict orthodox communities of Crown Heights in New York where the zaddik Menachem still lives on in revered memory, people say that his prediction that Chertnow would wind up in Satan's clutches and be exterminated from the earth was fulfilled because families that fail to live according to the law are doomed to annihilation at the righteous hand of the Lord.

The other version of events is closer to historical fact.

In the autumn of 1942 two heavy trucks transporting men in dark uniforms drove into the large square by the synagogue. The men were Germans, policemen in Reserve Battalion No. 101, fathers of families, too old to serve at the front. All were volunteers. Their profession was racial purification and their history was anything but glorious. They assembled the Jews in the marketplace. The commander made a quick calculation and saw at once that it would take too long to shoot them. The Jews were herded into the synagogue, and the doors were carefully locked and sealed. The battalion leader issued the order to burn Chertnow to the ground. The last of the flames died out thirty-six hours later. Nothing was left but ashes.

To Budapest

MIRIAM WAS A SIMPLE SOUL, a human being on the far edge of existence, invisible to history. She had a story and history of her own, but they left no trace anywhere. Today I'm the only one who even knows that she once existed.

The trip to Budapest, a rail journey through a wasteland, took more than fifty hours. Miriam slept almost not at all and ate even less, for the costs of the burial had used up the few groschen her father had left behind. On the train she sat squeezed between a nun and a portly colonel who tried in vain to engage his fellow travelers in conversation. She gazed out the window, watching the pastures and the trees flying past. The landscape was bathed in sunshine, and the luminosity of the sky was almost unbearable. The sun, the stifling air aboard the train, and the fatigue from her sleepless nights made her vision blur. Her thoughts wandered.

She tried to recall her sister's face. *There must be some way out for me, too, as totally isolated as I am,* she told herself. She promised God she would never ever again ask for anything, if only he would guide her safe and sound to Rachel.

On a summer day in 1897—I think it was the tenth of July—Miriam arrived at the Budapest-Nyugati western railway terminal, a colossal temple to architecture designed by the Frenchman Gustave Eiffel.

Budapest had more than a million inhabitants at that time and had established itself as one of Europe's most vital capitals, unapologetically pretentious, with no qualms about its ambition to surpass Vienna in everything essential —and why not Paris and London as well? People from all across the double monarchy found their way to this pearl of the Danube: Ruthenian peasants, Polish workers, optimistic Jews, Czech cobblers, Austrian bankers, Serbian pickpockets, Croatian pimps with tidy mustaches, and urbane con men. There were also innumerable beauties with rouged cheeks and pink lips, wearing elegant dresses and on the prowl for monocled gentlemen ready to open their bulging pocketbooks to have their fancies tickled.

The city seethed with activity in an air of cosmopolitan elegance. Not for nothing was the Hungarian capital called "America on a smaller scale."

Its world was new and old at the same time. The air was so charged with possibility that one could hardly breathe. Bright promises were not the only things on offer here. Under the bravely effervescent, carefree life of the city there was a dark side with, in the words of the writer Gyula Krúdy, "no real love, not a single honorable man, and not one respectable woman."

The train slowed and pulled into the station. Confused and exhausted, Miriam descended at the end of the line from the first train trip of her life into the most intense heat wave of the year. She would take only one more train ride during her long life, forty-seven years later, and that would be in an overcrowded cattle car, back to Poland to a site only a few miles from her birthplace, which became known by its German name: Auschwitz.

Ahead of her now were decades of isolation and hardship in a land steeped in prejudice and injustice, a country where she would never feel at ease or put down roots and would forever remain a foreigner.

All her possessions were contained in a small woven basket. She clutched it hard in her right hand as she left the train. She looked out at hundreds of people on the platform, a completely overwhelming sea of human faces. Some were well cared for and elegant, but most were bedraggled and perspiring in the heat. Young people, workers, women carrying their children, the elderly; all were trying to push their way through the crowd. She stopped dead, filled with dread because she'd never seen so many people. Just as she was about to be swept away by this mass of humanity, she caught sight of a man wearing the uniform of a conductor of the Imperial and Royal Railway. She approached him and asked in a quivering voice where the synagogue was located. Everyone in the city of Budapest spoke German. Almost no one understood Yiddish, Miriam's mother tongue. The conductor was jovial, however, and even more important, helpful. After several attempts he made out what she was saying, wrote out the address, and sketched a simple map in his notebook. Clutching the page from the notebook, she stepped out into the seething swirl of the big city.

An Encounter with the Metropolis

MIRIAM'S FIRST STAGGERING WALK through the streets of Budapest was overwhelming. The city roared, thundered, and hissed like a locomotive. Peddlers cried their wares, newspaper vendors shouted, and crowds surged excitedly in both directions along the endless, wide boulevards. The immense houses looked like palaces with their ostentatious superfluity of decoration and adornments, statues and recesses. She had never seen anything like them, and they made her head spin. Nothing was lacking and everything was displayed in overabundance: jewelers, tailors, fashion designers, hair salons, beauty salons, clothing shops, cafés, restaurants, flower shops, luxurious hotels, and theaters, one unbelievable establishment after another. She stood for a long time before each one along the way, craning her neck and gaping.

The people seemed respectable and elegant—gentlemen in their splendid suits and women in their colorful dresses. But she was struck by the way the handsome women rolled their hips in a manner that the folks back home in Chertnow would have regarded as truly scandalous.

Many decades later Miriam could still recall how unbearably hot it was that day. She made her way unsteadily onward for hours in the oppressive heat, perspiration dripping from beneath her firmly knotted head scarf.

None of those whom she asked for directions was particularly helpful; she felt increasingly worn and sick at heart. Most of all, she felt lost.

She became aware of her ravenous hunger only when she stumbled into a broad marketplace with vegetable stands, butcher shops, and food stalls. She stopped to catch her breath. She felt her heart pounding and her breast heaving. Her nose was assaulted by a great variety of smells: fat and drippings from a stand where two frying pans were sizzling, sweaty bodies, unidentifiable odors of fruit and vegetables. She found every one of assorted temptations on offer at the market intensely appetizing, even though she knew most of the food wasn't kosher. Her mouth watered as she stared wide-eyed at a fat butcher who had elevated his profession to a fine art, applying his gleaming sharp knife to the elegant art of transforming a length of meat into neatly trimmed slices.

Miriam wandered farther into the city. At a street corner a horse drawing a cart snorted directly in her face and the driver shouted at her to get back. She was so frightened that her knees almost gave way, but she managed to hurry farther along the street.

The streets were suddenly reeking of garbage. She found herself in a part of the city that was ugly and mean, full of tumbledown houses, a poverty-stricken neighborhood where the people were unusually pale.

In one barren street a stubby little girl with a strange face crossed her path. The child greeted her with a simple but serene smile, looking for all the world like a pilgrim who had just reached the gates of heaven after a long journey. Miriam felt a flash of fear and tensed as if she had caught sight of the devil. At home in Chertnow they'd lived near a family with a feeble-minded boy everyone in the town regarded as sweet but hopelessly dim-witted. On the other hand, she had never encountered anyone like that remarkable young girl. Today most of us would say that the child had Down syndrome, but that diagnosis did not exist in Miriam's world.

The girl took Miriam's hand in both of her own, as delicately as if she were a porcelain figure. Her gentle touch made Miriam shiver. The girl seemed to be thinking of a secret. She whispered something so quietly that Miriam couldn't understand her. She pointed upward, toward the pigeons sitting on the roof of the house.

Miriam took this as an evil omen. She suddenly feared for her unborn child. She had absorbed with her mother's milk the belief that even the briefest encounter with strangers of abnormal appearance could deform an unborn child in its mother's womb. She pulled away her hand and hurried off as fast as she could manage. When she turned to look back, she saw the girl standing at the same spot, smiling and waving to Miriam and to the pigeons in turn.

Time passed; fatigue overcame her. Her body felt heavy, as if her blood had turned into lead. She couldn't go a step farther. Thirsty and exhausted, she drifted into a daze. She felt that she was being sucked into the violent maelstrom of the city. She sat down on the curb, to keep from collapsing outright. Her eyes filled with tears.

A few feet away at the corner of the street a woman stood behind a crude stand, selling vegetables. She must have seen Miriam's misery, for she came to help. She gave Miriam water to drink. It tasted heavenly, but Miriam did not even have the energy to thank her. She felt all her forces flowing out of her body; she lost consciousness.

In a Room and a Half

IN HER DREAM Miriam had returned to an earlier period of her life in Chertnow and relived some of the horrors of her childhood, particularly including her terror whenever her father would grab her violently by her braided tresses, an anxiety that abruptly ended on the day a neighbor boy with eyes full of malevolence deliberately snipped them off for no reason at all. That malicious act had caused a great deal of excitement in the otherwise tranquil town, but it liberated Miriam and made her life easier. The memory of it made her waken with a start.

She was lying in a bed she didn't recognize. The pillow was hard and smelled sour. Her back ached, her neck was numb, and she looked around in consternation. She didn't know where she was or how she had gotten there. She could not remember anything that had happened.

Slowly she sat up in the bed and looked around with bleary eyes. The walls were peeling and the ancient furniture appeared ready to collapse. A candleholder with seven arms stood on a cabinet. There was a sack of potatoes and a kerosene burner. The place smelled of poverty and mildew. How long had she been asleep?

The woman from the market entered the room and smiled at her. "There was once a time," she said, "when our home was much more beautiful and a great deal cleaner. But it has gotten all too expensive to hire housekeepers."

She surveyed Miriam, and her face lit up with a friendly smile. Miriam could see that the woman had few teeth left and her face and neck were deeply creased and wrinkled. Her eyes were striking, though, and they danced with happiness. With evident satisfaction she enumerated the seven people who lived in the apartment of one and a half rooms that measured scarcely a hundred square feet.

"First, there's me—I'm Luiza. There's my very rheumatic mother, Erzsi, who is terribly afraid of losing all her hair and is always wailing about that. Most of the rest of the time she sits in that broken-down old armchair for days on end, thinking about the past, sighing, and waiting to be fed from what little we have. Sometimes she tries to tell my five children how things were in Transylvania when she was young. But they're too little for that and don't have the patience to listen to old folks."

Luiza's heart filled with joy as she told the story of her life. It was obvious that unlike Miriam she was never at a loss for words. She assured Miriam that she had become inured to the unremitting injustices of life and was endowed with a vitality that triumphed over everything. The only thing she could not stand was self-pity. "One shouldn't whine," she declared. "One must bear up to one's circumstances instead and fulfill one's destiny before finally giving up and disappearing forever."

Luiza said that she didn't believe in God but even so, every day she thanked her Maker for her good memory. It was the only thing about her that had always worked well and had never failed her once in her forty years on this earth. She was of the opinion that certain people are born with a special ability to remember things. She herself had memories of things that had happened long before her parents had first met, and of course she could recall everything, even the tiniest and most ridiculous details of the lives of every person she had ever encountered. As a demonstration of this unique gift she told stories about people, mostly those living in the same building. She freely acknowledged that she loved sad stories—the more tear-stained, the better. Sad stories thrilled her heart.

She told how folks in the building had been afflicted by heat and cold, deformities and hunger, poverty and sickness, in fact by all the plagues of the human condition. They were worn down and tired out. Some had given up hope, and some had fallen into despair over the pointlessness of existence. But there was still something nearly noble about them, something worthy of respect. They were good people.

"Nothing is really either black or white," Luiza said. "The truth is that the white often enough has some black in it, and the black is just something white that went wrong somehow."

Miriam listened to her and tried to come up with something intelligent to say. She compared the stories that Luiza told her about the neighbors' desperation and poverty with her own experiences. She was embarrassed. She felt that she had no right to bother Luiza with her own trivial life story from Chertnow. So she said nothing.

A New Life

THE AFTERNOON had given way to dusk. Luiza asked no questions of her. Miriam was relieved not to have to explain why she had left her village. Luiza's mere presence had a calming effect upon her. Not a single time since that evening when she'd met Jasja had her spirit been so serene. She felt appreciated, for no one had ever afforded her so much time and attention. Suddenly Miriam felt enormously comforted, and she shivered with release and a sense of freedom after her great adventure.

EVEN THOUGH she never said so, Miriam believed that she had been graced with a great favor when fate brought her together with Luiza. She had traveled to Budapest in quest of her sister, a home, and a family. She never did find Rachel. But with Luiza she found everything else she was seeking.

Luiza had partitioned off the bed in which Miriam was lying from the rest of the apartment with a length of dark cloth tacked to the ceiling. There, in that space of scarcely twenty square feet, Miriam would live with her daughter, Sara (my future grandmother), for more than a quarter of her life.

Release from Detention

I'LL HAVE MORE to say about Miriam and her daughter, Sara. Just now, however, something else has come to mind and a different story insists on being told.

ADI WAS ABOUT to turn fifty. All Germany was preparing to celebrate the Führer's birthday. They were planning for it to be the celebration of the century, even bigger than the 1936 Olympic Games in Berlin. The week before the actual day—April 20, 1939—he made a lightning visit to Frankfurt and had an indication of what to expect from the German people, who idolized him. The swastika reigned supreme over the city. The fifty thousand party faithful crammed into Wald stadium eagerly watched the airplanes circling above and scattering banners with swastikas. Cries of *Heil!* thundered out when the leader appeared upon the stage of honor. His fifteen-minute speech was a concentrated harangue. He praised the German *Volk*, those courageous men and women who feared nothing and were ready to offer their lives for the fatherland. That was all there was to it. The uproarious jubilation seemed never-ending. The sea of people wept for joy. Then the Führer left the stadium for several other meetings with the German people.

The idea came from Mathäus Frombichler. The two friends were staying at Berghof, the Führer's private residence in southern Bavaria, not far from the regions the Third Reich's battle-ready storm troops would plunge into a new world war only four months later. On that uneventful morning with clear skies one could look out the broad windows and see all the way to Salzburg in the north. An almost palpable melancholy lay over the kitchen. Frombichler was chopping onions for a salad niçoise for the day's lunch. Adi was scowling and cleaning his fingernails with a kitchen knife. He was appalled by the thought of his birthday, he said, because he hated the idea of getting older. He lay down the knife and grasped his genitals. His dissatisfied expression suggested that the object of his interest was tiny and flaccid. He commented sourly that he'd almost forgotten how to use the thing, because Eva was completely uninterested and as dried up as a hole in the desert. He no longer got anything from her except a good-night kiss on the forehead. Frombichler was quick to reassure him that this didn't mean that her affection for him had cooled. Adi heaved a sigh of resignation.

Two young soldiers stood watch at the door of his kitchen. They couldn't avoid overhearing the Führer, and they became as pale as the baguette the cook was chopping into the bread basket. Disconcerted, they fixed their eyes on the floor.

Fritz, Eva Braun's favorite German shepherd, was dozing beneath the kitchen table. He cut a tremendous fart that made Frombichler and Adi grin like schoolboys.

Adi dropped the subject of his love life and complained about the unexpectedly strong reactions worldwide to his annexation of Czechoslovakia. He was vexed that the only statesman who understood him was that clown Mussolini. Frombichler lifted an eyebrow. "Adi, maybe you should release some of the better-known prisoners from Dachau. Many people abroad are unhappy that authors and celebrities are prisoners there. Let a few of them out on humanitarian grounds for your birthday celebration. That should quiet the criticism of you out there in the world."

"That is unacceptable," Adi replied. "We can't set such criminal scum loose just because a few liberal MPs in London are whining. That would be a mistake, a very big mistake."

"But a necessary one. Adi, just think about it. I don't need to explain to you that Dachau is no ordinary prison. No one there has been tried or sentenced for anything. That's a stain on your reputation and on Germany. The London liberals can't stand the thought of cultural figures in jail, wearing stripes. They want them in somber, perfectly tailored suits. Put dark suits on them, let a photographer take a few pictures as they leave Dachau, and ship them off to England. That'll make everyone happy."

"You're talking like a moron, Mathäus! They're Germany's worst enemies. Jews, communists, homosexuals, Gypsys, trade unionists—"

"So release fifty of them. It'll be a symbolic act, and you won't miss any of them," Frombichler insisted. "We have plenty of prisoners in German jails."

After lunch Adi instructed Hermann Göring, his favorite, to draw up a list of the prisoners in Dachau.

Two volumes arrived the next morning with more than seventeen thousand names. Adi had gotten up on the wrong side of bed, and now he threw a real tantrum. He screamed that nitpicking bureaucrats were drowning Germany in a flood of paperwork. Frombichler calmed him down. Picking out fifty names would take no time at all, he said. He handed the first volume to Adi and took the other one himself. They began to page through them at random. "Bruno Bettelheim, psychologist and author . . . Hermann Broch, author . . . Alfred Cohen, dentist . . . Surely no one in London is weeping for a dentist. That's one Jew who'll have to stay in Dachau," Adi decided.

Hermann Göring carefully noted down the names of those to be released, regarding Hitler with almost religious reverence.

Frombichler's eyes fell upon a familiar name. His pulse accelerated. *This can't be true,* he thought. He cleared his throat. "Franz Scharf, cabaret artist," he said.

EARLY THE NEXT MORNING a guard came to the barracks to fetch my great-uncle. The soldier was a short man, not in the prime of life, but he was carrying a heavy rifle. Scharf was to report to Sturmbannführer August Behrendsdorff. "For special treatment, or something," he added darkly. My great-uncle panicked. His hands began to tremble and his mouth suddenly became dry. Behrendsdorff, an Austrian, enjoyed whipping specially chosen prisoners until their backs and rears were bloody; then he violently jammed blunt objects up their rectums and raped them. Everyone knew it. None of his victims had lodged any complaints, however, for the Behrendsdorff special treatment always concluded with a pistol shot to the nape of the neck.

Rain had fallen overnight, and the morning sky was dark and cloudy. My great-uncle knew his last hour on earth had arrived. His heart raced. He walked as slowly as he could. The soldier ambled along behind him and said nothing. The muddy path led through a gate topped with barbed wire into the area where the commandant's office was located.

The Sturmbannführer smiled pleasantly, rubbed his hands together, and offered him coffee. It was ersatz—not the real thing—and disgusting. But Behrendsdorff seemed not to be bothered by the taste of it.

"Do you know why you're here, Herr Scharf?" he inquired. Without waiting for an answer, he explained that the Führer in all his generosity had pardoned him. He was to take a shower, shave, and receive an issue of new clothing. He and various other prisoners would be driven to the railway station in Munich. The first train to Budapest left at six o'clock that evening.

"Are you terribly disappointed, Herr Scharf, that we're sending you home to your family?" Behrendsdorff gave a dry chuckle and sipped coffee. "We expect the gentleman to stop speaking ill of our leader. Tell people instead about German hospitality here in Dachau. Herr Scharf has received room and board from the authorities for a whole year, and we have asked nothing from him in exchange."

My great-uncle sat there in silence, plunged in thought. He didn't believe a word of this Austrian's farce. He thought this was part of Behrendsdorff's despicable routine of torture, beguiling his victim into believing he was about to go home. But a few hours later and with an immeasurable sense of relief, he took his seat on the train to Budapest, completely baffled by the pardon granted to him with no indication of who had secured it.

The Cook's Rescue Operation

MAREK HALTER, the French author who grew up in the Warsaw ghetto, made a documentary film not too long ago—I seem to recall that it was titled something like *Rescuers in Dark Times*—about individuals who had saved Jews from the Nazi extermination machine. It included an interview with Mathäus Frombichler, who had been awarded Israel's highest honor, a proclamation recognizing him as Righteous Among the People. The elderly cook described how he had gotten the idea for his rescue operation, one of the most remarkable of the Second World War, when he came across the name of his old friend Franz Scharf on the list of prisoners at Dachau.

Frombichler was notorious, for he was Hitler's half-Jewish cook. After the fall of Berlin the Russians arrested him in the Führer's bunker and held him prisoner. During the interrogation led by Captain Lev Kopelev he confirmed that Hitler was dead and the charred remains in the office were indeed the leader's. He gave an account of the last hours of the Führer, describing how Hitler had raged when he heard that the Red Army was less than a quarter of a mile from the bunker. Not even Hitler could believe any longer in a final victory. He waved a pistol wildly, his hair fell across his forehead, and he screamed that it was all the fault of Jews who had undermined the German nation. Frombichler was convinced that Adi was about to shoot someone. Others with them expected to see a nervous collapse. But then Adi mastered his emotions and asked for his favorite meal, salad niçoise, to be served in his office. When Frombichler brought it to him, Hitler invited him to stay and share his last meal. The three of them had lunch together. A couple of flies settled on Eva Braun's plate, and she waved them away with a grimace. They seemed to make her lose her appetite; she didn't touch her salad. She sat silent while the two men ate. The friends recalled the times of their apprenticeship in Linz many years earlier. Hitler rambled. He wondered how many of their Jewish classmates were still alive. The only name he could remember was that of Ludwig Wittgenstein. He could still see him very clearly, that rich little Jew who was two years younger than they were but who was permitted to attend the same class because everyone thought he was superintelligent. But he was no fighter. Hitler told how a couple of times after his father beat him, he turned around and took revenge by attacking other boys at school. Ludwig Wittgenstein was the one who usually got the worst of it, he recalled, because he was a puny little whelp who never defended himself. What had become of that Jewish wunderkind? They got up from the table after they'd finished the meal. Hitler shook Frombichler's hand and thanked him for their long friendship. Eva Braun kissed her husband's forehead and then swallowed poison. She died almost instantly. Hitler tried to commit suicide by swallowing a cyanide capsule, but the poison wasn't strong enough to finish him off. He writhed in torment. The pains in his belly were unbearable. He begged his friend to help him end his life. Frombichler picked up the pistol that lay on the table and aimed it with a trembling hand at Hitler's temple. He placed his finger on the trigger. "Shoot!" screamed Hitler. But the pistol was not loaded. Frombichler spat on the floor and swore. Increasingly pale, Hitler howled in pain and pleaded to die. Frombichler rushed out to the kitchen and grabbed a heavy cast-iron frying pan. With two decisive blows he crushed Hitler's skull. He stared at the body, then took several minutes to recite Kaddish for his friend. He went to the kitchen for kerosene. He emptied two full bottles over his friend and set the body alight. He stood by the flames, tears in his eyes. As he was leaving Hitler's bunker, he was seized by the Russians.

Eighteen months later Frombichler and twenty-three physicians were put on trial in Nuremberg for crimes against humanity. The physicians had carried out experiments in various concentration camps—lowering body temperatures to less than eighty degrees Fahrenheit, throwing women out of airplanes high in the sky, excising vital body parts without anesthetic, sterilizing adults, carving the embryos from the bellies of pregnant women, injecting black dye into children's eyes, spraying chloroform into the hearts of twins, disjointing dwarfs, murdering, injuring, and handicapping countless prisoners. A couple of the physicians were pardoned, several received long prison sentences, and eight were sentenced to death and executed.

Of course, there was no reason to put Frombichler in that group. He was no physician. But as a mere cook he could hardly be tried with senior military officers and politicians.

The trial went on for eight months. Hundreds of documents were introduced into evidence. Nothing established any guilt on Frombichler's part. His only crime—if it could in fact be counted as such—was that he had kept Hitler strong and healthy by providing him sustenance with tasty food.

In the final phase of the trial three witnesses appeared and testified under oath that the cook had saved their lives. Somehow he had arranged for them to be released from concentration camps and permitted to leave Germany. More than four hundred people owed their lives to him.

Frombichler was acquitted. The American judge Francis Biddle asked him to reveal to the court the details of his incredible rescue operation, and the cook happily did so. His account sent everyone in the court into gales of laughter. Frombichler explained that after the Führer's fiftieth birthday they'd made a pact, he and his friend Adi. Every time he concocted a dinner that aroused Eva Braun's libido so Hitler could exercise his male member and feel like a real man, Frombichler was permitted to consult the voluminous archives of the Gestapo and to choose two names from any of the concentration camps. Those individuals were immediately released. When the judge asked whether there was any special recipe that had saved many lives, the cook answered with a grin: "Five-sixths dark chocolate, licorice for the rest, spiced with a touch of anise. It worked every time." Frombichler sold his chocolate recipe to the Zurich-based enterprise Lindt & Sprüngli many years later. It made him a wealthy man. He retired to Burgenland and purchased his boyhood home close to Castle Biederhof. But his chocolate recipe, called Eva B. by the company, never reached the market. The Swiss health authorities never approved it.

Kolyma

ONE MORE THING needs to be added to this story, and that concerns Captain Lev Kopelev. He volunteered for the Red Army when the war broke out, and his superiors soon noted his intelligence, decisiveness, and courage. His fluent German and sense of diplomacy were great assets in the war when Hitler's fortunes changed and Stalin's troops went storming toward Berlin. Kopelev was assigned to interview captured officers. Few other interrogators had such command of the German language. Many of them compensated for their linguistic shortcomings with their fists. Some applied rifle butts. A number attempted to impress their superior officers by beating to death the people they were supposed to be interrogating, especially those of lower rank. But not Kopelev. He treated the Germans with respect and was always friendly. He never used violence, either psychological or physical, and he didn't enter into political discussions with prisoners of war. He much preferred to discuss the music of Wagner. He adored Wagner, although he found some of the scores fairly torrid and emotionally manipulative. In a quiet tone and without vaunting himself he demonstrated a profound understanding of the operas in which the master's tone and dramatic ethos had achieved their fullest realization: *Tristan und Isolde, Parsifal*, and *Die Meistersinger*. His interrogations turned into discussions of culture. By behaving in a manner completely different from what the prisoners expected, he won the trust of even the most recalcitrant adversaries and brought them over to his side. The highest ranked officers, usually of aristocratic background, were especially susceptible. They proved unable to hold their tongues and quickly revealed the secrets of the Wehrmacht. Kopelev was highly praised by his superiors and was decorated several times for valor. Unfortunately, his successes awakened the envy of his colleagues. Strange rumors about him began to circulate. At first they were mere whispers, but the accusations rapidly became bolder and more open, then turned into direct attacks. The charges were extremely serious. His interrogation methods were criticized. His patriotic loyalty was questioned. Some held that he was all too friendly with the senior German military. Others claimed that they'd heard Kopelev, a native of Kiev, speaking about Holodomor, the mass famine in Ukraine in 1932–1933 that took the lives of between four and five million, and that he had blamed Stalin for deliberately creating that disaster. Several reported that they'd heard him say that soldiers of the Red Army had raped more than two million German women and plundered even more homes. Kopelev was summoned to Moscow shortly after his interrogation of Hitler's cook. He was informed that the People's Commissiariat of Internal Affairs (NKVD) was going to decorate him with the Order of the Red Star, Third Class, for his accomplishments as an interrogator. He felt honored and proud. He wished his parents could see him. He traveled to the capital, never suspecting a thing. Not even when he was ushered into the presence of the generally feared Lavrenty Beria, the head of the NKVD who had sent countless men and women to their deaths, did Kopelev sense that anything was wrong. When he reached out to shake hands, Beria clapped handcuffs on him and glared at him with immense loathing. "Your disgusting fraternization with Nazis is a knife in the back to the party leadership that relied upon you," Beria said. "You are a traitor to the motherland. It will be a pleasure to see you hanging from the gallows." Kopelev was taken away by two guards. They went to the basement where a cluster of officials were waiting. Only then did he realize how grave his situation was. The trial took only a few minutes. A prosecutor read out the charges. His voice was so tense that Kopelev actually felt sorry for him. The allegations were manifestly ridiculous; Kopelev wanted to ask the prosecutor if he could respond and whether the man really believed that mishmash of lies he'd just presented. But he didn't have the opportunity; the judge immediately sentenced him to ten years of exile in Siberia for spreading bourgeois humanism and showing excessive sympathy for the enemy. "You'll have plenty of time to regret your crimes," was the judge's comment.

"Regret what? Treating Germans like human beings?" Kopelev asked. The judge wrinkled his nose in disgust and told the guards to take the prisoner away. Kopelev had absorbed with his mother's milk an optimism that not even adversity, profound injustice, and severe punishment could entirely quash. He firmly decided not to allow himself to fall prey to doubts about the infallibility of the party's justice system. He was particularly determined not to fall into the lassitude he'd observed in many of the German prisoners. He rejected despair. He would use the time in Siberia for some significant undertaking, even if for the moment he didn't know what that would be. He wound up in the same barracks in Kolyma as my great-uncle. The prisoners called it "the United Nations" because it housed representatives of all the peoples that lived east of the Elbe River. They all had nicknames. Kopelev was dubbed "Ruby" by the other prisoners. I have no idea why they chose that name. Perhaps because of his optimistic nature, or maybe because he had a hard inner core that nothing could break. My great-uncle mentions him in the manuscript he sold to the Genealogical Library. Ruby was the only one my great-uncle could carry on a cultivated conversation with, since no one else in the camp spoke a German as pure and rich in vocabulary as that of the former interrogator. They recommended books to each other—books that of course they had no possibility of acquiring. They carried on passionate discussions of Heinrich Heine's earthy humor and cutting, ironic verse, especially in *Germany: A Winter's Tale*, a book they both loved. They discussed Gramsci's thoughts about the path to a socialist society. They told each other stories to light up the darkness of the camp. Both knew that Scheherazade—the very symbol of humanity's desire to elude looming, tragic fate—told stories for a thousand and one nights in order to save her life. They shared their feelings and thoughts because the authorities wanted to silence them, because they knew that when the stories fall silent, death arrives. There's no indication, however, that either of them mentioned the only acquaintance they had in common: Frombichler.

At first glance all of this might seem to be extraneous to the history of the Spinoza family, so at this point I must not forget to mention the name of Lev Kopelev's book. He was released in 1954 and rehabilitated two years later. The experience in the Gulag never crushed his ideals or shook his belief in a more just and equitable society. He applied to join the Communist Party, and when he was accepted, the party gave him work at the university. In his lectures and discussions Kopelev praised freedom of expression in literature. He taught a younger generation that the truthful and courageous words of the greatest poets are weapons for peace. The motherland's brutal invasion of Czechoslovakia in 1968 finally shattered his illusions about the superiority of the socialist order. Without a thought for his own safety he campaigned in favor of human rights in the Soviet Union. He stressed that men of goodwill can resist evil rulers and even overcome them. The authorities' reaction wasn't long in coming. He was isolated and shunned at first, and then he was exiled. He wrote his book *To Be Preserved Forever* in Germany. He gives a harrowing description of life in the Siberian camps during the great terrors of the Stalinist era. The camp at Kolyma was one of the greatest horrors of the twentieth century, on a level with Auschwitz and Hiroshima. Kopelev tells of the fates of several of his fellow prisoners. I recognize his story about F. as that of my great-uncle. F. is a German-speaking Jew from Hungary, a cabaret artist first confined in Dachau and then forcibly conscripted during the war to work in copper mines in Yugoslavia vital to the German war effort. After the liberation soldiers of the Red Army picked him up on the street in Budapest and sent him to forced labor in the Soviet Union, where factories were standing empty because of all the men who had died in the war. F. proved too weak for such hard work and was sent to Siberia. Kopelev writes that F. was already in a weakened condition when he arrived after agonizing weeks of confinement in cattle cars, mired in filth and mad with thirst. Life in the camp with the freezing weather, forced labor, lack of sleep, illness, vermin, fear, humiliation, and suffering ravaged his body even more. By the time he returned to his home in Hungary, he was a man in broken health.

A Revised Version of History

I DON'T KNOW WHY, but another of my great-uncle's stories has come to mind.

Lavrenty Beria, he told us, still in strictest confidence, was Stalin's right hand, a cunning, enigmatic little man. He was reputed to be erudite; in fact, he was uneducated but widely read in a completely unsystematic fashion, for he reviewed all literary works and advised Stalin which should be prohibited. He also read all the unpublished manuscripts the secret police seized from poets and artists who more often than not simply disappeared as soon as they signed their forced confessions. Beria's wide-ranging and extensive reading had left him nearsighted, so he wore pince-nez. Worn leather scourges hung on the walls of Beria's office at the NKVD. This was where plans were prepared for the extensive purification of Georgia in 1937–1938, for the massacre of more than 4,400 Polish officers in the Katyn Forest in 1941, for the murder of Trotsky, for brutal relocation of large populations, and for the systematic use of torture, slave labor, and murder. He sent his fellow countrymen to their deaths for the most trivial reasons. Everyone was terrified of him, for his repulsive nature and horrific overreactions were common knowledge. His outbursts of wrath were legendary. So were his sexual appetites. He drove around at night in a large Volga sedan with dark windows, hunting for women; most of those he found never came home again. It was said that his perverse desires were not limited only to women. He was said to have a taste for young boys. Sasha and I were told that after Beria's death his closet was found to contain the chopped-off hands of hundreds of children. That private collection was so bizarre that it apparently displeased Stalin, who didn't care for such evidence of the victims of the regime. The infallible leader decreed that all traces of them were to be eliminated.

My great-uncle's stories usually incited my imagination. I could usually sit listening to him for hours, but not when he told us about Beria. Those stories scared me. All that talk about children's chopped-off hands seemed so terribly evil that I wanted to rush off to hide in the bathroom.

That night I had a nightmare. I was at our usual playground, alone in the twilight. All the other children had gone home. A black Volga sedan screeched to a stop right next to me. The driver wore round spectacles perched on his nose. He gave me a friendly smile and invited me to join him in the car. I wanted to refuse, but my throat closed up and I couldn't get a word out. Then the man said that my brother, Sasha, was waiting for me at home, in the closet, with a pile of candy. As he spoke, I could see that he had jaws capable of gobbling a child whole. He got out of the car to pick me up, and I suddenly saw he had no hands. He opened his arms wide to enfold me. I woke up with a start, soaked in sweat. I was frightened and relieved at the same time. The room was quiet and dark. Sasha and

Grandmother were sound asleep. I went to the window and peered through a crack in the blinds, watching for a black Volga sedan that never appeared.

The real Beria was a more complicated and composed person than the one my great-uncle described to us. This I learned from Kopelev's book. On the one hand Beria had millions of people murdered, out of "necessity," as he himself termed it. On the other hand, he was eager to reform the Soviet system. After Stalin's death in March 1953, he criticized the collectivization of agriculture, canceled costly projects, and advocated setting East Germany free and reuniting Germany. Even more important, he shut down and emptied much of the Gulag archipelago in Siberia; almost half of the prisoners were allowed to go home. It was thanks to him that my great-uncle was released and returned to Hungary. But a hundred days after Stalin passed away, Beria was arrested. Everyone knows he was liquidated. The circumstances of his death, however, are completely unknown.

My great-uncle also mentioned that the execution of Beria caused problems for the publisher of *The Great Russian Encyclopedia*. When subscribers had received the *B* volume of the reference work—sometime at the end of the 1940s—it featured an article about Beria that dutifully praised him as a great hero of the Soviet Union. After his fall, all of the subscribers received a letter from the publishing house instructing them to clip out and return the pages that mentioned Beria. In exchange they received an article with pictures of the Bering Strait.

Truth is stranger than fiction, my great-uncle always told us. When one knows what actually happened, one doesn't need to make up stories.

Love Is the Future

WHEN SECRET LOVERS Ariadne and Bernhard discovered that she was pregnant, everything in their young lives was turned upside down. They were afraid of the consequences. They feared that they would be separated. This was the first time either had been in love, the most glorious experience of their lives. Their love obliged them to look toward the future and rely on themselves alone. Love, Bernhard declared, is the enemy of tradition; it stands on the side of the future. Love *is* the future, Ariadne said. Love overcomes all, Bernhard answered her.

That very night they decided to run away from Biederhof.

The reason that Ariadne and Bernhard chose to set off to Hungary remains a mystery. Not even my great-uncle could explain it. Once he said it was because Ariadne had unpleasant memories of her early childhood in Vienna. Later he said he believed that the couple, both of them minors, she only fifteen and he seventeen, thought no one would think to search for them in the Hungarian capital.

The youngsters' first encounter with the city was encouraging. They happened to arrive during the great holiday celebrating the unification of Buda and Pest, each on its respective side of the Danube, to constitute the single city of Budapest. Singing crowds filled the broad boulevards, proudly waving flags and embracing. Even total strangers hugged each other. Ariadne and Bernhard immediately felt welcome, and they saw the unification as symbolic of their own union. She held his hand, the hand that gave her such feelings of security and happiness. In an outlying neighborhood they managed to locate a fairly intoxicated local mayor who didn't bother to ask the underage couple for any papers when he performed the ceremony that made them husband and wife. The world was bright and beautiful. The future lay before them.

When Rudolf heard that Ariadne had married Bernhard and had given birth to a son in Budapest only a few days later, he changed beyond recognition. Before this he had shown no interest in Ariadne and her disappearance; now he was outraged. As a prince and the patriarch of one of Austria's most ancient noble families, he could not bear the thought of his daughter marrying a Jew and giving birth to Jewish children. He was incensed with Jakob, even though the man had saved him from ruin, made the estate bloom, and taken charge of Ariadne. Dark images made Rudolf's head spin. He told himself that Jakob had schemed to steal his daughter. He ordered one of the servants to go the cellar to fetch a bottle of ancient vintage cognac; he emptied it in one long swig. Ariadne was a whore, he proclaimed, just like her mother, that heartless female who had lured him and played with him and exploited his generosity. He called for more cognac. He drank and carried on like a wild beast, he screamed and generally laid waste to everything and everyone in the castle. But he refused to receive Jakob, who was importuning him for a meeting to discuss the matter. Reeking of cognac, he swore at Jakob at the top of his voice. He cursed him and by turns called him a Jewish swine and a piece of rotten filth. He blurted out his adamant conviction that Jakob had been planning all along to get his hands on everything he owned by stealing away his daughter, locking her in his house, and setting her to copulate with his son. Rudolf's ranting voice echoed through the splendid halls of the castle. Dusk was coming on as he staggered onto the balcony and screamed for everyone to hear that he was not flattered in the least to have a Jewish son-in-law, and he knew what was behind this vulgar spectacle. He would by God make sure that Ariadne was no good catch; he would disinherit her so the Jews couldn't take over Biederhof after he died. In the middle of the night he had a public notary called in and dictated a new last will and testament. After he passed away, everything would go to his cousin Ludwig von Thurn und Taxis, the natural heir, since Ludwig with his blue blood was the only man on earth who could be trusted. He drank even more and went out on the balcony again. He bellowed that now his spirit could be at peace because he had changed his will and cut off that whore Ariadne. For a moment he stood there straight and tall, fumbling for the words to express his emotions. Blinded in the following instant by the first piercing beams of the morning sun, he lost his balance, fell over the railing, and crashed to the ground.

The funeral took place a week later. But by then Jakob and his family had already left the estate and fled to Vienna.

Three Other Siblings

JAKOB HAD FOUR CHILDREN. Despite their occasionally serious flaws and errors, each had inherited some characteristic of their father: Nikolaus had his financial genius; Claudia had his good heart; and Andreas had his ingenuity. But none of the children was blessed with all of Jakob's qualities. I'm no psychologist and so I won't try to compare them. But I know that only one of the children achieved the same human and intellectual heights that Jakob had reached: Bernhard, who had his sense of ethics, his authority, and his brain power. The fact that I concentrate mostly on Bernhard here shouldn't surprise anybody. He was my grandfather's father and he inherited not only the gigantic Spinoza nose; as eldest son he also received the family's secret treasure, *The Elixir of Immortality*, and in his own way carried on our unusual tradition.

But it's only fitting that I account for the other siblings who grew up in that tight-knit family but were so markedly different from one another. As adults they wound up widely separated, living in different worlds, not only because of the differences in their characters, ambitions, and talents, but also because rapid developments in those years caused kaleidoscopic changes in society and produced a spectacle of constantly shifting patterns that affected human relationships. But I think that the outcome was also related to an unusual attitude characteristic of the Spinozas since time out of mind. Family ties have always been important to us but only provided rules of appropriate behavior are strictly observed. The reaction to anyone who gets involved in irregularities or scandal, abandons the true faith, or enters into an unsuitable marriage is straightforward: The other family members shut their mouths, turn their backs to the offender, and exclude him from the community as if he'd never existed.

To give full justice to Nikolaus, Claudia, and Andreas, I would have to tell you about their daily lives, play back their conversations and arguments, describe the relationships between them and other people, and relate the events that affected their lives and determined their fates—childish quarrels, love affairs and marriages, births of children, illnesses and deaths. But unfortunately I have neither the time nor enough of the facts, let alone the talent with the written word that that would require. The only thing I can do is pass along what my great-uncle told us and hope the past will provide a glimpse of what really happened. Nikolaus followed in his father's footsteps. Although he was named for his great-grandfather, the French revolutionary thinker Nicolas Spinoza, he was interested in almost nothing but numbers from a very early age. His siblings found mathematics boring and were hard put to understand his passion. After attending business school he got a job at the Rothschild bank. Despite his respect for his father and deference to him, he knew very well that their motivations were different. His father's imagination was not stimulated by the prospect of making money but rather by the intellectual challenge of finding novel solutions to financial problems. For Nikolaus the work at the bank meant nothing in itself; he was obsessed by the desire to become a wealthy man. His results under his father's tutelage were outstanding, and he took over the direction of the Vienna branch while still in his twenties. He was an elegant young man and well regarded, a man about town who found plenty of willing female companions in Vienna. He had no intention of giving up his bachelor life—until he met the youngest daughter of a Bohemian baron. Beatrice was an adorably plump eighteen-year-old with a slight limp because one leg was shorter than the other, but she had a bosom that would have put the nymphs of Olympus to shame. He immediately fell head over heels in love with her. The scent of her hair and her warm skin intoxicated him almost as much as her father's wealth. Beatrice had no objection to his proposal of marriage. With a number of slick maneuvers Nikolaus duped his siblings and got his hands on the entire fortune left by their father. With those funds, supplemented with a hefty loan from his father-in-law, he bought a majority of the shares in the Rothschilds'

Österreichische Credit-Anstalt für Handel und Gewerbe. He shortened the name to Credit-Anstalt and within ten years was the proprietor of Europe's leading financial institution. Nikolaus was given a noble title by Kaiser Franz Josef and regularly appeared in the most elegant circles of the double monarchy. He was a guest much sought after by the leading salons of Paris, London, and Berlin. So it was that after suffering so many disasters, our family enjoyed a brief cruise on the tide of success. Our name was spoken with respect by opinion-makers and decision-makers all across Europe. We had changed teams. No longer were we respected as philosophers and writers; instead, the achievements of Jakob and Nikolaus had converted the Spinozas into high priests of the temple of Mammon. Nikolaus, king of finance, eagerly invested in enormous industrial projects, even though very few were located within the borders of the double monarchy. Boundlessly optimistic about the future, he provided generous loans to the British White Star Lines and became personally involved in the shipping enterprise's huge project to build three new passenger liners. The *Titanic*, the *Olympic*, and the *Britannic* would be the most impressive mechanical constructions of the age and would surpass all rivals in luxury and extravagance. When the *Titanic* made its maiden voyage, Nikolaus and his wife invited all their children and several important business acquaintances along for its debut crossing of the Atlantic. Spirits were high. Toasts were made with Cristal, Czar Alexander II's favorite champagne, from the vintage year of 1876. The dinner featured an abundance of gastronomic excess, consisted of eleven courses, and lasted four hours. The guests' bellies were hugely weighted down after the extravagant feast, so they sank in the cold sea like stones after the collision with the iceberg sent the unsinkable ship beneath the waves without a trace. None of Nikolaus's guests survived. His body was eventually found, much later. In his suit pocket were fifty ten-thousand-dollar bills bearing the bleakly smiling portrait of U.S. Secretary of the Treasury Salmon P. Chase, along with the curiously well-preserved menu card describing the eleven-course meal.

Claudia married young. She was only nine years old when she realized that Markus Frombichler, no one else, would be her husband. They were the same age, and their birthdays were only two weeks apart. They'd been playmates even before learning to walk and classmates in school after that. Markus's father, a peasant, lived near them on the Biederstern estate. When the Spinoza family departed for Vienna, Claudia and Markus promised each other forever to be true. Seven years later he traveled to the capital city to locate her. A young, tongue-tied, hesitant, bashful suitor appeared before Jakob. This individual, by no means a man of the world, requested the hand in marriage of his only daughter. Only a blind man could fail to distinguish how deeply in love the two of them were. Jakob advised Claudia not to marry him, however, for he couldn't imagine that she would ever be happy out in the countryside, married into a Catholic family and living among uneducated peasants. Furthermore, such a union would mean she would have to change her religion; Jewish faith and traditions, he emphasized, were not something you could trade for something else like a pair of gloves. Her mother's eyes filled with tears, and she murmured that no Jewish mother could imagine having someone like Markus as a son-in-law. Nikolaus predicted that his sister's life would be one of sorrow. Andreas laughed at her and said that those dumb peasants knew nothing about the real world. Claudia countered that her suitor Markus was no spoiled rich Jewish man's son with delicate white hands like her brother the genius; he was a man used to hard work, a man who knew and accepted his duty. And so what if his father was a peasant? "The Frombichlers are simple people," she said. "They've never solved any of the world's problems, but they've always lived on their little piece of land, taken care of their children, and been content with their lot in life." And as for religion, she declared, she had never believed in any God. Jewish or Catholic, for her there was no difference. Love was more important. The family heatedly debated the issue, and of course Jakob had the last word. I don't know how long the discussions lasted, but no amount of persuasion or argument could change Claudia's mind. She stood firm and married Markus. They had three children. Mathäus was the oldest, a difficult and ill-behaved child. When he was ten he tried to drown one of his young sisters in the well. As punishment he was sent off to live with his father's cousin in Linz and learn a trade. The cousin was a corporal in the Imperial and Royal Army and had no children. The man's wife was a poison-tongued old biddy whom Mathäus instantly despised. The only reason he didn't run away from the loveless couple was that among the other apprentices he'd made a friend, Adi. His sisters, Isidora and Hedda, married and emigrated to America. All trace of them vanished after the stock market crash of 1929. Claudia's marriage was a happy one and she felt content with her lot as a peasant wife. The only times that she felt a pang in her heart were when she thought of her siblings. They had turned their backs on her for marrying a non-Jew, and the family had disinherited her. Markus died a natural death in 1937. Five years later Karl Schneider, Markus's best friend and the police chief in the district, invited Claudia to his office for a review of her birth certificate, a mere formality. She didn't come home

that afternoon. Or the next day. Her life came to an end two
weeks later in Auschwitz. Hitler's cook, whom so many had
to thank for their lives, was not able to save his own mother.
Andreas was the youngest child and the family clown.
His brothers and sister called him "the carp," because his
lips quivered like those of the fish when he laughed at his
own stories. He had a wonderful gift as a storyteller. In spite
of all his untruthfulness, playful exaggerations, and elaborate mischief, people on the estate thought it great fun to
listen to his elaborately convoluted tales. Much to his family's horror, Andreas developed a fondness for firearms and
an attachment to Bertold, the man who, like his father and
grandfather before him, was the caretaker of the estate's extensive store of hunting weapons. The city that awaited the
youngster upon the family's relocation to Vienna made him
absolutely miserable. He hated bustling city life and missed
nature, the forest, and the hunting preserves, everything
about Burgenland's calm country idyll. Andreas dreamed
of studying physics at the Polytechnic Institute, but his
application was turned down. After three tries he gave up
and wrangled a position as an apprentice in the Austrian
Arms Manufacturing Company, the firm that produced the
country's finest hunting rifles. Firearms of that time were
still slow and clumsy. Andreas applied his ingenuity to improving the accuracy of the guns and shortening the time
required to load the ammunition. He was aware that in the
Prussian-Austrian war of 1866 to establish hegemony over
Germany, the Prussians had fired seven shots from a prone
position with their breech-loading Dreyse rifles in the same
time it took Franz Josef's soldiers to load their weapons in
a standing position and get off a single shot. At those odds
it was easy to see who would come out on top. Andreas
crafted a weapon that was rapid, accurate, and resistant to

humidity. He roused a certain amount of interest when he presented his weapon to the military high command, but the bureaucratic mills of the double monarchy ground slowly. The matter was evaluated and discussed, reports sent out to various other departments prompted new questions that had to be answered, time passed, and Andreas grew tired of waiting. Disappointed, he crossed the border and called on the weapons manufacturer Paul Mauser in the little German city of Oberndorf am Neckar. Mauser immediately perceived the brilliance of Andreas's system of rotating the barrels to load the ammunition and greeted it as a great achievement. No one had ever constructed a weapon that enabled the infantryman to fire fifteen shots in as many seconds, accurate to more than a thousand yards. Andreas signed a contract with the Mauser-Werke arms factory, and the improvements he had developed were immediately incorporated into Model 89, the new repeating firearm. The legendary infantry general Lothar von Trotha, preparing for his imminent expedition to East Africa, came to visit the factory to test the new weapon. He was more than satisfied. "With that superweapon we can carry out an absolute *Vernichtung* of the rebellious Africans," remarked the general. "*Vernichtung*," Andreas repeated after him, and commented that he liked the sound of the word—extermination. Shortly before meeting the general he'd happened to read a novel by H. Rider Haggard. The English writer's romantic tale, highly charged with eroticism, fascinated him with its descriptions of white men dominating women in the colonies and conquering Africa's treasures by virtue of their cultural and technological superiority. Enchanted with the tale, he asked for von Trotha's permission to accompany him to East Africa to study the performance of the new weapon in the field. For two years he served on the general's expeditionary staff. As villages were plundered and burned, a third of the population was murdered, and an equal number of the natives were maimed, Andreas sat in a comfortable military tent—tormented by insect bites, true, but well attended by two most obliging dark-skinned mistresses—and improved the weapon further by devising how to recapture the smoke and gas released as the shot was fired. The general's merciless campaign and the incalculable suffering of the Africans bothered him as little as the shrieks of the monkeys and the roaring of wild animals around his tent. He'd always found it easy to repress unpleasant thoughts. Of course he knew that all human lives have the same value and all individuals have innate rights. His parents had taught him this at an early age. But none of that was relevant to Africa, where he shared the general's view: The blacks were not to be viewed as human beings. Weren't their simple lives, deep ignorance of the world, and primitive beliefs and rites sufficient evidence of that? He and von Trotha bonded closely. They sat for hours by the campfire in the jungle, telling their stories. After their return from East Africa, the general introduced Andreas to his niece, whom young Spinoza later married. Andreas subsequently went with von Trotha to southwest Africa to put down the Herero people's rebellion against the colonial powers that treated them worse than dogs. His wife waved goodbye to him in Hamburg harbor. With a premonition he wouldn't come home again, she burst into tears as the ship disappeared from sight. The German troops were self-confident and arrogant in their expectation of an easy victory, and the general didn't plan for adequate supplies for his troops. The Namibian heat was unbearable. Herero fighters offered unexpected resistance and cannily exploited their knowledge of the terrain. After three months in the desert the colonial force's supplies of food and water were exhausted. More Germans died of tropical diseases and exhaustion than from the bullets of the rebel forces. Andreas was one of them. Stressed by hardships, he had a fit of fever. His legs gave way, he collapsed and couldn't move. A few hours later he was afflicted by diarrhea and bleeding. He despaired because he knew that his condition made it impossible for him to travel with von Trotha and his troops. He had a sinking feeling that he would never get out of the Omaheke desert. The general visited him. Andreas wanted to unburden his heart to the general but was unable to speak a word. Von Trotha thought about putting a bullet into his friend's brain to end his suffering, but he couldn't bring himself to pull the trigger. They left Andreas behind in a tent along with his two mistresses from the Nama tribe. That night the women slipped out of the tent and disappeared. He lived four more days, alone and abandoned in the heat, and finally died of thirst and exhaustion. Meanwhile, despite significant losses the general refused to negotiate a cease-fire with Samuel Maharero, leader of the Herero people. He wanted to write himself into the history books by confirming that Germany ruled over vast expanses of Africa. Determined that the cowardly blacks had to be exterminated, he ordered his troops to massacre defenseless old people, women, and children. Then they shot all of the male Hereros, whether they had carried arms or not. The machine guns constructed by Andreas grew so hot from gunfire that the German soldiers could scarcely touch them. Nor did the Nama people escape. The stink of blood filled the air across all of Namibia. Von Trotha was hailed in Berlin as a hero upon his return home from the first—but far from last—genocide of the twentieth century. A few months later, however, he was put on trial, according to my great-uncle, and found guilty. Not for having killed more than eighty percent of the Herero people and fifty percent of the Namas; instead, it was for physical abuse of his mistress in Windhoek, a white woman who was the niece of the German Imperial Commissioner for Southwest Africa.

A Brief Period of Happiness

NOW, WHERE WAS I? Oh, yes—with Ariadne and Bernhard. The young couple maintained a great distance between themselves and Bernhard's family because they feared that Jakob would try to block their path to happiness. Contacts between them and the family in Vienna were infrequent, and Bernhard refused to accept any assistance from his father, who repeatedly tried to explain to him how terrible it was to be poor. The young couple was proud of their independence, and they often spoke of their delight to be living in Budapest, far from their parents, where no one could interfere and tell them what to do with their lives. It didn't even occur to them to complain of the poverty that was their fate in Hungary.

Five years after their arrival in Budapest they already had three boys: Moricz, Nathan (my future grandfather), and Kalman. They also had a daughter, Hanna, the youngest. She was brought into the world by cesarean section in the seventh month, far too early, and weighed less than four and a half pounds. Ariadne was stretched out on the operating table with her life hanging by a thread because she had lost a great deal of blood, but a young doctor saved her life. The chief physician at the hospital for the destitute informed them little Hanna had a complicated heart defect, and he described a complex operation essential to keep her alive. He asked for five thousand imperial crowns for his own fee and said that he would need to hire an additional physician and two experienced nurses to assist him, all of whom would have to be paid. When the chief physician saw Bernhard's face turn pale, he added that at a private clinic such an operation would cost at least twice as much, perhaps more. At that instant, Bernhard would say many years later when he recalled the events, he understood the meaning of money in this world. He replied that he had no funds to pay the fees, but his daughter's life had to be saved. He asked for a few weeks to take out loans until his father could send him the money. He promised to pay; as proof of his creditworthiness he explained that his father headed the Rothschild bank in Vienna and was a wealthy man. The chief physician responded with a skeptical smile. All he had to do was glance at the young man's worn trousers and frayed shirt collar for conclusive evidence to the contrary. He told Bernhard that no one in Budapest would perform such an operation on credit. He expressed his condolences and vanished in the corridors of the hospital. Bernhard was close to tears. To hide this, he fixed his gaze on the cracks in the wall caused by the humidity. Two days later he buried little Hanna.

Ariadne remained in the hospital for ten days. She was plunged into unbearable grief. Her sorrow changed her. After she returned home she became more and more despondent and couldn't face the trials of daily life. She became quarrelsome—certainly a character trait she'd inherited from her father—and she perpetually found fault with Bernhard. She started in on him first thing in the morning before he went to work and picked up again in the evening as soon as he came home, in spite of the fact that Bernhard was taking care of everything. He was a real worker bee. He did the shopping, prepared the food, and made sure the house was clean and tidy. When the children were sick, he got up at night and took care of them. His fervid activity may have discouraged Ariadne from taking her share of responsibility for the household. She did nothing. Not only because she'd been blind from birth; she was indolent by nature and not particularly well organized. Bernhard took charge of everything and always treated her with affection, even when she least deserved it. He knew that her life, isolated all day with three small children in that miserable little apartment, was no bed of roses. She was subject to sharply changing moods. She would call Moricz a darling one second and then denounce him as wicked and vicious the next when he asked for something more to eat. Nathan, whom she scolded for his slow wits, suddenly became a genius when he played with Kalman in the afternoon so she could take a nap. Bernhard understood why she was so jealous. It wasn't because of any infidelity on his part, for he had no such inclination; for him, there was no one but Ariadne. She was quite simply of a jealous temperament and regarded Bernhard as her possession. Her attitude was greatly influenced, no doubt, by the fact that she had no one other than Bernhard—they had neither relatives nor friends to support them.

Pester Lloyd

PESTER LLOYD was the flagship of the German-language press in the Hungarian capital, a sober daily paper devoted to the issues of the day. Its finances were assured principally by the support of the liberal banker Siegmund Kornfeld, who in his youth had been Jakob's protégé in Vienna and at the age of twenty-six had been appointed by Albert Rothschild as head of the Ungarische Creditanstalt in Budapest. The newspaper's editorial offices and printshop were housed in a building in the northern section of the fashionable Lipótváros district. The editor in chief, the legendary Miksa Falk, moved with great ease in distinctly different social circles. He was Empress Elisabeth's confidant, and even Franz Josef would lend him an ear. Falk had a unique ability to hold many threads together at the same time, and he did all that he could to persuade his colleagues to share his adventures, instead of following the far more common approach of the time of dazzling others with one's knowledge and seeking to become the fair-haired boy of the newspaper. Falk always listened to others and inspired those around him with his ideas and suggestions. He was lavish with his praise and carefully moderate in his criticism. He couldn't tolerate florid style or the use of too many adjectives. "Fear of the adjective," he used to say, "is the beginning of style." All of his colleagues knew what he expected of them, so he never had to lecture them. The sharply downturned ends of his mustache gave him a rough, stern appearance, but he had a fundamentally friendly nature. Only those on the staff who were smug and excessively sure of themselves needed to fear the cutting remarks he used to deflate them.

Bernhard got a job as an errand boy at *Pester Lloyd* soon after arriving in Budapest. His wages were minimal, scarcely enough to cover room and board for his family. He was no stranger to hard work; he ran errands all day long with the same enthusiasm he applied to shifting heavy bales of newsprint. He was happy in the seductively feverish bustle in all departments of the newspaper. He loved the smell of printer's ink and felt a boyish excitement in using the paternoster elevator, a continuously moving succession of cages that linked editorial offices on different floors of the building. It gave him unheard-of satisfaction every day to be among educated men and women who selflessly devoted themselves to the less privileged sectors of society. He began to dream of seeing his own name on the front page of the newspaper. One day—in what he himself found to be a moment of pretentiousness—he wrote an article about the difficulties of the blind in the city of Budapest. He knew that the likelihood of the article being accepted was about the same as that of Ariadne suddenly gaining her sight, but he turned in his piece to the head of shift at the city desk. Several weeks passed and he had almost forgotten it, so he was surprised one morning to be called into the office of the editor in chief. For a moment he thought that he was going to be reprimanded or lose his job for some mistake. Instead, Falk greeted him courteously and apologized for having taken so long to read the article. He asked if Bernhard had published anything before, since if not, he would be making his journalistic debut the following Sunday on *Pester Lloyd*'s front page. His article not only met the newspaper's high standards but was also important because it threw light on a problem that—as far as he could recall from his many years in the newspaper business—no journalist had ever raised before. He asked how Bernhard happened to know so much about the difficulties of the blind. He couldn't believe his ears when he heard that the young man's wife was born blind. "Your wife!" exclaimed the editor in chief. He found it hard to believe that a mere youngster like Bernhard was already married. He was even more astounded when Bernhard explained that he was in no way a "mere youngster"; he was a full nineteen years old and already the father of two sons. "In that case," Falk replied, "a modest honorarium would be a welcome addition to the family finances." He offered the prospect to Bernhard of having a good number of articles published, provided they were as well written and insightful as his piece about the visually impaired, and provided his other work at the paper didn't suffer. Bernhard was deeply grateful.

Sunday arrived, and Bernhard's disappointment knew no bounds when he held the newspaper before him. The article was indeed there on the front page, but his name was misspelled. Instead of Bernhard Spinoza, a "Bernhard Spiritosa" was credited in the byline. He knew that *Pester Lloyd* was reputed never to make editorial mistakes, so he assumed that someone on the editorial staff had changed the spelling of his name out of pure spite. On Monday he went to the editor in chief and asked for a correction; he was directed to the chief typesetter. There he was informed that the typographer who had set up the article early that Sunday morning had dropped the line of lead type with Bernhard's name, and when he reassembled it in a rush he mixed up some of the letters. "It could have been worse," the chief typesetter commented laconically. Bernard couldn't understand the grizzled technician's failure to appreciate the awful fact that he had to swallow the indignity of seeing his first published article appear with a byline that misspelled his last name.

The misspelled name—the very first such disaster of its kind in the history of the newspaper—was the principal topic of discussion at the editorial conference on Monday morning. One bright journalist commented with a smirk that there must be some hidden meaning in all of this. He offered his own opinion—unaware, of course, of Bernhard's family relationship with Bento and Benjamin—that the last name of Spiritosa was a good one for a young man who was always smiling, and at any rate it was certainly better than

Spinoza, which brought to mind that dour old killjoy of a philosopher. From that day on everyone at the newspaper referred to Bernhard by the nickname of "Spiritosa," an expression in Italian meaning *humorous, witty,* and *spiritual.* A month later Bernhard received a letter from his mother that caused him even greater disappointment, if that was possible. She congratulated him on the publication of his first article. At the same time she expressed her joy that she had at last succeeded in convincing her husband, long a skeptic, to ask his former protégé, *Pester Lloyd*'s most important financial supporter Siegmund Kornfeld, to pull a few strings to get her son a promotion at the newspaper. He was crushed.

The Paternoster Elevator

ARIADNE HAD BEEN in a foul humor for a long time. In the normal course of things, even when she was most ill-tempered, after a few days she would allow herself to be awakened by Bernhard's delicate caresses and pat him on the head as a sign that the joys of the marriage bed could commence; when they got out of bed they were friends again. Several weeks had gone by since their most recent physical reconciliation, and that morning had been the worst yet. Ariadne had awakened in a more quarrelsome mood than usual. She bemoaned her fate and called him and the boys all sorts of insulting names. The boys began to cry, and she responded by smashing plates against the wall and breaking a windowpane. It took almost an hour for her to calm down enough for Bernhard to go to work.

Later that morning chaos erupted in the newsroom. People were shouting, women were weeping, and men were rushing around. Bernhard, who by then had worked for a couple of years as an assistant editor in the advertising office, was appalled at the commotion. The hubbub was everywhere, in all the editorial offices. Bernhard really had no desire to deal with any more problems that day, but his curiosity got the better of him. He got up from his desk and was just on the way out the door when the editor in chief appeared. Falk was deathly pale. His voice shook and his hands were trembling. He asked Bernhard to sit down. Bernhard had a premonition that something terrible had happened. Falk told him what had occurred, and Bernhard's life came to a sudden standstill. The body of a young woman had been discovered in the mechanism of the paternoster elevator. She must have stepped out of the open cage between two floors or lost her balance; in any case, she had fallen and been killed by the mechanism. Her head had been chopped off. As far as they could tell, the young woman must have been blind. They had reason to believe that she was Bernhard's wife.

Ariadne was Bernhard's whole life. He'd never had anyone else; he knew no other love. We should thank divine providence that Bernhard had three sons, for otherwise he would have simply given up after Ariadne's death. But though Ariadne was never out of his thoughts for a second, he knew he had to take care of the children.

Inside the battered suitcase that I inherited from my grandfather, in the thick jumble of letters, diaries from across the centuries, birth certificates, wills, and other papers documenting the history of the Spinoza family, I also came across a yellowing photograph, probably taken before the Second World War, with the image of a black granite gravestone inscribed in gilded letters: *Ariadne—my princess—you saw the world with different eyes. You are eternally missed.*

On the back of the photo my grandfather had written in tiny characters, *My only memory of Mama.*

Shortly after the funeral Bernhard received a summary of the autopsy. Ariadne had been pregnant. His eyes filled with tears. He realized that Ariadne, who almost never left home because of her blindness and had never visited the newspaper, must have been coming to ask his forgiveness for her behavior and to tell him she was expecting a baby.

The Best Cure

"*LABOR OMNIA VINCIT.* The quotation is from the great Roman poet Virgil," the editor in chief told him, "and it means: Work conquers all." Falk regarded Bernhard with the austere sympathy one offers to someone who has just suffered a catastrophe.

"I must be frank with you," he said. "You cannot go around here all day long at the newspaper thinking of nothing but your late wife. That's of no use either to you or to anyone else. You can't get her back again; she's dead. You have to accept that fact. The only appropriate way for you to honor her memory is by writing. The best cure for profound grief is work. Apply yourself to your writing again, and you'll see how your soul and spirit will rise once more. You'll gain a bit more courage every time you remove a worn-out word from your text and replace it with another that's less trite; you'll find a moment of pleasure when you discern just the right path through the endless galaxies of language."

The editor in chief said that Bernhard's article about the blind was the most vivid description he had ever read about the situation of the afflicted in Budapest. That text in itself was evidence that Bernhard was among those very few individuals born to write, he said emphatically, and therefore Bernhard had only one purpose in life: to take up his pen to battle to improve the lot of mankind. Falk explained that he himself came from a poor Jewish family, and his fundamental motivation was to advance the cause of social justice, for all too many people in Hungarian society bristled in opposition to his principles, summarized in the motto of the French Revolution: Freedom, Equality, Brotherhood, words first joined and proclaimed by Nicolas Spinoza. Bernhard's mouth twitched in a weak smile. He nodded.

"Your true inheritance is from your old grandfather Nicolas," Falk said. "It's your ability to see familiar things with new eyes and to describe them. The man who writes becomes a witness in the court of public opinion. Your words give others strength to lift themselves above their ordinary destinies."

The editor in chief taught Bernhard more than just how to manipulate language, hammer out sentences, and struggle with words. Falk was a master teacher, no mere mentor in journalism. He oriented Bernhard in Hungarian history and opened for him a tradition of humanism rooted in the writings of Cicero, Plutarch, and Seneca. He urged him to read Erasmus of Rotterdam and Michel de Montaigne. He exercised Bernhard's debating skills with lively discussions of economics and politics. He helped him make allies of some of the greatest contemporary authors and embrace the delights of the many destinies described in classic works of poetry. He taught him to breathe the atmosphere of books.

At the Café du Matignon

THEY'D AGREED to meet at the Café du Matignon in the elegant Faubourg Saint-Germain. Herzl had chosen the place. He'd been the correspondent in Paris of the Viennese newspaper *Die Neue Freie Presse* for four years, and so he knew the city well, especially the arrondissement where Alfred Dreyfus had lived and worked before his arrest. Herzl had followed the trial of the Jewish captain with great interest and had wholeheartedly backed the campaign in France to give justice to Dreyfus.

There was nothing Herzl looked forward to more eagerly than meeting Bernhard in person. Rivals and equally influential opinion-makers for the subjects of the double monarchy, they had followed each other's writing and careers with admiration for ten years. One was from Budapest and had moved at the age of seventeen to Vienna; the other broke away at the same age from an estate not far from Vienna and had settled in Budapest. They were twinned in some unusual way and constantly involved in similar issues and controversies. Perhaps it was for that reason that Herzl was sometimes called a kind of Bernhard Spinoza in Vienna, while Bernhard would hear himself referred to as a sort of Theodor Herzl in Budapest. Both were known for their prodigious productivity and exalted conceptions of the mission of the journalist. They were aware of their critical influence as shapers of opinion. Almost no other writers provoked such intense debates, demanded such radical political changes, and wounded and harassed the authorities as much as these two. It was hardly surprising that each had an important place in the consciousness of his readers.

Herzl and Bernhard had carried on a lively correspondence for many years, but they had never met. Herzl took the initiative and proposed the meeting in Paris. He was working on a book he was calling *The Jewish State*, in which, as a reaction to the anti-Semitism spreading in Europe in the wake of the Dreyfus affair, he argued that the Jews should establish their own nation-state. He had sent an outline of it to a handful of influential Jewish cultural leaders in the German-speaking countries. Their reactions were overwhelmingly positive. The only negative reaction and counterargument came from Bernhard. Herzl was eager to discuss the issues further with him, for he was sure that the encounter would be of great benefit to his work.

Bernhard arrived at the Gare du Nord on a bright and sunny morning in early May. He had hardly enough time to deposit his luggage at the nearby Hôtel de l'Europe on the boulevard de Magenta before setting off toward the Left Bank of the Seine where the meeting was scheduled to take place. He was pleased by the prospect of meeting Herzl. He recognized him as soon as he stepped into the Café du Matignon, even though Herzl's appearance was not quite as Bernhard had imagined. Herzl was taller and thinner. He had recently turned thirty-five, Bernhard knew, but he looked older. His long dark beard gave him the air of an Old Testament prophet. They embraced instead of shaking hands.

After a number of pleasantries Bernhard asked Herzl how he was getting along in the French capital. "Paris is the center of the universe," Herzl replied. He described his love for the beauties of the city but commented that the French were not always easy to deal with. They were arrogant, stubborn, fascinating both in their rigidity and their elegance, at times extremely spiritual, but even more often downright stupid. But the women of Paris were wonderful, splendid, and flirtatious. He confessed with a smile that he always fell mildly and hopelessly in love with every Frenchwoman he met, but they were unattainable, so the only brief moments of pleasure he experienced were those he purchased. *"O là là, cher ami,"* he said, "I could tell you amazing things about those establishments they call *maisons de tolérance* here in France." He noticed that Bernhard, who had vigorously de-cried the reduction of erotic experience to crude commerce and had demanded the closure of the brothels of Budapest, was moderately disconcerted by this topic. Herzl quickly changed the subject to French cuisine, which he consid-ered to be without peer anywhere. A beef bourguignon, he argued earnestly, provides a thousand times more nourish-ment than a dry Wiener schnitzel. "A good Parisian cook," he declared, "is your best physician." They shared a pleased laugh and went on to discuss more serious matters.

What did they discuss during the ensuing hours? The persecution of Jews and the way to remedy it. Herzl said that for two thousand years the Jews had been living in constant fear. They had been persecuted, discriminated against, hu-miliated, maimed, and murdered. Why? Because they were foreigners everywhere in the world and therefore seen as a different type of human being, people who could be mis-treated without a second thought. They had no country of their own to protect them and no flag to feel proud of. But once the Jewish nation-state was established, the situation of Jews everywhere would improve.

Bernhard replied that there were two Jewish traditions, each of them centuries old. The first he called "Masada" after the impregnable fortress on the shore of the Dead Sea where Jews offered heroic resistance against the far larger Roman army after the fall of Jerusalem in 70 BCE.

The Jewish rebels defended their last remaining lands for seven years. When all hope was gone, they committed collective suicide, dying as free men instead of living as slaves. The alternative he called "Javne" after the tiny village where the pragmatic Rabbi Johanan ben Zakkai founded a school at about the same time. That was where Judaism changed from a religion tied to a specific land with historic sites and holy places to a movable faith enshrined in a few books, a faith that could exist even beyond Israel, since one carried it along wherever one went. The hallmarks of the Javne model, he said, were knowledge, teaching, pragmatism, and peaceful coexistence—the only things that could guarantee the survival of the Jews over the long term.

Herzl did not agree. He declared that the Javne vision was fading, and the spiritual principles of Judaism would inevitably be corrupted because prejudice and social injustices obliged Jews to live in a world steeped in hatred of Judaism. He emphasized that it was not his aim to solve the Jewish problem by creating a spiritual center but rather by re-creating the Jewish nation-state after two thousand years of a sleep as deep as that of Cinderella. He stressed that at the same time he did not want to found a nation-state that resembled all the rest. He dreamed of a model state based on tolerance and equality, one that embodied the ideals that were Europe's contributions to the world but had been betrayed by the nationalisms of the day.

Bernhard interrupted him to say that the Jews' greatest contribution to the world was not monotheism but instead the law, the principle of universalism, the fact that the law applied to everyone and no one stood above it. Democracy could not exist without that principle, and the ideals of the French Revolution would be impossible to realize. The Jews' contribution was to preserve and defend the principle of universalism, the very concept that linked them across boundaries and hundreds of years of exile.

Herzl countered that exile was a dead end, a barren waste where Jews had been stumbling around for generations. They had lost their compass and direction. Many faithful Jews, in his opinion, had exchanged their duty to hold high what Bernhard called the flag of universalism for the legend of the Chosen People. In their attempt to compensate for their hopeless physical vulnerability, they believed in their own spiritual superiority to others.

Bernhard could see that Herzl found it difficult to accept his opinion that exile to a life in reduced circumstances was in itself the logical continuation of the Jewish contribution to the world. He was moved to confide to Herzl that he'd inherited from his father a book by the philosopher Benjamin Spinoza. It had been in his family's possession for more than two hundred years, he explained, and no outsider had ever been allowed to read it. The book contained reflections about some of the greatest issues of mankind. Shortly before he got on the train in Budapest, he'd read a passage that dealt with the true spirit of Israel; it had made a deep impression upon him.

He told Herzl that according to a legend recounted by Benjamin Spinoza, each one of the earth's seventy kingdoms was watched over by an angel named Fürst, or Prince. The angel guided the people and went before them to the throne of the Lord. The people of Israel were the only clan that had no angel, for the Jews refused to accept an intermediary in their dialogue with the Lord or to subject themselves to any ruling power that didn't originate directly from God. Benjamin Spinoza warned against calling for a Fürst or, rather, to be more specific, he warned of the miseries that would afflict a nation that worships itself and its own individuality and fails to recognize any other obligations. In the spirit of Israel, the philosopher had emphasized, the Jewish people should not express their collective egotism but instead embrace a truth beyond all nationhood, a higher realm which humanity is called to enter. Otherwise, the Jews would find themselves under the yoke of the Fürst— whether that Fürst is a human being or a small patch of earth or even an idol—and from that Fürst a god would be constituted. All of this has to do, Bernhard went on, with the Jews' mission to battle against the worship of idols and to preserve universal values. It can also be seen as a warning against establishing a nation-state that will come inevitably to resemble any other.

Bernhard looked expectantly at Herzl. He saw immediately that it was no use waiting for Herzl's reaction, because the man was leering and flirting openly with the elegant woman who had just seated herself at the next table, not paying the least attention to his revelation of Benjamin's secret book and the lesson of the mission of Israel. Bernhard cleared his throat to attract Herzl's attention. He said he was tired after the long journey, so perhaps it was time to finish up. They decided to meet the following day at the same time and in the same place to continue the dialogue, then went their separate ways.

Bernhard checked out of his hotel the next morning and took the train back to Budapest.

ELEVEN

The Communist

Jove

I'VE ALREADY MENTIONED that from the first to the very last my grandfather's marriage to my grandmother afforded him very few moments of pleasure. He regarded his wife as a creature of split personality. One face was enticing and the other was horrific.

The Sara who was impossible to resist turned her compelling brilliance upon him during a boat trip on the Danube one warm Sunday in the summer of 1918. Her face glowed with youthful beauty and suppressed desire, and he fell at once for her gaze and her sparkling eyes, for the bare golden brown arms revealed by her red polka-dot dress, for the immediate feeling of intimacy. This sudden stirring of attraction lured him into dreams of bliss. Accordingly, he proposed to her only a few days later, with no idea who she was or where she came from.

HIS FIRST DISCOVERY of the horrific side of Sara's nature came some months after their wedding night. With a listless expression and a sorrowful voice, she told him that she was pregnant. She had something to confess. She asked him to forgive her for not telling him earlier—perhaps she should have revealed her secret as soon as they met. Although he could expect her to be faithful, she could never give him her whole heart, because she loved another, a man who'd never come back from the Italian front. This declaration devastated my grandfather and would become—eventually, not immediately—an unending source of annoyance and provocation to him for the rest of his life.

I cannot imagine how I would have reacted if the woman I loved, already pregnant with my child, told me her heart belonged to someone else. I've avoided such risk, essentially because I've never loved any woman at all. Of course, I've been infatuated a couple of times, but I'm fundamentally shy, and I've always kept my distance. Whenever I met an attractive woman, I felt my cheeks burning, which bothered me, so I pulled back into my shell. I admit that at times I've felt I missed out, and I've yearned terribly to hold someone's hand; my life has been a lonely, wandering journey through a desolate, haunted landscape. I've been afraid to initiate a relationship, mostly because I've always assumed nothing can be more terrible than the moment when love dies. It's cruel and unfair to the children born to such a union. I've heard Grandmother out on the staircase telling stories to our woman concierge about her relationship with Grandfather and what came between them. My father was not one to complain. But I know it must have been hell on earth for him and his siblings to grow up in a home where the parents hated each other like the plague and were constantly quarreling.

The Housemaid

MARIKA ÓVÁRI—THAT WAS THE NAME of the housemaid Bernhard had just hired. She was twenty-two years old, short, and plump; her rounded figure nicely filled out her tight dresses. She was from the city of Kolozsvár in Transylvania and was of unknown origin. Her mother had sung ballads with a wandering cabaret troupe when she was young; now she was the housemaid to a baron from Romania.

Marika didn't know who had fathered her. She'd occasionally asked her mother about her father—who he was and where he'd disappeared to—but her mother refused to answer. Sometimes Marika suspected that her mother probably never knew the man's identity and that she'd been born as the unfortunate outcome of some obscure event. Even as a child she'd understood that her mother's life hadn't been free of such so-called accidents. Men were always clustered around her mother, swarthy men with hungry eyes who gave her money to spend time with her.

Marika's mother taught her very early on that broad hips and a prominent bosom were God's gifts to women, whose role in life was to please men in exchange for security of some form or other. She was fourteen years old when she discovered that she was especially talented in the art of love. To supplement her mother's modest wages, she took the initiative of dropping by one of the city's better brothels three nights a week and offering distinguished gentlemen the chance to satisfy their desires in her arms.

SHE ARRIVED IN BUDAPEST after selling her body in several villages along the way, and she had the good fortune to meet a young gentleman wearing a custom-tailored suit of the finest English wool, decked out with a heavy gold chain for his pocket watch. He appreciated Marika's professional services, and paid well for them. He also presented her to other young men of the better sort. Just as she began to enjoy this lively upturn in her profession, an ectopic pregnancy and the resulting complications obliged her to change jobs for a time. One of her clients helped her to secure employment as a housemaid for his aunt, the widow of Miksa Falk. Her duty was to prepare and serve the paralyzed old lady's meals. A few weeks later the widow died and Bernhard engaged Marika to manage the Spinoza household. He knew nothing of her background.

Why am I telling you about this housemaid? Because she was one of the causes—although an indirect one—of the strife-filled marriage of my grandfather and grandmother. As well as my emigration to Norway.

Initiation

MARIKA, WITH HER EXTENSIVE KNOWLEDGE and experience, quickly perceived that nineteen-year-old Moricz wasn't attracted to women. He liked to boast of his adventures and worldliness, but he had noticeably little to say about the lusts of the flesh. She caressed his cheek a couple times, apparently in all innocence. His lack of reaction was a clear sign that he had no desire to get to know her better.

Therefore Nathan, years younger, became her candidate for initiation in the arts of love. The perfect opportunity presented itself one chilly autumn day. Nathan was studying mathematics at Eötvös Loránd University and getting along extremely well. One morning he went to the window, pulled back the curtains, and saw that the street outside was still dark, even though the clock had already struck six. He was still drowsy. He was strongly tempted to forget about his classes and spend the whole day in bed. He went to his father, who unlike him was always an early riser; Bernhard was putting the last touches on an article. Nathan complained that he felt a chill coming on. He gave a few dry coughs and asked if he might stay home, since he had no particularly important lectures that day. Permission was granted. On the way back to his room Nathan caught sight of Marika leaning over, gathering sweepings from the kitchen floor. He stopped and stood there transfixed, his gaze fixed on her pear-shaped backside as he imagined the pleasure of taking a firm grip on that rounded rump. He left, closed the bedroom door behind him, lay down in bed, and drifted off in erotic fantasies. Once all the other family members had left, Marika went into Nathan's room without knocking. She immediately noticed the bulge under his blanket. His face turned red. After a moment of embarrassed silence, she offered to prepare a cup of chamomile tea with acacia honey, a reliable old Transylvanian recipe against the sniffles. Nathan had no objection. Fifteen minutes later she returned with the tea and settled herself on the edge of the bed. She said that where she came from, people used chamomile to cure all sorts of maladies, everything from toothaches to impotence. He didn't hear a word she said. The top two buttons of her blouse were open, and she exuded a pungent scent of femininity. He could think of nothing but her bosom. He wanted to touch her breasts. He could scarcely restrain his hands. He was quivering with desire and felt that he would give anything at all to be able to take her in his arms. She must have noticed this, for she slipped her hand beneath the blanket and gently caressed his upper thigh. Nathan felt a thrill go through his whole body. He flushed and stammered. Marika told him that if he thought she was not serious, he was mistaken. Without waiting for a reply, she pushed the blanket aside; with avid desire flaming in her eyes, she wrapped her lips around his stiff male member.

Nathan was dismayed by his first effort, which was over and done with in a matter of seconds. Marika wiped her mouth. He wondered what semen might taste like, but didn't dare say a word. She explained to him that physical love was a matter of natural aptitude; one was either born to enjoy it or else one never learned the art. She told him with great seriousness that their first experience together, as short as it had been, showed that many wonderful hours in bed were ahead of them; she promised to apply her talents for him, to become his tutor, and to give him all of the lessons he would ever need, for she found that with his well-developed organ, far superior to her expectations, he was created for the ecstasies of love.

She began caressing him once more a few moments later. When he was obviously ready to continue lovemaking, she positioned herself astride him. As they coupled, she whispered into his ear, "I'm all yours. Do with me whatever you want."

Later, when she got dressed, he stared furtively at her hips and was grateful she'd made a man of him.

Erotic Pleasures

FOR THE NEXT SIX MONTHS Nathan had only one thought in his head, and it had nothing to do with mathematics. He couldn't decide whether he was in love with Marika or only obsessed by her voluptuous body, but he was ready to do whatever it took, including selling his soul to the devil, to be alone with her and roll around in bed until he could do no more, for she was hot and greedy and bold and inventive and completely irresistible. The tension of their secret life together and the risk of being discovered simply increased his desire. The impressive performances she incited him to deliver—performances she said would put to shame even the most stiff-dicked he-men—made him immeasurably proud of his newly discovered manhood and inexhaustible energy.

Sometimes Nathan felt a touch of jealousy at the thought that Marika, never reticent about describing her erotic experiences to him in great detail, had met so many men in her life. Her perceptive feminine intuition included an uncanny sense for those small shifts in his mood. Perhaps she knew that his jealousy could easily deteriorate into suspicion, and she wanted to prevent that; in any case, at such times she would always murmur into his ear, "Nothing has any meaning to me except us, you and me."

Early in the new year Nathan noticed that his father was more cordial to Marika than he usually was with housemaids. From time to time he caught sight of his father staring fixedly at Marika and then hastily turning his eyes to one of his sons. Nathan reacted to the intensity of his father's gaze. He told himself in silence that his father was getting to be a bit of a dirty old man, harmless enough and not so surprising, considering that he hadn't been with a woman since he became a widower. *He would really be jealous of me*, Nathan thought and smiled to himself, *if he had any idea what Marika and I have been up to*.

Betrayal

ON APRIL 9, a day that Nathan would remember for the rest of his life, Emanuel Lasker came to the university. The reigning world master in chess had received his PhD in mathematics a few years earlier. He was scheduled to lecture on his latest contribution to algebra, something he called "polynomial rings." Students and teachers packed the lecture hall. The temperature in the room rose, and it became hard to breathe. Nathan had difficulty hearing Lasker, who was speaking in a monotone. He became distracted, and his thoughts began to wander. He thought of Marika. They hadn't been alone for more than two weeks. Was it only by chance? Perhaps she was avoiding him. Suddenly he had the impression that she'd been a bit unreceptive of late. Then he immediately recalled that in the hallway only a few days before, she'd whispered to him, "The only thing that matters to me is us, you and me."

He blinked and could see before him Marika's naked body stretched out on the bed. He felt a wild longing for her. He wanted to stroke her smooth skin, take her nipples into his mouth and suck on them, bury himself in her sex. He decided to leave the lecture, since he couldn't make out anything the grand master was saying, anyway. He slipped away and hurried to the tram line. When he finally arrived at the apartment building, he took the stairs two or three at a time, hurrying up to the fifth floor. He opened the front door carefully and stealthily, hoping to surprise Marika. As he stepped into the hall, he heard strange noises in the dining room. He froze, listening intently. Was that debauched moaning coming from Marika? Anxiety filled him and a foreboding shot through him—a premonition that what awaited him in the dining room was a discovery that would shatter his whole life. Should he turn around and leave? *This is your destiny*, said a voice within him. He took a deep breath and steeled himself. His face was pasty white as he tiptoed forward as quietly as he could. The instant before he reached the wide-open doors to the dining room, he heard Marika gasping, "Keep going. More. I'm yours. Do what you want with me." And then he saw how his father was thrusting his flabby lecherous body onto Marika, who sprawled there, willing and open. His father was moaning and slapping her breasts with the backs of his hands, producing sounds like those of a wet rag whacking a stone. She had her legs wrapped around his fat buttocks and was quietly gasping and raving.

Nathan stared at them, betrayed and disgusted. So this was his father, heaving like a wild beast, brutal and sweaty. He let out a deep, shuddering breath. They realized he was there and a deathly silence filled the room. A dire and disagreeable silence. Bernhard gave his son a desperate look, his shoulders hunched with anxiety and his whole stance a plea for understanding. An apprehensive smile appeared on Marika's face. Nathan said nothing and asked no questions. It was enough for him to look his father and Marika in the eye to understand clearly, once and for all, how things were between the two of them: This was obviously not the first time.

He had never seen his father naked before this. The sight of his father's erect penis deep in his lover's sex—this was unbelievable, unheard of. Nathan couldn't bear the spectacle of their copulating bodies. He turned abruptly and rushed out of the apartment.

He leaped down the stairs and paused on the street outside. He'd never in his life felt so lonely and abandoned. *This is worse than being flayed alive,* he thought, his heart torn with pain. He recognized the feeling of sorrow; it was the same grief that he had experienced as a child when he first understood—oh, perhaps it wasn't understanding but only some sort of awareness that slowly but surely filtered into his consciousness—that his mother would never come back. It was the same sorrow that had filled his chest when at the age of ten he'd been unjustly accused of stealing Turkish delight from Hermann Kohn's delicatessen and his father had refused to believe him and had beaten him and had never apologized even after his innocence had been confirmed.

He gasped for breath, blinked, and tried to summon strength from within. He couldn't understand how Marika could do such a thing. Couldn't she see how low she'd sunk by betraying him with his own father? How could she live with such treachery? Or maybe it didn't bother her conscience at all. Only then, as he asked himself these questions, did he begin to understand that Marika's whole life was based on pleasing men, embracing them, letting strange men take possession of her. He vowed that he would blot her out of his life forever. He couldn't imagine any treachery greater than his lover having sex with his father.

As for his father, Nathan was furiously angry and deeply disappointed. Something burst inside him. His heart pounded, and his head spun at the thought of his father's repugnant behavior. Behind all his high and mighty pronouncements about justice, his father was nothing but a horny old goat who couldn't keep his hands to himself. *The sultry air of pretense has been lifted,* he said to himself. The behavior of his father and his beloved had reached such a level of insanity and monstrosity that he was forced to respond. He was completely beside himself. Ever since the day he'd been accused of stealing candy, he'd known that one day he would leave his father behind, that one day he would no longer feel any affection for his father. Now that day had come. It was time to take the step toward freedom and maturity, for this was something he could never forgive. What use was forgiveness? It couldn't possibly undo the evil already committed. He realized in that bitter moment of defeat that he would never be able to look his father in the eye again. Suddenly he recalled the comment of a pimple-faced classmate whose family had thrown him out after he was caught stealing: "Anyone with the least sense of self-respect has to leave his father's house before he turns twenty and set out to explore the world."

A Reunion

I REALIZE that I'm jumping ahead in time, but I think it's appropriate at this point to mention that Nathan and his father never met again.

Marika, on the other hand, did turn up again, quite unexpectedly. That was in July 1919 during the final days of the short-lived Hungarian Soviet Republic.

A year before this, Nathan had given free rein to his fantasies about the utopia under construction in faraway Russia. Socialism was no longer simply a theory; it was on its way to realization in that country. He experienced a rush of warmth as he thought of the proud Russian people carrying on their bold struggle for freedom and justice. In Lenin he discovered exactly what he'd been seeking for so long: a father figure to look up to, admire, and love.

The appeal of the Russian Revolution immediately attracted him to the Republic of the Councils instituted by Béla Kun in Hungary. He joined the Communist Party and worked with all his might to support its agenda. For years after this Nathan fought against admitting that the imagined socialist paradise in the east had little in common with everyday life in Budapest. He assumed that Béla Kun was as infallible a leader as Lenin, so he defended Kun, whatever happened. He made all possible excuses for Kun's repeated political mistakes, terrible judgments, and plans that ended in disaster. When it came to the monstrous atrocities allegedly ordered by the leader with an almost disdainful indifference—including the slaughter of whole ranks of his opponents—Nathan dismissed them as crazy accusations almost completely out of touch with reason and reality. He also insisted that the claims the country was in a deep economic depression were baseless, and he said any economic crisis in Hungary was entirely the fault of the bourgeois class.

In the worst of the summer heat, Nathan was summoned as a member of the Federated Central Executive Committee to a meeting in the Executive Building to discuss the preparedness of the workers' militia and the division of responsibilities. The party leadership had received reports from reliable sources that the reactionary regimes of neighboring countries were planning the imminent dispatch of foreign counterrevolutionary troops to crush the Hungarian Soviet Republic.

To everyone's surprise, Béla Kun attended the meeting in the company of his secretary and without his defense minister. The rumor was that the secretary—generally viewed as hopelessly incompetent—was really his longtime mistress. Even respectable party members who stoutly rejected these insinuations, along with other attempts to tarnish the leader's reputation, found the whole thing a bit fishy: He supposedly had met her when she was a high-school student in their hometown of Kolozsvár and was working as a minor in a brothel, and now she was expecting his illegitimate child, even though he was married and had several children with his wife.

Nathan had never met Béla Kun before this, so he studied Kun with interest from his seat in the back row of the hall. The leader of the Communist Party was a stubby little fellow, less imposing than Nathan had expected. Kun's hair was cut short and his well-tailored dark suit could be that of an upper-class attorney. His bull neck and broad forehead, and especially his piercing gaze, reminded Nathan of a portrait of Robespierre he'd seen somewhere. The dark circles under Kun's eyes betrayed his lack of sleep; the unshaven jowls showed that he hadn't had the time to pay attention to his appearance. He looked like a peasant, and his Hungarian surname was in odd contrast with his Jewish origins. Nathan immediately noted Kun's peculiar tendency to emphasize certain adjectives, expressions he employed often and enunciated in a declamatory style so that each individual letter of the word was articulated and the ends of his sentences sounded almost like chanting. Béla Kun's eyes flashed and his voice thundered. He declared that he had no wish to make anyone's burden heavier than it already was, but it was the clear duty of every communist to demonstrate his heroism and resist hardship, even to the extent of laying down his life if foreign soldiers attempted to overturn the workers' revolution. He waved his arms dramatically; Nathan thought for a moment that Kun was about to pull a revolver out of his jacket and emphasize his message by firing a few shots at the bourgeois symbol suspended from the ceiling, a heavy crystal chandelier.

Several burly fellows were standing in front of Nathan, partly blocking his view. That was why he did not initially catch sight of Béla Kun's secretary. When he glimpsed her a couple of minutes later, he recognized her instantly, even though her face was more rounded and she had bleached her dark hair. It was Marika. He stared at her in astonishment. He was amazed that the delirium and pleasure she had given him so long ago remained so vivid that even now, although he thought he had forgotten her, his heart started racing and the member in his trousers rose at the memory of their playful lovemaking.

The meeting ended. Nathan went outside with the others and took his place in the receiving line to shake hands with Béla Kun, who had obviously doused himself with strong eau de cologne. The sharp odor tickled Nathan's nose and the closer he came to the leader, the more unpleasant it became. He managed to put up with the reek of it. He felt obliged to say something. An older party comrade had told him Béla Kun was particularly susceptible to flattery. "I was greatly impressed by your speech," he heard himself say. The leader smiled and was in no hurry to answer him, as if he was expecting additional praise. After a moment Kun said, "My comrade can count on the decisive victory of the working class. I will tear apart both heaven and earth if need be. Many barons and members of the bourgeois class will lose sleep before I finish with them." Nathan nodded in agreement. He wasn't looking to engage Béla Kun in polite small talk. All he wanted was to get close to Marika, to take that opportunity to look at her and just for a moment hold her hand in his. She stood at the communist leader's side. Nathan stepped toward her and suddenly saw she was pregnant. He looked deep into her eyes and extended his hand. He wasn't expecting her to fall into his arms, but even so he was a bit disappointed at her reaction. She pretended not to recognize him. For a few instants she looked at him warily but finally she took his hand. "Our leader," she said uncertainly, "is firmly decided . . . to eliminate all . . . types of injustice."

"Injustice," repeated Nathan absently. "Of course." Then he released her cold little hand and left the meeting.

Another Betrayal

GRANDFATHER HAD A YOUNGER BROTHER. I mentioned his name before: Kalman. He died young in tragic circumstances. Grandfather never spoke of him. When Sasha and I asked him about his little brother, Grandfather inevitably became annoyed and replied with scarcely concealed reluctance that he had no desire to dig into the past. We thought his refusal to say anything was because Kalman had been their father's favorite, completely spoiled, and that was why Grandfather never liked him. Or perhaps, we imagined, he was fed up with Kalman because he'd grown up hearing that he was responsibile for taking care of his insufferable little brother, protecting him and defending him.

A letter signed only with the letter *K* lay in the suitcase I inherited from Grandfather. It gave a different picture of their relationship. Kalman writes that they'd always been close, and for that reason his betrayal of Nathan was all the more painful. The betrayal, he confessed, was that he also was going to bed with Marika, even though he knew how deeply in love with her Nathan was. Kalman writes that he'd wanted to make a clean breast of it and confess his treachery, but he couldn't bring himself to do so, because he didn't want to hurt Nathan. Even so, he couldn't keep away from Marika, because the lure of the flesh was stronger than the restraints of his conscience. The letter concludes with a fervent plea for forgiveness.

In a postscript Kalman says their father surprised him and Marika in bed, and all hell broke loose. Very soon after that he was sent away to Fiume, the town from which the letter was written. He hoped Nathan would come to visit him someday.

Nathan considered his own attraction to Marika entirely natural, but he thought the behavior of his brother and his father was disgusting. What pained him far more, however, was that they'd both done things behind his back. It felt doubly humiliating to him that they'd regularly belittled Marika in his presence—Nathan remembered how nonchalantly they had made disparaging remarks about her—and had given the impression that they disliked her simple nature. Obviously, that had been nothing but a subterfuge to hide their physical relationships with her.

Nathan hated lies. That may have been partly because his brother Moricz never told the truth. Even when Nathan was a small child, lies would make him frantic. The most innocent white lie was enough to cause a rupture between him and the person who told it. That was why he vowed to say nothing about certain persons—his father, his young brother, and Marika—whom he had completely stricken out of his life.

Dreams by the Sea

KALMAN WAS BORN with a tremendously large nose, inherited from his father, and a troublesome affliction of the skin, ichthyosis, which was a genetic inheritance from his mother's side of the family. His body, especially his arms and legs, was covered with thick layers of skin crisscrossed with cracks prone to infections and bleeding.

Moricz suffered from the same skin condition although in a milder form. He felt guilty every time the family doctor came to examine Kalman and treat him with various creams. He thought he was the cause of the violent itching that tormented Kalman because he must have infected his little brother. This created strong ties between the eldest and the youngest of the Spinoza brothers.

Kalman was sent away to Fiume at the age of eighteen, in part because the dry inland climate of Budapest was the worst possible environment for a person with ichthyosis. Since Kalman's suffering increased in his late teenage years—at times he was terribly tormented by itching open sores on his knees and elbows—the family doctor recommended that he move to the Adriatic shore, because the coastal climate with its cooler summers and milder winters, and especially the salt sea and moist air, would offer a more effective alleviation of intense itching than all of the moisturizing creams in the world; the location itself offered the best prospect of relief from ichthyosis. The doctor was of the opinion that Kalman would be well advised to go into some maritime line of work. He himself had a nephew living in Fiume who had studied at the famous Hungarian Royal Maritime Academy.

Kalman's greatest hero was Louis Blériot. The French engineer was one of the pioneers of flight. In July 1909 he flew across the English Channel in an airplane he had constructed himself, a so-called monoplane with a three-cylinder, twenty-three-horsepower Anzani motor. The plane was called *Blériot XI* because the cross-Channel machine was the eleventh that the Frenchman had constructed. The thirty-seven-minute flight brought Blériot not only the thousand pounds sterling offered by the *Daily Mail* in London as a prize to the first pilot who succeeded in flying between England and France but also worldwide fame. *Blériot XI* established the principles in manufacturing, design, and pilot training for the empire of the air.

Kalman read about that pioneering French pilot in *Magyar Estilap*. The article fired Kalman's imagination. He was, if possible, even more enthused by the photographs of Blériot surrounded by journalists and admiring onlookers after his successful Channel crossing. He dreamed of becoming a pilot. He imagined himself as the Flying Jew. He saw himself crossing the Mediterranean and landing at Rishon LeZion, the first Jewish settlement in the Holy Land.

He saw his pioneering feat rewarded by the *Daily Mail* with a thousand pounds. He would use the money to build his own airplane, the *Spinoza XI*.

FIUME WAS THE PROUD SITE of Hungary's largest deepwater port and home to its most diverse collection of ethnic groups: Croatians, Serbs, Slovenians, Italians, Germans, Austrians, Montenegrins, Gypsies, Jews, Greeks, and Albanians lived side by side with Hungarians.

Kalman felt at home there, even though he hated the disgusting reek of fish from the canning factories close to his lodgings. Certain accounts maintain that he had a lengthy involvement with a Croatian girl named Silvia, the daughter of a foreman at the Ganz & Danubius shipyard. Bound as she was by every imaginable narrow-minded Catholic moral constraint, she is said to have been most unreceptive when he besieged her with his burning passion. She couldn't imagine engaging in sexual relations before marriage, so Kalman was reduced to the pleasures of the sort provided by the Serbian sluts at the brothel.

His studies at the Maritime Academy were a great success. He had the highest marks in every subject and stood at the head of his class. To supplement his allowance he would accept money from his classmates to help them with their homework. He wanted to save a lot of money, because he'd never abandoned his dream of constructing his own airplane. His generous nature got in the way, however, for he always volunteered to pick up the bar bill when he was out with friends.

Kalman's first thought every morning, when he was awakened by the piercing wails of the ship sirens in the harbor, was that he wanted to look down on Fiume from above, to glide through the air and observe the earth beneath him. His friends always laughed when he spoke of his dreams. They found them preposterous, wild fancies that obsessed him and made him lose his grip on reality, and they maintained that his prospects of ever flying were virtually zero. It would be smarter of him, they said, to give up the hope of conquering the skies and instead to devote himself with all his energy to assuring himself a brilliant maritime career. Whenever they pitied him for his unrealistic dreams, he merely raised an eyebrow as if hearing a lame joke. He replied emphatically that he had no doubts. He was as certain his destiny was tied to that of the celebrated Louis Blériot as he was that the sun would rise the next morning. He made no secret of the fact that he pitied his friends for failing to share the enthusiasm of people all over Europe for the greatest achievement of modern times, the creation of wings that enabled mankind to take flight. As for himself, he aspired to join those who dared to risk their lives for something they believed in.

One of Kalman's classmates read in the Italian-language daily *Fiume della sera* that on September 9, 1912, pilots from all of Europe would meet in Brescia for their fourth annual airshow at the airfield in Montechiari. Great feats of prowess were expected, and the principal attraction was the Frenchman Louis Blériot, who would be flying his three-seater dubbed the *Blériot XII*. The promoters were expecting thousands of attendees, some from as far away as England and America.

As soon as Kalman heard that, he decided to make his way to Brescia. He declared that he was the happiest man in Fiume and tried to persuade four of his closest friends to accompany him. He described the perilous infancy of flight, the Wright brothers, Gustave Whitehead, Clément Ader, and other daring pilots who were competing to be the first to craft a fully perfected motor-driven airplane. His companions listened with interest. They were concerned, however, that the hotels and private apartments in Brescia might not be able to accommodate all the visitors, and prices would shoot up. In hopes of recruiting company for his trip, Kalman promised he would help pay for lodging. That was the determining factor that enticed two of his friends to declare their willingness to go with him. All three applied for a week's leave from the Maritime Academy. When permission was denied, the two friends dropped out of his project. This was an unpleasant surprise for Kalman. Disappointed, he climbed aboard the train all alone the next morning.

Flight Lessons

IF THE PATHS of fate were not inexplicable, so that none of us can actually see his destination but is permitted only an intuition of it, Kalman probably would have turned around as soon as he got to Brescia, even though it was already late in the evening. He was about to take a carriage to the hotel. The coachman demanded two lire, paid in advance. Kalman discovered at that moment that someone on the train had picked his pocket, extracting his wallet and travel documents from his jacket as he stood there blissfully unaware. Everything had disappeared. But he was not about to lose the chance to see Blériot fly, even though it meant he would have to sleep on a bench in one of the city parks and go without food for several days.

Kalman spent the night on a park bench. He was awakened by the first beams of the sun that filtered down from behind the Basilica Duomo Nuovo. He discovered immediately that under cover of darkness someone had stolen the bag with all of his clothing that he'd been using as a pillow. He was furious. Eventually he calmed down and resolved not to let the theft spoil the great experiences awaiting him. At last he was going to see and maybe even meet his French hero.

HE HIKED for an hour and a half to get to the entrance of the famous airfield. The crowd pressed eagerly around the ticket office. Suddenly he was presented with the vision he had been dreaming of for years: For the first time in his life he saw an airplane take off, sail a hundred feet in the air, and then bank toward the grove of trees lining the right side of the airfield. The colors of the Italian flag were painted on the side of the aircraft. It occurred to Kalman that the red, white, and green stripes could just as well symbolize the Hungarian flag. He waved frantically at the airplane and yelled at the top of his lungs. He lost his balance. Never before had he felt such exhilaration. He hurried toward the broad gates as the airplane disappeared toward the horizon. A great mass of humanity was packed there. The men elbowed him and gabbled in foreign languages. When he finally reached the entry, a guard stopped him and demanded his ticket. Entry to the airfield cost five lire. He cursed the bastard who had stolen his wallet, but that did him no good. He couldn't buy a ticket for the simple reason that his pockets were empty.

He refused to lose heart, however, and decided there was no need to waste time just standing there. Still outside the enclosure, he began to work his way along the dark fence around the airfield. He had the idea that he might eventually get close to the hangars that way and get a look at the flying machines. After a few minutes of this, he glimpsed signs with the names of the aviators participating in the air show: Calderare, Curtiss, Pégoud, Voisin, Douhet, Fokker, Rusjan, Moore-Brabazon. The machines were positioned in the hangar behind drawn curtains. He sighed in relief when he caught sight of the name on the last sign: Blériot. Kalman arrived not a second too soon. An assistant pulled back the curtain and Kalman saw Blériot about to climb into the gold-colored airplane. He saw one mechanic bending over the engine and another stepping forward to grasp the single blade of the propeller. Not far away, three more mechanics stood watching the pilot, wide-eyed and alert. Blériot positioned himself to his satisfaction and then signaled the mechanic to turn the propeller. The motor caught on the third try, and the propeller began to spin. Kalman's ears seemed to catch the draft from the whirling propeller. Blériot's plane slowly rolled out of the hangar and disappeared behind a wooden hut in the direction of the airfield. Kalman could no longer see it, but a few minutes later the Frenchman's plane appeared in the air. It climbed to about a hundred feet and buzzed in a wide circle over the stands, greeted by the joyous shouts of the crowd. Blériot flew out over the field, banked away toward the wooded area, and turned in a lazy circle back toward the airfield. In the course of the following thirty-eight minutes he made four of these circuits. On the fifth tour, out of the sight of the crowd in the stands, the machine began to lose altitude on its approach to the hangars. Kalman stood craning his neck and saw the plane approaching at an altitude of scarcely thirty feet. Dazzled by the sun, he didn't see Blériot's airplane lose its right wheel just before it flew overhead. A second later Kalman was sprawled on the ground, his head crushed.

The winner of the Brescia 1912 grand prize, worth five thousand lire, completed seven circuits and flew a total of seventy-five kilometers in sixty-three minutes and eleven seconds. Louis Blériot received the most enthusiastic applause of all the aviators and was hailed as a hero, less for his expected victory than for the fact, discovered only after he had landed and come to a stop before the grandstand, that his plane had lost its right wheel. The Frenchman's perfect landing was regarded as an enormous achievement. No one except Blériot knew where the wheel had fallen.

That afternoon some people walking through the area behind the hangars discovered a young man lying in a pool of blood. They notified the police, who blocked off the area and hustled away the few curious onlookers. A physician soon arrived on the scene and determined that the man, between twenty-two and twenty-five years of age with healthy teeth and an enormous nose, had been killed by an airplane wheel that lay about ten feet away. The doctor closed the eyes of the dead man with the tip of his index finger; they'd obviously been open wide at the moment of his sudden death. The police found it impossible to determine the man's identity because he was carrying no documents. The only clue they discovered was a label discreetly sewn into his jacket and trousers: Elemér Polgár's Tailoring for Gentlemen, Váci Street, Budapest.

Commissioner Bussoli

LATE THAT EVENING the Brescia police commissioner, Enrico Bussoli, interviewed Louis Blériot about the accident with the lost wheel. The pilot expressed his regret at the death of the young man and said that the tragic event, due to an unforeseeable mechanical failure neither he nor his assistants could be blamed for, had occurred at a most unfortunate time for him and the French nation. His enterprise, Blériot Aéronautique, had a signed contract with the military of his homeland for no fewer than 125 flying machines of the same model. He was concerned that the fatal accident had the potential to call the deal into question or block it entirely, significantly prejudicing France's vital air defense. He looked deep into Bussoli's eyes and said quietly, almost in a whisper, that since the victim was a foreigner of unknown identity, perhaps an individual with a criminal history although, granted, he had apparently done nothing illegal—but considering that he was lurking around the hangars where he had no business to be, one could assume that he was up to no good—and since no one had reported him missing, perhaps the best thing to do instead of engaging in long months of fruitless investigation would be to take the case out of the files and quietly lose the documents somewhere in the back of the commissioner's desk drawers. This would certainly lighten the work load of the Lombardy police force and free them to devote themselves to solving crimes more serious than an innocent accident caused by a screw shaken loose by the vibration of the airframe. The police commissioner's face took on a thoughtful look. Blériot indicated after a short pause that he was quite ready to compensate Signor Bussoli generously for his cooperation. Demonstrating Italy's renowned hospitality, the police commissioner accepted the Frenchman's suggestion and promised to put an end to all journalistic inquiries concerning the identity of the unknown victim. The gentlemen shook hands on the deal and went off to a nearby trattoria to discuss the details over a couple of glasses of grappa.

Three days later, since no one had reported the dead man as missing, the body was transferred by night to the Cimitero Vantiniano and placed in an unmarked grave. Kalman received neither burial rites nor gravestone.

His worried friends met at Feral, Kalman's favorite tavern. Two weeks had gone by since he left and none of them had heard anything from him. This was unlike Kalman. Perhaps he had gotten a job with Blériot. Or met a woman. Maybe he had fallen ill. What should they do? The teachers had begun to ask after Kalman. After a long discussion and a fair number of bottles of the local Riesling, they decided to call on the rector the following day and tell him Kalman had gone to Brescia.

In mid-October Bernhard received an official letter with the elegant emblem of the Hungarian Royal Maritime Academy in the upper left corner of the envelope. Suspecting nothing, he opened the letter and was surprised to see the rector's signature. He carefully read the short text informing him that Kalman had been absent from classes for more than a month without permission. The official of the Maritime Academy responsible for discipline had decided in accordance with the prevailing statutes of the royal institution to dismiss Kalman, effective immediately. The decision was final and without recourse to appeal.

The letter astonished Bernhard. He thought it over and realized that in fact he had heard nothing from his youngest son since early September. Something must have happened. He began to suspect something was amiss and decided to go to Fiume.

His stay was brief; he remained for only two days. Neither his visit to Kalman's landlady nor his meeting with the rector of the Maritime Academy gave him any clue about his son's activities in recent months. He got a bit more out of Kalman's friends. They were obviously distressed. One chewed on his lower lip and another wrung his hands as they recounted the discussions preceding Kalman's trip to see the air show. Bernhard went to the police station to report his son as missing before he took the train to Brescia.

In Brescia he had a long discussion at the hotel where Kalman was supposed to have stayed, but nothing indicated that the young man had ever arrived. He questioned the employees of all the hotels and trattorias in the center of the city and heard the same thing, the story he would hear many more times: No one could recall having seen or met Kalman. Nor did his call upon the police turn anything up. Commissioner Bussoli proved to be the very soul of friendliness and told him with elaborate courtesy that tens of thousands of people had visited the September air show, a well-run affair staged without incident. He suggested that an ardent young fellow, as he imagined Kalman to be, might well have been struck by Cupid's arrow while sitting on the train sitting opposite some dark beauty. Perhaps he had followed a signorina off the train and was now, heedless of the rest of the world, enjoying his conquest. Bussoli predicted that the prodigal son would turn up any day now. His father could look forward to an affectionate reunion.

The police commissioner's theory that Kalman had simply fallen in love and lost his head sounded suspiciously pat and didn't reassure Bernhard. Not at all. Bussoli's spiel left a bitter taste in his mouth. Nathan had rushed away from home in anger and turned his back on his family because of a housemaid. But Kalman was not like his brother; he would never vanish without a word.

Cenotaph

DURING THE YEAR after Kalman's disappearance, Bernhard never gave up hope of locating him. He left no stone unturned and pulled every string available to him, but all in vain. The search for his son took up most of his time, and he aged prematurely; the dynamic newspaperman became a tired old man. He wrote almost nothing for *Pester Lloyd* anymore and found it increasingly difficult to keep up with contemporary events. He completely lost his earlier fascination for the obscure intrigues of society and the politics of the double monarchy, although growing nationalistic sentiment and insistent demands for secession made these more disquieting than ever. Becoming openly sentimental, something no one could have accused him of before, he sank into deep melancholy. He felt helpless, and it pained him beyond measure that he had lost contact with all of his children. The last he had heard of his black-sheep eldest son, Moricz, was that the young man was somewhere on the other side of the Atlantic, wanted by the Chicago police for serious fraud. Nathan was studying mathematics at the university in the German city of Erlangen, that much he knew, but all of the many, many letters he had sent to Nathan were returned unopened. As for Kalman, Bernhard felt a suppressed but distinct anxiety that he would never see him again.

Bernhard opened Benjamin's book, *The Elixir of Immortality*, in search of consolation. He had read it many times, but he'd always skipped over certain passages. He'd never found any reason to study the chapter on the history of the family that described a succession of future events the philosopher had sketched out in fragmentary fashion several

hundred years before. During his sleepless nights Bernhard
heard those voices from the past, the murmuring of his
forefathers and their sighs of disappointment at life's cruel-
ties. Only now did he realize what a rich treasure of love,
devotion, belief in God, and human dignity he had lost by
turning away from his family and its past, neglecting the
world that had meant everything to the Spinozas.

Benjamin writes of a noble author so intent on improving
the world that he completely forgets his family. Bernhard
was pained to recognize himself in that passage. For a time
he tried to make sense of the mixing of the blue blood of
the Biederstern princes and the blood of Arabella Braun;
he even turned to the study of Gregor Mendel's research on
genetics, a fascinating subject, because he wanted to find a
way to convince himself there might be some other explanation for the loss of his sons. It was no use; he was forced
to conclude that although inheritance is a significant factor,
neither chance nor events at birth or in childhood, nor even
developments in society at large, played more of a role in
shaping the relationships between him and his sons than
his own shortcomings and absence from their lives.

Benjamin's chapter on the schools of thought of the
ancient Greeks and their customs contains a passage that
haunted him:

> The ancient Greeks had a custom that merits our at-
> tention: for those who perished in fire, those engulfed by
> volcanoes, and those buried by lava, those torn apart by
> wild beasts or devoured by sharks, the populace of their
> native city would construct what they called cenotaphs
> or empty graves. For bodies are fire, water, or earth and
> the spirit is Alpha and Omega; these are the things for
> which one should erect a memorial.

One year to the day after Kalman had boarded the train in Fiume on his way to Brescia, Bernhard had a stone placed over the empty grave he had acquired in the Jewish cemetery. Engraved in the stone were three words: *Kalman Spinoza—missing*. Bernhard stood next to the empty grave for a long time, totally alone, his hands clenched, struggling to contain his tears.

I am the last of the Spinozas. Our lineage could very well have escaped dying out, but I have put no child into this world. I've never had any woman, not from a lack of interest in the opposite sex but because I've never been able to love anyone truthfully and sincerely. I'm lying in a hospital in Oslo, my body is riven with cancer, and soon the long saga of our family will reach its well-deserved end. Now, at the very end of my life, these memories come crowding forth. All the memories I thought had faded, slipped away, and disappeared in time have invigorated themselves; they live their own lives and the past comes burgeoning forth, our past so charged with meaning. I am devoting all the time and energy left to me to the attempt to keep previous generations from disappearing without a trace. I write down everything that comes into my head. It may be that these words of mine will serve as a cenotaph, an empty grave for the Spinoza line. Our bodies are perishable but our souls emerge suddenly from eternity, and I'm trying to raise a memorial over them.

Revenge in Vienna

ONE PASSOVER EVENING when Nathan asked why they'd never had a family reunion, Bernhard told his sons that their aunt was married to a dull-witted Catholic peasant of no interest to anyone, and their uncle living in a grand palace in Vienna had deceived his siblings and made off with the fortune left by their grandfather. This was a clear demonstration of Nikolaus's wickedness and the reason Bernhard wanted nothing to do with him; this was why the children had almost never met their relatives.

The memory of that remark came unsought to Nathan as he stood outside the door just after he had seen his father plunging himself into Marika. He didn't think twice. He decided to go to Vienna—not to visit his aunt in the countryside but instead to look up his uncle. For the time being he simply couldn't think of any better way to revenge himself on his father than to ask Nikolaus for financial help to establish his own independence.

Nikolaus received Nathan at once and embraced him with delight. He stood there for a time, looking at him, examining and noting similarities and differences. He said that it had grieved him all these years not to be allowed to get to know his nephews. He wished nothing better than to change the situation and reunite the family. Nathan felt unexpected relief at the warm welcome. A smile, the first smile since he came upon his father with Marika, appeared on his face. Nikolaus conducted him to an elegantly furnished salon and offered him a glass of dry sherry. As they sipped the amontillado he commented that in his opinion Bernhard had gone much too far when he cut all contact with him because of an unfortunate misunderstanding. Nikolaus said he was certain that Nathan was a reasonable young man capable of working out the difference between what he'd been told and what he could see with his own eyes. Nikolaus was pleased that the son of his favorite brother had come to him and now they could get to know each other.

Nathan stayed in Vienna with his uncle throughout the summer. Those five months were the happiest time of his youth. Nikolaus's family lived a completely different life from that he'd known in Budapest. They were incredibly wealthy, of course, and they lived like royalty. They had tennis courts and swimming pools; they went skiing in the Alps in the winter and sailing in the Mediterranean in the summer; they traveled regularly to Paris to shop for clothes; and several times a week they hosted superbly prepared dinners for prominent guests. They had great expectations of their lives and great demands. All this quite bedazzled Nathan at first, but before long he became part of it, oiling and parting his hair, dressing himself in tailored suits, appreciating and enjoying their dolce vita. Nikolaus spoiled him with expensive presents, including the gold Doxa pocket watch we boys later dreamed of inheriting one day, and took him to fashionable salons where Nathan was introduced to young beauties from aristocratic families. That spectacular world gave him a lifelong taste for elegance and fine clothing. He got along famously with the ruling class that his father had criticized in his articles for years. He considered his uncle a great man, nothing like the malicious portrait drawn by his father. Four decades later when he was in the process of rotting away in a communist jail, he blushed at the thought of how blind he'd been. It was many years before he understood the reason for the exaggerated generosity of his shameless, duplicitous paternal uncle.

Mathematics in Erlangen

IN AUTUMN Nathan returned to his study of mathematics, although not in Budapest. He didn't want to go back there.

His last memory of Eötvös Loránd University was Emanuel Lasker's lecture, and he remembered the grand master's passing comment that the most important mathematical research in Germany was being done by a young woman in Erlangen. Nathan had stupidly forgotten her name. But he had no desire to start something new, so he applied to the mathematics faculty of the university in that idyllic setting in a small town in northern Bavaria.

Emmy Noether—Nathan had never met anyone like that young Jewish woman. The daughter of a well-known mathematician, she was only a few years older than he was. At that time women generally did not have access to advanced studies, but she managed to write a groundbreaking doctoral thesis only shortly after her twenty-fifth birthday. Albert Einstein was among those who later praised her achievements, for he relied heavily on Emmy's analysis while working out his general theory of relativity. Researchers in particle physics considered her divinely gifted, and in the world of mathematics she was seen as one of the most promising talents to emerge in decades.

Many years later as Nathan looked back over his life, he commented that if Emmy hadn't been heedless of her appearance and so unattractive—nearsighted, big-nosed, with a flat chest and a high forehead—he would certainly have fallen in love with her. Already at their first meeting he sensed the immense power she radiated, a power that intimidated opponents of feminine attendance at the university and made older professors quake in her presence. But the students treasured the lectures that she delivered for seven years without pay because women were officially barred from teaching at German universities.

Emmy and Nathan were not meant for each other, but they established a friendship that grew ever deeper as time passed. During their three years of collaboration on the analysis of algebraic invariants, he often turned to her in hopes of finding guidance in all sorts of important matters, for he was convinced that she knew how to deal with almost anything. Mathematics was holy for Emmy, and she recognized that she was devoting her life to its research. She once told Nathan she'd thought of teaching languages before she discovered that the logical world of mathematics stood wide open to her. She could enter it anytime to rummage around and put things in impeccable order, while the rest of life was marred by chaos, governed by chance, and, in particular, ruled by men. She knew that as a woman she had absolutely no influence over them. Truth has a face, she said, but it has nothing in common with the reality that we human beings in our blundering errors see around us; truth has to be searched out in the structure of the world. She did not make any secret of her contempt for money or her antipathy for the reactionary Bavarian upper class with its deep disdain for women, Jews, homosexuals, and workers. Emmy had a deep abiding faith in the future, even though she was aware that a very long time would have to pass before the individual realized that his egotism must be subordinated to the welfare of collective society. Her views had a lasting impression on Nathan.

In Budapest Once Again

ONE DAY HE RECEIVED a letter from the legal offices of Gottfried & Gottlieb in Budapest. They informed Nathan that his father, Bernhard Spinoza, had succumbed to a heart attack and he was to contact the executor of the estate as soon as possible, preferably in person. Nathan had no feeling of loss; if anything, he was indifferent. He tried to imagine the death of his father. All he could see was the man's erect penis plunging into Marika's sex, and all he could hear was her inciting him with an excited voice, "Continue. More. I'm yours. Do with me what you will." He had a vision in which his father, sweating and panting as he stood up, squealed in pain, grabbed his chest, and collapsed headlong over Marika's naked body.

The attorney, Géza Gottlieb, told Nathan that a neighbor had found his father lying in the staircase between the fourth and fifth floors. The elevator had been out of order all day, and tenants had been advised to use the stairs. This had obviously been too stressful for him, and his heart could not take it. He was conscious the whole time. As he was being transported to the nearest hospital, he complained of chest pains. An experienced physician examined him and was preparing an injection. Just then Bernhard began bellowing in excitement, his face turned white, he gasped for breath, and he suffered a heart attack. Five minutes later he was dead.

Since Bernhard had not left a will and Nathan was the only one of the sons the attorney as executor of the estate had managed to contact, he was deemed to be the principal heir and was therefore entitled to take possession of the household, all the movable property, and the contents of the deceased's bank accounts.

Nathan was aware of the existence of *The Elixir of Immortality*. His elder brother had told him of it some years earlier. They'd met at the Café Gerbeaud at Moricz's suggestion. Nathan hadn't seen his brother for a long time and was confused when Moricz didn't come alone but instead arrived in the company of an Austrian acquaintance, someone he'd recently met through their cousin Mathäus Frombichler. The man's name was Adi and he had an odd, chilly air about him. Nathan instinctively distrusted him. Moricz recapitulated briefly for him what he'd been up to in recent years. Nathan was surprised at the changes in Moricz. His charm had utterly disappeared, as had his inimitable, captivating volubility. He showed no interest in Nathan's life and doings. He said he'd lived in Chicago for a while, but because the FBI had a warrant for his arrest in connection with a few minor oversights, he'd found it advisible to leave the United States. He'd been working as a Presbyterian missionary in Toronto when the Canadian immigration authorities had gotten on his case and made his life unbearable. So he came back to Europe. Of course Nathan understood that his brother hadn't been involved in innocent fun and games in North America, but he said nothing; he simply smiled to himself. For the time being Moricz was living in Vienna. There through the good offices of Frombichler the news of his father's death a few years earlier had come to his attention. He told Nathan about Benjamin's book, suddenly becoming much more animated—how he had come across it by chance many years earlier, hidden in a secret drawer on the bottom right side of their father's desk. He said that the book, which existed only in that single copy, contained many prophecies and wisdom older than time, all of it incomprehensible to him, along with the history of the family. According to tradition, he said, stressing each word, it was handed down through the family to the eldest son of each generation. He'd come to Budapest to claim it, since it belonged to him now. Adi and he were planning to sell the book to some German aristocrat with a lot of money and secret Jewish origins. Nathan sat there depressed by all this as the other two discussed how much money the treasure might fetch. Moricz was almost beside himself with the happy anticipation of collecting more than a hundred thousand marks if they—as Adi expressed it—had luck on their side and got the right sort of collector on the hook. Nathan realized that he must at any cost keep *The Elixir of Immortality* from winding up in the hands of his erratic brother and Moricz's unpleasant friend. He told Moricz to come pick up the book at his house the following day at lunchtime. He bowed his head and studied his fingernails as he waited for their reaction. Naturally he was relieved when his brother accepted the offer without question and didn't insist on setting off to collect the book right away. Nathan excused himself with the pretext that he had a doctor's appointment, which was in fact a little white lie. He got up and quickly went home to locate the book and put it some secure place.

WHEN I WAKE UP early in the morning, most of the time just before dawn, I feel myself getting weaker, and I sense that my time is running out. In my darkest hours I tell myself that I won't be able to finish what I've started here. That is a terrible thought, but hardly unexpected, for I've failed at everything I've ever undertaken. I'm pleading now with whatever powers may exist not to let me fail this last time. The fingers of my left hand have been paralyzed since the morning of the day before yesterday, because now the tumors have attacked that arm. I still have a functioning right index finger, however, that I can stretch out to snare and reel in all the loose threads of this tattered fabric.

MORICZ AND ADI were white with rage when they discovered that the hidden compartment in the desk was empty. Moricz shouted that Nathan was the mangy dog who'd stolen the book, and Adi threatened him with a pistol. Nathan's heart contracted with terror as he entreated Adi to put away his weapon and assured them that he'd never heard a word about the book, much less seen it. He suggested that they search the apartment, since it was inconceivable that their father would have removed it. Moricz and Adi needed no encouragement. They set to work at once, methodically examining everything in the house, opening every cabinet, pulling out drawers and dumping the contents on the floor. Over the course of six hours they thoroughly searched every nook and cranny, turned every room upside down, and intently went through every single book on every shelf, all without finding *The Elixir of Immortality*. Both were dizzy with fatigue. Nathan asked for help in putting the apartment back together, and Moricz burst out in a resounding roar of laughter, turned toward Adi, and brayed, "Didn't I warn you my brother was a comedian?" They left the apartment, vowing to come back the next day at the same time. Nathan slept fitfully that night and woke with a jerk at about three in the morning, soaked in sweat, with the sensation that an iron hand was squeezing his heart. When they next appeared, Adi carried himself in an aggressively threatening manner, waved his pistol several more times, and made a solemn vow to come back to Budapest some day, if necessary with a whole army of men ready to work themselves to death to find the Jew book. Moricz was swearing in Hungarian and German and cursing their father. Nathan was at a loss afterward to understand how he had managed to find the strength to conceal the book and not give himself away.

Socialism and Jove Boats

IT WOULD BE NO EXAGGERATION to say that Moricz's behavior stimulated Nathan to study *The Elixir of Immortality* in depth. The book's magical world, its subtleties, its brilliantly ingenious analysis, its beautiful use of language, and, not least, the epic adventure described in it all made a profound impression on him. As he read the history of his lineage, his heart swelled with pride that for centuries and centuries his family name had been borne by men significant in the evolution of Europe, even though they were unaware at the time that they constituted a relatively important part of God's great plan. He still frowned sometimes in disappointment at the book's failure to offer a clear account of how his ancestors felt and reacted and how they were affected by their pleasures and joys, the closeness of families and communities, duties and achievements, dreams and dashed hopes, in all their terrible vulnerability. Nathan wanted guidance for a world marked by the triumphs of violence: trenches on battlefields, grenades, poison-gas attacks, strife of man against man, suffering, and death. Books were of little value to him unless they served as signposts pointing toward the future and describing the new era awaiting humanity after the great wars ended. As he read Benjamin's book, he realized that the Spinozas had always valued the past above everything else. And the more he thought about it, the clearer it became to him that the future—not just his own future but that of everyone else—was far more important. He asked himself what could bring the greatest good to the greatest number. Peace, social justice, technological progress, and respect for human dignity were all part of the answer. His reflections led him to the form of society that offered the masses the promise and hope of all of those: socialism.

It would take many years for him to realize that the truth was a little more complicated than that.

While the war with its voracious appetite devoured millions of young men on its fronts, Nathan sat safe and sound in Budapest within the walls of his childhood home and found himself terribly bored in his isolation. Since the collapse of the empire of the czar in February 1917, he had been hoping that the Bolsheviks would storm onto the scene of history and lead the people to decisive victory. But not until November did the guns of the battle cruiser *Aurora* boom out over Petrograd with the message that the time had come for Lenin's Soviets to take power in the land. Nathan began to imagine thrilling developments: The events in the East would be the spark that set all of Europe and especially Hungary blazing with the prairie fires of revolution. But more than that—most of all—he was dreaming of something else entirely, for when he woke up in the morning he had nobody to wish him good morning and when he went to bed at night there was no one to kiss him good night. He dreamed of a woman to share his lonely days.

The people called them "love boats," with just a touch of irony, and they were immensely popular at the end of the war and during the years that followed. The cruises went out on Sundays, north toward the picturesque villages of Szentendre, Visegrád, and Esztergom, and when the weather was good, these pleasure trips offered beautiful views of Budapest and its leafy environs. Most of those on these boat trips were returned soldiers and young women who had lost fiancés in the war. Most of them bought their tickets not in search of love, the true opium of the people, but in the hope of whatever pleasure they could find. Chance encounters brought together the son of a professor and a scrubwoman's daughter, a devout Catholic welder and a Protestant flower girl, a young man of the lesser nobility who had lost his arm at the Italian front and a nearsighted converted Jewess. And Nathan and Sara. But I suspect that Grandfather and Grandmother realized from the very first instant—he with delight and she with sorrow—that despite their differences and their contrary views of the world, they were meant for each other.

A Normal Life

AS A CHILD I loved to play with my grandmother's sewing machine, an imposing construction of enameled wrought iron that stood in the bedroom Sasha and I shared with her after Grandfather died. As often as I could, I would run my fingertips over the plaque on the upper side where the manufacturer's name was engraved in elegant letters: Singer. It was framed by the manufacturer's golden yellow trademark and the plaque looked like a centuries-old coat of arms. I would also touch the shining vertical axles of the head assembly and drive wheel, forged of tempered steel. Most of all, I loved to press down the pedal, stamped out of sheet metal. This set the sewing machine in motion, thanks to a pulley that fit into a groove on the drive wheel and emitted a sound like that of a buzzing bumblebee. Once I was just about to break the needle because I'd been inspired to place a little piece of wood beneath the cylinder holding the sewing mechanism. At exactly that moment Grandmother happened to step into the bedroom. She gave me a resounding slap on the side of the head and shouted, "Isn't anything sacred around here? Can't I at least have my sewing machine to myself? Do you have to destroy the only thing I've ever owned in my life?"

The long-awaited day of Nathan's release from thirty-six months of prison in Vác and his return home ended in a battle royal. The fact is that he found to his dismay that, without informing him, Sara had allowed her mother to move into the apartment. Miriam sat there in the kitchen, white-haired and toothless. Nathan disliked her deeply. In his eyes she represented everything unchanging and backward in the world of the Jews. A humble market woman, she had sat behind her rickety vegetable stall in the market for the poor folk, and even after living in Budapest for twenty-five years she could hardly speak a word of Hungarian. The notion of sheltering her within the walls of his home was completely unacceptable to him. Sara tried to persuade him. She explained that her mother was ill, growing weaker by the day, and could no longer take her place in the market. She couldn't even pick up an apple with her frostbitten hands, twisted as they were with rheumatism. To make things worse, Aunt Luiza, who had worked like a slave all her life taking care of five children and a senile mother with no help from anyone, had suffered a stroke; since she was behind in the payment of her rent, the heartless landlord had thrown them all out onto the street. Aunt Luiza and her mother, Erzsi, were living with a neighbor for the time being. The poor women were subsisting on their pickings from the garbage and were close to dying of hunger. They had given up hope. Their misery beggared all description. Sara told him her mother had nowhere else to go. She needed a roof over her head. Turning her away was unthinkable. She also told him that she'd purchased a Singer sewing machine on credit and was trying to earn a little extra money by taking work from the dress shop home overnight to do late in the evenings. In the interim she was providing Luiza with food and an occasional coin or two. But since they were desperate, she intended, if Nathan would only agree, to let those two women move in with them. She feared that otherwise they would simply perish. Nathan threw a fit. He shouted that no one could expect him to feel any sympathy for those old women; he refused to have them hanging around his neck. All he wanted was a normal life with his wife, and he had no desire to have to feed three old mouths. Mother Miriam's eyes were full of tears. She stood there with her shoulders hunched and replied in Yiddish that she had no intention of remaining for one second in the same house with her son-in-law, a Jew without a shred of decency in his body, who refused to offer a helpless old woman a minimum of consideration and a scrap of bread. This provoked Nathan even more, although he didn't understand everything she was saying. He began shouting again, in transports of rage. Sara begged him to lower his voice so as not to awaken their little son, who lay sleeping by the oven. But he paid no attention to her. So she reared back and gave him as good as she got. The huge quarrel went on for more than an hour. Nathan's emotion eventually subsided and he finally gave in. Miriam could stay. As for Luiza and Erzsi, he needed a few days to think it over. He said that he felt very tired and suggested that they all go to bed. He was hoping that in the matrimonial bed Sara would become more tractable beneath his experienced hands.

Sara provided for her family with her job as a seamstress in a boutique where affluent ladies had their clothes made. It was in the center of the city, and she walked there every workday, all year around. It took her two hours to get to the shop and just as long to come home. By walking she saved the cost of tram fare, enough to keep the three old women alive. Only every fourth Sunday was she spared from leaving home at five in the morning and returning at seven in the evening. That was always the shortest day of the month, for it was devoted to cleaning, laundry, cooking, and sleeping. But Sara never complained. She considered that it would do no good. In any case, she had no time to think of herself because she was constantly busy with the needs of others. Five times in the course of as many years she became pregnant, however, even though Nathan was almost never home, and most of the time he was depositing his semen in the bellies of other women. With her five pregnancies she gave birth to two children who were healthy and survived, Carlo and Ilona.

After his time in prison Nathan found it hard to go back to ordinary life. The considerable inheritance from his father was long gone. He had no job, and it wasn't easy for an ex-convict to get work, especially if he'd been closely associated with the Republic of the Councils. He had his own family now and wanted to keep them out of the gutter, so he went on a long round of knocking on doors. His past followed him doggedly. Besides, the times were hard; not for nothing was Hungary called the land of three million beggars.

A Great Privilege

SÁNDOR FÜRST AND IMRE SALLAI were executed in Budapest on July 29, 1932. They had been sentenced to death two weeks earlier after a summary trial, charged with plotting the attack at Biatorbágy, the sleepy little village some twenty miles west of Budapest where the Vienna Express had been dynamited the previous year and twenty-two people died. Everyone knew the truth: Fürst and Sallai were innocent. They had watertight alibis. The perpetrator, Szilveszter Matuska, had confessed his odious crime; he'd even boasted about it. Huge protests were organized in many parts of the world, demanding that the two men be freed. All for nothing. The Horthy regime was absolutely determined to make an example by sending Jewish communist leaders Fürst and Sallai to the gallows.

It was purely by chance that Nathan, who for many years had been one of the most public faces of the Hungarian Communist Party, as it was called in those days, wasn't arrested along with Sallai and the other comrades when the police raided the secret headquarters of the banned party. Shortly before this, you see, Nathan had been infected by a venereal disease, and Sara wasn't about to put up with that indelicate affliction of her husband's. She'd learned to live with the fact that he frequented whores, but bringing home exotic illnesses was something else again. She had a fit of righteous indignation. She scolded him and swore and whacked him on the head with a frying pan. Nathan's usual placid self-confidence in crises was knocked out of him, and for once in his life he showed signs of something resembling remorse. He promised to reform and do better. Sara didn't believe him. She was certain that her obsessive whoremonger of a husband neither wanted to reform nor was capable of changing his ways. She demanded just one thing of him: to accompany her the next morning to Aunt Luiza's funeral. Nathan hadn't noticed the old woman's death, even though they'd been living under the same roof. He'd had more important things to think of. But he was relieved to hear that she was finally out of the way, so without thinking much about it, he agreed. He felt all the more relieved the following afternoon when he realized that as he'd been watching Luiza's simple wooden coffin sinking slowly into the grave, the police had been raiding the office where he usually spent his mornings and arresting all the comrades there.

Nathan's calm, impassive exterior concealed deep apprehension. He had a distinct foreboding that years of prison and
persecution lay before him. In his darkest hours he feared
for his life. He argued his case before the party leadership,
and in a lengthy discussion he offered a long list of justifica-
tions for taking refuge abroad. They concluded that the best
course was for him to emigrate to the Soviet Union. Alone,
of course, without his family. They were conferring a great
privilege upon him, since fundamental doctrine required
every communist to strive to bring about the revolution in
his own country. But Nathan was entirely too important.
He had a keen sense of what moved people, he was a brilliant analyst, and he'd mastered even the most obscure
points of Marxist doctrine, quite an unusual achievement
in party circles. They agreed that he was in great danger
of arrest, so they decided to smuggle him out of Hungary
that very night. He would wait in Berlin for a visa to the Soviet Union. Nathan was greatly relieved. At last he was on
the way to the promised land, escaping the shackles of the
bourgeois world. The implications for the future of his wife
and children were of very little concern to him.

Moscow Was No Paradise

NATHAN ARRIVED IN MOSCOW after five months in
Berlin, shortly before the long night of National Socialism
fell over Germany. He traveled in the company of eight German comrades, dedicated communists who'd lost the battle
against Hitler and were forced to flee in order to save their
skins. Six years later when Nathan at last had the good fortune of being allowed to leave the Soviet Union to return

home, not a single one of them was still alive. The revolution had devoured the best of its children, detaining them, brutally torturing them, and sending them to inhumane conditions in Siberian camps, then dispatching them with carefully aimed shots in the nape of the neck, a process very similar to that described by Chiara Luzzatto a hundred and thirty years earlier.

The first to disappear was David Goldstücker. Although originally from an affluent bourgeois Jewish family in Kopenick, he had served the proletarian revolution with his whole heart. He led an armed cell that waged many bloody battles with Nazi Brownshirts in the hot summer of 1932. They developed a warm friendship when Nathan stayed with him in Berlin, even though personal bonds between party members were considered suspect and therefore likely to be denounced as political factionalism, a mortal sin. Loyalty to the party demanded absolute obedience and an end to competing ties of friendship. Individuals could make mistakes; they could be led astray by those close to them. Not so the party. The party was infallible, and only those who believed blindly in the party as the perfect manifestation of revolutionary ideals in world history could be given the responsibilities of leadership. Nathan and Goldstücker did not give a damn for any of that cant. They took great pleasure in each other's company. When they were alone in private, Goldstücker was a cheerful man with a lively wit that delighted Nathan. He was also thick-skinned and phlegmatic, impervious to discouragement. His concept of the workers' paradise of the East corresponded exactly to that depicted in party propaganda. He believed that the Soviet Union was seething with eagerness and creativity, disciplined workers and enthusiastic peasants, and that a shared society was being constructed under the leadership of efficient engineers and irreproachable officials, all of whom took their inspiration from visionaries and were led by the selfless comrades of the party leadership. As soon as they reached the border, however, Goldstücker was presented with some food for thought. Grim Soviet customs officials opened all their valises and examined the contents with suspicion: every article of clothing was turned inside out, each book and piece of printed matter was laboriously examined. Nothing was neglected. Everything was inspected in detail and then tossed back into the suitcases. Everything, that is, except food, which—to judge by the hungry faces of the customs officials—wound up in their own pockets. Processing took an eternity. The train stood for a full day at the border station before it was permitted to depart for Moscow. Out on the endless Ukrainian steppes it halted countless times at ramshackle railway stations where platforms were teeming with terribly thin men offering embroidered tablecloths, icons, and jewelry in exchange for bread, and wasted women tearfully begged travelers to take their children, whose swollen bellies, sunken features, and arms and legs as thin as spaghetti made them look more dead than alive. Everyone from Berlin could see that the country that was supposed to surpass America with its current five-year plan, with goals the party leaders were promising to meet ahead of schedule, was in fact a primitive land suffering from general famine. They all saw this and understood it, but only Goldstücker had the courage to put his own conscience above the party's requirement of self-censorship. He dared to ask questions. In Moscow Nathan and the German party comrades were received by Stalin's protégé Lavrenty Beria, a stubby, bald, nearsighted man with a pince-nez. It was Beria's responsibility to receive the newcomers and help them get on their feet. The conversation with him went through interpreters because he spoke no German. At the very first meeting Goldstücker asked Beria to explain why there were so many hungry men, women, and children in the Ukraine, a place known, after all, for its flourishing agriculture. The interpreter politely discouraged him from raising that topic, but Goldstücker was not to be dissuaded. No one knew exactly how the interpreter worded his inquiry, but they all saw that Beria was displeased by it. He took off his spectacles and wiped them on his handkerchief. This was a delaying tactic, and he managed only to make the lenses even dirtier. It was clear he was in no hurry to reply. A dry rasping sound came from his throat. Eventually he overcame the temporary obstruction of his vocal cords and explained that the Ukraine, so long neglected during the rule of the czar, was undergoing a comprehensive restructuring. There were plans to construct five new steel mills to produce a full range of products, from ingots to rolled steel, a concept one had to admit was unique, considering that the United States had only one such mill, located in Cleveland. The total production of those five steel mills was calculated to grow to three million tons of rolled sheets annually. Goldstücker wasn't satisfied with the answer, but Beria adjourned the meeting before any further questions could be asked. At the next meeting, Goldstücker said he was haunted by the awful thought of all those starving in the Ukraine, so he was obliged to repeat his question. Beria explained that under the current five-year plan the construction of two enormous power stations had begun in the Ukraine, on the Bug River and on the Dnieper, and the country's largest plant for manufacturing locomotives and agricultural machinery was under construction in Dnipropetrovsk. Goldstücker didn't attend the third meeting with Beria. He didn't come the next time or the time after that, either. That's when Nathan asked Beria where the comrade from Berlin had gone. Beria replied that comrade Goldstücker had applied to travel to Donetskbackenet to attend the ceremonial opening of the Dneproges dam. Nathan asked when he would return. Beria avoided answering directly. It was cold down there in the southern Ukraine, Beria said, and comrade Goldstücker had caught a chill; he was in the hospital with an inflammation of the lungs. Not even the doctors there could predict whether he would recover. No further questions were asked. The mood became somewhat sorrowful and gloomy. David Goldstücker's name never came up again.

Moscow was no paradise; one couldn't dream one's way out of its reality. Six years of life in the Soviet Union cured Nathan of most of his illusions. But he held his tongue, even though he knew that the man who remains mute only serves evil. He felt undecided and unsettled. The dark shadow of terror lengthened within Nathan's soul at the same rhythm that Hitler built up his armies. The nearer war came, the darker were the images that haunted him. The vulnerability of the Jews in Europe, a constant preoccupation, kept him up at night. He thought of Sara and the children, whom he had essentially abandoned, and he feared for them. His own security was no better assured. Stalin's paranoia had taken over and decimated the leadership; only a handful of the comrades who'd been in the most senior party ranks were still alive. That knowledge became ever harder for him to bear. Not least because he knew that it would do no good to question decades of uninterrupted loyalty to the party. One rumor scared him to death: Béla Kun, whom he'd supported, had fallen into disgrace. Nathan knew very well what that meant. He asked permission to return immediately to Budapest to carry the fight to the enemy there.

For Different Reasons

NO ONE in our family ever wanted to talk about what had
happened during the war. Whenever Sasha and I asked
about that time, the adults bowed their heads, fixed their
eyes on the floor, and a painful silence settled over everyone. Mother and Father were especially unwilling; they
changed the subject whenever the war was mentioned.
Even my great-uncle avoided the topic—a curious complicit
silence from the man who accepted Shoshana's help from
beyond the grave to pry open not only the past but also the
hidden recesses of the human soul. Maybe they just wanted
to spare Sasha and me from the frightful things they had
experienced. For in the Torah it is said, "Let there be light,
God said, and there was light." The act of speaking of something endows it with life. We Jews are the people of the
Book, and our lives came out of the Word. So it would be
entirely reasonable to suppose that the adults in our family
were guided by the principle that speaking of something
gives it an existence denied by silence. A more likely explanation, however, is that they were trying to forget harrowing
memories. But memories resist banishment and they lived
with constant nightmares. Sometimes we were awakened
by screams in the night.

Once Grandmother told us—with a touch of enthusiasm
that surprised us, since we'd never heard a positive word
about Grandfather from her—that after his return from
Moscow, Grandfather was one of the heroes of the neighborhood. Everyone in our impoverished district knew him
and idolized him. This was extraordinary, considering that
Jews were barely tolerated in that part of Budapest. Some
folks hated us because they thought all Jews were as rich

as mountain gnomes. Others were convinced that on Fridays the Jews drank Christian blood. Some of them complained that the Jews couldn't be true Hungarians, because they always kept to themselves. Lots of envious people had a sense of cultural inferiority; they despised Jews because of the common assumption—far from true, Grandmother added—that Jews were super-talented and succeeded in everything they undertook. Her mouth twisted in a grim smile when she commented, "The people in that part of Budapest took great pleasure in denouncing their Jewish neighbors to the police, then taking a Sunday stroll down to the Danube to enjoy the matinee performance where whole families were shot in the head and dumped into the river. Then on Monday morning they took over their vacant apartments. But our neighbors never treated us that way. They hid us and protected our people even at the risk of their lives. The Gestapo was hunting your grandfather. They were determined to catch him. Not because he was a Jew, but for different reasons."

As a child one encounters so much that is beyond one's comprehension. Only now do I clearly understand what she meant by "different reasons." Our family lived within its own rigid set of principles. Some parts of this system were mystical and others were hidden, and the system was completely incomprehensible to outsiders. In the last analysis, our system was based on a covenant with God, the Creator of the universe, whose face we'd never seen and whose voice we'd never heard. The principles were extremely demanding and the penalties very severe. No Spinoza ever discussed the system; that was forbidden. But our silence was steeped in a belief in eternal life and in the sanctity of human life, because we knew that God had a great plan and we were playing an important role, and the Almighty could conceal himself in invisibility because we humans were his disciples on earth. That was the system that Hitler wanted to eliminate. That's why he was after *The Elixir of Immortality*.

Aunt Ilona

ON A DIFFERENT OCCASION shortly after Aunt Ilona died, our grandmother said she knew who had betrayed their hiding place. Father and Uncle Carlo were sent off to the labor brigades. The rest of the family—Grandmother and her mother, Miriam, Grandfather, and Aunt Ilona— went into hiding every night, always at different addresses. The family had to split up, because few people could shelter more than two outsiders overnight. One night in December 1944, Grandfather was in a safe house at 19 Rottenbiller Street. That night it happened to be his turn to take care of Miriam, but he had no desire to drag the old woman along with him. He persuaded his daughter to change places with him. A van with darkened windows pulled up in the dimly lit street at three o'clock in the morning. Several SS men, hefty fellows dressed in black and wearing armbands with skulls and swastikas, rang the doorbell at the home of Antal Gyurkovics, a humble welder who was a member of the clandestine Communist Party. When he opened the door, they shot him dead, brought out the women, and took them away in an entirely matter-of-fact and routine operation.

Miriam and Ilona wound up in Auschwitz. During the sorting process on the platform the old people were sent to the left toward the gas chambers and the younger ones were directed to the right. Ilona refused to be separated from her grandmother and held her fast in her arms. The guard wielded his baton, striking Ilona on the head and shoulders. A masculine-looking Jewish woman with whom Ilona had exchanged a few words during the trip in the overcrowded cattle car threw herself on the guard, trying to stop him. A tumult ensued. Several guards surrounded the women and beat them violently. They carried Miriam off and pitched aside the half-conscious younger women. The sorting process continued.

Her name was Eszter Heymann. Life together in the barracks made Eszter and Ilona inseparable. They shared everything, supported each other like sisters, and helped each other survive. After they returned, Ilona accused Father as if somehow it had been his fault she was sent to the death camp. She broke with the family and moved in with Eszter. The two of them opened a shop selling sewing notions. It provided a small but steady income. They were never apart, not even for a second. Neither ever felt a desire to have a husband or children. They lived together for almost twenty years. Ilona died because a routine operation went wrong, and the following day Eszter swallowed a whole bottle of sleeping tablets.

Grandfather's Refusal

AFTER THE LIBERATION it was dangerous to be seen on the streets of Budapest. Ragged drunken soldiers of the Red Army terrorized the city. Sometimes they forced people to strip naked in the street in the middle of the day and stole their clothes and everything of value. It might be disagreeable to fall victim to such uniformed thieves, but their victims were more fortunate than all those men forced into the backs of trucks and shipped in cattle cars to the Soviet Union for *malenkij robot*—"some easy work"—which in fact meant long years of forced labor in factories and camps. Soldiers broke into countless private homes under the pretext of searching for members of the fascist resistance and brazenly took away everything they could carry. They prized strong drink above everything else. One day the Russians might be moved to tears by the misery of the people and give their food rations to starving civilians; the next day they would plunder the houses of the very same people and rape even the most elderly women. Grandmother sometimes said that in a way it was just as well that her mother was sent directly to the gas chamber, since it spared her from living through liberation by the Russians.

In December 1948, two days before Hungary's communist regime was appointed, the Moscow-line party leader Mátyás Rákosi offered Grandfather the post of minister of the interior. His choice of Nathan Spinoza surprised no one. Grandfather had a solid reputation as an honorable and loyal communist. So it astonished quite a few when he stood at full attention with a bleak expression on his face and turned down the offer on the grounds of poor health. Rákosi didn't believe a word of it. He was furious. He refused to accept a "no" from anyone. He cursed and raved. He called Grandfather arrogant and conceited, though not to his face, of course. Grandfather's treachery was insignificant compared with the atrocities Rákosi had committed in the name of the Communist Party. He was a demon and a wild animal. All the comrades in the party leadership knew it. But they'd long been paralyzed by fear and weren't brave enough to do the right thing. They all knew Nathan Spinoza was as good as dead.

What made Grandfather refuse when he knew very well the personal risk he was running? Hypocrisy. Plots. Bribes. The slandering of honest men. Purification of the ranks. The knowledge that the Communist Party had the Russian occupation forces behind it but lacked the support of the people. The insight that Mátyás Rákosi, Stalin's most faithful disciple, was in the process of transforming Hungary into a miniature Soviet Union. He was well acquainted with the party's thirst for blood, and he could visualize the heaps of victims the new society would require. He refused to become the executioner. That wasn't the future he had dreamed of.

Uncle Carlo

UNCLE CARLO came back to Budapest after four years in a Soviet POW camp, so changed that he frightened the family. His body, previously thin and clumsy, had become muscular and athletic. There was something wolfish in his expression. It was clear he had been thoroughly brainwashed. There was a bitter undertone in everything he said. He fiercely hated the fascists who had sent him onto the killing fields as forced labor. He boasted that someone highly placed in the party had offered him a position with the security services. Grandfather gave his elated son a sharply skeptical look and with heavy sarcasm quoted a cryptic line from Benjamin's book: "A fish and a bird are capable of falling in love." Grandmother begged him to take a different job. Carlo replied that it was an honor to be accepted into the inner ranks and serve the party.

Carlo was proud that his first major assignment came from Mátyás Rákosi himself. He was to interrogate former foreign minister László Rajk, who as minister of the interior had forged the nation's police force into an obedient tool of the party. This loyal party member was accused of conspiracy for having collaborated with Tito and the CIA to overturn the Hungarian communist regime. He'd been deprived of sleep for several days. Now that he was properly softened up, it was time for Carlo to extract a confession. Carlo went methodically to work. He ripped off Rajk's clothes and slammed a pistol butt into the man's naked chest, shoulders, back, thighs, and genitals. Every part of the man's body had to feel and acknowledge Carlo's power as chief interrogator. He abused the foreign minister for more than two hours, then took a break and peered into Rajk's face for some indication he was willing to cooperate. Rajk remained silent, even though he didn't have much face left. Carlo stuck the barrel of the pistol into his mouth and threatened to pull the trigger. The response? None—not a word, not a gesture, not a blink. The interrogation continued. Carlo might just as well have abused the wall and told it to talk, for the result would have been the same. Rajk would not confess to any crime. Each succeeding day Carlo became more irascible at the effort required, and he intensified the torture. He was given a day off after two exhausting weeks. János Kádár took over. He was Rajk's best friend and godfather to his newborn son. Kádár explained that he was personally convinced of Rajk's innocence but the fact was that the party needed a scapegoat. For the good of the party, for communism, for the people, and not least for the welfare of his own family, Rajk had to sacrifice himself and sign a confession. That was the least one could expect of a true communist. In official terms his confession would result in a guilty verdict and severe punishment, but in reality he would be allowed to leave the country with his family the very next day to begin a new life in the Soviet Union under a new identity. Rajk was silent for a long time, so Kádár told Rajk his wife was sitting in jail suffering from milk fever and their little son was in the hands of social workers. Rajk then readily signed the confession that someone had already written out for him. He thought he'd get to see his family, but they hanged him that same night, no farewells allowed.

A year and a half went by before Carlo was again entrusted with the interrogation of a senior party official. Interior Minister János Kádár had been relieved of his post several weeks earlier "for reasons of health," but the all-powerful party leader Mátyás Rákosi told a party conclave he was still dissatisfied with the way things were going. He openly criticized both the newly appointed interior minister, Sándor Zöld, and his predecessor, Kádár. Terrified, Zöld went home, killed his wife, mother, and two small sons, and then put a bullet in his brain. Rákosi sent Kádár to Carlo. The man was of the same stuff as his late friend Rajk. Carlo pulled out all his nails and almost beat him to death, but Kádár didn't say a word. It may have been that he had nothing to confess. Or perhaps, as Grandmother maintained, Carlo was completely incompetent, as usual.

Days of Torment

THEY ARRESTED GRANDFATHER in the summer of 1951 and accused him of attempting to bribe two officials of the Department of Health and Welfare. The case was a complete fabrication. The prosecutor didn't elaborate and

presented no evidence. Grandfather had never met the officials in question and certainly had never done any business with them, so it was just as well they weren't called to
the witness stand. The judge noted for the record that my
grandfather had failed to prove his innocence and sentenced
him to eleven years in prison. The sentence was unusually
harsh, even back then. As it turned out, Grandfather spent
only six years behind bars. Dictator János Kádár pardoned
him in August 1957, his way of sending a friendly greeting
from the new party leader to an old party comrade.

Mother and Father took Grandmother and Grandfather
in hand. Or, at a minimum, they took care of the old folks
and let them live with us. One assumes that in their youth
my parents and paternal grandparents had possessed the
characteristic Jewish sense of humor, the ability to distance
oneself from troubles by making light of them, but life had
made them increasingly morose. I'd be hard put to claim we
had a happy childhood. Of course, my great-uncle brought
a note of cheer to my life and Sasha's with his tall tales and
his delight in Spinoza family history, but that didn't entirely
make up for the lack of warmth and affection.

Sasha was the apple of my parents' eyes. My mother's
nickname for me was "Ratko boy." I assumed this was a
term of endearment, and I was flattered that she never used
it for my brother. I was mistaken. Not too long ago I discovered that Anna Ratko was the Hungarian minister of health
from 1950 to 1953, and her first official act was to prohibit
abortions. It turns out that I was one of those unwanted
children born during her time in office.

Mornings of torment, days of agony. The hardest thing
is probably this fatigue that only death will cure. But I must
collect my forces and continue the story until the great final
silence descends upon me. I have to put it in words and

write as much as I can to keep away the silence, for once I stop putting my thoughts into words, my memories will wither away in my soul like a plant drying out in the desert, and our world will disappear, unnoticed by anyone.

Let's Live Dangerously

I'VE KEPT PUTTING OFF the story of my worst experience, the tragedy of my life. It happened on August 12, 1965. That was the day I lost my brother, Sasha, the boy I was closely tied to via the peculiar and mysterious kinship of twins. He died a terrible death, and it was entirely my fault.

I'll never forget that Thursday. The day was unusually warm. By nine o'clock the mercury in the thermometer outside the kitchen window was pushing toward ninety degrees. My morning had already been ruined by a quarrel with Sasha. We'd both wanted the last piece of processed cheese in the refrigerator. We adored those little triangular foil-wrapped wedges of cheese with the picture of a waving Teddy bear on the label. Sasha won the dispute. He grabbed me around the neck as I was on my way to the refrigerator and held me from behind in his iron grip. It hurt and I couldn't breathe. I was forced to give in. I was humiliated even further when he made me repeat after him that he was stronger, so he deserved to have the cheese. Sasha opened the refrigerator door and scornfully said I was a born loser. We didn't say another word during breakfast. Sasha silently lorded it over me, and I was close to tears. The physical pain of it was made worse by my feelings of misery and despair. After breakfast I went into the bedroom and sobbed my heart out.

My only thought after that was to get even. Everyone knew that Sasha was afraid of machinery. So I decided to try to lure him into going with me to the shut-down textile mill where I could lock him in the vast enclosure still filled with rusty old machines. Only a few days earlier, a couple of bigger boys persuaded me to enter the place and then called me a Jew and a heathen, a spawn of the devil. They roughed me up and kept me prisoner there for two hours. I never dared tell anyone in my family because I knew they would scold me and maybe even punish me for going into the old mill, because Father had explicitly forbidden us to go there.

Sasha accepted my proposal to go look for discarded old tools to sell to the junk man. He thought it was a fine idea, because he had been saving for a long time to buy a bicycle and needed another two hundred forints to convince the neighbor boy to sell his old bike. We set off for the decommissioned mill. Our spirits were high. We took a shortcut along the railway, which was behind a high fence. No one was allowed to enter the enclosure, a prohibition that simply pleased us all the more as we climbed the fence. I playfully suggested to Sasha that we could pretend to be Blondin, the French tightrope walker who was the first to cross Niagara Falls, as we balanced our way along the tracks. I was in the lead, showing him the way. We whistled and sang and laughed. Suddenly I heard a shriek behind me. It came from Sasha. I ignored him and just continued along my way. Sasha shouted that he'd lost his balance. I turned and saw that he'd stepped onto the ties, trying to keep from falling, but just at that moment the track mechanism shifted and trapped his foot. His shoe was clamped between two rail segments that moved to shunt traffic onto a different line. He couldn't free his foot, no matter how hard he tried. It was jammed tight. He must have been in terrific pain. He screamed again, louder. He sounded desperate. I looked up the tracks and saw a train bearing down on us at full speed. I panicked, couldn't breathe, and couldn't move. Sasha screamed and begged for help. I was only thirty feet from him but I couldn't move a muscle. My arms and legs had turned to lead. Sasha saw the train and screamed again, a heartrending shriek. The last words I heard were "Ari, save me!" The rest of his cry was drowned out by the whistle of the locomotive. The train was shunted automatically onto the other track and rushed by me, inches away. I was miraculously untouched. Nothing was left of my twin brother but his chopped-off right foot, still jammed between the tracks.

We never mentioned Sasha's death in our house. My mother and my father couldn't bear to speak of it. For a long time I couldn't remember anything at all about the accident, probably because I was in a state of shock. The strangest thing was that something happened to my voice. I tried to speak and call out, but my tongue flapped uselessly in my mouth. This terrified me. I told myself that surely my voice would come back, but it never did, no matter how many times I tried to speak.

There was an elderly man who lived on our street. People said that he was born deaf and mute. I was always scared of him because he looked so bizarre with his comical grimaces and the insistent gestures he tried to use to compensate for the voice he lacked. I vowed I would never do that. When I wanted to communicate, I wrote whatever it was on a scrap of paper. I worked for years to improve my handwriting and produce beautifully legible script. My own nervous scribblings had always been as illegible as bird scratchings.

One morning many months later, as I reached into the fridge and picked up a wedge of processed cheese in its foil wrapping with the label showing the waving Teddy, words echoed in my ears: *Let's live dangerously.* I sat down at the kitchen table and suddenly the memory of it was crystal clear. That was the last thing I'd said to Sasha as we set off to balance our way along the tracks. That little piece of soft cheese brought back the memory of everything that had happened on that terrible Thursday. It had sunk deep into my consciousness and hidden itself.

Sasha, let's be Blondin, king of the air. Nothing can stop us. Let's live dangerously!

Were those the last words I would say in my life? Did my voice extinguish itself after I called them out to my twin brother?

I realized in that moment that there must have been some reason for me to lose the power of speech. Some higher unknown power had decreed my fate. My crime of enticing my brother to his death had called down upon my head the wrath of God or some other power and inflicted on me this awful punishment. Because he who causes the death of his closest relation is doomed to eternal isolation.

A Norwegian Acquaintance

LATE ONE EVENING two years after Sasha's death, Father told us that we were going to Oslo. I couldn't believe it. We were living in a police state and borders were tightly sealed. I'd never heard of anyone receiving permission to travel to the West as a tourist.

Why on earth would we be going to Norway?

My father explained that a Norwegian acquaintance had invited us to visit and was covering all the costs. The paperwork had already been approved. Mother knew and smiled in satisfaction, while my grandmother and I peered suspiciously at my father. We'd never ever heard him mention any acquaintance in Norway. Father put passports with visas and tickets onto the table in front of us. Everything was properly stamped. All we had to do was get on the train that would be leaving early the next morning. Grandmother grew agitated, not because she was staying behind but because no one had informed her this was being planned.

It wasn't hard to guess why my father kept it quiet. He wanted to keep Grandmother from gossiping about our plans all around the neighborhood. There was too high a risk that some envious neighbor would try to interfere. Back then it was enough for someone just to whisper that you wanted to get out of Hungary for the police to revoke your permit and block the trip.

We packed that night. Father admonished Mother and me to travel as light as possible so as not to arouse the suspicions of the police. I didn't understand exactly what he meant. But I noticed that he was planning to carry with him the little suitcase I had inherited from Grandfather.

The next morning we said goodbye to Grandmother. She wasn't unhappy to see us go, as far as I could make out. She told my father and mother she understood why they wanted to leave the country. The communists had left everything in ruins. She gave me a kiss on the forehead, something quite unusual for her. "You'll have to learn to speak Norwegian," she told me emphatically.

A well-dressed gentleman met us at the railway station in Oslo. I couldn't believe my eyes. The resemblance was uncanny. If it hadn't been for the enormous nose of the elegant Norwegian, I'd have sworn that Grandfather had come back from the dead to welcome us. Our host was the

living image of him. He introduced himself in impeccable
German as Wilhelm Amundsen Gange. There could be
no doubt—even I could see it—that he was a very refined
gentleman. He helped us with our luggage and placed the
bags carefully in the trunk of his car. He and Father sat in
the front and carried on a lively conversation. I no longer
remember what they talked about. I had a weird feeling that
I'd met him somewhere before. The drive took only a few
minutes. He lived in a spacious apartment on the third floor
of an elegant building. It was just behind the royal castle,
which one could see through several of the windows in his
very nicely decorated residence. He pointed at the castle
and told us he worked there. He was the personal physician
of King Olav V.

My memory is failing me now. Was it the first or the
second evening that Wilhelm told us his story? Maybe it
wasn't until our third evening at dinner that he told us
that when he was small he'd wondered if his parents were
his real mother and father. Not just because he was short
and dark-haired and they were tall and blond. But because
he felt unloved, especially by his father, who sometimes
seemed to treat him as a leper or outcast. The feeling was
especially noticeable in the late 1930s when his father
was the first secretary of the Norwegian embassy in Berlin. He told his son not to visit because his appearance
wasn't Aryan enough. Wilhelm described his father as a
stern person, pompous and haughty, highly aware of his
own social standing. His mother came from a poor family
but had learned nothing about thrift during her years at the
bottom of society. She spent lavishly, which meant more
often than not that his father's ample salary was gone long
before the end of the month. That didn't appear to worry
her in the least, because her only interest was playing the

part of an elegant lady. The servants were left to take care of the household and their only child, so she could enjoy the luxury of sleeping late in the morning. Wilhelm wished he could have had smiling faces around him; he had to endure a great deal. No matter how hard he tried to please his parents, they were ill-tempered with him most of the time. They became even harder to put up with as the years passed, and he was secretly delighted by his father's professional reverses, particularly at the failed attempts to get an audience with Hitler. When Norway was occupied by Nazi Germany, Wilhelm smuggled Jews across the border to Sweden. He was certain that his German-loving father and mother with their mania for the Führer couldn't possibly be his real parents. They met a few times during the war; the atmosphere between them was always chilly. They glowered at one another across the table. His father's death shortly before the end of the war was, frankly, a relief. Now he could confront his mother with the questions about his origins. On May 7, 1945—he laughed heartily as he told us about it—both Germany and his mother surrendered, the latter only after strong pressure. She admitted that he was adopted. After Norway gained its independence, the couple had lived in Budapest where his father was a second secretary at the embassy. They'd tried for many years to have children and finally decided to adopt a newborn. His mother said they never knew the identities of the child's biological parents. Another twenty years would go by before Wilhelm discovered that she had been lying. He found his birth certificate among her papers after she died. The yellowing document named his biological mother as one Marika Óvári. The man she had reported as his father—without his knowledge or agreement—was someone named Nathan Spinoza.

Wilhelm quickly won my trust and devotion. He was something astounding and novel for me. And the exact opposite of my parents—stylish, courteous, full of zest for life, very wealthy, and astonishingly candid. He made no secret of his sexual proclivities. That was the first time anyone had spoken to me of physical love between men as if it were the most natural thing in the world. He also helped me see why the wisest thing for us would be to stay in Norway, start life over again, and make a new future for ourselves. He shared my father's view that life in the Eastern Europe of true socialism had become too precarious. Of course he'd read everything written on the subject and was astounded at the depth of my ignorance about the world around me. He explained that yet again the Jews had been made scapegoats and persecuted, this time in Poland. That type of behavior could easily spread to other socialist countries. I'd known nothing of all this.

We'd never have made it without Wilhelm. He helped my parents get a residence permit and a place to live, and he made sure that they got real jobs. He accompanied me to the session where educators considered whether I could be admitted to secondary school. They found the young mute completely unqualified. I was deeply shamed and felt like some mangy dog. After some searching, Wilhelm found an appropriate job for me.

Wilhelm was God's gift to us in our new country, but we didn't have him for long. He died in an avalanche in the Alps shortly before the following Easter. His death seemed to be a warning, a grim, tolling bell for the whole Spinoza family. We couldn't laugh anymore or take pleasure in anything. After more than eight long centuries full of grief and gladness, after undergoing so many trials and still surviving, we felt the future slipping out of our hands.

In Each Other's Arms

WE COULD ALWAYS PREDICT the mood of the woman who was our concierge in Budapest. Madame Lakatos was forever morose and contrary, and she had a surly phrase or a bitter comment for everyone who entered our building. Nothing happened in the neighborhood of my childhood without her getting involved. No one dared to say anything or complain, because we were all scared of her, even though she was tiny and frail. We knew she informed the police of everything going on in the neighborhood. Her assignment as an informant gave her the power to spew her gall all over her neighbors and any passersby.

Madame Lakatos despised everyone, with the single exception of my grandmother. I can't really explain why that was. Grandmother had a generous spirit, even if in her later days she tended not to favor her immediate family with it. She was the only person on our street who would regularly help the concierge, who had more important things to do than shop for food and clean an apartment filled with all sorts of bric-a-brac and permeated by the foul odor of bad tobacco.

Some months after our arrival in Norway we were surprised to receive a letter from Madame Lakatos. Perhaps it's rude of me to reveal it, but the concierge was only just barely literate. The letter was full of misspellings and grammar errors, written in preposterously formal language with mistaken phraseology that introduced unintentionally comic errors into the text. We would've laughed out loud if the news she was communicating hadn't been so terrible. She reported that shortly after we left the country, Grandmother had been reluctantly persuaded to allow Mr. Fernando to move into the apartment. There was nothing scandalous to this per se, the concierge stressed in her letter, since as everyone in the neighborhood knew, Madame Spinoza and Mr. Fernando had been fiancés before the First World War and had always adored each other. Rarely had anyone seen a pair so well suited. They started the day by quarreling, then they had lunch and an afternoon nap, and the sun had hardly set before they were back at their amicable bickering, right up until they went to bed, where they devoted themselves to renewing memories of old times before going to sleep. This could have gone on for many years. But one day after lunch, the concierge wrote, Madame Spinoza prepared potato soup with dumplings for dinner. Something must have distracted her, for she left the soup on the stove while they were taking their nap. Not long after they went to sleep, the soup boiled over and extinguished the flame, but the gas from the stove continued to seep into the room. Only many hours later that evening did the neighbors notice the strong odor of gas coming out of the apartment. They rang the bell, and when no one came, they called the police, who forced their way in. They turned off the gas and opened all the windows wide. The old couple was discovered in the bedroom, lying peacefully, embracing each other in bed. The all-knowing concierge reported that Fernando's lips were formed into a blissful smile.

Of course my great-uncle was smiling. He was happy that the woman he had madly adored was his—if not for life, at least in death.

TWELVE

The Heavy Smoker

An Unfilled Promise

MY MOTHER BEGGED ME just before she died to tell the world that during the war the Nazis had brutally murdered a pious young man, a certain Lipot, who along with several other young Jewish men had concealed himself in her parents' house. She wanted me to ask how God could allow such a thing. Guilt-ridden at having neglected my mother and impressed by the seriousness of the moment, I promised her that someday I would do so.

Ten years later, when the doctor told me right out that I'd been attacked by an aggressive cancer and he would have to cut out my larynx at once, I suddenly recalled the day my mother passed away. My heart began pounding and all my senses suddenly became more acute. I could see my mother on her deathbed muttering her last words and me promising that someday I would describe the isolated little universe that was our home on earth. Only at that moment did I become aware how many years had passed and realize that I hadn't fulfilled my pledge to her or done anything of any significance with my life.

I'd long been accustomed to a general feeling of dissatisfaction with my life. Bothered by that oppressive middle-age heaviness that nothing can alleviate—neither adventurous trips abroad nor the relative peace of everyday life—I silently grumbled a great deal, and from time to time I had sudden fits of anger. I cursed both God, who was always so remote, and my dead parents, who had never been close. But most of all I bitterly accused myself for failing to achieve anything worthwhile.

Books and Dreams

I WAS EMPLOYED at a book warehouse in Oslo from the
age of seventeen right up until I fell ill. Uncle Wilhelm had
gotten me the job. I drove a warehouse hoist for them for
more than thirty years, every workday from eight in the
morning until four-thirty in the afternoon, moving pallets
loaded with cartons of books, positioning them or taking
them down from the tall shelves that various publishing
firms rented from the warehouse. It was a simple, boring job
that required no effort on my part. It was perfect for me, for
I'd never exerted myself in search of the fruits of success. I
was lazy and didn't ever try to better myself in any way.

I've lived with the smell of books for all my life. Reading
them, on the other hand, has never interested me. My parents were great readers. They eagerly scooped up every new
book published in Hungary. That was their way of seeking
out some few crumbs of truth in a country where everything in public life was rotten with lies. All the shelves and
niches in our house were stacked with novels and poetry
collections. I never opened a single one; I was satisfied just
to look at the covers and rub my fingertips along the spines.
Perhaps that was a sort of protest against my mother and
father, my reaction to the perception that they spent more
time on literature than they did on me and were always
preaching about the virtues of reading. I preferred a thousand times over to listen to my great-uncle's stories than to
open some dusty old book, even though my parents regularly warned Sasha and me that Fernando was fooling us.

My lack of interest in books was mostly due to the fact
that reading required patience, a virtue I've never had much
of. During my years in the book warehouse I did become

accustomed to leafing through novels early in the morning, especially books by authors whose names I recognized. I picked up this habit after attending a party where I met an attractive young woman. She assumed that since I worked with books—I didn't explain that I was a hoist operator in a book warehouse—I'd certainly read *A Hundred Years of Solitude* by Gabriel García Márquez. For a moment I thought of confessing that, on principle, I'd always avoided books; but I felt a twinge of shame. Judging from the title, I thought the book she mentioned might well have some implications for my own life and certainly I should have read it. So I smiled and scribbled on a scrap of paper that I'd enjoyed it a great deal, especially the parts about Central Europe, because they brought back my own experiences and I was pleased to recognize my own world. My great-uncle used to say that it's easier to catch up with a liar than with a lame dog. The truth of his proverb was demonstrated to me that evening. The young woman unfortunately made no secret of the fact that I had not been telling the truth. That was when I decided I would start actually looking into the books in the warehouse, so I could avoid the humiliation of being exposed as a liar with a nonexistent education.

It was enough for me to page aimlessly through a book for a few minutes to get an idea of its contents. This was usually sufficient to set my imagination working. Driving a hoist is a lonesome job; one wears ear protection all day long to muffle the noise and block out the rest of the world. Even at lunchtime I would sit there alone. The other workers dismissed me as stupid and simple because I couldn't speak, and they rarely sought my company. After holding a book in my hands, I would give free rein to my imagination to go anywhere it wished. This made the mindless work much easier to bear. It became a habit after a while. As soon as I got up in the morning, my imagination went racing off on some giddy adventure that went on and on, right up until I fell asleep that evening. I could always find some new book with a scenario to explore. For example, one time a couple of days after picking up Franz Kafka's *The Trial* and skimming the back cover, I became a dazzlingly talented attorney—modeled after Perry Mason from the television program—and my eloquence saved the innocent Josef K. from a death sentence. Another time I stumbled upon a volume of Marcel Proust's series *In Search of Lost Time*, and for a whole week I envisioned the breathtakingly beautiful Countess of Guermantes lying in my arms and begging me to make love to her one more time. Dostoyevsky's *The Idiot* made me dream that I was Dr. Freud and had developed a miraculous treatment that could cure the mentally ill of the world. Finding Joseph Conrad's slim little book *The Heart of Darkness* just at the time that Mother Teresa received the Nobel Peace Prize stimulated me to fantasize that I was saving the children of Africa from deadly diseases and starvation.

Liberation from Life's Terrors

MY DAYDREAMS were different every day, but they had generally the same theme: I was a special individual whose achievements astounded the world. It never occurred to me that I was daydreaming in order to hold my sad reality at a distance. The truth is that my life in Norway has been miserable and lonely.

I never succeeded in becoming a member of any community in my new country. I never made any friends. I lived without a goal. I closed my eyes to affection, to pleasure, and to the temptations of life. I led a life of pure escapism and in my thoughts I was always on the way to somewhere else. My great mistake was never joining, never trying to blend in by being and behaving like everyone else. Choosing to go one's own way is a punishment in itself. People who live in isolation soon shipwreck themselves on the reefs of reality. I lived for myself alone, lonely, with no purpose and no ideals. My life was reduced to nothing but a way to pass the time.

It's a solemn but proud moment when one is struck by the revelation that one has thrown one's life away, the only life one will ever have. Even minor reverses used to leave me downcast for weeks on end, and when I was in a dismal mood, as I often was, I would fixate upon my misfortune, plunge into depression, and let myself slide down into the black depths. But not this time. I wasn't dismayed by my insomnia or my difficulty in swallowing or even by the ominous diagnosis of cancer of the larynx. On the contrary. I accepted without protest the knowledge that I was going to die soon, and strangely enough, death freed me from my fear of living. Death gave me the right to be myself and to break the contract forced upon me in my earlier life. I had nothing more to expect from life, so I might just as well do something astonishing that would defy the boring routine of my humdrum existence.

But what could that be?

No matter how frantically I sought the answer, I always got lost in distractions and trivialities.

THE OPERATION changed my life. Because of it, I underwent an odd transformation. I suddenly abandoned my daydreams and forgot my constant dissatisfaction with life. I woke up each morning with a feeling of gratitude and joy, just to be alive.

My inability to speak still tormented me. I've been mute for more than thirty years, of course, and I long ago got used to communicating by writing things on scraps of paper. But somewhere deep inside me a little hope had lingered, a hope that someday I might recover my voice. The surgeon's knife put an end to that hope. I tried to console myself with the thought that, after all, I'd probably never have found someone willing to listen. In all these years in Norway, you see, I never met a single person—except for Uncle Wilhelm —who was ready to embrace me without reservation and listen to the story of my life, so I could just forget about that. And now, as the past began to well up inside me, now that hope was gone, I was seized by the desire to tell stories about life's pitiless treatment of all those generations of my family.

Stories

I WAS BORN in a world where the past had more meaning than the future. The shining promise offered to others by the new day meant nothing to us. Our golden age lay behind us and was wrapped in deep silence. Oddly enough, no one in the family talked about the fates of our many family members, either because no one could bear to relive the past or simply because everyone wanted to shield us children from the suffering of the Spinozas throughout the ages.

We'd been struck by so many misfortunes. We'd been dogged by disaster as far back as anyone could remember.

Almost everything that happened in the world turned out to be disastrous for us. The Middle Ages. The Enlightenment. The French Revolution. Emancipation. World wars. Catholicism. Nazism. Communism. Liberalism.

Life in our family was based on principles that had never offered us security in the past and might always be subject to attack in the future. We were secular Jews who'd lost contact with traditional concepts of our faith and customs, Jews who never put down roots wherever we were living. That's why we were forever excluded from the benefits of joining any other community.

If it hadn't been for my great-uncle, a man who actually had no blood ties to us, Sasha and I would have grown up in that tyranny of silence. But Fernando knew how to conjure up our hidden legends and all the events and history that lay concealed deep within our genes, and he brought our heritage to life for us with his epic talent for storytelling. I'm convinced he understood what our family's willful suppression of our story was doing to us children, and he wanted to infuse us with vital force and courage by giving my twin brother and me something to be proud of: strong roots. That was why he taught us that the events themselves were to blame. None of it was our fault.

Nothing seemed more natural to Sasha and me than drifting off in our great-uncle's stories about those many things that happened long ago. His tales were sources of delight for us. He effortlessly created for us a whole world of yesteryear, painted with a sort of melancholy but happy exaltation that made Sasha and me a bit giddy.

Quite suddenly, then, those stories popped into my mind. Without warning they simply gushed out from the darkness within me. I realized that I was carrying an endless store of anecdotes, and I couldn't push away the powerful and ever more insistent need to communicate everything I had stored inside me. But how can one possibly tell stories without a voice?

A Nightly Dream

ONE NIGHT I had a strange dream. I saw myself sitting at a table talking with an angel and his two assistants. I'd never seen a creature lovelier than that angel, who was the incarnation of joy, full of the wisdom of life. Around the angel shimmered the whiteness of the silence of the Milky Way. That pure white, so unattainable and absolute, cast a special spell upon me. It whispered to me that the gleaming colors of the world of the senses that the Hindus call the Veil of Maya are no more than a subtle deception.

But then the angel's young assistant, a man with a heavy Russian accent, explained that the absence of color around the angel symbolized the pitiless void of the universe.

"Mankind alone can find the antidote to meaningless nothing," he said. "Human beings do this with their consciousness, with words and memories. Mankind's greatest gift is the ability to endow life with meaning."

I wanted to know if my own life had any particular meaning. But I never managed to ask the question, because the other assistant, an old man with a sharp profile, temperamental and full of passion, declared in bold, ringing Italian, "Il esplorazione!"—the voyage of discovery!

"The true voyage of discovery, the great adventure," he explained further, "is that of life and death. The traveler plunges into the soul of humanity. There he is carried in circles and tells all, he builds bridges of words to that inner silence he discovers within his fellow humans, anchored within his own family."

The scene in my dream shifted. Everything became dark. I sat alone at a table. I dipped my pen in the inkwell and began writing effortlessly. I filled up the white sheets of paper quietly, methodically, with a jumble of words, but soon a structure gradually began to emerge. I finished writing, and my words whirled away in the wind; humanity held its breath and the birds fell silent.

That dream was balsam to my heart. I awoke the next morning full of joy, with a new attitude toward life. New inner worlds had opened themselves to me. My understanding had been guided by a peculiar light and greater peace. I'd found the undiscovered land: stories. The purpose of my remaining months and days was to write down those stories.

Writing

WELL AWARE of the urgency, I devoted all my energies to deciphering the past so I could understand my own origins. Over the course of several weeks I devoured everything I could find: the documents about my family that I'd discovered in my grandfather's suitcase, of course, and the thousand and one utterly fascinating pages of Benjamin Spinoza's book, *The Elixir of Immortality*. Reference works and novels, as well; I read an enormous amount. My hunger for the written word and my ability to absorb it surprised me. My expeditions into the realm of fiction gave me great sustenance and the feeling that I was touched by genius; I had the impression that the momentous thoughts in those pages were my own, not those of others. In the refuge of good writing I felt shielded from my perishing existence. I believed in immortality.

OBSESSED BY THE THOUGHT that every human being is unique and that every event occurs only one time, I began for the first time in my life to write down the stories that I'd carried within me since childhood. Slowly at first and hesitantly, almost reluctantly, since I thought what little knowledge I possessed was all too insufficient and fragmentary to capture reality. Moreover, I didn't really know where the twisting path I'd begun would take me. I quickly discovered that language falls short when one tries to describe one's inner life; only the outer appearance of things could be adequately captured. I could clearly understand a subject and yet become terribly exasperated when I tried to put it into words.

WRITING THE PROLOGUE about my mother's death was agonizingly difficult. That passage took me far more time to write than anything else I wrote—a whole month.

Why on earth did I need so much time to craft that passage of less than eighty lines?

What can I tell you? I've always found writing extremely difficult. I've never had any real gift for it. I've always hesitated, doubting every word as I put it down. In the middle of a sentence I'm always in danger of losing the thread; I write, cross out words, rewrite, cross out words again—it never ends.

AND THEN CAME what they called *peripeteia* in Greek drama, the sudden change of fortune. A routine medical examination revealed it. The physician discovered a metastasis of the cancer. My traitorous blood had transported rebellious cells to the remotest regions of my body. I came face-to-face with the knowledge that my time was running out and soon I would be defeated by the rebellion of my own insides. On the one hand, I'd just reconciled myself with my upcoming death. *One family after another dies out,* I thought, *suns are lit and extinguished, and soon it will be my turn to go the way of all flesh.* On the other hand, I was tormented by the thought that once I shut my eyes forever, all those stories in me would be gone without a trace and all those who had preceded me would disappear forever.

I couldn't stand by and just let my ancestors disappear into the chaos of time. I faced one last decisive struggle.

THEN, WHEN I least expected it, I began writing quickly, relieved to find myself liberated from the torture of my wordlessness. From then on, I began to appreciate every day—in my head, in my spirit, and also in my body, not least in my body—how much that writing meant to me. The words literally poured out of me. My brain was feverishly occupied with my family lineage, everything I'd tried to suppress for years and forget completely. My dying ancestors danced around my head and jealously followed my writing; they were all, every single one, demanding their places in the text.

I could feel them close to me, and I could sense their warm breath as they leaned over my shoulder and read how I was giving shape to their lives. I could hear their whispered comments and their surprise when I put words in their mouths that they didn't want to acknowledge and when I gave away their secrets.

All of them were there except for my mother and father. All along, those two considered me to be a failure as a son, someone they could never depend on or be proud of. Much of our relationship remains unexplained, and for that reason I can't put down the details of their lives in a factual, accurate narrative. They knew that. That, I believe, is why they held themselves at such a distance. Undoubtedly my mother and father have been hoping that I would enclose them in the only thing they value: silence.

OFTEN I WOULD collapse into bed after two o'clock in the morning, only to be awakened by my inner clock four hours later so I could return to my task. I rarely bothered to get dressed in the morning; it took too much valuable time. It was more or less by accident that I had anything to eat or drink. No one and nothing else existed outside my narrative. The words made me forget everything else. The act of writing charged me with the energy of language, so that like Scheherazade I kept away the Angel of Death for a while longer.

WHAT I'VE WRITTEN here is not a confession. It's a narrative. This is what happened; things like these happen here in this world. Narratives like this one about the Spinoza family and millions of other family chronologies are the basis of history. They constitute the great story of mankind.

TIME IS FLEETING. Our past is gone forever. The future has no need of me. Tomorrow will be built by other people. I can shut my eyes in peace. My task on earth is complete. I've replaced the elixir of my ancestor Baruch with the only thing that can possibly give human beings immortality on this earth: our ability to remember.

I LEAVE NOTHING but my own words after me. Benjamin's book, the treasure of our family, I take with me to the grave. Ever a heavy smoker resistant to cure—I have an addiction that not even cancer could free me from—each time I finished writing a passage about our family history, I tore a page out of Benjamin's magnificent book, filled it with tobacco, and enjoyed a hand-rolled cigarette.

At this very moment the last page of *The Elixir of Immortality* is going up in smoke.